MW01139954

SEVEN BRIDES OF SOUTH DAKOTA

BOOKS 1-3 PLUS PREQUEL

KARI TRUMBO

Seven Brides of South Dakota 1

Copyright © 2017 Kari Trumbo

ISBN: 978-1076673824

All rights reserved under International and Pan-American Copyright Conventions

This is a work of fiction. Names, characters, places, and incidents are either the products of the author's imagination or are used fictitiously, and any resemblance to actual persons, living or dead, business establishments, events, or locales is purely coincidental.

By payment of required fees, you have been granted the *non*-exclusive, *non*-transferable right to access and read the text of this book. No part of this text may be reproduced, transmitted, downloaded, decompiled, reverse engineered, or stored in or introduced into any information storage and retrieval system, in any form or by any means, whether electronic or mechanical, now known or hereinafter invented without the express written permission of copyright owner.

Please Note

The reverse engineering, uploading, and/or distributing of this book via the internet or via any other means without the permission of the copyright owner is illegal and punishable by law. Please purchase only authorized electronic editions, and do not participate in or encourage electronic piracy of copyrighted materials. Your support of the author's rights is appreciated.

No part of this book may be reproduced or transmitted in any form or by any electronic or mechanical means, including photocopying, recording or by any information storage and retrieval system, without the written permission of the publisher, except where permitted by law.

A RUBY GLOWS

This book is dedicated to two women who have been with me from sentence one. Thank you, Margie and Connie for your unflagging support.

CHAPTER 1

Wedding of Josiah and Penny Hanover
Cutter's Creek, Montana, 1892

Pretty people gathered all around Ruby, talking to her,
including her in their merriment. That had never happened
before. Course, for the last year there hadn't been anyone
around *to* include her.

Her glance flitted all over the room as she pressed her ill-fitting
skirts against her legs. Josiah Williams had found her just a few
weeks ago, saving her from the wilderness. But parties, especially
weddings, were a much scarier wilderness to her. She took a deep
breath and gripped her knees.

Just sit. Don't run.

The lovely Lily Donaldson sat to her right, and the bride-to-be,
Penny Hanover, reclined on a chaise opposite Ruby in the front
solar of the Hanover home. Penny's mother, Sara, had decorated
the area in bunting and pine boughs with candles, and now they
were waiting for the groom and his family to arrive, along with
Reverend Bligh. Everything about Penny seemed to sparkle as she
talked and laughed with all the guests. She certainly deserved it

5

after all the confusion and pain of getting shot and losing her memory. But now Ruby's only friend was marrying Josiah. As soon as he arrived. Penny glanced over Ruby's shoulder toward the door.

Ruby touched her stomach to relieve the roiling beneath her hand. The more Penny laughed and joked about becoming a wife, the sicker Ruby felt. Weddings didn't bring out the best memories, but she pushed those down. It was Penny's wedding day, not her own.

Ruby's wedding, just a little over a year before, had been terrifying.

Again, the memories of that day rose to bang against her heart.

One morning, fourteen months before, her father dragged her from the room she shared with her seven sisters. She'd been seventeen then, but her naiveté didn't last long. An old man with a gap-toothed smile and his hat in his hand waited outside. He'd licked his lips and tossed his hat back on his head, reaching for her. Her father shoved her into the old man's arms and she screamed. The old man reeked of moonshine, the same stuff her father brewed.

Her father stood tall, shoved her closer to the man, even as she'd tried to run. He smiled at each of them.

"Father. Why? Why are you doing this to me?" Ruby cried.

He flinched then held out his arms. "Arnold Gresham, do you take Ruby Grace Arnsby to be your wedded wife? To have and hold, and all that," his voice boomed through the clearing around their small shack.

Arnold scratched his chin and held her at arm's length. She cringed and hunched her shoulders to cover herself as his leering eyes roamed slowly up and down her body, peeling back layers of clothing. He grinned wide, and she shrank back. "Yep, I think I do," he answered.

Her father held up his arms in celebration. "Good enough for me."

"Wait," Ruby screamed, fighting to get free of Arnold's fierce grip. "Don't I get a say in this?"

"Nope." Her father turned and disappeared back into the

house, slamming the door behind him. Ruby glimpsed her sisters peeking through the pink netting on their window, but then Arnold spun her roughly back to him, kissing her square on the lips, his sloppy wet mouth soaking her face.

That was the last time she let her guard down around him.

He'd never touched her again.

Ruby heard the room quiet around her, pulling her from her own troubling thoughts as Penny's gaze snagged on something behind Ruby. She turned to see who'd joined them and her glance caught on a man she'd seen talking to Josiah, Penny's intended, once before.

Her heart sputtered in her chest. It wasn't that he was incredibly handsome, nor incredibly plain. What made her stop in her tracks was that when their gazes met, his went from smirking and aloof to alluring and playful, and no one had looked at her like that before. His long dark hair brushed past his shoulders, but for the occasion he'd tied it back. He had a broad chest, swathed in a crisp white preacher-collared shirt under a black vest, narrowing to a lean waist. She couldn't stop staring at him.

Penny laughed and touched her arm, breaking his hold over her. "Ruby Gresham, this is the ever too-quiet Beau Rockford," Penny said cheerfully.

Standing on wobbly legs, Ruby held out her hand to him, hoping he didn't notice her nervousness. His gaze never leaving hers, he captured her hand and kissed her knuckles. Excitement and fear collided within her. She wanted to yank her hand away and drag him closer, the two disparate desires making her head ache.

Thankfully, he didn't smell like a drunk possum, so he was already better than the men she'd known in the past. But that didn't make him safe.

"The pleasure is all mine, Miss Gresham." He never looked away, not for a second. "Please, have a seat. No need to stand on formality for me." He waved his hand over her chair.

Ruby sat and waited for her knees to stop knocking together. She should tell him the truth. What did it really matter, though?

Marriage was for lovers, not for those too frightened to ever go near a man again. She would never, could never, let a man close to her. She'd run from her husband for so long, running had become a habit. One she wasn't sure she wanted to break.

Reverend Bligh entered the solar, escorting Josiah's family. Josiah's father limped in on the arm of his daughter, Carol. Penny and Lily had told her all about Carol; how she was sweet, but to not tell her anything you didn't want the whole town to know. Also, the sweet gossip was man-hungry. Josiah's father had some type of leg ailment. His face was unnaturally white and sweat covered his brow as he limped into the room. Reverend Bligh quickly retrieved a chair for him and he lowered himself into it. Carol took her place beside her father's chair, resting her hands protectively on his shoulders. She regarded Beau openly, where he stood behind Ruby's chair. Carol's gaze dropped to Ruby and her eyes narrowed to an icy stare.

My, what a fickle girl, Ruby thought, turning back to Penny.

Bill and Sara stood by the large picture window and Reverend Bligh motioned them over. They joined the Reverend, giving their daughter hugs and private words. Penny clutched her parents close. Soon enough, the reverend arranged both families in a wide arc around Josiah and Penny, starting with Josiah's father and ending with Penny's brother, Holston. Ruby's stomach fluttered and she glanced around for the nearest door. Beau's eyes on her set her belly fluttering in other ways. She was trapped on all sides. There was no escape.

Ruby stood between Penny and Lily. On the other end of the half-circle stood Lily's fiancé, James, and Beau stood right across from Ruby. His dark-eyed gaze captured hers and her insides suddenly felt like snow in sunshine, warm and melty. She didn't much care for attention from men so she'd have to keep that one as far away as possible.

Reverend Bligh began the ceremony with a few simple words of welcome that seemed to drone on forever.

Though it was chilly outside, the Hanover's home was stifling.

If she were honest, the heat alone wasn't responsible for the flush and weakness she felt.

The reverend spoke of happiness and fulfillment, and Ruby could only hope it held true for Penny and Josiah. It hadn't for her parents. Nor her.

The reverend's voice broke over her, "Josiah, you may now kiss your —"

Penny jumped into Josiah's arms and kissed him full on the mouth. The family around her erupted in cheers.

Bile rose in Ruby's throat and her head throbbed. Her breath came fast and darkness closed in on the edge of her vision. She closed her eyes and backed away from the happy scene playing out in front of her.

She needed air.

Penny turned with a jubilant yell and tossed her bouquet into the air. Ruby, who had turned in the same moment, couldn't stop the token of joy and wedded bliss from landing in the crook of her arm. She blinked down at the flowers, unsure of what to do. She swallowed, unable to breathe, the air growing thick, heavy, hideous.

Must get out.

She tossed the flowers to Lily and ran from the room.

CHAPTER 2

Beau wandered away from the celebrants and toward the hearth. Too much noise. The crush around Josiah, the one person he knew well at the party, was too much. Carol kept following him around like a lost puppy, and he'd rather avoid all contact with her if it was possible. She was young and it was no secret she was husband hunting. She and most of the town girls like her, were one of the reasons he always left Cutter's Creek for winter. Freedom was all he'd ever wanted. He'd have to leave town soon, or risk being snowed in. Then he'd have to avoid Carol all winter.

He glanced at the door, wondering where the beautiful Ruby had run off to. He frowned. Where had she gone? One minute the bride and groom were kissing, the next … She'd turned a sickly pale color, her eyes brimmed with tears, then she tore from the room. Not the typical reaction to a wedding kiss. He didn't put much stock in marriage, but the idea had never made *him* ill.

He rested his forearm on the mantle, leaning against it, staring down into the dancing flames and bright red coals of the fire.

She'd be pretty in front of the firelight, her red curls shining.

Ruby certainly wasn't the typical Cutter's Creek gal. Frankly, she looked uncomfortable in the dress she'd put on for the occasion, and she'd scratched at her hair as if wearing it up were foreign to her. Aside from her uniquely red hair, the only other notable thing about her were those blue eyes. More blue than he'd ever seen. He glanced at the door again, hoping to see Ruby walk through it.

What could be taking her so long? Why hasn't she come back?

He approached the door and touched the handle. He heard a soft squeak from the other side. Beau leaned forward, pressing his ear to the polished wood. The sound came again, followed by a hiccup. He turned and took stock of the people around him. Everyone was on the other side of the room, engrossed in Penny and Josiah. No one would miss him for a minute.

He stuck his finger in the recessed handle and gave the door a slight nudge, opening the sliding pocket door just enough to peek through. He caught a glimpse of a rose-colored gown and deep red hair. Ruby sat on the floor, knees to her chest, cradling her head in her arms, her skirts draped in a circle all around. Her shoulders quaked slightly, and the soft locks of her hair that draped her shoulders trembled with the movement. The sight of her crying did things to him he'd never experienced before.

What had bothered her so much she felt she had to leave, going out there to cry in secret? He wanted to go and ask her. On the other hand, he didn't want to disturb her.

Then again…something about her tugged at him. He couldn't leave her.

Beau pulled the door open a little more, slipped through, and closed it behind him. He maneuvered over to the wall where she sat and slid down next to her, feeling her jump as he landed.

"Oh." She sniffled. "I didn't expect anyone to come after me." Her bright blue eyes, rimmed in red, stood out against her pale skin. And the backwoods accent he'd heard so much about was tempered with her obvious attempt to cover it.

Beau peered back at the door, then stretched his legs out in front of him. "I was waiting for you to come back and join the party. I finally gave up and decided to join you out here instead. I couldn't just let you sit alone. Care to talk about what's bothering you?"

Her eyes widened and her lovely mouth opened for a moment, then snapped shut. She shook her head, her curls bobbing around her softly curved neck.

He had nothing to offer her but an ear, and he happened to have one to spare. "I'm leaving town in a few days, and I don't know anyone but Josiah. I ain't got no one to tell. I'm no gossip, anyway."

Ruby turned her face away then dashed the back of her hand under her eyes, wiping the tears from their wet tracks on her cheeks. He fought the urge to draw her glance back to him.

"Weddings just make me cry, is all. I can't talk too much, or you'll realize I ain't cultured." Her eyes widened further, and she gasped. "See, I already ruined it." Her lip quivered again, and despite the fact that he generally hated female tears, hers hit him as more personal than annoyance.

Her glance stayed far away from him and she played with the hem of her skirt like a child caught in a lie.

"You didn't ruin anything, Ruby, and I didn't expect you to be cultured. Josiah said he found you out in the middle of nowhere. I don't know how you survived all on your own for so long." He searched for the right words to say next. He'd always struggled with knowing just what to say. Eventually, he'd developed the habit of saying nothing at all. A habit that wasn't helping right now. He folded his hands together and rested them on his stomach. "Where were you from?"

Ruby sniffed and he pulled his handkerchief from his pocket and handed it to her.

"I'm from Yellow Medicine. My kin's still there, I think," she replied.

"I know quite a few people from there. I've done some work there as a wrangler. I never met a Gresham family, though. Sorry I didn't get to meet them, or you, when I was there."

Ruby furrowed her brow and crossed her arms, draping them

over her knees. "I guess you could say we stayed away from town. I only remember going into Yellow Medicine a few times."

That wasn't uncommon. Families often lived off the land, but he wanted to know more. "Aren't you a might young to be living on your own without your family?" He kept his gaze focused out over his feet. He didn't want to accuse her of anything, but her silence made him uncomfortable, which wasn't usually the case for him. He was treading into uncharted territory.

"I was…kidnapped, and held for a while, until Josiah found me and brought me here." Ruby flinched then leaned forward, her gaze focused on the door across the hallway that led back to the party. She tensed like she wanted to dart through it, away from him.

Watch it, take it slow.

"I see. I'm sorry for you. If you decide you want to go back to your family, let one of the Hanovers know. I'd be happy to find you a chaperone and take you back to Yellow Medicine. Not that I want to see you go after just meeting you."

Ruby's eyes widened again and she sucked in a deep breath, holding it until he was sure she'd faint. She was terrified. Poor thing. Probably scared of what her family would think of her being gone so long.

Beau clenched a fist then flexed his hands, willing his body to relax. Just sitting beside Ruby, knowing her heart was full of fear, did something to him he didn't want to name. He had to get out of there. He pushed himself up to standing and walked back into the party, leaving her be like she wanted. He didn't mean to be rude, but he couldn't stay beside Ruby any longer.

Just like he'd always thought, he was better off alone. No one to worry about impressing. Josiah and James could have married bliss, well, James could in time, when he and Lily finally got around to saying their 'I do's'. But, as long as he avoided pretty redheads, he'd just be fine alone.

~

RUBY WATCHED Beau's back as he slid through the pocket doors. He glanced at her for just a moment. His blue eyes and the slight slump of his shoulders betrayed his sadness before the doors closed with a thud, dampening the sound of the party on the other side. She pressed her hand against her forehead, her tears now used up. She'd lied, run, and felt alone for so long that this new life filled with friends was like a strange new second skin over her old bruised and broken one. The problem was, the new skin didn't fit.

She stood up, straightened her ill-fitting dress, and hesitated. At just eighteen years, it was as if life had passed her by. There was no one to watch out for her besides herself. She couldn't count on anyone. She sighed and turned toward the stairs leading up to the temporary room the Hanovers had let her use. It'd be best for her to disappear for a while, especially after embarrassing herself in front of all the guests, but that wasn't possible. She had nowhere else to go.

She made it to her bedroom without encountering any of the staff Penny's mother had hired for the occasion. She'd never had a room all to her own before and it might be the one thing she enjoyed; a little open space. Growing up, she'd shared her room with all seven of her dear sisters. Every single one had been a treasure and her heart ached with longing to see them again. The chance of that happening, though, was slim. Her father had been quick to marry her off at seventeen and now, a little over a year later, another of her sisters was probably forced into an unwanted marriage. Which meant she'd never see Jennie again.

Ruby pulled her worn-out dress from under the bed. She pressed her face against the mattress, reaching as far as she could, she found her bonnet and bag. Penny's mother told her not to worry about her dresses, that Ruby could wear Penny's while she was here, but she suspected they were just embarrassed by their worn state. She opened her carpet bag, realizing now just how filthy and battered it was compared to the white coverlet on the bed.

Pulling out the one dress she owned, Ruby viewed it critically. The fabric was thin. It was threadbare by the knees because she'd knelt to clean the cabin and pluck weeds from the small garden. A tiny burn near the shoulder reminded her just what happened when an unhappy man got too close.

When he couldn't catch her one evening, Arnold had thrown his pipe at her. She could still feel the burning tobacco as it dislodged from the pipe and seared her dress and skin. She touched the matching scar under the fabric of her new dress.

Ruby knelt on the floor, digging farther under the bed. No man would ever rule her again. She pulled the shotgun out, opened, then checked the barrel.

If they even thought about it, she'd kill them first.

CHAPTER 3

Beau stood in the door of the Cutter's Creek Sweet Shoppe. He'd never liked going in, especially after Penny had been shot, but his feet were dragging and a hot cup of Arbuckles was just what he needed to warm up.

Josiah had pestered him about staying and continuing to work with him moving freight, but he'd never done one thing for so long before. Now, he had to consider his options. He'd agreed to do all of Josiah's deliveries for a week while he and his new wife got properly acquainted. That time would be up in just a few days and he didn't know where to go next. Josiah would have very little to do in just a few weeks, with the snowy season approaching.

Beau yanked off his hat and tossed it onto a table. Turning the ceramic cup face up to signal he'd like some coffee, he scanned the room to find Martha, the shop owner. She wasn't in sight, so he tapped the table with his finger to get her attention, wherever she was. His eyes swept the room only to find the dark blue eyes of Ruby staring at him as she tentatively made her way toward him.

She wore her hair up loosely, her deep red curls shining in the sunlight from the front window. Her bright white apron cinched neatly around her small waist showed off gently rounded hips. He closed his eyes then opened them again, reminding himself to look back up at her face. She tilted her head to the side and held up the coffee carafe.

"Would you like coffee or tea, Mr. Rockford?" She whispered, her strangely polished voice shaking slightly.

He leaned closer to her and smiled, hoping it'd calm her nerves. "It's no secret I'm a coffee drinker, never could stomach that English stuff."

A shadow of a smile teased her top lip as she poured the fragrant black coffee into his cup. "Would you like anything else, sir?"

His shoulders slumped and he reached for his heart feigning a sulk in the hopes of earning a smile. "Sir? Am I that old? Mr. Rockford if you must, but Beau'd be even better."

One side of her mouth quirked. Almost a win. "Would you like a scone, Mr. Rockford?"

He shook his head. "You sound different. What's wrong with the way you talk?" He leaned back and regarded her, wishing she'd go back to being the Ruby he'd talked with at the wedding. She took a step back and her face fell as she glanced over her shoulder.

When she turned back to him, the pinched lines of her face tore at him. "Martha doesn't like the way I talk. She gave me a list of things to learn to say and I'm not supposed to say anything else. She says I sound too... I don't know the words she used." Her cheeks reddened to match her hair.

He sighed, wrapping his hands around the warm mug. It wasn't his affair. If Martha wanted to run that kind of business, it should be her choice, but that didn't mean he had to agree with it.

"I'm sorry to hear that. If I can't get you to talk with me, then, I think this'll do just fine. Thank you, Miss Gresham."

A darkness settled over her as she wandered off to another table. Her careful speech drifted across the room, sharp to his ears. He'd liked Ruby's frank way of speaking.

Since she'd found a job, did that mean she'd be staying in Cutter's Creek? He furrowed his brows and released his cup to drum his fingers on the table. He'd have to see if he could find her family the next time he went to Yellow Medicine. If she had been kidnapped, as she'd said, they might miss her as much or more than she missed them. If she were with family, she could talk any way she wanted to.

In a few weeks, the snow would pile so deep in the higher elevations that delivering anything, even with Josiah's ox cart, would be difficult. Ruby had probably thought ahead and taken the job to stay through the winter. She could go home after that, and if he was still here, he'd offer to take her. A heaviness pressed on his chest. He shook his head to clear his thoughts then donned his hat. He dug a few coins out of his pocket and left them on the table; for the coffee and for Ruby.

He strode past the Hanover house and back a few houses to his father's small shaker-box home. His father, Marshal, sat in front of the fire, wrapped in a quilt. "May? Is that you?" his glassy eyes searched the doorway.

Beau sighed and hung his hat on the peg by the door. "No, Pa. It's Beau. You sent May to live in Maine with your sister, remember?"

"What?" he rasped, holding his hand to his ear. "Speak up and stop mumbling. You're always mumbling. Can't hear a word out of your mouth. Go get May and tell her to make me some of that soup she's so good at."

"I can't do that. She's not here," Beau said, standing in front of his father. How he wanted to be frustrated, but not with his father, only with his weakening health.

The old man sat back in the chair and took a harsh breath. "This cold will be the death of me. Stoke up the fire, Beau, will you?"

The room was already roasting but he knew better than to question his father. He spread out the glowing coals and put a few more logs on. He took off his coat and hung it up next to his hat, the room was now so warm he certainly didn't need it.

There was an unopened letter on the table. He'd gotten it two days before, but the name on the front had been marred by the damp weather and he didn't know who it was from. Uncertainty ate at him. He didn't know if it were for him or his father. If it were for his father, he wanted to respect his father's privacy. But if it were for him… He couldn't wait any longer.

He tore the end off of the envelope and pulled out the small sheet of paper. It was folded neatly and thin enough to see through. The script was neat and clipped, but not familiar.

October 1, 1892
  Dear Beauford,

I'm writing chiefly to make you aware that Aunt Cici is about to be remarried and is no longer desirous of my company. I will be coming home on the train as soon as you are able to wire the fare. She has been a dear and is quite sad to see me go, but at her age, she wants to enjoy the freedom she now has without worrying about seeing to me or showing me off to society, which I detest at any rate.

  I miss you and father terribly. My studies here have been pleasant. Though, I know, I will never in all likelihood find work at a law firm in Cutter's Creek. At least I can say I completed my training and can, therefore, hold my own.

  I must keep this short, please wire the necessary funds or send the train ticket along with your reply at your earliest convenience.

  Respectfully yours,
  Maybell Rockford

Beau blinked down at the words and groaned. May was too smart for her own good; could talk her way out of just about anything, and was adept at hearing everything she shouldn't but missing everything she should. There was no way father could keep an eye on her. Most of the time he didn't even remember he was still in Cutter's Creek. Beau dug into his cigar box on the mantle and took out a little of the money he'd been saving. He shoved it into his vest pocket. If she needed a ticket he'd better get it to her.

Now, he might not have a choice about staying in town. He hated the idea of being cooped up in Cutter's Creek all winter long, but having May here would mean he'd have to.

He tossed on his coat and hat and stomped back out of the cabin, slamming the door behind him. The mercantile was only a few blocks away and he could take care of this chore quickly. He entered and waited for Holston to finish with a fabric order for Carol Williams. He turned away from the counter and tried to avoid her, the woman was never quiet. She daintily cleared her throat and he turned back, groaning to himself. She'd never let him alone.

Carol sashayed up to him and laid her gloved hand on his arm. "Why, there you are, Beau Rockford. Wherever have you been? I haven't seen you come around half as much, now that Josiah is married." She stuck her bottom lip out a little, licking it slowly.

"Miss Williams." He nodded his head to her and backed away, letting her hand fall off his arm. He moved forward toward Holston.

Carol stepped in his way. "If you aren't busy, you should come over tonight. I'm making a lovely dish for father. I've not gotten used to only cooking for the two of us so you'd be more than welcome." Her eye lashes danced up and down.

Beau backed against the counter. "Thank you, kindly. But, I need to take care of dinner for my Pa." He pulled the money from his pocket.

"Are you sure? I could send a bowl home with you for your father. It'd be no trouble at all." She leaned against him.

Beau moved over and she lost her balance for a moment, groping for the counter.

"Sorry, Miss Williams. I really do need to finish my business here and get back to my Pa. He's not feeling well." His neck grew warm under her narrowed eyes. He was sure Holston laughed at him behind the counter. He just couldn't handle attention from

Carol, or just about any woman. He felt ill-equipped, as if neither his brain nor his tongue worked quite right.

He shook his head and regarded Holston, pushing the money forward. "I need to wire some money to my sister in Maine. The bank says you have the only working telegraph in town and that you'd know what to do."

Holston took the money and counted it, finally glancing up to meet his gaze. Laughter brightened the other man's face. They both turned as the bell over the door chimed Carol's exit. "You actually handled her well. She's a bit eager."

The receding heat came back full-force. "She just don't take no for an answer."

"I'll get this taken care of for you right away, Beau. Is May coming home?"

Beau nodded. "Looks that way." He tipped his hat and went back out into the cold.

The sign above the boarding house caught his eye. 'Fresh hot soup. Every day!' "Well, looks like something is finally going my way today." He said aloud, adjusting his course to the large house on the corner.

CHAPTER 4

Ruby dropped the last of the cups in the soapy water and rolled up her sleeves to wash them. She'd worked hard her entire life, but this job just didn't fit. Martha had been nagging her all day, even when it seemed she'd done nothing wrong. Martha needed someone to help her after Penny got married and quit, so taking the job seemed perfect at the time. It was obvious now, though, that Ruby couldn't fill Penny's shoes.

Martha entered the room, clanking more cups together. "Ruby…I've had a few people complain…again. We call it coffee, dear, not belly wash, black water, or…," She winced, "brown gargle."

"Martha, I'm sorry, I—"

Martha held up her hand for quiet. "We serve bacon and eggs in the morning, not overland trout and cackleberries." The word dripped from her mouth like drool from a dog.

Ruby shook her head and dried her hands. "I'll hang up my apron. Thank you kindly for letting me try. I…guess I'm just not cut out for this work."

Martha's forehead creased and she crossed her small arms. "I'm sure there's something you can do where you don't have to talk, but it just isn't here. I counted out your pay and left it by the till, good evening." Martha dunked her hands into the water as Ruby went for her coat. She and Martha had never gotten on particularly well, but the dismissal still felt harsh.

Since staying with the Hanovers would've been strange after Penny left, she'd moved in with Lily. The whole upstairs had been converted into rental rooms, owned by James Cahill's aunt. Now she'd have no way to pay her share of the rent, which would mean she might have to leave Cutter's Creek.

She trudged across the street to old Mrs. Cahill's. Ruby found Lily sitting in the window, reading.

"Oh Ruby, you're home a little early, good. James and I are going out tonight to plan our wedding. We're thinking spring, that way David'll be about a year old so we can include him. Won't that be wonderful?" Her eyes had a faraway glaze over them and Ruby knew she wasn't expected to answer.

She dropped down on her bed and tucked her skirts around her legs. Though the room was papered in yellow and cheery, she couldn't manage a smile. What in the world could she do now? Going home was certainly not an option, despite what Beau had offered. At least he'd never be able to find her family with the name she'd given him. There were no Greshams in Yellow Medicine, and no one in Cutter's Creek knew she'd been an Arnsby. She didn't want Beau to ever get near her family, either. Pa wasn't one to mess with. The only one who could tangle with Pa was Ma. And even Ma couldn't keep him from tossing Ruby out when the time had come.

Lily laid her hand on Ruby's arm and she flinched.

"Ruby? Is something wrong?" Lily sat next to her on the bed. "I've been talking, but I don't think you heard me? I was asking if you wanted to be part of my wedding?"

Ruby shook her head. "Oh, I'm sorry Lily. I just don't know. I didn't do well at Penny's wedding. I wouldn't want to ruin yours, too."

Lily smiled then laughed. The tenderness in Lily's eyes made her want to run; there was always something behind a kindness, something she had to avoid like a sickness.

She laid a gentle hand on Ruby's arm. "You did no such thing. While I don't know what happened, because you left the room, it wasn't as if you had an episode in front of everyone…like I did."

Ruby's head popped up. "You? But you always say the right thing and act with manners and such. I don't."

"I stood up at James's first wedding because I was imagining it was me he was marrying." Her lovely eyebrow arched. "Can you top that for embarrassing?"

"I lost my job today because I don't talk like everyone else in town."

Lily scoffed and shook her head. "That isn't your fault, Ruby. Martha's so used to having Penny in there she doesn't remember what it's like to train someone new. Penny has worked there ever since her family moved back from Pleasant Valley."

"I heard tell they might be going back."

Lily nodded. "All of that is speculation. The Hanovers don't share anything with people until they're sure, because they're opposed to gossip. I'm sure we'll know when we're supposed to know. Now, about the wedding…"

Ruby shook her head. "I don't want no part of another wedding. I'm sorry, but I just don't see no reason to hitch your wagon to a man if you don't have to."

Lily patted her arm. "Just wait, Ruby. Someday you'll meet a man that'll make your heart ache from wanting to be with him. He'll say just the right things in just the right way, and you'll feel, from your head to your toes, that nothing will be right unless you're with him."

Flashes of Arnold's gap-toothed leer waded behind her lids. "If your heart hurts, take some ginger water and lay down for a spell. Don't go getting hitched. Makes no sense to me."

Lily smiled and a twinkle lit her eyes. "You know, Ruby, the Moore family is looking for a nanny for little Malcom. You could be yourself, because he's just a baby, and you'd be able to help a family. Mrs. Moore isn't feeling well and Heath Jr. works all day. You'd be such a benefit to them."

Ruby turned away. "I don't know. If the people of Cutter's Creek didn't like me pouring their coffee I can't imagine they'd want me anywhere near their babes."

Lily stood and straightened her skirts. "Well, you never know until you ask. You'll have to find something." She gathered her reticule and pulled the key from it, handing it to Ruby. "I won't need this as I'll probably get home in the evening. You might want to go check with the Moores."

Ruby grabbed the key and waited until the door clicked shut behind Lily. Alone again. She'd been alone for five long months after her husband passed away. Course, that might be counted as her fault, too. Her husband had always managed to consume enough of her father's hooch to be as worthless as a holey nappy every night. For the whole eleven months that she'd been married, she'd never once slept anywhere but the rocking chair. She'd gotten up before her husband every morning, leaving her husband never the wiser.

One night, it had been bitter cold and he'd run out of drink before he could drown himself as usual. He'd gone out to get more and hadn't come home. That wasn't rare and always a blessing. The next morning, she'd found him leaning against a nearby tree, cradling his bottle, frozen solid. She'd been shocked he could freeze since she was sure more alcohol ran through his veins than blood.

She should feel sorry, but she couldn't. Her husband had tormented her from the moment she'd laid eyes on him until the moment she'd rolled him into a ravine, never to be seen again. Part of her wished she'd taken the time to burn down the old shack they lived in. Sure as shooten' she'd never offer to go back.

The room closed in around her as she considered what Lily had said. There weren't many jobs for her. The Silver Dollar Inn might let her work there, but they also might have the same issue with her Martha had at the Sweet Shoppe.

I wonder who Beau will get his coffee from now.

Ruby pulled on her wool coat, slipping the key in her pocket. It wouldn't hurt to talk to the Moore family. If she were turned away, she'd take that as a sign from God that she had to go back to Yellow Medicine...and to her family.

CHAPTER 5

Cutter's Creek, Montana
Early December, 1892

B eau stuffed his hands into his pockets, slowly shifting his weight from one frozen foot to the other. He'd spent a month working in Yellow Medicine and only returned to Cutter's Creek last night. Not a single person he'd talked to in Yellow Medicine had heard of Ruby, and the only Gresham anyone had heard of was an old drunk no one had seen in months.

He scratched his chin and tipped his head to the sky as first flurries, then snow, pelted him. He'd known a storm was coming. The weather had changed rapidly and he hoped his sister's train would arrive soon. If it was delayed, she wouldn't have the money for lodging. He stretched his neck to see around the small train platform and spied a puff of steam in the distance, as the engine traveled the trail cut through the foothills.

Beau was exhausted but wound up, he didn't like being stuck in town when his body and mind ached to be anywhere else — he couldn't just leave Pa, though. Beau needed someone to watch out for him. May would just have to agree to stay home with Pa. Beau was itching to be on the move. He'd been ready to cut ties with Cutter's Creek for some time. But then, who'd watch May? He wished he knew the answer. He shook the snow from his hat and waited. Blasted cold.

The train rumbled to a stop at the platform and Beau watched for May to make her appearance. He grumbled, ready to quit the train station and get somewhere warm. He'd already been there long enough. She'd left Maine a month ago, and had been traveling by rail to get home before the winter weather hit.

Just as he began wondering what she'd look like after a month confined to a train, his boisterous, dark-haired sister stepped onto the platform. She wasn't alone, though. She was walking arm-in-arm with a man in a tailored suit, neither the worse for wear.

Beau approached the pair and she released her companion's arm, throwing her heavy muff at the poor shocked bloke, and bounding into Beau's arms, almost toppling him.

"Beau, you need a haircut. You look like a pirate from a dime novel." May laughed. "We'll have to clip you tonight, no way I'm standing for that."

Beau frowned and ignored her, casting his gaze to the man she'd been with. "Who's this with you?" The gentleman waited a few feet away, his eyebrow arching over a gold-rimmed monocle and his lips turning down in distaste.

"Oh, this is Mr. Emerson Caruso. He's a lawyer I met the very day I got your correspondence. He's hoping to spend a brief period in Cutter's Creek on business. Now I can work for him while he's here. Isn't it perfect?"

May, working with some stranger? She wouldn't have time to look after Pa if she were working.

"May, what about Pa? You can't work and take care of him." Beau glared over her shoulder at Mr. Caruso. The man hadn't even made his acquaintance and he'd already made a muck of things.

May touched Beau's cheek and tugged the hair by his ear. "You mean like *you've* been caring for Father as you travel all over, doing whatever it is you've decided you do? It's time for you to settle down and find a respectable job, Beauford. Maybe even a wife."

He ground his teeth. "It's Beau, and I've done what I can to keep Pa fed and in his house."

May rolled her eyes. "Of course you have." She snapped her fingers. "We'll need a wagon. We each have four trunks."

Beau felt the hair on the back of his neck bristle. "Four! Where in blazes do you plan on keeping all that? It isn't like Pa built an extra wing onto the house while you were gone!" Beau set his jaw. May was always able to set him off, and if he wasn't careful, she'd do it again.

She crossed her arms and narrowed her eyes at him. "Then I'll just take *your* room. It isn't as if you need it. Mr. Caruso will be staying at the Silver Dollar until he can find a place to set up a temporary office."

"Why does he need an office if he ain't staying?" Beau threw his hands into the air. "Never mind. I'll go borrow the ox cart from Josiah, that ought to be big enough." He couldn't keep his agitation at bay and it was good that he could walk away before May made him say more he'd regret. Maybe.

"I am *not* riding in an ox cart," Mr. Caruso finally spoke up, his cultured and clipped eastern accent punctuating each word. His brow furrowed, swallowing his monocle in the deep recesses of his eye socket.

Beau turned away from the pair and rubbed his forehead. How could May think inviting that man to live in Montana was a good idea? He wouldn't last the winter. Course, May had been away for two years, she might've softened so much she wouldn't survive, either.

She was the exact opposite of Ruby.

Ruby Gresham. Why couldn't he stop thinking about her?

Earlier that day, he'd stopped by at the coffee shop to grab a cup and chat with Ruby a little, but Martha said she hadn't worked there in a month. He hoped she hadn't left town. She hadn't gone home. He'd been in Yellow Medicine and hadn't seen her come by stage, but he hadn't been watching for her, either.

He'd asked around about her as he'd worked a few odd jobs, and the fact that no one knew anything made him even more

29

curious about Ruby. Everyone he'd spoken to had high-tailed it as soon as he'd mentioned her name. He hated to admit it but... maybe she lied.

It wasn't far to Josiah's, and the ox cart was in the barn behind the house. Beau spotted Josiah's large new house at the end of the street. It was the perfect place for a new wife.

Beau sneered to himself. There was a time he thought Penny would make a good wife, if he'd wanted to take one. That thought didn't last long, not with Penny and Josiah being inseparable since Josiah helped Penny's family move to Cutter's Creek. Penny was Josiah's. Stealing a man's woman was as bad as stealing his horse, you just didn't do it.

Beau led the team of oxen back to the railroad station and the waiting couple, still on the platform.

His sister resumed her fussing as soon as she saw him approaching, crossing her arms over her chest and tapping her foot as the snow gathered around her. He swallowed a laugh at the thought that the snow would never cover her mouth, it moved too much.

"Beau, I think you're doing this just to be contrary! You knew Mr. Caruso didn't want to use the cart, yet here you are. I declare, you must be the most difficult man in all of Creation."

He gave her a forced smile as he climbed down. "If you're going to do something, do it well."

He walked past the duo, ignoring Mr. Caruso's glare and mumbled words. A mountain of trunks sat next to them. All eight trunks were bigger than Beau had expected. Did May suddenly think she was royalty? Who in their right mind needed so much?

May had left Cutter's Creek with one carpet bag and come back with an entire life.

He raised a questioning eyebrow at the lawyer but decided against asking for help. The uppity man wouldn't lift a finger. May told him which trunks were hers and Beau put them in first so they could drop off the others at the inn. He refused to carry the other man's trunks up to his room. Mr. Caruso would have to pay someone at The Silver Dollar to do it.

The snow came down in earnest now, coating everything in white and cold and quiet. Beau just wanted to get everyone where they needed to be so he could get home and stoke the fire for Pa.

I won't be able to check on Ruby during this storm... Not that he knew where she was. Last he'd seen her was at Penny's parents' house and he had no reason to go there.

Beau dropped Mr. Caruso at the inn and the man descended the cart without even a thank you. Rushing into the inn, he snapped his fingers as four men appeared and unloaded his trunks. He stood to the side to supervise.

"May, I do hope I'll see you soon," he called up to her, approaching the cart.

May smiled down at him. "Be sure to stop by for a few meals. I'm sure the Silver Dollar is busy."

Beau cracked the whip over the oxen before Mr. Caruso could answer and May lost her balance, grabbing hold of him to steady herself. She glared over at him, looking like she wanted to box his ears, but held tightly to the seat. He pulled to a stop in front of Pa's house and May waited with her hands in her lap for him to come around and help her down. Beau grumbled as he shimmied down the wheel of the huge cart and went around the back. May stood and he grabbed her around the waist, swinging her down in one motion. She shrieked in protest.

"Beau! You can't do that. You don't go swinging women about like they're a sack of potatoes." She pulled her hand out of her muff and readjusted her hat.

He grunted. "Well, I wanted you out quickly so I can get these trunks in the house. I still have to get the cart back to Josiah's and walk all the way home. I'm in a hurry. Snow's coming down fast." He gestured to the air, astounded that such a smart woman couldn't figure all this out.

"Beauford Edward Rockford, stop being so selfish." May crossed her arms and huffed a *harrumph* that billowed over her head.

"Just go in the house, and keep your things out of my room. With this weather, it looks like I'll be sticking around for a while."

She stomped up the walk to the house. "Pity. I was hoping you'd leave so I *could* have your room." She tossed over her shoulder.

Beau heaved each of the four trunks into the house and left them in the front room. Pa and May sat in front of the fire, chatting the entire time. Neither bothered to say a word to him, which was fine. He didn't care. Pa would be happier with May there to care for him and make sure the soup was just as he liked it. Maybe he hadn't watched over Pa as much as he expected May to, but it'd be good for both of them. It would ground May, and Pa would be well-fed.

He climbed back onto the cart and drove it to the end of the street where he could turn it around. The snow in the street buried the base of the cart's wheels by at least two inches just in the short time he'd used it. It took some doing but he got the cart back to the barn.

Josiah was there, waving to Beau as he drove the oxen in.

"Beau! Good to see you. Want to come in and share some stew? Penny sure can cook." He jumped to action, helping Beau unhitch the oxen.

"I just dropped May at home. I need to stake my claim to my own space, since I plan to stick around a bit. She came home with a passel of new clothes and I don't know where she's gonna put 'em. She also brought some lawyer, because Cutter's Creek needs one." Beau shook his head and wished again that May would consider things before just doing them. "Course, I don't think *Mr. Emerson Caruso* will last the winter."

"Why do we need a lawyer? That doesn't make sense. He going to fight cases against himself?" Josiah squeezed the bridge of his nose. "Your sister always did have grand ideas. Crazy as all get-out, but grand."

"You don't have to tell me," he muttered. Suddenly, a thought occurred to him. "Hey, have you seen Ruby Gresham lately? She was here when I left, but I haven't seen her since I got back."

Josiah laughed and led one of the oxen back into its stall. "You ain't been back but a few hours, have you, and you're already asking about her?"

"I don't see how that matters. Nothing ever changes much in Cutter's Creek." Beau led the other ox into its stall. He hunched his shoulders against the cold. His coat was soaked. Josiah had seen right through him. He had to stop thinking about the alluring redhead.

"That's where you're wrong, Beau. Things always change. You just never notice anything because you aren't here. Now, Ruby's been working for Heath Jr. His wife has been sickly and they have little Malcom to take care of. Ruby's been watching the baby and helping Maddie, his wife."

"Heath is married? We went to school together." Beau scratched his cheek and counted in his head how many of his school mates were now pairs.

"Yup. You're the only holdout, Beau. So, when are *you* going to settle down?" Josiah hit him with a heavy glance and waited.

"I don't need to marry anyone. No one wants to get hitched to a man who can't sit still. I don't like to be in any place too long, and I like the freedom to move more than I like any woman."

"You just haven't met the right one. Once you do, you'll want to put down roots."

Beau grunted as he heaved the heavy cart back into its place and tipped his hat. "Evening. Enjoy your dinner." Beau didn't want to listen to Josiah go on about getting married. He'd get enough of that at home with May.

Josiah laughed as Beau tromped out of the barn. He'd have more than warm home fires that night. Somehow, that thought had never called to him, but now, he could see red curls shining in firelight, waiting for him. just like Penny waited for Josiah.

He grit his teeth and strode down the street. Even if he did fancy Ruby more than other women, no one wanted to live a life without a hearth.

CHAPTER 6

Ruby hadn't wanted to attend the Christmas Social at the little red chapel. Social gatherings always made her lack of social grace stand out like a purple ox. However, she'd heard a rumor from Maddie that Beau was back in town after a month-long absence. She hadn't been able to think of a single good reason to seek him out, so she'd strapped on her courage and said a prayer he'd make an appearance.

She'd been working for Maddie Moore for a month, but Maddie had insisted she take the night off, as she couldn't go herself. Little Malcom had weaseled his way into Ruby's heart and she hated even one evening away from him. Her arms ached to hold the child. Since she'd never have one of her own, it was a passable replacement.

So far that evening, she'd spent most of the event with Carol Williams who, despite her actions at the wedding, was now warm and friendly. It could have something to do with the dark handsome stranger who couldn't take his eyes off Carol from across the room. He was a doctor from the east, there to help Carol's father. The woman fairly glowed whenever she looked over at him. However, when it came time to ice skate, Carol deserted her to go frolic with the others. Ice skating was one thing Ruby had no interest in learning. So, she remained where she was, away from the crowd, watching people gather coats and skates near the doors of the sanctuary.

As the crush of people thinned, she strolled near the door, avoiding the remaining couples filtering out of the little chapel but not ready to go out in the cold. She sat on one of the pews the men had pushed against the wall and watched as guests claimed the last of the food and then cleaned up the tables.

Her skin tingled, someone was watching her. She glanced around the room rubbing her arms to dispel the feeling and spotted a cowboy standing in the corner. She'd noticed him earlier and thought he'd seemed familiar but she'd been whisked away by Carol before she could give him much notice. Now that she had a minute to look at him, she was almost certain it was Beau.

He glanced up, his hat revealing the barest shadow of a beard, then the long dark hair and finally those eyes so dark she couldn't name their color, at least until she got a closer look. Heavens, when had she decided to get closer? Her pulse raced as he pushed himself away from the wall, staring straight at her. Thank the Lord she was sitting; her knees wouldn't hold weight. Her hand ached to reach for him as Beau strode up beside her. "Care to join me outside for a little fresh air, Miss Gresham?" He held out his hand.

Her breath caught in her lungs and she couldn't answer. She stood and placed her hand in his, gazing up into his face, memorizing every handsome angle in case he disappeared again. His hair had grown even longer since she'd seen him last, and he had it pulled back with a leather tie. Close enough now to see his eyes, she saw they were dark blue inky pools. His hint of dashing beard made Ruby warm right down to her bones.

"I think I could use some fresh air," she squeaked.

He placed her hand on his arm and directed her toward the door. Reaching for her cloak as they strode by, he draped it over her shoulder, his hand lingering for just the briefest moment before he clasped her hand back around his arm to lead her outside.

Her resolve to stay away from men after her disastrous

marriage easily crumbled beneath Beau's unpracticed charm and earthy appeal. All he'd had to do was walk back into her life and here she was, clinging to his arm. He smelled of cloves and wood fires, and she tucked herself into him, dragging his scent into her lungs.

They stopped by the door, let a few people by, and he gazed down into her eyes. Heat flushed her cheeks but she couldn't break free of his stare if she'd wanted to. He led her out into the night as a soft smattering of flakes fell around them, their glittering softness brightened by the moonlight as it dashed through the clouds. Carol and the other skaters were already long gone on their way to the river for the skating part of the Christmas Social, and soon, Ruby and Beau were alone outside the chapel, the other townsfolk drifting away.

Could she trust Beau? She stole a look up into his eyes through the snow on her lashes. His face was mostly hidden in shadow. Though she'd tried avoiding his gaze, she knew he'd been watching her, his eyes never leaving her. No, he definitely couldn't be trusted, but then, neither could she. She'd left her husband to die under a tree.

"Pretty night," she whispered to break the silence.

He led her to a bench behind the church, far from the gas lights of the street. The trees surrounded them and, though they were in the middle of town, the wooded area gave the impression of a glade. He brushed the snow off the bench so she could sit.

"Yup. If you like snow, Montana is the place to see it." He helped her sit then took the seat next to her.

"I'm sure other places have snow. I don't necessarily want to stay here forever, though I don't know how I'd leave." The words wandered out of her and she wished she could pull them back. Where would she go beyond Cutter's Creek?

Beau shifted on the bench. "I guess I always just figured you'd stay here. What with your family living so close and all. Your family *is* close, isn't it?"

What a strange way to ask her that question. "Why yes, in Yellow Medicine, as I said." Her stomach tightened. He was getting far too close to the truth and, though Josiah knew more than anyone else, she wasn't ready to share her past with anyone, not even Beau.

"I think I'd better get back to my room. I shouldn't be out here with you, alone in the dark." Ruby stood, preparing to run for the safety of her rented room ... and the loneliness waiting there for her. She pulled her cloak tighter around her shoulders.

Beau reached out to stop her. "Ruby, stay for a minute. If you don't want to talk about your family, I won't ask. It's been a whole month..." There was a pleading in his voice she didn't understand ... but it was one she recognized.

She wanted to spend time with him, too.

She stopped and turned back to him. "It's a long story, Beau. I told you I was kidnapped, and that's mostly true. But, my family wouldn't want to see me again. So, it does no good to talk about them. I don't belong anywhere. Not Cutter's Creek, not Yellow Medicine."

Beau drew her back down next to him on the seat, her heart racing at the warmth she could feel from him. What if he kissed her? If he did, she'd run. It's what she wanted to do. She couldn't let him get that close, but...

He placed one hand on her back and she flinched, pulling away from the brief contact. He bowed his head for a moment and sucked in a deep breath, then tugged her to standing, taking her hand in his. He walked her a few feet from the bench. Though no music played, he led her in a slow dance.

She hadn't let a man so much as help her across the street, yet Beau held her close in his arms. And ... she had to admit, it was nice. Ruby hesitated only a moment before she raised her hand to his shoulder. It was a broad, strong shoulder. The strength of it evident beneath her fingers even through his thick wool coat.

She'd never danced before, but he led her easily. They didn't speak about family or future; words weren't necessary and neither was music. They danced in the moonlight, to a tune only softly falling snow could play.

They danced like that, beneath the moon and snow, until the

owls hooting above reminded her it was late. Lily might worry if she made it home first.

Beau widened the space between them and gazed down into her face. The flickering torches from the area set up for the skaters by the river a block away cast a faint glow behind him, but Ruby could only make out his glinting eyes and his mouth. His gaze was penetrating, piercing her skin and into her blood. Again, the urge to run shot through her, but a stronger feeling emerged from deep within her, begging her to stay.

Beau took her hand, still gripped in his, and kissed the sensitive skin of her knuckles. The heat of his breath sent a shiver down her body. It was a sensation she'd never felt before.

"I'll see you home." He led her down the path and back to the church, then into the street. Though it was only a short way to her room, she wanted to fill the silence. He'd danced with her; a new and intimate experience, yet they'd hardly shared a word. Though she felt like she knew Beau, she didn't. Not really.

"Are you going to stay? I understand you don't normally, but with the weather … I thought, maybe?" She paused in their walk, hoping to keep him to herself for a few more moments.

"I have to stay. The weather crept up on me, took me by surprise, but also my sister seems to have embroiled herself with the new lawyer she brought with her from Maine. Pa isn't well enough to keep a good eye on her. I hate to be a chaperone, but if anyone needs one, it's May." He drew his arm around Ruby briefly to get them moving again.

"Is that what brought you to the social tonight? Your sister?" They were almost to her door and she wished, just this once, she lived farther away.

"That was *one* of the reasons. I'd been on the lookout for someone and was hoping to see them there."

Ruby stopped at the stairway along the outside of the house, leading up to her apartment. "Did you find them?" She held her breath, strangely hoping he'd been looking for her. His hat hid his features and she wanted to see him, to know what he was think-ing. Without taking the time to consider what she was doing, she reached up and took it off, revealing his face in the soft moonlight.

"Yes, I did." He took the hat from her but didn't put it on. "Did you have a good time?"

He was so confident and quiet, subtle and thoughtful. Everything her husband hadn't been and everything she suddenly wanted.

She stepped close to him and perched on her toes, kissing his rough, stubbly cheek. Because, even though she'd never willingly kissed a man, it seemed like the most natural thing in the world to do. "I did. Good night, Mr. Rockford." She dashed up the stairs, leaving Beau and his lopsided grin behind.

BEAU TOUCHED his cheek and couldn't keep the smile from his face any more than he could keep his blood from pumping. The town around him was cloaked in darkness, not that it mattered. Most everyone was at the river ice skating, including his sister and Mr. Caruso. Mr. Caruso had started coming to dinner every evening, Beau had begun to wonder about the nature of the relationship between May and the lawyer. Now he knew. His sister had as much as told him to leave them be, that she hated society soirees and was happy to have Mr. Caruso's attention without such events.

Yet, she'd gone to the social with him.

Beau slapped his hat back on and slowly walked toward home. He'd used the occasion of the social to watch Ruby in plain sight. He'd always been able to fade into a crowd; it was probably one of his better talents. Ruby had laughed and chatted with Carol all evening, and he hadn't wanted to talk to her while in the presence of that overbearing gossipy child. And Ruby hadn't danced a single dance with anyone at the social, which had made him want to fix that as soon as they were alone. He'd approached her when most of the people had left so they wouldn't be noticed.

Ruby... How well she'd fit in his arms, and when she'd leaned up and kissed his cheek … his heart had beaten so loud in his ears, it was as if he were on another night delivery with Josiah. Still, minutes after Ruby left him, he could feel the whisper softness of her lips on his skin and her warm breath fan over his ear.

Now, he had to decide. Would he stick around and see where things might lead with Ruby, or move on as he always did to avoid the disappointment. Women never wanted to roam like he did and they always misunderstood him. They wanted to have houses and start families. He'd never seen much value in that particular Biblical edict. Multiply. He'd always left that up to his friends. So, which was more important, his freedom to roam the wilds or his heart soaring in his chest?

Then there were the secrets. Ruby was certainly hiding something. Why would a kidnapped woman not be welcomed back into her family? It made no sense. Her family should be worried about her and she should want to go back to them. She couldn't be more than twenty. He'd known women to live at home longer than that, in fact, Lily, the woman Ruby lived with, was twenty-two and had just moved out of her parents' home.

He had to find out more about Ruby without doing anything to hurt her. She didn't want to talk about it. That was plain enough. But if he could get back to Yellow Medicine between snows, he might be able to find someone who knew something of her family. If she was wrong and they wanted to see her, their reunion would make a fine Christmas present.

He strode into his Pa's house and stomped his feet by the door.

"Hey boy, come on over and stoke up the fire a bit. Are you staying for the next few days?" His father held out his hands and rubbed them in front of the glowing fire. He was sitting close to the flames but also covered in a thick wool blanket.

Beau knelt in front of the fireplace and prodded the coals with the metal poker, sending up a flurry of sparks. He put in two more logs and then warmed his hands.

"I think I'll be heading back to Yellow Medicine soon." He didn't bother to turn to Pa, in a few minutes, he wouldn't remember what Beau had said anyway.

"You doing another delivery with Josiah?" Pa's voice cracked.

Beau turned to see his father's eyes clearer than they'd been in a long time. "I haven't worked with Josiah in over a month. He doesn't have much work in the winter, so I'm working whatever jobs are available in Yellow Medicine."

"What's so special there? There are jobs available here, *and* a warm bed for you. You could work with the railroad or at Cahill Lumber. Not to mention you could help me keep an eye on May. I certainly can't. Caruso seems genuine enough, if a little shifty. I don't know that he plans to stay in Cutter's Creek and I don't know for sure what his intentions are with May. She starts working for him soon, once he gets his office set up. I don't like that she'll be there working with him when his apartment's right above the office."

Beau had the very same concern. So, did he stay because his father asked him to, or go to find out more about Ruby? This was why he'd always wanted to get out of town, no responsibilities but those he signed on for.

"You asking me to stay?" He turned back to the fire and used the small bellows to stoke it.

"I'm asking you to find out what Caruso's up to. If nothing, then go on to Yellow Medicine and whatever keeps you there that's more important than family."

Beau let the fire heat his face until it hurt. Pa was always good at using words like a scythe. Heavy, sharp, and capable of slicing to the bone.

CHAPTER 7

"Ruby, I'm surprised you aren't married and having little ones of your own. You're so good with little Malcom. He's really taken with you." Maddie lay draped across her settee with her feet up, the picture of the contented lady of the house.

Ruby felt heat rise to her face. She'd never known how to deal with a compliment. "I don't think there's much to it. I just sit here and play with him. He's an easy baby to get along with."

"On the contrary. Many women would find what you're doing boring or a waste of time. I, however, am so blessed by the time you're able to spend with us. Dr. Pierce tells me I should try to avoid having more children because of the strain it would put on me. Heath is quite disappointed, as he came from a large family, but at least we have a boy to pass on the family name."

Ruby smiled and slowly waved a wooden rattle in front of Malcom. "I came from a big family, too. I have seven sisters. You'd think that'd make me want to have a big family, but I'm satisfied alone." How hollow the words sounded to her ears.

"Only eight of you?" She laughed. "Heath's parents adopted six children, then had six more of their own. Heath was the first son they had together which is, of course, why he's a junior."

Ruby closed her eyes. "And did they have enough to provide for all those little ones? Sometimes I wish I'd never been born so at least my sisters would have had more." A knot formed in her throat. The ache for her sisters was like a hole in her heart.

"Heaths parents didn't spoil their children, but they were provided for, yes. I'm sorry that wasn't the case with you, Ruby. You're already forging a life separate from your parents. You obviously have a calling with children, and you're following the Lord's lead and helping to raise my little Malcom."

Ruby opened her eyes and shook her head. "I don't have a calling. Only special people get a call. Lily just told me you needed help and I needed the work."

"Oh, that isn't true, Ruby. Some people get many calls, not just one. When I was younger, before I married, I was called to write letters of encouragement to people without ever telling them who I was. Later, I'd hear that a mystery note had brightened someone's day."

"So, why does being married stop you from doing it if the Lord said you should?" Ruby flinched at the accusation in her voice. She'd only been curious.

Maddie's face crumpled. "Well, I don't know what my husband would say, and after having Malcom, I just don't have the energy anymore. Maybe those are just excuses. I *should* talk to Heath about it."

Ruby changed Malcom's nappy and laid him down for his nap, signaling the end of her work day. The cook took care of making the meals and a maid cleaned for them. Ruby was no doctor, but she was sure Maddie wasn't sick or frail at all, just bored with everyone doing everything for her. She was neither pale nor wane. She never seemed to flag when she had to get up to do things if no one was around to do them for her.

Ruby tossed her wool coat over her shoulders to head for home. She'd gotten it when she'd lived with Penny's parents. It had been one of Penny's old ones. All of Ruby's *new* clothes were

Penny's cast-offs. She'd never made enough to pay for more than her share of the rent and her portion of food, so new clothes were a luxury she couldn't afford. Penny had never asked for them back, so Ruby continued to use them.

She rushed up the stairs to the small apartment she called home. It only had a pot-bellied stove, which was difficult to cook on. There also wasn't much room to store food with two women living in the small space that was little more than the upstairs bedroom of James Cahill's aunt's house.

The close quarters brought to mind the tiny room she'd shared with her seven sisters. They had played and worked together, gathering food and firewood, cooking, farming, anything to keep Pa happy. When she cared to think about it, she couldn't figure why her father had given her to such a horrible man. She'd done her best her whole life to please him, but he'd never bothered to be pleased with any of them.

That cabin with Arnold outside of Yellow Medicine had been another time when she'd had to suffer through tight living quarters and lack of privacy. He'd had a one room cabin with no neighbors. Nowhere to hide.

The wedding her pa had performed never seemed quite right to her, so she'd never considered it binding. But now she was stuck. She'd given Arnold's name to Josiah when he'd found her by the river a few months back, mainly because she didn't rightly know who she was anymore. Ruby Gresham or Ruby Arnsby – did it really matter? Once Beau found out she'd been married or had been living with a man, he wouldn't want her at all. Men wanted pure women, not whatever it was people would call her. Though she'd never been touched, she certainly wasn't pure.

The room closed in around her; it felt like she could reach out and touch each wall if she spread her arms wide. Oh, to have space! She'd never dreamed of being rich, but to have enough room to breathe, that would make her wealthy. Her father had said she'd have done best as an Indian, in the wide-open spaces. Maybe he was right.

The bell just inside the door rang and she crept to the window to see who'd like to come up. It was usually one of Lily's friends. Beau stood there in the snow. He turned up his collar against the wind and glanced up to her window, kicking the snow off his boots as he waited. She ducked out of view then shook her head at her foolishness. Beau was as good an excuse as any to get some fresh air. She yanked on her coat and dashed through the door and down the stairs.

Beau stared at her, his expression blank but eyes warm with appreciation. "Good afternoon, Ruby. Care to join me at the Silver Dollar for a little supper?" He held out his arm for her.

She clasped it and he covered her hand with his warm one, returning the slight squeeze.

They fell into step together for the short distance to the inn. Ruby glanced over at him, quickly wondering what his intentions were. He led her into the inn dining room, then pulled out a chair from a small table in the corner and sat across from her, his eyes never leaving a table across the room.

"Beau, did you have anything you'd like to talk about?" She moved her head to block his line of sight. It was so strange after such a long absence that he would see her twice in as many days.

Beau laughed. "I'm sorry, Ruby. I'm here watching my sister, but didn't want Mr. Caruso to get suspicious about it. If they come over to the table before they leave, I'll introduce you."

"Oh." Her heart sank. He hadn't really wanted to spend the dinner hour with her as she'd hoped. He was merely using her as a good reason to be there. She was serving as a convenient cover for his spying. "I see."

Beau glanced down at the day's offerings on the small menu card in front of him then up at her, oblivious to her concerns. There was a distance to him that hadn't been there before, a coolness in his look that gave her pause.

"I'll probably be going back to Yellow Medicine in the next few days or so, but I hope to make it back to Cutter's Creek before Christmas. If not, I don't want you worrying about me."

Worry? Why would she worry? Did he think she cared? Did *he* care?

Lord, I can't make hide nor hair out of my feelings for this man...

"I'll try not to worry." She ran her finger down the few options printed on the menu card. The Silver Dollar Inn was usually a little more expensive than she was willing to spend. She frowned at the least expensive option: squirrel. After Arnold's death, she vowed she wouldn't eat it again. It was the easiest thing to get out there by the secluded cabin, so she'd eaten a lot of it in her short life.

Beau pointed at the most expensive offering, a cut of beef served over potatoes with a brown gravy. Just the description made her mouth water. But Beau wasn't courting her, he shouldn't have to spend that much.

Beau pointed to the beef on her card. "I really like this choice. Do you mind if I just order one for each of us? Easier that way."

"Oh, I hadn't thought..." She felt the heat rise up her face. Asking about a man's money was rude, even *she* knew that.

He reached across the table and lay his hand on top of hers. Warmth spread through her at the simple contact. "Don't worry, Ruby. I asked you here with the intention of treating you. I know it isn't a fine restaurant, but it's the best Cutter's Creek has to offer, and I might not see you for a while."

She couldn't quite make herself look away from his eyes. "I suppose a few weeks isn't all that long. I do have my job to keep me busy."

Caroline Tufts strode up to the table and poured them each a cup of coffee, then set the carafe in front of Ruby. "What can I get for you two tonight?" She smiled, planting her hands on her hips, and glanced back and forth between them.

"We'll take two of the beef plates; please and thank you for the coffee." Beau tucked the little menu cards to the side.

"Ah, going to make the lawyer pay for the most expensive dish?" She laughed.

Beau's eyebrows bunched and he glanced over Ruby's shoulder for a moment. "I don't know what you mean." Ruby turned to see the lawyer sitting with May a few tables away. He had slightly fleshy cheeks and an expensive suit. He waved at them and laughed.

"Did you want to add some wine to the bill, too?" Caroline snickered.

Ruby shook her head without thinking. She had no intention of drinking anything stronger than the coffee.

Beau cocked his head, an annoyed yet resigned grimace on his face. "Are you sure, Ruby? If he wants to buy us dinner, we should enjoy it."

"I had a few sips at the social, but I don't usually even do that. You go ahead, if you'd like." She frowned and laid her napkin in her lap, using it as an excuse to avoid meeting his gaze. Oh, how she hated strong drink.

"Ruby, if my having a drink bothers you, I won't."

Caroline shook her head and turned from the table. "Two moo's, coming right up." She hustled away, stopping at a few tables as she went.

Beau tapped the table with his fingertips. "Ruby, can you tell me a bit more about your family? I know you didn't want to talk about them before, but I have a hard time believing they wouldn't want to see you. I searched for any Greshams I could find when I was in Yellow Medicine and I couldn't come up with a one. How long has it been since you've seen them?"

Ruby sighed. She wanted to enjoy her dinner with Beau, not relive those terrible last moments with her family. Her sisters might miss her, but her father surely wouldn't, so why bother searching? But maybe if Beau found them, she could at least *see* her sisters. Seeing them again would be wonderful. That meant there were seven reasons to tell Beau the truth. The Good Book said she should tell the truth anyway, or at least that's what her Ma had said.

"You didn't find any Greshams in Yellow Medicine because there aren't any ... anymore. The man my father forced me to marry, Mr. Arnold Gresham, was the last one."

Beau's eyes widened and he pushed his chair away from the

table. "Marry?" He clenched his fist as he slid it slowly back to him and under the table.

Ruby glanced around at the eyes all around her now staring at them. "He's dead, Beau. I'm a widow ... at least, I think I am."

"Just what's that supposed to mean?" He tensed and sat ram rod straight in his chair, then shook his head, throwing his hands up. "No, no I don't want to know. What was your name before you were *married*?" His voice was low and tinged with wariness.

Ruby hunched her shoulders and dipped her head as she'd done all her life to fade away from the watchful eyes around her. She should've known Beau wouldn't understand. She should've known better than to hope he would care. She wasn't as pure and perfect as the snow outside. "Arnsby," she whispered.

Recognition flashed in his eyes. "I recognize that name. Big family of girls a few miles outside of town."

Ruby nodded. "Yes, eight of us."

Caroline returned with two plates, heaping with food. Then she refilled their mugs with coffee. "Anything else I can get you two love-birds?"

Ruby flinched and Beau frowned, grating a, "No," through clenched teeth.

He folded his hands and prayed for the meal then began to eat in silence. If he didn't want to know about her marriage, what more could she say? Maybe he wouldn't bother coming back to Cutter's Creek? It was probably for the better. She had to take care of Malcom and help Maddie, that job would only get more difficult as he grew and she couldn't do a good job if she was distracted with Beau.

A lovely woman with rich dark hair approached the table with the man who had laughed earlier. "Beau, are you going to introduce us to your companion?"

Beau turned red as a beet and glared up at the woman. "Ruby, this is my sister May and her escort, Mr. Caruso."

May held out her hand and Ruby took it in weak fingers. Ruby glanced at the door but escape was just too far away.

"Ruby, I don't remember you from before I left. Did my

brother finally order a mail-order bride, and how has he kept you secret?" She clapped her hands together. "The ladies' guild at the church will love to hear about this!"

Ruby's stomach settled somewhere down by her feet. The beef no longer seemed appetizing, in fact, her hunger had flown right out the window.

"Excuse me, I think I need to be going. Beau, enjoy your dinner. Have a nice trip…"

Should she express how much she wanted to see him when he returned, when it seemed rather obvious he didn't share such feelings? "Perhaps I'll see you when you return." It wasn't a question. She didn't have the heart to pose it as one. Before he could stand, she jumped to her feet and tossed her coat on, running out the front door.

She gripped her elbows and took deep breaths, desperate to keep the tears at bay. The breathing had always worked in the past, but now, the hot tears fell over her lashes and onto her cheeks, the cold December air biting at her as she rushed to the comfort of her locked room.

BEAU WATCHED HELPLESSLY as Ruby ran from the inn. He couldn't beg her to stay, especially not in front of May. "Why'd you have to scare her away? I'll be leaving soon and I just wanted to have dinner with a friend. Why'd you have to interfere?"

"I could ask you the same question, Beau. There's nothing going on between Mr. Caruso and me, so no reason for you to be here. I'm helping him start his practice, nothing more. He's here on business but may decide to remain here permanently. That's all you need to know."

"What do you mean? He's already set up an office and has an apartment. I thought he was staying." Beau shot the lawyer a glance and the man joined them at Beau's table.

May plopped down in Ruby's vacated seat. "I guess I can tell you, it isn't like you ever talk to anyone anyway."

49

Mr. Caruso threw his hands up and strode away, mumbling about confidentiality.

May rolled her eyes then fixed them on Beau. "Mr. Caruso was the family lawyer of one Calvin Masters. He's a lumber tycoon in Maine. Amazing fellow, or so I've heard, but I've never met the man—you know how I feel about social gatherings." She shook her head and pushed Ruby's plate to the center of the table.

"Anyway. His wife, Mrs. Ivy Masters, disappeared one day. He'd never paid much attention to what his wife had bought or didn't so they never knew if she took anything with her. She may have been kidnapped, but he always suspected she just ran." May leaned in closer and whispered. "Personally, even if I knew my spouse ran, I'd tell everyone it was kidnapping. Wouldn't you?" She leaned back in her seat. "Here is where we get into the juicy gossip. Her family says that Mr. Masters threatened them, that if they were harboring her, he'd ruin them. Problem is, if they were honest, not a one of them saw Ivy. Only one of her distant relatives couldn't be reached for questioning; Mrs. Camden." May sat back with a smug expression.

"*The* Mrs. Camden…as in, *Willow Street* Mrs. Camden?" Beau still couldn't see what this had to do with his sister or Mr. Caruso, but it wasn't like he could chase Ruby into the street. She was long gone.

"Yes! That's why I went with Mr. Caruso to the Christmas social. We had hoped that Ivy, if she's here, would feel safe enough this far away from Mr. Masters to risk showing herself. But it wasn't like we could just saunter up to Mrs. Camden and ask her. We've been keeping an eye on her, though. She'll slip eventually, then we'll know where Ivy is."

"It isn't like women usually run from their husbands. Have you ever thought there might be a reason she left?" He took a bite of his beef, but it was cold and had lost its appeal.

May rolled her eyes again and heaved a heavy sigh. "It isn't like we want to drag her back kicking and screaming, Beau. There is a huge reward for finding her. *Finding*. Not returning. Remember, Mr. Caruso is Mr. Masters attorney, so he knows all the loopholes in Mr. Masters' plan. Plus, what we've planned isn't half as bad as what her *husband* did. Right before we left, Mr. Masters posted a bounty for her return. He had all manner of nasty people coming to see him about it. Between his practice, his classes, and these vagabonds, Mr. Caruso couldn't wait to leave town and check out this lead."

Beau shook his head and dropped his fork, having lost all interest in his expensive meal. "Seems to me, to prove you've seen her, you'd have to put her in danger. Don't seem right, especially for money."

"That's your opinion. I'm of the opinion that she said marriage vows and should be held accountable to them, even if her husband is using horrible methods to find her. Perhaps he loves her so much he's desperate."

"You and I both know some people don't say their vows willingly, and still others say them without knowing what they're getting into. Better to not say them at all."

"I'm sure her family wouldn't have agreed to the marriage if Mr. Masters wasn't a good match. That's none of my business, but the reward most certainly is."

"I think I'm going to ask Caroline if I can take these plates over to Ruby. I can bring them back later. Excuse me." He stood. leaving his sister at the table. Spending time back east had changed her, and maybe not for the better. He frowned, searching the dining room for Caroline. He spotted her at a table by the window overlooking the street.

She smiled up at him as he approached. "Beau, what happened? You were sitting there with that pretty lady then all of a sudden she was just gone."

"Sisters'll do that," he grumbled rubbing the tension from the back of his neck. "Do you have a basket or something I can carry these plates in? I promise I'll bring them back. I just want to make sure Ruby eats something."

"Oh, for you, of course." She bustled back into the kitchen and came back with a large basket. "This was the only one I could find that'd be big enough." She brushed past him and back to the table.

May and Mr. Caruso had left. "I don't know about that sister of yours." Caroline pinned him with a stare.

"Yeah, I don't know about her, either." He shook his head. "Caroline, if you'd been away from your family for a year and a half, would seeing them again be a good Christmas gift?" He'd hoped to find Ruby's family and bring her back a note or something, to let her know they missed her. It might encourage her to go home.

Caroline laughed. "I don't think I could go that long. I have a mighty big family."

"Thank you, Caroline. I'll have this back to you soon." He grabbed the basket and rushed out into the cold.

Ruby had to have gone back to her apartment, there was nowhere else for her to go, unless she'd gone back to work. Though he didn't want to, he'd try her place first. Instead of ringing the bell, he toted the basket up the stairs and rapped lightly on the door to her apartment. He'd never been in there, of course, and he wasn't quite sure where they'd eat, but he still wanted to share a meal with her. He wanted to spend as much time with her as she'd allow before he had to rush out of town.

Lily opened the door a crack and peeked out at him. "Oh, Beau! Goodness, we aren't used to having anyone come all the way up and knock. Come in, it's too cold to stand outside."

Beau ducked into the small room and stood by the door, unsure of what he should do next. Ruby turned away from him and he could see her shoulders quaking.

"Ruby…" he said, taking a step toward her.

Lily directed him over to their small table. "Did you bring a picnic, Beau? Isn't that so sweet? I'll sit over on my side of the room and let you two chat. I won't even listen." She strode over to Ruby and put her hand on Ruby's shoulder, bending her head close to Ruby's. They talked quietly together for a minute. Beau turned to remove the plates from the basket and place them on the table but he couldn't shake the feeling they were talking about him. This wasn't quite what he'd had in mind when he'd thought about inviting her to dinner, but now that he'd talked to May and Mr.

Caruso, he was pretty certain there wasn't anything romantic between his sister and the lawyer, far from it.

Ruby approached the table and her red-rimmed eyes tore at his heart. He took a step closer to her and she backed away, her eyes widening, stopping him where he stood.

"I'm sorry, Ruby. My sister ... well, I just wanted to spend a few minutes with you before I left town again." He pulled out her chair.

Ruby considered him stiffly, then she sat, rigid, and allowed him to push her chair in. She studied her plate, but didn't move to pick up her fork.

"Is there anything I can say or do to make you smile?" How hard did a man have to work for one smile?

Ruby sat up straight and avoided his eyes. "I'm surprised you came back. You seemed to want to run from the table as soon as you heard the word 'married'. I just saved you the trouble. If you'd bothered to listen to me, you'd have heard —"

He held up his hand. He didn't want to hear any more about her marriage. It tore him up inside to know that she wasn't who she'd said she was. "It was just a shock, is all. I guess, well, it doesn't matter now." He pushed his food around. So much for eating.

"I think you should finish your meal and then go. I hope you find what you're searching for in Yellow Medicine, because you'll not find it here." The biggest tear he'd ever seen trickled down her cheek. He tossed his napkin down on top of his plate and scraped his chair on the floor as he shoved it back.

Beau stood in front of her as her shoulders quaked, and a need rose up in him that he'd never experienced before. He took her elbow and guided her to her feet, wrapping her in his arms before he could convince himself not to. Her head fit perfectly in the crook of his neck.

"Whoever he is. He's a lucky man." Beau turned from her, grabbed his hat and left before he could make a bigger fool of himself.

CHAPTER 8

Ruby hugged herself to retain some of the heat Beau had
willingly given, then all to quickly took away. Arnold
was dead; of that she was certain. She'd pushed his
body, frozen like a moonshine icicle, over the edge of the ravine
because she couldn't dig a hole. As for him being lucky? It had
been torture living with Arnold Gresham. She'd been ready to tell
Beau the truth back at the inn and now here, but he hadn't wanted
to hear it.

Ruby turned to face Lily. "If you're still hungry there's no sense
in this food going to waste. I don't want it."

Lily stood from where she'd been reclining on her bed. "Why
don't you tell me what's *eating at you*. I've never seen Beau intentionally talk to a woman … not ever in all the years I've known
him. And an *embrace*? That tells me he considers you pretty special.
He is a wonderful guy and I've prayed he'd find someone like you.
Why're you fighting him, don't you find him attractive?"

Ruby flopped back into her chair and buried her head in her
arms along the backrest. It was a poor attempt at hiding the heat
crawling up her neck. "Of course I think he's handsome, who
wouldn't? But it doesn't matter what I think. He doesn't want me

because of Arnold. Maybe neither of us talk enough for our own good. I just don't understand him."

Lily sat in the chair Beau had vacated. "It just seems to me both of you are longing to be with someone, and just maybe that someone could be each other. Especially now that Carol Williams is quite wrapped up with some new tall, dark Texan. I saw her staring at him at the social. She used to only have eyes for Beau."

Ruby shook the image of Carol chasing after Beau out of her mind. "I asked her about that man at the social. Now that you mention it, she didn't even look for Beau, even though I'd heard a rumor he was home and asked her about it. She changed the subject. I guess I'm glad of that."

"Why? If you don't want him, shouldn't Carol be able to chase after him if she wants?" Lily's eyebrow rose.

"If Carol has her eye on this other man, Beau shouldn't matter." Ruby clacked her jaw shut. She couldn't explain why she wanted Carol as far away from Beau as possible any more than she could explain what had happened between them at dinner an hour before. She only knew her heart wasn't having any of it.

"Beau mentioned he wanted to spend a few minutes with you before he left. Is he leaving again?" Lily said.

Ruby nodded, desperate to keep her hands from shaking. "He said he'd try to make it back before Christmas." Ruby stood and then threw herself onto her bed.

"Perhaps you should think of something you can give him for Christmas so that he never wants to leave again?"

Ruby pushed herself up on her arms and glared over her shoulder at Lily. "You have no idea. There's no way I can give him what he wants. I'd love to go back to before all this began and run away instead of living a day of what I did. I did everything I could to keep *that man* from ever touching me, but what does it matter? I lived with him so it's just as bad as if I'd given myself to him." She lay down on her back and covered her face with her arm. If Beau would only listen, if he hadn't been so angry, but he was and now he was leaving.

"I think you ought to talk to Reverend Bligh and see what he tells you. Even a leper could be made clean, Ruby." Lily placed the plates, still loaded, back into the basket and swung into her coat. "I'll be back after a while. I think you could use some peace." She strode out of the room, quietly closing the door behind her.

As much as Ruby wanted to talk to Reverend Bligh, she couldn't do it today. Just having Beau show up and ask her to dinner had set her spirit soaring. Then the realization that, as much as he'd asked about the truth, he didn't really *want* the truth, had crushed her. All she wanted now was to forget Beau Rockford.

~

BEAU STOMPED into the house and slammed the door. May came rushing to the front then stopped when she saw him.

"What's got your dander up?" She frowned. "You'll take the whole house down with all your ruckus."

"Maybe I'll just take my ruckus and go." He smashed his hat back on his head.

"Brother, will you just sit down," she huffed.

Beau dragged himself to the kitchen table and allowed May to plop him into a seat. She ducked into an apron and fixed him a cup of coffee.

"So, you have my attention." She set down his cup and put her hands on her hips. "I'm making soup for Pa, it's his favorite and he's in a snit because I told him what I told you about Mr. Caruso. He chooses to believe otherwise."

"You'll have to convince him. I'm not going to be around. I need out of this town. Everything is closing in around me. Getting to where a man can't breathe."

Her face softened and she clicked her tongue. "Oh, Beau, there's plenty of room. The air isn't your problem and you know it. Spit it out, you need to talk to someone."

He glared at her. "She's married. That's what's the matter."

"Who, Ruby?" May sat down and leaned her elbow on the table, propping her head in her hand.

"Of course, Ruby. Who else?" He snarled at her. Women and their infernal talking.

"She doesn't act like a married woman. You said she's been living here since Josiah and Penny were married, that's over two months."

"That's what confuses me, she said 'he's dead ... I think'." He scraped his eye lids with his hands. "I don't even know what that means. Does she think he's dead? How does she not know if her husband is alive or not?"

"Sounds to me like you heard wrong, brother." She narrowed her eyes at him.

"I most certainly did not. That's what she said. I was so confused; I didn't want to hear anymore. It's bad enough that I was starting to enjoy the company of a married woman, but then to think she's just living here without knowing..." He shook his head. "I don't even want to think about it. I'm going to go hunt for her family. She finally told me her family name and I'm pretty sure I met them last time I worked in Yellow Medicine."

"What do you aim to do and why do you care anymore?" She got up from her seat and stirred the soup, avoiding his glare.

"I aim to take her home for Christmas. Her family should miss her. She can go back and live with them."

"Wouldn't that work out just perfectly for you?" she snipped. "You're not fooling anyone, Beau. You want her far away because you're flustered and confused. That's what you always do. Instead of just asking her to explain herself, you got rattled and left. Women don't like that. It isn't that we don't understand you, Beau, it's that *some* of us need to talk—not to just fill the air with noise, but to know what's happening in someone else's head. No one knows Ruby's mind better than she does, excepting the Lord, of course."

"Well, maybe I don't want to share my life with someone who jabbers at me all the time." He leaned back in his seat, knowing that would get to her for a change.

May threw her head back and laughed. "You? You want to get married, just like every other man does. It's only right. In fact, you're supposed to. Paul said it's better to get married than be wanting. It'll lead to sin."

"She kicked me out of her apartment, May. She doesn't want me around. For someone who's supposed to like to talk, she sure didn't want to."

May threw her hands in the air. "If you acted anything with her like you just did with me, I don't blame her. Stomping, pouting, yelling, those won't endear you to anyone, Beau."

"She's *married*, May." He laid his head in his hands, unable to shake that fact from his brain.

May sat next to him and laid her hand on his shoulder. "Did it ever occur to you that I work with a lawyer who can easily check the public record and find out about Ruby and her husband? If she's married, all the paperwork will be on file. It might take some poking around to find out where she was married, but once we have that, then you'll know. Since just asking seems like such a chore to you."

"Fine, you do that. But don't you dare let Ruby know you're sticking your nose into her business. I don't need her even angrier with me."

"I work with a lawyer; confidentiality is my middle name."

"That is exactly why I'm worried."

CHAPTER 9

The bitter cold numbed her toes through her boots and wool stockings as Ruby rushed to the Moore house. She was late for work and Maddie would need her more than ever today. Ruby had grown terribly attached to little Malcom and loved sitting on the floor with him and just playing the afternoon away. She'd never been allowed such a luxury growing up. The problem was, the longer she played with little Malcom, the more she ached for a child of her own.

Ruby entered the house and went to the sitting room straight away. "Ruby, I was getting worried. Come on in and have a seat by the fire." Maddie reclined on a settee and watched longingly as Malcom played on the rug near the raised hearth.

"Tell me, Ruby. What are your plans for Christmas day?"

"I'll be here. I have no plans for the holiday, so it's no bother spending the day here." Ruby hung up her coat and muffler then knelt on the floor with Malcom.

"Come now, you must have somewhere to go. Celebrating Christ's birth should be done with family. At the very least, you should go to the chapel and enjoy the candle light service and listen to the readings all day."

"I'm sure I'll find something, if I'm not here. I don't have any family. Lily doesn't either, but I think she's spending the day with James and his."

"I'd ask you to come here as a guest, but most of Heath's family will be here and the house will be full to bursting. All of Malcom's aunts and uncles will want to hold him so you wouldn't have anything to keep you busy and probably wouldn't know anyone anyway."

Ruby nodded. "What do you need me to do today?" She tickled Malcom behind his chubby knee. Listening to him squeal and squirm in delight filled her with a warmth she cherished.

"I have a few presents yet to wrap and put in the tree, the bread pudding needs to get soaking... I have *such* a list. Perhaps you could help me when Malcom goes down for his nap, I'd surely like appreciate it. The cook is doing most of the work, but Heath has said I can do a bit."

Ruby wouldn't let herself get too close to Maddie, she felt like a governess, just part of the hired help. Spending time with the dear woman away from the safety of Malcom's nursery made Ruby wary.

"If you're sure you'll need me, I can try. I don't know how to wrap anything." She wrung her hands.

"Oh, it's quite easy once you learn how. You don't have to fret, Ruby. I know you try hard when you're here and I think you do a wonderful job with my son. We think the world of you."

If only the one she wanted to think highly of her, actually did...

An unfamiliar woman's voice in the back of the house drew Ruby and Maddie to the kitchen. A young woman stood just inside the door, talking with the cook, Chef Chen. She was wrapped in a long cloak that covered her completely. Maddie stepped forward and invited her in.

"I'm sorry to bother you. I'm making dinner and I'm short on flour." The woman stated from the depths of her deep hood.

Ruby cocked her head. Though she was newer to Cutter's Creek than most anyone, she'd never seen this woman before.

Even the servants at the two wealthiest houses came to the mercantile or walked about town.

Ruby stepped forward and peered under the hood of the cape. "I'm Ruby Gresham, don't think I've had the pleasure of meeting you."

The woman pulled her hood back from her face and her glance darted from Ruby to Maddie. "I..." She stopped, then clutched Ruby's hand. "Ivy, I'm Ivy Masters, pleased to meet you."

BEAU HUNCHED over in the cold, flipping his collar against the biting chill. At least most of the ride to Yellow Medicine was through the cover of trees. They'd shelter him from the wind. His horse wouldn't appreciate the work, but they could make it the whole way in one day if he left now. He tossed the wool saddle blanket on Rex and cinched the saddle tight, waited for Rex to breathe, then finished the job.

Rex blew and shied as Beau rode him out into the cold. He patted the horse's neck and glanced back into town one last time. When he got back, he'd be ready to ask Ruby about her marriage and what it meant. From the house, his sister waved from the window, then ran out to him in the cold.

"Beau! Beau!" She waved. "Wait. I talked to Caruso and he had an idea. While you're in Yellow Medicine, ask around about her husband. You're a tracker, go find him. If you find him or his grave, there'll be no need to go hunting for her paperwork."

Beau scowled. Meeting Ruby's husband was the last thing he wanted to do.

May shivered. "Don't give me that look. If he's dead as Ruby thought he might be, you could let her know for sure. She may be worried sick about the man."

"Right." The horse danced to the side, feeling the tension run through his rider. Beau patted Rex's neck again and forced himself to relax.

"I'll find him. Let's hope Ruby was right," he grumbled, then immediately regretted it.

May laughed. "Remind me never to wish your kind of charity on anyone." She dashed back into the house.

May was right, as usual. He had no right to wish the man dead, just because he wanted to get to know Ruby more. If she'd married Mr. Gresham, he couldn't have been that bad. Beau shoved his hat lower over his ears and hunched his back against the wind, directing Rex into the forest headed for Yellow Medicine. He had to learn more about Ruby's past, but leaving Cutter's Creek without talking to Ruby and patching things between them felt like the worst mistake of his life. He'd never both wanted to go, and hated to go, so much all at once.

His sister's relationship with Mr. Caruso had held him up in town and now he only had a few days before Christmas to learn what he wanted to. There wouldn't be much time to find work and make a little money.

The one good thing about the long ride in the cold was that it gave him time to sort out his thoughts and feelings about Ruby. He loved her quiet presence and how her smile lifted some of the weight off his shoulders. He pulled the reins to halt Rex and sat still for a moment. He couldn't believe he'd actually thought *those* words...

He loved her...

His own mother had felt just like Ruby about strong drink and had always quoted Titus; *"...teach the older women to be reverent in the way they live, not to be slanderers or addicted to much wine, but to teach what is good."* While Ruby wasn't old, in the short time they'd known each other, she'd taught him much about himself. Ruby was a good woman, and if anyone could handle the life he'd set out to live, it was her. She'd already lived on her own for months. But that was putting the cart a mile before the horse, he'd have to find out about her past first.

The Yellow Medicine livery was right on the edge of town. He had to get Rex inside with some oats, a good rub down, and then a blanket. Best take care of that quickly so he could then warm *himself* up. Hopefully the inn wouldn't be too full. Once Rex was bedded down, Beau paid for his keeping for the next few days and strode over to the inn. The main room was fairly empty; a good sign.

Beau rang the bell at the front desk. A man in a black suit and a white preachers collar wandered in from the lobby while he waited.

"What are you doing traveling about in this weather, son?" He held his hand out. "They call me Parson Level."

Beau smiled and gripped the man's hand. "Beau. I'm on the hunt for a family. Got a girl who went missing a while back and I want to reunite them."

"Wish I could help. I'm just passing through. I travel to little towns all over that don't have a preacher and teach as I can."

"Ah, a circuit preacher. How far d'you go?" Beau rubbed at the stabbing throb in his fingers as the warm blood mingled with the cold in his veins.

"This is about as far west as I go. I head east to Deadwood, then south to Abilene and back around again."

"That's a lot of miles. Deadwood you say? I've always wondered about Dakota."

"It's beautiful. Rolling hills like here, but covered in pine, spruce, and birch trees. Right now, it's a lot of miners and mining towns. Deadwood is an interesting place. In most other towns, you have a bad side of town where the saloons and," he frowned, "*houses of ill repute* are. But, Deadwood is mixed; a respectable business will be on the main level and you never quite know what's going on upstairs. I'm needed more there, but there's only one of me and all the little towns expect me back."

"Sounds like an exciting place. Is there only work in the mines there?"

Level laughed. "Don't know. I don't go there searching for work." He patted Beau on the shoulder and walked away just as the inn keeper strode up front.

Beau watched the preacher leave. Deadwood could make a new start for him. A fresh place to stretch his legs.

"Sorry to make you wait." The front desk man turned his book toward Beau to have him sign in.

Beau paid for a few days and went to his room to warm up and make a plan. He'd met the Arnsbys outside of town when he'd been asking around before. That'd be his first stop. They'd hopefully tell him more about Ruby and what had happened to her. After that, he should know enough to be able to find Mr. Gresham. May he, with a bit of luck, rest in peace.

Beau sat in front of the fireplace in his room and let the heat pour out over him. The ride had taken longer than he'd wanted, with drifts of snow along the stage line. It wouldn't be any better in a week when he went back. He certainly didn't want to think about bringing Ruby right back on that trail all the way here, but if her family wanted her, she should go. His gut clenched and he shook his head at his selfishness. She wouldn't be *too* far away in Yellow Medicine, but Cutter's Creek had always been where he'd gone when he wanted to go home. Ruby leaving didn't sit well.

He went down to the saloon attached to the inn and watched some men play a few hands as he ate dinner. He had to be careful where he sat. Some men didn't take kindly to other men watching too closely. They'd probably think he was helping one of the other men cheat. The preacher wandered in and sat down on the other side of the small table.

"You sounded awful interested in Deadwood earlier. I'll be heading out that way again in the spring. Got to hole up here over the colder months because of my rheumatism."

Beau nodded. "I might just take you up on that. If the timing is right, I might be thinking of making a new place home, at least for a while."

"I'll be staying at the inn until April, then I'll light out. If you're here when I leave, you can follow me. I don't usually travel slow, but if you have a heavy wagon, we'll make it work."

"I'm much obliged, sir." Beau massaged the bridge of his nose. Maybe the old preacher could help him figure out what Ruby meant. It was possible May had been right and Ruby wasn't married, though it made not a whit of sense. "I've a question for you. How do you know for sure if a marriage is legal?"

The preacher scratched his jaw. "Now that's a question." He leaned forward and wove his hands together on the table. "We live under both the laws of God and the laws of man. Under man's laws, a man and woman stand before someone who has taken an oath. They sign a contract and that contract is recorded, then they're married. Under God's law, you're married when you consummate a union, which is why a marriage can be annulled if it can be proven there was never a marriage bed. Though, that's a pretty shaky determination. We don't do such things anymore; we must take people at their word." The preacher eyed him. "You got marriage on the mind? That trip won't be easy for a bride."

"I don't know. I've never wanted to get married. My lady friend, Ruby, she didn't seem to know if her husband was dead, but now I'm wondering if maybe she's unsure she's married at all. It'd make more sense. That's why I asked."

"Are you sure you aren't just hopeful she isn't? Are you looking for a loophole, or permission?"

"Truth. That's what I want." That and understanding…why did all this matter to him? He'd been fine on his own, so why did Ruby make him want things he'd never thought of having. A home, a wife, children…

"Well, in that case, I pray you'll find it." He stood and left the table. The men were still playing cards at the next table over. One player showed a full house. Was that a sign? Maybe he could hope.

CHAPTER 10

Maddie stepped in front of Ruby and pulled Ivy into the house, closing the door. "Land sakes, it's winter out there!" She held out her hand. "I'm Maddie Moore and you're welcome here anytime you need anything. Where're you from?" Maddie turned and whispered something to Chef Chen, then turned back to Ivy.

"I came in on the train during the blizzard and I'm working…" her glance shifted all over the room and if it was possible, she grew even more pale.

Ruby put her arm around Ivy and pulled her in closer to the stove. "You don't have to say a thing."

Chef Chen handed Ivy a tin cup full of flour.

"Oh, thank you. I know I won't need more than this and I'll return with a full cup soon." She grabbed the cup and rushed back out into the cold.

Ruby stared at the door. After a long moment, she finally realized Maddie was speaking to her.

"…so odd. We don't normally get strangers in Cutter's Creek. Don't you think it's strange, Ruby?"

Ruby shrugged then flinched at the unladylike response. "Why, no. Just a few months ago, I was new to Cutter's Creek and it was a mostly welcoming place."

"You've been here so much that I'd forgotten you haven't always been here. Why, you don't even sound the way you did when you started working here." Maddie smiled at Ruby, and Ruby felt a warmth spread through her. It was strange…feeling at home somewhere that wasn't actually hers to call home.

"I've been reading a lot of Lily's books, and working with you has helped me talk like other folks. I don't want to teach Malcom to talk like I used to."

Maddie nodded. "He spends so much time with you, that's a good idea. If I'm not careful, he'll call you mama first." She laughed humorlessly.

Ruby laid her hand on Maddie's arm. "Maddie, you don't really need me. Why don't you play with him and teach him?" As much as she wanted the job with Maddie, if her being there hurt Maddie or Malcom, she'd leave.

"I can't do it on my own because the doctor said I mustn't, so Heath required I hire someone to do the job. Though it's one I wanted more than anything in the world." Maddie turned away and her voice softened to a whisper. "If it weren't you raising my son, it'd be someone else. At least I can get along with you, Ruby." Her shoulders fell and she left the room.

Ruby didn't know what to say to her. Maddie's pain made her uncomfortable, she'd rather not see it at all. She followed Maddie to her settee. "I'll go back in with Malcom, he should be up any minute." She turned to leave Maddie to herself.

"You don't have to leave, Ruby. I'm sorry. It's just…when I married, this wasn't what I pictured at all. I had visions of meeting Heath at the door with his favorite meal. Playing with our children in the wildflowers at the edge of town, like I used to do as a girl." She shook her head. "Heath makes a good living, but not near enough to afford what he feels he must to support me. I've become a burden to the family."

Maddie dabbed at her nose. "Malcom won't be awake for another half hour yet. Why don't you help me prepare these pine cones for the fire so we can have the wonderful smell and pop during our Christmas get-together. *This* my husband will let me do, but I don't want to do it alone."

Ruby glanced at the door, wishing Maddie would let her go, but then sat down in the seat Maddie indicated. "Your husband does all of this because he loves you."

"Oh, I know. I just wish there was another opinion. Everyone has trusted Dr. Peirce for so long, but I feel like I could do so much more than I do. It's so very frustrating."

"Could you take up something to keep you busy, that maybe wouldn't be too taxing?" Ruby sprinkled cinnamon on the pine cone she held, the sap stuck to her fingers as she turned it.

"I asked Heath if I could write letters as I used to and he didn't even want me to do that. What is less strenuous than writing letters?" She sighed. "You see? It's hopeless."

Ruby set down the cone and regarded the woman who she was beginning to think of as her friend. "I think you should talk to him, and I'm not much for talking, but there are times that words need to be said. If you grow weak, then you could stop."

Maddie shook her head. "I don't want to push him. He's already taken the time to talk to me about writing the letters. I don't want to make him cross with me by bringing it up again." She sprinkled clove on her own pine cone, the warm scent mingled with the pine, filling the room.

"Perhaps we should pray for a new doctor in Cutter's Creek, with a new opinion." Ruby smiled. "In fact, I think that prayer might be answered already. There's a doctor from Boston in Cutter's Creek right now. Carol told me he came to help her father. Perhaps he'd be willing to give you an examination?"

"Do you think he would?" Maddie's chin lifted ever so slightly and she squared her shoulders just a bit.

"I don't see why he wouldn't. They only live a few houses away. After Christmas, we should go down to the Williams's and ask the doctor if he'd be willing to take a look at you. That's the only way you'll ever find out. Though, I hate to start a disagreement between him and Dr. Peirce."

Maddie frowned and tilted her head thoughtfully. "I suppose that'll have to be considered, but it gives me hope. If I want to find out if I'm as fragile as they say, I need to ask."

~

BEAU DIRECTED Rex along the worn trail to the small house about two miles out of town. Who could forget a house that small, where, a month back, a seemingly endless flow of girls had come out the door upon his arrival. Now, that he thought back on it, the older girls had been mighty frightened by his visit. He hadn't taken the time to consider why before.

This time around, Mr. Arnsby sat on the front stoop smoking a pipe. It was far too cold for anyone to be out. If Beau wasn't there on a personal mission, he'd be in his warm room at the inn.

"What can I do for ya? I ain't got anything made up right now. I'll have to get your name and you'll have to wait. Bad crop this year." Mr. Arnsby remained in his seat.

"Mr. Arnsby. I don't know if you remember, but I came to call about a month ago. I was asking about a Ruby Gresham. You told me then that you hadn't heard of her."

Mr. Arnsby pulled his pipe from his mouth and leaned forward, his head hung low between his shoulders. "I don't remember you."

"I think you do. I think you know Ruby Gresham pretty well, or at least you did."

Mr. Arnsby shoved the pipe in his mouth and shook his head. "How's my girl?" he whispered.

Beau dismounted and fought the urge to yank the man out of his seat. He had to keep calm, give the man a chance to speak, or he might never learn about this Arnold Gresham and where he might be.

"Do you care? You didn't when I was here before. If you had, she could've been back with you by now."

The man's head swung up. "You challenging me, boy?"

Beau planted his feet and gave the man a hard glare. "I guess I am. You lied to me, and Ruby told me she was kidnapped. If

69

you cared, you would've asked about her when I was here before."

"You don't know anything. I got *eight* girls. Not one boy. Eight mouths to feed and no one to pass on my name. When Ruby's time came, someone made an offer and I took it. It wasn't like we could be too picky, and he promised to take care of her. He ain't come back here in quite some time, though."

"Ruby thinks he might be dead. Where are the marriage papers filed?" He couldn't stay here much longer or he'd do something he'd regret. While his own Pa had steadily gone more forgetful in the last few years, Beau had always known his Pa cared.

"Arnold Gresham? Dead? Nothing could kill that coot 'less she kilt him."

A new, unwelcome sensation crept up his spine. Beau rested his hand on his hip. "Where'd he live and where are the papers filed?" Rex pawed the ground, he heard the tension in Beau's voice.

"I don't know what you're talking about, papers. Gresham lived down by the river, east of here in a shack by Snake Rock."

"I was told that in order for a marriage to be legal, you had to file papers. If she was married, where are Ruby's marriage papers filed?" He raised his voice and a blond head appeared in one of the front windows.

Mr. Arnsby frowned. "Ain't no papers. Never was. I said the vows. Gresham wouldn't have agreed if we'd a had the law out here to do it. It was just as legal as me 'n the missus."

Ruby wasn't legally married…and she'd been shoved into a life with—from what he'd gathered on his last trip—an old, mean drunk. Disgusted by the man reclining on the stoop, Beau slipped his foot into the stirrup and pushed himself up. He glared back at Mr. Arnsby from his saddle.

"You want to see your daughter? Think she'd want to see you?" Why did he even ask? As far as he was concerned, the careless, heartless father didn't deserve to see Ruby again.

"Why, you want to get rid of her, too?"

"No, I just thought since she was your daughter, you might want to see her and make sure she was well. I can see you don't."

Arnsby laughed. "I just want 'em out of my hair. You lookin' to marry? I got one that's ready and no one to claim her yet; name's Jennie. Bit feisty, though." Mr. Arnsby wiped the spittle from his chin with the back of his hand.

Beau's stomach clenched and he couldn't quite bring himself to call the man sir. "No, I'm not." Beau turned his horse and headed toward Snake Rock. No way would he ever tell Ruby about his trip out to see her father. She didn't need to relive what that man put her through…what he allowed to happen to his own flesh and blood. He couldn't imagine the horror of being sold like cattle. Now, there was an even bigger problem.

How could he go about telling Ruby that he knew the truth? How could he convince her he still wanted to court her, and more than that, wanted to help her and her sisters out of their predicament? He'd have to tell her he'd visited her father. He wanted to swear, instead he cast his eyes to the sky, saying a prayer for peace. There had to be a way around the situation, otherwise he'd have to tell her.

Beau followed the trail to the east then veered along the river. He took the path and followed it, finally reaching an old hovel just as the sun set. Inside, he found a dusty and abandoned room. It hadn't seen people in quite some time. He returned outside and led Rex into a small lean-to, giving him some grain he'd stored in the saddle bag before they'd left. Then he took his own rations into the house to start a fire.

The hut wasn't air tight and the wind from the hills blew in under the door and banged at the windows. The fire in the hearth danced with the drafts, but if he sat close enough, he was almost warm. There was one bed along the wall and it was nothing more than a pallet of old pelts, and the smell was *ferocious*. A small table sat along another wall with two chairs, and alongside the hearth hung the cooking equipment.

Too wound up to sit still, he stood and took in the room. Something behind the stew pot caught his eye. He walked toward it. It was a small white corner of paper sticking out from the Dutch oven. He lifted the Dutch oven from its hanger and removed the lid. Inside was a hand drawn sketch of eight girls. On the bottom in small print was the name Ruby Arnsby, then she'd crossed out the last name and wrote in *Gresham* in stilted ugly letters. It couldn't have been her handwriting.

He studied the picture and each solemn face. Ruby had missed her sisters enough to draw them, but why did she leave the picture behind? Had she run from this place, from Arnold? Beau saw no sign of Ruby ever living there. No dresses hung from the hooks, in fact, there was only one hook by the bed. The house wasn't equipped for two occupants, with the exception of the table.

He glanced over at the pallet and shuddered. It wasn't big enough for two, but there wasn't anywhere else to sleep. Could he face Ruby knowing what she must've gone through in that tiny, filthy cabin? She'd be doubly crushed to know that she'd been forced to live with Gresham out of wedlock, that she'd never been married by law. He refused to let his gaze fall on the pallet again, instead curling up on the floor in front of the fire and praying his mind would quiet enough for him to sleep.

CHAPTER 11

The next morning, Beau did a thorough search of the cabin, but apart from the pallet of pelts, came up with very little of use other than a growing sick pang somewhere deep inside him. The man Ruby had thought she'd been married to must have been a drunk, as glass bottles and ceramic jugs littered the area all around the small cabin. But for all his searching, he couldn't find any sign that a man had been in that cabin in a long time. Every bottle outside the shack was weathered, the hay in the lean-to was gray with age. Either Gresham had moved on, or Ruby was right and he was dead. Either way, the man had no legal hold on her. That was the only piece of information he'd learned that he could take with him.

From the cabin, he was much closer to Cutter's Creek than he'd be if he went back to Yellow Medicine, so he directed Rex toward home. Toward Ruby. He only had today and tomorrow before Christmas and he had to make things right with her by then. The trail was more out in the open, so colder, but not as windy as it had been, so Rex ate the miles quickly. After a few hours, Cutter's Creek came to view. Ruby would be at work at the Moore's so he'd go home and check on his Pa and May first. He didn't want to say the wrong thing, so he'd consider his words carefully before seeking Ruby out.

Rex was happy to see his warm stall and Beau had no trouble getting him bedded down. He draped a thick wool blanket over Rex then left the lean-to to go inside where he could rest a bit.

May met him at the door, concern worrying her brow.

Beau continued in, knowing his time of rest stopped at the threshold. "May, you've got something on your mind. Out with it." He pulled his cup off the hook on the wall and poured himself some hot coffee.

"Mr. Caruso received a telegram from the Masters family."

"Ah, more on the elusive Ivy?" He raised a brow, lifted the cup to his lips and let the steam warm his face. He had enough to worry about. May's moneymaking scheme to find Ivy Masters was the last thing on his mind.

"The elusive Ivy is free, and quite well-to-do by Mr. Caruso's account. Problem is, no one's been able to find her. We're almost certain she doesn't live with her aunt, though her housekeeper is tight-lipped, so it's possible... There's no place a socialite could hide in Cutter's Creek. It's quite baffling. She should stick out like green leaves in February."

"What do you mean, she's free, and where does that leave you and Caruso and your scheme to get rich?" He inspected her over the rim of his cup.

May huffed. "It wasn't a scheme. They were offering money and I intended to provide what they were asking...in a manner of speaking. But, it doesn't matter now. Mr. Masters put an advertisement in the paper searching for his wife, offering a sizable reward. The authorities are not sure if it was the ad for a bounty on her that led to his death or if it was just some of the shady men he commonly associated with."

Beau frowned and sighed. He'd had about enough of shady men. "Sounds like just the kind of husband you should send a woman back to," he said, sarcasm dripping from his words. "I sure hope you make a good, Godly match May. I hope you never feel like you have no way out but to run off and hide."

May rolled her eyes and sat across from him. "Heaven knows, no man could keep up with me. I'll just stay here and help Mr. Caruso. I have a good job. I don't need a husband."

"Speaking of Caruso, why aren't you working?"

May took in a deep breath and let it out slowly. "He's deciding whether Cutter's Creek is a good place for him. It's a little small for his taste and now that there's no reward for information on Ivy… In fact, the family wishes she'd just stay gone. Mr. Caruso isn't sure if he'd ever do enough business here for a permanent move to be worth it."

"So if he goes back, what will you do?" Beau set his cup down. He'd planned on her being here. He couldn't consider moving to Deadwood if she was going to leave. There'd be no one to look after Pa.

"I have nowhere to go back east, Beau. As much as I love it there, a woman alone can't rent an apartment or buy a house, at least not easily. I can't stay with Aunt Cici anymore…"

"And if Caruso would offer you marriage, would you go with him?"

May narrowed her eyes at him. "Why do you keep insisting there's something between us? I have to admit, I'll be sad if he leaves, especially because I'll have no income, but I won't be heartsick."

"If you change your mind, you need to let me know. A place in Dakota is calling my name."

"Dakota? What in the world can you find there that isn't here? There's even less people there."

"That's exactly the draw. Less people to expect anything out of you."

He held tight to his cup and kept his voice steady. The less May knew how angry he was over Ruby's cabin, the better. "I found out Ruby's marriage wasn't legal. They didn't say vows in front of a preacher or sign anything."

May drummed her fingers against her chin. "I don't know the law here in Montana, but in some states, if a couple remains together for a while, they are common law married. But I don't think Ruby's old enough to have been with anyone that long."

"I also found out she has seven sisters, and her Pa is trying to get rid of them however he can. But most likely the same way he got rid of Ruby."

"Marry them off? That's barbaric, but what could *you* do? There aren't enough jobs or places for them in Cutter's Creek… and not many husbands either, truth be told."

"I thought about trying to find seven men who'd marry them, but I'm not even sure all of them are marrying age yet."

May shook her head. "That's quite the problem. There are plenty of men in need of wives, just not here. In the East, they have agencies that match up marriageable women with men in search of wives. But it doesn't make much sense to send them east to an agency, just so they can come back west." She resumed her tapping against her lips, the gears turning in her head.

"I can't tell Ruby that I know. If she finds out I confronted her father and he didn't care about her… Well, I just don't know how she'd take it. Maybe she already knows he's a scoundrel, maybe not."

May frowned. "I know how I'd take it. But how are you going to help those girls without telling her? Especially if they aren't marrying age? Ruby might be about twenty, though if she's lived a hard life, she may look older than she really is. If she's the oldest, her siblings could be quite young yet. Do you want the responsibility of taking care of a gaggle of young girls?" Her eyes widened.

"No, I surely don't. I don't even know that I want to have responsibility for the one yet, much less the other seven. I just know it ain't right."

Beau pulled the picture he'd found in the Dutch oven from his vest and laid it out on the table. "I can tell her I found this in her old shack and her husband was nowhere to be found. The place hadn't been used for a long time. I'll ask her to tell me about them.

With any kind of luck, she'll ask for my help. She might even have an idea how to help her sisters, since she knows how her father thinks. I don't know where they'll stay, though...there ain't room at Ruby's apartment and they can't stay here..."

"It's a good start of a plan. And Beau...?" May looked at him, her bright eyes sparkling.

"Hmm?" he asked, uncertain he wanted to know what else she had to say.

"It's good to hear you speak up now and again." She squeezed his shoulder and left him at the table.

The clock on the mantle struck four. Ruby would be on her way home soon.

～

RUBY WRAPPED her coat tightly about her. Maddie wanted her to join the family for Christmas, but only because Ruby had nowhere else to go. The idea of spending time with the extended Moore family had her more nervous than a trapped rabbit. She didn't like the idea of being stuck in a house with a bunch of family she didn't know. They'd expect her to talk and be friendly, and every time she opened her mouth, she felt plum silly. But turning her boss down without a good excuse would be difficult. Maddie had been more than a little emotional lately as Malcom crawled for the first time, babbling and smiling. Fighting the invite had seemed rude, but now Ruby wanted to hide at home.

She trudged toward the party. In the swirling snow ahead, she saw a tall man walking toward her. She recognized the coat and hat right away. Beau was home much sooner than he said he'd be. She quickened her pace to reach him.

He moved in front of her to block the wind, and she was grateful for the warmth. "Ruby. Fine afternoon for a walk." Beau smiled anchoring his hat to his head as the wind tried to steal it.

"Fine if you want to get blown away." His presence calmed her nerves. But why was he back so soon? What did he find out?

"Let's find somewhere warmer." Her skirts swirled around her feet, sending cold chills through her wool stockings.

He nodded, indicating the Sweet Shoppe. "I know it isn't your favorite place, but the coffee's hot."

She followed, glancing up the street toward the Moore home. She probably wouldn't be missed, anyway. As soon as Beau closed the door behind them, the heat of the potbellied stove in front and all the baking ovens in the back warmed Ruby. Beau chose a table near the stove and held out a chair for her.

"Thank you." She sat and waited for him to do the same. "You're back early. Did you find anything?"

Beau motioned for Martha. "Yes, I did. Let's get something hot and I'll tell you about it."

Martha came over and laid her hand on Beau's shoulder. "Why, I haven't seen you in here in a month if it's been a day. What can I get you?" She didn't spare a glance for Ruby.

"We'll each have a cup of coffee, Martha. Thank you, and thank you for being open on Christmas Eve, there wasn't anywhere else to go."

"You should be at home, celebrating with family." Martha narrowed her eyes and folded her arms over her chest.

He turned to face Ruby and Martha scuttled off, returning with a steaming enamel pot before he could say anything else. She flipped two ceramic cups over and filled them.

"Let me know if I can get you anything else." She glanced over her shoulder at them as she walked away.

"I told you I was going to Yellow Medicine, and I did. I met someone who told me that your place was out by the river. It took me a while to find it, but I did. It had been abandoned for some time, but I found this." He pulled a folded sheet of paper from his vest and spread it out in front of her.

Ruby covered her mouth as a deep burning rose within her. The picture, drawn so long ago, reminded her of each face, voice, and manner. She hadn't allowed herself to think about them for so long that seeing their figures drawn onto paper felt like a physical cut to her heart. "Those are my sisters," she pushed the words past the tightness in her throat. "You found the shack." She touched each precious face and wiped at the tears gathering at the corner of her eye.

"I noticed that you drew them all as children, including you. How old are they now?" Beau's rumbling voice reminded her that they sat in a coffee shop, not a place to cry. She wiped her tears with her kerchief and took a deep breath, taking the edge off the pain in her heart.

She pointed to the figure on the far right of the page. "I drew us from oldest to youngest, this is me when I was ten. Next is Jennie, she was ten as well, just eleven months younger than me. Then Hattie and Eva, they were twins and were both eight. Frances was the next youngest at age six. Lula was only four. Nora and Daisy were both babies at two and just born."

"Why did you draw all of you so young?"

The drawing made them feel closer than she'd felt to them in a long time. She held the drawing to her heart. "I drew this when I was ten and had it with me the day I was taken. Mama said that after Daisy she wouldn't have no more babies. She took something that'd make her womb shrivel. I don't know what it was, but it worked. I was taken seven years later."

"So how old are all of you now...if you don't mind me asking?" Pink crept up his neck and she bunched her hands in her skirt to keep from caressing his cheek.

Talking about her sisters made the ache for them grow, but there wasn't anyone else she could trust more than Beau. "Well, I'm eighteen—"

Beau's eyes grew as wide as saucers. "You're *how* old?"

"Old enough." She frowned. What could he possibly find amiss about her age?

"I guess I just thought you were...I mean you act much..."

"Don't finish that sentence." She narrowed her eyes at him.

"Yes, ma'am. You were telling me about your sisters." He leaned back in his chair, hiding a lopsided grin behind his coffee cup.

She smiled, too. "Everyone is seven years older than when I

drew that picture. Jennie would be seventeen, she'll be eighteen in a few months. Hattie and Eva would be fifteen, Frances thirteen, Lula eleven, Nora nine, and Daisy would've just turned eight."

She turned the paper and glanced down at it. Her heart leapt into her throat, and she swallowed down the tears that followed after it. "This picture doesn't tell the whole story, though. All of us —at least the older ones—tried to earn our father's affections. We knew he was capable. He loved Ma…at least some of the time, but he wouldn't love us. We were mouths to feed that didn't seem to work hard enough. No matter the job, a boy could've done it better, faster…" Ruby met his gaze. "I don't think Ma told him she didn't want any more babies. I think she took it upon herself to stop it. I don't think it was right, but Pa would've kept trying until he had a boy, no matter how full the house got."

Beau reached across the table and lay his big callused hand over her smaller equally callused one. A slow burning heat started where he touched her and fanned up her arms and straight to her belly.

"I'm sorry. Seems to me a child should be loved by their parents. I know it don't always happen, though."

"If I could get my sisters away from him, I would've. I don't know how, but some day, I will. If it's not too late."

"If they were a little older, it'd be easier, but eight…that's still mighty young."

"I wouldn't put it past my father to try to marry her off by age twelve. It isn't unheard of. I'd be surprised if they are all still there. If his distiller isn't making enough, he'll marry the older ones off. Saves him the mouth to feed and he gets a few coins for his trouble."

"Distiller?" Beau cocked his head and waited, his thumb whisking back and forth on her hand, sending pleasant tremors through her.

Ruby closed her eyes and along with them closed the door in her heart that she'd opened when Beau showed her the picture. Beau needed to know what her pa did, he didn't need to see all the pain she'd stored up for years in fear of what Pa could do, and had done. "Pa made whiskey. But, I didn't know it until I was married. That was how Pa and Arnold met. Pa sold him whiskey until Arnold couldn't pay anymore, then Pa told Arnold he'd forgive the debt if he took me to wife. Arnold later said it was the worst decision he ever made 'cause Pa wouldn't give him any more credit." There, she'd admitted to someone what her pa was; a bootlegger who traded his daughters for debt.

Beau squeezed her hand and she started at the gentle pressure, having forgotten he was holding it.

"I'm sorry, Ruby. You don't have to talk about it if you don't want to."

Ruby closed her eyes. Of course, he wouldn't want to hear about her time after she'd been taken. If only she could come right out and say she'd never let her husband near her. Had managed to elude him for nine long months. Just the thought of talking about something so private sent heat into her face.

"I'm just glad I'm no longer married to him."

"How can you be so sure? I went to the shack and it was empty, but couldn't he have moved somewhere else?" Beau's fingers rubbed over the top of her hand, sending a pleasant shiver up her arm.

"I'm quite certain he didn't move, because he froze to death and I chucked his carcass into a ravine. He was a dirty rotten, drunken, scoundrel and maybe I should feel remorse, but I don't. He took me as payment for his debts. I was a possession to him. How do you forgive such a thing?" Her voice quaked but she lowered it to a whisper to avoid the ears near their table. Martha might be nice to others, but Ruby didn't know if she'd gossip or not.

"Forgiveness isn't about him, Ruby. What does he need it for? He's dead. When you forgive someone, your Father in heaven will forgive your sins. It isn't easy. It isn't supposed to be. But maybe it's easier to think about now, when you're far away from both of them. Neither Arnold nor your father can hurt you anymore."

Her heart ached for her sisters as that small door within her opened once more—just a crack; she missed them terribly. All those years, in that tiny room, it was just her and her sisters against

Pa. She could count on them and they could count on her. Now, she had no one... "No, but my Pa can still hurt those I love." She pulled her hand from his and stood, pushing in her chair. "Thank you for the cup of coffee, Beau. I have to get to the Moore's, I'm terribly late."

CHAPTER 12

The cold wind blasting in her face sucked the air from her lungs. Ruby gasped and yanked her scarf over her face. The gale kicked up snow around her and her heart raced as she tried to see and breathe. She took a step back and someone grabbed her arm. Ruby swung around to see who had laid a hand on her. A woman wrapped in a long dark cloak and hood stood behind her, her head bowed.

"Are you all right. You looked like you might fall." Ivy lifted her head enough to let Ruby see her face.

"Oh, I'm sorry. I didn't mean to scare you. This wind. It steals your breath."

Ivy twisted to glance up and down the street. "Come to my house for tea while I make dinner. I'm living with the Williams's and their house is very quiet right now. I'd love the company."

Ruby knew she should get to Maddie's, but her curiosity was piqued and she hurried to follow the shrouded figure. The wind prevented any talk during the short walk to the Williams's, and getting home would be a long walk from one end of town to the other. She hoped the wind would calm before the evening.

Ivy pushed open the back door and invited Ruby inside. The

kitchen was small and warm, with a large cook stove and work table in the center of the room. Ivy pulled out a stool for Ruby to sit on. She removed her coat and scarf, hanging it next to Ivy's.

Ivy glided over to the stove and moved the kettle to the front. "There. Now we can talk. Montana is bitter cold. I thought I was used to cold and snow from living in Maine, but this is different. It's as if the very air is made of all that's cold."

"I've never lived anywhere but here and Yellow Medicine." Ruby rubbed her hands together to stop the pain in her fingers from spreading.

Ivy placed a cup and a tea diffuser in front of Ruby then put the pot of water on to boil. "I'm guessing Yellow Medicine is nearby? I'm not from around here. I only came to Cutter's Creek a few weeks ago."

"What brought you all the way to Cutter's Creek from Maine?" Ruby wrapped her hands together wishing she'd sat a little closer to the stove.

Ivy busied herself pumping water into a large stew pot and then hefting it over to the stove. When she finished, she turned back to Ruby. "I'm sorry. The water takes so very long to heat. I didn't actually set out to stay in Cutter's Creek," she began. "I only meant to visit for a short time, then keep going to California. The blizzard that kept the train from running made it impossible to leave, and now I have a job here. I'm not sure how long I'll stay, but Cutter's Creek is nice enough I don't mind staying until I can go the rest of the way."

"What is so important in California? If you like it here, why not just stay?" Ruby felt a kinship with Ivy, some shadow or secret they both had.

Ivy went to a bin and pulled out enough onions to fill her arms. She set them on the table and sat across from Ruby with a large knife. "In California, there are enough people that I can get lost and not enough people I'll know if anyone I recognize shows up." She sliced into the first large onion and the scent stung Ruby's nose and eyes.

"The same could be said of Cutter's Creek. I've only seen you twice. It's like you're hiding."

"I am, though I don't want to hide anymore." She laid the knife down. "I noticed a couple who followed me here and haven't left yet. I was rather hoping they would."

Ruby leaned forward in her seat and waited as the pot whistled for Ivy's attention. She stood and wiped her hands on her apron, then poured them each a cup of steaming water, finally returning to her seat. Talking to Ivy was much like talking to Beau, both would say what was on their mind when they got around to it, and with as few words as possible. It was one of the things she liked about them both, she never had to worry about her own hesitance to speak bothering them.

Ivy settled back into slicing her onions. "I mean Beau's sister and the lawyer, Caruso, of course."

"How did you know about Beau…and his sister…and Caruso? How did you know his name? I've never seen you except at Maddie's."

"You've probably seen me in town, but didn't notice me. Mr. Caruso was my husband's family lawyer. He was easy to spot, but difficult to avoid on the train here. Though, I managed to go unnoticed for the month-long trip by wearing my mother's deep mourning, including her veil. She helped to hide me for a time until we could manage to get to the train ticket window without detection. It was during that month I learned to hide."

"As to the rest of your questions: winter is wonderful. I can go out as often as I like and bundle up my face. No one knows me from any other woman in the street. Since most people walk hunched over in the cold, they don't notice me, anyway. There are a few people I avoid, like May and Caruso…and others, but for the most part, as long as I'm covered, I can roam."

"What will you do when it gets warm?" Ruby dunked her diffuser into her steaming water and let it steep.

"I'll leave for California. The road will be easier by then."

Ruby closed her eyes. Ivy needed to know the truth before she wasted time planning to leave as soon as the snow melted. "You don't know Montana. The spring is a dangerous time by road. Mud slides. I'm not sure which is more dangerous, going in the winter and risking frostbite or staying until spring and dealing with the swollen rivers and mud." Ruby opened her eyes and glanced up from her tea in time to see Ivy's face go deathly pale.

"Ivy, what are you running from? You can tell me."

Ivy shook her head. "No. I can't tell anyone where and what I've come from. Everyone expects you to just stay, to just be a good woman, a dutiful wife. I couldn't stay another moment."

Ruby sighed. "Did he drink?"

Ivy's head swung up and her pinched face and narrowed pain-filled eyes answered Ruby's question.

"Was he a mean drunk?"

"No, he was just mean. The drink just made him invincible."

Ruby slowly nodded her head. "You won't get any judgment from me." She sipped her tea and fought the urge to wrinkle her nose. As much as she wanted to like tea, like a lady should, she hated the stuff. It had the distinct appearance of swamp water and smelled about the same.

Ivy laughed and went to the wall near the stove, lifting a small crock. She pulled a stick out from it and honey oozed off the tip. "Let me sweeten that up for you a little." She wound the honey around the stick then dipped it into Ruby's tea, stirring the honey off. Then she tossed the stick into her wash water.

"That should make it taste better for you. I'm sorry. I'm used to everyone drinking tea and it's difficult for me to get used to the custom of drinking coffee."

"You drank it all the time?" Ruby frowned and sipped the tea, it was only slightly better now, but not enough that she'd want it more than on a visiting occasion.

"Well, maybe not all the time. Tea is costly. But whenever you drink coffee, we'd have taken tea instead." Ivy went back to slicing onions, her head tipped in a thoughtful manner.

"Is he dead, is that how you left, or did you just leave and hope to lose him forever."

Ivy dropped the knife and Ruby jumped. "I don't think it's a good idea to keep asking these questions."

"I'm sorry. I was looking for something in common between us. My husband froze to death when he was in a drunk. Then, Josiah Williams happened by one day, months later. Since I didn't shoot him on the spot, I decided to come with him to Cutter's Creek."

"You were going to shoot him? Why?" Ivy's hand steadied and she went back to slicing her onions.

"He was trespassing. He was in a snit about Penny at the time and came out to the river to do some hollerin'. He plum scared me to death."

"When you relax, you talk differently, more natural. Why is that?"

Ruby sighed. "I guess I always felt like no one wanted the real Ruby, so I just try to fit in with everyone else."

"I'm sorry for interrupting you, go ahead and finish your story." A tear from the onions ran down Ivy's cheek. At least Ruby hoped it was from the onions.

"That's about all there was. Josiah came and when he convinced me he wasn't there to hurt me, I invited myself to go with him. Living in that shack wasn't easy and Cutter's Creek has become home now."

"I don't expect it was." Ivy gathered the sliced onions and put them in the pot of hot water.

"You fixin' to make onion soup?" Ruby asked, wondering what else would go in the pot.

"Yes. The onions here are small, but flavorful. It should make a good soup. I'd ask you to join us for dinner, but it isn't my place to ask, and I've heard Carol mention how they don't have much extra. I'll be putting in a few doves to roast in a bit, but they are so small, they don't take long. It's Christmas Eve, so Carlton wanted something a little nicer."

"I understand what it's like to be wanting. Do you think you could do me a kindness?" Ruby felt like a wretch for asking for a favor, but she couldn't see any other way. When Ivy nodded, Ruby continued. "Maddie, the lady I work for, was told she shouldn't do much after she had her baby. In fact, the doctor said she shouldn't even have any more babies. She thinks he's wrong. Could you ask your doctor friend if he could examine her? Please?" Ruby peered down into her cup and couldn't force herself to take the last few sips, she glanced at the bottom of her cup flecked with floating leaves.

"I'll ask Dr. Gentry. I know he's some type of specialist for Carlton's leg. I don't know if he does work like a regular doctor."

"Maddie would sure appreciate another opinion, if he'd be willing to give it."

Ivy's expression softened to concerned. "Will you continue to work there if Dr. Gentry says she's perfectly healthy or will you lose your position?"

Ruby stopped, then slowly gathered her coat and scarf to give her time to think of an answer. "I don't rightly know. I don't think she'd need me anymore. But, for some reason, I'm just not fussed about it."

Ivy nodded and stirred the pot. "I'll get the message to him. Stop by whenever you want, but please don't tell anyone I'm here. It'll have to remain our secret."

Ruby smiled at her new...*friend*...and let herself out into the blustery afternoon.

CHAPTER 13

May swished her way into the sitting room and sat next to Beau on the worn couch. She had changed from her day dress into an evening gown.

"You're going somewhere on Christmas night?" He turned to face her.

"Yes. Mr. Caruso is having a small party at his office. I am, of course, invited. There'll be a few people there he hopes will become clients. It may help him to decide if he'll stay in Cutter's Creek. It should be a fun time. Why haven't you gone out to visit your Ruby today? It's Christmas, don't you think she'd like to see you?"

"I saw her yesterday. She ran off and I haven't wanted to see her much since."

"Leave it to my brother to scare away the only woman who shows him any interest. Except Carol Williams, who gives every man over the age of seventeen her attention."

That stung. At one point, Penny had held his attention, but she was now happily married. Now, he never even thought about her. Ruby had said she was late in getting to the Moore's for their Christmas eve celebration, but he wasn't sure if she'd spend

Christmas Day with the Hanover's or the Moore's, and he couldn't remember if he'd actually asked her or not.

"I don't think Ruby has any interest in me at all. Every time I see her, she's running away."

May frowned. "That's because that's all she's known for over a year. A hunted deer doesn't stop running when it gets away from the hunter. It thinks everyone it sees after that is also a hunter."

Beau nodded. "So, if you're so smart, how do I let her know I'm not a hunter?"

May leaned into him and whispered. "That's the whole problem, Beau. You are."

Beau shook his head. "I was in that cabin. I'm nothing like that man. Even after months of neglect, that cabin had a smell and *feel*..." He closed his eyes and swallowed the anger rising in him. "I can't let her go back to that."

"I doubt she wants to. But if her father's as bad as you said he is, and her husband, who actually wasn't her husband at all, was as bad as her father is, it only stands to reason she'd question your every action and every word from your mouth."

"I haven't even said anything!" He shot to his feet and strode over to the fireplace.

"Now that doesn't surprise me a bit. How about you go over and just talk to her. Find out what her favorite color is. What does she like? Instead of bringing up all the things she doesn't want to talk about and re-live. Who wants to sit with someone they like and spend that time talking about things they don't like? Stop bringing up unpleasant things, it'll make her lose interest. Just enjoy a few minutes with her. If you like her, that shouldn't be hard."

"I don't just sit and talk, May. You know that." He rested his arm against the mantle and let the warmth seep into his arm. Even thinking about things to say terrified him. He'd rather volunteer to go on another midnight delivery with Josiah Williams than to have to sit and talk to a woman, even Ruby.

"You can be the silent type once you win her. Now is the time for action!" May stood up and approached him, laying her hand on his shoulder.

"If I agree to go see her will you go to your party and leave me be?" He wouldn't turn to look at her.

"You don't want to listen to me, but you must. You'll lose her if you don't. As much as I love you, brother, it has to be said, there is no other woman who will put up with your wanderlust. And what other woman will put up with your long, brooding silences?"

He turned away from her and grabbed his coat from the hook by the door. "Fine. I have nothing to give her, but if you insist, I'll go out and see her."

May smiled at him and clasped her hands. "Good. You can walk me to the law office on the way."

He cocked his head and looked at her with new eyes, he'd just played right into her hand and she'd come out with a full house. "You could have just asked. You didn't need to trick me into leaving the house."

"Yes, but this was so much more fun, and now I know how you really feel about Ruby." She laughed.

"Why do I get the feeling you really wanted to be a lawyer?"

May wrapped her coat around her, careful not to ruin her hair or squish her dress. "I refuse to incriminate myself."

He opened the door for May and was immediately happy the night was cold, clear, and calm. He offered his arm and May took it, walking beside him.

"So, now that you know how I feel about Ruby, why don't you tell me the truth about Caruso?"

May smiled up at him. "He's a wonderful man, but I can't get too attached. As I told you, he's received word that Ivy's husband has died and the Masters family needs him to return to be the executor of his will. He'd like to stay and bring Ivy back, as he knows she stands to inherit a large sum of money, but it could also be dangerous for her. Her husband's family isn't one to be questioned. Just defying them to stay here the winter will make them angry. Even if he gains enough clients to stay here permanently, he will always have to watch over his shoulder."

"So, if he stays, he'll be inviting some nasty people to Cutter's Creek?" He slowed their pace to hear May's answer.

"Yes, and Ivy isn't enough reason to risk his job and his life. If he doesn't get enough clients, there won't be anything else here to keep him."

Even in the faint light of the gas lamps along the boardwalk, he could see her normally smiling face fall and her body stiffen.

"It sounds like you need to take a little of your own advice, May." He whispered, opening the door to Caruso's office. It had a short hallway that led to an indoor stairway up to the second floor with the office door to the left.

"I don't have enough sway over him to keep him here, Beau. Unlike Ruby's interest in you, Mr. Caruso doesn't return my feelings." She patted his hand. "I'll ask him to walk me home, though."

Beau nodded but his thoughts were already elsewhere. Ruby's small apartment was only a few buildings away, but visiting her there was objectionable, especially since he knew she'd be there alone. He'd only been there the once before and Lily had been there. But, she'd be celebrating Christmas with James. Beau had heard word they'd marry in the spring. There was nowhere in town he could take Ruby. Everywhere was closed for the evening.

He stopped in the middle of the cold, empty street and peered up at her window. There was a weak light coming from inside, so she was home. If he went up there, did that make him a hunter? It certainly made him a cad. He grimaced. He'd have to ring her bell and have her come down, but then what? They couldn't just stand in the street.

"Are you gonna just stand there and stare up at her window, or are ya gonna invite her down for pie?" came an old, cracked voice from the shadows.

"Mrs. Cahill?" He squinted into the darkness along the boardwalk. Mrs. Cahill lived right on Main Street and didn't have a porch like others, but the boardwalk went right by her house.

"Who else'd be sitting in front of my house? Go on. I ain't gonna sit here all night in the cold." She tapped her cane impatiently on the boardwalk planks.

Beau jogged over to the stairs and glanced heavenward. "Thank you, Lord," he said as he passed the bell and ran straight up to Ruby's apartment. He knocked and heard shuffling on the other side of the door. Ruby opened it as she wrapped a shawl around her shoulders.

"Oh, Beau. I wasn't expecting anyone."

She wore a simple day dress, not something she would've worn to a party. Her hair was down and flowed over her shoulders in tempting, deep red curls. She gathered her hair and pushed it over her shoulder, a sweet pink tinge crept up her face.

"Mrs. Cahill invited us over for pie. Would you care to join me?" He stepped forward to block her from the cold air and she backed away.

"I was just about to get ready to turn in for the night. I..." she turned from him and her body tensed.

"Please, Ruby?"

"I thought Mrs. Cahill was over celebrating with her family. She was going to walk Lily back in the evening, but Lily isn't back yet."

"You could come down and ask her. If Lily is too tired or James can't, I can go over and get her...it isn't far."

Ruby's lips formed the shadow of a smile, then fell. "That'd be kind. Let me wind my hair up and I'll join you downstairs in a moment."

He wanted to protest. Her hair was much longer and prettier than he'd first thought.

When did I let myself imagine what her hair'd be like?

"If you must. It'll just be me and Mrs. Cahill, and I suspect she'd rather talk with you."

A muffled sound, suspiciously like a chuckle, came from Ruby's throat as she turned back to him. "She doesn't like talking with anyone. I don't know why she'd invite you over, and I doubt there's any pie."

"Well, now I'm heartbroken. I was looking forward to a piece." Beau felt a smile crack his face.

Ruby grabbed a ribbon from a small table and quickly braided her hair, tying the bit at the end. "I guess you can take me down, I'm ready now and you let all my heat out."

"Oh." He shook his head. He'd let himself get distracted by her shiny, long hair. "Why don't you go on down and save me a seat? I'll throw a log on your fire so it's warm in here when you come back up."

She glanced nervously behind her. "No, I think it'll be fine once we close the door." She walked past him and her scent filled him. There was no way pie could smell better, not even fresh from the oven.

Ruby led the way down the narrow stairs and waited at Mrs. Cahill's front door, her breath a puff of delicate cloud around her as she waited. Beau knocked and Mrs. Cahill ushered them in.

"I couldn't wait outside anymore. Too cold. Take your coats off, if you like, or leave them on. Pie is on the table. I'll be back in my room."

Ruby's eyes grew large and she clutched her coat about her. "But, don't you want to sit out here with us?"

The old woman turned and smiled a big toothless grin. "Of course not. It isn't right for you to be anywhere all alone, but no one said you couldn't sit by my fireplace. I'll be in the back of the house in case this young man tries anything...but I know he won't. He's a good boy. Bank my fire when you're done."

Beau snorted. At least one woman in the room trusted him. "Thank you, ma'am." He put his hand on Ruby's back and led her over to the table, pulling out her chair for her.

She slid her coat off her shoulders and sat, waiting for him to join her. The pie had seen better days. He wasn't even sure when it had been made, but he wasn't there for the pie, despite what he'd told Ruby. She picked up her fork and poked it as if she thought it might come to life.

She glanced up at him conspiratorially and whispered. "I warned you."

He picked up his own fork and cut a bit off the end. The crust was about as hard as a day-old biscuit, which worried him. "What do we do with it?" he whispered back.

"I think this might be the same pie she offered Lily and I the day I moved in. That was two months ago."

"Wouldn't it mold?" He wanted to choke. What kind of strange magic did Mrs. Cahill use to make this pie?

"I don't know. Lily warned me, but I didn't listen. I thought it'd be rude to say no. I was sick for two days afterward."

He pushed it around with his fork. "I don't think either of us wants to get sick."

She laughed and a warmth spread over his face. "I'm sure we can think of something."

"Why don't we go sit by the fireplace. I'm still a little cold." Ruby shivered.

He stood, picking up both plates and carrying them to the living room. He scraped the pie into the fire and it smoked and sizzled.

Ruby strode into the room and paused in front of the fire. "I don't think it'll burn. If that pie fought hard enough to avoid mold, it isn't going to give up against some flames."

He pulled the poker from the hook and broke the pie apart as best he could. She sat down on the floor next to where he was squatting in front of the fire. Having her so near made his head turn to mush, he could hardly remember his own name. He breathed in deeply and tried to remember what May said he should talk about, what did he need to know beyond what he already knew?

"Ruby, what's your favorite color?" *Oh, you're such an idiot.* Of all the questions May had given him, why did he ask that one?

Ruby laughed a nervous titter. "I don't rightly know that I have one. Do you?"

Now there was something he'd never considered. "I don't think I have one, either. Though I'm partial to the color of the sky as the sun comes over the trees in the foothills."

"That's beautiful." Her voice was soft and slipped its way through his senses.

He leaned back and pulled his legs out from underneath him, moving so he was still next to Ruby, but not too close. "That color is pretty close to your hair." He focused on the fire, if he turned to look at her she might run, and he couldn't take her running from him again.

"My hair is horrible. No one remembers a thing about me except my hair."

"I'd imagine they also remember your name…" He poked the pie one last time and it belched sparks at him.

"Funny story. I was born bald. My ma desperately wanted my hair to be like hers, so she named me Ruby in the hopes it would be."

"I guess she got lucky…and I'm really glad she didn't name you Bluebird."

Ruby laughed and his chest swelled with the sound. He'd do about anything to hear it again.

"I don't think it works that way, but I won't tempt the Lord by using that name for any of my children."

"Do you think you'll have a lot?" He glanced back at her, wondering what she'd say. He'd come from a small family, it was just him and May, but Ruby had been one of eight.

"I guess it'd be up to the Lord, but I'd like to keep it at just a few…if I ever get married." She drew circles on the rug in front of her with her finger.

"Do you think marrying is out of the question?" he refused to give credence to her first marriage and he couldn't help leaning toward her, hoping she'd respond encouragingly.

"I hope to…someday. When the right man comes along, a man who doesn't hate me for my past."

He laid his hand over hers and a jolt of something delicious shot up his arm. "The past doesn't matter, Ruby. If someone loves you, they love you for who you are *now*, not who you were *then*. You wouldn't be the woman you are without everything you've been through."

Her deep red curls tempted him and he took gentle hold of her braid, tugging the ribbon free of its hold. She gasped and reached for her hair, but he'd already undone the binding. He dropped the ribbon and lifted his hand to her hair again. Each strand was softer than a horse's muzzle and he couldn't stop until he'd reached her neck, massaging out the last of the woven braid. He fanned her locks out over her shoulder.

"You have beautiful hair, Ruby."

She stood up quickly and grabbed her shawl. Cheeks flushed and eyes wide, she stammered, "Merry Christmas, Beau. I need to go make sure Lily made it home. Good night."

Beau tried to stand before she could get to the door but he heard it close with a thud just as he made it to his feet.

CHAPTER 14

"Forgive me, Father, for I have sinned. Forgive me, Father, for I have sinned..." Ruby chanted the words all the way to the small red chapel at the corner of town.

Her mother had been Catholic and she'd taken Ruby and her sisters to mass twice, that she could remember, at least. The little church was not Catholic. So, for the most part, she'd stayed away. Until tonight. Tonight, she needed to go to confession, because her heart was doing things it shouldn't, and her body was wanting things it had no business wanting.

Candlelight inside the small church building danced along the windows, and the familiar scent of incense greeted her as she approached. How would a Protestant church deal with confession, did they even have confessionals? If they didn't, where could she go? She opened one side of the large double doors and slipped inside. It was quite dark, with only the candles on a tiered table at the front for illumination.

The man she recognized from Penny's wedding as Reverend Bligh approached her. "Good evening. What can I do for you?"

Ruby looked around the chapel, but then glanced back at the reverend.

"Strictly speaking...I was raised Catholic and I'd like to...," she whispered, "use the confessional." Reverend Bligh cocked his head to the side, and his face transformed with a bemused smile. "I'm sorry, miss. This isn't a Catholic chapel. We don't have one of those here."

Ruby clutched her cloak closer. Her mother had warned her about Protestants and their false teachings. "Where can I find a priest?"

The reverend laid his hand on her shoulder and she was surprised to find that it didn't make her want to run through the nearest wall.

"Please, have a seat. I don't have a confessional, but I do have a wife waiting in my office. She could sit behind the curtain I use to change before service and you could sit outside it. She'll never know your name, and you've never met her before. Will that suffice?"

"Yes, but, she isn't Catholic. How will I be absolved?" Ruby felt a growing dread within her as if the world were going to crush her at any moment.

"Ruby, the Lord hears you, no matter where you are or who you're speaking to. Why would an omniscient God need to use one of His own creations as His ears? He knows your thoughts and He knows your hurts. I'll be right back. Have a seat."

"But...what about the candles. I saw the candles, so I thought..." Confusion and embarrassment roiled through her.

"You saw what the Lord knew you'd need to see to come in here tonight. The candles were for this evening's Christmas service. Anyone who had a prayer for supplication or thanksgiving lit a candle. I gave a sermon on how our prayers are a pleasing aroma to the Lord, and I sprinkled incense over the flames."

That was it. It hadn't just been the candles when she'd come in, but the scent had reminded her of the masses she'd attended as a child.

The Lord knew what I needed to see and hear...the Lord...knew me...

Ruby turned to ask him another question, but he'd disappeared into a room off the sanctuary—his office, Ruby supposed. Ruby sat and stared up at the wooden cross in the center front of the building. While her family had never been devout by any means, and if the church had known who her father was, they wouldn't have allowed them in at all, Mother taught them as best she could. Ruby had learned the rosary at a young age, though she'd never been diligent about practicing.

The room was warm and Ruby removed her cloak and laid it gently on the pew next to her. There was a small kneeling bench in front of her and she knelt.

Lord, I don't know what to say. I'm here in this Protestant house, are you here, too? Can you hear me? I don't know what to do. I care about Beau more than I can explain, but he don't deserve me and all the trouble I've been through. He says the past don't matter, but I don't see how that can be true. Help me to see...

"Miss?"

Ruby raised her head and Reverend Bligh laid his hand on her shoulder. "Come with me, child."

"Ruby Gres...Ruby Arnsby. I'm Ruby Arnsby." She held her head high, feeling the weight of that old name slip off her.

"Pleased to meet you, Miss Arnsby. Come with me."

He led her up the aisle and to the narrow door in the back of the sanctuary. He pushed the door open and ushered her in. The room was lit by an oil lamp sitting on a desk. Just as he'd said there would be, a tall curtain hung from the ceiling nearest the back wall, creating a small nook.

"Come and sit, child. Tell me what's on your heart." A voice came from behind the curtain.

Ruby sat on a nearby chair and took a deep breath. "Forgive me... I don't know how to address you. I know you aren't a Father."

The curtain laughed. "No, I'm certainly not. Why don't you just tell me what's bothering you without worrying how to address me?"

Ruby nodded then laughed nervously. Reverend Bligh shut the door, leaving the two women alone.

"I told your husband my name was Ruby Arnsby. That's the

first time I've used that name in a long time. Two summers ago, my father convinced one of his clients to marry me as a way to forgive that man's debts to my father. He performed the ceremony right there in the yard. I didn't want to go, and never...I never... He never..." How could she explain?

Mrs. Bligh cleared her throat. "I understand. Go on."

"I never thought I'd be rid of him, but I prayed for it. I prayed for a way to be rid of that awful man, but I never meant for him to die."

"He didn't die by your hand, did he?"

Ruby straightened. Though she'd chastised herself for leaving him in the cold, she had never come right out and said it— "Of course not!"

"Good. So, something happened and now he's gone."

"Yes. He froze to death. Recently, I learned my marriage wasn't even legal. It never felt *right* to me. Am I ruined because I lived with him for so long? I know I need to be forgiven for praying to be rid of him..." she paused, her thoughts rattling around in her head. "I don't know what else. Yes, I do. I need to be forgiven for wishing Beau'd kiss me. Because I do, and I shouldn't."

For long moments there was silence from behind the curtain. "I don't need to forgive you for anything, child. You haven't done a thing to me and you just asked the Lord for forgiveness. How do you feel?"

"How do I feel?" Ruby stared at the curtain and felt the tension in her face. "I feel like I want to run back to Mrs. Cahill's house and kiss Beau silly. That's how I feel."

Mrs. Bligh laughed so hard Ruby thought she'd fall out from behind the curtain. After her guffaws subsided, she asked. "Ruby, do you love him?"

"Love? He makes me feel like I've never felt before; silly, like there's bubbles in my belly. When he touched my hair tonight, I couldn't breathe. I wanted..." She felt the heat rise to her cheeks.

"Those are wonderful feelings, dear, but they aren't love. They're the *tools* the Lord uses to help you *find* the one you love. You'll know you love him when you'd willingly sacrifice your life for him. You'll probably never have to make that choice, but you'll know it."

"So, that's it? I'm forgiven? Just like that?"

"I don't think you did anything wrong. It's natural to pray for a way out of a terrible situation and you're of an age that one man should make your heart sing. Keep yourself pure for him and then kiss him silly on your wedding night."

"But he doesn't see me as pure. I lived with a man for nine months. There's no way he'd believe nothing happened. Why would he ever want a bride he thought was all used up?" She wrung her hands in her lap, the tension in her shoulders making her neck ache.

"Now, that's a sticky situation."

Ruby heard Mrs. Bligh move on her seat behind the curtain.

"I know. I can't exactly tell him I'm a, that is, I'm not..."

"Yes. I know Beau, and that isn't something he'd be comfortable talking about, in fact, most men wouldn't. My advice to you, dear, is to spend time with him. As much as you can without letting carnality steal your intentions. Let him know, by your godly words and deeds, that the Lord preserved you just for him."

Ruby nodded. "I can do that. Thank you, Mrs. Bligh."

"You're welcome, Ruby. I hope at some point you'll feel comfortable enough to talk to me face to face. But until then, if you ever need to talk again, just let my husband know."

Ruby emerged from the warm church and the chill night air caught her breath. The street was empty and she could see from where she stood that Mrs. Cahill's home was dark. Mrs. Cahill had now gone to bed and Lily was not yet home.

Ruby suddenly realized she was out in the night alone. She scanned the street nervously. Thank goodness it was only a short distance to her home. She spied a couple, hunched together, walking up the street on the other side.

She shivered under her cloak. She held it tightly around her as she stepped out onto the street. Three men jumped from the shadows, grabbing her before she could scream.

"Thought you could hide away in the church, did you? There's a bounty on your head and I intend to claim it."

One of the men pulled a rag from his pocket and shoved it in her mouth, then yanked a flour sack over her head. Ruby's world plunged into complete darkness. She kicked and squirmed, but the men tied her hands behind her and pulled her up off her feet. Soon she was tossed into some type of wagon. The beating of hooves and the rumble beneath her told her she was on the move. Which way and how far, she couldn't guess. She wiggled to get free or to at least get the gag out of her mouth, but the material was thick and rough. She couldn't budge it.

What would they do to her? There wouldn't be a bounty on her, she wasn't worth anything! If it wasn't her they were after, would they let her go? She flopped, banging her hip against the hard planks below her.

I thought the Lord led me to go to that church. Help! The voice inside her screamed, just as the wagon came to a stop.

Hands gripped her painfully numb shoulders and yanked her out of the wagon. One of them tossed her over their shoulder and every one of her muscles protested. Men all around her spoke in muffled words. She couldn't tell if there were now more of them or still just the three. She tried to stop her ragged breathing but the thought of what they might do to her made it all the worse. They carried her bouncing up a few steps, then she was unceremoniously dropped onto a chair. Seconds later someone yanked the flour sack off her head, pulling some of her still-loose hair with it.

The room around her was near dark, but she could make out two men and a rough fireplace to her right. The rest of the room held little, nothing of note but some old ripped curtains on the one window by the door.

"Oh, no." A man dressed in black, with ragged teeth jumped back, his eyes wide. "We got the wrong girl. Ivy's got yeller hair."

"You oaf. She could've colored it." A skinny man with oily hair approached the chair, reaching for her hair, and she shied away. He pulled at it and glared at her scalp. "Don't see any yeller parts."

"I think we got the wrong gal. She had a hood on and it was dark, Boss." The man in black crossed his arms.

The boss dropped his head in his hand and the first man yanked the gag from her mouth.

"Water?" she choked.

The younger man filled a small tin cup with water and put it to her mouth. She downed it in a single gulp.

"You ain't Mrs. Masters, are you?" The boss squeezed the bridge of his nose and frowned down at her.

Ruby scowled at him. "Of course not, and you don't even have to take my word for it. The lawyer in town knows what Mrs. Masters looks like because he works for Mr. Masters." She shifted in her chair trying to get feeling back into her arms.

"You mean to tell me that we can find her and collect the bounty without going all the way back to Maine?" Boss glared down at her.

"I won't help you." She promised Ivy she'd keep her mouth shut. They wouldn't find out about Ivy from her. Ivy's husband had to be even more frightening than Arnold if he'd been willing to send out bounty hunters to find her.

"Oh, you'll help us, all right." He laughed. "Or you'll never go home again. Just because you ain't Mrs. Masters don't mean we can't make money off you."

She hadn't considered that. She tipped her chin defiantly and Boss laughed.

Boss thumbed toward the door. "I'll need a night to think about this, Skunk. Put her in the cellar and we can go have a chat with the lawyer tomorrow."

Skunk grabbed her arm and hoisted her out of the chair. He shoved her outside and yanked the door to the cellar open. "You won't freeze, probably." He untied her wrists then shoved her down into the hole. She groped for anything to hold on to as she fell, tumbling down the stairs into the dark recess as he shut the door over her head.

Ruby ran up the stairs and pounded on the door. "Don't leave me down here!" Something heavy fell against the door from the other side.

"You quiet down in there." She peeked through a crack in the door and the man's foot came toward her, kicking the door and raining dust down on her.

Ruby sat on the stairs letting the small shaft of moonlight fall across her face. She couldn't force herself to go further into the cellar. The deep blackness was thick around her, clawing at her. A scratching sound came from the depths of the room and Ruby shrieked, pounding against the door. The man had left, leaving her without a guard. It almost would've been better if they had, because then she wouldn't be alone.

Her breath couldn't fill her lungs. She felt light-headed and her hands shook.

"Please, let me out of here! I can't stay in here!" She pounded against the door. When no one came, she sat on the very top step and clutched at her throat, her cloak choking her. She blinked to clear her vision and a halo of light formed around the shaft of moonlight, then solidified into an intersecting point. If she gazed up at it just right, the light became a cross.

Her racing heart slowed.

The Lord is my Shephard; I shall not want... Ruby repeated the verse, never taking her eyes off the cross.

I will make it through this night.

CHAPTER 15

Beau lay in his bed examining the ceiling. He'd been awake most of the night thinking about the feel of Ruby's hair, and what it had cost him. He shouldn't have touched her. But it had been too tempting. He had to remember she felt *hunted*. He didn't want her to feel like prey but rather like a sought-after prize. In his mind, there was a big difference. One was precious, the other, just dinner.

He sat up and sighed as he rested his head in his hands. Ruby was on his mind more and more often. He knew the remedy and it wasn't what he'd ever planned to do. He'd seen men bitten by the marriage bug before, and he had all the symptoms. Problem was, the woman he wanted to be his bride wasn't the usual woman. She was so skittish, and the words he felt he should say…they'd send her running. So, what was a man to do?

He heard a distant knock and the sound of May's booted feet on the wood floor as she went for the door. He yanked on his clothes and ran his hand through his hair. May stood in the sitting room, offering Mrs. Bligh a seat.

"Good morning, Beau. I was wondering if I might have a private word with you?" She stood.

Beau's sister and father were already sitting at the table breaking their morning fast. They wouldn't miss him for a few minutes.

Mrs. Bligh's face brightened as she waited for him. "We could go over to the Sweet Shoppe for a cup of coffee."

He nodded and slid on his boots, then grabbed his coat as he followed her out the door.

He couldn't figure what he'd possibly done to warrant a visit by the preacher's wife. "I don't mind saying, this is a little strange for you to come to my door. Have I done something wrong?" Beau gazed down at the short, older woman, with the round, friendly face.

"Not at all, Beau. Frankly, I wasn't sure if I should talk to you at all, but after sharing with my husband, we both thought it'd be a good idea. Did Ruby Arnsby happen to seek you out last night? I know it was late, but she seemed rather eager to see you." Mrs. Bligh glanced up at him, her eyes twinkling.

"Ruby...*Arnsby*? No, in fact, last I saw her, she was running from me. I sometimes get the feeling she wants to see me, but then other times...well, I'm sure she'd just rather be alone."

Mrs. Bligh waited for him to open the door to the Sweet Shoppe and when he did, she slid into the first available seat and waited for him to do the same.

"There's where you're wrong, Mr. Rockford. She'd much rather spend time with you, but she's frightened."

"She told you that?" He felt heat rising up his collar, so he waved to Martha to distract Mrs. Bligh.

"She told me she felt...certain things, but I'm not at liberty to share the particulars. However, I do want you to know something—"

The door slammed open and Beau turned as Lily rushed in.

"There you are!" Lily exclaimed. "She's gone, Beau! I went to bed before Ruby came home last night, but she never did come home. Her bed isn't disturbed. Everything is just how it was. Maddie Moore hasn't seen her. She's just gone!" Lily's voice cracked and she grabbed ahold of the chair for support.

Mrs. Bligh patted the table next to her. "Sit down, dear."

Lily obliged. Beau had never seen Lily so disheveled; as if she'd left her house before she finished getting ready.

"Now," Mrs. Bligh continued, "I saw Ruby just last night at the chapel, or rather heard her. I did not *see* her. Since we know she was there and that's the last place any of us saw her, let's start there."

Beau left a few coins on the table for the coffee and held the door for Lily and Mrs. Bligh. They inched their way to the little chapel, searching the ground for any hint of the missing woman. It hadn't snowed in days and the area around the chapel was trampled with hundreds of foot and hoof prints. They couldn't make hide nor hair of the prints in the snow.

"I should have followed her when she left Mrs. Cahill's. A woman shouldn't be walking alone at night. If I hadn't been so prideful..." Beau clutched his hands into fists. He was always doing something wrong when it came to women.

Mrs. Bligh laid her weathered hand on Beau's arm. "Young man, I know you don't want to hear this, but the Lord needed Ruby to seek out the chapel last night. Ruby has a hole in her heart that only the Lord can fill. In fact, she can't love you proper until she heals from her past. You can help her by seeing her for the woman she is."

"But...I do. I don't care about where she's been or who she was."

The old woman's eyes gleamed. "Good. That's a good start. I think you should tell the sheriff. Both of you. I'll be praying for Ruby's safe return." She strode up the stairs into the chapel, leaving Beau and Lily in the street.

RUBY BLINKED against the light on her face and raised herself off the stair she'd slept on. She stretched her tight shoulders and neck. Thankfully, it was the day after Christmas and too cold for any type of bug or snake to trouble her down in the dark cellar. She shivered and pulled her cloak covered in twinkling frost tighter around her. The sun shining through the crack between the two doors allowed her to see a little further into the cellar. It was empty of any food. Neat shelves hung along three of the walls and crates lined the floor. In the light of day, the room itself was not frightening, but being trapped was. At least down here they couldn't harm her.

Shuffling footsteps approached the door and she backed down into the cellar to keep from getting hit by anything they might throw down. Skunk flung open the door, scurried down and, grabbed her, then shoved her back up the cellar stairs and into the house.

"We've decided to bring the lawyer out here to tell us who you are. If you really are Ivy, then we can collect our money. If you're not, the boss has other plans for you." He shoved her into the chair she'd sat in the night before, and tied her arms behind her back. Ruby didn't even want to think about the *other plans*.

She searched the room for a way to get them to untie her. If she could make a run for it, she might be able to find her way back. "Excuse me, I need to use the necessary."

The man's eye's bulged. "They's a pot over in that corner." He pointed.

Ruby rolled her eyes. "And how am I to use it, tied to this chair?"

Skunk scratched his head and scrunched his face at her. "Are you tryin' ta escape? 'Cause if you are, you'll get me in a heap a trouble."

She squirmed in her seat. "No, believe it or not, women sometimes have to go, too."

He turned red from his neck to his scraggly hairline. He untied her and backed away, watching her with wary, mud brown eyes.

"Do you plan to stare at me the whole time?" She couldn't keep the agitation from her voice.

He turned his back as she approached the filthy corner. Aware of the awkwardness of her situation, she finished quickly. It hadn't been as urgent as she'd made it out to be, but he didn't need to know that. She scrambled to the fireplace and grabbed the poker, holding it out like a sword.

"Now, you're going to let me go. I'm not Ivy and I've got no business with you. You let me go and I won't even tell Sheriff Brentwood where to find you."

"That shouldn't be hard, since you don't know where you are." Skunk sneered.

"If you think I'm too scared to use this, you'd be wrong." She steadied her breathing and focused on controlling her shaking hands. Freedom was her only chance. Once she was free, she could get back to Ivy and warn her.

"I ain't scairt of no bitty girl." He lunged for her.

Ruby pulled up on the poker, but it only grazed his cheek. He didn't even wipe at the small scratch it left.

"See, you can't do nothin'."

The door swung open and Boss walked in carrying wood. He dropped everything and drew his gun, pointing it right at Ruby's chest.

"Skunk, git that gal tied back up. What'd you let her loose for?"

Ruby backed away from him but Boss cocked his pistol and all the fight left her. Skunk took her hands and yanked them roughly behind her back, wrenching her shoulders painfully. He tossed her into the chair, tying the bonds even tighter than he had the first time.

Boss gathered the wood he'd dropped and stacked it beside the hearth.

"I went into town this mornin'. That lawyer you said would be there, wasn't in his office today. I'll have to wait to see him. In the meantime, guess you get to stay." It wasn't just his words that terrified her, it was the dark leer on his face.

CHAPTER 16

"I think Mrs. Bligh was right. I wouldn't know where to start." Beau directed Lily to the sheriff's office.

"I'll go talk to Sheriff Brentwood if you think it'll help. I don't know much other than that she didn't come home."

"Are you absolutely sure she didn't come in late and leave early?" Beau directed their steps to the small brick building in the middle of town.

"Yes. The room is small and I'm a very light sleeper." She blushed and glanced at her feet. "I had to be to avoid riling mama."

He patted her hand. No one in town had ever truly understood what went on in Lily's house growing up, but everyone had whispered about her mother, Crazy Candy. Some of the whispers were more cruel than others. In early fall, when her mother had kidnapped James Cahill's son, everyone began to understand just what poor Lily had been living with her whole life. Since then, her parents had moved outside of town and very few people ever saw them.

"Thank you." He stopped and held the door for her, ushering Lily into the small front room of the sheriff's office.

The office held a small desk piled high with papers and a hallway that led back to the two cells.

"Hello?" Beau called, and the walls echoed back at him.

"Well, I guess that's why Brentwood isn't here. He's in his fifties; guess I'd be at home with my wife if there wasn't anyone to watch here, either."

Lily turned to leave when the door swung open and in sauntered Sheriff Brentwood.

"Morning. What can I do for you folks?" He pulled out the chair behind his desk and plopped into it, throwing his hat on a stack of papers.

Beau led Lily to the chair and he remained standing, his feet unable to stand still for long. He didn't know why, but he couldn't shake the feeling that for every minute, Ruby was getting further away. He wove his hands together, flipped them outward, and pressed until all his fingers popped. Lily jumped, flinching at the noise.

She took a deep breath. "Sheriff, Ruby, the young lady that lives with me, didn't come home last night. It isn't like her to just disappear. We spoke to Mrs. Bligh and we think she may have been the last person to see Ruby."

Beau stood behind Lily's chair. "She was with me before she went to the chapel. We were at old Mrs. Cahill's for pie. Then she left, saying she had to check on Lily."

Lily glanced at him over her shoulder and blushed. "James walked me home. It was rather late... Now that you mention it, there was a small group of people in front of the chapel as we were walking. We didn't pay them much mind. We were talking about our wedding."

Sheriff Brentwood leaned forward in his seat. "Did you notice anything?"

Beau came around and lowered himself into a squat. "Do you remember anything, Lily?"

She closed her eyes and frowned. "There were three men and one woman. It was too dark to see much of anything. I only knew there was three men because they were in pants. We were on the other side of the street and it was quite dark. I only looked at them for a moment. I'm sorry, that's all I remember. It might not have been her. I didn't see a struggle and I can't imagine she would've left with three men willingly."

"Unless..." Beau shook the thought from his head. "No, he's dead."

Sheriff Brentwood cleared his throat. "I'll decide what is and isn't important. Out with it."

Beau rose to his feet and returned to pacing behind Lily. "She said her husband was dead, that he froze, and I guess that holds true because I couldn't find a trace of him."

"But, perhaps this husband is still alive and could be the one who took her?" the sheriff asked, his eyes keen.

Lily shook her head. "Her husband would've made her go back for her gun, it was his. She said that it was the only thing he ever had worth anything. She leaves it under her bed and even takes it outside of town to shoot it once in a while. I peeked under her bed, it's still there."

Beau continued pacing. "No, it couldn't be. She said he was dead. We looked over by the chapel. We couldn't find any tracks. It was a muddy mess from the last snow and there are footprints every which way."

Sheriff Brentwood stood. "Lily, you go on to work and let Mrs. Bligh know we'll investigate this. Beau, you wait here until I get a small posse together. We'll ride out in an hour."

An hour later, Beau had saddled his horse and was waiting for Brentwood and his posse by the chapel. He was itching to get a move on.

Brentwood arrived with five men and reined in next to Beau. "All right men. As I said when I rounded you up, Ruby Gresham is missing. She was last seen by the chapel last night around ten, so they've got about twelve hours on us. Judrow, Jefferson, Carlson, you take the west end of town and work your way out. Me, Rockford, and Cahill will take the east.

They all turned and slowly made their way out of town, their eyes pinned to the ground. Once in a while, Brentwood would stop and ask passersby if they saw anything or knew of any suspicious looking men around town. No one saw or knew anything.

"Beau, go check that cabin she lived in, just to make sure it wasn't that husband you mentioned."

Beau pulled up on the reins. "But, he's dead. Ruby took care of his body. It'll be a waste of my time."

"Are you part of my posse or not? I've got to make sure we check everything. If it isn't her husband, it could be someone who knew him. We need to eliminate each lead." Beau sighed and turned his mount back toward town. It'd take hours to ride back to the cabin which meant he wouldn't be there when they found Ruby.

Brentwood hollered over his shoulder, "If you see anything, stay back. Don't be a hero without someone there to back you up."

Beau nodded. Staying hidden, even in plain sight, was a skill he'd honed to perfection. Not that it mattered, Ruby said Arnold was dead, which meant this trip would be a waste of his time.

RUBY'S STOMACH grumbled loudly and Boss sneered at her. "Now, that ain't even ladylike."

She hadn't eaten supper the night before, since she decided at the last minute not to intrude on Maddie's Christmas. She'd sat at home reading until Beau had knocked.

Boss stood up and shoved a piece of jerky in her mouth then returned to his chair. The sound of approaching horses made Boss jump and walk to the window. He held up two fingers.

"You get her mouth shut, y'hear?" He let the shabby curtain fall back into place.

Skunk came up behind her with a length of rag and held it over her mouth. She squirmed against him but the more she fought, the tighter he held on. The dry jerky in her mouth worked against her, keeping her from being able to swallow or yell. Boss opened the door a crack to talk to the men outside. Ruby jumped in the chair to make noise, then threw her head back into Skunk's stomach and twisted to the right, freeing her mouth for a moment. She spit out the remainder of the jerky and screamed.

The men outside shoved the door open, pushing Boss back into the cabin. Skunk shoved her forward and the chair tipped then fell sideways onto her arm, just missing the hearth. She ignored the pain shooting from her elbow to her shoulder and twisted her head to see Sheriff Brentwood and James Cahill cuffing Skunk and Boss. James walked to her, lifted her chair, then untied her. She massaged her wrists and gently touched her tender arm.

Hot needles shot through her hands as the blood rushed to her fingers. Her arm would be bruised mightily, but it'd be all right.

"Ruby, do you know where the third man is? We were told three men took you."

She shook her head. They weren't going to hurt her. She was free, but where was Beau?

"I don't know. There were three there last night, but I've only seen these two." She rubbed her arm gingerly.

"We'll have Dr. Peirce take a gander at you when we get back, if you want. Why don't you sit here while we finish taking care of these dogs?"

"James? Where's Beau? I would've thought..." she whispered.

"He was with us at first, but Brentwood was worried your husband had taken you and sent him to check the old cabin."

"But that doesn't make sense...I told Beau Arnold was dead."

James's eyes crinkled. "Beau told him that, but Brentwood is the boss in a posse and Beau seemed a little unsure."

Ruby shook her head, anger blinding her. "He's always going to worry Arnold's out there. Isn't my word good enough? If it isn't, then maybe he isn't good enough for me." She stomped outside for some air.

Ruby paced in front of the cabin.

He doesn't trust my word. I told him Arnold was dead, why doesn't he believe me?

She'd worn a clear path in the snow and mud when Brentwood and James came out of the cabin with Skunk and Boss. Sheriff Brentwood put them in the back of the buckboard Ruby assumed the men used to transport her to the cabin. Then he helped her into the front seat. He tied his horse to the side and climbed up next to her.

Sheriff Brentwood didn't say much on the trip back to town, which suited her just fine. She didn't have much to say to anyone. A bath and something to eat would go a long way toward scraping the last twelve hours from her memory. Though she knew it was silly and she was happy just to have been found, Beau's lack of faith in her had shaken her deeper than she thought it could.

After a long ride, they arrived in Cutter's Creek. Ruby didn't wait for the Sheriff to help her down.

"Sheriff Brentwood, if you don't mind. I'd like to go—" She fingered her snarled and grimy hair, "make myself right again, and get some rest. Can I come to the office tomorrow to give you my statement?"

Brentwood nodded. "Yes, ma'am. You do that. We caught them with you red-handed, so I don't mind locking them up without getting anything signed. You just stop by tomorrow."

She returned his nod and strode up the boardwalk toward Mrs. Cahill's. Each stair up to her apartment seemed to drain her. By the time Ruby reached the top, she could hardly move. There was no room in the small space to take a bath and not enough privacy for one, anyway. She heated some of the water from the bucket Lily had drawn that morning and used it to scrub her face and hands. It occurred to her to go to the inn and pay for a bath, but then she'd have to leave her apartment.

She changed into her nightgown, got into her bed, and curled under the covers. That's when she realized she was shaking, and not from the cold.

She'd been so close to dying, so close to something more horrible than she could imagine. She might not have made it home to her warm bed again. Would anyone have noticed? She wasn't sure who asked the sheriff to find her, but she couldn't believe it was Beau.

She'd no sooner got comfortable than Lily burst into the room and ran for her, throwing her arms around Ruby's shoulders.

"You're home! They found you!"

Ruby scooted out of reach and Lily sat on her bed.

"It was you, wasn't it, who told the sheriff I was missing?" The room felt terribly cold and Ruby yanked her blanket up around her. Lily stood and got her thick wool shawl from where it hung on her headboard. She wrapped it around Ruby's shoulders. "I was the one who went to find Beau, yes. It was Mrs. Bligh who suggested we go to the sheriff, though, if we hadn't found anything, I'd intended to go to him, anyway."

"I figured as much. Did Beau seem worried?" She tried to catch Lily's eye, but Lily rarely sat still. She was now flitting over to the potbellied stove to fill it with wood.

"Of course he did. He was worried sick about you."

"So worried sick that he left the search party to go off on his own." She knew it was childish to pout, especially when he couldn't defend his actions, but a little sulking felt good.

"Ruby, he turned as white as a sheet when I said you were missing. I only knew you were back because James found me at the chapel and told me. Oh!" She clapped her hands to her cheeks. "You must be starving! Let me run down to the inn and get you a hot meal. I'll be right back." She thrust her arms back into her coat sleeves and left the room in a rush.

Ruby's belly gave a rumble and she frowned, tucking herself back into the covers. The little stove glowed red from across the room, but Ruby shivered despite the sheen of sweat across her brow. She fluffed her bit of pillow and rested her head on it, closing her eyes.

A while later, something stirred her from her almost-slumber. She heard laughing and recognized it immediately as Arnold's. Clutching the covers, she pulled the coverlet over her head. The laughing continued, *louder*.

"Go away. You're dead and I don't believe in spooks. Leave me alone." She pressed her hands to her ears.

The voice cackled louder. "I told you I'd get you, girl. I knew one day you'd let your guard down and put that gun away. I had to bide my time, but I got 'cha."

117

I don't believe in spooks. I don't believe in spooks. Lord, he's dead, make him go away!

"You leave me be, Arnold! You can't hurt me no more!"

The door swung open and Lily ran in. "Ruby? You're yelling so loud I can hear you outside. What's wrong?"

Lily pulled the covers back and Ruby hid her face from the light.

"Oh, you poor thing." She helped Ruby sit up. "You were gone all night. Do you want to talk about what happened?" Lily balanced a tray with a steaming bowl of soup on Ruby's lap.

"No, I surely don't." Ruby picked up her spoon but her hand shook and she dropped it back on the tray with a clatter. The scent of carrots, onions, chicken, and broth wafted to her nose and she inhaled deeply.

"I saw Beau while I was getting your soup. I let him know you'd been found. He asked to see you, but I told him you weren't up to a visit right now."

Ruby held out her arms and flinched at her plain nightgown, and nodded. "That's true."

"He seemed so worried. I don't think he was thinking straight and he looked pretty gruff."

"You got all that from looking at him?" Ruby managed to spoon a little into her mouth and the flavor burst on her tongue, spreading its warmth through her head. The ghostly laughter she'd not been able to shake finally died away.

"I spoke to him briefly. When I told him you'd been found, he said, '*no thanks to my help*'. He was pretty sulky about it."

Ruby spooned more soup into her mouth to avoid answering right away, savoring every drop. Lily laid her hand on Ruby's arm.

"I think he'd hoped he'd be the one to rescue you, but he had to go because the sheriff told him to. He was thinking out loud at the sheriff's office and mentioned your husband. I guess the sheriff couldn't let that lead die."

Ruby let the spoon clang into the ceramic bowl. "Even if Arnold was alive, I'd never, *ever* go back to him."

"Beau didn't know that and neither did the sheriff. You haven't talked to anyone about your life before Cutter's Creek, so how can you expect us to just understand?"

"Beau doesn't know because he didn't want to. He wouldn't let me finish telling him when I was trying to be honest with him. When he found out I'd been married, he told me he didn't want to know any more."

Lily squeezed her arm and Ruby yanked it away. "Is it so wrong that just once I wanted a man to think highly of me? To think of me as a treasure, instead of just…"

Lily knelt on the floor by the bed. "Ruby. He does. I've known Beau all my life. He was with me all through school, and I don't think I heard him say more than a smattering of words all those years. He talks to you even more than he used to talk to Penny. He seeks out your company. I know you don't want to, but please, give him another chance."

Ruby handed Lily the tray. "He has to trust me."

"What're you going to do?" Lily pushed away from the bed and stood.

"I don't know, yet. But I've only got until the weather warms up."

"You're right about that. He'll duck out as soon as he's able, especially now that May is back to care for their father."

A small part of Ruby wanted to just give up; Beau didn't trust her and maybe never would. But then, the feisty part of her took her by the shoulders and shook her. He'd been disappointed he hadn't found her himself, perhaps as disappointed as she'd been when she realized he hadn't been one of the men there to rescue her. That was something she could cling to.

CHAPTER 17

"Are you just going to walk a hole in the floor or are you going to go over there and ask what needs to be asked?" May thrust her wooden spoon at him.

He danced out of the way just as she tried to whack him with it. "It isn't right for a man to go to a woman's apartment when she might be alone, especially when she doesn't want to see him," he mumbled.

"Fine." She whipped her apron up over her head. "I have no such issue." She handed him the spoon. "Don't let it burn." She whisked past him and grabbed her coat.

"Wait!" he called. "If you'll be there then it isn't a problem if I am."

May laughed and grabbed a thick towel, pulling the soup off the stove and leaving it on the hearth. "All right. Let's go over and see how Ruby's doing."

He flung on his coat and tried to keep up with May. "Why are you in such a hurry to see her?"

"Because my brother is smitten with her. I want to get to know the woman who was able to climb *that* mountain." She lifted her skirts as she picked her way across the frozen, rutted street.

"May, wait! You can't say anything to her. She don't feel that way."

May stopped in her tracks and Mr. Jorgensen had to pull up hard on his lines to keep his horses from running her down in the street. May didn't seem to notice.

"Beau, you wouldn't know the first thing about how women think. You've been running from anything feminine for so long she could walk up to you, kiss you silly, and tell you she loves you, and you still wouldn't know for sure."

Beau felt heat rush to his cheeks as he glanced around to see if anyone heard May. Then he took her hand, tucking it into his arm to hold her back. "I'm not quite as daft as you think."

"We'll see."

He stopped at the base of the stairs leading to Ruby's apartment. "May, behave yourself."

She pulled her hand from his arm and rang the bell, then ran halfway up before he could stop her. "I always do." She turned and winked at him then ran the rest of the way, knocking as she landed on the last step.

Beau squared his shoulders. It wouldn't take much effort to rush up there and push his sister right over the edge of the landing...not that he would, but at least then she wouldn't make the situation any worse. He'd failed Ruby and she was probably hopping mad about it. *He* would be.

The door above him opened as he took the first step. "May, so good to see you!" Lily's voice floated down to him. He'd be outnumbered.

"Beau is tagging along. He'll be up in just a moment."

Lily peered down the stairs at him and he ran up the last few steps so she wouldn't have to hold the door open. The room was stiflingly warm and he pulled off his coat, draping it over one of the chairs. May did the same. Ruby sat at the table, her hands and face pale. She was wrapped in two thick cloaks. She stood but focused on her hands clutching the table in front of her.

Beau stepped forward and took her hands in his, they were like ice. "Ruby. I'm so glad to see you back. You had me worried."

She pulled her hands from his and sat back down, wrapping the shawls tightly around her. May pulled up a chair. "It's a good thing they didn't get far. What did they want?"

Beau laid his hand on May's shoulder and squeezed. "She probably doesn't want to talk about it, May."

Ruby glanced up. "They were on the hunt for someone else. When they realized I wasn't the one they were after, they waited to decide what to do, that's what gave the sheriff time to find me."

Beau couldn't hide his flinch. He couldn't blame anyone but himself. He'd had to leave the search to check something else. Something pointless. Something that took him away from the one woman he'd wanted to save.

"Were they searching for Mrs. Ivy Masters?" May leaned forward in her seat.

"How did you know?" Ruby's brow wrinkled.

"Mrs. Masters may not know it, but there's a price on her head. She's worth about $10,000 alive, only $2,000 dead. Or, she was. Her husband was murdered, so the bounty is now void. We're still searching for her, but only to award her the proceeds of the will. The amount is undisclosed and *much* higher than her bounty. Her relatives would like nothing more than if Ivy were never found. Then they wouldn't have to share their fortune."

"So, you aren't going to turn her in?" Ruby tucked a lock of hair behind her ear then hunched deeper into her shawls.

"You sound like you might know something about the situation." May stared across the table and Beau held his breath.

Ruby frowned. "I know where Ivy is, but like I told the bounty hunters, I won't tell you anything until I can be sure it won't hurt her. I'd like to talk to Ivy to see if she wants to be found, inheritance or not."

"How is it that we've been hunting for her for over a month, yet you already knew where she was?"

The shadow of a smile crept across Ruby's mouth. "She was hurt in a way that only someone who shares that hurt would understand. She saw that in me." Ruby sought his eyes and, more than anything, he wanted to wipe the pain off her face. He wanted to give her new memories by helping her forget the old. He blinked and she'd glanced away. He'd make it up to her. In some way. He would.

I'll rescue her sisters for her.

He smiled. "May, I think we should let Ruby recover in peace. Why don't we say our goodbyes?"

"But, but, Beau. I'm talking to Ruby and I need to know about Ivy," May blustered.

"You heard the lady. She isn't going to tell you a single thing until she talks to Ivy, so you'd best let her rest up so she can." He stood and pulled out May's chair so roughly she almost lost her balance. May threw an evil glare over her shoulder. He pulled her coat off the back of her chair and draped it over her shoulders, then pulled his own coat on over his. "I hope to see you soon and as right as rain, Ruby." He strode over to the door. "Coming May?"

May glared at him as she shoved her arms into her coat. "Yes, brother." She elbowed him in the ribs as she stomped by. He held his stomach and tipped his hat to Ruby and Lily, securing the door behind him.

"What was that all about. We'd just begun a good visit. They hadn't even offered us anything to drink yet." May stomped down the street.

"Couldn't you see how tired she looked? She wasn't glad to see us and she wasn't going to tell you anything else about Ivy. She doesn't know you and if she knew about your original plans for Ivy, she certainly wouldn't tell you anything."

May had the grace to blush. "I've thought about that a bit. I've only ever known people who cared about me so it seemed a bit odd that she'd run away, especially from a rich husband. But Emerson's been telling me about the Masters family, and if it had been me in that situation, I don't know that I would've stayed."

"So, when did Mr. Caruso become just Emerson?" Since May changed the subject, he'd go along with it.

"Emerson is still Mr. Caruso at work, but we do talk some at lunch and after office hours."

"I thought there was nothing between you two?" He tried to catch her eye, but she moved too quickly.

"I said he didn't show any interest. He may not stay in Cutter's Creek. Since I must stay for Pa's sake, it wouldn't do any good for me to form any attachment to him, but that doesn't mean I can't enjoy the time I have with him while I have it."

"And what if he does stay?"

"Then perhaps I will see what he feels, if anything. I know you think of him as cold, but really, the Ivy plan was mine, not his. The Masters family has always provided for him, but he sees Cutter's Creek as a possible way of escape. We'll just see if he takes it."

"Give him a reason to, May."

"Now you sound like me." She crossed her arms over her chest.

"It wasn't bad advice," he shrugged, hiding a grin.

"Do you think they are gone and do you think they'll follow me if I go talk to Ivy right away?" Ruby chewed her finger nail.

Lily sat down on her bed. "I'm sure I don't know. Do you think it's wise to go out when you're ill?"

"It isn't that I want to, but if it means that Ivy could finally be free, I'll do it." Ruby stood and the room spun, she fought to keep what little she ate in her stomach. She stumbled back to her seat. "Just maybe not this minute."

"That's what I thought. Give yourself another few days. If you're not better by tomorrow, I'm going to ask Dr. Peirce to come see you. Oh! That reminds me, I heard that Maddie went to see Dr. Gentry earlier today. In his opinion, she's just fine. He wasn't sure what Dr. Peirce saw that made him think she was unwell, but he couldn't find anything."

"So, I'm without a job, again." Ruby let her head fall into her hands.

"If you haven't been fired yet, then don't worry about it. You love little Malcom and they can keep you on as a nanny."

"They don't need a nanny. Maddie would love to sit with her baby and play, she just hasn't been allowed to. Now she can, and that's wonderful." Warmth spread through Ruby's chest. "And watching little Malcom made me feel something I never thought I would."

"The feeling of wanting children?" Lily moved to the table, sitting next to Ruby.

"Yes. I never wanted them before, since I come from such a big family. I thought I had my fill of little ones."

"I know what you mean. I was an only child and feared having any of my own, but I am so smitten with James's baby, David. He even calls me 'Lily-mommy', which would be frowned on if anyone but his father and mother heard, but I love it. I can't wait to be his mommy for real."

"I'm glad you'll have that chance." Ruby closed her eyes and tried to imagine what a family would be like, but try as she might, Beau was the only man she could picture as her husband. Beau, her sisters, and her. They could be a family. If only she could rescue them from the same fate Pa had dealt her.

"You'll have that chance, soon enough. It didn't seem to bother you one bit when Beau showed up just now."

"I had no idea he'd come and certainly not May, though she was only here because she suspected the whole thing had to do with Ivy."

"Now, here's the question." Lily stood and put her hands on her hips. "Do you trust me? If you do. I'll go out tonight after dark and bring Ivy here so you can talk to her."

"If it wasn't safe for me to wander at night, what makes you think you'd be safe?" Ruby's heart raced and she clutched the edge of the table.

"Well, if she's in hiding, she isn't going to come out in the daytime, is she?" Lily said. "It isn't like I want to go out, especially after you were taken. But those men were caught and I don't see any other way."

"I've been to see her during the day once before. I'll go tomorrow, after I speak to Maddie about my job."

"If that suits you." Lily frowned. "Would trusting me have been so hard?"

"She asked me not to tell anyone. I can't break her trust."

"Ruby, you have to learn that there are some people in this world who aren't trying to hurt you and take advantage of you. By the same token, if you look for bad people, you'll always find them."

"Lily, you've never been traded like a cow. You've never had someone you thought loved you, cast you away."

"That isn't true. Your hurts aren't so much different than mine. I was terrified I'd be ostracized right along with my parents, but the people of Cutter's Creek understood. You have to open up. If you don't let people love you, and learn to love people, imperfect as they are, you'll always be lonely."

"I'll go as soon as I'm feeling up to it." Ruby ducked her head, avoiding Lily's gaze.

Lily sighed loudly. "If you want to sit here and wallow, then so be it. I'll be back later."

The door clicked shut behind Lily and the laughing in Ruby's head grew louder. She covered her ears and it grew louder still.

"You won't win, Arnold. I won't let you."

The voice just laughed harder. "I already have."

CHAPTER 18

"May, I need to find somewhere to put the Arnsby girls."
Beau strode back and forth in front of the fire.

May laid her open book in her lap and set a ribbon on her page, closing it and setting it aside. She cocked her head slightly. "There aren't many homes in Cutter's Creek that'd be big enough to comfortably house that many girls. You could practically found a school with all of them."

Beau frowned. "That isn't helpful, May."

"Well, Mrs. Camden has enough room, but she'd never agree to it. Dr. Peirce has a few rooms, but he needs them. The Moore's have a large house and might be willing to take in some girls, but I don't know that anyone who has the room would be able to afford that many extra mouths to feed. Most folks here have only stored enough food for their own families for the winter."

Beau stared into the fire. "I have a little money squirrelled away, I only used a bit of it to bring you back here. I'd hoped to use it to move to Dakota, but Ruby and her sisters are more important."

"Oh, the Williams's! They have lots of room in that lovely old house of theirs. It reminds me of the Queen Anne style homes in

Maine. Honestly, it'd have to be the Moore's or the Williams's, all other homes in Cutter's Creek are too small or too full."

"I can't go talk to Heath about this, word might get back to his wife who'd then tell Ruby. It's important to me that I surprise her. I failed her by not finding her myself, I need to make it up to her."

"Well, now that Dr. Gentry is here you can go visit the Williams's. There's an announcement in the paper about the impending marriage of Dr. Gentry and Carol Williams. They are to be wed on the New Year."

"Carol is getting married?" He couldn't believe it. It hadn't been that long ago she'd been chasing his coattails and he'd been running in the opposite direction.

"Yes, sometimes these things move fast." May laughed. "Now that Cutter's Creek doesn't have to worry about their young men, perhaps the good doctor can also keep her from wagging her tongue. If he can do that, she'll make him a good wife."

"*Harrumph.*" Beau returned to pacing in front of the fire. "So, I can choose between a couple getting married in days, or a family where Ruby works…"

"Go, talk to Heath first. Let him know it has to remain a secret. If they are unable to do it, you can always go right over to the Williams's house and try there."

Beau donned his hat and coat. "Best get it squared away. I'm not looking forward to the trip to Yellow Medicine this deep in winter, but this can't wait."

While the streets of Cutter's Creek were generally bustling in the summer, the winter was another story. People tended to stay indoors unless they were forced outside. The less people had to open their doors, the less heat they lost. He knew all this yet it still shocked him to walk outside and find empty streets. It didn't help that it was closing in on the dinner hour. If he hurried, he could catch Heath before he sat down to eat.

He knocked on the front door and tried to hide his surprise when Maddie answered.

"Beau! I haven't seen you in quite some time. Heath just got home. I'll take you to him." She stepped back, letting him in and taking his coat.

She led him to the back of the house, to a small office where Heath sat opening his mail. He glanced up and nodded, smiling at Maddie.

"Hello Beau, thank you dear." He stood and kissed her on the cheek, then closed the door as she left. "I haven't seen you in some time, Beau. Are you hoping to work at the mill? Cahill is looking for a couple men. I could surely get you in." He gestured for Beau to sit.

"I might take you up on that, since I've got to stay here all winter, but that's not what I came to see you about." Beau scratched his chin and tried to think of a good way to ask someone to take in what'd amount to seven orphans.

"Did you want to join us for dinner and talk about it? I'm sure Maddie won't mind. Since we let the cook go this morning she's been cooking constantly." He laughed.

"I don't know that that's such a good idea... You know Ruby, of course."

"Well, yes. Maddie knows her better than I do, but yes."

Beau leaned forward in his seat. "Ruby doesn't know that I'm here, and I'd rather she didn't find out. She has seven sisters and they are in a bad way. I plan to bring them here to Cutter's Creek to live with Ruby, but she doesn't have the room in her tiny apartment. Do you have room here, just until spring? We could find some other place for them by then."

Hopefully, they'll be with me in the house I'll get for Ruby and her family...

Heath shook his head. "Seven? That's a lot of extra mouths to feed, Beau. Maddie was just given a clean bill of health, and I'd like her to not be worn out by watching extra children."

Beau closed his eyes and let his head drop a bit. "Would it change your mind if I paid Ruby's wages?"

"I'm sorry, Beau. I don't mind telling you it scared me when Dr. Peirce said Maddie shouldn't tax herself overmuch. We still don't know why he said that, so we don't know if it could happen again. I have to think of my wife first."

"I understand. Thank you for talking with me about it." He stood and shook hands with Heath.

Heath nodded. "I wish I could help in some way, but we just can't."

Beau left the room and Maddie met him by the door, handing him his coat. "My, that was a short visit. Are you sure you won't join us for supper, Beau? It's no trouble at all."

"Thank you kindly, but I've got a few more errands to attend to before I can sit down for a meal."

She smiled, opening the door and letting him out. That left him with one other place; the house he didn't want to go to. He'd made it a point not to go to the Williams house after Josiah had gotten married, mostly because of Carol Williams. Even if she was getting married, she wasn't yet, and he didn't want to put himself within her reach.

The lateness of the hour meant he'd have to delay his visit until the morning.

He might have to delay his plan, anyway. With the doctor and Carol getting married, they'd leave on a honeymoon. While they couldn't go anywhere besides the hotel for a honeymoon, Beau couldn't leave Mr. Williams in charge of so many girls.

Those Arnsby girls might have to wait until mid-January for their rescue. That didn't sit well with him.

RUBY PULLED her cloak on over her dress. After a full night's sleep and a good, hot meal, she felt much better. First, she'd go speak to Ivy, then she'd make her report to the sheriff. Hopefully, the men who kidnapped her would stay jailed until the circuit judge could come for a trial. Though, with the weather, they could sit in the jail for months, not that she minded, as long as they were far from her and Ivy.

The sun warmed her black cloak as she strode down the street.

It had brought others out to enjoy the day. Ruby nodded or waved to a few people she knew, hoping none of them would notice her going to the Williams's back door. She dashed a glance behind her as she turned down the street and all the way to the end. No one followed her and there was no one in the street to see.

She knocked lightly. The door opened a crack and a dark blue eye appeared.

"Oh, Ruby. Come on in out of the cold." Ivy opened the door and stepped back.

Ruby came in and embraced Ivy before hanging her cape on the hook by the door.

"I had to come as soon as I could. I'm not sure if you heard, but Christmas night I went to the chapel for a word with the reverend. When I came out, three men took me, thinking I was you."

"Oh no! Not here! They couldn't be here already." Ivy covered her mouth with her fingertips.

"They were caught when I was found. But, when May Rockford came over to find out about it, she told me that your husband —" she looked toward the kitchen door and lowered her voice—, "isn't searching for you anymore. And, should you want it, there is a large sum that you'd get by way of inheritance."

Ivy's face twisted in anger. "I don't want a single cent from that family. Not a one. All I want is for them to leave me alone for the remainder of my days."

"I think you should visit that lawyer, Caruso. Maybe he could write something up that says you won't take the inheritance if they leave you be?"

Carol walked in, smiled, and pulled out a chair next to Ruby. "I had no idea you two were acquainted! Ruby, how are you? I haven't seen you since the Christmas social."

Ivy set down a cup in front of each of them and turned back to her work, her movements harsh and angry.

"I was just talking to Ivy for a bit. How are you? I hear there is to be another wedding in Cutter's Creek next week."

Carol clasped her hands in front of her and sucked in her breath. "Yes! Manning proposed Christmas day and he doesn't want to wait. It'll be a small ceremony at the chapel. You're welcome to come."

Ivy set the tea service down on the table; she seemed unruffled except for the shallow crease across her forehead. "Ruby brings me news that may or may not allow me to go to your wedding, Carol."

Carol squealed and bounced in her seat. "Really? That'd be wonderful! You won't have to hide anymore?"

"Perhaps, though with what I've been through it's difficult to believe it isn't a trick to make me reveal myself."

Ruby laid her hand on Ivy's. "You once told me that Caruso was honest enough. May works for him and she is Beau's sister. I don't think she'd steer you wrong."

"Be that as it may, after hiding and running for so long, it's difficult to believe that it could be over…just like that."

"I don't think you have anything to lose by talking to Mr. Caruso, in fact, I'll take you over there if you wish, so you don't have to go alone."

"Thank you, Ruby." A subtle smile lightened Ivy's eyes.

Ruby turned to Carol. "Carol, I need to ask something of you. Normally, I would never, but the situation is dire. I couldn't help but notice that you have a large house and only the few of you. Will you and Dr. Gentry remain here or will you want a place of your own?"

Carol smiled and reached for her tea. "It is a beautiful house. Our plan is to stay here. Though, the house is much too large for Father to maintain alone and Manning intends to take over Dr. Peirce's practice in the coming year. He'll begin working with Dr. Peirce in February."

Ruby drummed her fingers on the table. "I'm about bursting with something I need to tell. I want to take the stage to Yellow Medicine and get my sisters, but they need a place to stay once they get here. Carol, do you think you'd have room here if I were to pay for room and board? They're used to work and could help with cleaning and even starting a garden in the spring."

Carol raised a dark eyebrow. "I'd have to talk to my father, but I can't see him turning homeless girls out in the cold. There is nowhere else big enough in Cutter's Creek, except for the inn, and that'd be expensive."

Ivy sat next to them. "Aunt Amelia's would be big enough, but she'd never accept strangers in her house."

Carol nodded her agreement. "Ruby, when do you think you'll go?"

Ruby sighed. "I'd thought to go as soon as the next stage heads for Yellow Medicine. No one will miss me because they will think I'm still in my apartment, getting better. I don't know how I'll do it, or even how I'll face my pa, but I know my sisters can't stay there any longer. I just have this feeling they need to get away, and fast. Jennie is eighteen now, older than I was when Pa married me off to Arnold. If he does the same with Jennie, I may never see her again."

"Well, that won't do." Carol shook her head. "Just how are you going to get them away?"

"Well, fact is, he don't want them. I was hoping he'd just let me come get them."

Ivy reached over and squeezed Ruby's arm. "We'll pray they'll be easily delivered from him."

"I'll wait to go until I hear from you, Carol." Ruby glanced at her.

"Well, since it hasn't snowed in some time, the next stage could go out any day. I'll go talk to him right now. He's been doing much better since his fall."

Ivy nodded. "It's true. His appetite is better and he talks more now than he did when I started. He reminds me a lot of my own father, before he passed."

"I'll return shortly." Carol stood and left the room.

Ivy poured more steaming water in Ruby's cup and pushed the crock of honey toward her. "Do you really think I should go see the lawyer?"

Ruby dunked the infuser into her cup thoughtfully. "I do. I think if you have the chance to be free, you should take it."

"And if it's just a ruse to flush me out?"

"I know you're scared, but I don't think there's anything to be afraid of."

Ivy frowned, then nodded. "All right. I'll go, as long as you go with me. I've not faced Mr. Caruso alone before. My husband had always been present."

Carol burst back into the room. "Ruby! Father says he'd love to fill the house! You can bring them whenever you wish!"

Relief, bright and hot, rushed through Ruby. "Finally, some good news." She smiled. "If it's agreeable to you, I'll take Ivy over to see Mr. Caruso. I'd like to help her before I head out. I've heard the ride to Yellow Medicine in the winter is treacherous and I'd feel better about setting out if this was done first. I also need to talk to Maddie and make sure she's all right."

"By all means! It's early so Ivy will have plenty of time to finish dinner, and I can work on it while she's away."

Ivy's eyes widened. "Please, don't. I want your father to get better, not worse." She laughed.

Carol rolled her eyes and flounced from the kitchen.

CHAPTER 19

Beau strode into Mr. Caruso's office. He'd been inside the building before but had never ventured into the office itself, only staying in the hallway to wait for May. The office was wood-paneled, with book shelves along one wall. May's small desk was attached to Mr. Caruso's on the right. She sat straight-backed in her seat taking dictation from Mr. Caruso.

Both stopped working as he strode in. "Beau, welcome." May stood and led him to the client seat in front of Mr. Caruso's desk. "What brings you by?"

"I was wondering what it'd cost to have a contract drawn up?" He tried to avoid eye contact with May.

Mr. Caruso pulled a sheet of paper from his desk. "What kind of contract?"

Beau felt the heat rush up his neck. He'd hoped May wouldn't be at the office, but he should have known she would be, since she hadn't been at home. "A…marriage contract."

May squealed and jumped in her seat. Mr. Caruso shot her a scathing glance then set his pen down. "Beau, that isn't how it works. We have a form that we fill in when a marriage takes place.

You can have the reverend do your wedding or wait for the circuit judge."

"No, I'm not looking for a wedding contract. I want a *marriage* contract, saying I agree to stand by her and provide for her, that I'll never take advantage of her. That I...think the world of her."

May wrote furiously, the scratching of her pen disrupting his thoughts. He glanced over at her, then back at Caruso. "So, what would that cost?"

Mr. Caruso leaned back in his seat. "Well, that isn't something I've seen. Would she then hold the agreement, and what would her recourse be if you do not follow through? A contract is a serious thing, Beau."

"I know it is. Binding. I want her to know that she doesn't ever have to fear anything from me. As far as what she could do if I break it..." His blood ran cold in his veins and he suppressed a shiver. "I'd say she could leave me and ... I'd let her go."

Mr. Caruso nodded. "Being as that you're a *friend*, Beau, I'd write up such a contract for you for one dollar, not a cent more. I'm not even sure the contract will be worth more than the paper it's written on, since it isn't like Ruby has the power to contest it."

"That ain't the point. I want her to know I'd be willing to sign a contract saying she could leave if she wants to. She won't ever be trapped, again."

"I understand. It'll take me a day to make sure I get the wording just right." He glanced at May. "You took down notes of what he wanted, I presume?"

May nodded and handed him the sheet of paper.

"Thank you, May." He folded his hands over the note. "You can come back tomorrow and make sure everything is just as you want it."

Beau stood. "Thank you." He shook Mr. Caruso's hand as the door opened and Ruby and another young woman he'd never seen before came in.

Mr. Caruso dropped his hand and gasped. "Ivy Masters...."

∼

RUBY'S EYES widened as Beau leapt toward Mr. Caruso's desk and flipped over a sheet of paper. She cocked her head at him as he stood up straight, raking the back of his neck with his hand and peering at the floor.

"Ruby, didn't expect to see you here. I was just going..." He glanced at Mr. Caruso. "I'll be back tomorrow."

Mr. Caruso nodded and Beau wove his way through the small office, brushing her arm as he walked by. His scent wrapped around her and she closed her eyes, savoring it. He was gone before she opened her eyes again.

Ivy stepped forward and pulled her hood down. "Emerson Caruso, I *hope* it's good to see you." She hesitated then held out her hand.

He accepted it and bent, brushing her knuckles with his lips. "Mrs. Masters, you have my deepest condolences on the loss of your husband."

Her blue eyes widened. "So it's true," she whispered. "I'm free."

"You are, indeed." He dug through a few papers on his desk and handed her a letter.

She skimmed it briefly and handed it back, Ruby stayed near the door, waiting to see what she should do.

"So, why haven't you left? The letter said you are required to execute the will. The Masters don't take kindly to being ignored."

"No one knows that better than you and I." He sat in his chair and indicated that she should sit as well. "May, why don't you take Miss Arnsby into the hallway for a bit. Mrs. Masters and I have a bit of private business to discuss."

May nodded and stood. Ruby didn't know what to do, she'd agreed to stay with Ivy, and how did Caruso know *her* name?

Ivy nodded her agreement, and Ruby followed May out of the room.

May closed the door behind them and stood in front of it like a guard on duty.

Ruby walked to the chair beside the hall door and sat. "I don't suppose Beau was just visiting you before I came? He looked mighty nervous."

May strode past her to the base of the stairs. "You mean as nervous as you do now? I'd love to tell you why he was there, Ruby, but I'd lose my job. What he's doing is a good thing, that's all I'll say. Come with me." She started up the stairs.

"Up there?" Ruby squeaked. "We can't go up to Mr. Caruso's apartment!"

"And why not? Believe it or not, I go up there all the time."

"May Rockford, are you...?"

May frowned, rolling her eyes. "No, Mr. Caruso and I are not acquainted in *that way*. Like you and your former husband, or whatever he was, we've been alone for some time and nothing has happened. As much as I sometimes wish otherwise."

"May!"

"Oh, don't sound so shocked. The good Lord made desires for a reason; I desire the man. Didn't say I'd actually do anything about it."

She strode up the remainder of the stairs and opened the door. "Are you coming? Surely it's fine if it's just the two of us up here."

Ruby waited and rubbed her brow. "It don't seem right to go in a man's space."

May strode down the stairs and yanked Ruby up behind her. "Come on, there's something you have to see."

Ruby lost the fight and followed May. She stopped just after the threshold and waited as May dashed to a back room and returned with a book. She opened it and pulled out another, smaller book from the hollowed out inside.

"Ruby, do you believe my brother loves you?"

Ruby backed out the door. She couldn't answer that question, didn't want to examine it too closely.

May rushed over and yanked Ruby back into the room, and closed the door. May pushed her down onto the plush sofa in front of the large window facing the street.

"Now, answer me. Do you believe my brother loves you? Notice I didn't ask what you think. I already know the answer."

Ruby shook her head. "No, I don't."

May handed her the small leather book. "These are the things he has said to me, just about you. I keep them here so Beau won't know, and so I can give Emerson a few hints. My brother is more romantic than I thought possible, but only about you. You're the only woman who could bring him out of his shell. In fact, if you look at the last page, you'll find a note he wrote Christmas night… He was so sorry for scaring you away. Please, don't take that lightly. He loves you. You have my word."

"You don't understand, May. He doesn't trust me. You can't love someone you don't trust."

"Ruby, dear. You don't know me from Eve, that's why I gave you the book. Read it yourself and find out from his own words."

"But you wrote this. How do I know he said it?"

May winked. "I guess you won't know until you read it."

She looked at the small journal and clutched it close. Whether his words were written in the book, it didn't matter, she loved him. She couldn't imagine life without Beau.

Ruby rushed out of the room and down the stairs, her thoughts flying. She'd only ever ridden a horse when Josiah had brought her to Cutter's Creek. She couldn't control one on her own. She'd have to pray the stage would go through today and hope it hadn't left yet.

She ran up the stairs to her apartment and flung the door open. Lily shrieked as Ruby ran in.

"What are you doing, flying in here like that?"

"I've no time to talk. I have to catch the stage." She tossed her carpet bag on the bed and stuffed her few dresses inside. She reached into the pocket of her one evening dress and pulled out the few dollars she'd managed to save. It wouldn't be enough, especially if her father wanted some type of payment. Also, she'd have to pay for eight passengers on the return stage. She didn't have near enough.

She pulled her shotgun out from under the bed and set it down. It was the only thing of value from her former life, and though she didn't want to hold onto it because of who'd owned it, it had kept her safe for so long it was like an old friend.

"If I can save the money when I return, I can buy it back," she whispered. Ruby turned to Lily. "I'm sorry. When I return, I'll be staying with my sisters at Carol's. Can you manage here without me?"

"Well, of course, but Ruby, I really don't think you should go. It'll be dangerous. You should tell the sheriff or take Beau with you. You shouldn't even ride the stage in the winter."

"No. I need to do this on my own." Ruby checked the barrel of the gun out of habit, then set it back on the bed.

She swung out of her cloak and tucked it into the bag. It was the only piece of clothing she'd ever bought for herself. It was a butter-soft black wool, but she'd give it up in a heartbeat for her sisters. Grabbing Penny's old coat with the fraying elbows, she pulled it on around her. Ruby hefted the shotgun and the now-heavy carpet bag and left before Lily succeeded in changing her mind.

CHAPTER 20

Beau sat in front of the fire waiting for May to get home for supper. She'd gloat about his visit to Caruso. She was later than usual and he wondered what Ruby was doing at the lawyer's office to keep her there. Why'd Ruby need a lawyer? It made no sense.

Someone banged on his door and he jumped to his feet. The pounding continued and Lily almost fell into him as he yanked it open.

"Beau! You have to hurry. Ruby's going to get her sisters, she just left for the stage. I don't know when it leaves."

He grabbed his coat and rushed out, putting it on as he ran. She couldn't leave on her own, she'd be in danger of every two-legged varmint in the area. The stage coach station was on the other end of town, down by the railroad. As he turned the corner onto the main street, he could see the driver climb up onto the stage and tap the top of the coach with the butt of the whip to let the passengers know he was about to leave.

"Stop!" Beau couldn't catch his breath. The driver ignored him and pulled a timepiece from his coat pocket. He tucked it back in, pulled on his gloves, and cracked the whip above the draft horses heads, sending them off with a jump.

"No! Ruby!" He yelled, running to the spot where the coach had been. "No," he rasped, holding the stitch in his side.

"Beau?"

He stood up straight and turned to see Ruby, holding her carpetbag in both hands.

"I ... missed the coach," she stammered. "What are you doing here?" she asked.

Words escaped him. His heart soared, and the stitch that had stolen his breath a moment ago was replaced by something wholly different, but left him just as breathless. He strode up to her, taking the bag from her hands and setting it by her feet. He cupped her soft face in his hands and she glanced at him, confusion in her eyes. Wisps of her hair blew across his knuckles, tickling and tempting him. Her face fit so perfectly in his hands and he pulled her closer until he could see each beautiful fleck of gold fire in her eyes. He kissed her temple, enjoying the hitch of her breath as his lips touched her silky skin. Then he kissed each of her cheeks. She turned her head to meet his mouth, and he pulled her against him as their lips met for the first time.

She was warm, inviting, intoxicating. She drew away, and he wanted to gather her into his arms again, but her expression tore at his heart. She was not afraid, not of him, anyway.

He covered her mouth with his finger. "I know you want to get your sisters. I do, too. Will you let me do this for you? He'll let me take them, he offered to let me take Jennie when I saw him last."

She squinted at him and tilted her head. He moved his finger and she asked, "What do you mean, *'when you saw him last'*?"

"I should've told you, but I didn't want to upset you." He paused, forming the words slowly. "I saw your father the last time I went to Yellow Medicine, that time I found your cabin. Can you forgive me for keeping it from you?"

"He didn't care, did he?" Her lip trembled and he pulled her close, tucking her head under his chin.

"It don't matter if he did or not. He's a fool. And you know what? I'd like to take you with me when I go to get your sisters. I want you to show him what a strong woman you are, that you didn't need him and your sisters don't need him, either."

She wrapped her arms around his waist and he tightened his hold on her, convinced he could never let her go.

"We can't travel alone without being married, though. I was going to wait until Caruso was done with my contract before I asked you, but you rushed me a bit." He let out a soft chuckle, then a heated thrill rushed through him. "I'd like to make you my wife, Ruby. If you'll have me?"

She clutched the back of his neck, pulling him into a kiss that lit a fire in his heart and quickly ignited every part of him.

As she broke the kiss and met his gaze, her eyes danced with deep emotion. "I'm sure the preacher is in."

RUBY COULDN'T BELIEVE she was a married woman. For real this time; for the first time, as far as she was concerned.

She sat on the bench of the buckboard Beau had borrowed from Josiah and held onto his leg, since his hands were busy. He kept glancing down at her hand, and she could feel the tension in his muscles, even through the thick dungarees he wore. They hadn't been dressed for a wedding, and had to pull two people off the street to be witnesses, but it was done. Mrs. Bligh chuckled through the whole service and made kissy faces at her, right before Reverend Bligh had pronounced them husband and wife. Ruby took Mrs. Bligh's silly faces to mean she should kiss her new husband good, and she had. If he weren't driving, she would again. She'd never dreamt kissing could be so enjoyable.

Now they'd spend their wedding night at the inn in Yellow Medicine, with seven young girls... For once, she was a little disappointed she wouldn't be alone with a man. She squeezed Beau's leg and he turned and stole a kiss, quickly turning back to driving the team. Her insides fluttered. She was Ruby Rockford and soon she'd be caretaker of a whole passel of Arnsbys. Beau said it'd be easy to get her sisters, and she hoped he was right. She prayed her father was sober and not in the mood to fight.

The road was rutted; frozen mud and the buckboard bounced them around. She held tight to the side and to Beau. He'd never let her fall, but it was a whole day's ride and they had gotten a very late start. He slowed the horses and let them walk for a bit. He glanced over at her and nestled her closer to him.

"Are you cold?" His breath fanned over her face and she snuggled in near to his side.

"Not now." She smiled up at him.

He reached behind him and grabbed a blanket, handing it to her. She draped it over their legs and tucked it beneath her to trap the heat. Her stockings and petticoats provided some warmth, but the cold had seeped through. Beau held the lines in one hand and draped his other arm around her.

"I need to let them rest a bit and I…uh was wondering…since it's going to be so late when we get to Yellow Medicine and I already have a credit at the inn…" He ducked his head away from her.

She reached under the blanket and put her arms around his waist. "I think my sisters will still be there tomorrow morning." He sighed and kissed the top of her head. She smiled. The Lord sure answered her fears and worries in strange ways.

It was full dark when they pulled into Yellow Medicine, and she helped Beau unhitch the team, mostly she just kept him company, since she hadn't any idea what to do with all the leather straps and rings. Beau was nervous or cold and his hands fumbled with the buckles. He spoke to the liveryman about his credit. The liveryman wrote something down and then Beau took her hand, leading her into the warm inn.

He waved to a man in a preacher's collar then he approached the front desk to speak with a man there. He nodded and handed Beau a key. Ruby's heart tripped at the sight of it, her shyness returning in spades.

Beau gently took her hand and led her up the stairs, holding her carpet bag in his other hand. Reaching their room, he unlocked the door and pushed it open, then led her in, closing the door behind them.

She faced him and he captured her lips against his own crushing her to him, but not near enough to suit her. She wrapped her arms around his neck and he ran his hands up her sides and down to her hips.

She didn't want him to say a word, didn't want him to ask any questions. If he did, it might ruin all the feelings rushing through her. They could talk about what she had done, and hadn't done, in the morning.

CHAPTER 21

Beau woke with lovely red hair spilling over his chest, and a lovely wife tucked in beside him, breathing softly. He slipped his hand under her head and kissed her gently. Her eyes fluttered open.

There were millions of things he wanted to say, but there wasn't much time for talking. "We should leave soon. We've got a long ride ahead of us if we want to make it back to Cutter's Creek with your sisters."

She wiggled up close and kissed him on the nose.

"I could wake up like that every morning." He smiled.

"I can see to that." She rested her head on his chest.

It took them a while longer to get down to breakfast but they hoped the trip out to Ruby's parents would go quickly and smoothly. As it was, they'd probably have to bunk at his Pa's house that night as it'd be too late to take them over to the Williams's house. They ate in a rush and got the team hitched for the ride out. It was only a few miles to the Arnsby place.

Beau lifted Ruby onto the buckboard and she settled herself next to him. He couldn't say much, and hoped he didn't have to. He was concerned about seeing Ruby's pa again. Though Ruby sat comfortably next to him, he could feel the tension in her arm next to his. She had to be even more nervous than he was.

Beau navigated through the thick trees over the narrow trail. As they got closer to the cabin, the horses shied and side-stepped as the smell of smoke surrounded them. Beau glanced over at Ruby, the fear etched on her face tore at him. He jumped down and grabbed the halter on the lead horse. They pulled against him, but he led them along the path as Ruby held the lines.

They came into the clearing to find black smoke billowing out the windows of the small home.

"Ruby, set the brake!" he called as he ran for the house. Ruby pulled the brake and wrapped the lines around it. She climbed down and rushed after her husband. Her mother and sisters stood outside the door, staring at the flames.

Ruby touched her mother's shoulder and the red-haired woman turned, gasped, and yanked Ruby into an embrace.

"What are you doing here, Ruby?" she yelled over the deafening fire.

"Beau and I came to get the others. Where's Pa?"

Her mother peered at Beau then shook her head. "I made him move the still into the cellar. He complained about it, but did as I asked. Two days ago, it started to smell right awful. Thank the good Lord the girls and I were out here gathering wood when the whole place just..." She shook her head, again her face twisted in pain.

"You take these girls and get them out of here."

"Ma, I can't just leave you here." Ruby grasped her mother's arms.

Beau stepped forward. "Ma'am, I'm sorry to meet you like this, but I'm Ruby's husband, Beau. I'd be happy to take you back to Yellow Medicine or back to Cutter's Creek with us, if you'd like. You can't stay here. It's the middle of winter. You'll freeze."

She shook her head. "Argus was my life. What'll I do without him?"

Beau appreciated the stubborn tilt of Ruby's head. "You still have us. There's room for all of us in Cutter's Creek, and I've missed you so much."

Ruby's mother held out her hand to Beau. "Maeve Arnsby, I'm pleased to see that my daughter wasn't as cursed as her father said she was."

Beau turned to the fire, it had eaten away most of the house, the roof had collapsed.

"I can try to put it out with buckets of snow, ma'am."

Maeve shook her head. "It's no use, Beau. We were standing here for quite some time, not knowing what to do. All the buckets were in the house, melting snow for water. The house is gone, though we should wait here until the fire dies down."

As much as Beau wanted to just leave it all behind and get Ruby out of there, the house was close enough to the trees that it'd be dangerous to leave it.

Beau wrapped his arm around her and squeezed, then went back to the wagon and grabbed the blanket out of the back. He wrapped it around the four youngest girls who were standing in a huddle. They'd be frozen if he didn't do something for them quickly. Though the fire was large, after being outside for so long, the girls were shivering.

Ruby took them over to the buckboard and got them settled on the seat, while he searched the garden and found a shovel. By the house, he found several large rocks, hot from the fire. He picked one up with the shovel and took it back to the buckboard, leaving it under the blanket Ruby's sisters were using.

As the fire died down, he and Ruby examined the inside without getting too close. The cabin that had been her home was now just a hole in the ground, with black charred boards sticking out of it. Everything was gone.

Maeve and Jennie moved to stand next to them.

"It's time for my girls and I to start new lives," Maeve said, her voice weak but her tone determined.

Beau led the women back to the wagon. Ruby waited while he got them all comfortable in the back, then he helped Ruby up and put another warm rock under the blanket. Seating himself, he took the lines.

"It's already getting dark. We should head back to town and start our trip back to Cutter's Creek in the morning."

Ruby nodded. Beau's throat tightened at her silence. She'd been strong in front of her mother and sisters, but now that they had a minute, he wanted to give some of his strength to her. She buried her head in his shoulder.

When they reached the inn, Beau gripped Ruby's small waist and lifted her down from the wagon.

"I'd like you to go inside and get two rooms, we'll have to split us up, five of us in each room."

Ruby nodded and waited as he helped each girl, then finally Maeve, down from the back of the buckboard. When he turned around again, Ruby was already inside. The day had turned from the best of his life, to the worst. Though Ruby's father had done a horrible thing by sending her off with Arnold, Ruby had still loved him. He could see it in the pain in her eyes.

He gave the wagon lines to the liveryman, then went inside to join the women. He found all nine of them sitting in the room he and Ruby had been in the night before; Maeve and the younger ones on the sofa, the older ones sitting in a circle around their mother's feet. Ruby was by the hearth, lighting a fire. He took over so she could go to her mother.

Very few words were said all evening and no one mentioned getting anything to eat. As the evening wore into night, Maeve took four girls with her and went into the next room, leaving he and Ruby with three of the older girls. Ruby got them situated on the sofa and the rug in front of the fire, then she turned to him. He held out his arms and she rushed into them. He stood holding her for a few minutes, giving comfort and accepting love.

A few hours later, Beau heard Maeve enter the room and begin waking the girls. He nuzzled Ruby awake. She rubbed her forehead and her face pinched.

"You need a shave." She reached up and scratched his chin.

"I'll do that when we get home, so let's get there." He kissed her and pushed himself off the bed.

Maeve collected all the girls. "I don't know how we're going to do this. We have nowhere to go, no clothes… How are you going to provide for all of us? Argus was never able to make enough, even with his business."

Ruby got to her feet and tidied her hair. "Ma, don't worry. I've got a bit of money and I don't mind sharing. We already have a place for you when we get there. We'd already planned to come get the girls."

"I just don't see how you're going to provide for all of us." She bit her lip.

"We'll worry about that when we get to Cutter's Creek." Beau nodded and counted each head as he took in the whole room. Ruby had told him all their names, but he could only remember the oldest was named Jennie, because her father had mentioned her the last time he'd been there. She had dark blond hair like her father. Hopefully, she wouldn't have the same temper.

"Let's go down and get a few bites to eat, and then we'll be on our way. It's a long drive back."

Beau made sure everyone was as comfortable as possible for the ride. He hoped no one bounced out the back with the ruts, but better that the road was frozen then full of snow or mud.

He tried to drive around the worse areas as best he could, but everyone was glad when the gaslights of Cutter's Creek came into view. Beau heard Maeve's sigh of relief.

He drove down the first few blocks of houses, then turned down the street to Carlton William's home. Beau climbed down and stretched the numbness from his legs. He strode up to Carlton's front door and knocked. Ivy answered and smiled.

"Good evening, Beau. Are these the girls?" She peered out into the night.

"Yes, and one extra. Their mother, Maeve, will be joining them, if that's all right with Carlton."

"I'm sure it is. Why don't you just bring them right on inside? I've spent all day preparing a few rooms for them."

Beau went back out to the buckboard. Ruby had already helped the younger girls down so Beau lifted the older ones. He brought Ruby, and all the others followed.

Ivy led the three oldest girls to one room on the second level, then the four younger girls to another room. When she came back down she introduced herself to Maeve.

"I don't have a room ready for you yet, but we do have plenty of space. Dr. Manning and Carol are on holiday at the inn, they were married yesterday. Carol won't mind if you use her room for the night."

"I thank you." Maeve appeared much older and more tired than when he'd met her just the day before.

"I wasn't sure when to expect you so I'll go to the kitchen and get you something to eat. I'm sure you didn't stop along the way."

Maeve shook her head and Ivy led her up the stairs to Carol's room, leaving Beau alone with his very tired, but happy, hopeful bride.

"Should we stay and make sure they are comfortable, or can I take you home, Ruby Rockford?"

Ruby blushed a pretty pink. "I think I'm ready to rest. Take me home Beau."

LOVE RUBY and Beau's story? Please leave me a review. From here, you can either continue reading in the Cutter's Creek series to find out what happens with Ivy Masters, or, if you want to know what happens with Ruby and her sisters, follow that story in Dreams in Deadwood.

DREAMS IN DEADWOOD

I dedicate this book to the writers who have helped me so much along the way: Melissa, Kit, Lynda, and Julie just to name a few. I always thought writing was a solitary venture, until I put pen to paper and realized that I'd be nowhere without the friends I hold so dear.

CHAPTER 1

Black Hills of South Dakota
May 1892

Jennie smelled a change on the air as she peered out the back of the covered wagon at the slowly passing spindly trees. Her ma had always said she had a weird sense about coming danger. If only she knew better how to predict it. But it was a fickle gift at best. Something or someone followed them—maybe not close enough for her to see—but they were there, nonetheless. She shivered as a bead of perspiration rolled down the back of her neck, reminding her they were out in the open. Easy prey.

She'd turned eighteen just a few days before. Or was it a week? She'd lost count of the days. Her older sister, Ruby, drove their wagon and Ruby's husband Beau drove the other. There hadn't been room for all nine of them to ride in one. Her mother had stayed behind in Cutter's Creek and Jennie was still sore about it. She searched the trees one last time for a sight of anything moving, but the feeling had now dissipated to a low tingle in her blood.

They stopped to camp for the night. As they prepared and ate their supper, they listened to the old circuit preacher, Reverend Level, tell them stories of the Wild West. He was the one leading them to Deadwood, South Dakota. Jennie had been ignoring the tales for the last week or more. They hadn't even reached Deadwood, and she already hated it, had a feeling deep down within her that it couldn't be a good place, not for her or her sisters. Nothing about this trip had been her idea. She'd have stayed back in Cutter's Creek if she could've. But Ma had told her to go, told her to watch her sisters. So, she'd obeyed. She always obeyed.

The campfire burned down and Ruby led the smaller children to one of the wagons and got them tucked in on the feather tick in the back. She and her two younger sisters, Hattie and Eva, the twins, would share the tick in the other wagon. Sometimes Ruby joined them, sometimes not. She didn't speculate where Ruby slept the other nights. It wasn't any of her business.

Jennie climbed in the back of the wagon and pushed Hattie over a bit, so she had room to squeeze in. Hattie swatted at her hand and mumbled something but rolled closer to Eva. It was a wonder how people could travel all across the country in one of these. She'd probably die first. It was hard work for those doing the leading or driving, or even walking, but for those just riding, it was dull.

A prick of fear had her sitting up and listening. Coyotes sliced the silence with a high-pitched sound. Half bark, half howl. Then came the crack of a twig in the distance and she held her breath, listening. The rumble of Beau's voice interrupted the cry of the coyotes and she strained to hear what he was saying.

An unfamiliar man's voice said, "Been walking for some time. My horse went lame a while back and I lost him a few days ago. I'm trying to get to Deadwood."

Beau answered, "Let me stoke the fire for you. We're pert near full-up on seats, but the preacher we're trailing's got room in his cart, if you don't mind listening to him talk. You'll have to ask him in the morning. He's early to bed and early to rise."

"I'd listen to *spooks* if it meant I could get off my dogs for a bit."

The man's voice was scratchy, like he was old or had sat by a fire too long.

Beau laughed and Jennie heard them move to where the fire had been between the wagons. Jennie crawled to the opening of the canvas and peered out, avoiding her sisters. She watched Beau and the stranger from the shadows, careful to keep her fingers from view. The stranger looked blonde, though it was hard to tell in firelight. As he took off his hat she gasped at his ragged face. It was buried beneath a thick beard and smattered with dirt. He could be young, or old. It was difficult to tell. His clothes were quite worn and dirty, but they fit him well and the saddle he carried was made of a good leather. She could see the shine of it in the firelight. He had to have been strong to carry it for so long.

"Where'd you come from?" Beau asked. His stance wasn't necessarily welcoming. While he'd offered the stranger use of their fire, he also rested his hands on his hips, close to the gun always on his belt.

"California. Tried my hand at the pan and lost everything. Heard there's a mine in Deadwood that's hit it big and looking for help. Maybe—if I can't find a spot—I'll head over to Keystone or Hill City."

"You go ahead and warm yourself by the fire, the coffee's cold now, but it'll heat up fast."

Jennie gasped and backed further into the shadows as Beau strode toward her. She didn't want to be caught listening. He veered off to the other wagon and rummaged quietly in the back, returning to the fire with his find. Jennie inched back to the opening, moving carefully over her sisters' feet so she didn't wake either of them.

"Here's a bit of tack. It's all I can find in the dark and I don't want to wake the girls. You can bed down under that wagon." He pointed right at Jennie.

"Thank you, kindly. I'm Aiden Bradly, by the by."

"Beau Rockford, and you're welcome to stay, just steer clear of my girls." His hand moved ever so slightly south and rested on the butt of his gun.

Jennie heard the slight threat in Beau's voice and shivered. For some reason, now that she saw the stranger she'd felt coming earlier, he didn't bother her a bit. Though he was set to sleep right beneath her, he'd be below her and could do nothing. She crawled back to her spot and pulled the covers around her ears, cuddling in closer to Hattie. The morning would come soon enough and then she could see what this Aiden really looked like. Man…or beast.

AIDEN STARED into the fire and toed off his boots. It wasn't near warm enough to go without, but he'd been walking for days straight and his feet were tender where the blisters had broken. Then the boot had rubbed the sensitive new skin raw. He was happy for the smell of the pine wood as it burned, covering the stink wafting from his feet. He'd learned that if he could get them clean, then dry, he'd be fine by morning. But he'd need new boots before long and his money clip was looking pretty lean.

Beau had left him a cup, indicated where the wash water was, and then turned in for the night. He didn't intend to stay up too long either. But he had to attend to a few things, or he wouldn't be much help to this family in the morning. He drank a little of the lukewarm coffee and let it sit in his mouth as he took a bite of tack. It was the only way to soften it enough to chew. His stomach was grateful. He'd had to abandon most of his provisions when he lost his horse, taking only what he could carry.

He glanced behind him at the two large covered wagons and wondered just how many *girls* Beau had. He said a prayer that he hadn't come upon one of the wagon trains he'd heard about back in the Rockies. Cat wagons, where women were brought in by the cart full to work in the brothels. Sometimes they stayed in the wagon as a moving brothel. That couldn't be it though. Beau had mentioned a preacher…hadn't he? Aiden shook his head. He couldn't remember what month it was. He was just happy to remember Beau's name.

Finishing the bit of tack, he plunged the cup in the wash water and carried it back to his seat by the fire so he could see what he was doing. He washed his sore feet, then bound them with two bandanas from the pack he'd carried. He carefully banked the fire and limped over to the wagon Beau had indicated. Laying his saddle down as a pillow and his blanket to cushion the ground, he curled up as tightly as he could to keep warm and fell sound asleep.

CHAPTER 2

Jennie's eyes flew open and she held her breath. Something wasn't right, but she couldn't place what it was. She glanced next to her and clutched the blanket at her neck. Both Hattie and Eva were still fast asleep, and it was still quite dark beneath the canvas of the wagon. In the distance, she heard Reverend Level whistling a hymn as he built the morning fire, but that wasn't what had woken her. She was used to his morning noise.

As she lay there it came to her: snoring. Deep, heavy snoring right under her. She crept to the end of the wagon, untied the canvas so she could slip open the back, released the bolts holding the tongue up, and gingerly released it. Careful not to catch her dress on the rough wood, she slid onto the tongue and peeked under the wagon. Her long braid slid down over her shoulder and hit the ground with a soft thud. He was curled in a ball and grass blocked her full view of the man lying there. Aiden. It hadn't been a dream. And he looked even hairier up close.

A giggle escaped her lips before she could think better of it. She slapped a hand over her mouth, losing her balance on the back of the wagon tongue. She tumbled out, landing with a snapping sound then crumpled to the ground on her head and shoulder.

Aiden sat up with a start, slamming his head into the bottom of the wagon. "Tarnation! Who's out there?" He blinked, looking around with wide, sleepy eyes.

Jennie wished the grass in the hills was longer…so she could hide in it. She lay on her stomach, hoping he was too sleep-addled to see her.

"You ain't hiding from anyone, girl. What're you doing laying there staring at a man? It ain't right." He shook his head and wiped the sleep from his soft hazel eyes.

Jennie glared at him. "Well, sleeping under a lady's wagon ain't right, either." She sat up and crossed her arms.

He laughed. "If I see a lady, I'll be sure to ask before I sleep under her wagon." He rolled back onto his pack and began snoring again, almost immediately.

Insufferable man! Jennie rubbed her head then climbed back into the wagon and secured the tongue in place. She was now wide awake, might as well help the reverend if he needed it. If she stayed, she'd just wake up her sisters, if the man's infernal snoring didn't wake them first.

Since all their belongings had been lost in a fire, Ruby had found each of them two dresses and one nightgown. Jennie chose her blue dress because it went the best with her eyes. She only took her braid out on bathing days, and they wouldn't stop for a bath for at least another few days, so she didn't worry about her hair.

She climbed out the front of the wagon, over the seat and down the wheel, sneaking a glance at Aiden as she walked toward the reverend. Men were, frankly, a rare sight and this one wasn't much to speak of with his reddish shaggy beard and scruffy hair.

"Good morning, sir," she called quietly.

The short reverend with his bushy shock of white hair poked his head around the side of his small cart. "Good morning, child. I don't usually see you about this early. Was I too loud this morning?"

"No, sir. The man sleeping under my wagon snores." Her father had done that, especially after a binge of testing his own whiskey. She hoped Aiden wasn't anything like her father, especially about the drinking. Beau would have him gone in a jiffy if he did. Her sister Ruby didn't abide alcohol, which meant neither did Beau.

"Is that a knot on your forehead? What'd you do, hit it on the side of the wagon?" He approached her and touched her forehead gently, his kindly old gray eyes inspecting her head.

She flinched, not realizing how bad it hurt until that moment.

"You'll have to ask Ruby if she has anything for that. It'll bruise up fast." His brow furrowed and he tapped his chin. "You must've really hit it hard."

Jennie covered the spot with her hand and closed her eyes. How could she hide that from everyone?

"Hmm," the preacher mumbled. "Let me see what I have here. Don't think I've ever seen you girls wearing bonnets, but I think I might have one somewhere here... I often meet up with poor young girls in my travels. Sometimes, they are so poor they can't afford anything. A new bonnet brings a smile to their faces." He stood up straight and smiled. "And sometimes it makes their parents a little more likely to listen." He turned and fiddled in the back of his wagon, moving things around, finally pulling something free. "Here's one that might work!" He handed her a cream-colored bonnet made for a child. She pulled it on and tied it under her chin, looking up at him and praying she didn't look as silly as she felt.

"Well, it doesn't hide it completely, you'll still need to ask Ruby if she has a remedy." He nodded. "Want a cup of coffee?"

Jennie nodded. "Thank you, sir." She sat by the fire and rubbed her hands together, waiting for the reverend to return from behind his cart.

"I get the inkling you aren't pleased about coming on this trip." He sat next to her on a stool and handed her a cup, then took a deep sniff of his coffee.

"You *inkled* right. I'd rather have stayed in Cutter's Creek with

Ma. I miss her. I'll probably never see her again." Jennie shifted her feet closer to the fire. The deep yearning for home felt like a hole the size of the hills inside her.

Reverend Level laughed. "From what Beau told me, she was rather taken with a man named Carlton Williams."

Jennie shook her head and sighed. "She said there was a better chance for me to find a good husband here than in Montana. But that's foolish. There're even less people in Dakota than there is in Montana. She just wanted me to keep an eye on the littles is all."

"I don't think your ma lied to you. I think she *does* believe you'll have more choices in Deadwood. They run mighty low on good women there."

"It sounds to me like they run just as low on good men. Gambling, drinking...and all that other stuff that comes with it. I left a good little town to go to a den of demons." She clutched the coffee tighter to keep from shivering at the daytime thought of the things that had been keeping her awake some nights.

"Now, now. Don't think that way. Deadwood might have its fair share of trouble, but any new town will. Goodness, Dakota only became a state in '89, just three years ago. Everything's new in South Dakota."

"Except the Indians."

He chuckled mirthlessly. "Well, yes, there's that. But you've got to remember, we've been buying up land they used to hunt on. If someone came by your house and moved into your garden, you'd be hopping mad too."

Reverend Level stood up and stretched onto his toes. "I've used those grounds twice. You can toss them when you're done. I need to take my morning stroll and have some time with the Lord. Best make some noise to wake your crew. I'll be clicking out when I get back."

Jennie nodded and tossed what was left in her cup into the bushes. She turned to see Ruby just emerging from under the wagon, Beau right behind her. His hand lay possessively on her hip. Both were in the same clothes as the day before but something about that scene was too intimate. She turned away, her face flaming hot. How Ruby could allow a man's touch after watching their parents and after what she'd been through before finding Beau, well, the thoughts couldn't be borne.

Jennie cleaned up the preacher's camp then went to help Ruby, Hattie, and Eva with their own. She caught Ruby's attention who then strode up to her, narrowed her eyes, and tugged the bonnet off her head.

"Girl. What did you do to your head?" Ruby reached for Jennie's forehead. Jennie stepped back out of reach but not out of sight.

Jennie yanked the bonnet back up, but too late, Aiden joined the growing crowd standing around the ashes of last night's fire. Heat crept up her neck.

Aiden laughed. "She took a dive out of the wagon this morning and hit her head."

She wanted to stomp his foot, but she'd have to move to do it. Oh, she'd get him. Ruby pulled the bonnet back a little.

"I'm afraid I have no ice to bring down the swelling." She gingerly touched the raised knot. "It's hot to the touch too. What happened? Did you have a dizzy spell?"

Jennie shook her head and left the group to go help the littlest ones get ready. She heard more laughing, mostly Aiden, and her cheeks flamed again. That man was fast becoming a nightmare. Perhaps her initial feelings of worry were correct.

Frances, Lula, Nora, and Daisy all grumbled as Jennie pulled on their dresses and checked their braids. She could smell the smoke of the fire and knew the simple breakfast of biscuits and honey would be done soon. It wasn't a normal biscuit because they had no butter or milk, but they'd never had those things when they'd lived with Ma and Pa in Yellow Medicine, either.

If Pa had lived, he'd have married her off by now. Probably to a drunk just like he did to Ruby. Except Ruby had managed to get away after her husband died and found a good man, a man who treated her like a prize.

She helped the younger girls get their food and did her best to stay far away from Aiden and his foul teasing. Beau laid his hand on her shoulder as she did the breakfast dishes.

"We're pulling out in a bit. I'm checking the wheels and straps to make sure everything's in shape for a good go today. Mr. Bradly offered to drive the second wagon so Ruby can ride beside me. I know she could drive, but I'd rather she not have to."

Jennie flinched at the thought of the scruffy stranger joining them. "Are you sure he can be trusted? He just showed up and you've invited him to join us? He could be anybody."

Beau smiled and slid his plate in the water. "He could be anybody, or somebody. I guess we'll just have to find out."

Beau strode away and Jennie shook her head. "He could also be a snoring jack mule that laughs when he shouldn't." She picked up a plate to scrub it as another plopped down in the water, splashing her. She looked up to see Aiden's hazel eyes twinkling at her.

"Jack mule, now that's a new one." He tipped his hat to her and turned away. She noticed he limped slightly, and the ire melted out of her. According to him, he'd been walking for days and he'd been helpful that morning with Beau and Ruby. If he drove, her sister wouldn't need to. Though that also meant that she would be riding with him all day. When Ruby drove, Jennie would sit up front with her to help pass the time. Now she couldn't do that. She'd have to sit in the back and listen to Hattie's snipping and Eva trying to placate her.

Jennie herded the youngest ones to the wagon Beau and Ruby would drive, then climbed into hers. She laid on the feather tick and looked at the dark soiled canvas above her. The ride would be even more dull today since she couldn't sew or do anything else. The rocking of the wagon wouldn't allow it. Beau worried about Indians, so she couldn't even get out and walk.

"Hey, lumpy! Why don't you come up here and keep me company?" Aiden glanced back at her through the opening in the canvas.

She groaned and closed her eyes, pretending to ignore him.

Oh, how every word from his mouth made her chafe. Even being bored would be better than riding next to him.

"Hattie, is your sister hard of hearing?" He laughed. "I ain't sitting that far away."

Hattie laughed and leaned close to Aiden, propping her arms on the short back of the wagon seat. "She heard you. She's just pretending she didn't. I'd sit up there with you."

Aiden threw back his head and laughed. She could admit—though she'd deny it—he did have a nice laugh. Full, like a man's laugh should be.

"Sorry, sprout. You're a little young to sit up here with me. Not that she's much older, I'd wager." He glanced at her again, a mischievous twinkle in his eyes.

Hattie turned around and sat with her back to him. "*She's* just turned eighteen."

"Well, that's practically an old maid in these parts." He patted the seat next to him as if he knew she were watching. Her ire rose even more. How could he tell?

Jennie sat up, then stood, bracing herself on the bows holding the canvas against the rocking of the wagon, then stomped to the front. She climbed over her sister and onto the seat, sitting as far away from Aiden as she could manage. Impossible man. Why couldn't he just leave her alone?

"There, I'm here. Will you stop talking about me now?" She fixed him with a hot glare.

"That bonnet don't quite hide the knot on your head." He glanced at her head then back to the path. "The whole one side of your head's all purple."

If that was how he was going to treat her, then she'd get him just as good. "And your boots don't quite cover the stink of your feet, either." She gripped the side of the seat and turned away.

"No, I expect not. Guess we're both a sight." He flicked the lines.

"I didn't say anything about sight… I said they stink."

"I did the best I could with the bit of water I had. Didn't want to soak them in the dish water." He glanced at her and there was that twinkle back in his eyes. She couldn't tell if he was pulling her leg or not.

"You wouldn't really...?" She turned toward him her stomach turning at the thought of him putting his feet in their wash basin.

"Why, course not!" He laughed, softening his face to pleasant hills and valleys, plunging into the hairy mass of his beard. A beard that looked out of place with his eyes, which were without lines. He had to be younger than she'd assumed the night before when he'd wandered into camp.

Jennie shook her head. He was a maddening man and she'd not let him get any closer.

He put the lines in his left hand and reached over with his right, tugging on her braid. "I thought plaits were for young girls. I ain't ever seen an eighteen-year-old wear plaits."

"Are you going to poke fun at everything about me? How about my nose? Does that suit you, Mr. Bradly?" Her hands shook. How did this stranger make her so angry without even trying? She'd always been somewhat forgiving and placid, but every word he spoke made her want to stand up and throttle him.

"Now, that you mention it, your nose is right pretty." He nodded as if the decision was final on the matter, which made her fume darkly.

Jennie stood and climbed back into the wagon, finished with him. At least for a while. If she stayed in the front, she was liable to push him off the seat and wave to him as she left him—and his beard—in the dust.

CHAPTER 3

Aiden watched as Jennie abandoned her seat. She was a feisty one, so much fun to rile up. Just like Da used to do with Mam years before. He, his two brothers, and one sister had all worked hard on the farm, but there had always been moments of fun. Teasing was how they'd shown affection.

As he'd gotten older, it had taken more than teasing to keep him happy. He'd wanted something more than just silly words to cover up work worn hearts. He wanted to provide for his family, so they didn't have to work their fingers to the bone anymore.

A prospector had stopped at their farm on his way west. He'd convinced Aiden to leave home and come with him to find his fortune. They would strike it rich and he could come back and give his parents everything... Except that hadn't happened. He'd followed the old coot all the way to California. He'd worked and worked, and all they'd found was a few flakes. The prospector disappeared one night, the gold along with him.

California had left a bad taste in his mouth. But he'd heard if you could stand the cold and if you weren't afraid of Sioux aggression, there was gold in the Dakotas. He'd fair laughed at that. What would the Sioux want with him? The prospector had taken everything but his horse and his saddle. He didn't really want to fight Indians for anything. He suspected if he left them alone, they'd do the same. But, if he wanted to ever have anything to bring back home to his Da, he'd better get there and give it a try.

Though he didn't put much stock in *gold fever*, he could feel they were getting close to Deadwood. Deep down in his soul, he could tell there was something special about Dakota. It felt like he was right up in the clouds as he drove over the hills. Then the hills had become steep and hard to cross. Some they'd had to try to stick to valleys, but the valleys seemed to become hills of their own, as if they were trying to keep men away from their hidden treasure.

That morning, Beau had introduced him to each of the girls he'd mentioned the night before. He'd heard the story of how Beau and Ruby rescued the girls from unfortunate marriages. It was noble and all. It meant that the girls were safe to talk to, because they weren't free to marry. Which meant he could just be himself. He'd avoided taking a bride because his only passion was finding gold and making his da proud. Then, he could go home.

Aiden peeled his hat from his head and wiped the sweat from his brow. Though he was thankful to be off his feet, sitting in front of the wagon put him right in the burning sun. At least there was real heat. California had been cool and wet on the mountains. He smacked his lips and felt the cracks along the edges. A dipper of water appeared by his head. He glanced over his shoulder to find Jennie and her lavender eyes standing behind him. He wondered how long she'd been there while he reminisced about times best left in the past.

"I thought you might like to wet your whistle." She hung her head and held out the dipper.

He wound the lines around his leg then took the dipper and drank deeply. He could have taken about three, but he didn't want to be greedy.

"Thank you. I was mighty parched." Her eyes brightened and she tipped her head as he picked up the lines again.

She took the dipper back then appeared near his shoulder again. Her skirt brushed against his back.

"Sure is hot today." She moved away from him, like a tentative child when offered a piece of candy. There was a quiver in her voice. As much fun as it was to tease, it bothered him that she was nervous around him.

"Yup, sure is. Probably best if you stay back there. Might be a bit cooler out of the sun." He was hoping it would challenge her to do the exact opposite as was her habit so far. True to form, she climbed over the back of the seat and sat next to him, folding her small hands into her lap and swaying with the motion of the wagon.

"You like being contrary, don't you?"

Jennie shook her head. "I always do what I'm told. It's just *you* I don't listen to."

He snorted to keep from laughing. "I think we got off on the wrong foot... or head. I'm Aiden Bradly and I'm from Kansas. I moved to Cal-if-ornia when I was a young pup of just nineteen. I lived there for a year, then started my trip to South Dakota. What about you?" He focused on the lines and traces leading up from each ox, hoping that if he didn't look at her, she might just stay and talk.

"I'm Jennie Annette Arnsby from Montana, and I've always lived there. My Pa burned our house down when I was seventeen and my sister came to get us so we'd have somewhere to live. We lived in Cutter's Creek all winter and lit out in the spring. My Ma stayed behind. I don't want to be here, but I was told to go. And, like I already told you, I do what I'm told."

"Except with me." He smiled and pulled up on the lines. Beau's wagon stopped ahead of them and Aiden looked forward to resting his arms and stretching his legs, too. But it also meant the fragile hold he had on conversation with the little butterfly would end quickly.

"You don't count. You ain't family." Jennie climbed down the wheel and jogged away.

~

It took every bit of resolve she had not to turn and look back at Aiden. She didn't want to know anything about him except that he made her as mad as a hornet every time he opened his mouth. Except this time. He hadn't teased her. He'd tried to start over. When he was teasing her, she could give it right back, but when he was just talking … it made her feel like her insides were quaking.

Jennie collected the girls and brought them to the front of the wagon where she caught Beau and Ruby locked together in a kiss like she'd never seen before. She backed away but her sister's giggles made Beau jump away from Ruby as if she were on fire. He turned as red as Ruby's hair.

Beau wiped his mouth with the back of a gloved hand and pointed off into the distance. "See the birch trees? There's a stream over there. You girls go over and get cleaned up. The men will go later once camp is set."

Jennie had enjoyed the few times they'd stopped to bathe in the past, but now she'd be taking a bath with Aiden just a few yards away. Her belly did a strange flip at the thought. He wasn't family. Neither was the reverend. But somehow, Aiden was different. She held out her hands and the girls took them. They headed back toward their wagon.

"Both your dresses are dirty. We can wash one of them while we bathe. If the sun dries them enough, we can get both clean."

The girls nodded and ran back to the wagon to get their clothes. Jennie collected her own dress and the soap. She stuck her head into the back of her wagon.

"Hattie? Eva? There's a river. We're to go down and get cleaned off first."

Hattie threw her book across the bed and glared at Jennie. "What is the matter with you?"

"I'm sure I don't know what you mean. Get your clothes and come on."

"Aiden's been trying all day to get you to talk to him and you've done nothing but give him trouble. If you think there'll be a bunch of good men to pick from in Dakota, you're wrong. You didn't listen to all the stories, but Level told us there are a lot of men in

Deadwood that need the gentle hand of a woman. Best to take one you know will be good to you."

Jennie shook her head and glanced heavenward. "I know no such thing. And men need help everywhere, Hattie. But now you need to listen to what Beau said or you'll still be down there when the men go down to clean up."

"And why would I worry about that?"

Jennie felt the heat rush up her neck. Hattie had always acted the flirt. She turned and left Hattie to sit in the wagon. She'd come when she was ready.

There were thin white trees all along the river. Their leaves were small and made a wonderful rustling sound as the wind passed through them. The river made a pleasant soft noise that you didn't notice unless you really listened for it. Like a whisper. Ruby and the younger girls were already in their drawers and chemises, splashing in the water. Jennie ran to the edge and handed Ruby the soap. The faster they got the dresses washed, the faster they could lay them out to dry before they got themselves washed up.

The sun sparkled off the gently running water and glittered as the girls splashed one another. Jennie inched into the cold river and helped Ruby and Eva scrub the stains from the dresses. Hattie joined them a few minutes later but didn't join in the fun. Soon, all eight dresses were hanging from low bushes and eight sisters lay in the sun to dry themselves. Jennie glanced over at Ruby and her gaze froze on Ruby's waistline.

She assumed her sister had continued to wear a corset, but now, quite visibly, Jennie could see she wasn't. She only wore the corset cover to make it look as if she still were.

"Ruby..." Jennie whispered, "are you in a family way?"

Ruby rested her hand on her stomach. "I'd rather wait a little longer to tell everyone, if you don't mind. Beau will need to buy me the special stays when we get to Deadwood." Ruby gave Jennie a conspiratorial wink.

Having a baby was a great thing. Jennie couldn't figure why Ruby would want to keep it a secret. They grew up in a very small home, with only two bedrooms. Though most of the girls knew what happened when you were married, none would talk about it. The most affection they'd ever seen was between Beau and Ruby, and it still left them embarrassed. Ma and Pa had barely even touched in the out and open.

Curiosity got the better of Jennie and before she could stop it, the words tumbled from her mouth. "Ruby ... do you like being married?"

She opened her eyes and glanced at Jennie. "Why do you ask?"

"I don't know. Ma and Pa never seemed to like each other until everyone was abed at night. But you and Beau can't seem to get enough of each other."

"Well, I suppose that's true." She closed her eyes against the bright sun and smiled, her cheeks a warm pink under the heat of its rays.

"Why?" Jennie had to know. How could she ever find what Beau and Ruby had, and not what her Pa had expected of her?

"Beau and I want the same things. We want space and time with each other. We want to spend every minute together, and we want to make sure all you girls have choices you wouldn't have had before."

"So, love is just ... things in common?" Jennie wrinkled her nose and sat up, reaching for the brush to attack the snarls in her long blond hair. Love didn't sound like much fun, if that's all it was.

"It isn't just that, Jennie." Ruby sat up and grabbed the brush from her, motioning for her to turn around. She started brushing the ends gently. "I can't even explain it. It's like when he's around, I can face anything because together we're stronger than we are apart. Before Beau, I was afraid of so many things. Now I know I can be strong, because he's by my side."

Jennie enjoyed the soft rhythm of Ruby brushing but stopped her when she started separating it into strands for braiding.

"I want to try it a different way. Maybe, more like you. I'm only a year younger, it's probably time."

"I suppose, Ma tried to keep you looking younger hoping Pa would forget you were marrying age. Let me show you how to

175

wrap it up." Ruby slowly brushed through her own hair, then wrapped and twisted it until it was in a pretty knot at the nape of her neck, adding pins to keep it in place.

"I think I can manage that. Thank you, Ruby." She worked at her own hair while Ruby left to check the dresses. Jennie struggled to get her hair the same, twisting and changing it when it didn't feel right. It wasn't as easy on the back of her own head as it had been to watch Ruby do it.

Hattie plopped down next to her. "If you aren't going to be nice to Aiden, I will. I'm not even two years younger than you, I'll be seventeen before the spring's gone."

Jennie shook her head. "Beau isn't going to approve of Aiden. Not as young as you are. You can ask him if you want, but I heard him tell Aiden to stay away from us." She didn't have pins with her, so she wrapped her ribbon around the knotted hair and tied it, hoping it would stay up until she could get back and finish it. It was a way to get Hattie to leave her alone, by looking as if she were too busy to listen further. Really, she just didn't want to hear Hattie any longer.

Hattie pinched the fabric of her chemise and drawers to check if they were dry. "Well, I'll ask him anyway. I'm not opposed to being married and he seems like a good man."

"You've known him for a half a day. How can you know if he's a good man or not?" Jennie narrowed her eyes at Hattie. She had Jennie's full attention now. Hattie had always been the only sister to be mildly excited, even from a young age, at the prospect of marrying one of Pa's clients. They'd always thought it was because she was too young to understand, but Jennie wasn't sure anymore. Hattie seemed to have a pretty good grasp of what went on between men and women and was excited at the prospect.

"He smiles a lot and treats Beau and the reverend with respect. That's all that matters, right? I can teach him the rest."

Beau's voice echoed through the trees "Are you ladies about done?"

All the younger girls shrieked and sat up covering their bodies with the petticoats nearest them. The older girls knew Beau would never get close enough to see them. "We'd like to wash up before it gets dark," he called.

Ruby answered. "We'll be back in just a bit." She stood and gathered the dresses from the bushes and helped each of the younger girls get dressed quickly. Nora and Lula fought over the brush and Ruby took it from them, admonishing them to behave.

"We need to hurry. I'll get your hair in order when we get back to the wagons. We need to make some supper so it'll be ready by the time the men come back."

They arrived at the camp to find all the wagons had been pulled in a rough circle, and Level's horse and their oxen had been unhitched and were tied to nearby trees. In all the days they had traveled, they had never unhitched during the day.

"What's going on, Ruby?" Francis reached out and took Jennie's hand. Change always made her nervous. Her sweet face wrinkled in worry.

"I'm sure I don't know. I've been down at the river, same as you."

Beau flipped his change of clothes over his shoulder as he strode toward them. Ruby held out the soap. He stopped and laid his hands on Lula's and Francis's shoulders.

"I talked to the reverend. We'll follow this river, Level says it's called Whitewood, all the way to Deadwood. It's only a few more hours away. Tomorrow will be our last day on the trail."

The girls jumped up and down while Ruby hugged Beau. Jennie kept moving. The journey would be at an end, and then what? Supposedly, there were a lot of men in Deadwood. Men outnumbered women there a full ten to one, which meant it was dangerous. Her Pa had also told her stories of Wild Bill Hickock and Calamity Jane, though she was pretty sure both were dead now.

Jennie's stomach tightened and she felt sickly. The town which had seemed so far away, she never considered they'd actually reach it. Now, it was on the horizon and she wasn't so sure she wanted the journey to end. Ruby moved toward her and touched her shoulder.

"You don't seem all that happy to be nearing home."

She stepped aside out of Ruby's reach. "It isn't my home. I never wanted to leave. First you yanked me from Yellow Medicine and planted us all in Cutter's Creek. As soon as we met a few people and started feeling like we belonged, you yanked us out into this wilderness."

Ruby frowned and shook her head. "I don't think you'll find much in the way of wilderness in Deadwood. From what I hear it's a bustling town. Bigger than Cutter's Creek, for sure."

Jennie's breath came fast as she tried to hold back what she wanted to say to Ruby. What she'd wanted to say for over a month as they'd been traveling. The words tumbled from her mouth as she lost her control. "And that's what you want? A big town with a wild past? I don't want that. And I don't want to be here."

Ruby crossed her arms over her chest and her mouth flattened. "I'm sorry you feel that way. I wish you'd have told us when we left over a month ago. You could've stayed behind."

A girl her age could not stomp her feet and it would do no good anyway, but her feet itched to show her anger. "No, I couldn't. Ma wouldn't let me. She said there was nothing for me there and it wasn't good to break up sisters."

The lines on Ruby's face softened and she touched Jennie's arm gently. "She's right. You've been together for so long. Wouldn't you have been sad never seeing Hattie, Eva, Francis, Lula, Nora, and Daisy every day? Wouldn't even missing one bother you?"

An unstoppable tear streamed down her cheek. "I would've been able to see Ma."

Ruby sighed. "The railroad is growing. Deadwood has a thriving railway that probably could take you right back to Cutter's Creek if you just can't stand to be here. But won't you give it a try? For us?"

Jennie narrowed her eyes and set her jaw, yanking away from Ruby's touch. She would never understand. She'd wanted to come out here, to follow Beau wherever he went, but not her. "I will give it three months. If anything happens to me or my sisters, we're going back to Cutter's Creek, to Ma."

"And are you taking them? What if they want to stay?" Jennie could see the small blue vein on Ruby's forehead pump angrily.

"Why would they want to stay in a gambling shanty-town full of drunken miners and prostitutes?"

Ruby turned on her heel and strode off to the wagon. Her shoulders were set and her pace furious. She hadn't meant to hurt Ruby. It was just that her life suddenly felt like it did when she was back with Ma and Pa in Yellow Medicine. Back when she feared every day, wondering what would happen next. Cutter's Creek had provided security and Jennie wanted that feeling back. Somehow, the prospect of Deadwood didn't feel as promising.

CHAPTER 4

A iden tried not to watch Jennie, who sat away from
everyone else at supper looking rather forlorn. Something had happened while he was at the river, something
that got her in quite a fuss. The whole group finished eating and
Ruby stood to put the water pot over the fire to heat for washing
the dishes.

Aiden waited by the wash bin for Ruby to notice him. She
turned to him and smiled, taking his plate and dunking it in the
water.

"Ruby, I hate to ask but I don't have a glass to use for shaving.
I'm feeling mighty shaggy." He scratched his thick beard and
wished he'd been able to get rid of it before meeting up with them.
"Do you have a glass I can use?"

Ruby smiled and glanced toward Jennie then back to Aiden.
"Beau has the only one and I think he'll be using it soon. There
probably won't be enough light when he's done." She scrubbed at a
pot then paused, glancing over her shoulder once again at Jennie.
"Ma used to have Jennie shave Pa. She's quite good. I can ask her.
If you'd like? I'll be warming Beau's towel over the water for the
dishes. I'm sure we have another towel we could heat."

Aiden felt his belly tighten. Exchanging words with Jennie was one thing, but if she was allowed to shave him, she might just cut him long, wide, and permanent.

"I'm not so sure that's a good idea, ma'am. But thanks all the same." He turned to sit. He'd teased her a bit too much to feel comfortable with her holding a blade anywhere near him, especially not at his neck.

"Oh, it really isn't a bother. Jennie! Come here, please."

He closed his eyes, knowing he was heading for a fight. All he wanted was to look a little less like a grizzly bear when they rolled into town.

He could see the apprehension in Jennie's eyes as she walked past him to Ruby.

"Yes, Ruby? What is it?"

"Mr. Bradly doesn't have a mirror to shave with. If I get him set up with a warm towel, can you give him a good shave?"

He stood and shoved his hands in his pockets. "It isn't any trouble. I can do it when Beau is done." He knew, even before turning toward the sun, he'd never make it. There was no more than an hour of good light left, probably less.

Jennie smiled and narrowed her eyes to mere slits. He swallowed the lump in his throat.

"Now, Mr. Bradly. There won't be near enough light by then. It's no trouble at all. Why don't you sit yourself down right here?" She pointed to a stool next to the wagon. The leather strop used for preparing the blade hung nearby. A steer waiting to be branded probably didn't feel any less fearful.

He shook his head and crawled under the wagon to get his saddle bag. He dug out his leather shaving kit. It contained his razor, cup, soap, stone, and brush. It could take a man a long time to learn how to use a straight edge and not end up a bloody mess. Did this tiny girl really know what she was doing? Did he have any choice but to find out the hard way?

He froze where he stood, his heart beating like a rabbit's. The side of Jennie's mouth lifted in a sardonic smile. She knew what she was putting him through and was enjoying every second of it.

She took the kit from him and gently pushed against his chest, pressing him backward onto the stool.

He pushed against her hand with his chest as he tried to stand back up. "You know. I'm thinking the beard doesn't look that bad. Maybe I'll just wait and visit the barber when we reach Deadwood." Jennie wouldn't move and he wouldn't push her away, so he fell back onto the stool and against the wagon.

"Oh, this won't take but a few minutes and you'll look like a new man, Mr. Bradly." She laid the hot towel over the side of his face and wrapped it so it covered everything but his nose.

"I'd be happy to take your dollar, though."

"A dollar!" The towel suffocated his voice, but he heard her laugh.

Then he heard it. The sound of the straight edge against the strop. Each long, slick *schlick* chilled his blood. He hadn't teased her that bad, had he?

She came back and massaged the towel into his cheeks, then removed it. Then she took scissors to his beard, clipping it close. He kept his eyes trained on her but wouldn't move to say a thing. He wouldn't let her know he held onto the stool for dear life.

When his beard was trimmed short, she brought over another hot towel and again draped it over his face. He knew in his head that this was the way of it. It took all these steps to get a good shave, but each step brought him to the edge of reason worrying over that blade. But more over that girl.

"I'll get your soap ready. Good thing you bathed earlier, or I'd have had to pick birds out of it."

He wanted to laugh. If she were in his shoes he'd be doing the same thing, but he couldn't quite find his humor.

He heard Ruby finish up the dishes and there was the sound of that strop again.

That has to be Beau...

Beau laughed. "Look at you, getting the treatment. I couldn't get Ruby to give me a shave... not sure I'd trust her to." He laughed then there was a loud *thwack* — "Ouch! Why'd ya hit me for?" Beau yelled and laughed. Aiden heard shuffling all around him as if Beau and Ruby were chasing each other about the camp.

The towel once again disappeared from his face and lavender eyes appeared before him. Jennie stood over him and tilted his head back, then left to right, inspecting him. His neck felt mighty exposed. She tucked the warm towel around his neck and worked the lather in the cup with the wet bristle brush. She rubbed the soap on in deft circles, massaging his face even more. He may have enjoyed it had it been the barber, but this girl … he barely knew her.

She flexed her pretty lips into a frown as she hovered over him, pulling on parts of his face. Her body lightly pressed against him as she pulled the skin near his ear taut. It was the first time he'd ever wanted to back away from a pretty woman.

She stood up straight. "Now, I need you to lay your head back and open your mouth like you're a drunk, sleeping."

He blinked at her. Could she possibly be serious?

She pushed his head back a little further, forcing his mouth open, leaning the back of his head against the wagon. "Now, relax. I've done this more times than I can count, and I never bloodied my Pa."

He sat up. "Are you sure about this? Really, I'm happy with the trim."

She pushed him back against the wagon. "Shush now. I need to concentrate. We've got to get this done while we have good light and I've never done this on someone sober. So, sit drunk."

He complied and tilted his head back as she asked. She pulled the top of his cheek up with one hand and he held his breath as he heard the crackle of the blade cutting the hair. She bit at her lip as she did short strokes down his face. He let himself take a breath as she lathered him back up for the second pass. He forced himself to watch her face and not think about what she was doing to him. She sure was pretty when she nibbled on her lip like that, though.

The angles of her cheeks were stark, as if she hadn't eaten enough, though they were just beginning to flesh out a bit. She was slender and delicate, especially in the hands. Her golden hair was the color of ripe wheat and now that he'd teased her about her plaits—which he'd liked—she wore it back in a standard womanly bun. Her eyes were almost lavender, the color of some lilies his mam had in her garden. Her figure, he couldn't much tell. Her dress hung loose about her as if it had originally been made for someone stouter.

Finally, she took to his neck which had been the part he'd dreaded the most. He couldn't make himself think about anything beyond the scrape of each pass of the blade. He held his breath and lightheadedness threatened to take him down, but he fought it. After a few minutes, Jennie disappeared then came back with a basin of water.

"Here. You can splash this water on your face. It's cool."

He did as he was told and rinsed the heat and remaining suds off his face.

"Now. Let's see how I did." She stood in front of him and laid her hands on either of his cheeks. He reached up to pull them away. What was this girl doing, getting so close? He glanced up at her and saw something he never expected to, warmth. Jennie liked what she saw, and he squared his shoulders, forcing a smile he hoped was less uncomfortable than he felt. He couldn't quite bring himself to remove her hands.

"Thank you, Jennie. I'm sorry I doubted."

She gently rubbed her thumbs over the top of his cheeks, and he closed his eyes to enjoy the softness.

"That'll be two dollars."

He laughed. "That's a mighty expensive shave. Next time, I'll just wait for the barber." He dug in his money clip and pulled out two dollars, handing them to her.

She folded them and tucked them into a pocket of her skirt and turned away to clean up his shaving tools. Beau stood a few feet away, about half done with his task, and Ruby eyed him with a slight smile. He wasn't sure what to do with himself now. But it felt like he was the show just sitting there.

Little Daisy eased up to him and touched his knee. "Tell us a cowboy story?" She looked up at him with plaintive eyes almost the color of Jennie's.

He ruffled her hair. The sweet child had his heart already. "I'm sorry, little one. I'm no cowboy. I'm a prospector by trade and those are no stories for little ears."

Jennie met his gaze as she turned from rinsing his brush. "If it's such a dastardly profession, why do you choose to do it, Mr. Bradly?"

She had him there. What could he say? The fact was, mining wasn't what he wanted to do, but what else could he do that would make enough money to keep the promise he'd made to his family when he'd left?

"Sometimes a man does what he has to do so he doesn't break his word. If a man ain't worth his word, he ain't worth much."

He couldn't sit around the fire any longer. The questions brought up things he'd rather keep buried. Like how he'd been suckered and wasted a whole year. He couldn't go home empty handed. His da would never forgive him for leaving to find his fortune if he didn't at least bring something back with him.

JENNIE WATCHED as Aiden wandered away down to the river. She hadn't meant her question to sound so mean. She'd wanted to know more about him. Shaving all that hair off his face had revealed handsome, young angled cheeks and a strong chin. Coupled with his clean face, it had transformed him from a miner who looked like he came from a shanty town, to a man who could run off with her desires. If she'd let him.

She hadn't been able to help herself when she'd finished. There was nothing quite as soft as a man's cheeks after proper application of the blade. Her Ma used to cup her Pa's cheeks just as she'd done to Aiden. She often wondered what her Ma thought about when she'd held his face like that. Now she knew. When a man's cheeks were as soft as butter, it brought all sorts of things to mind that made her pink around the edges. Ma had said there was nothing quite like kissing the cheek of a young man fresh after a shave. Now that she'd shaved someone other than her Pa, she could see it was the truth.

Jennie put Aiden's kit back in the leather bag he carried everything in and then she replaced it in Aiden's pack. She couldn't stop glancing at him off in the distance, sitting on a downed dead tree.

If she moved quickly, she could go apologize before dark. She'd have to be back to the wagon by sunset. "Ruby, do you mind if I wander for a minute?"

Ruby turned to the sun and squinted, shielding her eyes. "Go ahead, but don't wander far. And thank you for helping Mr. Bradly."

Heat rushed up her neck. "It wasn't anything and I got two dollars out of it."

She would do it again too. Even without the money. Her hands itched even now to feel his soft skin under her fingers and knew it would never happen. She slowly made her way to him, sitting next to him on the dead log.

He didn't notice her presence, or if he did, his expression didn't change. He stared off across the field of grass that led to the river. She fidgeted with her sleeve as the sun plunged lower on the horizon.

Jennie sighed and paused as she gathered her courage. "I'm sorry if my question bothered you. I didn't mean for it to."

Aiden shook his head but didn't look at her. "I got bigger things on my mind than making people think I'm something. I've just got to mine enough so I can get home. It ain't like I want to do this forever."

"So you haven't been bitten by gold fever?" Jennie sat forward to look at him, but he glanced away from her. Her stomach fell at his refusal to meet her eyes.

"Maybe I did at first, but the fever has long since cooled. My Da said it would. But I figured if I worked hard and brought back a haul, it wouldn't matter."

If what his father said mattered so much, that made him honorable. The more she learned about him the more Hattie seemed right. He was a good man. "So, you're hoping to strike it rich in Deadwood then take your riches home. Where did you say home was again?"

"Kansas, and yes. I don't even want to be rich. Gold is twenty dollars an ounce right now. I wouldn't need much."

"Well, I hope you find what it is you're searching for in Deadwood. I'm scared pert near out of my hair to go there. It makes sense that you want to go, but everything I've heard about it scares me. What if..."

He held up a hand to stop her, but the harsh lines of his face would have done the job. "Don't start down the road of *what if*, Jennie. Live life as it happens. You can't sit there and worry about tomorrow or you'll make your worries come true."

"I try to have faith that things will work out just fine, but people get hurt. I've been through enough to know that Deadwood could bring back all the things that scare me to death. Everything we left Montana for. Strong drink—and the drunks that come with it, being sold off to anyone who sees fit to ask..."

"You don't really think Beau and Ruby would do that to you, do you? I may not have been with you but a day, but I can't see them doing that."

"No, I don't. I think women are so rare they'd be a temptation to snatch right off the street."

He didn't look at her but laid his heavy hand atop hers between them on the log, sending a pleasant shiver up her arm. "I think you've heard a few too many stories. Tomorrow you'll see the real Deadwood. Yes, it's a town in the west. And yes, there've been some amazing characters who've passed through. But that doesn't make a town what it is."

"I've told Ruby I'll stay for three months. If anything happens to me before then, I'm going back to Cutter's Creek."

He turned his hazel eyes on her. The heat of his gaze and his hand covering hers made her heart trip. She'd met men in Cutter's Creek but most of them had been married. She dearly hoped that her thoughts didn't turn to pudding every time she was near one. Of course, if they didn't that would mean Aiden was different. She didn't really want to think about that, either.

He whispered into the twilight. "I hope you give it a chance, Jennie. Deadwood needs ladies to pretty the place up as much as any town." He pulled his hand from hers and she immediately wanted the contact back. He stood and walked off toward the river, leaving her feeling cold even in the warm May evening. Jennie didn't feel welcome to follow. He had to have some war going on in his mind to talk to her without the teasing that usually came with it. She almost wished for the teasing again, if it meant he'd hold his shoulders back and smile again.

As the evening wore on, a chill descended on the camp and a light drizzle fell. Jennie helped with the rushed camp cleanup. Once she was done, she put her foot up to climb into the wagon but paused. Under the wagon lay all of Aiden's things but it was empty of the man himself. He hadn't returned yet and he had no blanket other than the horse blanket he used to lay on. If she didn't do something, he'd get sick from the cold and damp weather. She dug through her trunk and found the blanket her mother had knit for her over the winter. She'd kept it perfect and refused to use it, thinking keeping it nice would somehow keep her mother closer to her. Now, she laid it out over the thick wool blanket so he wouldn't be frozen in the misty evening air.

It was dark inside the wagon and wet outside of it. There was nothing to do besides sleep which was what Hattie and Eva decided to do. Soon they were softly breathing but Jennie couldn't. She sat up, listening for Aiden to return. Though it was now full dark, and something howled in the distance, Aiden didn't return. Reverend Level would tell her to pray about it so she clasped her hands and closed her eyes, but words wouldn't come. She'd never been one to talk to the Lord. Didn't even know if He would just listen to her. Perhaps if Level prayed the Lord would hear?

Jennie climbed out over the tongue and picked her way around puddles to the reverend's wagon wishing she'd thought to grab a blanket to cover herself with. Beau stood at the corner of their other wagon, cradling his rifle in the crook of his arm and protecting it from the rain. Staring off in the direction Aiden had disappeared.

"Jennie, what're you doing out in this? You'll catch your death. Get back to the wagon and keep dry now."

"But Beau, what about Mr. Bradly?" She swiped the rain from her eyes and searched the dark, hoping to see him. A coyote called in the distance and the sound was like running feet up her spine to the nape of her neck.

"I got Aiden's gear from under the wagon and gave it to Level. He doesn't have much room in there, but I can't have him staying with you three. It ain't right for you to be out here looking for him either."

She didn't move. "Has he returned at all?" She clutched her arms, shivering. The early spring rain was bitter cold, but she just had to make sure he'd come back. He'd left after her remarks and her guilt was a heavy chain around her.

"I'm keeping an eye out for him. You go get in that wagon now, young lady. I'm not going to tell you again." He pointed the way as the rain picked up, dripping off the brim of his hat.

She scooted back toward her wagon so he would think she'd gone in. But she still needed to speak to the reverend. She couldn't possibly get more wet or cold than she already was. She'd have to be careful and speak quietly or Beau would hear her and then he'd be angry. She'd never tested him and really didn't know what he'd do if he weren't obeyed.

The reverend sat in the back of his wagon just inside out of the rain and he looked up when she peeked around the door of his wooden buggy. It was like a large wooden box on wheels.

His old white eyebrow raised in question. "To what do I owe this late visit, Miss Arnsby?"

She gasped, reminded that she shouldn't go calling on anyone after dark, but especially not an unmarried man. Even if he was old. "I'm sorry. Please forgive me. I just wanted to ask that you would pray for Mr. Bradly's safe return."

His other eyebrow rose to join the first. "I already have. But now my question for you is, why don't *you* just pray? Surely you know that your prayers are heard by the Father just as easily as my own?"

If she weren't frozen, she'd blush. She tried to keep her teeth from chattering to alert Beau. "I don't know much, I'm afraid."

He nodded and his eyes were sad. "Would that I'd given you a Bible instead of a bonnet. Come see me tomorrow, child, and we can make a good trade."

She nodded then turned around and went back the way she came to stay out of Beau's sight. She would have to change when she got into the wagon and pray it didn't wake up her sisters. Warming back up would take a long time. But what of Aiden? If he hadn't returned, he'd be freezing, soaked all the way to the skin. What would keep him away in this weather?

If you hadn't scolded him about mining, he wouldn't have left. She knew it was true right down to her toes. Sometimes an apology wasn't quite enough. She'd already been in a poor mood about Deadwood and she'd taken it out on Aiden. How could she make it right?

A coyote howled again, and Jennie quickened her pace to the wagon. She climbed up and changed quickly, her fingers shaking in the cold. He'd be all right. He had to be. She closed her eyes tightly and tried to keep from shivering. If she woke Hattie, she'd have to explain why she was all wet.

Okay, Level, here goes. *Lord, I don't know how to do this, so I'll just ask. Please keep Aiden safe and bring him back to the wagon train... Amen.*

Most of the prayers she'd heard had been a lot longer with thee's and thou's. Those words meant nothing to her. She hoped it wasn't required to sound like that.

There came the barking of either a dog or coyote. It came nearer until she heard it within the camp. Her skin tingled a warning and she hid under the blankets. Then voices. First Beau and then Aiden. She smiled as her heart leapt. There wasn't much of the night left. Now that he'd returned, she could relax.

She had just closed her eyes when something large hit the side of the wagon, swinging all the hanging dresses above her head in a great arc. A picture fell from the side of the wagon where it had been tacked up and Hattie and Eva screamed.

CHAPTER 5

Aiden struggled against the rope tied around the scraggly mutt's neck, but it was wet and slipped out of his grasp. He'd found the dog while wandering in the cedar scrub to clear his thoughts. The old yellow dog was tall and came up to Aiden's knees. He was a scrapper and had no intention to mind. The mutt ran for Jennie's wagon and jumped toward the toolbox on the side. He landed atop it and growled down at Aiden. A wave of screams erupted from inside and Aiden could imagine their terror. He hadn't considered when he'd found the mutt that it would be a danger to Beau and his girls.

The dog had to be under his control before it hurt someone. Edging closer he lunged for the rope, yanking the dog off the toolbox. He tied it to the wheel and scrambled for the dinner bones Level had left by the ashes of the fire. They'd stayed long enough in that camp to hunt a little, so there were fresh meaty bones. It was only a few jack rabbits, but the dog was starving and would have the bones devoured quickly.

Aiden threw them at the dog, and he snapped them up. Not even allowing them to hit the ground and growling when Aiden stepped too close.

"Aiden, what have you brought back with you?" Beau stood behind him, his voice a low rumble. Now without his rifle, he crossed his arms over his chest. Aiden didn't need light to tell him Beau wasn't pleased about the addition. The rain dripped off them both as they faced each other and Aiden shivered, just noticing the biting cold.

"He was being followed by a pack of 'yotes. I helped him get free, but he hasn't been especially thankful yet."

Beau gestured at the dog under his wagon. "And what do you hope to do with him? He's gone wild. Can't even get near him." Beau's face may have been hard to read in the dark, but his voice wasn't. He was doing just what Aiden would do if he had a passel of girls to look after. Protect them.

He glanced back at the dog now curled up in the center of the wagon, the only dry spot left. "He'll calm down. I think I'll call him Jack."

The dog lifted his head and stared at him then leaned forward. His hackles rose and he growled a low rumble that shouldn't sound half as menacing as it did since the dog was near dead with hunger.

"Don't seem like he likes that name." Beau came alongside Aiden and he knew he had to be strong. He'd been pushed around enough as a young man, but no more. Beau would respect him if he stood up and respectfully did what he had to do.

"Maybe not, but that's what I'll name him. Thanks for bringing in my pack. I had no desire to sleep on a wet bed."

"You probably will anyway. You're soaked and there's nowhere to change. Level's little cart is hardly big enough to change your mind, but it's dry."

"Much obliged." Aiden knocked lightly on the side of Reverend Level's rig then climbed in. It *was* small, especially with everything hanging from the ceiling and wall. He toed off his boots near the back and curled up on his wool blanket. Atop his saddlebag was a folded up knit blanket that was not his. He didn't want to get it wet but it sure would be warmer than going without. He unrolled a measure of his bedroll and covered himself with it then he pulled up the knit blanket.

The wind blew the pots and kettles above his head together, softly clanging and plinking above his head. The noise of the rain and the song of the pots lulled him to sleep.

It seemed like he'd just shut his eyes when Level shook his shoulder. "Good morrow, Mr. Bradly. Are you in need of anything?" he spoke out of the darkness and Aiden blinked wildly to remember where he was and who spoke to him.

He took a deep breath and yawned, recognizing the reverend. "No, sir. Just trying to catch a few winks before the sun comes up."

"Men don't take long walks in the rain for no reason. Either they are compelled by duty—such as searching for a military foe or chores on a farm—or they are compelled by a negative spirit in their head. We have no farm and are under no threat of military action as far as I can tell. So, Mr. Bradly, what is weighing so heavily on you?"

Aiden sighed and scratched his temple. The reverend wasn't going to let him go back to sleep, as much as he wanted it. At least he cared enough to ask. "Sir, all I really want to do now is sleep."

"So, after finding a lost dog out in the wild you have now figured out all of your problems and you can rest easy? Oh, that life were that easy for me. Perhaps I should keep my own ears open for a dog."

Aiden inspected the pots and other oddities Reverend Level had hanging from the inside of the rig but kept silent. Chasing a dog wasn't going to make him feel any better about what he'd done with his life so far and he couldn't go home until he'd fixed it. The dog was lost and beaten up. Just like him. He couldn't just leave it there to die.

He heard Jack yipping and his eyes flung open. Jennie was in that wagon and would be scared out of her wits. Had Beau told them about the dog or just gone off to bed? He hadn't even expected Beau to be out waiting for him when he'd returned to camp, though maybe he hadn't really been. He might have been watching for coyotes. They didn't generally go for prey they had to work too hard for, and didn't like people much, but it was never a good idea to take that for granted.

He listened hard for the sounds of fear in the night, but all he could hear were the distant yips of the coyotes and the occasional growl of his own Jack.

"If sleep is what you need this morning, I'll leave you until the sun is up, but I do want you to think about the demon chasing you, Mr. Bradly. If you don't douse it, it'll enflame you."

Aiden blinked up at the ceiling as Level climbed out of the rig to start his morning. Now he had plenty to think about.

JENNIE HAD NEVER HAD a dog in her life, and she was sure after this night she'd never want one. Every time any one of the three of them moved, the dog laying under the wagon would growl. At least she hoped it was a dog. It sounded more like a wolf. She tried closing her eyes and just ignoring it, but the fierce sound kept her tossing until the light of dawn glowed around the wagon.

She grumbled as she dressed then stuck her foot out the back of the wagon. The dog yapped and lunged at her ankle, clamping onto her skirts and yanking her hard. She screamed as she lost her grip and tumbled to the ground, hard. The dog barked and growled. Its hackles raised on its back.

"Jack, no!" Aiden ran at the dog as it sprang at her. Her heart raced and she gasped, covering her face as it latched onto her just below the elbow. Pain raced up her arm. She couldn't think. Couldn't breathe.

I'm going to die.

Weight like she'd never imagined landed on her. She heard herself scream and then the weight vanished. She pulled her legs up to her chest, covering herself as best she could. Her hands shook as she swallowed back tears.

There was a commotion, yelling, but what they said she couldn't hear distinctly. She felt a strange pounding in her head. The pain blocked her hearing, her vision, everything but the beat of her heart. Strong arms wrapped around her and lifted her off the ground as if she were a child. Caring arms like she'd always dreamt of when she *had* been a child.

"I got you... He was tied... I never thought..." Aiden's voice drifted through the pain. She raised her head opening her eyes and they focused on him. His eyes raked over her, stalling on her arm. He set her down on the tongue of the wagon, still nestled against his chest. He tore the fabric from her wrist all the way to her shoulder. She shrieked in protest, but the damage was done.

Her head swam at the sight of the blood running over her arm. It wasn't much. He'd only bitten once but she'd never really seen her own blood before. Ruby rushed toward her with a bucket of water. Ruby's pale face worried her, and Jennie couldn't stop her breath from rushing ahead of her, making her head swim. She leaned against Aiden's strong chest to steady herself.

Ruby set down the pail at Aiden's feet. "It's cold. I didn't have a chance to even put it over the fire but it's clean, far as I can tell."

Beau came forward. "Why don't you let Ruby handle this? We should take care of that dog."

Aiden lifted her arm. "I learned a few things about doctoring from the prospector I was with in California. I'll get the dog tied closer to me as soon as I do this."

Beau took a step closer. "I don't think you catch my meaning, Aiden. Let Ruby handle this and get your hands off her."

Jennie wanted to wrap her good arm around Aiden, to hold him close. His strength had fortified her and now Beau was taking him away. She looked to Aiden for help and his eyes bore so much pain. He showed her how to hold her arm bent and then turned on his heel and left. She swallowed her protest. Her words had done nothing but damage yesterday. She hadn't seen him return last night. Hadn't been able to ask if he was all right. What if he just walked the rest of the way to Deadwood and she never saw him again?

"No!" Jennie yelled when Ruby touched her arm. "Aiden, don't go!"

He turned back toward her and waved as he gathered his

saddle and the dog's rope. She ignored Ruby as she watched him get gradually smaller.

"Looks like I'll be driving the wagon into Deadwood. I don't think Beau meant for him to leave. Something's been eating at Aiden since last night and I think Beau was a little sore about spending so much of the night waiting for him in the rain when he would've rather been in the wagon."

Jennie closed her eyes. His teasing had been in fun and now it was her fault he was gone. She'd known that beast was under her. It had kept her awake all night. She should've been more careful climbing out of the wagon.

"I know it's silly but I'm going to miss him Ruby."

"I know. Beau told me you came out to check on Aiden last night. Beau trusts him enough to let him travel with us, but I'm not so sure he thinks Aiden is good enough for you."

Jennie's heart clenched in protest. "That isn't his decision. I didn't go from letting Pa pick who I would marry to your husband doing it. *I* will decide. No one else. You said yourself yesterday that it was important to you. Was that a lie?"

Ruby avoided her question and her eyes. "You think there was marriage in your future? I didn't think you two were all that close. Heavens, it's only been a day."

"We weren't. Not at all. I'm just saying it shouldn't be up to you or Beau or Pa or anyone else."

Ruby wrapped a bandage around Jennie's forearm and tied it near her elbow. "I don't think you'll have to worry. The bite was surprisingly shallow. I've never seen a man move so fast as Aiden when you screamed. I think he *flew* across the camp to get Jack off you."

Jennie looked down at the bandage, running her hand down her arm as she shivered. "Why did he bring that beast into our camp?"

Ruby collected the damp and soiled cloths. "I'm sure I don't know. He didn't say much to anyone when he came in last night. All we know is that he was late, and he brought the dog with him. Beau said he got it away from some coyotes."

Jennie searched off into the distance but he'd long since disappeared from view. Beau strode out from behind the other wagon, his face dark.

"We need to eat quickly then get back on the trail. Level wants to be in Deadwood by noontime."

Ruby touched Jennie's knee. "Just rest back here. Hattie and Eva are enough help. One of the girls will bring you something to eat. I'll mend your sleeve later, after we wash the dress."

Jennie nodded, not really caring about any of it. She'd wanted her first experience of Deadwood to be with Aiden, since he'd been excited about their arrival. She'd thought he would somehow make the fear in the pit of her stomach go away. Now, she'd have to face Deadwood, alone.

CHAPTER 6

Aiden's feet swelled after just an hour of walking and he could go no further. "Jack, hold up. I've got to rest a bit."

The dog bounded back to him and sat a few feet away, cocking his head.

"Why'd you have to bite Jennie? If you had to get angry with anyone it should've been me. I'm the one who tied you up. She didn't do a thing."

Jack sat and stared at him, panting. "I don't have any rations, boy. You'll have to go off and hunt on your own and I guess I gotta hope you come back." He tugged the rope and Jack pulled on it. When he got Jack close enough he untied it and Jack ran in circles, then laid down by his feet.

"Go. I know you need to eat. You're skin and bones. I'll be just fine." He peeled his boot off his foot and sucked in his breath as they throbbed. The oily stuff that had been coming out of his feet was thick and shiny in the sun. The smell turned his stomach. He hadn't been able to take care of them the night before when he'd gotten back so late. "Doesn't look like I'll be going anywhere soon, boy."

The dog whimpered and inched closer.

"You didn't act this nice back at the camp. What was the trouble?"

He heard the sound of wagons approaching and hung his head. Beau was the last person he wanted to see. And Jennie would never want to see him after Jack had attacked her. How could he explain to her that Jack was like him? He'd been run off, abused, chased, starved, and finally just run. Jack needed him. And life was a little less hopeless if something needed him. Aiden glanced behind him toward the sound of the wheels against the rocks under the sparse grass. He didn't recognize it. It was an old buckboard with an ancient man tottering at the lines.

"Ho!" The old man yelled down. "Who goes there? Need a lift to town?"

"I do. Can my dog follow?" Aiden glanced up and winced as he shoved his foot back into his boot.

"Don't see why not. You headed to Deadwood? Looking for work?"

Aiden laughed as he climbed up and Jack jumped in the back. The old man didn't seem to notice or care. "Yes, and yes."

The old man held out his hand. "Boom's the name. I work with a small mining outfit in Deadwood. It's hard to get work on the big mine. Men don't want to leave once they git a spot. But our outfit finds pay dirt often enough to keep our few miners working."

Aiden nodded. "That's what I'm looking for. Are you sure they're hiring?"

The old man threw his head back and cackled. "Yup, cause it's my claim. Deadwood's about two hours away by this route, but I was out checking a few things in Preston, then at the big load in Lead. Good thing I happened by. It ain't a good idea to be walking out here alone. Deadwood's been a town for almost twenty years. But we still keep our eyes open. This *is* Indian country."

The man's condescension made him chafe. Everyone assumed that since he was young, he didn't know anything. His da had been the same way. He'd never planned to be out walking alone anyway. When he'd left his first claim back in California, he'd *planned* to stick to the stagecoach trail. Then his horse died. Then, he'd *planned* to stay near the river, until the river he'd been following dried up. He'd met up with the Rockford group later. But then he'd been a fool. Now, he knew what his problem had been. He shouldn't have been *planning* at all.

"You know, Boom, I think I was meant to meet up with you today. I'm Aiden Bradly, and I know gold and how to stir it from the earth."

"Good to hear, son. We don't want 'em green."

No one ever did.

JENNIE SAT NEXT to Ruby as they pulled the wagons out of the circle and formed a line with Reverend Level in the lead, Beau following, and Ruby tagging behind. Jennie wouldn't miss the inside of the wagon one bit. She'd always thought sharing one room with her sisters growing up in the tiny house had been difficult. But it was nothing compared to the cramped covered wagon.

Jennie held her arm tight to her chest. Every bounce and shifting of the wagon sent a fire up her arm. She watched the ever-changing horizon as they slowly climbed over swells and maneuvered through valleys. When she was sure she couldn't take the sight of another evergreen tree, a city grew up in front of them squished between three tall hills and surrounded by deadfall.

Ruby pulled up on the lines and stood, shading her face. Jennie sat in awe and gasped, shading her eyes from the pressing sun. The town was made of *stone*. There wasn't a shanty in sight and no tents either. It was a bustling city, bigger than Cutter's Creek and far larger than anything she'd ever seen.

"They made it of stone... Like a castle from one of those stories you read to us in Cutter's Creek." Jennie could hardly get the words past her throat. An excitement she hadn't expected built inside her. All the rocks were light colored and glinted back at her in the sunlight.

Ruby glanced at her, a twinkle in her eyes. "The city of Deadwood has had a lot of time to grow. You'd have known that if you'd have listened to Reverend Level instead of going off on your own, deciding how much you hated the idea of coming here."

"I'm sorry now I didn't pay more attention." Jennie swallowed hard. "It isn't at all what I expected. What're we going to do once we get there?" Jennie gazed up at Ruby. Now that they were here, new worries attacked her. Where would they live? Did they have supplies? What if goods were more expensive?

Ruby handed Jennie the lines and stretched her back gingerly then sat back down, ready to catch up to Beau's wagon.

"The first thing Beau needs to do is get us lodging for a night at a boarding house or hotel. Then he'll need to find work so we can talk to the land office about housing. We had some money saved for the trip. But we didn't know how much land costs here. I'm not afraid to work. I've heard there are laundries and restaurants here. Not just saloons, gambling houses, and other places we have no business talking about."

"I'm sure all of us are willing to work." Jennie glanced back at Hattie. Jennie had an inkling that Hattie—more than anyone—would be more willing to work *any* job. She shook off the feeling and prayed what she hoped was a proper prayer for forgiveness. Thinking such things about her own sister would only cause strife.

"I'm just not sure what work we'll find. Just keep your eyes open and pray for something to make itself known. Beau has always been good about finding work wherever he is but that was when he was alone. Now he needs work that'll provide for his whole family."

"I guess since Ma and Pa made do with so little, I never thought about what it costs to have a family. I bet it was hard going from one man to a family of nine…"

Ruby smiled absentmindedly and flicked the lines, now in a hurry to get close to Beau's rig. "He's learned to trust less in himself and more on the Lord in these last few months. He's responsible for all of you and doesn't take that lightly. I'm sorry you felt he took your choice away from you when Aiden left. It wasn't his intention to make him leave. He just needed Aiden to understand—in the same way *he* had to learn—that you're all precious and take special care. He wants you to be able to turn to him like a father. Without ever asking you call him that or forcing you to treat him as one."

Her heart lurched in her chest. Beau wanted to be a real father to her so much more than the man who'd actually carried that title. "I never thought of it that way. I was thankful for you, and for him, but I never took account of what it cost both of you. What will you do when...? I mean—" She glanced down to Ruby's waistline suddenly worried that when a baby came, they wouldn't want the burden of her or her sisters.

"We'll be a family of ten," Ruby whispered as she leaned in close and flicked the lines once more. The oxen powered ahead, and Jennie groaned as the jolt jerked her back in her seat. As they navigated through the thoroughfare of people and animals, they had to slow way down. Ruby concentrated on avoiding everything with the heavy wagon.

They pulled their small train down the main street and stopped in front of an inn. Reverend Level and Beau climbed down stiffly and went inside The Grand Central Hotel. Jennie and all her sisters waited outside.

A handsome younger man in a suit walked by and tipped his hat to Ruby and Jennie. The longer they sat in the street, the more men stopped and just stared at them.

She didn't see a single woman around them. So at least some of her fears had been warranted. There were many men bustling about doing business. The city was huge, with many blocks of housing and businesses climbing up the face of the nearby hills. But she didn't spy a single swishing skirt.

The younger man approached their wagon and leaned against the buckboard.

"Hello ladies. Welcome to Deadwood. Name's Roy." He wore a smart gray suit and black satin string tie with a light Stetson perched on his head, shading eyes just a little too beady to suit Jennie's taste.

Beau strode out of the hotel and stood next to Roy, shooting him a glance that would've had her moving fast had it been her in Roy's shoes. He elbowed his way to the wagon, holding out his hand for Ruby. "I have a place for us but let's get a little lunch. Then I'll take you to the house we'll rent until we can get our own homestead."

He stepped back and looked at Roy. "Can I help you with something? Don't you have somewhere to be, mister?"

Roy held up his hand and stepped back. "No, no. I thought you were someone else entirely. Good day." He tipped his head and strode off.

Ruby let Beau help her down. "Strange fellow, though it seems we've attracted quite the notice."

Jennie scanned the street around them. Some men were outright staring while others tried to make it less obvious.

Ruby touched Beau's arm. "I don't think it's safe to leave all our things out here in the street. We should get all our belongings put away and then get lunch. With all of us, it won't take long." Ruby sighed and glanced back up at the seat. "I was looking forward to a short break but with as busy as it is here, I'll do whatever you think is right, Beau."

"How about we compromise? The owner of the hotel has a small livery in the back, and he said we could use it until we get ours cleaned out. I'll move the wagons back there while you ladies wait here."

Ruby shook her head. "If it's all the same to you, I've been kidnapped before and don't intend to let it happen again. We'll follow you. Then go in the back of the inn."

Beau kissed her on the nose. "Sounds good. We'll get these moved then join the reverend inside."

Beau and Ruby maneuvered the wagons through the busy, crowded street and around the block to the small stable in the back of the inn. Unlike out front, no one stood around to look at them back there.

Jennie laid down on the feather tick with the younger girls and waited for Beau to secure the oxen and give them some hay and water. She couldn't help but wonder what had happened to Aiden.

She'd hoped they'd have caught up to him before reaching Deadwood, but they'd seen nothing of him. She'd wanted to apologize for Beau. Perhaps even convince him to stay, though maybe not his dog. They were both in Deadwood but would they ever see each other again?

Beau called for them and they went into the inn to get lunch. When they'd finished, he walked them two blocks from the inn to a house the size of the one they'd left in Cutter's Creek. It had huge front windows, a wrap-around porch and enough room for all of them. Ruby and Beau walked arm-in-arm ahead of the group, smiling at one another.

"How did you get this for us? Why didn't the man at the inn just let us rent a room?"

"I explained to him that we'd be looking for a home and there were quite a few of us. He didn't really have the space for such a large family and for what could be more than a day. So, he suggested this. It was his mother's home, but she passed recently, and he hasn't had a chance to sell it. He'll rent it to us until he can find someone."

"And do we intend to be that someone?" Ruby asked as they waited for him to open the door.

"I guess we'll wait and see what the inside looks like and how much they want to sell it for. If I can find a good job soon, it might be possible."

Beau pushed open the door and they entered onto gleaming wood floors that led to a large fireplace. On the other side of the room was a large dining area and a table with enough chairs for all of them. Along the right wall was a staircase that led to the second level where the bedrooms were. Along the back wall, behind the stairs, was the small but serviceable kitchen.

Ruby stood in the middle of the room and held her arms out wide, slowly spinning in a circle, smiling when she finally stopped. "It's perfect, Beau."

Jennie felt the same way. After living in the tiny confines of the wagon, a home where you could stretch your arms out wide and not touch anything was a blessing. Lula yelled from upstairs,

"There's beds up here. Almost enough for all of us to have our own!"

Beau took Ruby in his arms and danced her around the large room. Jennie turned away from their affection.

"Will you work in the mines, Beau?" Jennie turned back toward the couple, her question stopping their celebration.

"I don't think so Jennie. I've never worked in a mine before and its dangerous work. The railroad is big here. I've done that, cattle work, worked with horses, and moving freight with ox carts. I'm sure I'll find something to do. I feel it. Right down to my bones. This is where we belong." He smiled down at Ruby.

If only Jennie felt as sure.

CHAPTER 7

Boom drove Aiden to the outskirts of Deadwood, then bypassed the town and went around to a small area with what seemed like endless rows of tiny decrepit homes. It was the shantytown Jennie had been so fearful of. The one he'd assured her didn't exist. It wasn't supposed to, at least that's what he'd heard. All along the edge of the shantytown was a row of houses painted red. He'd live in his very own red-light district without even being near the railroad. Aiden shivered. He hoped wherever Boom led him was far away from the cribs.

Boom pulled up in front of a shanty with a sagging roof and no paint. It looked only a little bigger than an outhouse. A foul smell surrounded him, and he held the bile in his throat at bay. There was nowhere for the men to empty chamber pots or spittoons, and litter had piled up in public areas. Even at the California claim, he and the prospector had been neat. Looking about him now, it was a wonder they didn't all die of disease.

"The last guy that had this one didn't take such good care of it. It's got a cot, a stove, and a table. Don't need much else. I'll pick you up tomorrow morning. Work starts early."

Aiden climbed down, grabbing his saddle from the back of the wagon, and keeping the pain in his feet barely under control. Jack jumped down, sitting by his feet and they watched as Boom turned his wagon and headed toward Deadwood in the distance. Aiden limped to the small run-down building. As he opened the door, he noticed there was no lock on it or any way to keep people out. The bed was a nearly flat tick that had seen better days. He'd have to search for miles to find enough material to fill it. He pulled back the shredded curtain that covered the one crate on the wall for storing food and dishes. It held one dirty plate, cup, and bowl. There was no food, no kindling or wood for the stove and he had no way to get into town except to walk. He didn't even have an ax to cut wood.

He glanced out at the sun. It was only around noon but getting his new home in order would take most of the day. He knew it would take a few trips but he grabbed a flour sack he found on the floor and called Jack to follow him.

Though there were a lot of trees, the ground was surprisingly free of twigs. Just under the sparse grass was a layer of rocky gravel. It was sparse and coarse so he wouldn't use it unless he had to.

Aiden searched in several areas about the camp but came up with very little he could use. Finally, he settled on the grass—the very stuff he'd hoped to avoid—hoping that as it dried in his mattress it wouldn't rot or get prickly. He brought the grass litter in and stuffed his tick full. When he'd finished, he was tired. His feet burned.

Peeling off his shoes once more, he noticed the odor which had bothered him before was now much worse and his sweat was not only oily but thick. He shook his head and lay on his new bed looking up at his sagging, uneven roof. A prayer formed on his lips, a prayer that it wouldn't rain before he got a day to repair it. Then, he fell into a deep sleep.

His hand was wet, that was his first thought as he woke up to Jack licking him. It was dark in his little cabin and he sat up, looking out the window. All around him, shanties were lit up with men spilling out all over. Music and male banter reached him through his thin walls. He would never make it to town and back and he hadn't gotten wood or extra leaf litter and twigs for kindling. He rifled through his pack and found a few dollars. He hoped it would be enough for a meal in town and that he could find his way back out to his new home in the dark.

Every step he took sent pain further up his legs. Though he hadn't gone far, he rubbed the sweat from his brow and took off his coat. Had it been this hot when he'd arrived in Deadwood? It sure seemed warm now. He pressed on though his feet throbbed. With each step he had to hold his breath, which meant he made nary any progress at all.

Jack whined and ran ahead then scampered back for him. But as hard as Aiden tried, he couldn't go faster. Full night came and the trail became difficult to see. Aiden tried to lift his feet with every step but they were like lead at the end of his legs. He tripped over a large stone on the side of the road and tumbled down the embankment into the ditch. Jack scampered down, licked his face, and ran off barking.

"I didn't leave *you*!" he yelled. His voice hoarse. He tried to pull himself up, but ferocious heat engulfed him. His body began to shake and he closed his eyes, collapsing in a heap.

"STOP FIDGETING, Jennie. What's gotten into you this evening? This house is snug and safe as a bank, yet you're wringing your hands and pacing. You're making me nervous." Ruby planted her hands on her hips and glared at her.

Jennie couldn't explain it if she tried. Something had her wound tighter than Carlton William's clock back in Cutter's Creek. She'd checked that both doors were locked and looked through the whole house for what had her in a turmoil but came up with nothing.

"I guess I'm just nervous to be in a new place is all. I'm sure I'll settle down after a bit."

"You're going to open up the bite on your arm if you don't. If you can't help me here in the kitchen, go find something to do. I can't get anything done with you pacing about."

Jennie left the kitchen and went back up to the room she now shared with Hattie and Eva. The house was fully furnished—which was good—because they hadn't brought much with them. It wasn't a large room, but it didn't matter. The bed was big enough so she wouldn't be crowded. There was a desk to sit at. And, she had a place to hang her dresses, if she ever had more than two. Jennie picked up the dress she'd changed out of and discarded on the floor. Aiden had ripped it right up the seam. The dress had been large on her anyway so she could repair it using the extra fabric.

"Jennie! Come on down here!" Beau yelled from below.

Jennie tossed the dress on the edge of the bed and ran down the stairs, holding her skirts away from her flying feet. At the base of the stairs, she stopped and gasped. Jack sat at the front door waiting for Beau to open the screen and let him in. He whined pitifully and lifted a huge paw in the air, gently jabbing at the wood as if to knock.

"Jack... Where's Aiden?" She glanced around the room but he was not there.

Beau opened the door and allowed the scruffy dog inside. The mutt approached her slowly and she sat on the stair, her heart racing in her ears. The dog laid his head in her lap and whined. She pulled back but his soft brown eyes stopped her.

"You're sorry, eh? So, where is that master of yours?" She gingerly laid her hand on the dog's head and he scooted closer, looking up at her.

"Aiden had gotten mighty attached to that dog after saving it. I don't think he'd leave our train for the dog, then let him go. I'll go with Jack and see if we can track him down." Beau opened the drop down of the secretary's desk by the door and grabbed his gun belt from inside, fastening it on. He pulled the gun from the belt and filled each chamber, then slid it back into place. Grabbing a few extra bullets, he put them in his leather munitions pouch.

"Come on, Jack. We need to find Aiden." Beau opened the

door and the dog lifted his head off Jennie's lap. He nipped the bottom of her skirt and pulled.

"No boy, I can't go out there. But I'll be waiting right here when you bring him back." She patted his head. He whined and pulled again.

"Jack," Beau called, and the dog reluctantly let go of Jennie's skirt.

She watched as the two disappeared into the night. Ruby locked the door behind them.

"I'm surprised you didn't hear the commotion. He started scraping on the door as soon as I sent you out of the kitchen. He must've tracked us by scent because he couldn't have known we were here."

"He must've been a good dog for someone." Jennie replied. "Now I hope he's a good dog for Aiden."

Ruby stood behind her and gently gripped her shoulders. Jennie realized she was shaking.

"Beau and Jack will find Aiden and bring him back here. Though with the way they parted, I don't know if Aiden will come here or not. Maybe you could make yourself busy cleaning up that servant's room down here behind the kitchen? That will give you something to focus on. Also, that'll be a good place for Aiden if he decides to stay. Far away from all of you." She peeked around Jennie's arm to the other girls in the parlor.

Jennie couldn't help the tear that ran down her cheek as she searched the darkness out the window, knowing Aiden wouldn't be found so quickly. "Or in case he has no choice..."

"Well now, I wasn't going to say that but we both know Aiden was having trouble with his feet and he walked a long way today. Beau wouldn't let me look at him. From what he described to me; he might have some sort of infection." Ruby shook her head. "Men and their infernal ways. If I'd been able to look, I could've told him right away if they were just sore or if they needed tending to. I have to finish supper now or we'll never eat. You go get busy."

With Ruby's red hair and no-nonsense words, she reminded Jennie of Ma. So, she didn't complain about being told what to do.

Jennie stopped at a small linen cupboard and grabbed clean bedding then opened the servant's room.

The house was equipped with room for one servant. Not even a couple could fit in the small space. The bed was little bigger than a cot but had a mattress stuffed with feathers so the lady must have cared for whomever had been doing her chores and cleaning. Jennie dusted the few pieces of furniture with a wet rag and made the bed. She'd added oil to the lamp and opened the window to let in a little air when she heard Jack barking again.

Jennie couldn't keep to the room and finish. Had Beau found Aiden? She ran out to the kitchen in time to see Hattie unlock the door. Jack raced into the house and skidded across the shiny floor. Beau struggled under the weight of an unconscious Aiden over his shoulder.

"Beau, the room is ready back here." She called and moved out of the way in the narrow passage leading to the back room. Beau shuffled past her and she heard a grunt and the moan of the ropes holding up the bed mattress as Beau dumped Aiden onto it. She peered through the door and saw Beau working to pull off Aiden's boots, but they wouldn't come off. Ruby pushed her aside as she bustled in with a pair of scissors.

"We've got to cut them off." Ruby knelt beside him.

"Ruby, I don't want you to have to do this." Beau refused to move and laid his hand on her shoulder.

She shook his hand off. "Beau, you know I respect and love you, but I can do this. I need to see what's going on so I know whether I can treat him or if we need to call for a doctor."

He held up his hands and stood back, giving her space. Ruby had to use both hands to cut through the heavy leather of Aiden's boots. The closer she got to his feet, the more restless he became until Beau had to hold him down. She pulled the scissors away and set it to the side. Beau came to the end of the bed and peeled the boot away from the tender skin of Aiden's ankle then off his foot.

The smell of Aiden's swollen red flesh hit Jennie's nostrils and she gagged. He had no sock left whatsoever and the inside of his boot had rubbed his foot raw. Jennie went to get a basin of water and soap while Ruby worked on the other boot.

Jack laid quietly in the kitchen and rested his head between his paws. She knelt down and patted him on the head. "Aiden must've shown you a pretty good turn for you to change your ways so much. Thank you for helping Beau find him." She stood and tossed down the bone Ruby had pulled from the stewpot along with a few bits of pork fat. While Jack ate his dinner, Jennie finished warming some water and brought the basin back to Beau and Ruby.

"Oh, Jennie. Thank you." Ruby wiped her brow with the back of her wrist. "It isn't good. I hope we can get this infection under control." She turned to Beau. "I need you to go get the vinegar from the kitchen."

"Aren't they pickled enough?" Beau's eyes grew wide.

Ruby ignored his attempt at humor. "It isn't for pickling. In this case, I want to clean the wound and I don't have any alcohol to do it. The vinegar should work instead."

"Or burn his foot right off his ankle..." Beau muttered under his breath as he left.

"Ruby, do you think he'll be all right?" Jennie came into the room and looked down at Aiden's pale face. Her heart ached for him. If not for her, he would've ridden with them in the wagon and his feet wouldn't be as bad as they were. She winced as she looked down at his ravaged feet.

"Oh yes. He just walked too far on boots that wore his feet away. I don't know how we'll replace his boots, but I suppose we'll have to. There was nothing for it, I had to cut them off."

"It's good to know. He wants to get to work so he can return to his pa. He can't do that if he can't walk." She set the basin down next to Ruby then straightened. Her hand seemed to move as if it had its own mind, first resting on his shoulder then up to his still-soft cheek, lingering a little longer than she knew she should. But being in the same room with him again felt more right than she could explain. Would he wake up and tease her or want to leave right away?

213

"Why don't you grab that stack of rags and bring them here." Ruby interrupted her thoughts with a gruff command. She gathered the strips of cloth and knelt next to Ruby.

Jennie whispered softly. "You can go finish in the kitchen. I'll tend to his feet. It's the least I can do. I should've known better than to jump out of the wagon with a growling dog underneath it."

"It wasn't your fault you got bit." Ruby snapped and picked up the cloths, moving them from her.

"It might not be my fault, but I should've known better. He didn't know I wasn't an animal coming to get him. Jack was scared."

Ruby stood and washed her hands in the smaller basin by the door. "I'll be in the kitchen," she tilted her head and her eyes said she could hear everything, "just on the other side of this wall. If you need me."

Jennie nodded and washed her hands then carefully pulled one of Aiden's legs off the bed, dipping it into the warm water. The soft cloth soaked up the water from the basin she'd brought, and she wrung it out over his ankle to wet the whole area. His foot was heavy and slippery as she gently lathered a cloth with the soap and dabbed it over the sore area, careful not to scrub. As she dipped his foot back in the water, she heard a sharp intake of breath and looked up at his beautiful hazel eyes, wide with surprise and pain.

"Didn't think I'd see you again so soon." His voice rumbled in the small space.

Jennie felt heat rush from her neck to her ears then smiled, dabbing his foot dry with a clean towel. He sat up in the bed and lifted his other leg into the water. He winced and sucked in a long breath.

"That really stings." He moaned and leaned against the wall.

Beau strode in holding a jar. He wore the look of a concerned parent as he handed it to her. "Here you go, Jennie." His hard face nodded to Aiden. "Aiden," he said before sitting in the one chair, a presiding force in the room.

Aiden rubbed his eyes and his stomach rumbled loudly. "What's in the jar?"

Beau laughed. "Jennie's going to pickle your feet, so we don't have to smell them anymore."

Aiden's face turned red. "Well, if you give me my boots, I can be on my way. You don't have to put up with my *feet* no more." He shoved himself forward to sit up but wouldn't yank his foot from her.

Jennie washed his other foot as Aiden and Beau bantered. She tried to ignore the irritation in Aiden's voice but it hit her deeper inside than she had any right to feel. If she could find a moment of peace to apologize, that need to speak with him would surely go away.

"You ain't going anywhere Aiden. My wife says you have an infection in your feet. You need to sit for a couple days to let them heal. You also need some new boots because she had to cut them clean off. They wouldn't budge."

Aiden glanced from Jennie to Beau, his voice exploded around her. "You cut a man's boots off? I need those!"

Jennie carefully poured the vinegar over his feet and his body tensed as he pulled away from her. He threw his head back against the wall with a *crack*.

"I'm sorry," she whispered. "It's done now. I just need to wrap them up."

Beau stood. "You'll have to stay here a couple days to mend. While you're here, this's your room. You'll stay on the main level of this house and won't go anywhere near the stairs, understood?"

"Yes, sir. Not like I can walk anyway." Aiden responded bitterly as he tried to lay back on the bed. He struggled with his feet still on the floor. Jennie lifted first one then the other for him and finished binding them. His soft, calm breathing left her sure he'd fallen back asleep. She gathered the leftover rags and basin of dirty water, balancing it against her waist to leave him be and let him rest. As she walked by he reached out and grabbed her hand. She gasped and jumped at the light pressure, sloshing the water a bit.

"Jennie, I'm so sorry about what Jack did. I didn't know he'd do that. I wasn't thinking. I tied him under the wagon I was sleeping under." He grimaced. "Is your arm all right?"

She nodded, staring at his hand touching hers, trying to memorize the feeling for later when he was gone again. "Yes. Ruby said your quick action saved me from getting bitten worse. Thank you."

"I'm surprised you let my fool dog in the house after what he did to you." He pressed his thumb into her palm and her belly did a strange quiver.

"It isn't *my* home and all of us knew if Jack found us without you, something was wrong. He wouldn't have broken free of you to find us, so he had to have been looking for us to help you."

"I'm glad he was there, or I'd still be in that ditch. Probably until morning when who knows what would have happened."

"You'll stay, won't you?" She closed her eyes and squeezed his hand, hoping against hope that he wouldn't run again.

"I'll stay until I can get new boots. I had a job lined up and I'm afraid I'm going to lose it."

She set the heavy basin on the table. "Tell Beau. Maybe he could work in your stead, so you don't lose your place?"

Aiden shook his head and his face hardened. "It's mining. Beau already told me he wants to avoid mines. He doesn't want to get bit with the fever. Too many pretty girls to provide for." His eyes softened and he smiled up at her, pressing his thumb in the palm of her hand once more. "I think I need a little rest. Thank you for bandaging me up. I'm sorry..." He turned red as a beet and glanced down to his feet.

"It's okay. It wasn't your fault. Rest now." She reluctantly released his hand and turned down the wick on the lamp then left him to rest.

CHAPTER 8

Aiden lay in his bed and listened to Beau, Ruby, and all the girls talking. He tried to remember the last time he'd eaten and far as he could tell, it had been the noon meal two days before. A shadow darkened his doorway.

"Are you awake, Aiden?" Jennie's soft voice made him smile and the smell that came with her had his mouth watering.

"I am."

She came in balancing something in her arms, slowly making her way the few steps to the edge of his bed. She set it down then pulled out a card of flexibles to light the lamp. It was black as pitch in the small room, but he could see Jennie in his mind's eye with little trouble. The lamp bathed the room in soft light and her gentle features came into focus. She replaced the hurricane and smiled at him. Though he was distracted by the stew sitting on the table beside him and the wonderful savory smell wafting from it.

"I heard your stomach making a fuss before and figured you could stand some supper." Jennie pulled up the chair next to his bed. "I'll stay while you eat. I already fed Jack so don't worry. He isn't starving."

Aiden pulled himself up and sat against the wall, reached for the bowl, and balanced its warmth on his chest. Jennie handed him a spoon and he took his first mouthful. Ruby sure could cook, that was fact. He closed his eyes and savored the bite.

"I talked to Beau about your job. He isn't sure what he can do about it because he has to go find his own job tomorrow. He's hoping to find something soon."

Aiden finished his bite and swallowed. "I'm guessing I'm not in a hotel, so this must be a house. How did all of you get into a house so quick?"

"The hotel manager didn't want to deal with all of us taking all his rooms. He had this house available, but it'll be for sale. We don't know how long we'll be able to stay."

Aiden frowned. "My pack is back at that old shanty and it isn't locked. I have a little in my money belt. I don't think I have enough for new boots. If I don't have those, I can't work in the mine."

She pulled the two dollars he'd paid for his shave from her apron and left it on the table. "Maybe you aren't supposed to. Isn't that dangerous work?" Jennie grabbed a cup of water and held it to his mouth.

She looked so worried about him. He didn't deserve anyone as pretty as her to pay him no mind. Aiden took the cup himself and drank then handed it back to her. "Dangerous or not, it's what I know. And I need to keep my promises." He ate a few more bites as he tried to think of a way to explain it to her without digging deep into his family and why he left. He'd been so young and foolish then. He didn't want her to think of him like that. A man had to act like a man, but he hadn't then.

"What promises? I don't understand why you must do it if there're other jobs available. Why would you risk getting hurt?"

Aiden shook his head. He didn't want it to matter to her, whether he got hurt or not. "Those promises are between me and those I made them to. At some point, I have to go back and make what I did right."

Jennie's eyes pleaded with him to share with her, but he couldn't do it. He couldn't say what he knew would make her run. It was selfish to want her attention for the brief time he'd be there, but his da had always said he was selfish. This just proved again his da was right.

"Money is money. No matter where you earn it. You're hurt and you can't work in the mine for a while. Once you heal a little, why not try working somewhere else? Somewhere safer?"

"Mining's all I know. You just wouldn't understand."

She clutched his arm and the warmth of her hands sent shock waves through his thin shirt all the way to his skin and much deeper.

"So, help me understand! Why can't you at least think about doing something else?"

She will never understand and it's better to keep my promise. Then, return home. He pried her hand from his arm and set his jaw then looked away from her and closed his eyes. "As soon as I can walk, boots or no, I'm going back to my home outside of town."

He heard her gasp and felt her knee nudge the bed as she stood and left. *You can find someone else, Jennie. Someone who isn't beholden to a promise and a family that will never love him.*

JENNIE CLOSED the door behind her and leaned against it. She was trapped inside this big pretty house. Back in Cutter's Creek or even in Yellow Medicine, if she'd needed a minute of peace, she could leave the house and go for a walk. She couldn't do that here. It wasn't safe to go out walking alone. Though she could probably take Jack, even that wouldn't deter someone who really wanted to take her. Ruby would never allow it.

She trudged up the stairs and flopped on her bed, no longer hungry. Her sleeve had to be repaired or she'd only have the dress she was already wearing. The bite on her arm throbbed but she ignored it. Picking up her small sewing kit, she focused on the sleeve's torn edge. Holding the needle tightly, she agonized over the stitches to make them perfect.

Hattie sauntered into their room and pulled out the chair by the small desk. She sighed loudly. "I just can't believe we're stuck here in this house with *nothing* to do. Beau made a long speech at supper about how we're to stay in the house while he's out looking for work and should only leave with him. He's decided this house won't work for us since we're used to our freedom, but we must stay here until we can get a homestead. He fears we may not be able to file for a homestead without filing for a claim, but he doesn't know for sure because he hasn't checked with the land office." She rolled her eyes. "Why did we come here again?"

Jennie didn't want to argue with Hattie. Didn't even want to talk to her. "We're here because it's a brand-new state, and Beau likes new places without lots of people. And Ruby would do about anything Beau said." Jennie tried to ignore Hattie and concentrate on her stitches. Over the last month, Hattie had been steadily getting under her skin. Her complaints were only making Jennie more furious.

"Well, Deadwood certainly doesn't fit that. It's bigger than where we came from!" Hattie stomped her foot.

"I don't know, Hattie. Why don't you ask him? I'm sure he thinks he's doing what's best for us and he's certainly giving it more thought than Pa ever did."

"Yeah, but at least Pa *wanted* us to get married. I don't see how we're ever going to find someone if we're forever stuck in the house."

"Reverend Level will start his preaching this Sunday. Beau and Ruby will take us over to hear him preach. Then you'll get to meet some of the townspeople."

"You have an answer for everything, don't you? Why are you so glum? Did Aiden finally tell you to skedaddle with your grumpy ways?" Hattie laughed loudly, leaning forward in her chair.

Jennie gasped and tears stung her eyes. She certainly hadn't meant to be grumpy with Aiden. He was healing. "How could you say such a thing?"

"Oh Jennie, I didn't mean anything by it. You know it. It's just that every time you turn around, you're all sulky. You catch more flies with honey than vinegar." Hattie winked and grinned.

"Maybe I don't want to catch flies at all." She shoved the

needle into the fabric and into her finger. She groaned, clutching her finger into a fist.

"You aren't fooling anyone." Hattie stood up and strode across the room, standing in front of her and narrowing her eyes. "Did you think no one noticed you dashing from Aiden's room up the stairs to avoid all of us? Don't you think we all knew exactly what happened? That you spoke your mind and you pushed him away ... again. Men aren't hard to understand, Jennie. They want what they want. You either stand with him or you stand against him. I guess you just need to figure out if Aiden is worth standing for, or if you'll step aside."

"You seem to forget that he hasn't paid you the slightest bit of attention, Hattie." Jennie glared up at her. She was not going to let her anywhere near Aiden. Not when it was obvious he had no intention of sticking around anyway. He'd head out as soon as a new gold rush hit.

"Only because he's still hoping you'll settle down and pay attention. A man'll only wait so long." Hattie flounced her hip out and turned.

"What about Beau? You are two years younger than me and he hasn't given you permission to even *look* yet."

Hattie's arms stiffened at her sides and her fists clenched into quivering balls of anger. "He didn't give you permission either, Jennie. He just never held you back. If you don't want Aiden, step back. Because I know a good man when I see him. If I don't get him, I'll find another way out of here. I'm ready for life, Jennie, and *this* ain't living."

"He'll be gone in two days and you'll never see him again, Hattie," Jennie screamed jumping from the bed. She wanted to throttle her sister but she'd never listen anyway. Hattie had always been stubborn.

Hattie winced and turned her head back to Jennie. "How could you have done such a thing? He's a good man, Jennie. Don't let him go."

Jennie threw the dress down on the bed and Hattie turned to face her.

"My whole life, the only thing that's ever mattered is getting out. All Pa ever wanted was for all of us to come of age so he could get rid of us. Now I have a choice. I don't want to marry just because I can. I don't want to marry just anyone. Look at Ruby. The man Pa found for her nearly killed her!"

"Then she found Beau. Marriage doesn't have to be terrible, Jennie. In fact, it looks like it could be a lot of fun."

"Ruby picked Beau! That's completely different. I didn't pick Aiden and he didn't choose me, either. He isn't the man you think he is, Hattie. He's been bitten by gold fever. As soon as Beau knows that, he'll make him leave."

Hattie screwed up her face. "He didn't choose you? Is that what you really think? When you jumped out of the back of the wagon yesterday morning, I heard him scream and I jumped to look out the front. He was running toward our wagon with a look like I've never seen before. He was terrified. You didn't see him cradle you in his arms when he reached you. But *we* did. You might not want to admit it but that man cares about you and you'd best consider that before you talk to him again." Hattie turned and left the room.

Jennie sat on the edge of the bed. A man shouldn't care about her. None of them. She wasn't ready for something as important as a man's heart.

CHAPTER 9

Aiden let his head bump against the wall behind him, the sound keeping time with his heart. His feet throbbed their protest at the end of the bed. At least the vinegar had taken care of the smell. He'd been sure his feet were rotting. While they still hurt, they felt better. He threw back the covers and stared at them. Jennie had wrapped them in clean bandages and Ruby had come in to tell him the boots couldn't be repaired. He'd need new ones.

He shook his head wondering what Boom must have thought when he was gone without word or even a note. Maybe Boom couldn't read anyway. Course, if he made it to his feet maybe he could get back to the shanty. Aiden picked up one leg and let if fall off the side of the bed. As his foot hit the floor a searing pain ran its way through his foot and up his leg. He bit back a yell. Jack poked his head in the door and tucked it low, growling at Aiden.

"It's okay, boy. It's just time for me to get out of here."

Jack growled again and Beau appeared behind him at the door. He crossed his arms over his chest and waited. Aiden scowled and lifted his other leg, letting it fall beside the other.

"So, that's how you'll handle this? You'll run? Here, if you're going to be as stubborn as a mule, let me help you." Beau strode into the room and yanked Aiden to his feet by his elbow.

Pain shot up Aiden's legs and sweat erupted all over his body. The pain burned and throbbed. Balance fled him and he wobbled, tottering beside the bed. He threw his arms out but there wasn't anything to hold on to besides Beau—and he wouldn't give him the satisfaction of granting him help. He fell back onto the bed with a bitten off curse.

"Want to try again? Goodness knows there's nothing more important than getting back to your *home* so you can catch a ride to the mine tomorrow morning. Never mind that we've welcomed you in since we met you. Are you a man? Are you going to let a few words from Jennie stop you? Get up. Leave."

Aiden clenched his teeth against the wave of nausea, then shook his head. "What do you know about it? Did she go running to you after I told her I was leaving?"

"She didn't have to. The walls are thin. I'm going to say what she was too smitten to say. You don't need to work in those mines to fulfil any promise. You can stay here, work hard, and go pay whoever it is you need to. Deadwood is a booming town. Miners spend money here. But, if you're going to return to mining, you leave Jennie alone. I won't have her mourning over you. She's had it tough enough."

"I *am* a miner. It's what I know." It even sounded hollow to his own ears and hearing that Jennie was smitten had hit him hard in the chest. He'd hoped he'd read her wrong. But if Beau had noticed, then he was right. He didn't want to carry her heart. He couldn't even be trusted with gold. "I don't want to disappoint Jennie. But the fact is, this's who I am. She can accept it, or she'll have to find someone who'll live up to what she wants. Maybe that isn't me."

Beau crossed his arms and stood back, giving him space to think. "It could be. The choice is up to you. You're welcome to stay." He turned and walked out of the room, returning a few minutes later to drop an old pair of boots by the bed.

"Jennie told me the money by the bed was for boots. They're

old, but they'll do until you can buy another pair. Ruby also insisted you take this pair of socks she knitted." He tossed them on the bed. "Let us know your decision." His angry footsteps stomped down the hall, leaving Aiden alone.

He looked at the empty door then felt something cold and wet touch his hand. He patted Jack on the head without looking at him. He could make the decision to just leave, but they sure were making it hard. They wanted more from him than even his parents had. The pressure laid heavy on him.

The dog lifted his head sharply, planting his cold wet nose against his wrist. Aiden frowned. "You want to stay. Don't you, boy?"

Jack laid his head on Aiden's lap, his eyes shifting all around.

"What if I don't belong here? I might cause more trouble staying here than I started a year ago when I left home."

Jack's dark brown eyes stared up at him as a small area of drool formed on Aiden's pants.

"I can't go home until I prove I was right. There's money to be made in mining."

Jack shifted and laid down at Aiden's feet. Even the dog had given up on him.

"Don't turn your back on me, Jack. It's important."

Jack lifted his head slightly and tipped his nose down. The dog was rolling his eyes.

Aiden threw up his hands. Even his dog was on Jennie's side.

JENNIE HEARD Beau and Ruby talking in the kitchen which was situated beneath her room. Beau hadn't yet left to look for work that morning but would soon. Jennie wouldn't go down and disturb them. They got so few moments alone. The front door closed with a click and Jennie pushed herself up out of the bed. Hunger gnawed at her. She hadn't gone back down to eat the night before after her argument with Hattie.

If Aiden wanted to go, she wasn't going to watch him make

that choice. She'd also heard the argument between Beau and Aiden. The whole house had. Her feet dragged getting ready, unsure if Aiden left or not and praying he hadn't made that choice on her account.

She wrapped her robe around her dress to ward off the chill in the house and padded down the stairs. Ruby waited in the kitchen, looking quite green as she stood by the pail on the dry sink.

"Ruby, what is it?" Jennie rushed over and hugged her older sister close as she quaked.

"I'm so sick. Never felt so sick in my life." she sniffed. "I don't know if there's something wrong with me or the baby. Beau wants to take me to visit the doctor when he gets home."

Jennie led her over to the table and sat Ruby down, then rushed to get her some coffee. Ruby hated tea so perhaps the warmth of something familiar would help calm her stomach. She set the steaming cup in front of Ruby then ducked out of her robe and strapped on her apron. "You sit, I'll take care of breakfast. I'm so sorry, Ruby. Just rest."

Ruby rested her head against her hand and stared down into her coffee. "I'm not that far along, but we're hopeful that it's just a bug." She laid her hand on her stomach and shook her head.

"Well, don't go thinking you did anything wrong. People get sick all the time. It doesn't mean there's anything wrong." Jennie rested her hands on her hips and swallowed back her own tears. It was bad enough Ruby would have to hide her illness from the others—because they didn't know—but she shouldn't feel bad about crying in front of Jennie. "Ruby, just remember what Ma used to say. Every life under heaven has a purpose. I don't know what's happening, or why, but I do know that He can give you hope."

"He did." A tear slid its way down Ruby's cheek.

Jennie turned, unable to blink back her tears anymore. It confounded her why the Lord might give then take away, but the Lord had His reasons. She'd just pray that the sickness had nothing to do with the little life growing inside Ruby. She cracked eggs into a bowl and cooked them up, dishing up portions for all her sisters and for Aiden, in the hopes he was still there.

She looked over her shoulder at Ruby and her sisters as they slowly filed into the kitchen and sat at the table, ready to eat. She left her own plate at the table and took Aiden's into his room.

He opened his eyes as she walked in then pushed himself up on his elbow. His hair was tousled with sleep and he was showing a bit of orange shadow around his jaw.

"It smells wonderful."

She waited for him to finish sitting up then set the plate on his lap. "I need to change your bandages. We worked hard to clean them up, wouldn't want the infection to get worse."

Aiden sighed. "Jennie, go sit with your sisters and eat. I won't go running off on you." He laughed. "Probably best if you have breakfast before you deal with a man's feet anyway. Might not want to afterward."

Something about his freshly risen appearance and his humor sparked something within her and built to a sweet glow. "Thank you, Aiden. I'll return in just a bit."

"I know *you* think I am, but I'm not a complete monster. Go. I'll still be here when you get back." He laughed and picked up his fork.

He couldn't have been more wrong about how she felt for him. Jennie took a few steps toward the door but stopped next to his bed.

"I never said you were any such thing." She leaned down and ran the back of her fingers down his bristly cheek. She had to know what the stubble felt like against her hand. It wasn't soft anymore. Yet the slight contact set her pulse racing.

Aiden reached up and captured her hand, holding it against his cheek. "You're too sweet, Jennie girl, to be wasting any of your time on me." He let go of her and fixed his focus on eating.

Her soul soared as she left the small room though it was short-lived. As soon as she saw the pinched look on Ruby's face she reined in her feelings.

Jennie sat down at her seat and forced a smile. "Hattie and

Eva? Do you think you could work with Francis, Nora, Lula, and Daisy to get the upstairs finished today? I promised Ruby I'd work with her on a project down here. We want to keep it quiet for Aiden so he can rest."

Hattie sent her a scathing look. "I don't see why we should be stuck upstairs where it is sickeningly hot. Can't we explore the town today?"

Ruby shook her head. "No, Beau is concerned that until we know more about what's expected here. We should stay inside."

"So, we're trapped in here?" Hattie crossed her arms. "At least back home we had the freedom to move."

Daisy laid her hand on Hattie's. "It's fine. Let's make our bedrooms as nice as they can be. Maybe when Beau gets home, he'll take us out to see the town."

Hattie frowned. "I wouldn't count on it. If he finds work, he'll get home late and tired." She pushed out her chair and stomped up the stairs.

Jennie interrupted. "I know that Beau and Ruby will be gone for a short while after, so he won't be able to take any of us out after supper."

Daisy folded her hands in her lap. "I'll go work on my room until it looks like what we left behind."

Ruby stood and pushed in her chair. "Thank you, Jennie and Daisy. I'm not feeling well. I'll be lying down for a bit."

Jennie watched Daisy and the others file up the stairs. When everyone was gone, she strode back to Aiden's room. He'd moved his plate off his lap and onto the small table by his bed. His head rested against the wall behind him. She took the plate out to the kitchen but returned quickly. If she could change his bandages while he slept, it might hurt him less.

She padded softly to the end of the bed and knelt by his feet. It took more patience than she realized she had to untie the bandage on each foot without moving him. Unwinding the long bandages would involve lifting his leg. She used some folded blankets and a spare pillow to raise his leg and lifted it as gently as possible. Jack whined at her feet.

"Shush, Jack. You're going to wake him up," she whispered, her hands trembling.

Aiden cleared his throat and she jumped, dropping his foot to the bed. He sucked in a deep breath as his heel dug into the cot.

"Aiden, you scared me." She backed away from him, putting her hands behind her back. She felt like a child caught stealing.

He moved his feet around, glancing at them briefly then up at her. "They feel much better. I'm not sure what Ruby used on them yesterday but other than being tender when they touch anything, they seem fine. Now, I just need those boots Beau found for me. He'd brought them in here last night, but they've disappeared."

"Just where do you think you're going?" She stepped forward and continued to unwind his bandages.

"I'm going home. I decided this morning—after listening to you and your sisters—that I've missed out on real riches. I haven't seen my brothers or sister in over a year. They have what makes life worth living. Not anything I can find here. I just have to swallow my pride, admit I was wrong, and ask my da to take me back." He laughed humorlessly. "Should be easy, right? But you should be happy. At least I won't be in the mines."

All the breath rushed out of Jennie's lungs and she couldn't speak for a moment as she unwrapped Aiden's other foot to avoid the hurt welling inside her. It was so foolish. He was going to go home where he belonged. Not with her. He was right, she should be happy. He wouldn't be in the mines. But for the life of her, she couldn't be. His feet looked fine. There was only so long she could use that as an excuse for her silence. She'd have to say something. The silence around her was weighted with his expectation of her answer.

"I guess if what you were looking for isn't here, then you should go," she whispered against the lump in her throat, clasping the strips of cloth tightly in her hands to hide their trembling. "I'll get those boots for you. Wouldn't want you to have to wait around here too long." Her voice lodged in her throat.

She tried to flee the room, but Aiden reached out and grasped her hand. Drat the cramped room that allowed him to reach her!

"Jennie, what's the matter? You're never this quiet. I thought you'd be happy. I'm not going back to the mines. It's what you wanted."

She wouldn't look down at him. "I'm sorry. I have a lot of work to do. This is a big house." She pulled free of him, a little more forcefully than was necessary, and left the room as a tear escaped down her cheek. When Beau had found Aiden again, she'd thought he would be around long enough to convince him he didn't need to work in the mines. Now that he'd decided against mining, he would leave her behind.

Stuck in Deadwood.

CHAPTER 10

Aiden lifted his feet one at a time and flexed his toes. They weren't painful or achy now. He just had to get his boots. Jennie hadn't come to see him in the two days since he'd told her he was going home. Since then, no matter who came in to feed him, they didn't bring them. He couldn't leave the room without them. While he wasn't a man of great manners, walking around the house barefoot wasn't an option unless you were a toddler. Jennie's distance—and the fact that she hadn't brought the boots like she'd said—bothered him. Her distance had forced him to think about her far more than was good for him.

He gingerly put one foot then the other on the floor and tested his weight on them. Finding them as good as ever, he stretched up on his toes then back down. Standing felt wonderful after lying in bed for days. He found the socks Beau had left with him near the ointment at the end of his bed. He slipped them on and relished the warm comfort of new wool socks. He walked to the door of his little room and Jack yipped at him.

Aiden patted the dog's head and moved further out into the short hall that led to the kitchen. Ruby stood by the stove stirring something in a large pot.

She glanced up and a smile played at her lips. "Aiden, so good to see you up and walking about. I was resting a bit the last few days myself and took that time to knit you some more socks. I'll get them for you."

She tapped her spoon on the side of the pot and rushed to the stairs, returning a minute later with another pair of black socks. He held them for a moment, feeling their thickness. He hadn't had a new pair of socks in longer than he could remember and now he had two.

"Thank you, Ruby. I won't forget your kindness." He sat at the table and she set a cup of coffee in front of him. He felt better now that he was up and moving.

Beau came in and kissed Ruby on the back of the neck. "Aiden, I have those boots near the door." He dug around and pulled out the old pair of boots he'd brought before. Beau dropped them by his feet and waited as Aiden tried them on. They fit as well as any other boots he'd ever had before, which wasn't great but expected.

Ruby turned and smiled. "Jennie tells us you plan to head out soon. Heading home. That's wonderful."

"Yes, ma'am. I'll need to work to earn a railroad ticket. But then I'm going home to my family."

"That's good to hear. But you'll have to keep in touch. You feel like family now." She turned back to the stove.

The words struck him. It was true. Beau and Ruby felt like family and he would miss them. The younger Arnsby girls had all wound their way into his heart like little nieces. Jennie though, as hard as he tried, he couldn't picture her in the same way.

Beau sat at the table across from him. "They need a type-setter at the paper where I work. It'd be easier for you if you can read."

"I can." He stood and tested the boots, flexing his toes within them, glad there were no rough spots to poke holes in his new socks.

"Then you can come with me tomorrow morning. It's messy work but nothing like the mine. If you can carve, they may even have you making the blocks. That would earn you more money quicker."

"I don't aim to make this a profession. I just need to work long enough to earn my way south."

"It shouldn't take too long. Maybe a month or so. You're welcome to stay here as long as you need. You know that."

He tried to keep his emotions in check. A month was a long time. Too long. If he let himself think about Jennie for a month, he'd be too attached. Either way, he had to find out what a ticket cost and see if his pack with the little money he had left was still where he'd left it. "I'd like to go back to the cabin Boom gave me before I ended up here. I left my bag back there."

"I'd take Jack with you. I've heard there are two places you want to avoid in Deadwood, the shanty town and Chinatown. Whether either warning is true, I don't know. But that's what people tell me."

"I'll keep that in mind." He whistled for Jack and headed for the door. "Thank you, Beau, Ruby." He plopped his hat on his head and tipped it to her.

Beau smiled. "Don't thank me yet. You haven't put in a day of work."

Aiden let Jack run around the front of the house as he closed the door. The fresh summer air buzzed with expectation. He'd been chained to that room because of his feet for too many days. The sun was high in the sky and he realized Beau must have come home during the midday meal. He'd lost all track of time. Even with the small window in his room, the light never seemed to fully make it into the space. Tilting his face back, he closed his eyes and let the sun warm his face. The weather was so much different than Kansas or California. It was like the best of both.

He made his way down the streets, following the glimpses of the shanty town he could see as he went by rows of homes. The closer he got the older and more decrepit the houses appeared. He walked by a few homes that were little more than burned out shells. Blackened boards stuck out at odd angles from deep craters. Some houses were still upright, but gray with soot, the glass in the windows long gone, and tattered curtains fluttering in the breeze. He shook his head. That was the mark of enough devastation to make a man pick up his family and leave...if the families who'd lived in those homes even survived.

As he walked down the rows of tiny homes in the shanty town not a soul was in sight. Every working man was off in the mines. There wasn't a woman or child, no dog or even chickens to be seen. Even the cribs were quiet. He searched for and finally found his small place. The door remained open, hanging precariously off the makeshift hinges as it had when he'd gotten there.

He pushed the door further open and saw the tick he'd spent the day filling was now flat and clothes he didn't recognize hung on the pegs on the wall. Boom had already given away his home to someone else, so where was his saddle? He searched through the few things inside, but his saddle was gone, probably sold.

A coldness lay on him as he closed the door behind him to leave. His da had got him that shaving kit when he'd finally started taking on whiskers. The pack and saddle itself had been a gift from his older brother. He'd carried it for more miles than he could count because it was all he'd had left of his family and he couldn't leave it behind. Now, his travels away from home had cost him everything. His snide insistence that the world held something better than what he'd had rang hollow in his ears. How would they ever forgive him?

He trudged back to Deadwood with Jack on his heels. His shoulders slumped and he passed Beau's house as he walked further up town. There were shops, barbers, grocers, restaurants, and other businesses that he only noted in passing. What he needed was the railroad station. Deadwood's rail system wasn't old, but it'd been carrying mining equipment for a few years. It had only recently connected with three other nearby rail systems to take passengers to and from Deadwood, making it more appealing and accessible. Though his only interest was in how to leave, and if those few rail systems connected with a major one to get him home. He searched the fare board and found what he was looking for. The new lines didn't go many places. He'd have to connect at another larger station farther south.

It would cost him thirty dollars to get home. If he could get the pay Boom had told him about as a miner, he could leave within two weeks. If not, he'd be here longer. There was just no way to know what Beau's job would offer until he showed up to check it out. Thirty dollars was a daunting amount when he currently made nothing. And four weeks was a lifetime when he had to leave quickly or risk caring too much. If he cared too much, he might not ever go home and make things right.

The walk back to the large house was a short one. His feet had already begun to throb. The front steps would make an excellent place to rest out of the way of the ladies in the house. While mining might not have been good for him, his body was in good condition because of it. Swinging a pick for a year on the prospector's claim had worked fine for him. He'd been younger and foolish enough to think the old man would give him his share. But here...miners were under contract and the experienced ones could make as much as seven dollars a day. He was sorely tempted to find Boom. But there was always the possibility Boom would be no different than the old coot in California.

He let himself fall comfortably on the steps of the porch back at the Rockford's and let the sunshine on him. Jack sat next to him and rested his head on Aiden's leg. He stroked the dog's ears but let his mind wander. During the day the city of Deadwood was an amazing ruse. It looked much like any bustling western town. They lived on the edge of the municipality where a few stores were still wooden with high false fronts painted white with bold black lettering announcing their business to the world. Men in white aprons, sleeves rolled high, helped farmers bring cattle into the back for butchering. He'd walked by just about any business a man could imagine.

The door clicked behind him and he heard the rustle of petticoats swish toward him. It was strange how Jennie could use the very same soap as the rest of her family, but he could tell without turning that the scent of rose soap clung to *her*. He turned and she joined him, sitting a few feet away on the other end of the step. Her hair was the same color as a flake of gold, and it shone just the same in the sunlight. She laid her hands in her lap and searched the area around them. Jack got up and went to her, plopping down by her side and licking her face. She laughed and patted her lap. Jack immediately obeyed and laid his head down for some attention. That dog was stealing his girl.

"How's your arm?" he mumbled, at a loss for what else to say.

She stopped petting Jack and touched her forearm. "Fine. It wasn't as bad as it looked at first. He's so good now. It's hard to imagine he did that."

"I think he was just scared. He'd been rescued the night before. The camp was new with different noises... I'm so sorry, Jennie."

She turned her face away and brushed a strand of hair behind her ear. "You already apologized, and I forgave you. It wasn't your fault. When do you think you'll go?" Her face didn't change but her body did, and Jack noticed the change as much as he did. He whined at the sudden tension in her shoulders and back.

"Well, that all depends on that job Beau has for me. If I can make what I would've in the mine, less than two weeks. If not..." he shrugged, he couldn't lie to her about his desire to go quickly. She would take it wrong and part of him still wanted to stay with the golden-haired beauty next to him. Even if it was dangerous.

She turned toward him. "And will you go work in the mine if you can't get that much with Beau?" Her face was set, just as it had been when he first joined them. She'd already shut him out and counted him as gone.

"No, that isn't my plan. I'm not strong enough to say no. If I started in the mine, it would be too easy to think just one more day and I'll be richer, just one more day until I strike it big. I may go home with nothing in my pockets for my da except an apology. I've got to pray that's enough."

She nodded. "So, what you really want *is* in Deadwood, you're just not willing to let yourself go for it. Temptation is a terrible thing."

He clenched his hands to keep from reaching out to her. No one knew about the difficulty of temptation more than him at that moment. He glanced away from her. "The cost of searching for gold is much higher than buying it. I see that now. Is Ruby going to be all right?" He ran his hand up the back of Jacks fur and scratched his neck, using the dog as an excuse to inch closer to Jennie.

Jennie hid a smile as she tucked her chin. "Yes, the doctor says it's pretty common to get sick. We didn't know. Mama never got sick with us."

"What do you mean?"

Jennie cocked her head to the side and smiled faintly. "I guess I can tell you, since she finally told the family. Ruby is in a family way."

For some reason her words came back to him and he wished he could've been included in the celebration. She must have told them when he was out of the house or he'd have heard it.

Jack rolled off Jennie's leg and turned over between them. His lips flopped open like a lopsided grin. Jennie laughed and her face softened.

"I've never seen a dog do that before." He couldn't take his eyes off Jennie and he said a prayer she didn't notice. "I wish I knew where he came from. I guess he's mine now, though I don't know if they'll let him travel by train."

"Maybe you'll just have to leave him here... with me." She glanced up at him, her eyes asking for much more than the dog.

He wanted to give her assurances, but he couldn't. If da didn't forgive him he'd work hard until he could earn forgiveness. Jennie was too good a girl to make wait. He'd never considered coming back, though, maybe it was possible. He still couldn't give her hope where there might be none. "I can't do that. Might be tempted to come back and get him. Like you said. Temptation is a terrible thing." He stood up and strode into the house before Jennie could make him admit more than he wanted to. Talking with that girl always made him feel as if more was being said than he meant, and he hated the tight feeling in his chest whenever he thought about what to say. He hated it even more when he left her.

∼

JENNIE BUSTLED around Ruby in the kitchen keeping busy. Nothing seemed to relieve the knot in her stomach. Aiden had said he'd be gone within two weeks. After that she could relax again. Every time she got near him and worse if she opened her mouth, her stomach would get too fluttered and her heart would speed up. Then her hands felt clammy and she had to mentally stop herself from wiping them on her skirt. She worried about her hair being just right or if her dress was just so. She tugged on her bodice, the pins she'd placed earlier to hold the dress so it would fit poked into her skin.

Jennie shook away the tense feeling in her hands and opened the oven to check the bread. Aiden would be joining them at the table that night and she'd already known she couldn't eat in front of him. Especially if her stomach wouldn't cooperate. The bread was done, and she grabbed the metal handle that would click into the groove on the bread pan so she could pull it out. Once it was out, she set it up on the cooling rack to finish.

Ruby and Jennie had been working in the kitchen for a few hours when the door opened, Jack barked, and Beau came in.

"Hello, lovely ladies." He swept Ruby into his arms and kissed her soundly. Jennie turned away as the heat crept up her cheeks. Her parents had never shown such displays and it made her nervous. It seemed inappropriate to look yet they were right there in the middle of the room.

"You're home a little early." Ruby glanced out the window. The sun was still high in the sky.

"Mr. Carmichael was glad to hear we would have another worker, at least temporarily, and he sent me home a little early today. With Aiden there to help I might be home at this time every day for the next few weeks."

"Well, good. I'm glad of it. Get washed up then sit down. We can be finished by the time you're done." She turned back to Jennie. "Why don't you go let Aiden know it's supper time?"

Jennie wiped her hands on a towel and lifted her apron over her head then hung it on the wall. She felt the knot inside her coil tighter as she strode to his room. She knocked and the knot tightened further, making it difficult to breathe.

"It's open," he called from inside.

Jennie pushed the door open and stood in the doorway. The room was lit with a candle and Aiden sat at his small table reading.

"It's time to eat. Best get washed up." She backed out of the doorway.

"Jennie, come in and look at this." He motioned her into the room.

She hesitated and her chest felt as if it would collapse under the pressure. She strode forward, forcing herself to put one foot in front of the other until she was beside him.

He pointed to a photograph of Deadwood from a few years before. "I found this in the desk. Probably a gift to the maid or whoever stayed in this room. It was used like a diary. They kept track of all the news, the railroad coming, Crazy Horse, Wild Bill Hickock, and the building of the Grand Central Hotel—it's all here." He looked up at her with the wonder of a child at Christmas.

"I keep praying Deadwood has moved beyond all that, but you want to *keep* that history?" She took a step back, unable to think clearly with him so near.

He closed the book and his expression fell. "You have to understand the history of a place to appreciate it, Jennie. A place is like a person. It has a past that makes it what it is. Deadwood had a rough beginning and it won't be tamed quickly. This is a mining town and it probably always will be. That Homestake mine will keep America in gold for a long time, mark my words. And where there's gold, there's miners. That's just a fact of life."

"Why are you so interested in the history here if you're leaving?" She rested her hand on the back of his chair as her legs urged her to run.

"Because it's interesting. This book was written by someone who loved Deadwood and was proud to see the growth. There were things they didn't like. The caravan of prostitutes for instance, including Madam Dirty Em, for one."

Jennie felt heat rise up her collar. She wasn't ignorant of what went on between husband and wife or what happened in brothels, but it wasn't usually brought up in conversation.

"I'm so glad. You can take that book with you when you go home. It'll help you remember us and maybe you can pray for us and ask the Lord to help Deadwood." She turned to leave the room, but he took her hand and heat shot up her arm, enflaming her face, trailing warmth all the way to her heart.

"I'll pray that, at some point, you'll see the beauty of the place you live. Even if you don't appreciate every last thing about it. I'll be out in just a few minutes." He regarded her hand in his and stroked the side with his thumb, sending shivers through her. The tension inside her squeezed until she was sure she couldn't take another moment. He pulled her hand closer, glanced up at her, catching her gaze. He drew her hand closer still until she was sure he'd kiss it. She held her breath and couldn't look away if she tried. He sighed and closed his eyes then let it go and turned away.

She was left with warmth rising in her and nothing she could do would quench it. How could she teach her body that wanting a man would lead to hurt? She wouldn't let anyone force her to marry. Beau and Ruby had even promised. But she didn't want to get married at all, especially with a man whose vice could be as bad as her own Pa's had been. Not for the first time, she wished her mother were there to tell her what to do.

CHAPTER 11

Aiden woke early and joined Beau at the table for breakfast before they'd head down to the newspaper for work. He finished off his eggs and set his fork aside. "You don't strike me as a newspaper man, Beau." He'd yet to form a friendship with the man. They'd shared too many heated words for that. But it would have to change if they were to work together.

Beau glanced up and finished chewing. "I'm not. I've never done this before. I've always worked with horses or cattle in the past. The railroad for a time, but there's too many people there. A man can't think."

"Well if that isn't what you want to do, why are you doing it?" He leaned back and waited.

"Why? I don't know if you noticed, but I have a lot of mouths to feed and I can't provide for them if I'm not in town. It might be what I love, but I love those girls more. Fact is, cowboy work don't pay any better than what I'm doing now but, the jobs just aren't here. So, working for the paper was a good substitute."

Aiden could well understand the draw. It was something to keep in mind for himself. If he ever took a bride, he'd have to think about her and maybe later the *leanbh* she'd have. "But don't you miss it? Don't you wake up every day and wish you could go do what you want?"

"Of course. This is only temporary. When I can secure a position that will provide a place for them, I can consider going back to it. But they can't live in a bunkhouse. So, for now, I don't want to be gone for days at a time."

Aiden laughed. "You ain't been married that long, then, huh?"

"Only since the day after New Year's. So, a little over five months. We've had the girls with us since the day after we were married. But until we left for Deadwood, they stayed with their mother at a different house."

A jolt of shock ran through him. "Their mother? I just assumed she was dead since she wasn't here."

"Naw, Maeve is back in Cutter's Creek. She and a man named Carlton Williams—where the girls were staying—seemed to have come to some kind of agreement."

"So, will they want to go back and join her?" An uneasiness fell over him, thinking Jennie wouldn't remain where he left her. Even if he wasn't nearby, he liked knowing right where he could find her.

"There was some talk of it, but we won't go anywhere until the railroad has more options. I'm not making that trip by wagon, again."

Aiden nodded and drank the last of his coffee. "I don't blame you. That wasn't an easy trek."

"We'd best get a move on. Don't want you to be late on your first day."

"Do you have any idea what he might be paying? I've got to pull together thirty for my trip."

"I can't guarantee you anything. But I can tell you that I get a dollar a day."

"A dollar! It'll take me three times as long working for the paper as it would if I went to work at the mine for the least they pay experienced miners!" His fist clenched and he held back from slamming it into the table. He'd never be able to leave in two weeks. Not at that pay.

"There's no guarantee you'd get that pay. You may know your way around a mine in California, but that don't mean anything here. There's a pecking order and you're at the bottom. You'd have to work your way up just like everyone else. At the paper that starts at a dollar a day."

Aiden wanted to argue. A year's worth of picking should account for something, but the fact was he couldn't prove it. While he could probably easily work through the ranks, he didn't want to be there that long. If he had to make a dollar a day anyway, it might as well be at a job where he could come home at night.

Both men stood and Aiden put his plate next to Beau's then grabbed his hat and the lunch pail Ruby had left for him. So, he'd have to stay a month for sure. At least he'd make it home to Kansas by harvest. Would his da even allow him back after all he'd said and done? He was a disgrace, an embarrassment.

Beau strode through the door and Aiden followed for the short walk to the newspaper office. Mr. Carmichael stood behind a high counter, waiting for them. His hands were covered in ink and he wore a white smock over his clothes.

"Ah, you must be Aiden Bradly. Beau told me you're looking for some temporary work. Well, we've got the work. Temporary or no. The miners might have started this town but some of us are here for more than the gold. I'd like to see this town prosper and the *Deadwood Times* is the best way to highlight the areas we'd like to enrich."

Aiden nodded. He couldn't agree more. Though setting letters into the molds didn't seem like much work. Mr. Carmichael led him back to the press.

"This is where you'll do most of your work. The press needs to be maintained to run properly. It must be cleaned between uses and the plates need to be made before each run. All those jobs will fall to you and Beau. Can you handle it?"

He nodded. "Yes, sir."

Mr. Carmichael left, and Beau grabbed a rag and cleaning solution. "They did a print run yesterday. So today we clean the machine."

Aiden grabbed a rag and took a deep breath. This work would have to do until he made enough to go home. He scrubbed the machine as he calculated the days remaining of his time in Deadwood.

~

JENNIE TOOK to knitting as soon as her morning chores were done. Beau had argued against them visiting around the town yet. All of the girls stayed indoors and did chores or other tasks that left Jennie's fingers itching for something to do. Beau had brought home a few bolts of fabric and some of the others were sewing to keep busy.

Jennie counted her stitches and started on the heel. She didn't understand why she wanted to be around Aiden but also wanted to avoid him at the same time. He'd leave in a month and she could only hope everything would calm down then. But what if it didn't? What if the feeling of expectancy, the need to be with him, only got worse after he left? What would she do then? It certainly wasn't possible to go with him.

Jack lay at her feet and nudged her toe with his nose. She knew he needed to go outside. Since the others were busy, she knew it was up to her to let him out.

"Come on, boy." She took Jack to the back door and opened it. An old man stood by the fence between both houses.

"Ho, there! Who are you? I don't recognize you. How many girls you got in that house, anyway?" His voice cracked.

Jennie stepped outside and glanced at Jack then took a few steps toward the man. "I'm Jennie and we've lived here for a little over a week, but we tend to stay inside." Something told her he wasn't safe to talk to and shouldn't know just how many of them there were.

"Hmm, and how many of you are there?" He scratched his chin.

"Well, it doesn't really matter. Beau and Aiden make sure we're well taken care of."

"Beau and Aiden? What, do they keep an eye on you?"

She bit her lip and checked to see if Jack was finished. "I suppose. They're working right now."

"That's interesting. A fella could get used to having such pretty neighbors." He touched his hat and walked back to his house.

Though she wore long sleeves, Jennie could feel the prickling of the hair on her arms and she rubbed them as she called to Jack. Something about that old man made her uneasy. Jack bumped her leg as he ran back into the house and Jennie followed.

She closed the door and barred it, letting her unease lift as the heavy plank fell into place. As she strode through the house, someone knocked on the front door and Ruby stood from her mending to answer it. Jack growled and barked. Ruby swung the wood slat for the peep hole and stood on her toes.

"I don't recognize him." She turned back to Jennie. "Beau said not to open the door for anyone but him, the owner of the house, or Reverend Level."

Jack growled again and sat in front of the door.

Jennie shook her head. "We shouldn't open that door with Jack acting that way."

Ruby nodded. "You're right." She opened the peep hole once again and yelled, "I'm sorry. Please come back later when Mr. Rockford is home. Thank you!"

Jennie couldn't hear what the man said in reply, but Ruby turned quite red and swung the peep hole closed quickly.

"What an incredibly rude man." She shook her head and stepped far away from the door as if she could dodge the words the man had said. "I'll be all the happier when we get out of town. Beau has a lead for work on a cattle ranch. He never expected that to be an option out here. He tells me ranching is fairly new to this area and they're looking for experienced men."

"So, where does that leave Aiden?" Jennie asked, hoping Ruby wouldn't dig too deeply into why she'd want to know.

"Well, if he can learn quickly it'll be a good job for him. If he wants it."

Jennie wondered what it would be like to live on a ranch, free to roam again. But Beau and Aiden had both just started. If they left, it might mean trouble for the paper. "That's true. What will the newspaper man do?"

Ruby shrugged her indifference. "I'm sure he'll do whatever he did before we pulled into town. Beau thinks it'll be safer for all of you out on a ranch where you can leave the house, do some chores, have life pretty much like you did in Cutter's Creek."

"It'd be nice. Hattie will be happy because a ranch means cowboys." Jennie laughed.

Ruby joined her. "That's true. I don't think Hattie will complain one bit. She even asked me if I could make her dresses a little tighter and more to the fashion. She wants to show off a bit."

"That reminds me. When I'm done knitting socks for Aiden, I should take these two dresses of mine and finally tailor them to fit me properly. The pins are bothersome. I didn't do it on the way here because the wagon was bouncy. But now that we're here and can't leave, it seems like I should take the time to do it."

Ruby smiled and patted her arm. "I think Aiden would love to see you in a dress that actually fits." Ruby pinched the arm of Jennie's dress and pulled it out about three inches. "Puffy sleeves might be in style but only if they're made that way, not because the gown was made for someone much larger than you."

Jennie tugged away. She'd only pinned the dress at the waist, but now she could see the rest of the dress looked silly. "We knew finding dresses for all of us would be difficult. I'm just glad I have them."

The doorknob wiggled and Ruby ran back to check. She smiled brightly and threw open the lock, letting Beau and Aiden in.

Beau took off his hat as he walked in the door. "I love coming home for a meal even if I'm still eating from a bucket." He swung the pail that Ruby had packed for him that morning. "Mind if we eat here?"

"Not at all! We just had the strangest visitor. I think he thought this was a women's boarding house." Ruby flushed red again.

Jennie pulled out two glasses from the cupboards then pumped water for Beau and Aiden. It was a good excuse to stay in the kitchen and sit across from Aiden. "How was your first morning?"

He glanced across the table at her and gave a half smile. "It's work, that's for sure. I'll be making quite a bit less than I would've in the mine, so I'll be here a month or so. What do you think of that, Jennie-girl?" He reached across the narrow table and gently tugged on her ear.

She shook her head as her face flushed at his attention. "It isn't up to me at all. You do what you need to do and we'll be here."

She stood and turned away to stop the fluttering in her belly. She could handle two weeks of the mounting tension, but a whole month... Just sitting with him made her want to drum her fingers on the table. She had too much energy and nowhere to let it out.

"How are your feet?" She began washing the counters without paying any attention to them.

"My feet are just fine. You and Ruby did a good job with them. Thank you."

Beau set down his sandwich. "I'm waiting to hear back from Ferguson about the foreman position at that ranch. That would pay much better than the newspaper."

Aiden finished his bite. "Do they have room for me, too?"

Beau sat back and regarded Aiden. "I think you're old enough to pick what you want for yourself. If I get the job, he already told me he needed a couple extra hands. You'd be welcome, since I know you can ride. If I had to guess, pay would be about the same. If you stay here, expenses would be the difference. You'd have to rent somewhere and pay for your meals. If you take a job out there, your room and board would be covered like it is now."

"That's a big draw, since I want to save every cent." Aiden rested hands covered in black ink on the table. He'd washed but the ink wouldn't budge. She glanced up to his eyes to find him staring at her and she turned and went back to her counter. The tension in her belly twisted tighter.

"The choice is yours. But you don't have to worry yet because I haven't heard from Ferguson."

Aiden nodded and downed the rest of his water. "We'd best get back to it."

Beau finished his bite and washed it down. "Yup. Thank you, Ruby, for letting us mess up your table."

She stood and kissed him on the temple. "You can dirty my table whenever you like."

Jennie wiped the crumbs while Ruby saw the men out.

After they'd left, Ruby returned and crossed her arms over her chest. "I'm tired of being cooped up in here like a nesting hen. I wanted to come here for the wide-open spaces, and I haven't seen a single thing besides the doctor's office."

A sweat broke out on Jennie's forehead and her stomach turned from tight to sour. "But Ruby, I don't think it's a good idea to go out. Beau will find us a place with peace and quiet and *then* we can all enjoy the out of doors again."

"I just want to go to the store, buy some flour and salt, and come right home. I think there's a mercantile just a few blocks down from here. If I can't walk a few blocks we have no business in this town. If you'd rather stay here, then do so. I'll take Jack."

Jennie stood in indecision. It would be good to get out of the house, but if anything happened to Ruby the others would be left alone until Beau and Aiden returned. Ruby reappeared with her hat in her hand.

"Well? What do you say? Are you coming or staying?"

Jennie glanced down at her feet, the overwhelming cloud over her pressed down hard. "Why don't you take Hattie with you? Two are better than one, but I'd best stay here with the younger ones."

"Wise plan. In case anything should go wrong—not that I expect it to—you'll be here." She called up the stairs for Hattie and turned back to Jennie. "Do take a few minutes this afternoon and work on your dresses. It would be worthwhile. You'll just have to trust me on that."

Jennie refused to think too long on Ruby's words. She and Beau spoke in whispers every night, but she didn't take to listening to them. She sighed as Ruby and Hattie left, clicking the lock into place. The heaviness in her chest nearly crushed her as she prayed they would return safely.

CHAPTER 12

Aiden followed Beau into the house, wiping his feet by the door as Jennie ran into the room. Her eyes were wide with tear streaks down her face. All the air in his lungs slammed into his chest at the sight of the fear in her eyes.

"Don't take off your boots! Ruby left just after lunch with Hattie to go to the market and hasn't returned."

Beau turned back to the door and shoved Aiden out of the way as he rushed out.

Aiden searched Jennie's face. Her forehead was lined with worry and she clasped her hands in front of her.

"Oh, Aiden. What if..."

"Shh." He pulled her into his arms and held her close, willing her to stop trembling. She fit just perfectly in his arms and her shaking seemed to dissolve as he held her close. "I've got to go help Beau. He'll need me. Don't hold supper. Feed the others." He allowed himself to brush his lips over the top of her head then he pulled himself away and followed Beau.

"I'll wait up. Please find them!" she called after him.

He dashed outside, smiling when he heard her lock the door

behind him. Aiden ran and caught up to Beau a few blocks ahead of him.

Beau slammed his fist into his hand. "Why would she leave, Aiden? I told her to stay put. I just don't understand how the house could get under her skin so quickly."

"Well, didn't you say you used to take odd jobs just to get out of town? Maybe she's cut from the same cloth? How long could *you* stay pent up in the house?"

Beau shook his head. "I should've made time to go shopping with her. I don't know what I'll do if I don't find her."

"We'll find her. Jennie said she went to the mercantile. Where is it?" He stopped and glanced up and down the street.

"It's a little farther down but there's no chance she'd still be there. It's been hours since lunch."

"I think we should go see if she made it there at all." Aiden pushed him further along the street but kept his eyes open for any sign of bright red hair. That hair might be worth a fortune to a madam. Beau pushed his way through a clutch of men by the front door and strode up to the front counter.

"Excuse me, I'm looking for someone who may have come in here earlier. She's about six inches shorter than me, dark red hair, with a younger blond about the age of sixteen."

The shopkeeper scratched his chin. "An old man came in after they paid for their purchases to help them home. Don't know where they went to after that."

"An old man... was he in a preacher's collar?" Aiden rested his hands on the counter to keep from clenching them.

The shopkeeper laughed. "No, he surely wasn't."

"Come on, Beau. Let's ask around in the street. Someone was bound to notice something." He pulled Beau's arm and could feel the tension. Beau didn't look outwardly scared, but Aiden could tell he was in knots. *He* would be.

Beau wiped the side of his mouth with the back of his hand and followed Aiden out of the mercantile. "Ruby wouldn't have accepted help from just anyone. She isn't that trusting. Hattie tends to want to attract attention and that's what scares me. Hattie may have put them both in danger."

"I think Hattie has too long been a child in the middle of a big family. She wants people to notice her away from her sisters." Aiden looked up and down the street and dodged between passing wagons, leading Beau through town. "I guess I should've paid more attention to her when she was looking for it. I didn't want to give her the wrong idea."

Beau's bottom lip disappeared as his mouth flatlined. "I don't need anyone giving attention to Hattie just yet. Not for any reason."

Aiden stood as tall as he could and noticed a squat building on the other side of the street. It gave him an idea.

"Where're you off to?" Beau asked, his voice high.

"The stagecoach station. If Ruby and Hattie were taken, the scoundrels wouldn't keep them here in Deadwood or we'd find them right away. I'm going to check and see if any women left on the stage this afternoon."

Beau yelled over the din. "Pray they didn't. Those stages make a lot of stops. If the girls were taken, they could force them off anywhere and we'd never find them."

A sick feeling left Aiden trembling all the way down to his boots. If they ended up down in one of the cribs in the shanty-town... No, he wouldn't even give that thought credence. A few men hung around the front of the station. It was a low, one-story log building, with a plank roof. It looked like it had been thrown up in a pinch and then was just left to run as it was. Aiden rushed through the door into the dark interior. A man with a corncob pipe sat on a stool behind a counter reading a newspaper. He glanced up at them and set down his reading.

"What can I do for you? Stage won't leave again until morning."

Beau pushed forward next to Aidan and spoke first. "I'm looking for two young women. A redhead and a blond that may have been taken by stage out of town."

"Been taken? I don't know what kind of establishment you think I run here mister. I don't like what you're suggesting."

Aiden cleared his throat. "Two ladies are missing. We're looking for them. That's all he's saying, sir." He shot a warning glance at Beau. Riling up the locals would only make the job more difficult.

"A young blond lit out on the three o'clock stage to Lead. She was leaning and pawing all over the man she was with, though. Don't sound like she was *taken* anywhere."

Beau shook his head. "That wouldn't be our girl. She may want attention but not that badly. And, she'd be with Ruby."

Aiden nodded and touched his hat. "That doesn't sound like our blond. Thank you for your time."

Beau and Aiden left the dark building and continued their search. "Let's go talk to the reverend, then the hotel owner. They are the only two people we know in town. Maybe they heard something."

Aiden scoured the street for familiar faces as he kept up with Beau. He pushed his way into the hotel and rang the bell at the front desk. An older man came out from a small door behind the counter.

"Beau, can I help you?" He pulled on the garter around his arm and shifted his gaze from one man to the other.

"I hope so, Lance. When I came home today, two of my girls were missing. They went to the mercantile and never returned. Has anyone said anything to you or have you seen them?"

Lance scratched his head. "I haven't heard anything, Beau. I'm sorry. I'll keep an ear out. I hope you find them."

Aiden cocked his head to the side and frowned. "I don't suppose you've seen Ferguson around?"

Beau glared at Aiden. "What does that have to do with anything?"

Lance scratched behind his neck and gave a noncommittal shrug. "I saw him this morning. Not sure why it matters."

Aiden rested his hands on his waist. The man's eyes were too shifty, as if he were hiding something and this wasn't the time to let something like that slide by. "It matters because if Ferguson mentioned he was thinking about hiring Beau, it would mean you would lose the rent on that big old house."

Lance's eyes flashed and he slammed his hands down on the front desk. "Hogwash. I'll be selling that house soon. I wouldn't do anything to anyone." He crossed his arms over his chest and glared at them.

"Come on, Aiden. Let's go check with the reverend." Beau pulled Aiden's arm as he left the hotel. "We aren't going to get anywhere with Lance. If we don't find anything else, we can always go back to check the hotel again. But... I've got this terrible feeling she isn't here anymore." Beau trudged to a small house on the edge of town.

"I didn't even know where the Reverend lived." Aiden looked around at the small houses shoved together without an inch of space between them, yet clean, with tidy painted fronts in a row.

"I wouldn't say he lives here..." Beau turned back to him. "He stays here while he preaches. I'm not even sure if he's still here or if he's moved on." He strode forward and knocked on the door of one of the homes.

A little old woman answered. "What can I do for you, sir?" her voice waivered and she stared up at him.

"Is Level still here? Or has he moved on, ma'am?"

She stepped to the side and opened the door further. Beau stepped inside and Aiden followed. Reverend Level sat on a chair next to the couch. Someone lay on the couch, red hair peeking from beneath a blanket.

Beau rushed to the couch and knelt in front of his wife. He brushed the hair back from her face to reveal a dark knot on the side of her head.

Level cleared his throat. "Just who I was hoping to see. A friend brought Ruby to me earlier. She was screaming in the street and someone hit her over the head. My friend took exception to anyone treating a lady like that and removed her from the situation. Ruby has quite a lump on her head, but we've been caring for her as best we know how."

"I can't tell you how glad I am that you have her. Did your friend mention any other women? Her sister Hattie was with her." Beau pulled the blanket down and touched her hands and shoulders gently, checking for injuries. Aiden stepped forward and winced. Her temple was a vicious purple.

"He didn't mention anyone with her. Just that she was screaming which drew his attention. Then he saw her get hit. I don't know what transpired that he ended up with her. I didn't ask for specifics."

Beau laid his head against Ruby's. "We'll never find her. She could be anywhere."

Level stood and patted Beau on the shoulder. "I will pray for her and so should all of you. I didn't know Hattie was missing, or I would've asked more questions. I can seek out information tomorrow. Perhaps I'll find out more."

"Thank you, Reverend. I'll get her home and let her sisters take care of her. If you think she'll be okay to move?"

"You'll draw attention to her without a cart. You may use mine. Allow me to hitch up my horse."

Beau nodded. "Thank you, sir."

The old woman approached him and gave Beau a cloth. "For her bump." She touched her own head.

He brushed Ruby's red hair away from her face and laid the cloth over the large bump. Beau cradled her head in his hands and kissed her forehead and cheeks, mumbling something Aiden couldn't hear. Until a few days ago, if he'd seen that he would've called the man a fool. Weak. Now he knew better.

Aiden shook his head. "What in the world did he hit her with?"

Beau closed his eyes. "I don't know. Something weighty enough to do this. I don't even want to think about what would've happened if Level's friend hadn't heard her scream."

"Odd that he didn't mention the friend's name." Aiden sat in the chair the reverend had vacated.

"Maybe the friend asked that he not say who he was. We don't know. I trust the reverend. If he doesn't want to tell us, I'm all right with that."

Aiden nodded. "I think I'll run back to the house and let the girls know. Level's cart is pretty small for all of us and it's a short walk."

"Good idea. Have them get our bed ready for her." Beau continued tenderly combing Ruby's hair with his fingers. Aiden prayed they'd find Hattie. His stomach met his boots when he thought about telling Jennie what had happened.

CHAPTER 13

Jennie sat at the table with the rest of her sisters, drumming her fingers and waiting for any noise at all from outside. Eva laid her hand on Jennie's arm. "Do you think we should do anything while we wait? What if they don't come back tonight?"

"Please, don't say that. They have to come back and they have to find Ruby and Hattie." Jennie stood and collected two of the plates from the dinner that no one had touched.

Drawing hot water from the reservoir on the side of the cook stove, Jennie lathered some soap on a rag to wash the dishes. Eva brought in the rest of the plates and slipped them into the water. "I'll dry for you." She picked up a towel. Eva hated change and had always been the sister who tried to keep the peace among all of them. She was generally so quiet that everyone would forget she was even there.

Jennie needed the quiet ritual of doing the dishes to let her mind settle. So, having the quietest sister help her was the best option. She'd been too upset to eat. Why hadn't she tried harder to stop Ruby? While she'd sometimes thought about what things would've been like if Ruby hadn't brought them with her, she

257

knew Ruby had sacrificed a lot to do it. She and Beau were newly married, and both were filled with a wanderlust that normally might make having a family difficult. But they had agreed, even before they were married, that Ruby's sisters would be with them.

Jennie shook her head as she wrung out her washcloth. "Thank you, Eva. I'll dump this outside, then we should get ready for bed."

Eva nodded. A knock sounded on the front door and they both gasped and ran for it. Jennie lifted the wood slide of the peep hole. "It's Aiden!" she yelled, her spirit soaring with hope.

Jennie swung the door open and saw the weary smile on his face. She ran into his arms without thinking and he wrapped them around her, holding her tight. "Let's go inside and I'll tell you what I know." He whispered in her ear as he placed his hand on her back. Warmth spread over her, strengthening her. He indicated that Jennie and Eva should sit on the couch then knelt in front of Jennie.

"We found Ruby with Reverend Level. She was hit over the head and has a pretty bad bump. She won't be able to work for a few days once she wakes up."

He searched Jennie's eyes and she wanted desperately to know what he was trying to tell her.

"Hattie's gone. She wasn't with Ruby and we have no idea who took her, much less where. Level is going to ask around tomorrow and we hope to find out more. Beau is pretty shaken up about it."

Jennie shook her head, her thoughts spinning out of control. She reached out and clutched Aiden's hand. "No, she can't be gone." Jennie felt tears well up and made an effort to slow her breathing. The more she tried, the worse it became until her stays bit deeply into her and the tears fell anyway. "This is Beau's fault. He brought us all out here. He knew the danger and still brought us out here!"

Aiden stood and yanked her up off the couch and into his arms, tucking her head under his chin. "Don't say that. Beau couldn't have foreseen this. He told Ruby to stay in the house and for whatever reason, she decided not to. But whatever your feelings, Ruby needs you to get her bed ready and manage the house. We'd planned to tell you all we're moving out to the ranch next week, but now everything's on hold."

Jennie pulled away from him. "We can't leave now! What if Hattie finds her way back and looks for us? She'll never find us out on some ranch. She'd look here first."

Aiden backed away. "It isn't for me to say, Jennie, or you. You'll need to do what Beau and Ruby decide."

"And what about you? Where will you go?" Jennie crossed her arms, all the mixed feelings inside of her swirled and flashed, turning to an anger she couldn't manage.

"If Beau'll have me, I'd like to work out on the ranch for the next month until I can earn my money to go home. I can help Beau keep looking for Hattie if he wants, but we'll probably just take it to Seth Bullock. If anyone can find her, he can."

"What makes you think he's got time to look for one missing girl? He's got this whole mess of a town to look after." Fury knotted in her stomach at the injustice. They may never see Hattie again. Oh, how she hated Deadwood!

Aiden pulled her back into his arms and she clutched the fabric at his neck, letting her tears soak his shirt. The last thing she'd said to Hattie hadn't been kind. They hadn't gotten along at all in the last few weeks. She should've listened to Hattie more, tried to understand more.

"It's going to be okay, Jennie-girl. We have to hope and pray that she's found and she's all right. That's all we can do."

She nodded and clung to his strong frame. His muscled arms held her close. They were a comfort she didn't expect.

"You two go on up and get Beau and Ruby's room ready. Send the other girls down so I can warn them. Level and Beau should be here soon."

As usual, Eva had been so quiet Jennie had forgotten she was even there. Heat crawled up her cheeks at what Eva had witnessed. She didn't want to let go of Aiden. Resting in his arms was the safest she'd felt in weeks. But he was right, her sisters needed her to be strong now. So she must. She pulled away and

259

rushed up the stairs, sending the remaining four sisters down to talk to Aiden.

She'd never been in Beau and Ruby's room before. They hadn't had much in the way of privacy since their wedding night, so all the girls had a silent agreement that their room was off-limits. They needed someplace that was only for them. She pushed open the door and stood just outside. Even knowing she'd been told to enter, she didn't want to. Jennie stepped inside and cupped the side of the water pitcher. It was cool, but not cold. There was nothing in the bowl, so she didn't need to refresh anything.

She turned down the blankets and opened the armoire then pulled out a sleeping gown for Ruby. She heard the front door open and rushed back downstairs as Beau carried Ruby into the house followed by the reverend. A white cloth wrap covered half of Ruby's face.

Beau carried her up the stairs and Jennie glanced around the living room, not sure what to do next. The reverend was on the couch and her younger sisters sat silently, their faces white and eyes wide. Aiden stepped in behind her and led her over to a chair. Her legs were stiff, as if they were frozen solid.

Level clasped his hands in front of him and bowed his head. "Lord, we seek your guidance today. We don't know why terrible things happen, but we know we are not promised an easy time, only peace. We need your peace now, Lord. The peace that will help us understand that you can reclaim all situations for good. We ask that my query tomorrow is fruitful and that if it be your will, young Hattie would come home quickly. Amen."

The group mumbled an 'amen' in response.

The reverend stood and pulled his vest down tight over his stomach. "Jennie, you'll have to take care of Ruby for a while. She won't be capable and, frankly, she might not be willing for a while. She might blame herself for Hattie's disappearance. Be gracious to her. Help her." He turned to Aiden. "You said you were moving out to the Ferguson place next week?"

Aiden nodded. His steady hand remained on her shoulder. "Yes, that's right."

"I think you should go. Do your work on the ranch and let the sheriff and his men handle this. It's what the town pays them for. I had meant to be moving on here real soon. But if I find out anything tomorrow and it will help for me to stay, I will."

Aiden said, "Thank you, reverend. We'll take what help we can get. I didn't know Hattie all that well, but I aim to help however I can before I leave."

The reverend cocked his head. "Where're you headed?"

"Kansas. That's where my family is. I need to go back to settle a few things."

"It's good to keep with your family. Except when you can't." He raised his eyebrows, smiled mysteriously at Aiden, then left.

Eva, Francis, Lula, Nora, and Daisy all moved to the couch next to Jennie or sat at her feet. They were silent, but each girl needed to be close to the others. Jennie touched each sister on the arm or head. "We'll get through this. We Arnsby's always do."

Eva gripped Jennie's hand. "What if Hattie never comes back? What if we never find her? She's my twin, like half of me." Eva's mouth quivered.

Aiden sat on the arm of the couch. "Please don't think that way, Eva. We're going to do our very best. It's only been a few hours. She couldn't have gone far. If we need to get the sheriff involved, like Reverend Level said, then we will. I'm sure they'll find her. We need to keep working. As much as we all want to, we can't just stop and spend every waking minute looking for her. Beau and I will go out and check a few of the... less savory establishments tonight. If she isn't there, we'll talk to the sheriff in the morning. If he directs us to the marshal, so be it. We'll do what we need to, to find her."

Eva shook her head. "They won't find her. Hattie was looking for a chance to get out. She wanted to see the world and meet all sorts of men. She wanted attention. Ma never knew it, but Hattie used to steal Pa's moonshine. When we first arrived in Cutter's Creek, Hattie had the sweats and the shakes. I didn't know she'd been nipping from Pa that much, but she was hooked. You'll find her where there are men and booze."

Jennie gasped. "Eva don't say such things. From what Aiden was told, she was taken and that's what I'll believe until we learn otherwise. It isn't right to condemn our sister when she isn't here to defend her reputation."

Eva shook her head. "What reputation? She won't have one after tonight. You were there. You were next to her on the floor of the hotel the night of the fire when we lost Pa. I remember you asking Hattie if she had enough blankets because she was shaking like a leaf. Don't you remember how she avoided Ma for over a week? I don't think any of us knew the real Hattie until we got to Cutter's Creek and found out she *wasn't* very nice at all."

Jennie closed her eyes. Eva's words rang true. Hattie had been quite docile while they lived at home and frequently liked to be alone in the small lean-to next to the house. She'd become angry as soon as they'd gotten to the hotel that first night. And from then on...

"While you may be right, Eva, let's wait to pass judgment. We all know living in that tiny house with Pa and his ways was hard. Hattie may not have found a good way to handle it, but it was a way."

Beau trudged down the stairs. "Jennie, Ruby is awake and she's asking for you."

CHAPTER 14

Jennie raced up the stairs and into Beau and Ruby's room. She knelt next to the bed. Ruby's face was shocking, and it took all Jennie's concentration not to flinch and gasp. "Ruby? It's Jennie. I'm here."

"Jennie?" Ruby reached out and groped for her hands as if she couldn't see. "I'm so sorry I didn't listen to you. It was a set up. Hattie had been talking to the man next door for a few days when she'd let Jack outside. She'd told him to watch for her if she ever got free of the house. I don't know what he offered her, but the plan never was to take me, only her. She wanted out. If I'd taken you instead, she would've left with him while I was gone. Then the girls would've been alone. I wasn't bothered at all until Hattie left me and climbed into a wagon with the man who'd knocked on our front door this morning and another man who looked a little familiar." She squinted. "But I don't know why." She shook her head. "I screamed for her to get down. I grabbed for her and then he kicked me. I fell back and would've been trampled by his horses, but a man grabbed for me. When he did, something else hit me above the eye and I don't remember anything after that. Maybe the horse kicked me." She gingerly rubbed the spot above where her face turned a harsh purple.

Jennie combed the hair back out of Ruby's face and tears welled up inside her, pushing their way free. "A friend of Reverend Level saw you and that's where Beau and Aiden found you. I can't believe Hattie would just run off…"

"I knew she was unhappy. She wanted to get out, see the town, investigate. I could tell that something wasn't right, but I didn't know what. I'd bet Ma knew. I wish she would've warned me. I could've kept a better eye on her."

"Oh Ruby, what'll we do? She could be anywhere. Do we go after someone who doesn't want to be found? She's only sixteen." Jennie's stomach turned sour as terrible, worrying thoughts flooded her.

"It won't be up to me. It'll be up to Beau. This's his household. Ma gave us complete control."

Jennie rested her chin on the bed to hide her face and calm herself. "We should've been able to choose between staying and going. I think most of us would've chosen to stay."

"That's exactly why we didn't. Ma couldn't provide for you and Mr. Williams certainly couldn't either. He's not young and he can't work. Ma and I both agreed I would take you because Beau is capable of taking care of all of us. Even when we have a family of our own, you will still be just as loved and cared for."

"You don't think she'd try to go back to Cutter's Creek, do you?" Jennie knew the answer before she was even done asking the question. Hattie wanted freedom. That meant from Ma too.

"No. She didn't want to be with Ma any more than she wanted to be with me. She wants someone like Pa who'd provide her the hooch and leave her alone. Trouble is, I don't think she'll find anyone who'll leave her alone."

"You knew?" Jennie sat back away from the bed. How had Ruby known and no one else but Eva?

"Yes. Ma told me as soon as we got off the wagon when we arrived in Cutter's Creek. I'd seen how Hattie was shaking. I was worried she'd caught her death of cold.

Jennie let that idea roam in her head. "I'm worried about the men, too. Just how far will Hattie go to get what she wants?" A pain wedged itself deep in her heart. She knew what Hattie would do. She'd practically spelled it out with their last argument.

Ruby reached out and squeezed Jennie's hand. "I need to rest but I wanted to tell you what happened before I forgot." She gently rubbed the angry bruise on her head. "Please, don't tell the other girls. I don't know how much they know, and I don't want them to feel any less for Hattie. If she does come back, we need to love her not condemn her."

"Eva already told everyone about Hattie's drinking. The others seemed quite ready to believe it. I think the only one in the dark was me."

Ruby laid her head back against the pillow. "I'm sorry to hear that. I wish Eva had confided her fears to me. Since they're twins, Eva was probably more observant of Hattie than any of us."

Jennie pulled the coverlet over Ruby and left the room.

Oh, Hattie. Why didn't you focus your attention on Aiden for a little longer? At least then you'd still be here. She knew Aiden had paid little attention to Hattie or any of her sisters. He knew their names, but the only one he ever spoke to was her.

Jennie wandered to the edge of the stairs and stopped, listening to Beau and Aiden as they spoke below her on the landing. She leaned over, grasping the wall for balance.

"Ruby told me Hattie wanted to go and that she left by wagon. She isn't around here. I'd rather not visit any of these places. Especially if the only fruit that would come of it would be rotten," Beau remarked.

Aiden sighed. "I agree. If she wanted to go bad enough to take a wagon with some stranger, you aren't going to find her next door. I *do* think we should get the sheriff or the marshal involved."

"I agree, Aiden. I can't fathom what we did that would've made her run, but I pray the Lord's with her, and we'll find her safe. I'm afraid Hattie has no idea how big and cold the world can be."

Jennie's feet thudded down the stairs as she struggled against the weight of moving at all. She'd misjudged Hattie completely. Beau and Aiden turned as she descended the last few steps.

"I'm sorry for listening." She searched their faces for any hint of anger. Finding none, she went on. "I think you're right. I didn't want to believe it, but once Eva pointed out Hattie's changed behavior. I couldn't help but notice. I hope the sheriff finds her, but perhaps being on her own for a bit—of her own choice—will help her to see what a blessing family can be."

Aiden nodded and approached her. "Beau and I will be working tomorrow, and Ruby is not to get out of that bed."

Jennie's hands felt clammy and she wiped them on her skirt. "I've never run the household. It's never been my place."

Aiden smiled at her and caressed her chin, lifting it slightly. "Now, that isn't the spitfire I met on the trail who fell out of the wagon 'cause she was so curious. That isn't the girl who gave as good as she got every time I teased her."

Jennie closed her eyes and stepped away from his gentle touch. She couldn't think straight looking up into those penetrating eyes. "Life was easier then."

"Jennie Arnsby, you are a strong and capable woman. I have no doubt you'll be just fine. You don't have to be perfect."

Beau stepped forward. "Thank you, Jennie. I know I can trust you to look after the place. And please keep the girls from bothering Ruby too much. I think she'll be back on her feet even before a doctor would want her to. That's just her way."

Jennie turned from the men. "That it is. She's as stubborn as a goat. We all are, I'm afraid."

Aiden touched her shoulder and she turned to him. "We'll move out to the Ferguson place in three days. One way to keep the girls busy and not dwelling on Hattie is having them pack their things."

"There's so little to pack." Jennie shook her head. "I'll find something to do and we'll keep an eye out for Hattie. Maybe she'll change her mind and come home."

Aiden pulled her into an embrace. She held on to him tightly, accepting the strength and comfort he offered. "Don't let yourself dwell on it. I don't want your heart to break further." She felt his warm breath fan over her head and his lips pressed against her hair. Her heart tripped over itself but before she could even think to pull him back, he was gone.

Aiden turned and followed Beau out the door and the house went silent. She hurried to the back door and let Jack in before he could scratch a hole in the door. Holding it open, she searched the fence for any sign of the old man who'd spoken to her. The back door of the other house swung in the wind as if the house was abandoned. She wouldn't search the house for Hattie. But if anyone were there surely, they would secure the door.

Jack nuzzled her hand and whined for attention. She took Jack back inside and knelt next to him. "You'll help me tomorrow, won't you? I used to be strong, like Aiden said, but I've lost my way. I'm scared to make a wrong move or miss any sign my sisters are hurting."

Jack leaned into her, enjoying the scratches behind his ears and whining happily.

"Well, at least I know you'll help me watch the door."

CHAPTER 15

J ennie helped her sisters into the two wagons as Beau and
Aiden loaded their trunks. Ruby squinted into the sun and
pulled on a hat, tying it off as she strode from the house to
the lead wagon. Beau insisted she not drive the three miles
to the Ferguson ranch, so she'd ride with him. That meant Aiden
would be driving the other wagon with her, Eva, and Lula.

Aiden rushed back into the house and returned to the wagon
with a flour sack. He laid it under the seat and climbed up next
to her.

"Are you ready for our next adventure?" His eyes twinkled.
For a man who had no intention to stay, he sure enjoyed acting as
part of the family.

"I don't know anything about ranching, but I'll be happy to go
outside and enjoy a day again. Jack will like being able to run free.
I don't think he wanted to stay in the house that much." Jennie
couldn't wait to have the room to stretch her legs when she wanted
and just get outside and breathe fresh air.

Aiden paused and his brow crinkled. "I'm sure you're right. I
know we talked about it last week, but I don't think I can take him

on the train to Kansas. If I were riding it'd be different, he could just come with me. But I don't have a horse of my own and I can't afford one."

Jennie nodded. "I wish I could keep him, Aiden, but it isn't my place. You'll have to talk to Beau. It'll be his house." She couldn't look at him, couldn't let him see the hope she had that he'd come back, even if it were just for the dog and not her.

Aiden nodded and his jaw hardened into a flat line. "We'll be living on a ranch with quite a few men... You won't go running off on me... Will you?"

Jennie had to grip the side of the wagon seat or risk falling out in her shock. He'd never been quite so bold. "Aiden, I don't plan on running off with *anyone*. That just isn't the life for me."

"Good." He flashed a dazzling smile that left her belly fluttering. "Now that that's settled..." He flicked the lines to keep up with Beau's wagon. "Let's talk a bit. I've saved up enough working with Beau and doing extra work the last week, but I'm not quite ready to leave yet."

Jennie craned her neck to look him in the eye. "How did you manage to work enough to save a month's worth of wages in one week?"

"I talked to the boss. Whittling the blocks for the pictures was expensive work and takes a skilled hand. It paid more. I offered to do it." He shrugged a shoulder.

"I thought leaving was all you could think about? You said you weren't a man if you didn't make right whatever went wrong back home."

"That's true. But I'm worried my da won't take me back. I've failed. Which is exactly what he predicted. I told him I'd be this great prospector and make all this money. He'd always been so proud of my brothers. I wanted him to be proud of me. I'd be more than happy to work for him to earn back his respect, but there won't be much to do until harvest. It would be best if I returned right when they need me. If I come before and there's no hard work to do, they may not welcome me back."

Jennie couldn't think of a single reason she wouldn't take back her own family. Even her pa—who had been a reprobate—wasn't excluded. While she'd not want to live with him, she'd never wish him gone. "Do you really think they'd turn you out over a misunderstanding?"

Aiden frowned but didn't look at her. "I don't know. I can't say for sure. I just know I'd give about anything to take back the things I said before I left. I didn't even let my mam know I was leaving. I was in such an all-fired hurry." He shook his head. "I just hope they can forgive me, is all."

"I think you'll be surprised. Just like if Hattie would come home even now after only being gone a few days, we'd take her back immediately. She'd be forgiven for running off, for scaring us, and even for putting Ruby in danger."

"Not every family is as forgiving as yours Jennie."

She sighed and allowed the rocking of the wagon to pull her from side to side. "I'll pray they forgive you and that you have a wonderful homecoming." *But I'll also pray that you want to return...someday.*

"I sure am going to miss you." He moved the lines to his left hand and touched her cheek gently with his right. His eyes were soft, and tenderness welled within them.

She felt heat rise up her neck. "I'll miss you, too. How long do you think you'll be gone?"

He turned back to watching the horses. "I don't know. Right after harvest comes the winter. It can be slow in coming in Kansas or it can hit hard and early. It'll be colder here sooner than there."

"But if you're riding the rails it shouldn't matter... Right?" She needed to hear that he wouldn't be gone for too long. Somewhere between yanking on her braid and kissing her head...she'd fallen for him. Though he had to leave, it wouldn't be easy letting him go.

"If I aim to help Beau on the ranch, I really need to have my own horse. That means I'll be working for my da, if he'll have me, until I can earn one. It could take a while."

"But... what if the job with Ferguson isn't open when you come back? It isn't like you can expect him to hold it for you."

"I know. I guess I just hope Beau will want to hire me as soon as I'm able to return. I'll do my best. You know that, don't you?"

"I know you spend an awful lot of time looking at that Deadwood book and the rest of your time talking about returning to your folks. I don't fit in there anywhere. I don't love Deadwood. It took me away from a place I'd learned to think of as home. It took my freedom for a time. And it took my sister from me. I'm stuck in a place I detest because my sister's husband likes it."

Aiden shook his head. "None of those things have anything to do with Deadwood. They would've happened anywhere. If Beau had chosen anywhere else you still would've had to stay inside until he learned that it was safe for his womenfolk to walk about. He was being a good protector and provider."

"That's easy for you. You're a man. You can walk about and do whatever you like."

"Not really. We have to work and bear the burden of making decisions. It isn't easy on us, either."

Jennie wanted to cross her arms, but she had to hold onto her seat on the bumpy trail.

"Why do you like to argue with me so much, Jennie-girl? I noticed you are sweet as apple pie to everyone else. But with me, you get sour as vinegar."

Jennie ducked her head to hide her embarrassment. It wasn't that she didn't like him. On the contrary, she liked him far too much. It was more that she felt secure with him, a freedom to be herself she didn't feel with anyone else. "I don't do any such thing."

"Whatever you say." He glanced over at her and gave her sly smile that said he could see right through her.

"You think you know me so well? You don't know one whit about me."

"Oh, really? I know you want to have a say in everything. You always feel like because there are so many voices, yours isn't heard. I know that when you're nervous you tend to cut people off rather than face it. You don't like to confront people and you tend to put more weight on people's words than they mean." He narrowed his eyes and nodded. "Like when I said I couldn't find real riches here in Deadwood, that I'd have to go home to find them… You thought I was talking about you. I wasn't. As God as my witness, you're sitting next to me on this wagon which proves you are completely portable." He flashed her another glance then turned back toward the worn path.

"You're wrong, Aiden. I'm no treasure. If I'm gone, there are seven more just like me." She looked away from him, afraid he would see how much her own words hurt.

"That's not true one bit, either. Just like when you said Hattie had needs the rest of you didn't. So do you. I aim to find out what those are before I go."

"Why? You're leaving Aiden. You may never come back. What if you're so happy with your family that you realize what you had here was fool's gold?" Her hands shook and she dug her fingers into the seat to keep them still.

Aiden pulled up on the lines and the horses came to a stop, pitching her forward until she locked her knees. Two heads popped up from the bed of the wagon behind them.

"You are not fool's gold, Jennie Arnsby. And if I knew for certain that you wanted to be with me, I'd ask Beau to court you proper before I go."

The two girls behind the seat erupted in gasps and giggles. They ducked back behind the seat in a fit of whispers.

Aiden sighed and reached out for Jennie's hand.

Jennie scooted back from him. "Well, I don't want you. I don't want a man who's going to leave, and I won't split up my family any more than it already is!" She turned and climbed into the back of the wagon. Leaving her family after all they'd suffered wasn't possible. Losing Aiden would be horrible, but she couldn't lose her sisters. She glanced at Aiden's back. He slouched down in his seat and flicked the lines, nudging the horses faster to catch up to Beau and Ruby's wagon.

∼

AIDEN GLANCED behind him every few minutes, but Jennie wouldn't even gaze up at him… At least, not when he was looking. He could feel her eyes boring a hole in his back. He scratched the back of his neck then stood up bracing his foot against the buckboard for balance. There were fences ahead, and fences meant people. They might have a mile or so to go but they'd be there soon.

He flicked the lines and followed Beau diagonally up the side of a hill. His stomach flipped as visions of Jennie or one of her sisters falling out of the rig and tumbling down the hillside flashed through his mind. They called them the Black *Hills*, but they were steep. The wagon slid on the loose rocks and the small granite chunks that marked the trail. Aiden pulled to the left and the horses veered off the trail to the right onto a level spot cut into the side of the hill, stopping them from slipping farther.

Aiden wiped his brow and let his breath catch up. There hadn't been any mangled wagons at the bottom, and he didn't want to be the first. Beau had made it around the hill and was out of sight. Aiden flicked the lines and pulled right. The horses responded quickly, pulling them back onto the makeshift trail. The wagon lumbered around the bend. The closer they came to the top, the more the trail was made of little more than loose rocks.

As he turned the bend, a level area with a huge house and many outbuildings came into view. He followed Beau's wagon to the front of the house and stopped just behind it. He held the lines but turned in time to see Jennie helping the others out of the wagon. She didn't bother waiting for him.

He shook his head. That woman ran hot as fire and cold as ice. Somehow, she'd wheedled her way into his blood. Beau strode out of the house, followed by a man with salt and pepper hair and a thick mustache. Aiden met them as they stepped off the front porch.

The older man held out his hand. "You must be Aiden Bradly. I'm Brody Ferguson." He gave a firm shake then turned, spreading his arm out wide. "What's visible here on the ledge is about a tenth of the area I've got. You saw some of the fence coming in, but we've got enough land for pasturing. Beau, I see you traded your oxen for horses. That's good. You can't ride the range on no ox." He laughed. While Aiden couldn't tell which state he'd hailed from, his slight drawl pegged him as a former Southerner.

Beau chuckled. "That's the truth. Bradly, here, might only be staying for a few weeks. He's got business to tend to down in Kansas."

"Will you be returning after your business or is the trip permanent?" Brody asked.

Aiden glanced at the women standing by the other wagon and crossed his arms over his chest. "I don't know for sure, sir. If I'm needed, I won't be able to return."

Brody nodded. "The job will always be here. I'll need men until this place folds. Which I hope'll never happen. You get your business tended to then send me a wire and tell me if you're coming back or staying there."

Aiden nodded. Leaving his new boss so shorthanded left a bad taste in his mouth. But without knowing if his da would welcome him back he couldn't make any promises.

"You should get your horses put up for the night. I'm sure they're tired. I've got a few in the corral you can take. Saddle 'em up and I'll show you around the place. We won't be back until supper. You'll all be eating with us tonight. Lefty had to go buy some provisions in Lead. It's a little closer to us than Deadwood but we're considered part of Deadwood."

He pointed to a spot behind the house. "That log house yonder with the red door, that's your place, Beau. Aiden, I don't have a bunkhouse built yet. But I do have a small cabin my ma used to live in about twenty yards behind the log house. That one's yours."

"Thank you, sir." Aiden tipped his hat and he and Beau led the teams to the large stable.

"Beau, tell me something… Are *all* the Arnsby girls stubborn?" Aiden brushed the dust from the horse's mane.

Beau shook his head. "Aiden, you don't know the half of it. Have you finally got up the gumption to ask me to court Jennie?"

"I'd like to, but she said no. Said she doesn't want to if I'm going to leave. I want to come back. I like it here. Jennie's a formidable woman but if I can't break through that layer of anger... If she don't want me here... I don't see any reason to leave my da if he needs me."

"Let me tell you a little something about those sisters. Their pa threatened them with sorry marriages from the time they were very young. He wanted them all gone. Would've traded every last one of them for one boy. With the exception of Hattie, not a one of them is interested in getting married."

Aiden frowned. "Beau, you're married to one. Obviously, they aren't *that* opposed to it."

"For Ruby, I had to prove I wanted her heart and that I'd do anything—including let her go—to show her how much she meant to me."

Aiden led his horse to the stall and poured some oats in a trough. "I'm not following you, Beau. You let her go? What does that mean?"

"Ruby was as timid as a rabbit any time she was near me. She ran away from me at every turn. I finally had to prove to her I wasn't hunting her down, but I'd do anything for her. Including saving her sisters from their father. Which we did."

"Well, I can't rescue everyone. I know bringing Hattie back would help but I wouldn't even know where to begin."

"It isn't that easy, Aiden. You need to talk to her, find out what it is that's the most important thing, then help her get it."

"That ain't going to be easy."

Beau laughed as he closed the gate for the last horse. "If it was easy, every man would be married. Let's go pick out a horse. Don't want to keep the new boss waiting."

"You really think I can get her to stop running?"

"If you're intentions are honorable, and you keep trying...yes. And Aiden, don't you go laying your lips on my Jennie again until you get permission to court her."

He smiled as he approached them. "Can I have permission just in case?"

Beau raised a warning eyebrow. "Just in case, what?"

"Just in case she changes her mind."

Beau's let his eyebrow fall. "I'll give you permission to court. But that's as far as it goes for now."

Aiden smiled as the afternoon sun lit golden pockets through the trees. "Yes, sir." The day was looking better by the minute.

CHAPTER 16

Jennie paced back and forth in front of the empty stove. This house was smaller than the last two but would fit them just fine as long as she didn't need room to breathe or think. But there was the problem. She needed to do both and there just wasn't enough space. There was one large open room for a parlor, dining area and kitchen, a door separated the one bedroom on the main floor which would be for Beau and Ruby, and a large one room loft for all the girls. They even had a dresser, which they'd never had before, but that was the extent of the house.

Ruby rested in her room after the trip. The younger girls had put away their clothes. Jennie was restless with nothing further to do. She'd seen the whole cabin and wanted to explore but none of the men had bothered to tell the women if they could. They'd arrived hours ago, and the soft light of evening poured through the windows. She needed air or she'd suffocate on the spot.

Aiden's cabin was empty. He hadn't had a chance to unpack since he'd had to work right away. She could go and spruce it up for him. He'd gotten used to her fussing over him back in Deadwood so it would be no bother to make sure his tick was ready and that he had water to wash up with when he returned. It would give her something to do and get her away from the walls that were moving in on her with every breath.

She slipped out the back door so she wouldn't disturb Ruby and Jack followed her. When the door was shut and she began her walk he jumped and barked, chasing every scent and enjoying his new freedom.

"You'll have to stay over at Aiden's now. You're not my dog, Jack."

His large fuzzy head tilted at an odd angle then he scampered away.

Jennie came to the small cabin in short order and pushed the door open. Inside, every bit of space was used. A corner for the bed, the cook stove sat along one wall, with one small cupboard for eating and cooking utensils. She closed the door behind her and smiled at the sweet space, taking in the tiny kitchen area. *It isn't like he'll use that. I'm sure he'll eat with us…until he leaves.*

The coverlet on the bed was dusty so she took it outside to the clothesline and hung it over, beating the dust out with a long stick. When she'd freshened it up a bit, she took it back inside and made the bed. The wash bowl next to the bed was dry so she pumped some water for him, careful not to spill anything on the floor or it would be difficult to sweep.

She heard a squeak and turned as a large man filled the door-way. His long coat billowed out around him and his hat shaded his face. With the sun behind him she couldn't see who it was, and she gasped. Trapped inside Aiden's cabin.

"Jennie-girl? What're you doing in my house?" He swung his hat from his head and tossed it on the table. As he stepped inside, she could see heat and confusion warring in his eyes.

Jennie breathed deeply and licked her suddenly dry lips. "I thought…you might like it if I freshened the place up a bit. I'm sorry if I was intruding." She stepped to the side and dashed for the door. His lean arm snaked out and caught her around the waist, tugging her close to him.

"Jennie-girl promise me you won't ever go into a man's house alone again unless you're married to him. I don't want to see you hurt and other men might not be thankful as I am."

"Well, of course I won't just go into a man's home. You must not think very much of me if you do." Strange that she had no desire to fight against his hold even though what he'd said made anger bubble like acid in the back of her throat.

His voice dropped to a whisper next to her ear and she shivered. "Oh, I think far too highly of you. But right now, I need you to scoot out of here before anyone sees you or we'll both be in trouble." He swatted her on the behind with his free hand to get her going.

Of all the insufferable things a man could do, she blustered and fussed, making him laugh. He turned around so she couldn't see his face.

"Aren't you gone yet?"

"Mr. Bradly. I'll thank you to keep your hands off me." Her heart raced as he slowly turned and strode up to her each step painfully intent. He put his hands behind his back and leaned down. His breath fanned her cheek and she closed her eyes. Her skin tingled and she gripped her own hands behind her back to keep from grabbing the front of his shirt and dragging him in closer. His scent was straw, leather, and work and it had never thrilled her more. He pressed his lips against hers and her breath caught in her throat, pulling back as the pleasant feeling of anticipation burst through her. She flung her eyes open.

"You didn't say anything about my lips." He laughed.

She gathered her skirts and rushed out the door, his laugh chasing her down the trail.

Jennie rushed through the log cabin's back door and washed her hands, splashing cool water on her face.

Ruby laughed and all her embarrassment came back. Had Ruby seen where she'd come from? "Jennie! Where have you been? I looked around for you but didn't see you anywhere."

Jennie turned and dried her face with the towel. "I was..." Aiden's words of warning rang in her ears. "I was just looking around outside."

"Well, you weren't here to hear Beau's warning. They spotted some strange hoof prints up on the north hill pasture. He asked that we stay close to the houses. We're free to roam about here but not to wander too far."

"I won't wander. It is beautiful out here...reminds me a little of Cutter's Creek." Anything to keep Ruby from asking about the heat that wouldn't leave her face.

Ruby glanced out the window and her face softened. "It does. I love the green of the trees, and from the top of this hill, it's like you can see for miles."

"That's true. Cutter's Creek was at the base of the mountains, but we're higher here, like you're a little closer to God."

Ruby turned back to her. "Jennie, I had a lot of time to think while I was resting. I'd be lying if I didn't tell you that Eva told me about your argument with Aiden on the way here...and what he offered. I'm worried you'll pass up the opportunity to be with him because of Hattie. Please don't let her choices ruin yours. If I could go back and change anything, I would've insisted Ma come with us. Hattie may not have run away from her, but we'll never know for sure."

"Ruby, this wasn't your fault and you can't go back so it doesn't do anyone any good to think on it." Jennie turned and splashed her face one last time to make sure any visible sign of Aiden's kiss was gone.

Ruby stepped toward her and rested her hand on Jennie's shoulder. "Jennie, I want you to think about something, deeply. You've based all your ideas on marriage on Ma and Pa, but they aren't your only guide. Think of Beau and I. Marriage can be a beautiful thing."

"I'm sure it can be... When you want it. I've been afraid of it for so long. How do I just change how I feel?" The thought of Aiden's lips on hers just a few minutes before sent heat crawling back up her cheeks. What would that kiss have become if she hadn't jumped back? They had been alone in his home...

"You first have to *want* to change. Then you make decisions that slowly take you out of where you're comfortable. Love, in the beginning, isn't comfortable. It can be exciting and a little scary."

"I've spent the last year changing. I just want to find somewhere I can do my work and be left alone." Jennie had to get away from Ruby. Ruby would never understand that she *did* love Aiden, but she couldn't let herself hope until he returned. She rushed up the ladder in the loft to change for supper. The longer Aiden was here, the more everyone would try to push them together. He certainly made her pulse race when he got close or when he teased her. But feelings just weren't enough. Ma had talked about the feelings she'd had when she first met Pa. *She'd* ended up living in a tiny house with eight girls and a husband who brewed moonshine. Feelings couldn't assure her Aiden would return. Until then, his parents came first.

She pulled her work dress over her head and changed into her one nice ecru lace dress. She buttoned the front up the high neck and looked down at it. While it wasn't elegant, it fit her well after her alterations. She helped Lula with her braids and gathered the girls to come down. They would go over to the main house for supper as a family.

Jennie held her skirts close to her and climbed down the ladder from the loft. When she reached the third rung from the bottom, someone grasped her waist and swung her down. She turned and Aiden's hands squeezed her waist gently, fitting comfortably and almost encircling her back and belly.

"You look beautiful, Jennie-girl." He beamed down at her and she froze, not sure what to say or do. He'd shaved and put on a shirt she didn't recognize. It was clean and white and looked so nice with his brown leather vest. His sandy red hair was just a bit too long and she wanted to push it behind his ears.

Beau cleared his throat and Jennie jumped away from Aiden for the second time that day. Aiden chuckled and offered her his arm.

"Care to walk with me?"

If she refused, she'd look rude in front of everyone... If she accepted, it was almost an acceptance of his pursuit. She hesitated, then reached out and touched his arm. For now, she would avoid *saying* she accepted him.

He grinned at her and swept her from the cabin. When they were outside and a few steps ahead of everyone else, he laid his hand on hers.

"Thank you for freshening up my cabin. I should've said so when I got there."

Jennie tried to pull her hand back but his held hers firm. "As I recall, your lips were too busy with other things for the task."

His hazel eyes darkened to the color of a beautiful glade. "Aye, and don't tell me you wouldn't rather have that than a thank you." His voice was thick, intimate. She shivered.

"That's what I thought. It was just such a pleasant shock to find you there. A man doesn't expect to find a beautiful woman waiting for him unless he's married to her."

Jennie watched her feet as she walked across the sparse grass. "I was only trying to be kind. I didn't even mean to be there when you returned."

"I'm not complaining. In fact, I'm hopeful someday I can come home to you every day."

Jennie shook her head. "Aiden, stop. I enjoy your company. More now than I did at first, for sure. But I'm not interested in marriage. Not now… or ever. I've always seen marriage as a threat, something held over my head. I'm not going to choose it, ever." That's what she'd keep telling him, so it didn't hurt so terribly when he left. Maybe if he believed it, so would she, but it didn't stop the words from tearing something within her.

Aiden held her hand on his arm as they stepped onto the porch and waited for Beau. She saw the confusion in his eyes. He stepped away from her and a coldness filled the space like a wall. She swallowed back the words to bring him back to her. The sooner she got her heart to forget him, the better off they would both be. *He was leaving.*

Beau led Ruby and the five other sisters onto the porch, Eva trailing silently at the rear. Beau knocked and a Chinese woman opened the door.

She spoke with clipped words. "Mr. Ferguson is waiting. This way." She closed her eyes and bowed her head slightly. A few silver strands ran through her thick black hair tied back in a large bun. Her tiny feet made soft swishing noises under the strange robe she wore, like a long coat, as she led them in short steps to the sitting room. Jennie knew the woman was Chinese because there was a group of Celestials settled in Deadwood, but she'd never actually seen one.

The woman stopped in front of a set of large double pocket doors and gestured inside. Jennie hesitated for a moment, wanting to know more about the woman but would her host think her rude for her curiosity? Jennie tilted her head to the side and waited as the others entered the room.

"Something wrong, young one?" the woman asked.

Mr. Ferguson approached them, smiling. "This is my house-keeper, Mrs. Chen. She lost her husband a few years ago and has been with me for some time. She used to work in the laundry seven days a week, twelve hours a day. It wasn't right. So, now she's here."

Jennie held out her hand. "It's nice to meet you, Mrs. Chen."

She looked at Jennie's hand and nodded then turned to the back of the house, leaving them.

Mr. Ferguson put his hand at Jennie's waist and directed her in the room. "Don't take her lack of reaching out as a refusal to get to know you. Lei was treated very poorly in Deadwood and is still suspicious of people. Her people work hard in the laundries and mines, but folks are scared of what's different.

Jennie whispered, "What happened to her feet?"

"That's their custom. I don't know the whole story. Just that many of the women there have those tiny feet. In fact, those that don't are often unmarried and ridiculed."

"Strange." Lei came from a life completely foreign from her, one not embraced by others in the community. Hadn't Beau said Chinatown was dangerous? Lei certainly didn't seem so. She wanted to follow Lei instead of sitting in a boring dinner, talking about cattle.

"It is, but strange isn't always bad. And, while I don't share the fears of some of the people in Deadwood, I do understand. Before they moved west many of them heard of the dangers of *different* people. They've been taught to fear those who believe differently, have different rituals and ways. Without more people willing to cross the lines we create our worlds will remain shared, but separate."

Lei appeared at the end of the hall and slowly made her way toward them, stopping just a few feet away. She bowed her head and waved down the hall as a short man pushed a cart laden with plates.

"Thank you, Mrs. Chen. You need not serve us. You may have the rest of the evening off. Thank you for staying."

Lei nodded and folded her hands in front of her as she made her way past them and back to the front of the house.

"Isn't it difficult for her to move around?" Jennie wanted to know more.

"While she does have some difficulty, especially by the end of a day, she likes to remain helpful. I've offered her other jobs that would keep her off her feet. This is the one she wants to do the most. Now, let's turn our thoughts to something else, like the ranch. The Bar F was one of the first ranches near Deadwood. The railroad just started moving cattle this far northwest and I was glad to finally be doing what I wanted to. I'd heard all the stories about Deadwood and was fascinated. I came up here thinking I would stake a claim, strike it rich, and live out my days in luxury." He laughed.

Jennie shifted her gaze to Aiden who was, for once, ignoring her and paying attention to Mr. Ferguson. Kindred spirits looking for wealth from the earth. She mentally shook off her pique that he could be so easily turned.

Mr. Ferguson's glance landed briefly on each guest. "The good Lord had other plans for me. I had the money to buy up four claims, all connected, not a single one of them had any dust that I could find but it was prime land for cattle. I helped out a friend who had a reasonably good find of copper and he shared some of his earnings from selling his claim with me. Which is how I was able to buy my cattle. I paid him back after the first year. Now, I don't need gold. I have a commodity that's even more rare than gold up here. Beef."

Aiden smiled. "So, you've been here a few years. Is the weather good for ranching?"

"Well, that remains to be seen. I've seen some wicked storms up here, but they don't come around every year. Everywhere you go there're dangers to ranching, but cattle aren't much different than bison. They do have less hide, though, so you've got to move them into more protected areas when the weather starts to turn."

Aiden glanced at Jennie and caught her watching him. She dropped her gaze to her lap, her stomach tightening like a child's windup toy.

"Mr. Ferguson, it sounds and looks like you have a great spread here with a lot of potential. I wish I could promise you that I'd be able to come right back from my travels. I wish I didn't have to leave at all."

His words slammed into her ears and she snuck a glance at him to see a mischievous smile directed at her. The room was suddenly stifling in her high-necked gown.

"Now, Aiden," Brody leaned on the table over his crossed arms. "I understand why you want to go and why you might not come back. Don't concern yourself with it. I'll be showing Beau around for the next few days. After that, he'll be in charge of the hiring here. He's the one you'll need to prove yourself to if you return."

Beau sat up as the man from outside the door pushed a cart into the room and set heavily laden plates in front of each of them. Jennie eyed the foods in front of her and didn't recognize most of it. She'd never seen so much food on one plate before. It overwhelmed her senses. Was she truly supposed to eat it all? She glanced around the table and her sisters were doing much as she was, unsure of what to do next. Brody folded his hands and bowed his head and they all followed. He said a short prayer over the food and then lifted his fork.

Ruby leaned over to Jennie and whispered in her ear. "It's

beef. Beau bought it for me once. It's good, try it. You may not get a chance again for a long time." She straightened and started on her own meal.

Jennie reached for her knife and cut off a small bite. While the taste was similar to the venison she'd had growing up, it wasn't quite the same. She took a few more bites and knew she'd love to eat it again, given the chance.

The meal ended and she and her sisters were excused to leave. Ruby stayed with Beau, so Jennie and Aiden led the girls back to the cabin. There wasn't much to say during their walk. Their argument from earlier hung in the air like a wet sheet dividing them. Jack met them halfway and circled them barking. Then he ran off returning quickly, enjoying his freedom from four walls. Jennie turned and Aiden leaned over, patting Jack on the head.

The girls giggled as they ran into the house and watched from the front window. Jennie remained outside, waiting to see what Aiden would say or do. His revelation at dinner had been shocking, but perhaps no more than hers before. He smiled as he walked alongside her, past her house and under a tall spruce tree. He turned her to face back toward her house and looked up at the sky. The stars overhead were bright and the air was cool and calm, so fresh and clean after life in the city.

"So, what did you think of dinner?" He tucked her hand under his arm and held it there with light pressure as he gazed up at the stars. As she turned to see what fascinated him so in the sky her neck tingled with his warm breath. His gaze had drifted much further south than the heavens.

"It was pleasant. I learned a lot about the Chinese people of Deadwood."

"There's always more to learn. I know if you get curious, you'll find a way to learn more. I'm happy to see you take some interest in Deadwood, even if it isn't a typical one."

She didn't want to argue with him. Arguing over something so unimportant seemed silly and they'd already wasted enough of that day fighting. He'd only be with her another few weeks.

She shivered and stepped away from his arm. "Take me for a

walk? I'm not supposed to go past the buildings alone." It seemed the perfect excuse to stretch the evening for a few extra minutes.

He gazed down at her, the darkness shadowing his face. She stopped, holding her breath. Perhaps she shouldn't have asked.

"I don't think it's a good idea to take you beyond the buildings or anywhere into the dark. A man has to know his limits, Jennie. If you want to see the stable and the buildings, I'll show them to you in the morning."

She hadn't even considered what people might think of them wandering in the dark alone. But the sky was so perfect, the air so crisp. She'd been inside a house for too long. A short walk couldn't hurt.

"Are you always so concerned with what other people think?" She continued along the worn path toward the stables, ignoring his warning.

He sighed and turned to follow her. Exasperation thickening his voice. "There isn't anyone out here to see us. Which is part of the problem. I was thinking more of my *own* temptations."

She slowed her pace. "Well, maybe it would be best if I didn't go with you then." If she let herself be alone with him in the barn would he take liberties and kiss her again? Would she mind if he did?

He laughed as he came alongside her. "I can probably keep myself in check for a few minutes. Can you?" He tugged gently on her ear lobe and ran off into the stable.

Jennie clutched her skirts in hand and ran after him, laughing as she skidded to a stop just inside the door of the lighted barn. There was nothing to the left or right. It was as if he'd just disappeared. There was a row of horse stalls just to her right, most of them full. She leaned over and glanced down the row, then crept to the next. This row had empty stalls, the perfect place for him to hide.

She gingerly tip-toed over the rough concrete block floor, careful to check each stall. Her heart pumped in her ears as she waited for him to jump out and scare her. That would be just his way. She'd almost reached the end when a few blades of straw rained softly down on her head. She peered up as Aiden sat on a beam above her. His thickly muscled arms held him for a moment as he swung down then he extended them, releasing his body from the rafters above. He landed right in front of her and she gasped, nose to nose with him. His hazel eyes swept over her face, stalling on her lips, then he turned from her and scraped his hand over the back of his neck expelling a huge breath. She wanted to stalk over there and yank him back. She wasn't done with him yet.

"We shouldn't be out here. Brody showed us the tracks of unshod horses out in one of his pastures. Could be Indians or someone trying to look like Indians to stir up trouble. I should get you back home. It was foolish of me to bring you out here."

He grasped her arm and tugged her along with him. She lost her footing and slid along for a moment until she gained her feet and yanked herself free.

"Just wait one minute! You haven't shown me anything except that you know how to hide." Her breath ached to be free of her stays. She was breathing too hard to calm herself.

He returned to her, just a bare few inches away. "You don't understand, *M'fhíorghrá*. I can hardly stand to breathe if I'm not with you. But I know you'll never want to be with me. So, I have to stay away. You're tearing me apart."

He closed the distance between them and nuzzled her ear. She leaned in closer, a sigh escaping her before she could pull it back. She let his breath fan her neck and the tension in her own belly tightened.

"What does that mean? what you called me?" Her voice was barely a whisper as she tilted her head to let him explore her neck further.

He nibbled below her ear, leaving a trail of heat. She'd never experienced anything so delicious.

"It's what my da always calls my mam." He took a step closer and his voice caressed her as sure as his hands on her shoulders and his mouth on her neck. "My da and mam's parents came to America to escape the Great Famine in Ireland. They found jobs in New York and raised their children together." He stopped and stepped back from her. His eyes hotter than his touch. "No one was surprised when my parents married. They'd been together their whole lives. What my grandparents *didn't* expect was that they would pull together the few dollars they could and move to Kansas." He shifted his body and laid his forehead against hers, breathing deeply. Her body pulsed, fanning a flame deep inside her. He was far too close and yet not close enough. She told her fingers to keep still but they wound their way around his waist against her will.

"My parents told us that leaving New York hurt our grandparents greatly, but there was nothing for them there but poverty. They weren't expecting their son to do as they did...leave without warning."

His words were full of so much pain and torment. She was tormenting him, keeping him from his purpose. "And that's why you have to go back." She breathed in the clean scent of the soap he'd used, the hay all around them, the oil he'd used on his leather vest. All the scents swirled about her, pressing themselves into her memory. Because, though he wanted to come back, it was never a guarantee and he *needed* to go home to be the man he wanted to be.

"Yes. I was young and foolish. I truly thought I could find better than what they gave me. If I didn't feel like I had to do this, I'd stay here. I would've not only asked Beau to court you, but I'd ask him for your hand just so I could be sure no other man could *ever* take you from me. Please understand, Jennie. This is something I feel like I have to do, like my soul is calling me home."

She stepped out of his arms and took his hands in hers. "If you're being called home then you should go. Perhaps you'll feel tugged back here. But if you don't..." She couldn't finish. Her words choked her. She rushed past him out of the stable and into the night. Her tears ran down her cheek, blurring her vision. She didn't know the lay of the land well enough to run home from the wrong end of the barn and Aiden soon caught up to her.

He took her arm and turned her around, holding her close. "It will be all right. I'll be here for the next week to show Beau I can learn quickly. That way if I return, I can just jump right back into work."

He threaded his hand behind her neck and held her close. She clutched his vest in one hand and wove her other in the hair at the nape of his neck, but it couldn't dispel what that one word did to her heart...*if*. He held her close, her forehead to his lips, until her tears ran dry. He kissed the tears from her eyelashes then let her go.

"It's late. I'm sure Beau and Ruby are back by now. I need to get you home."

She nodded, unable to speak.

He led her to her door and opened it for her. She stopped in the doorway.

"Good night, Aiden."

"Good night, *M'fhíorghrá*."

CHAPTER 17

Aiden strode into the barn just as the morning rays peered through the windows. The sunlight held bits of dust and warmed the stable floor as the horses stomped, wanting their freedom out in the pasture. He could understand their plight. He felt tied to returning to his parents. But like them, he didn't have a choice. He could only pray his da would let him free after. Even if it meant working to return every cent he'd promised before he left.

Beau glanced up from the saddle he was fixing. "Morning. You're on time. That's a good start. It'll be easier in the future if you don't keep Jennie out so late."

Aiden heard Beau's meaning loud and clear. "Yes, sir. What are we aiming for today?"

"Brody asked us to head out to those prints we saw yesterday. See where they lead. You up for a day in the saddle?"

Aiden nodded. "I better be if this's what I aim to do."

"Yup. You'll find yourself in the saddle more often than not. Brody said you should take Blaze, that roan down the second row. After the trip out yesterday with the heavy wagons, he didn't think any of the horses we brought were up to the task of riding all day."

Aiden nodded and went to the tack room. An old man sat on a bench oiling a saddle.

"What can a get for ya?" He looked up, his pipe hanging loosely from a jaw without enough teeth.

"I'm looking for a saddle for Blaze."

The old man laughed dryly, and he caught his pipe as it fell from his mouth. "That one, right in front of you is the only one that'll work. He likes to flip ya. So be sure you're cinched good before ya' mount."

Aiden nodded. Testing the greenhorn was the way of things. He'd been tested when he started prospecting and he'd expected it here, too. Give the new guy the toughest horse, or the ugliest job, and see how well he could do it. Even if he's horrible, if he didn't give up, he'll eventually be good. That was just the way of it.

He cinched the saddle and waited to the count of twenty-five. Then, pulled it tighter. He tested the stirrup and it didn't slide. Blaze turned out to be a good mount. Easy to read. He took his cues well as Aiden took him for a trot around the corral. He patted Blaze on the neck and waited for Beau to mount and ride out.

They rode along the ridgeline for a while then cut north down into a valley. In the mud, along what had been a shallow creek during the snow melt, they found the tracks from the day before.

"This can't be Indians. It'd be too easy to find them," Beau said, dismounting and bending to take a closer look at the tracks. "They're excellent trackers and they wouldn't ride their horses down the one spot that would leave a trail. And if there had been water then, from the melt, it would've washed them away."

Aiden joined him next to the creek bed and squatted for a closer look. The middles of the tracks were damp. The edges were dry and deep. Too deep for a horse without a rider. It had been wet when the horses went through. "I agree with you. But why would people go to the trouble of finding unshod horses to walk up this muddy spot just to stir trouble?"

"My guess is, they're planning to rustle a few cattle and hope Brody blames the Indians. If he does, he won't go looking to get them back." Beau shaded his eyes and gazed farther up the creek bed. "They were headed this way. Let's follow carefully and see if we can tell where it leads. My guess is, once this line of mud meets a lake or another river, we'll have lost them."

Aiden wiped his brow with his bandana. "I'm sure you're right, but if Brody wants us to check it out, then we'd best do it."

They mounted and followed the prints to a wash where the creek had become deeper. It carved a deep muddy groove between two hills. The hoof prints ended there.

"They came up on the grass right here. We'll ask Brody who owns the claim next to his. He can check with them and see if they've spotted the same signs."

"Or if they have an abundance of unshod horses." Aiden smirked, turning his horse back toward the ranch.

"There's always that chance but let's hope we have better neighbors than that." Beau turned his horse as well. Blaze followed with little direction and Aiden used the chance to keep an eye out on the ridge for anyone watching them. They'd made it back to the area where they'd first spotted tracks when Aiden heard a crack. Pain exploded in his shoulder spreading flame through his arm and chest.

"Get down!" Beau yelled.

Aiden tried to reach for the reins, but a black ring formed all around him, closing in on him. He felt his head meet the ground as he tumbled off his horse.

JENNIE HEARD A SHOT. It was faint but it made her jump. She'd expected to leave the shooting behind when they'd left Deadwood. Someone pounded on their door and Ruby rushed to answer it. She pulled the door wide and Brody stood outside panting and bent at the waist from his run.

Brody clutched the door jamb with one hand and his gut with the other. "Has Beau come back yet?"

"No, sir. They left early this morning and didn't come home for the noon meal."

Brody shook his head. "I'll have to take Lefty with me and see if we can find them. I heard a shot coming from the ridge where I sent them. I don't think Aiden was armed, only Beau."

Jennie's heart sank into her feet. *No!* "Ruby, what should we do? What if one of them is hurt? How should we get ready?"

Jennie turned in a circle, thinking of all the things they might need but unable to move from her spot to go get them.

Ruby touched her shoulder. "First, you're going to take a deep breath. Then you're going to go put clean sheets on my bed. No matter if one, both, or neither of them were hurt, we want to be ready and the only bed available is ours."

Jennie nodded, took a deep breath, letting it clear her mind, then dashed for the linen cupboard. Lei had made sure everything in their cabin was ready for them. Jennie grabbed what she needed and stripped Ruby's bed, remaking it with the clean bedding. She leaned out the door. "Do you think one of us should ride to Deadwood for a doctor?"

Ruby had begun heating water and she called from the stove, "No, not until we're told to. I don't know what Brody does out here for medicine, but it'd be a long ride all the way back to town. If it were a bad shot, they wouldn't live long enough for us to get there and back again."

Jennie felt sick and waiting made it worse. She paced in the living room until Ruby sent her outside. She walked to the stable. If she knew how to ride, she could go out herself and find out what was going on. She heard three more shots, all close together, and ran to the back of the house, watching the ridge behind the corner of Aiden's house.

Within a few minutes she saw three riders and a horse clear the ridge and race toward her. One of the riders had another draped in front of him. He looked dead. Jennie sank to her knees. *No, Lord. No. Please don't take either Beau or Aiden… I'm begging you.*

The horses bore down on her, racing toward the safety of the ranch house and buildings. She ran back to the house and through it, avoiding Ruby as she dashed through the front door. Brody slid to a stop near her, tossing gravel and dust in her face then dismounted. She couldn't take her eyes off the man draped over the front of his saddle. She knew the brown oil coat and saw the growing red spot down the sleeve. Tears erupted behind her eyes and her hands shook.

Brody broke through her frozen thoughts. "He's alive. Open that door, girl. So I can get him in and patched up before he bleeds out."

Jennie shook herself and ran for the door as Brody heaved Aiden over his shoulder and carried him into the house. Ruby rushed into the bedroom and Brody laid Aiden on the bed as gently as possible. Aiden sucked in his breath and flailed as he hit the mattress. Jennie came close and brushed the sweaty hair from his head. He was shivering even with the heat of mid-summer and her heart ached to take away his pain.

"How do we get his coat off without moving his arm?" She looked to Ruby, but Brody answered. "Go to the main house and ask Lei for the medical bag. I have a scissors inside that'll cut it. I had to move him more than I'd like just to get him here without any extra holes. I don't want to risk that ball causing any more damage."

Ruby dug through her bag and came up with the same scissors she'd used to cut Aiden's boots. She handed them to Brody as Jennie turned and ran from the house. The longer she stayed in Deadwood, the more she hated it. It took Hattie and now it could take Aiden too. She pounded on the door to the house and it seemed to take a full minute for Lei to get to the door. She opened it slowly and gave Jennie a strange look.

"Mr. Ferguson not here. You go find him." She pushed the door against Jennie.

"No wait! Mrs. Chen! Mr. Ferguson asked for his medical bag. Aiden's been shot!"

The woman hesitated then nodded. "You go."

Jennie glanced back at the cabin and then at Lei as she padded softly across the floor and out of sight. Jennie dashed back to the cabin, her lungs on fire, praying that Lei understood and would bring it.

"Lei is on her way with the bag, I think." Jennie gasped and bit her lip. She wished she'd been able to get better confirmation out of the woman.

"Good. She's as good as any assistant I've had. Now, as soon as she gets here, I want you two out. Nothing you say will make me change my mind on that. I'll have all the help I need with Beau and Mrs. Chen. Understand?"

Jennie touched Aiden's cheek. "But…"

"No."

Jennie closed her eyes against the fear of losing him. Not to Kansas or his parents where he might return to her but something much more permanent. She leaned over and kissed Aiden's forehead her heart beating a terrible rhythm.

She whispered for his ears only. "You better not leave me Aiden Bradly."

Mrs. Chen entered the log cabin without knocking and appeared at Brody's side.

Brody nodded to Ruby and Jennie. "Now go."

Beau had been standing in the corner. He came forward and kissed Ruby on the head then gave her a squeeze. He whispered, "I'll tell you what happened later."

She kissed him on the cheek then ushered Jennie from the room. They sat on the couch in front of the empty fireplace.

"What if he doesn't make it Ruby?" Her feet wanted to get up and pace, but Ruby held her fast to the seat.

"That's a good question, Jennie. What *if* he doesn't make it? What would you do?"

Her throat clogged at the thought. "I know it doesn't do any good, but I keep praying God would take me instead."

Ruby draped her arm over Jennie's shoulder and pulled her close. "A wise friend once told me love had nothing to do with all those wonderful feelings you get when you're near one another. It has everything to do with wanting the very best for that person. Even risking your own life to save them…"

"Are you saying I love him?" Jennie tucked her head under Ruby's chin.

"Jennie, that's what love is. When you would rather hurt than see them hurting. When you would brave your worst fear for them. That's love."

"My worst fear is marrying a man and then finding he's just like Pa."

Ruby brushed the hair from Jennie's eyes and stroked it back into her bun. "Do you really think Aiden has hidden who he *really* is from you? Do you honestly think he could be hiding something that dark from all of us?"

She thought about all the times he'd teased her and challenged her and infuriated her, but not once had he intentionally hurt her. Even when he'd said something that had cut her deeply, he'd told her she'd been mistaken and explained himself.

"He's been talking about courting you almost from the start, Jennie. He felt something between you as soon as you met. Beau wasn't ready to give him permission right away. But after he saw you two together the day you gave Aiden his shave... Beau told me he would approve if Aiden ever decided to ask again. He didn't until we got here though. Why is that?"

Jennie flung her head into her hands and sobbed. "I told him not to. I didn't even know he'd still gone to Beau. If he was leaving and never coming back, I didn't want to be stuck here loving someone I'd never see again."

"You pushed him away at every turn. Don't you see now that if you'd taken the time to let him court you while you had the chance, you could've gone with him to Kansas as his wife? You could've met the family that's so important to him he's willing to leave the woman he loves for them. You could have been the great treasure he promised them."

Jennie let Ruby's words wash over her heart. She refused to believe them until he professed his love himself.

"But I didn't want to." Jennie wiped the back of her hand across her eyes. "I don't want to leave my family. We've already lost Ma and Hattie. I'm not splitting us up any more. Even you said, on our way to Deadwood, losing just one of us would be difficult. Why are you so ready to see me go now?"

"Jennie, don't you see? Families may grow apart and live in other places but that doesn't mean they love each other any less. I lived away from all of you for over a year and my love for all of you only grew stronger." Ruby touched her knee and Jennie glanced up to meet her gaze. "And it isn't like you'd never come back. Aiden wants to be here.

"You could write to Ma any time you wish. I have the address in my Bible. If you'd go with Aiden, you'd never be farther away than a letter. Now that they have the train in Deadwood you could always visit."

"A letter…" Why hadn't she thought of that? She didn't have to lose him at all. "Aiden could write his parents a letter instead of going!"

Ruby grabbed and held fast to Jennie's hands. "Don't be disappointed if he still wants to go, Jennie. He knows his family better than you do. While it may seem to be the perfect solution. Maybe he feels he *has* to go because something important is waiting for him there. If you love him, you have to let him lead. That might mean letting him go."

Her shoulders sunk. "None of that will matter if he dies."

A loud holler came from Ruby's room followed by Brody yelling instructions to Lei and Beau. Jennie sprang to her feet and Ruby clutched her hand tightly.

"Brody said no. You stay right here."

"He needs me, Ruby."

Ruby glanced at Jennie. "I think you'd best put together a pallet for Beau and me out here. It'll keep you busy. I don't think we'll be sleeping in there for some time."

Jennie sighed then nodded as she glanced back at the bedroom door one last time. "I best do that so I can keep my mind off what's going on in there. At least if he's yelling, he's still alive."

CHAPTER 18

Aiden felt a cool cloth wipe over his brow and he heard...*humming*. He recognized it as a hymn but the more he tried to name it, the more he couldn't string two thoughts together. It didn't help that the pounding in his head was worse than the night the prospector introduced him to whiskey.

He opened his eyes and glanced around, squinting at the searing light pouring in the one window. Nothing looked familiar, until his glance fell on beautiful violet eyes smiling down at him. His left shoulder throbbed, and he couldn't even think about moving it. He reached up with his other hand and wrapped it around the back of Jennie's neck. She slid down to her knees on the floor, nearer to him. He pulled her closer and she did not protest as he claimed her lips.

Energy surged through him and he drew her tightly to him. She couldn't get close enough. Pain throbbed down his arm and she pulled away, laying her beautiful head on his chest. He let his hand rest against her neck holding her, his fingers tracing the soft wisps of hair at her nape.

"Aiden, I'm so glad you're awake. I was so scared."

He moved his hand to her head and relished the feeling of her against him. "You can't get rid of me that easy."

She laughed and sat up, running the cool cloth over his forehead again. "You've had a fever. We were so worried about you. You're still so hot…"

He cupped her cheek and she closed her eyes. "I don't want to leave you behind, Jennie. Please say you'll come with me."

She shook her head as she pulled back and a wavering smile covered her lips. "We could write them a letter, Aiden. I could even write it for you, now. You don't ever have to leave." She waited with expectant eyes for something he could never give her. And it broke him.

He trailed his thumb in circles in the soft hair by her ear. "I'm so sorry, Jennie. It can't be that way. I *have* to go. I won't be able to sleep easy until I go back and tell my folks how sorry I am. You can't do that in a letter."

Her face crumpled with a swallowed sob and her eyes shut tight against her tears. "I almost lost you once. Please, don't make me lose you again." She leaned into his hand, letting the tears drip down her cheek and onto his thin undershirt.

"You don't have to lose anything. Don't you see? If you come with me, we'll always be together."

She shook her head, dislodging his hand from her hair and he let it drop. "No, I can't go knowing I may never come back. And if you decide to stay, I can't come back alone."

"You'd do that? You'd rather be with your family forever even if it meant you wouldn't be with me?" His chest tightened as he waited for her to meet his gaze.

"I could ask you the same question and I'd think we'd both answer that it isn't like that. I *can't* leave them. Over the last half-year, everything I've ever known has changed. The only thing that's stayed the same are my sisters. Hattie has already done enough damage. I can't leave my sisters, too. If you go and I stay, then I hope you'll be more likely to come back."

He closed his eyes and saw that she was right. They both needed their families for different reasons. She'd been here next to him while he'd recovered. That was *something*. But what if *his* family didn't understand? What if they wanted him to work to make up for leaving them? Or, it was possible they didn't miss him at all. The pain would be great, but then he could come right back. But not as the man he hoped to be.

Fabric whispered next to him as Jennie stood. Her cool lips pressed against his head. He sighed and when he opened his eyes, he was alone. Whose bed was he in and how long had he been there? Had they found who'd shot him or was the scoundrel still on the loose? Brody came through the door and pulled up a chair.

"You've been down for quite a while. That little gal out there got a few gray hairs on account of you."

Aiden rubbed his shoulder and flinched. "I didn't sign up for this when I offered to go with Beau."

"You surely didn't. I got a good look at him. He didn't even bother to hide. Pretty sure he thought you were me since you were riding one of my horses and we're about the same size." He shook his head. "I rode back to Lead and got the sheriff. He didn't want to take my word for it, but Beau was able to get a good look at him as well. He gave a description to the sheriff that closely resembled my neighbor, Jed. It was enough. Maybe we'll find out why he took a shot at you when the circuit judge comes through."

Aiden nodded. "So, when will I be able to get up and start earning my keep again? I have to get to Kansas so I can make good with my family. Then I can come back."

"You sound surer of your return now than you were before."

"I am. If I explain to my family I have a gal waiting here and she's more precious to me than gold... I think they'll send me back."

"Well just remember, if they don't need you, you send a letter. Don't leave that gal waiting on you. It wouldn't be right." He patted Aiden on his good shoulder then went around the bed to check the bandages on his other. He made contemplative noises as he poked around.

"Yup, all the angry red around the wound is finally turning pink and puckering. The wound has scaled over well and isn't draining anymore. I think you'll keep your arm."

Aiden sat up and stared at Brody. Was he serious?

"I'm just funning with ya. There was never a question. I was an army medic with Custer. I got injured before the battle of Greasy Grass and was sent home as soon as my injury healed enough. You aren't the first bullet wound I've tended." He pulled the blanket up over Aiden and stood. "Glad to see you awake. I'll send Jennie back in here with a little soup. Then I think Beau should help you up so Ruby and Jennie can freshen this room. Then you can rest. Beau has set aside the money for you to go as soon as you're well enough. When I see you not only awake but walking around, we can talk about getting you a ride to town."

Aiden nodded. Brody didn't seem like the kind that would take well to taking orders, even in the army. He laid back against the wall as Brody left, letting his eyelids close while he waited. Unless the soup was already made, he'd have to wait a while for it anyway. The smell of old bandages, waste, and uncleanliness filled his nose. He hadn't been aware of it until Brody mentioned cleaning the room. He'd been too full of Jennie to notice. Now that she was gone the stench wouldn't leave him.

Aiden shifted to get off the bed and stopped as pain tore through his arm. He held it close to his body and used his other side to pull himself to the edge of the bed. He pushed the covers off and realized they'd taken off everything but his drawers and thin undershirt. The door handle clicked. He swung the blankets back over himself, wafting the stench into his face. It was enough to make his stomach curl.

"Jennie. I can't eat in here. I'm powerful hungry, but if I eat in here, it won't stay down."

"I don't blame you." The side of her mouth slid up and a mischievous twinkle lit her eyes. "I'll take this back out to the table and come back to help you up."

"No!" He shook his head. "I can't have you help me get dressed."

She laughed and a sweet pink tinge rimmed her ears. "Fair enough. Beau is home for lunch. I'll have him come in and help you." She swept out of the room and Aiden sighed.

Beau laughed as he came in. "I'm not sure what's funnier, that she just got you good or that you believed it."

Aiden frowned. "You shouldn't mock an injured man. Not a fair fight."

Beau put one hand under Aiden's right arm, the other under his elbow. "Jennie got your clothes cleaned and patched a week ago, though your coat was pretty well ruined."

"I'm sorry to hear that. The longer I stay with you, the more clothes I lose."

Beau led him over to the chair. Aiden sat and got to work putting on his own dungarees. He slid on a clean cotton under shirt to replace the one he'd been wearing and put his arm through one sleeve of a clean shirt and draped the other over his shoulder on the other side, leaving it open for movement.

"That's good. Let's get you out of this room." Beau helped him to his feet once again and he pushed one foot in front of the other, moving his upper half as little as possible. Jennie waited at the table for him. She let her eyes roam over him possessively and he couldn't say he minded. He sat next to her and she pushed the bowl over to him. It warmed him to know that she understood he'd want to feed himself.

He lifted the spoon to his mouth and the soup was as sweet as honey to his tongue. Being without for so long made him appreciate the richness of the meal. He let the broth and vegetables sit in his mouth for a second, enjoying every bit of the flavor, then he swallowed slowly. His throat protested and he reached for a glass of water. The cool water trickled down after the scratchy food.

Beau sat across from him. "Aiden. I'm not sure if anyone said anything yet, but my pay was more than we needed with our food included. I put the money aside for you. As soon as you can, you'll be able to go home. There should be enough there for your return trip too."

Aiden nodded and set his spoon down, reaching for Jennie's hand. "I want very much to go and do what's right and pray I can return." He lifted her hand and gently kissed Jennie's knuckles.

CHAPTER 19

Jennie stood on the porch as Aiden strode to the wagon and
tossed his satchel in the back. A great fissure cracked her
heart wide. His good arm reached for the seat of the wagon
and lifted his leg to climb up. He was leaving and though
he said he'd come back, what if he didn't? Could she really live
with him never knowing just how she felt?

"No!" Jennie yelled and tore away from Ruby's grasp on her
shoulder. Aiden turned and brought both feet back to the ground.
He opened his arms for her. She ran to those welcoming arms and
he lifted her right off the ground with his one good arm. Jennie
folded herself around his neck and clung to him, her chest burning
with tears. He pressed his lips to hers in a kiss that claimed her
very soul, sweeping every ache into her center then exploding
outward, claiming all that was her as his own. His lips told her
more than his words. He would return for her.

Slowly, he let her slide down until her feet touched the ground.
But she didn't let go. Couldn't let go.

"You'll take care of Jack for me?" He rested his head against
hers and cupped her cheek.

She covered his hand and let her tears stream over them. She didn't want him to think of her as weak, but inside the pain crushed her.

She nodded. "I will."

"You'll take care of my best girl?" Aiden murmured to the dog.

She raised her gaze to meet his. It immediately destroyed her resolve not to beg. "Oh Aiden, don't go."

"I promise I'll be back, Jennie-girl. *M'fhíorghrá*."

"You'd better." She held his hands over her face for a moment longer then let him go. He gently pulled her into another tender kiss then turned and climbed into the wagon. Brody reined the horses into a trot and Aiden turned and waved to her. She raised her arm and watched until he was out of sight then ran into the house and up into the loft. Her insides were as empty as a rain barrel in the desert. She lay on her bed and wrapped her arms around herself, holding on as tight as she could.

Eva rushed in after her and climbed onto the bed. "He'll come back, Jennie. He will. He promised."

"I know. But he's leaving… My heart is riding away from me and I wasted so much time worrying."

Eva rubbed her arm. "Be thankful you discovered your feelings before he left. How many women gave up their men to war, thinking they'd come back? It's okay to be sad. But if you mourn too long you'll only make the waiting all the longer."

Eva climbed off the bed and left the room. Jennie wiped her eyes. If she hadn't realized what Ruby said was true, Aiden might not have cared to ever come back. If he'd thought he had no chance, he may have stayed away. She'd come so close to losing him. Jennie sat up on the bed and went to her writing desk.

Dear Ma,

I know it's been some time since I've written to you but there are things I want to talk to you about. I miss you so much. I've met someone who has me tied up in knots.

His name is Aiden Bradly and he's a little older than me. He used to be a miner but is now helping Beau on a ranch outside of Deadwood. Someone shot him and I thought I'd lose him. Until that happened, I knew I felt something for him, but it wasn't until I thought I'd lose him that I knew —

Jennie paused, holding the pencil above her paper. *Knew what?* She thought she loved him, but did she really? Ruby's words and even Eva's were a balm, but she needed her mother.

She continued:

...that I love him. There, I said it. But I need you so much. I'm so confused.

I miss you so very much and need your guidance. We all need you. I know Ruby told you Hattie ran off, but we feel so torn. I know I'm asking a lot, but if you could come just for a visit. I think it would help. I don't understand what my heart's telling me and I'm so worried I'll make a foolish choice.

Sincerely Yours, Jennie

She read the letter over again. It was very short for the cost of a stamp. But what she really wanted—what she'd always wanted—was Ma with them. Ma had always held the family together and she could fix it now. She folded the letter and put it in an envelope, taking care to write the name and address as clearly as possible.

Ruby climbed the ladder and sat on the chair next to the bed Jennie shared with the youngest two sisters. "I'm a little surprised at you, Jennie. We've seen Aiden hold your hand or maybe give you a small peck but that was quite a display for your sisters.

"Because Ma and Pa were very private, Beau and I have tried to keep our affection under wraps. We don't always succeed but we don't want them feeling uncomfortable with us."

Jennie turned to hide her discomfort. She'd felt what Ruby was hinting at when she'd caught Beau and Ruby kissing. She twisted her apron in her hands. "There's nothing wrong with what I did, Ruby. I'll miss him and I don't regret one thing."

"You didn't let me finish. I was going to say, perhaps it would be good for the younger girls to see more affection between Beau and I. So, when they reach your age, we don't have the same issues with them that you and Hattie have struggled with."

"Hattie... I wrote to Ma about her. I even asked her to come." She glanced at Ruby to see what she'd think. Ruby probably wouldn't stop her, but she should have asked permission first.

"Jennie. Do you really think she will? She was so enamored

with Carlton. I don't think she'll come out here. She raised you girls the best she could, and she was worn out after protecting you from Pa and his anger for so long."

Jennie let her shoulders fall. "I don't know if she'll come or not, but she won't if we don't ask." Jennie knotted her hands together in her lap. "What'll I do if he doesn't return?"

Ruby smiled and laid her hand over Jennie's. "You'll go on, just as you did before you knew him. Your life will be different, for sure. But you'll move on because you must."

"Did Beau say how long it would take him to get to Kansas?"

"I think he said it would take about five days. It's slow going through the hills. The rails can't travel any faster than fifteen miles per hour. Not much faster than a horse and carriage."

Jennie sighed and tapped her pencil against her desk. "I've never ridden a train. I just thought it would be…better."

"Trains will get better and faster. You'll see. In the meantime, I wouldn't expect Aiden back before a month. In that time, you can sew up some lovely dresses and start making things for when he returns and for the home you can make together. If he stays here and you marry him, you may have to live with him in that tiny cabin. At least until he can buy land and build you something else."

"I don't care where we live as long as he doesn't have to leave again."

"That's another thing you need to think about. What if he only comes back to collect you and whisk you back to Kansas? Or, like mail-order brides, perhaps he'll just wire money for a ticket and have you meet him there."

"I told him I don't want to go."

"Why ever not? You don't even like Deadwood. You could have a fresh start."

"A fresh start far away from anyone I've ever known."

Ruby smiled. "Jennie, that's what a woman does. In fact, the good Lord built us to do just that. To leave our father and mother and cleave unto our spouse. He equipped women with the ability to make friends in almost any situation. You'll never be alone for long."

"But…"

"Stop making excuses. You'd best be ready for whatever happens."

AIDEN WATCHED from his seat in the third car of old #52 as the miles crawled by. He'd gone from hills and valleys to more sharp lowlands where the railroad filled the area with rocks, gravel, and sand to make a straight path. Now the land was flattening out into prairie. A vast green sea opened in front of him and he couldn't quite tell where the green faded to blue to meet the sky. He sighed and slouched back into his seat. The ride had only been a little over a day so far and he couldn't shake the need to see Jennie. If he could turn the train back around, he would.

A small voice whispered *home* in his ear. But Kansas hadn't been home for a long time. He couldn't even be sure what he was going back to. Would his family even still be there? There was no way to know except to go. He'd already decided, as soon as he admitted to his parents that they were right, that he'd been foolish to leave, he would ask for their forgiveness. Then he'd head right back into town and get on the train. Nothing would keep him from running straight back into Jennie's arms.

The train squealed along the track. Just the day before he'd gotten the worst headache of his life from that sound. But the longer he was forced to ride the more he got used to it. As much as a man could. It was a little better if the window was closed but only if all the windows near him were closed too. That was rare. In the summer heat everyone wanted the windows open for a breath of air. Even if it meant the dust, smoke when they cleared the ash, and the awful whine of the wheels on the tracks came through the windows.

He thought about his older brother, Hugh. The good son. He'd always been there for Da and Mam. He'd done the work of two men when they were younger, and Aiden had always disliked him for it, holding a grudge. His brother tried to make him look bad, but now he knew that he'd just worked harder than Aiden. He'd been sure Da loved Hugh more. Now he knew that wasn't true. Hugh hadn't caused as much trouble as Aiden had. So, what appeared as more love was just less correction. He could see that now, looking back on his boyhood. If he'd known then what he knew now—that if he'd just minded his da—he never would've wanted to leave. He wouldn't have needed to. But then he never would've met Jennie.

Aiden sat forward in his seat as if struck by a lightning bolt. If he hadn't been a wandering fool and if the old prospector hadn't stolen his share, he never would've met the best thing that'd ever happened to him. He wove his fingers together and laid his head down in them. *Ok Lord. I see now. You can redeem all situations. But what about this? What about with my parents?*

He gazed out the window as the train entered yet another small town and slowed to take on and let off passengers. He watched as men came home to waiting wives with children. They embraced on the platform outside his window. Happiness. Tears. If only that was waiting for him. He'd—yet again—been the bad son and could expect correction. A heaviness lay over his heart and he tried to shake it off without success. He reaffirmed his resolve to continue. If men ignored the hard tasks the Lord asked of them, perhaps He'd stop asking anything of them at all. No, he had to do this *because* it was difficult. To prove, at least to the Lord, that he could listen and obey.

CHAPTER 20

Jennie glanced behind her. No one followed her from the cabin. She needed to get out and away from the crush of people stuffed into the tiny space. She'd taken to wandering to Aiden's cabin and sitting outside it with Jack. Somehow, she felt closer to him near the cabin that had only been his for a short time. She sat on the ground, leaning against his door and threw a stick for Jack to fetch. She turned her head to the sky as a giant rain drop splatted onto her nose.

She scrambled to her feet and rushed into the cabin. She hadn't set foot inside since Aiden had warned her not to enter a man's space. Even though he'd been gone for over two weeks she could still smell the scent of his soap, the oil he used to clean the gun Brody had given him, and the fresh straw he'd filled his tick with before he'd left. She lay on the bed and held his pillow close to her, breathing deeply. A sob choked her. She closed her eyes and could see his face clearly.

The journal he'd found in the tiny servant's room at the house in Deadwood was now on a small table next to his bed. Curiosity overtook her as rain splashed against the windows. She flipped it open to a page on Pearson's first discovery of gold near what would eventually become the city of Deadwood in 1875. The following year, a few gunfighters attempted to clear out the gold rush riffraff. John Reid would claim he'd civilized the town. Jennie laughed at the idea of a gunfighter civilizing anything.

Outside, the rain now came down in sheets and Jennie grabbed the flexibles from the mantle and lit Aiden's lantern so she could keep reading. In 1876, the town grew from 'a group of miners and riff-raff' to a platted town. At that point, the diary took on real life. Instead of blurry photos taken from a pinpoint camera, the writer had cut clippings from a newspaper. She traced the fine print with her finger as she read of Crazy Horse and Sitting Bull, the birth of the Deadwood's sister city Lead, and how it grew from almost nothing overnight.

The book that Aiden had cherished enough to save linked her to him in a way she couldn't explain. And she read the pages as if she needed them to survive. She began to see why it had fascinated him so much. Deadwood had a rich history that wasn't all about gamblers, miners, and prostitutes, though they definitely had their roles.

She read how the *Deadwood Times*, the very paper Beau and Aiden had worked for, lobbied for a tax on prostitution to help clean up the city. And how much of the town burned to the ground in the fire of 1879. She sighed, closing the book and rubbing her eyes. She glanced out the window and realized she'd been there for hours. Ruby and everyone would be worried about her. She placed the book back where she'd found it and blew out the lantern.

Jack sat by the door and rushed out into the drizzle as soon as she opened it. Jennie held up her hand so she could see through the rain and picked her way over the puddles to her house. She said a little prayer that they had all stayed inside waiting for her as there wasn't far she could go.

She pushed open the door and quickly closed it behind her, leaning against it.

Beau stood in the kitchen, his arms crossed over his wide chest and his brow deeply furrowed. "Where can you have possibly been for the last few hours that you didn't hear Ruby and I calling for you?"

Jennie glanced down at her feet and felt the heat crawl up her face. "I was over at Aiden's cabin when it started to rain. I thought it would be over quickly, so I went inside to wait it out. Then it started pouring. I had nothing to do so I was reading a book about Deadwood...and lost all track of time."

"You must've had a one-track mind. That cabin isn't more than twenty yards away."

"I'm sorry. I hope you didn't worry too much."

"Oh, we were worried but not half as worried as your Ma."

Jennie's head snapped up and that's when she saw her mother, Maeve, standing behind Beau with a smile on her face.

"Ma!" She ran forward, pushing her way past Beau and into ma's waiting arms. "You came! But how did you get here so quickly? I only sent that letter two weeks ago?"

"The mail runs fast now that the trains carry it. I bought my ticket as soon as I got it and the train took a little over a week through the hills. If my daughter asks me to come, I come." Maeve held her close. "Now, what's this I hear about Aiden Bradly?"

Ruby came forward and pulled out a chair for Ma. "Aiden is a young man we met on our way to Deadwood. He has steadily earned Beau's trust."

"It isn't Beau's trust I'm concerned with. It's how my daughter feels about this young man that matters."

Jennie sat down next to Ma. "He and I didn't get along at first. We were at odds, you could say. Then we found out he hurt his feet and I had to tend to him for a time. That's when he stopped teasing me so much and started talking to me."

Maeve laughed. "Men sometimes tease girls they like. Not cruelly, I mean, but they do."

"I was just starting to think about him more often when he told me he was going to up and leave as soon as he got the chance. Then all I could think was that I wouldn't ever really matter to him...like you did to Pa."

Maeve reached out and took Jennie's hand in hers then she

glanced into the face of each daughter standing all around the table. "I want to tell you something. All of you. I loved your father for a time. Toward the end...he wasn't the same man I fell in love with. Love makes us blind to human faults. But know that if Aiden loves you, he's blind to yours too."

Jennie watched as Ma shook her head and the creases beside her eyes seemed to deepen. "About the time Hattie and Eva were born he changed. He really thought that once we had a girl, we'd certainly have a boy. He went into a terrible rage and moved us out of Yellow Medicine. Away from everyone. Two girls were more than enough. Four was an outrage. He accused me of some terrible things, believed it couldn't be his fault we had girls. That's when loving him became hard."

Maeve pulled her hand away and rested her elbow on the table, cradling her head against it. "By the time Francis was born he was out of money that he'd saved when he sold our house in town. He needed to find some way to make money or we'd all starve so he built his first still. It wasn't long until all manner of men came to our door at all hours, looking for your father...and moonshine."

Ma closed her eyes and her forehead was deeply lined.

"I don't tell you all this to make you afraid of marriage. What I *would* tell you, is this. If I'd looked at who your father was before we were married, if I'd *really* looked at his character, I could've seen the man he would become. I let his charm blind me. I was caught up in his fascination with me, and his kiss."

The younger girls giggled into their hands.

Jennie frowned. "But how? How do I look beyond the feelings? How do I know if I've found a good man?"

"When he hurts you, does he give a hollow apology or none at all, and does he do the same things again anyway?"

"No, not at all."

"That's good. I also like that Beau trusts him." She glanced at Ruby. "Despite what I said earlier." She smiled up at Beau. "Men don't usually feel the need to hide who they are from other men. So, if Beau trusts him then Aiden most likely has hidden nothing from you. But lastly, I want him to pass the mother test. I talked to

Mr. Ferguson on the ride here and he's agreed to let me stay in the big house until Aiden comes back. If I like him, I'll give my blessing and I'll return to Cutter's Creek after you're married."

Ruby sighed. "That's wonderful, but what about Hattie?"

Maeve shook her head. "Hattie's had her own demon for a long time. Longer than any of you know. She'll come home when she's ready. Even if you find her, it has to be when she's ready or you'll push her further away. Ah, my girls. It's so good to see you. I've missed all of you these last months and I can't wait to tell you all that's happened with me. But first, we should eat our supper and get a rest. It's getting late."

Jennie gasped. "You didn't eat? I'm so sorry for holding you up."

Ruby stood and rested her hands atop Jennie's shoulders. "We all need a break from the walls sometimes, Jennie. Just let me know before you fly away next time."

CHAPTER 21

Having finished her chores, it was time to spend the afternoon with Ma on the couch in the small parlor of their cabin. She sucked in a deep breath as she searched through the large stack of fabric before her.

Maeve touched a white linen. "What a generous thing for Mr. Ferguson to do."

Jennie smiled. "I wasn't expecting all this, that's for sure. He said it had been stored in his mother's cabin and he found it after she passed."

Maeve opened and measured a white cotton against her arm. "These will make some lovely sheets for your bed."

Jennie glanced at the floor. "Yes, well…"

Maeve laughed. "Let me tell you what's been happening with me the last few months. Carlton and I have become dear friends. We attended a few weddings and a summer barn dance together."

Jennie eyed her mother. Carlton Williams could barely walk. Dancing would be out of the question.

"I see you looking at me like I'm lying. I said we went. I never said we danced. We aren't like that, anyway. Carlton gets weak some days. His daughter is there to care for him since their housekeeper, Ivy, left last winter. But I do hope Aiden returns quickly so I can rejoin him. Carol isn't one for being a nurturer."

Jennie glanced out the window behind them. "I hope he returns soon, too."

"Let's get started on your hope chest. You're getting a late start. I never thought I'd be helping any of my daughters put one together. I'm so happy I could be here."

"I'm afraid the other girls will be jealous if you don't come back for them, too."

Maeve held her needle up to the light and threaded it, running the thread all the way to the other end and tying it off. "That'll be a while. I don't think Hattie is destined for marriage. At least not now. Though she and Eva are twins, she still acts quite young. But I would like, once Carlton is gone, to come here to stay with you. I didn't think it would be quite so lovely or as nice as Montana."

Jennie picked up a soft flannel and rubbed the light fleece fabric against her cheek. "I didn't want to live here at first. I missed Cutter's Creek, and you. I didn't think I'd ever like it. But the longer I'm here, the more I can't imagine ever leaving. It's more than just that my sisters are here now. It's like the Dakota's are part of me. The Sioux called this land the *Paha Sapa*, their holy lands. I can see how they think that. The land, the air, the water, it all gets inside you."

Maeve nodded as she whip-stitched the edges of a sheet. "I believe it and I also believe with all my heart that all my girls will find happiness here. Even my wayward child."

"It isn't your fault, Ma."

One side of Maeve's mouth turned down. "There're only so many places you can seat blame. Hattie should never have had to learn to escape her own life. But she did. She did because of *my* choice to be with the man I'd chosen."

Maeve draped the fabric out over her and sighed deeply, her glance darted from Jennie back to the fabric. "Just be sure to make room for me wherever you call home. I need to be with Carlton for now, but I'll be alone once he's gone. His daughter, Carol, is sweet now. But I don't see her welcoming me forever. I'm sure she and her husband will start a family of their own soon and fill that big house."

"Won't you want to stay with Ruby and the girls?" Jennie laid out the flannel to cut pieces for some sleeping gowns.

"Not if they're still in this house. I'd feel as if I was intruding here. I suppose I could ask Mr. Ferguson if I could live with him in his large house." She laughed. "I doubt he and his housekeeper would mind."

Jennie smiled. "I guess we'll ford that river when we get to it. You aren't yet ready to move here permanently."

"No, I'm not. At least there's a lot I can do in the short time I'll be here."

CHAPTER 22

A iden tossed his pack over his shoulder and nodded to people he'd briefly met as he climbed off the train. The little town of Belvue was an hour's walk—if he couldn't find anyone headed that way to ride with. He shifted his hat and glanced around. Women in colorful walking dresses waved to one another in the street. Men chatted on the corners or carried loads as they did their work. Dust rose from the street as wagons, horses, and men went about their day.

The easiest way to find a ride would be to start walking and see who came along. He smiled and nodded to anyone who managed to catch his eye as he made his way west to the edge of town. The open prairie spread before him with a rope of worn dirt for a road. After about twenty minutes of dragging his feet down the roadside, a wagon came up behind him.

"Ho there! You headed for Belvue?"

Aiden nodded. "All the way, if you go that far."

The man moved over on the seat and Aiden tossed his pack in the back and climbed up.

"Not many people visit Belvue. Going to see someone?" He flicked the lines and the swayback old mares plodded forward.

"Yeah. I'm going home. Name's Bradly, Aiden Bradly."

"Well, if it ain't..." He laughed. "Your pa been talking about you for a year. He had an accident last winter though. Ain't been the same since."

Aiden's gut tightened. "Is he all right?" He held his breath, waiting for the man's reply. It had been almost two months since he'd decided to come home, but even before then. His da had needed him.

"As all right as he *can* be. Crushed part of his back. He don't work no more. Walks with a cane."

Aiden's head sagged between his shoulders and his anger with himself burned hot. He should've been there. "I'm sorry to hear that. Are Hugh and Peader still there helping him?"

The old man brushed his chin with his leather-gloved hand. "Hugh is, but not Peader. He was with your pa when the accident happened. He tried to save your pa by pushing him out of the way of a rolling wagon piled high with flour. They were both hurt. Peader had gangrene set into his leg. They tried to take it, but he never beat the infection. I'm sorry."

Horror and grief collided within Aiden. He'd been selfish and run off then tried to justify it because he'd met Jennie. He shook his head. He'd have to see the state of the farm when he got there. Leaving to return to Jennie may be impossible. Jennie felt an ocean away and moving further by the second.

"Sir. Why don't you drop me off at the edge of town? I think I need a walk."

"Now son, this wasn't your doing. You can't get down on anyone. Bad things happen. That's just the way of it. It would've happened just the same if you'd been here or not. 'Cept it might've been you that yanked your father out of the way. Then you'd be cold in your grave. Things work the way they do for a reason. It ain't your place to ask why. Just how."

"What do you mean? What's the difference?"

The old man gazed over the vast prairie dotted with small houses. "Big difference. If you get stuck wondering why, you end up missing it. If you ask how, the good Lord can use the change. Well, then you're getting somewhere."

"I don't see how this can serve the Lord. I got a gal waiting for me back in South Dakota. If my family needs me, I may never see her again." He felt his blood rage in his veins. His brother was gone forever. He hadn't even known because his family hadn't known where he was to send him a letter about it.

"Well, if she don't love you enough to understand then maybe she ain't the woman you thought she was."

"But her family's there too, and they mean a lot to her. How can I make her choose my family over hers?"

"You haven't even been out to see your family yet and you're making plans. Maybe they don't want you there. Maybe they're so used to just living day to day that they can be just fine without you... Or maybe your brother is tired. Maybe he's ready to sell out to a pushy ranch owner who's ready to give them a hunk of cash. Maybe you're here to convince them to move on? You don't know why you're here yet."

"Someone wants our land?"

"Yup. Paul Turbin."

Aiden watched as his own driveway touched the horizon ahead of them. The old man pulled up on the lines and held out his hand. "I wish you luck, Aiden Bradly. Pray and listen."

Aiden climbed down the side of the wagon and grabbed his pack. "Thank you. I'll do that. Wait, I didn't get your name?" The old man waved and turned back, the squeak of the wheels and the jangle of the traces continued down the road.

Each step was familiar. Each large rock embedded into the ground brought back memories of running down the worn trail on the way to and from school. Hugh had never raced. He'd been too old for such fun, but he and Peader had. Peader. The loss hit him hard in the gut and he stopped. The farm held so many memories.

"I should have written... Then they could've told me." He kicked a stone off the path. "I don't deserve to even eat a meal with them."

He cleared the slight rise and his home lay before him. An old barn sat to the side of the house and a newer machine shed lay beyond that. Someone sat on the porch on the old rocking chair. He stood and Aiden recognized Da, although he was now stooped, and his once bright red hair was white. He slowly made his way off the porch and toward Aiden.

He'd been worried about this moment for two months and now it was here. His da could curse him and tell him to leave and never come back. Aiden wanted to get the confrontation over, but he had to apologize before his da had a chance to say anything. Then maybe there'd be a chance at forgiveness.

Da stopped a few steps from him, his face flushed and hands shaking. Aiden waited. Da held out his shriveled arms and looked Aiden in the eye with all the pain of a man who'd had everything but life taken from him. "My son."

Aiden rushed to his da and embraced him. "I'm so sorry, Da. You were right. About everything. I was a fool. I should've stayed."

His da grasped his shoulders in hands that were surprisingly strong. "None of that matters. You're home. Come, your mam will want to see you right away."

Aiden tossed his bag back over his shoulder and followed, feeling for the first time like an outsider on the land he'd grown up on. His mam rushed from the house, then gathered her skirts in her fists to run and meet them. He caught her in his arms and held her tight. When he released her, she cupped his face in her hands as a tear ran down her weathered cheek.

"Is it really true? Are you really home?" She reached for her apron to wipe the tears from her eyes.

"I'm back," he said, wishing he could tell them everything. Their joy at his arrival was so strong he couldn't bring himself to tell them about Jennie. Would they hate her for taking him from them again?

"Come. I've got supper on the table. Hugh will be so glad to have help again."

They walked with him to the house and opened the door. His chest clenched at the sight. The house hadn't changed at all. Ma's patchwork quilt lay folded neatly on the back of the old couch. Under that quilt was woodwork that he and Peader had carved up when they'd gotten their first knives…and gotten a tanning shortly after. The fireplace was as clean as mam always kept it with the smell of bread baking in a hanging pot inside. Not once had they run out of bread as children. He could count on a thick warm slice any time he'd been hungry. His stomach rumbled at the thought and mam clapped him on the shoulder and laughed. He winced and rubbed the still sore wound.

"What happened?" Da asked?

"I was shot. I was working for a cattle rancher near Deadwood and his neighbor wanted more than his share. I got in the way." Aiden tugged at the shoulder of his vest to cover the spot. He didn't even want to talk about Deadwood. It would lead to too many questions.

Hugh strode into the house and stared at him for a moment then turned to wash his hands, black with oil from working. "So, the favorite son returns. Did you bring us the famed largest gold nugget you've ever seen, *dearthàir*? Did you come bringing anything but another mouth for me to feed?"

Da jabbed his cane into the floor and growled. "Enough! I'll not have fighting. This is a day of rejoicing! My son is home!"

"Forgive me Da, for not joining in your celebration. The threshing team that was supposed to be here next week has been held up by the weather further south. From their telegram, they're at least a week behind. If the rains come, they won't be able to get into the field at all."

Aiden shifted in his seat. "Why don't we use the old thresher. We could get it done together."

Hugh arched an eyebrow. "You hardly lifted a finger to help when you lived here. There's no way I'm going through the work of getting everything up and working just to discover it's too much for you. That'd be a waste of time."

Da held up his hand. "It's time to eat. Your mam has worked hard to prepare us a good meal. Let's not spoil it."

The four of them sat at the table but his mam placed an extra plate where Peader used to sit. She held the plate for an extra moment then shook her head and went back to bringing the food to the table.

Da sat at the same seat he'd always occupied. "Since you haven't asked, I'll guess someone told you about Peader."

"Yes. An old man gave me a ride to Belvue and as soon as he found out who I was he told me what happened. He also told me about Paul Turbin." Aiden glanced at Hugh to gauge his brother's thoughts.

Hugh shook his head. "I want to finish the harvest... After that... I make no guarantees. This isn't family land. We've lived here one generation. The rest of our family are still in New York."

"Do you want to go back there?" Aiden couldn't understand why Hugh would even consider going back. They'd left for a reason.

Da knocked his cane against the floor. "No. I won't go back. I don't have the strength to help Hugh anymore, Aiden. But you do. You can save the farm from Turbin's clutches."

Aiden sighed and scooped some turnips onto his plate.

"What's the matter? Now that you're here, you don't want to commit to work? Just like it used to be." Hugh sneered.

Aiden slammed his hand down on the table. "You don't know what my last year has been like."

Hugh narrowed his eyes. "And you don't know what it's been like here. Because you left and never bothered to tell us where you were." He leaned back in his seat and crossed his arms over his chest. "So, you said you got shot up working on a ranch near Deadwood. Isn't that where they found gold a few years back? Not surprised you'd be there. Did you get shot protecting a claim? Prospectors are miserable low-lifes who'd just as soon steal from you as they would work." He spat the words at Aiden.

Aiden shot to his feet. His brother only knew one prospector, him. So the slight hit home. "You shouldn't talk about what you don't know and will never understand."

"Are you challenging me, little brother?" Hugh stood and

leveraged his hands on the table, leaning forward and staring at Aiden.

His brother had at least forty pounds on him and a few inches, but anger could take you a long way. "Yeah, I guess I am." Aiden leaned forward toward Hugh, his muscles tense and ready.

Mam slammed her spoon down on the table. "Boys! You mind yourselves at my table. I'll not have you two throwing your muscles around here. Eat your supper then take it outside."

Aiden sat down. "Yes, Mam."

Hugh scowled at him. "After we eat, brother."

CHAPTER 23

Aiden massaged the sore muscles of his hands. Throwing hay was a lot different than throwing an axe but he wouldn't slow down. He couldn't. Not with Hugh dogging him at every turn. He'd been back for a little over a week and, though his body was sore from the work, the field was in before the threshing team had even come to town. It had been long hours in the hot sun, but his brother hadn't said a word. So at least supper time was quiet.

He strode into the barn and over to the horse he'd been riding, Sol.

"So, the favorite son finally appears. Day starts at sunup, brother." Hugh tossed a saddle blanket at him.

"Cut the *favorite son* nonsense. We both know it was *you* da favored."

"How dare you come back here after being gone so long? All I heard for a year was moaning about the son that left. What about the sons who worked day in and day out to make the farm work? One of those sons gave his *life* for this place. But it never mattered since you were gone."

Aiden held his anger in check. He'd never been favored, had

always been a breath away from the woodshed. Hugh would never know that humiliation. "He never loved me! I was always in trouble. I left so he'd never have to deal with me again and so I could become a better man. I left so that when I came back with enough wealth that Da wouldn't have to work so hard he'd finally see *me*. Not the oldest son who was trusted and would take over everything. Not the youngest son who was allowed free rein. But as *me* the one who tried so hard to be seen at all that I would do *anything* for it. You don't get it. He praised you for everything." Aiden couldn't keep his voice in check. He slammed his hand against the wall and the tools hanging above his head shifted and clinked together.

Hugh turned his back on Aiden and leaned against the horse stall. "I wasn't allowed to play. Even as a child. I was always in his shadow. Always had to learn something new and I had to do it right the first time. While you and Peader were out fishing and having fun, I was learning how to plow. How to work."

"At least he showed you! I had to learn from you, from someone who hated me!"

"I never hated you! I wanted to *be* you! Until you came back, I had da convinced it was a good idea to sell to Turbin. I'm only thirty-three years old and I'm tired, Aiden. I want to be married, have a family…and I can't because I work all the time. I feel guilty if I take a day off. But if I don't do it the work won't get done. This farm grew as we brothers did so all three of us would help and prosper when we came of age. I can't do the work of three anymore. I won't."

"Hugh, I never planned to saddle you with all this. I didn't leave to make you work harder."

"That may not have been your intent but that's exactly what happened. I'm going over to Turbin's to try to get him to hold his offer. You try to convince Da that it's a good idea. If you don't succeed, I'm leaving anyway. We've got plenty of family in New York that would help me get on my feet."

Hugh mounted his horse and rode away. Aiden watched the

open gate for a minute then turned at the sound of muffled footsteps behind him.

Mam folded her hands in front of her and regarded him with soft eyes. "Why do I get the feeling there's more to your story than what you told Hugh? You've been here only a few days, but I can tell you've changed. You yearn for something that isn't here." She laid her hand on his shoulder and the sadness in her eyes tore at his heart.

He didn't want to hurt Mam, but he ached for his Jennie. "Do you remember how you told us you and Da fell in love and decided to move away from your family to give your new family a better chance?"

"Of course I do." Her face softened and she patted his shoulder gently.

"I met someone in Deadwood. Jennie Arnsby. She reminds me of you a little. The way her temper gets her sometimes. But mostly she's as sweet as can be. I miss her, Mam. I miss that girl so much it hurts."

"Why'd you come back, Aiden?" She pulled him over to some bales of straw and sat him down.

"I felt like I needed to. Like I had to tell Da that he was right and that I was sorry for the things I said and for leaving the way I did."

"You did that the very first thing when you got here. Colin told me it was so. But why didn't you tell us about this young woman? Didn't you think that would bring us even more joy? To see you happy and married? Da and I thought you came home because your fervor for that life had finally diminished."

"Mam, I'd like to take a little extra time and convince Da to listen to Hugh's plan. Then, I want you to think about coming back to Deadwood with me. I could build a house near the ranch where I work, big enough for you and Da, Rachel, me and Jennie."

"And all the grandkids, don't forget those!" She smiled and patted his leg.

"Do you think Da would consider it?"

"I think he will, but I worry about Hugh. He's had quite the burden this last year. I thought he'd be happy when you returned, but perhaps it was just too late. I'll talk to Colin for you, you can talk to Hugh. New York is not where he wants to be. My sisters and brothers still live in poverty." She closed her eyes. "He doesn't know what he wants. Only that he wants away from here."

"I'll talk to him, Mam. But please, even if he chooses to go to New York, will you come with me to Deadwood?"

She crooked the side of her mouth. "I hope your bride and I get along."

CHAPTER 24

Jennie scanned the stack of gowns, towels, sheets, night clothes, napkins, curtains, and other things laying on her side of the bed. It was all meant to go inside the beautiful cedar chest Beau had made for her.

The cedar bushes were all over the pastures and Brody had asked Beau to remove them. He had. Then he'd brought the thick trunks to the mill in Lead to be hewn down into boards.

Jennie ran her hand over the lacquered top. It was beautiful. She'd never owned anything like it.

Maeve slowly climbed the ladder and sat on the bed next to all the clothing. "I'm so sorry I couldn't be here long enough to meet your Aiden. I'll try not to think less of him for not returning right away so I could."

Jennie closed her eyes. "I hope we didn't work this hard for nothing. After the third week I started to lose hope. Now it's been five weeks since he left and not even a note."

Maeve kissed the top of her head. "Dear, sweet Jennie. Don't lose hope. While it would've been nice if he'd written a letter telling you what was keeping him, we don't know what trials he's going through. I hope that you'll write me as soon as he does return."

"He has to come back first." Jennie lifted a few things and laid them gently in the chest, the scent of cedar a welcome change from the scent of the ranch.

"Don't worry. He *will* return and then all these things will be ready to use. You'll see. Goodbye, dear. I'm getting a ride into Deadwood with Brody. He's quite a nice man. Not as nice as Carlton, mind you, but nice." She stood and held out her arms.

Jennie stood and hugged her mother tightly. "Thank you. It meant so much to have you here. It would've been an endless five weeks without you."

"Yes, I'd think you'd have worn the pages near through on that Deadwood book of Aiden's." She winked.

Jennie smiled. "He told me to find something I love about Deadwood. Turns out, what I loved was him."

Maeve nodded and swung down the ladder. She waved one last time as she closed the front door. Jennie sat back down on the bed and picked up one of the handkerchiefs she'd made for Aiden. She hadn't known his middle initial or even if he had one, so she'd embroidered it A.B. in pretty blue floss. The stitches were neat even though they'd worked quickly on each and every piece. Her sisters had even helped with a few of the less intimate items, like tablecloths. Jennie touched the soft linen to her face then pulled it away as a tear fell. She didn't want to have to wash and press it again.

The sound of the wagon rolling away made her stand and go to the window. She'd searched the horizon every time she'd heard one for the last few weeks. This time it was her mother leaving. Going home to Cutter's Creek. If she'd had her way back in late April, when they'd left, she never would've met Aiden. Many other things wouldn't have happened either, but meeting Aiden tempered the more painful things.

Slowly, she packed each item in the chest and closed the lid. Beau would have to bring it back downstairs, as she could barely lift it empty. Where he'd put it remained to be seen. If Aiden were back, they could just store it in his cabin. He wouldn't care to look inside it so it would still be a gift when she opened it for him. But she couldn't ask Beau to put it there before Aiden returned.

She climbed down the ladder and curled onto the couch. Beau and Ruby had lightened her chores with the amount of sewing she'd been doing with Ma. But now that she was gone, she'd get right back to her normal chores.

Soon, I'll have my own house and there'll be no one to help me with my chores. "But only if he comes home," she muttered.

Jennie opened the Deadwood journal to a news clipping from September of 1879. *A fire erupted from an overturned kerosene lantern and quickly spread to a nearby hardware store where barrels of gunpowder exploded into a massive inferno that left over two thousand people without shelter.* Jennie read further and her eyes grew heavy. She moved to the rug in front of the fireplace and pulled a blanket over her, rubbing her eyes to stay awake. She didn't want to be found napping in the middle of the day, but Ma's departure had left her exhausted.

Flopping the book back open in front of her, she ran her hand down the column until she found her place and began reading more about the bakery where the fire began. The words merged together on the page and she stared into the fire in front of her. The flames burst in and out of focus. She felt as if the fire pulled her into its depths then shoved her out.

Her lids closed and when she opened them again, she was surrounded by fire. A towering inferno lay in front of her. It was the house from Deadwood.

She ran inside and the bright orange flames danced all around, singeing her skin and clothing. Something was inside the house, but the painful heat kept pushing her back. She slipped past the flames, but they chased her back to Aiden's room. Instead of Aiden, Hattie was there, a shell of the girl she used to be. Hattie looked up at her, her eyes empty of emotion, her dress torn and tattered. She poured a bottle of alcohol onto the flames around her own bed and laughed. "You can't help me now. I'm too far gone."

CHAPTER 25

Aiden's hands slipped on the side of the wagon. The closer he came to Jennie, the more he wanted to jump from the wagon and run. He had to see her. His heart beat erratically in his chest and his muscles wouldn't relax. Five weeks was five too many. He shook his hands, one at a time, to relieve the tension.

Colin elbowed his wife. "Martha, do you think the lad's nervous?"

She smiled back at him. "I'd say he is. He's never been good about writing letters. I'd bet he's worried what she'll think when he walks through the door."

His parents had always been able to read him well. He was just glad Hugh had decided to stay in Deadwood to find work because Hugh would go out of his way to make Aiden even more nervous. Even after the evening they'd spent in the barn just before they'd left, he still knew how to rile Aiden. And enjoyed it. The wagon leaned as they started the trail around the hill up to the ranch house. Colin pitched to the side as the wagon tilted. Martha screamed and Aiden reached back and caught him before he fell out. His sore shoulder wrenched painfully but he wouldn't say a word. Complaining would do nothing.

Colin laughed. "I managed the whole trip and now that we're here, I almost hurt myself."

Aiden could read the pain in his eyes. He'd been so strong before. It had to be hard to be reduced to shuffling around with a cane. Brody navigated the last turn up the hill and the house appeared before them. Aiden chuckled as his parents gasped over the site of the large house. His happiness was short-lived as Brody pulled the wagon to a stop. Aiden heard terrible screams of pain that made the hair on his arms stand on end. They were coming from Beau's cabin. Ruby ran from the barn toward their home and Aiden jumped from the bed of the wagon, making it to the door before Ruby.

He threw open the door to see Jennie reaching into the fireplace. The arms of her gown were alight, and she was screaming. Her eyes were open but unseeing, as if she were blind.

Aiden ran to the fireplace and yanked her out, smothering her in his arms to put out the flames. He grabbed a blanket from the couch and wrapped it around her, hoping to kill any remaining embers. Jennie shook in his arms and he tilted her head up. Her vacant eyes stared at the ceiling above him.

"Jennie?" he kissed each of her eyes. He searched her face for some sign of recognition.

Ruby touched Jennie's shoulder. "Jennie?" She shook her and Jennie continued to look at the ceiling. Ruby picked up Jennie's scorched hand, already swelling and turning a bright pink. She led Aiden with Jennie to the table and brought over a pitcher of clean water. She dunked Jennie's hand in it and Jennie screamed, yanking it out.

Jennie looked down at her hands, then at Ruby. "What...? What happened?"

"Aiden pulled you out of the fireplace. I think you should tell *us* what happened."

"Aiden?" Jennie turned and her eyes locked onto his chest then moved slowly up to his face, locking on his eyes. "You're home...?"

333

"I am." He wrapped his arms around her. "I've never been so scared in all my days. I don't ever want to hear you scream like that again." He pulled her close to him and she shuddered and wrapped her arms around him, her tears wetting his shirt.

He kissed the top of her head. "I'm home to stay, Jennie-girl. In fact, I've brought my family with me so neither of us has to sacrifice the love of our families to be together."

She backed away from him. "Oh, Aiden. You missed my mother! I waited and waited but she had to leave earlier today."

"I didn't miss her. I saw Brody at the train station with a lovely lady and he introduced me to your mother right before she boarded her train. I wish I'd been able to get back quicker but there was a lot of work to do on the farm before we could sell it."

He reached for her wrists, avoiding the hands that were now swollen to twice their size. "I want you to soak those in cold water while I go take care of my parents. You'll get to meet them soon. Let Ruby take care of you. We'll all hear what happened after I get my parents settled so they can rest."

Jennie nodded and Ruby took her back into her room to see to the burns on Jennie's arms and hands. Aiden shook his head and glanced at the fireplace. If he'd gotten there any later, it may have caught her hair and the damage would've been much worse. Why would she stick her hands into the flames and what was wrong with her that she didn't see him? The questions weighed like rocks on him.

Martha waited next to the wagon. Colin had already gone inside with Brody.

"I hope whoever that was is all right now. I've never heard such a noise." She shuddered.

"Yes, she's fine now and her sister Ruby's taking care of her. I'll get you settled, then you can meet Jennie tonight at supper. Does that sound good?"

Martha nodded. "That's fine. It's been a long journey. We haven't traveled so much since we came to Kansas. I'm ready for a rest."

Aiden put his hand at her waist and led her up to Brody's house. He opened the door for her. Mrs. Chen waited just inside.

"Mrs. Bradly?" Lei tilted her head.

"Yes, I am." Martha held out her hand.

Lei inspected her hand for a moment, then reached out and shook it. "Your Mr. Bradly is resting."

Aiden waited for his mother to go upstairs, but as soon as they stepped out of his sight, he ran back outside and over to Beau's house. He didn't bother with knocking. Jennie couldn't wait.

His eyes filled with the sight of her as he slammed the door open. She sat at the table holding out her arms, wearing only a chemise with her stays and a skirt. Both women jumped when the door hit the wall and Jennie moved to cover herself, but Ruby grabbed her upper arms and held them wide.

"You're covered enough. I need to get this salve on you right away or you'll scar. Stay put." Ruby glared back at him. "Aiden, I have a door for a reason. Kindly turn your back so I can get this done."

He blinked and forced his mouth closed. His beautiful Jennie was all shades of pink and red with harsh white lines around the reddest parts. He slowly turned away from her and his heart sunk. Would she be scarred? Did it matter?

"Jennie, while I finish wrapping your arms why don't you tell Aiden and me what happened. Is it like when we were kids?"

Jennie's voice was soft. "Yes. I think so. I know I used to walk in my sleep and wake up in strange places. It hasn't happened for a long time though."

"You used to sleep so deeply that you could walk around the house, eyes open, and we didn't know you weren't awake. None of us knew if there was something wrong with you or not. But then you grew out of it," said Ruby.

"I was reading the Deadwood book of Aiden's. It was a journal someone had left behind. I was reading about a fire and Ma had just talked to me about Hattie. I guess my mind confused the two in my sleep. I remember seeing her in the house in Deadwood. She was in a huge fire and I wanted to save her. She poured something on the flames, and they erupted all around her. I tried to pull her out…and then I was standing in the kitchen with my hands in cold water. It hurts so bad." Jennie's voice shook and Aiden clenched his fists to keep from rushing over to comfort her.

"Aiden, Jennie is covered now. You can turn around," Ruby said.

Aiden spun and ran over to Jennie. He came behind her and wrapped his arms around her shoulders to avoid touching her burns. "If you walk in your sleep, we'll find some way to heat without fire. Something. When we're together I'll protect you. I won't let this happen again."

Ruby stood up tall and slammed her hands to her hips. "Aiden Bradly, that might be the worst proposal I've ever heard. And don't you dare make another sound until you talk to Beau. You have to ask *him* first."

Aiden pegged her with a smile he felt right down to his toes and squeezed Jennie closer. "I don't have to do any such thing. I asked her mam when I met her at the train. She not only gave her blessing. She laid a kiss on my cheek for good luck."

Aiden came around to the front of Jennie's chair and knelt in front of her. He didn't want to hurt her hands, so he laid them on her knees. *"M'fhíorghrá*, I promise to love you forever. Will you marry me and love me too?"

She lifted one of her bandaged hands and touched his cheek so gently. A timid smile touched her lips. "I will. I'll love you always, Aiden."

He laid his head in her lap and every fear he'd had of not measuring up lifted. He was himself. That was more than enough for his Jennie.

"Now that's better." Ruby grumbled as she left them, closing the door softly behind her.

CHAPTER 26

S*ix weeks later*

JENNIE SAT in the back of the wagon with Colin as they drove down the peak of Ferguson hill. Colin poked her gently with his cane.

"The lad says you need to close your eyes." He laughed.

Jennie shook her head, used to his teasing at this point. Now she knew where Aiden got it. "I've been waiting for a month while he and Beau have been working. I can't close my eyes. I want to see it!"

He laughed harder. "Feeling cramped in that little cabin, eh? You should've seen the little place Martha and I had when we first moved. Not much more than two walls leaned in on one another."

Jennie's leg danced up and down as she nervously waited for the wagon to descend. At first, she'd been disappointed when Brody sold them the land at the base of the hill. The very edge of his property. They would live right off the road without any of the views the upper homes boasted. Then Aiden had brought her down and showed her the spot. The area at the base of the hill reminded her a little of Montana and it was nestled in a small valley between three hills. Protected, sheltered.

They curved around the hill and she could see the roof. It was much bigger than she'd thought it would be. A two-story home with white painted boards and green trim. It had a porch big enough to sit on and Aiden had even planted some flowers along the front for her. Jennie couldn't speak. All the words she could think to say were trapped behind the lump in her throat.

Aiden came out of the house and closed the door behind him, beaming as the wagon came to a stop. He looked perfect standing on the porch of their home. A feeling of peace and contentment washed over her. She'd never fear change again. Not as long as they were together.

"Mrs. Bradly, what do you think of your new house?" He held his arms wide for her.

She jumped from the wagon and rushed to him, throwing her arms around his neck. He lifted her and swung her around. "Let me show you the inside." He opened the door and led her in.

Jennie stood in a large living room, already furnished.

"I don't understand… Where did this furniture come from? It isn't new but it isn't from the cabin." She turned to glance at him then back at the couch covered with a hand sewn quilt.

"It was my parents'. They had it all shipped here when we moved. It's one of the things that took so long to arrange before we left. Hugh helped me move it out and get it set up."

"Hugh? I haven't seen him since the wedding. I thought he'd be gone to Lead by now."

Hugh appeared from the back room and touched his hat. He was so like Aiden but darker and taller and so quiet. He hadn't said more than a handful of words to her since they'd returned. Where Aiden had the light red hair of his father. Hugh had his mother's dark hair. Even when he smiled there was a brooding secret behind his eyes and he never laughed.

"Thank you, Hugh. Without your help, I would've had to wait

even longer to be in my house." She squeezed Aiden closer and winked.

Hugh shook his head. "Aiden had to hurry or he would've missed my help. I'm headed to Lead this afternoon. I'll be there for a while. Bullock is sending me on a special job to find your Hattie. He thinks she's in Lead…and that she probably couldn't leave if she wanted to."

Jennie gasped and covered her mouth then dropped her hands and hid them in the folds of her dress. They were still discolored from the burns and they embarrassed her to no end. She'd seen the doctor in Deadwood. He didn't know if they'd ever heal completely. Only time would tell. In the meantime, she covered them.

Aiden put his arm around her shoulder. "Godspeed, brother."

Hugh nodded. "I'll need all the help I can get." He tipped his hat. "I'll go help Mam and Da move their things in then I'll be off. You probably won't see me for quite some time."

Hugh left and Jennie turned to Aiden and returned her hands to his neck.

"Thank you, Aiden. It's perfect."

"It wasn't perfect until you walked through the door. Now, it's home." Aiden leaned forward and tugged her down on the couch onto his lap, kissing her until she felt it down to her toes.

As always, her heart soared. She drew back and cupped his cheek. "Aiden, I do believe you need a shave." She laughed as his eyes grew wide with apprehension.

"I don't have two dollars, Jennie-girl." He gently twisted the hair by her ears, uncoiling it loose from her bun.

Jennie laughed and leaned forward, whispering in his ear, "I've never kissed a man fresh from a shave." She watched him scuttle to their room for his new shaving kit. She couldn't help but remember the shave she'd given him after she'd first met him and how she'd wanted to kiss him even back then. But she hadn't. She'd been so afraid to live.

While Deadwood would never be Cutter's Creek. With Aiden by her side, it would always be home.

HISTORICAL ELEMENTS

Dreams in Deadwood takes place, of course, in Deadwood South Dakota, just three short years after South Dakota became a state. While the whole story is a work of fiction, I've done my best to include little bits of Deadwood history within the story. Here are a few examples:

The *Deadwood Times* mentioned in the story was actually called the *Deadwood Pioneer-Times*. The editor was known for showcasing areas he thought could be enriched within the city of Deadwood and was a big supporter of taxation on prostitution. You can find old issues online at https://www.newspapers.com/newspage/93970696/.

Deadwood began as a mining town, a western boomtown that practically grew up overnight. With mining towns—and the single men that worked them—came the gambling, saloons, and bawdy houses that the Old West is known for. At the time of this story, men quite literally outnumbered women 10 to 1, and wandering the street without a chaperone wouldn't have been recommended for a young woman.

This story takes place in 1892, just 15 short years after the Black Hills war, also known as, the Great Sioux War of 1876.

While fear of the Indians may not have been forefront on people's minds, it was close enough in history that the fear was real. I tried to convey that by mentioning it but not making it a main focus of the book.

Seth Bullock would later become famous for his friendship with President Theodore Roosevelt, but prior to that he was known for taming Deadwood. Or at least giving it a good shot. Some would claim Deadwood still isn't tamed. The day after he arrived, the notorious Wild Bill Hickock was shot and, because Deadwood had little more than a camp court at the time, his murderer went free. For a time. Bullock deputized citizens to help him and he was later sworn in as sheriff. Would he have taken any interest in a missing girl at the time? I can't say. But I *can* say, judging by the historical record, he probably would have appointed Hugh to do the job.

The city itself has changed drastically over time. Deadwood has suffered three major fires that decimated much of the town. In fact, it was one of the first towns in the west to enact building codes requiring brick buildings, which is why the old parts of Deadwood, if you visit today, are all brick. Those are the buildings that survived.

I'd like to take a moment to specially thank the Adams Museum and the Adams House in Deadwood, South Dakota for creating my fascination with Deadwood. I highly recommend a visit to these places on your next visit to Deadwood.

Would you love to visit Deadwood? Every year I venture to South Dakota for Wild Deadwood Reads, an opportunity for authors and readers to hang out together in the beautiful Black Hills. You can find out more at http://wilddeadwoodreads.com/

Sad to see it end? Join my mailing list to keep up to date on when the next book will be released! You can sign up HERE.

Get the next book in the series, Kisses in Keystone now. ORDER MY COPY

KISSES IN KEYSTONE

I dedicate this book to Carley and to Michelle, who battled addiction and continue to win every day. I know I couldn't have begun to write this book without watching you succeed. Special thanks to Michelle for taking the time to talk me through what Hattie would've experienced.
Thank you for helping bring Hattie to life.

CHAPTER 1

Keystone, South Dakota
July 1893

I *need a drink!* Hattie groped under her bed for the dark amber bottle of whiskey that should've been there, just under the edge of her bed. She refilled it every night before coming up to her room for *work*. Finally grasping the cold, smooth surface, she breathed a sigh of relief…until she lifted it. The bottle felt far too light to her hand and her thoughts crashed back through the floor. She'd finished it the night before. Her world spun out of control at facing the day—even just the morning—without a nip. Life was deplorable without the drink to take away the harsh reality of life at The Red Garter Saloon in Keystone Though, it was little more than a two-story shack thrown together to ply money from the miner's fingers before it even got warm in their palms.

She'd never meant to end up here. Just a year ago, she'd been with her sisters on the way to Deadwood. She'd needed a drink then, too. So bad she could taste it. The bitter followed by the burn. When they'd reached Deadwood, she'd met their next-door neighbor. He'd told her about his son, Roy, who was looking for a sweet pretty girl. She'd been so naive. She'd thought he meant his son was looking for a girl to settle down with. But that hadn't been it. He'd wanted her all right, but then he'd sold her to The Red Garter and continued to collect her *earnings*.

She pushed herself off the bed with one bruised arm. As she turned it over, her gaze followed the bruise around to her forearm. Every day was a new set of marks, a new ache. Her chemise was torn down the front and the coverlet lay in a pile on the floor. Hattie groaned as the realization of pain throbbed its way through the clearing fog in her mind. *No!* She wanted to scream, to run, to do anything but stay here. And worst of all, she didn't want to remember. A flimsy robe hung on a nail near her bed and she yanked it on. Though it did little to hide her tattered clothes. Her skin prickled in gooseflesh, but she couldn't feel the cold. Only the sharp need that the empty bottle couldn't quench.

Roy had promised her fine clothes. Had promised her wealth. Had even hinted at love when he'd first met her at the stagecoach station in Deadwood. And she'd been more than ready to give him anything he wanted for that first drink. The other passengers on the stage had clicked their tongues when he'd pulled out a silver flask and offered it to her, but she hadn't cared. She'd laughed at the gasps as she tipped it back for a healthy swig. She'd needed it. Had waited so long... And it had been the best whiskey she'd ever tasted.

She couldn't remember a time when she hadn't taken what she'd wanted from her father's stash. When he burnt the house down, that had been the end of both her father and her affair with his moonshine. Then she'd had to deal with the nightmare of need.

She sat at her mirror and gasped at the dark purple splotch across her cheek. Lady Ros always provided them with enough creams to keep the bruises hidden from the men who'd inflict more damage later that night. Her body was constantly healing from some violence. Hattie pulled open the drawer of her mirrored table and took out the small canister of cream makeup, setting it gently on her dressing table. Then she pulled the drawer out all the way and reached back inside. She found her small clutch of bills still hidden there. The greenbacks made a pleasant sound as they flicked through her fingers. It wouldn't do to have them out too long, lest anyone see them. But she had to know they were there. The only hope she had. It took her three tries to count the pile before she was sure she'd gotten it right. Seventy-five dollars.

There was a harsh, insistent knock on her door and the lock clicked out of place. The lock that had kept her in all night. She cursed, a bad habit she'd picked up recently, at letting someone sneak up on her. She shoved the money back in its spot and slid the drawer back in place as quietly as she could. The door swung open and Roy strode in, kicking the door shut behind him.

His fine cotton trousers looked strange against his bright white clean shirt open halfway down his chest, revealing a filthy undershirt.

"You look horrible this morning, Hattie. Best get your face made quickly before anyone sees you." Though, her face couldn't look too bad. It hadn't kept him from staring at her and licking his thin lips. He sat down on her bed and finally let his eyes wander elsewhere as he lifted the bottle. "My, you've been going through this quicker than ever." He tipped the bottle over and shook his head as he rolled eyes too weak to control her, yet she'd let him. "I promised I would take care of you, Hattie, and I have. But you need to take care of yourself a little too. You have to stop drinking so much. Lady Ros has complained to me that when the men come up here after a long hard day, you just lay there. Sometimes you sleep. They are paying customers."

Bile rose in her throat. She bit the back of her lip to keep from screaming. Roy *couldn't* get angry with her. If he did, he'd take away the only thing that made this bearable. And even that was questionable. This *wasn't* what he'd promised her. This wasn't taking care of her.

Her tongue felt like a pillow wedged in her mouth. "Take care of me? Just how do you s'pect you take care of me? You sold me. Just like my pa always threatened to do. That was the whole reason we left him. So I'd have a choice." She turned from him but kept her eyes on his in the mirror as she opened the small jar of cream makeup. He couldn't be trusted enough to take her eyes off him.

"You did have a choice. You *chose* to believe what you thought you heard. You have a job, clothes, food, a roof over your head, and enough whiskey to drown a mule. Who do you think pays for all that?" He stood and narrowed eyes at her that she'd thought, for a very brief time, were handsome.

"I do," she said through gritted teeth then closed her eyes at the glint of anger in his. Even seeing them diffused in the mirror wasn't enough to keep the burn off her neck. "I do, because you take every penny I make," she mumbled.

He leaned over and grabbed the bottle again then cleared the small room in three steps, slamming it down on her table. "And if you want to keep having all those things, you better make yourself presentable and a little more gracious." He gripped her shoulder in a bruising fist and whipped her around to face him. He bent to look her straight in the eyes and she suppressed a shudder.

"You'd best be careful, or I'll have Ros put you in the back room where you can't say no." He cupped her chin and regarded both sides of her face. "I wouldn't pay good money for you anymore." He slid his hand down around her neck and she held her breath, fearful he'd choke her. He ran his finger along the back of her neck, the silky fabric of her robe heightening the chilling sensation. He smiled at himself in the mirror and peeled the front of her robe down, letting it hang by her arms.

"You can't leave this room without your makeup and your hair under a wrap until the dinner hour. There's some lawman downstairs asking around about you. Ros will never let you go, so don't even fantasize about leaving. Course, I could keep you busy up here until he's gone." He turned her back to the mirror and she watched in horror as he lowered his mouth to her shoulder. He kissed the back of her neck up to her ear and tugged on the robe, but she held her arms tight against her.

She clenched her jaw tight and gritted through her teeth, "I won't do a thing until you fill that bottle and bring it back."

He bit down hard on her ear and she cried out and flinched away. "You drive a hard bargain. I'll be right back."

Hattie searched her room once again for something she could use to keep Roy away. He was relentless. But as always, her room was bare of everything. She had little but the dressing table, the bed, and a small armoire with a few dresses in it that were far too revealing for her to ever where outside the Red Garter. Roy had taken the dress she'd shown up in the first night. She pulled up her robe and tied it closed. It wouldn't matter in a few minutes anyway, but at least she'd tried.

Roy walked in and swung the door shut then turned and locked the four separate locks on the inside. "I filled it half-full. You don't need more than that and that's all you'll get all day." He handed her the bottle and she couldn't help but drag it straight to her lips. She had to do something to help get her through the day. The burn she expected didn't happen. It was like he'd poured a few fingers in a glass full of water. She coughed on the unfamiliar drink. Not that she'd had the best whiskey since coming but it was better than nothing. This swill was worse than nothing. It was cheap moonshine like her pa had made but at least half strength.

"What is this?" She slammed it down on the table.

"That's what I'm going to give you until you can get back to a reasonable amount. You're a drunk, Hattie. A filthy, rotten, little sheet-scraper, drunk."

She was exactly what he'd *made* her, and his words burned. "And you're a—"

She didn't see the slap coming until it lit the back of her eyes and her cheek burned with a deep fire. Hattie screamed and shot to her feet, knocking him back. She grabbed the bottle and heaved it at him as he scrambled away from her. It went wide and exploded against the wall, leaving a huge circle of whiskey and an arc of dark glass all over the floor.

"I'm tired of your outbursts." He cleared the distance between them in two strides and, clutching the robe, he yanked her to his body. "I'll teach you to mind."

A harsh slamming on the door stopped Roy's words and he

shoved her onto the bed. He strode to the door and unlatched all the mechanisms then yanked it open to reveal a tall man with broad shoulders that filled the doorway. His appearance was unexpected. Her gaze caught on the badge on his chest, shiny even in the dim light of her cloudy window. She couldn't tear her eyes away. Was this the man Roy said was looking for her?

"What's going on in here?" He looked at her, then Roy, then back at her and held. She wanted to clutch her robe around her. Which was silly since it felt like just about every man within at least five miles had lain with her.

Roy smirked. "Nothing at all, sir. We're just sharing a little... companionship, you might say. Why don't you leave us be?"

The lawman didn't bother looking at Roy. "You Hattie Arnsby?"

She needed him to know who she was, but her mouth worked slower than her mind. She nodded and tossed her legs over the edge of the bed. A feeling she hadn't had in the last year sparked in the back of her heart. Hope.

Roy growled and stepped in front of her. "It's legal for her to be here. You've got no call to come in here."

The lawman scoffed and tilted his head to see her. She was sure he'd smile, but it never appeared. For some strange reason, that left her off-kilter like a set of stairs not quite plumb.

"If she's Hattie Arnsby, then there is. Hattie was taken from Deadwood against the wishes of her guardians. They want her back."

Hattie's heart raced in her chest. She hoped she could return home, but the shame of who she was had held her back from even trying.

"You'll never get her out of here. You aren't the law here."

"You don't think Deputy Peterson would be fool enough to ignore Sheriff Bullock, do you?"

Even Hattie—though she'd let her mind get washed away by drink nightly—knew of the formidable Seth Bullock. No one messed with him. He'd managed to tame Deadwood, as much as it could be tamed, without ever shooting anyone. He was a living legend. She pulled her robe tightly around her and considered running behind the lawman while Roy was distracted. But how would she get past Ros's muscle men downstairs?

Roy strode up to the lawman and pointed a finger into his chest. Hattie held her breath and waited for Roy to be knocked across the room as it appeared the cowboy-styled lawman wanted to do just that.

"I still don't know who you are and why you think you can just barge in here. Hattie came with me of her own free will and now she works here, for me."

Hattie shook her head, her matted blond hair rough against her cheek. Her words tumbled free before she could think them through, "He tricked me. He told me he cared. I don't want to be here anymore. I *am* Hattie Arnsby. Take me home, whoever you are."

He tipped his hat to her. "Good to find you, Miss Arnsby. Sorry it took me so long. I'm Hugh Bradly and I'll get you out of here as quickly as I can."

CHAPTER 2

Hugh hadn't sworn in a long time, but he wanted to now. He knew what Hattie would look like. Her sisters, Ruby and Jennie, had both described her as looking much like Jennie, blond with a straight nose and tiny bones. What was the word Jennie had used? *Petite.* They said she'd look younger and have a fire in her eyes. Catching Hattie's gaze, he wanted to swear again. There was definitely a spark there, but it was near burnt out. She'd been used and it scorched his gut because he knew how young Hattie was. The fool in front of him either didn't know or didn't care. Men like him took advantage of the new laws in the state of South Dakota. It wasn't lawless as people thought. Just too new to have enacted the ones they needed. Bullock was doing his best to bring justice to the area, but he couldn't do it alone.

He shrugged off his coat and handed it to Hattie. She blushed, which was shocking since she'd probably seen about everything in the last few months…excepting maybe kindness.

"Do you need anything else from this room?" He looked around him to keep from staring at the girl in her flimsy night-

354

clothes. He'd never frequented saloons much less the rooms upstairs, and he'd had quite enough of The Red Garter.

"I have this, if you need it." Hattie's quaking voice angered him all the more. If he could shove that rat out into the hallway, she might not be so afraid. Hattie pulled out a drawer and reached behind it, pulling out a small bundle of cash. The man jumped for it. Hugh stepped in his way as Hattie dashed it behind her back. "You just leave this alone, Roy! You can't have this! You got all my wages. These were tips and they're mine!" she screamed.

Hugh held Roy at arm's length but his arm fairly itched to yank back and send him flying into the wall. "You just keep away from her. She isn't your concern anymore."

Roy snickered and rested his hands on his hips. "You think so? You think you can just walk out of here with her because you say so? I think you're trying to steal her. You'd better have more than your little badge if you think you can just walk in here and take her. She isn't going anywhere and I'm going to talk to Ros." He pushed past them and stomped away, leaving Hugh alone with Hattie in a room that smelled of strong drink with a hint of perfume. It was enough to gag a dog. He glanced at her. "You ready?"

She drowned in his large coat. He was reminded she'd only just turned eighteen in the last few days. She was no longer a child. Her last months of childhood were stolen by grownup vices.

"Yes. I've wanted to leave from the very first moment I was brought here." She gazed up at him, clutching the roll of bills in front of her.

"Good. Do you have a bag or anything?" He couldn't imagine her traipsing through town in what she was wearing. Maybe they could use some of her cash on a dress or at least some fabric. He couldn't travel with her looking like that. Just the amount of calf and ankle she was showing under his coat would have people staring.

"No. They took the one dress I could call my own. As it is, they could accuse me of stealing what I'm wearing. It isn't really mine."

She had to wear something. He couldn't parade her about town in her birthday clothes. He took out a half-eagle and slapped it on her dressing table. "There. That should more than cover that tattered bit of cloth they gave you for a nightgown. Shameful really, that they couldn't even cover you when you weren't working." He regretted his words as soon as he saw the stricken look on her face. She hadn't asked for any of this... Well, maybe some of it. If what he'd heard from her sisters was true. And judging by the shaking in her hands, it was.

"You don't understand." She blinked back tears and the deep bruise on her cheek tore at him even more. "I'm always working."

"Not anymore." He turned from her, pushing his unwilling feeling of pity to his stomach. He had to worry about getting out of here first. Then deal with her story. Let her sisters heal her. "Let's get out of here before Roy brings back Ros's men. I'd rather just walk out then have to threaten anyone."

He went first, leading Hattie out of her cell and down the stairs avoiding the looks of the other painted ladies peering out at them from behind heavy doors. It didn't even matter to him if they were jealous of Hattie or if they'd chosen the life they led. They made it down to the saloon before two of Ros's burly men met them, arms crossed and ankles wide, blocking the mouth of the staircase.

"Ros wants to know why you think you can steal from her?" The biggest man regarded them with squinting eyes and lowered his hands, ready to fight.

His badge would only get him so far in this little town. Hattie just had to stay close to him and he could get her out. Let Bullock handle the rest. "I didn't steal anything. I left money for the few scraps of clothing Hattie's wearing upstairs on the table."

The man snickered. "I ain't talking about her clothes. Hattie was paid for. She's under contract to work here until Ros decides she isn't worth the upkeep."

A sick dread crawled up his spine. "Did she sign it?"

"Don't matter. It's binding." He took a step closer, resting one huge hand on each side of the railing and blocking them in. His chest was the size of a wine barrel.

"Who signed it?" They had to get out of there quickly. A crowd grew around them and Bullock wanted to avoid confrontation without backup as much as possible. Hugh had worn his barkers, but they would do no good at such close range and might hurt innocent people. Well perhaps not *innocent*, but those not involved in Hattie's kidnapping.

"Ain't none of your affair, lawman. Miss Hattie, you git right back on up to your room." He glared over Hugh's shoulder at Hattie and he could feel her grip his vest tighter.

"Don't move, Hattie." He glanced back at her then focused back on the brutes. "I have a letter from Sheriff Seth Bullock, stating that Hattie is to be brought to Deadwood. Do you really want to stand in my way? Do you want to bring him here?"

"Bullock ain't the law here." The man spat a dark wad in the direction of the spittoon and took another step closer shoving his foot on the first stair.

Hattie scooted up close to his back, pressing herself against him and cowering. How many times had she hid from these fools? He squared his shoulders. There had to be a way out of this. At least temporarily.

"Your contract isn't valid if she didn't sign it. If you don't like it, you can take it up with the judge... He should be coming along in two weeks. Until then, we'll stay at that little cabin just down from the Keystone mine. The owner's been letting me stay there. If you can provide proof that Hattie agreed to come and that she's old enough to sign that contract, then I can't stop you."

Hattie squeaked in indignation behind him. He had to keep her quiet if they were going to get out of this. He reached for her hand and placed it in his as he squeezed it gently.

The man looked back at the other waiting at the base of the stairs. They'd obviously never been questioned before. Taking them both on alone would be more than foolish, it might be deadly. He'd most likely lose, and they'd take out their trouble on Hattie. She had enough marks on her to last a lifetime.

A woman with red-stained lips and a purple silk robe that was in much better repair than Hattie's strode into the room. Her dark hair was pulled back into a loose bun with two sticks poking through it. Everyone went silent as the diminutive woman approached the two henchmen.

"What's going on here? Why isn't Hattie back up in her room by now?" She glared at Hugh.

He almost laughed at the pale woman who commanded her small army around her. But that wouldn't get him the desired result. He moved to rest his hands on his hips then quickly changed his mind when they brushed against Hattie's.

"Hattie was taken from her home. I've come to take her back. It's as simple as that. I have a letter from Sheriff Bullock saying he wants her in Deadwood. If you won't let her go free, the circuit judge will have to decide."

"Then I guess he will because I'm not just letting her go. I paid for someone to be in that room and there will be. She wasn't old enough to sign a contract, but her guardian did. It's perfectly legal."

Now she'd rubbed him wrong. "Maybe you haven't heard the news, but slavery is illegal. Even here. You aren't allowed to just buy people." Hattie's hands clenched just over his hips and he felt the soft pressure of her forehead against his back.

"Prostitution *is* legal here, Deputy. I don't think you have a leg to stand on. Fine. You stay in your little shack and enjoy Hattie's company. But in two weeks, you'd best be prepared to bring her back and pay for all the time you've had her. She ain't free. Oh, you'd also better have a sizable account. She's a sot. She's been drinking almost two liters of whiskey a day." She swung around, her robe billowed out around her, followed by her two men.

Hugh sighed. He hadn't really wanted to stick around Keystone any longer than he had to. It would be good to get back to Deadwood and see Da and Mam again. And even his brother, Aiden. Now that they were away from the farm in Kansas, he wanted to get to know him better. He'd never admit it to Aiden, but he was the reason Hugh had rekindled his faith. A faith he'd need if he was going to stay in that tiny shack with Hattie. But he'd signed on to bring Hattie home, so stay he would.

"I'm free?" she choked into the fabric of his vest.

He turned around and she fairly jumped into his arms. He hadn't prepared for it and the wisp of a girl almost bowled him over down the stairs. She was far too tiny—skinny would be a good word—and her fierce hold on him made her tremble.

"Yes. For at least the next two weeks, you're free. I need to wire Bullock and get someone here to back me up. In the meantime, we need to get you to that shack and away from everyone here."

She nodded, pulling away from him, and tucked his coat tighter around her body. The motion saying more about her fears and insecurities than she'd ever have to voice. He wished he'd thought to bring her some clothes, but it hadn't been on his mind. Find her. Bring her home. Those were his first thoughts every morning for the last eleven months. He'd thought he'd been close a few times. The search had finally made him understand the draw Aiden had seen in gold mining. When you found the treasure you were seeking, it made your heart race in your chest with a kind of joy he couldn't name.

He put his hand at her waist and directed her out of the saloon and into the bright sun. He had one horse, but he could walk. He'd offer it to her, but he couldn't ride with her dressed like that.

She squinted into the sun as she looked up at Daisy and shook her head. "I've never ridden. I wouldn't even know how to get on."

He smiled. Perfect. "Then we'll walk." He held out his arm and she looked at it for a moment, her face pensive.

A tear traced its way down her sunken and bruised cheek. "No, mister. I don't deserve your arm." She turned and headed north, leaving him to catch up.

CHAPTER 3

Hattie pulled Hugh's oil coat closer around her and let the heavy weight comfort her like a wall between her and everyone else. She hugged her arms close to her body to keep it closed.

Though it was before noon, the dusty streets of Keystone were bustling with life. After being trapped within the confines of the saloon, the town felt wide open. The owner of the hotel stood outside on his wide veranda, his lean gray suit shining in the sun as he wiped the sweat off his brow. He was so engaged in his task of sweeping he didn't notice her until she'd almost passed him. When he saw her, his eyes snapped wide and his broom touched nothing but air as his body continued the sweeping motion. A child chasing a ball stopped dead in his tracks and stared at her. As she walked down the street, other people stopped and took note of the dove who'd dared leave her cage. Her feet seemed to slow of their own accord, the weight of their gazes making her feet as heavy as a whet stone. Hugh stepped up behind and put a comforting hand between her shoulders.

"Come, this way." He led his horse along behind him and directed her down the street past the sea of spectators. Her stomach clenched as she recognized some of the faces they passed. One man, Mr. Henches—if she remembered correctly, though she doubted they gave their real names when they visited the Red Garter—stopped in front of Hugh and glared at them both in turn.

"You there." His voice rose above the bustle of the street until everything was silent around them. It was like a free show and she was the entertainment.

"Finally taking out the rubbish. Good riddance." He spat at her face. She flinched away, but not fast enough. Her hands trembled as she wiped it from her cheek. Hugh pushed ahead of her and landed a punch to Mr. Henches' mouth, knocking him back onto his hind quarters. A dribble of blood marred his lips under a bushy mustache.

"In case it escaped your notice, she isn't in cuffs. She isn't my prisoner. Stand aside or I *will* take out the rubbish." Henches pushed back to his feet, his face pinched in fury. Hugh shoved him out of the way and Hattie grabbed on and clung to the arm she'd refused a few moments before. Now she was hoping they could just leave before anyone else stopped them. Hugh gathered her close to his side and took up the reins as they finished the long walk down the block and to the edge of town. The eyes burning into her back left their mark as surely as if they'd actually hit her with the stones they had on their minds. Though prostitution was legal, it was a dirty little secret. No one liked having to admit they indulged, even when the next man on the street probably indulged just as much.

Hugh flipped the reins over the hooked horseshoe on the outside of the last building, the mercantile, and drew her up the stairs.

"I'll be just a minute. Will you be all right here?" His eyes glanced briefly at his coat around her and his dilemma was clear as the mountain sky. Did he leave her outside to the wolves, or take her inside and risk being thrown out?

She nodded and hid beside the horse, hoping that most people would be at work. Not leaving or entering town where they could see her. Hugh stepped inside for only a few minutes and she was proper glad he did. She didn't belong out in the open, dressed as she was. But what choice did she have?

Hugh strode back down the steps a few minutes later and turned to her, his eyes lightened. "I just sent a note to Bullock. He can send one of his men to tell your family you've been found. We might need one of them to come here if the judge wants proof you're too young to sign anything and that you were taken from your home. They've got the next two weeks to come up with a document that you signed. They know anything signed by Roy won't hold up—unless you married him—then there might be some trouble."

Her stomach twisted into a knot. That first night when he'd taken her from Deadwood, she'd wished she would be his bride. Then the first few weeks at the saloon, he'd even teased her with *someday. Someday* he'd have enough money and she could be his bride. She'd never have to lift a finger. Now, she was glad he'd never followed through. He was a horrible man and marrying him would've tied her to the saloon forever. She concentrated and tried to remember if she'd ever signed anything. But those first few days were, thankfully, somewhat blurry. She'd cried a lot and relied on Roy. He'd convinced her she had to do the job for him, that he would love her if she did. He hadn't. He'd loved her body and the money she made for him. But never *her*.

"I never married that no-account, lousy cur. I don't recall ever signing anything."

Hugh flipped the reins free of the post and frowned.

"Mister, aren't you afraid of what people will think of you? Taking me out of town...alone? *Me?*" The shard of hope she'd had back at the saloon smashed into a million tiny pieces. No respectable man would allow anyone to see him taking a prostitute into his home.

The sound Hugh made may have been a laugh, but it could just as easily have been a cough. "No, these aren't my people and I don't care what they think of me. I'm not saying they aren't good people, but those I love are in Deadwood. Far from Keystone. No one knows me here, and they won't remember me after I've left."

Hugh glanced down to her as he moved them around a bend outside of town and up the gentle slope to the cabin in the trees just out of sight of town. For the first time since she'd left Deadwood, she felt her age. She'd counted the days and knew she'd turned eighteen just a week before, meaning her twin Eva had also celebrated a birthday. Celebrated... Hattie hadn't celebrated anything in a long time.

Hugh touched her back with a hint of gentle pressure then dropped his hand, bringing her thoughts back to the present and allowing them to just walk. He was silent, far too quiet for her nervous thoughts. What would they do once they got to the cabin? He couldn't possibly be worse than Roy had been, but she really didn't know. She'd trusted him. But now her stomach roiled. Her hands shook more than they ought, even from nerves. The sun was far too bright, and her head throbbed with its intensity. She covered her face with her hand, but it didn't help. The sun seemed to pulse and burn brighter.

"Mr. Bradly, I really need..." She shook her head. He wouldn't help her. Not like Roy had, and did she want him to? Roy had taken every advantage. Every help he'd given her had come with a kingly price tag. Eventually, all that had been left of her was despair.

"I know what you think you need, Hattie. You won't feel strong enough to get past it for a while, maybe even the full two weeks or more. You might always crave it. Part of your mind will always think it needs it. But you are stronger. You need to be at your full strength and wit when we go before the judge."

"I don't feel stronger." She stumbled, the throbbing in her head intensified to a drumbeat.

"You won't for a few days. I could get you free of Madame Ros. I can lay hands on every man who looks at you for a second longer than I'd like. But I can't free you from *this*. In fact, for a little while, it'll feel like I'm keeping you in more of a prison than she ever did. You might even hate me when I hand you back to your family. But since I have to keep you here for a few weeks, I'd like to hand you back to them even better than the way you left them."

Heat rose through her and she bit her lip to stop from crying out. "I'll never be the same, Mister. Never."

He stopped and touched her arm. His touch was so different from any that had been forced on her. It wasn't meant to enflame, not her or himself. He wanted to give comfort, not take anything. "I didn't mean it like that. I was talking about the drink. I won't minimize what you've been through. I can't make that go away. But I can help you over this mountain."

Hattie stared up at a large cleft of white rock jutting out of the mountain above them and suspected it would be much harder to overcome *her* mountain than the one looming over them now.

CHAPTER 4

Hugh slowed his pace as they approached the small cut-log cabin tucked into the spruce trees, hidden from view of anyone but the Lord. He'd have to keep that in mind. What in blazes had he been thinking, agreeing to have this girl stay with him here? Her shoulder barely reached his chest, but her hand still clung to his arm. The closer they got, the more she stumbled. Though she hadn't said a word about food, she probably hadn't eaten in who knew how long. Her energy was flagging—if he was reading her pace correctly.

He'd been staying at the cabin for the last week, since he'd gotten the lead from a miner on his way to the Homestake mine in Lead. He'd told him about a girl in Keystone that sounded like Hattie. In the beginning, Bullock had thought Hattie had been taken to Lead. It was a company town for the Homestake mine but had since tried to shed its skin and change into a more civilized town. Much of that was due to the wife of one of the primary owners of the mine, Phoebe Hearst. He'd gone their first, but that had been months ago. He'd almost lost all hope of ever finding her. Had even prayed for a while that maybe she had found a home, husband, and happiness, and that's why he couldn't find her.

Instead, she'd been in the tiny town of Keystone, tucked away in the hills.

Hattie hadn't been in Lead, though, he'd spent weeks wasting precious time looking. Now, here she was. And his excitement had gotten the better of him. He should've waited to message her family until she was ready, but he'd been specially deputized to take on the task of finding Hattie, a job that he'd failed at, until today. Hattie didn't know it yet—and he'd have to tell her soon—but her brother in law, Aiden, was his brother. Not close enough to be relation, but close enough that he cared deeply about finding her and bringing her back. Hattie's twin sister, Eva, had been heartbroken with missing her. It had staked him deeper than he'd allowed anything to touch him in a long time. He'd made a promise and Hugh never went back on his word.

Hattie stopped abruptly. Her hand fell from his arm and she sat on the side of the trail. His coat swallowed her, making her look even smaller. He'd have to make sure she was fed better. Ros and Roy had let her waste away to bones. The dark areas under her cheeks made the rest of her face ghastly pale, excepting the blackening bruise on her cheek. How could a man call himself a man and do that to a woman? And one who couldn't fight back neither.

"Can you make it? It's only a few more steps." He held Daisy's reins and gave Hattie her space, something that little room at the saloon wouldn't have afforded her, much less those who'd joined her there. She'd probably had precious little space for months.

Her face was drawn and a sheen of sweat covered her forehead. He yanked his neckerchief off, took a step closer to hand it over, then retreated. When she didn't reply, he stepped back a pace more. She might be as worried as he was about how they were both going to fit in that small cabin without tripping over one another.

"There are two rooms in there... So, you don't need to worry. I've got food in the cabin, if you're hungry." He searched for something else to say, something that would make the wariness on her face soften.

She dabbed at her head and neck then folded the kerchief

neatly in her lap. "I don't know that I want to go in there. Why should I trust you? I don't know you. How do I know I haven't just walked into a worse situation than what I came from?" The stubborn tilt to her head was the only hint of the girl he'd been told about. The one with fire in her eyes and a wit to match.

"You're right. You don't know me from anyone else and you shouldn't just trust everyone." He bounced on the balls of his feet and glanced at the cabin. How could he find a way to earn her trust in just a few minutes? She had to get inside before she fainted. Sakes alive, he didn't want to have to carry her in that state. His thoughts stalled. "Maybe if I tell you who I am, you'll find it a little easier to follow me in there. But first, I'm going to let you rest and take care of Daisy here." He patted the horse's neck and backed away. Like a skittish horse, she needed to be left alone, then worked with for just a bit at a time. Too much and you might get kicked. As long as he gave her plenty of space, she'd figure out he wasn't looking for what all those other men had been looking for.

She sighed and glanced at the neat square in her lap. He tugged his canteen off the saddle string and handed it to her. "Here, rest and have a drink. It was a bit of a walk. I'll make you something to eat when we get inside. Then you'll feel better."

She took the canteen and nodded her agreement, though she didn't say more. Her eyes were glassy, and her face flushed. There had been a few men back in the little town of Belview, Kansas, where he'd grown up, who'd been heavy on the bottle. Problem was, he'd never seen them try to quit. He wasn't sure what Hattie would have to go through to give up drink, but it wouldn't be easy. He led Daisy up to the small lean-to shelter attached to the house and got her some fresh hay and a scoop of oats. Since Hattie was waiting for him, he hurried through the job.

When he rounded the house, he found Hattie with her legs bare up to her knees and spread out in the sun with her eyes closed. The sun turned her hair a pretty golden color. She'd be almost pretty after a bath, some food, and time to heal. It was hard to see what she actually looked like under it all. He forced his eyes up to the trees and cleared his throat. The dry brush under her crackled as she jumped, pulling her legs under her. He let his gaze fall back to her, but she stared at her hands in her lap, avoiding him.

"I promised you the truth." He sat down a few feet from her and plucked a blade of grass, running it through his fingers to pull the right words from his scrambling thoughts. The truth was multi-layered, and he wasn't at all sure what she'd remember tomorrow. Best to stick with the basics, the easiest things to explain again later. Why should she trust him in the small cabin after what she'd been through? Because she had to.

"I know you're nervous and that's fine. I understand." He tossed the grass away and plucked another blade. It wasn't working to put his thoughts in some order.

"I won't ever try anything with you. I know your family and respect all of them too much to ever do that. Not to mention, it's just plain wrong."

Her head flew up and her blue eyes popped with electricity. "How do you know my family so well? I've never met you before today." The side of her lip curled up slightly, then faltered. "I'd remember."

Hugh sighed. "Let's start with your sister, Jennie."

"What do you know of my sister?" Hattie narrowed her eyes at him and pushed herself back from him a few inches. He was having the opposite effect he'd wanted. By mentioning her sister, he'd made her wary.

"I'll get there." He had to explain quickly, or he'd lose her. "Your sister Jennie was married last year."

"Married?" Hattie sighed and closed her eyes. A serenity washed over her dull face, transforming it. "She beat the curse," she whispered, almost too quiet for him to hear.

"She married my brother, Aiden."

Hattie's eyes flung open and she stammered. "Your brother...is Aiden Bradly? They're married?"

He had to laugh at her look of shock. He'd been just as shocked to learn that his brother had found happiness when all he'd ever wanted was gold. "That they are. And happily, I might add. Or, at least they were the last I saw them."

"Good." She let her eyes drift closed again. "I was worried she'd let herself get in the way."

He wanted to point out that was exactly what Hattie had done, but he held his tongue. It wouldn't do any good to make her angry now when they'd just started building an understanding. "So, you see. When I went looking for work, I found Sheriff Bullock. He'd heard of Aiden and he'd known about you from before. He thought it would be best to put someone out looking for you who had a real stake in finding you. That was me."

Hattie leaned forward and rested her chin on her hands her eyes still closed, and her forehead still as wrinkled as a day-old shirt. "So, I'm important to you. And I can trust you because my sister is your brother's wife."

"Yes, that and it would be despicable to take advantage of you."

Her face pinched further and he was sure she was in pain. "You mean, like Roy and every other man who came near me within the last year?" Her voice was bitter, ragged. He couldn't blame her.

He sighed. Roy was territory he didn't want to cover. She'd made the choice to go with him, according to what he'd been told by her sister Ruby, who'd been there. But she was also young, much too young to be making choices like that. Much too young to have been put in the position she was.

"I don't want you to think about him anymore. He was a dirty, rotten, yellow-bellied rattler. He tricked you because he knew your weakness."

She hung her head and picked at her jagged fingernails. "I've had a lot of weaknesses, mister. More than I can tell you about. Help me into the house, will you please? I'm really tired and my mind isn't working the way it should."

She tried to stand, but her legs wouldn't hold her up. He clenched his jaw and lifted her easily to stand. She let her head fall against his shoulder. Poor little bit of a girl. She needed to eat some good food and get some rest. She had the battle of her life ahead of her.

"Call me Hugh, little lady, it looks like we'll be here for a bit."
She couldn't walk and he knew it. "Forgive me." He whispered as
he lifted her in his arms and carried her the last few feet to the
house. She didn't say a word or try to get away from him, just laid
there. He couldn't keep his own heart from thudding around in his
chest as her legs draped over his arm where his coat didn't cover.
He'd have to get her more to wear. Soon.

CHAPTER 5

Hattie reached under the bed before she even opened her eyes, groping for the friend she felt she needed more than air. Her brain was too big for her skull and she wasn't even sure she could open her eyes. The cure was easy…if she could only find it. Blast Roy. Had he taken it? She reached further under the bed and fell out, hitting her head against something on the way. She bit back a scream that would have people running for her room. Not to mention the noise would surely send her over the edge. She forced herself to open one eye—just a slit—and the floor was unfamiliar, as was the bed. The light was different, and the air was…warm. Midday. She'd overslept and—where was she? Her heart pounded to match her head and she opened her other eye to glance around the room. Everything was unfamiliar. She clutched her chemise closed as she pushed herself against the table.

A dark-haired man who was too tall to be Roy stood by a cook stove, heating something in a pan. Then it hit her. She couldn't smell food or hear it cooking. Her head was full of a rushing sound she couldn't explain. She touched her head where it had hit, shooting needles of pain through her head and down into her neck.

371

Hugh.

Now she remembered. He'd rescued her and he expected her to go without. Just as her family had when they'd left Yellow Medicine after their home had burned down. He couldn't understand her need now but he'd have to learn.

Slowly, she became aware of everything in the room. The sound started quiet, then grew in intensity. First, Hugh scraping the pan back and forth across the metal stove. That had to have been what woke her up. Then came the scent of whatever he was cooking. She ran her tongue along the inside of her mouth and lips, but it did little against the feeling that she'd chewed on a sock for however long she'd been asleep.

She stood on legs that didn't want to hold her weight and slowly made her way toward him. His coat lay draped over a chair and she slid it on, buttoning the top few buttons to hold it closed. Carefully, she pulled out a chair so it wouldn't scrape and make more noise, then sat down and waited for him to notice her. He turned and jumped a little when he saw her so close.

"There you are! I was worried you'd sleep right through lunch. How are you feeling?"

His voice was too loud in the small cabin. Too cheerful. She'd learned quickly at the Garter that people who asked that question in that way didn't really want an answer. They *needed* you to lie and then turn the question back to them so they could tell you everything that was troubling them. Just as much of her job had been listening to men complain about their wives as it had been any of the other jobs she'd been required to do.

"I'm sure I'll do just fine." Though she wasn't sure at all. Her head hurt like her skull was trying to escape through her teeth, like she'd get sick. Her pa had always joked she could hold her liquor against any man. Where her sisters had avoided Pa at all costs, she'd spent as much time with him as he'd let her. He'd let her a lot more after he'd discovered her nipping his 'shine.

"Well, that's an optimism I wasn't expecting." He set down a plate of eggs, bacon, and toasted bread in front of her.

The smell of the eggs lit into her nose and her stomach threw itself against her throat. She wanted to eat. Needed to eat. And it looked so good, but even the smell was too much. She stood from the table and the room swam in circles around her. She had to get out before she embarrassed herself further by messing up the floor. A floor she didn't have the strength to clean.

Hugh set his plate down and grabbed hold of her elbow before she fell. "Whoa there. Take it slow." He tried to help her sit back down but she fought against it, pushing against him.

He cocked his head to the side and his soft warm eyes calmed her a little.

"Start with the bread. If you can manage that then try whatever sounds good."

She stared down at the plate. When was the last time she'd sat down for a meal and didn't just nibble whatever was left over from others? It was the night Roy had taken her to Lead from Deadwood. They'd arrived in a pretty stage. She'd clung to his arm and giggled when he'd said things to her she'd always considered *naughty*. Private things that should've been shared between a husband and wife. It made her think he cared about her. He'd plied her with that flask over and over and she'd been too besotted and happy to reject it. After six months of being without, it was warm in her mouth and had a pleasant burn all the way down her throat. He'd brought her to Lead, taken her to the hotel restaurant for a fancy meal where he'd complimented everything about her. Then he'd gotten a room.

There had been another bottle waiting inside by the bed and he'd pushed her to have even more. She'd enjoyed every drop. Then, when she was feeling quite good, he'd pushed her against the wall and lifted her skirt. It had been shameful. She didn't even fight. In fact, she'd been so sure he'd take her to wed the next day that she'd tried her best to enjoy it. Not that she could remember much.

He'd told her the next day that she was made for that kind of work, convinced her she'd loved it. She was ruined anyway, and he didn't want a wife just yet. He'd pointed out how she didn't even say no, so she'd wanted it. That made her a whore. Though she'd joked with her sisters how much she wanted to be married she couldn't remember wanting *that*. She still didn't want it.

She sat back down and pushed the plate away with shaky hands, letting her head fall onto her arms folded on the table. She couldn't embarrass her family further by going back. She was a prostitute. Just as Roy had said. Even now, she'd go back if it meant he'd let her have what she needed. One drink would take away the pain in her head. One drink and she could eat again... "I can't go back home Hugh. I'm sorry. I've done so many awful things and I don't ever want to go back. I don't belong anywhere."

To his credit, he didn't reach for her. He didn't try to comfort her with his touch which she didn't want.

"We all do things we regret Hattie. You have a choice to keep doing what you regret or step away. I'm bound by contract to bring you back to Deadwood, but what you do after that is up to you and your family."

He sighed and pushed the plate back toward her. "I'm going to heat some water for you and get you a bath ready. Then I'll go back into Keystone and see what I can find for you to wear. You can't wander around in my coat."

She felt the rough canvas of his coat against her skin. He shouldn't be expected to pay for her clothes. She'd saved her money for just that type of thing, that and escaping. Once she had something to wear, she could go back to Keystone and hide until Hugh left town. Her family might be sad about her disappearance, but it'd be better for them than having her return. No decent family tree wanted a branch like her.

She picked up the bread and nibbled on the edge. Though she didn't eat often she couldn't remember the last time she felt hungry either.

Hugh stood and went back to the stove. She continued to work on her piece of bread, barely taking in anything. It felt like sawdust in her mouth. He returned with two buckets of water. There was a giant copper boiler on the wall that took up the two burners when he set it on the stove. He poured the water in slowly. Then he took a washtub that looked like it was meant for clothes and set it on the floor next to the stove. His eyes were soft and apologetic when he looked at her.

"I wish I had a bigger tub for you, but this cabin is small. So, there's one tub for washing both clothes and people. I hope it'll do."

She nodded and watched him leave to refill the buckets once again. It wasn't anything she wasn't used to. Growing up, she'd only had the use of a small washtub for bathing. Hugh came and left again more times than she could keep track of. He filled the tub a little over half full, then grabbed some towels and heaved the steaming boiler off the stove and poured it into the tub, creating a steaming bath. He set the bar of soap on the table and a dry cloth for her. Then he donned his hat, tipping it to her slightly and left.

She tossed the bread back on her plate. Her stomach still fought the idea of eating. The coat slid easily off her shoulders and she set it to the side, taking great care with the nicest thing she'd worn in longer than she could remember, shivering at the loss of its warmth. It would take more skill than she had to mend the torn sleeping chemise. The top had been ripped wide open. She tossed the robe and the chemise to the side, slipping down into the water, squeezing herself into a tiny ball to fit. But the warmth was like sun against her frail skin; she needed it. She hadn't realized how filthy she felt until the warm water seeped into her. The steam rose all around and cleared her nose and head. She would've never had the strength to get the bath ready for herself. How kind of Hugh to go to town so she'd feel comfortable in the small cabin.

She'd do well to remember that it was only a matter of time before he let her down. They always did. But if she left quickly, she could always remember him as the kind man who hadn't taken advantage. *If he lets me go...will he be letting me down?* She shook her head and leaned up for the soap. That kind of thinking would get her nowhere.

There had to be some kind person in Keystone who'd be willing to help her. But first, she had to figure out where she could go. Perhaps home to Ma in Cutter's Creek? The water lapped around her, soothing the bruises on her arms and legs. She wrapped her arms around her knees and let her head fall forward, curling herself into a ball. Here she felt warm and safe, and gloriously clean. The first she'd felt that way since...well, it didn't matter. Not anymore.

CHAPTER 6

Hugh took his time saddling Daisy. Keystone wasn't far and there was no telling how long it took a woman to bathe. He didn't even need his horse for such a short walk, but saddling would use up some time. His mam had always done that kind of thing when he, Da, and his brothers had been out working all day. If it took that long to get a woman smelling nice, well maybe it was worth it. But it presented a problem. How would he get the clothes in to her when he got back?

He'd made her a promise and so he'd figure out a way. His horse ambled slowly into town, forcing him to focus on the task. He didn't want trouble with anyone in Keystone, but if they took issue with him or what he'd been sworn to do, well he'd rectify it. The first day he'd checked out the town, he saw a small house with a placard that read *seamstress* on the front. Keystone was growing. It was close to Hill City. There were copper, pyrite, graphite, and quartz mines. And the Big Thunder which, of course, drew miners from all over the area because of its gold. Keystone was relatively new and had just sprouted up as more of a town than a mining camp. It still held that rough edge, as if it didn't want to settle down just yet.

He tethered Daisy near the small white house which sat across from the boardinghouse at the end of town. Where Battle Creek swung around behind them like a scarf. The home had a short set of stairs to the porch. It was clean and neat and looked new, like most of the other buildings in Keystone. He stood outside the door as a feeling of unease crept over him. He'd never gone into a dress shop and this one was in a woman's home. He certainly didn't belong anywhere near a dress shop. Would she display *all* of women's finery or just dresses? Would she even let him in? He'd only thought of Hattie and her need for clothing and privacy. He'd been so focused on getting Hattie some decent clothes, he hadn't considered what his rushed plan would require.

A woman opened the door and regarded him with a question in her gaze. Rather than ask her question, she quirked her lips in a smile. He couldn't thank her enough for that. She wore a tailored dark blue walking suit and her hair was put up intricately. It looked like waves cascading around her head. She shook the confusion from her face and offered a full smile, opening the door slightly and holding it in welcome.

She led him into the sizable parlor with headless dress forms all around. Dresses hung from them in various stages of completion. "I'm quite booked sir, but if you need something small, I can probably accommodate you." The elegant woman folded her hands in front of her and waited for him to explain why he'd interrupted her day.

She backed further into the room, allowing him a full view of everything she was working on. She was a busy lady. He hadn't realized she wouldn't sell something Hattie could wear today. That might pose a problem. He sucked in his breath to collect his words and glanced around him. The home had high ceilings and soft red wallpaper. All the headless women forms around him made him nervous, as if he were surrounded.

He cleared his throat but kept his gaze on the forms. "I have a young lady staying with me...friend of mine...who lost her clothing in a tragic accident. Everything's gone. She needs, well, whatever women need. Can you help me?" He felt heat rush to his face. Hattie's disappearance had forced him to do many things he never thought he'd do. This was another thing on that list.

The seamstress cocked her head and smiled in an over-bright way that made him jumpy. Like she was up to something.

"Come with me." She turned softly on booted feet and walked down a dim hallway, then through her kitchen to the back of her home. She dodged through another narrow door to a back room. He glanced back and forth at the forms and shook his head. They had no eyes, but he felt watched. And just where was this woman taking him? Going into the back of a single woman's home, what was she thinking? He followed her at a distance, keeping track of just where he was. She strode through the door and waited for him, standing over a trunk. When he came fully in the room, she began pulling out garments and tossing them into other trunks. Bright colors, lace, ribbons and ruffles flew over her shoulder as she tossed garments out.

She straightened, holding two dresses and white garments he didn't want to inspect too closely. "How old is your friend, if I might ask?"

Young, far too young to be out wandering in the hills. "She just turned eighteen."

"Ah, so is this someone a new spouse, perhaps? It's generous of you to go to such trouble. I daresay most men wouldn't." She set the two dresses on a table and folded them. "Now, you will need underclothes."

"Wait, no. She isn't my wife. She's just..." The woman would probably hear about Hattie soon enough. But if she hadn't yet, he wouldn't risk her not selling the dresses if he said anything. "Just a friend of the family."

"Well, your *friend* will need underclothes. I have some marvelous fabrics here to choose from."

No. He didn't want to have anything to do with choosing Hattie's underclothes. An unmarried man had no business knowing what women's underthings looked like. He took a step back out of the room. "I'll let you pick that out. I wouldn't know the first thing..."

The seamstress laughed. "I'm sure not. I have some around here that never sold but should be perfect." She dug around in the trunk some more and took some white and other colorful garments from the depths. She brought all the items to a table along the wall. The table had a large roll of paper bolted to it. The woman pulled a long portion off then cut it, wrapping the gowns and other bits up carefully for him. She tied a string around it and handed it to him.

"Don't worry about payment. The dresses are all samples from a few years ago. They're from well before I ever came to Keystone and they've no use to me here, since I don't do fittings anymore. Not to mention, they're a few seasons out of fashion."

He dug in his pocket and pulled out a half-eagle, handing it to her. "Please, take this for your trouble, ma'am. You've done me a kindness I won't forget."

She regarded his hand for a moment with a frown then accepted it, tucking the coin away into her skirt pocket. He slipped the large package under his arm and strode out of the shop, back into the sun, breathing a sigh of relief. His watch hung on his belt and he flipped it open to see he'd hardly taken any time at all. But there wasn't much more he could do in town. He hoped Hattie had been able to finish her ministrations. He didn't want to think about what would happen if he came back too early. Spending too much time in Keystone was a bad idea, so he tied the package to the back of his saddle and turned Daisy for home.

Arriving back at the shack, he found the door open and his heart lurched. His search for Hattie had taken eleven long months. He didn't want to think about starting over. If someone from the Red Garter had come to get Hattie, he'd go right back there and rescue her again. Blast it. They'd told him to take her!

He swung down from Daisy, snagged the package off the saddle, and ran into the house, his eyes taking in the whole scene in an instant. The tub sat on the floor, just where he'd left it. The water was a dirty gray, so she'd used it. He swung around and there, curled in a ball on the small couch, lay Hattie. Her hair was a golden yellow where it flowed down the side and almost to the floor. He took a step closer. Quietly, so he didn't alarm her. She had dark smudges under her eyes and the dark purple bruise down the side of her face seemed brighter now that her face was a clean milky white. Her bare arms also held many bruises, roughly the shape and size of a man's hands. He clenched his fist around the package. What kind of savage could do that to a girl? He grimaced because he knew the answer. He'd met a few of them.

Even in her sleep, she gripped the edges of the flimsy sleeveless underdress he'd first found her in. He turned and went to the bed she'd slept in earlier. It was little more than a cot, but better than the floor. He picked up the thick quilt and brought it to her, covering her as much for her warmth as her modesty. As soon as the cover hit her, she snuggled deep inside and sighed.

He turned toward the table, where the plates from their luncheon still sat. She'd managed a little of the food he'd cooked earlier. At least a few bites. Every bit would help her regain what she'd lost. He took the plate outside, tossed the leftovers into the trees, quickly washed the few dishes using a little of the left-over clean water from the kettle, then took care of Hattie's bath water. He glanced back at her. She didn't seem unwell, but it was an odd time of the day to sleep so hard. Course, with her previous occupation, she'd probably slept during the day, staying awake at night for her...*work*. Getting her back on a normal rhythm was another thing he'd have to help her through, but first the biggest one.

He'd never been much for drink. His da had told him stories of an uncle in New York who had trouble with the bottle from a young age. It eventually killed him, leaving his wife a widow. Da had said it was best to just leave the stuff alone, and he'd taken almost everything his da said as gospel.

Hattie shifted a bit then her eyes fluttered open. They were dull and sunken in her face.

"I'm sorry. I tried to wait for you, but I was so tired." She yawned and tried to hide it under the blanket.

"It's fine. Now that I know you're all right I should go tend to Daisy, then I want to show you what I brought for you."

She smiled slightly but wouldn't look up at him. Had she already begun to resent him? He'd tried to do right by her since finding her. But when he saw just how hooked she was to the bottle, he knew she might end up hating him forever. If Hattie had the mind to, she could get up and look around freely without him there. He took care of Daisy quickly, setting up a line for her by a tree and taking his saddle back into the lean-to. When he returned, Hattie had put away the blanket and wore the flimsy robe she'd been wearing under his coat. It was threadbare and did little to cover her.

He handed her the large, brown paper-wrapped package and her eyes grew large. She looked almost afraid to touch it.

"All this is for me? I don't think I've ever gotten a gift so large." Her hands trembled as she hesitated then lifted it from his hands.

He pulled her money out of his wallet and handed it back to her. "She wouldn't take payment. So it *is* a gift."

Hattie took the money and set it aside, then carefully untied the string and unwrapped the paper. She gasped and pulled out the lace drawers and then lavender stays. Heat rose up his neck at the sight, and he turned and made his way into the kitchen. She laughed at him but then her laughter quickly turned to squeals of delight. He'd never heard her make such a happy sound. When he turned back around, his breath caught at the bright smile on her lovely face. She was holding up a pretty burgundy dress.

"Oh, do you think it'll fit?" She held it up against her and suddenly he was worried it wouldn't and she'd be disappointed. Both in the gift and in him.

"Don't look so worried Hugh. I know I'm a spindly thing. I can sew it right up. Thank you."

He gulped back a smile. "Why don't you go behind the curtain and try it on? See what you think?"

She clutched it to her chest. "I think I will!"

CHAPTER 7

Hattie laid out all the pretty items on the bed, cataloging everything in her head as she inspected them. How had Hugh known just what a woman would need? Roy had never cared about what women wore outside of the Red Garter. What she had now would more than double what she'd left in Deadwood, if they'd kept her few things.

The new fabric was as soft as a cloud against her skin, and she cinched, tied, and buttoned until she had every piece on as it should be. There was no mirror in the small cabin for her to see how she looked. She suspected the practical cabin was meant for a man. It didn't seem big enough for a family. Thinking on the mirror again, she realized the only place she'd ever had a glass was in Keystone, and since then her reflection had turned into something she hadn't wanted to see anyway.

She pulled out the second dress and flicked the wrinkles out. A brush landed on the pile. It had been wrapped in the dress. She grabbed it up and held it in her shaking hands. Oh, how good it would feel to brush her hair and put it up again. She stepped out from behind the curtain, the brush clutched tight to her chest.

Hugh gave an appreciative nod. "You look much better. What's that you've got?"

She held it out to show him. "She put a brush in the package with the gowns. But my arms are so tired, I don't think I can make it through all the snarls." Her chest heaved with unshed tears. She hated being so weak. She'd always been strong, had always been able to count on her own strength.

"THAT WAS a surprise she didn't tell me about." He pulled out the chair for her and indicated she should sit.

The last time she'd let a man stand behind her, Roy had bitten her. Her hand touched the tender spot on her ear. She had to make a choice. Realize Hugh wasn't Roy and trust him, or live assuming every man was out to hurt her. He waited patiently for her to decide whether to sit. Hugh hadn't done a thing to her. He'd even let her sleep in peace. He wouldn't hurt her now.

Decision made. Her hands trembled as she sat in front of him. He reached around her for the brush and his hand gently brushed her cheek. She flinched and drew away as he took it from her clenched fingers. No man in her life had ever been kind. With perhaps the exception of Reverend Level who'd led them from Montana to South Dakota, but he had been aloof at best to her and her sisters. He'd never spoken directly to her and certainly never given her anything. Even Ruby's husband Beau had always looked at her with suspicion.

Hugh gently tugged at the snarls in the ends of her hair and took his time, slowly working his way up to her roots. At first the tugging was almost more than she could bear, but as he continued and the tangles released, each brush stroke was like a sweet caress. When he got to her scalp, he gently ran the brush down its length, as if he was as sorry as she was to be done with the task.

"I'm sorry, Hattie. I hope I didn't hurt you too much," he said quietly as he handed her the brush over her shoulder then turned from her. How could she answer that? His kindness made what all the other men had done all the more heartbreaking. And she'd let it happen just to get her hands on what she'd needed, or *thought* she needed. Blood pounded in her ears. How would she get more? What did she have to do to end the agony in her head?

She stood and faced his broad strong back. He wore trousers and a neat vest, the fabric across his shoulders was far too taut. Taking a deep breath, she held it then let it out slowly. She didn't want to do this anymore, but the drink called her. If using herself was the only way to get it, she'd make sure Hugh knew she could accommodate if she had to. Roy had told her she was good at it.

She stepped forward and ran her finger down the soft satiny fabric on the back of his shirt. Instead of calming him and making him pliable, he sucked in his breath and held it, his whole body tightening into steel.

Hugh turned in an instant and grabbed her hand. "You don't need to do that Hattie. You aren't that kind of woman anymore."

Her lip trembled. His hand was firm but didn't hurt her. His eyes hard, but not at her. How could she be so weak? Couldn't she even go one day without?

"Hugh. I don't want to want it anymore." She searched his eyes for help. He let go of her wrist and stepped back from her.

"I know Hattie. There's none here and I'll do my best to help you. But I can't fight that battle for you." He turned his face to the window. "And I won't be swayed either."

He'd known what she'd been doing, and it was mortifying. Did he really want to help her out of some strange unwelcome sense of duty, or did he just find her hideous? She wanted to be strong, but in the same breath was the realization that she wasn't. She wanted a drink. Was desperate for it.

There were so many things she wanted to say. She'd never asked him to fight for her. He wasn't much more than a stranger to her. Yet there was something unnamed between them. She certainly hadn't done anything to earn respect, but he respected everything about her. The hair on the back of her neck still tingled from his ministrations and her gaze flitted all around the room for something to think about other than him and the ever-present need for a drink. Saliva filled her mouth at the mere thought of it.

She turned to sit quickly, and the chair tipped as she pulled it. Her heart raced in her chest at the loud thud against the floor and Hugh appeared at her side and righted it. He didn't touch her, but her skin felt his nearness. Every muscle within her tensed. He looked down at her and if he were any other man, she would've expected him to crush her close and take what he wanted. But he didn't. He wouldn't be *swayed*. His eyes softened, and he rested his hand on the back of the chair.

"I won't hurt you Hattie. I'm sorry I didn't go to the mercantile and get you some pins for your hair. I know women like to wear it up, but I didn't even think about such things."

Of course he wouldn't. But it warmed her heart to know he thought about it now. She scooped up her hair and brought it over her shoulder. The ends were quite rough after going so long without a brush. "I'll just braid it and use the string from the package to tie it."

He turned and went to the kitchen, digging through a small box within a trunk. An amber bottle caught her eye from inside the box and her heart skipped a beat in anticipation. She stepped closer to the trunk.

Hugh pushed it out of the way. "I know I saw a scissors in here to cut the string. There's a bit of thread and a few needles in here too, though the dress looks good on you without you doing anything to it." He grabbed something within the box and produced a scissors. She remembered a time when she'd thought all things intimate were to be welcomed and she would've used the opportunity to sidle up to Hugh to give him a little contact as a thank you. He *was* handsome after all, but she couldn't act as she used to. Not now. Not after what he'd said. She reached out, careful to keep herself well enough away from him.

"Thank you Hugh. I wouldn't have known that was there." She went outside for some fresh air and a little space from the man who seemed to fill the whole cabin. She held out a lock of hair. Her shaking hands made the ends quiver. Her heart pounded within her chest. The scissors felt heavy as she lifted them to her hair and with the shaking of both hands, she couldn't even manage to squeeze them together.

Hugh appeared by her side and dropped down on the grass next to her. "Are you trying to cut your hair?"

She nodded and held out the scissors, shaking in her hands.

"Let me." He took them from her. She rubbed her hands together to calm the tremors. Though it didn't help. He gently drew her hair over her shoulder to her back and combed her mass of hair straight with his fingers, sending pleasant tremors down her back. The pointed end ran along her back as he cut a straight line across the bottom. She held her breath.

"The more I think on it, the more I want to get you back to your family quickly. You're just too young to be out here."

She let her breath out in a rush but held as still as she was able. "I'm not concerned. There are plenty of women my age who are married and having babies."

"I wouldn't push yourself into life any quicker than you've already been pushed." He stopped and the tip of the scissor raised from her back. "What drove you to accept Roy's offer?"

Anger rose white hot within her. He hadn't been there. He couldn't know what it was like. She tried to bottle it, but like bicarbonate and vinegar she couldn't help but bubble over.

"I was trapped. Trapped at home with a pa who didn't want us. Then in Cutter's Creek in a house where no one wanted us. And finally stuck with my brother-in-law on that wagon for over a month to get to Deadwood. And you know what? He didn't want us either. I never wanted to leave my home. I looked to get married and have a family of my own!"

His voice didn't waver. Nor did he raise it. "You're forgetting. I've met Beau. I know he cares for you and all of your sisters. He thinks of himself as your father."

He hadn't seen Beau watching her to make sure she never got into trouble or setting his jaw when he thought he'd caught her at something. "He doesn't care about any of us except Ruby." She spat out between clenched teeth.

"Why can't you admit it had nothing to do with Beau or anyone else? It was you. You wanted all the whiskey you could manage, and your family held you back."

She lurched to her feet and flung herself around to face him. "And does your revelation make you so smart? Yes, that was part of it. If I was married I could do what I wanted. Roy's father told me he was looking to marry, and I believed him! *I believed him.*" Her failure hit her square in the heart, and she couldn't breathe. Her breath held in her lungs until it choked her and finally escaped as a sob.

Hugh stood and his hands gently grasped her elbows, stabilizing her. But nothing could stop her seething anger at Roy and herself. She wanted to hate Hugh, but as much as she tried, she failed at that too.

Hugh's voice was little more than a whisper above her head. He held her arms but didn't pull her close, didn't take what she wouldn't offer. "He tricked you and used you. I'm sorry. I pray that Bullock or one of his men get here soon and we don't have to sit here and wait for a trial. I want to see you back home, with your family. Where you belong."

"What if I don't want to go?" She fixed him with the angriest glare she could manage even as her lip trembled.

He dropped his hands from her elbows and a chill replaced his strength. "I signed up for the job to bring you home. I guess you'll have to go."

CHAPTER 8

T he next night, Hugh gathered sticks for kindling from around the small clearing near the cabin. He needed to keep himself from thinking too much about what Hattie had said the night before. She'd changed so much from how her sisters had described her. The last few months had stolen most of her pluck. Though she'd given it a good try. The worst was yet to come. Giving up as much drink as she was used to could kill a man. He didn't want to think about what it could do to her. She was only a bit of a thing.

Her golden hair had been as soft as flower petals between his fingers. When her bruises healed and she started eating again, she would be a fair pretty sight. He just couldn't allow himself to keep thinking about her. He'd done nothing but think about her as he'd tracked her. It was a difficult habit to break. Though, now that he'd met her, his thoughts about her had changed. She'd been sharp and snappy with him all day, so he decided to give her some time. That was another reason he was outside in the clearing and not the cabin.

He deposited the kindling by the small hole he'd dug for evening fires and arranged it like the spokes of a wheel in the bottom. Then he strode to the wood pile and collected enough wood for a few hours of burning. Hattie hadn't come out since he'd cut her hair that morning. She'd looked so tired and stricken after his resolution to take her home no matter what.

He strode to the door and waited, listening. There was the quiet shuffling of soft feet on wood. He still needed to get her shoes. He gently opened the door to find Hattie bent over, franticly searching through the medicine box in the trunk he'd opened earlier. She was panting and her skin had gone from ashen to apple red. The items she'd taken out fell haphazardly back into the trunk with a loud clatter.

Her mouth dropped open and she blinked at him momentarily before falling to her knees. A sob erupted from her. He came inside and closed the door. Should he be angry or act as nursemaid? What would she need? Hattie's narrow shoulders shook and as he got closer. He saw the amber bottle in her lap. It was a tincture for muscles. He'd used it after a long bout of wood splitting. It had been in there earlier, but he hadn't paid it much mind. He stepped closer and the strong smell of the medicated whiskey wrinkled his nose. He held out his hand for it, but she clutched the bottle closer, flinching away from him and covering her face. He couldn't bear watching her cower like that. Having her even consider that he might inflict the same damage other men had curdled like milk and vinegar in his gut.

He squatted in front her and her eyes flashed as she shoved herself away from him. She tried to knock him away from her, but her arm was weak. There was some of that fire he'd been looking for.

He forced calm into his voice. "Hattie, you don't need that. Hand me the bottle." He reached out again, but she cradled it beneath her chin. Wrestling it from her would only make her angry and he didn't want to be a brute. She'd had enough of that for ten lifetimes. She'd never trust him again if he didn't do this with as much grace as he could muster. She had to come to trust him or he couldn't help her get out of Keystone. *Lord, help me to say what needs to be said.*

Her breath came too fast and her hands shook more than he'd seen them. He reached out and took her elbow, drawing her to her feet. "Come outside, Hattie. You need some fresh air. You can rest in the shade."

She shook her head, swinging her thick braid back and forth on her back. Her refusal to speak got to him. Much more than he expected it to. He closed his eyes for a moment and took a deep breath. "Come." He took a quick step behind her and lifted her to her feet, waiting until she was steady. He led her out the door, determined he wouldn't reach for that bottle. Not yet anyway. Leaving her to sit on a cut log, he crouched in front of the fire pit with his back to her as he tried to coax the small flames, blowing on the kindling. If she let go of that bottle, he wouldn't know it. But he suspected she'd rather boot him into the fire. She had to understand he trusted her as far as he could. She made a soft noise and he turned to see her rocking back and forth on the stump she sat on.

Her cheeks were as red as the sunset against skin too fair to bear the color. It gave her a sickly look. The wisps of hair by her temples lay damp against her ears. Her eyes were wide yet unseeing. The curve of her mouth tipped and moved quickly. Soft words escaped, but he couldn't hear what she said. He turned back to the fire and continued blowing on the kindling, giving her the space she needed, but staying close by. As he stood the bottle flew past him, smashing into the fire and exploding in a ball of flame. He jumped back to avoid the erupting wave of heat.

Hattie swung her gaze to him. "I didn't *want* to drink it, Hugh. I didn't." Her shoulders quaked under the admission. He collected her from her stump and wrapped his arms around her, pulling her close to his chest for her own protection and his. He didn't know what else to do to help her.

"I'm proud of you," he whispered into her hair. Her pulse slammed through her and into him. Her tremors wouldn't abate, and he drew her back and looked down at her. She shrank back from him and he let her go. He hadn't meant to frighten her, only to comfort. Blast. How could he have forgotten so quickly that she was still tender from her time at the Garter? She probably would be for a long time.

Hattie sat back on the stump, her eyes staring into the fire, far from him. "Hattie, not all touch is bad. I won't take advantage of you. I made a promise and I don't take that lightly."

Her eyes darted all around, but not at him. "It'll take more than a few days' worth of kindness to convince me of that. Roy could be kind if he wanted something too."

The words struck him hard. Of course she'd compare him to Roy. But how long until she didn't? How long until she compared men she met to some other yardstick? His gut clenched. Someday, those blue eyes would look on some young man with adoration. They would be a beautiful clear blue, not dull and expressionless. Her hair would be shiny, and her skin like a porcelain doll. If he stayed with his brother at the ranch—and she with her sisters at the same—he'd be there to see her choose that man. He turned away from her, swiping his hand across his forehead as he shook the thoughts from his head.

He couldn't afford to think of her as anything but his brother's sister-by-law. No matter how much she needed him. And she did. Though she was strong-willed, he'd yet to see her eat more than a few nibbles of bread and perhaps a bite of bacon. He'd tried to give her an apple or even tempt her with rice pudding. She'd turned green at the mere words.

Hattie slid to the ground and tucked her feet under her, her shoulders tight. He could see it even through the loose-fitting dress. Soft evening light fell around them through the sparse canopy of trees and the gentle night sounds mingled with the pop of the fire. Distantly, they could hear the raucous noise of the saloons in Keystone. A piano played and a woman sang a bawdy song. He looked at Hattie over the fire and the hunted look she gave him spoke volumes. He wished they could have been further from town, but that would lead to other dangers. He'd placed his stump on the other side of the fire. It would've been better to be closer to her, and he again reminded himself that she needed space.

He leaned back and watched the flames, his tired mind eager to drift away, until hoof beats interrupted the quiet moment.

A rider rode in and swung down from his mount even before the horse had fully stopped, spraying loose rock and gravel. A glinting badge bounced against his chest in cadence with the click of his spurs as he strode straight toward Hugh.

"You Bradly?" called the rider as he passed Hattie.

She clutched her knees closer but did not run. Hugh gave her a steady look, praying she stayed put.

Finally, he turned toward the stranger. "I am." He stood and met the man by the fire.

"I'm Deputy Cobble, from Deadwood. Bullock sent me with this urgent note." He pulled a folded paper from his vest.

He took it and the man turned back to his horse.

"Leaving so quickly?" He hoped Bullock wasn't pulling him away, leaving Hattie to fend for herself. He'd turn in his badge before he abandoned the job it had taken almost a year to finish.

"Read the note. It'll tell you everything you need to know." Cobble mounted his horse and was off into the darkness. The sound of his hoof beats bounced eerily off the hills around them.

The stark white paper in his hand stood out against the dark around him. He feared taking it to the fire to read it. What if it wasn't something he could share with Hattie or something he'd need time to talk to her about? She'd want to know anyway, and he couldn't expect her to trust him if he couldn't return that trust. He slipped the note into his pocket. Whatever it was, it would have to wait until the morrow when he had a free moment to think.

CHAPTER 9

Hattie smelled the smoke from the fire the night before still clinging to her hair and dress. The night had worn her out so thoroughly that after the fire had burned to coals, she'd just climbed into her bed without changing into the sleeping shift Hugh had brought with the dresses. The tight stays bit into her side and her chest burned with a cough, but her body couldn't move from its spot.

She'd tried to lift her arm twice, but it was as if they were weighted by rocks. Her chest felt heavy and each breath was a chore. Gooseflesh rippled down her arms, yet she could see a sheen on them where they lay over the coverlet. Her tongue felt as if it were made of bread dough. Though she couldn't think on that overmuch or her stomach would wage a war against her, or try to. She hadn't eaten for almost two days. The thought of food alone could send her to the privy, but now she was stuck. There would be no getting to the necessary or anywhere else.

She closed her eyes against the steady chop of Hugh's ax. The *thunk-thunk* echoed through the cabin from outside. It would've been rhythmic if her head didn't feel as if Hugh were whacking *her* with the ax. She pushed with everything she had and managed to roll to her side, a groan escaping her lungs at the effort. Would anyone ever care about the weakness and pain she was enduring? She was ruined, a drunkard and a prostitute. Drunkard. Prostitute. Those were words she hated, but there were no other words to describe how far she'd fallen. Her body convulsed.

Hugh had been there for her yesterday morning, even after their argument, helping her out of bed. Though she'd been mortified by it, he'd helped her with her stays and buttons up the back of her dress. Her fingers had shaken too much to do the job and she couldn't walk around in her chemise. He was just too good to even lay his hands on her and he hadn't. Even if she'd been a true flirt and actually wanted his attention, he'd already said he'd never touch her.

He'd received an important note last night. Important enough that Bullock had sent a rider all the way there to deliver it. But he hadn't read it in front of her. She'd waited until the last bit of flame had died into coals and he'd led her back to the house with her eyes so tired she couldn't see. But he didn't read it once they were inside, either.

It had taken a long time for her to fall asleep, despite her exhaustion, because she couldn't stop thinking of Bullock's messenger. Hugh couldn't know she was as on-edge about the possible trial as he was, or more so, because she didn't ever want to go back. No, she *wouldn't* go back. No matter what.

Hugh strode in and stood just inside the door, blinking his large blue eyes until he saw her. She still hadn't seen him smile and this morning was no exception. His chin, covered in dark stubble, was set in a hard line. He ran his hands up and down the front of his trousers and approached her little corner with caution.

"Do you need help up?" He leaned against the beam separating her space from the rest of the cabin and waited until she admitted him, but she couldn't, not today.

She tried to reach up but couldn't make it and gave up after just a few inches. At least she'd been able to accomplish that much.

He watched her hand intensely then glanced up to her eyes. "Perhaps today is a good day to let you rest. I'll make you some broth. Maybe that'll sit in your stomach and help you get strong. I need you to be strong, Hattie." He paused and the room filled with his unsaid words. They were at war in his head. She could see as much as sense he had something important to say and he was weighing the proper way to do it.

"Just say it, Hugh. I'm too weak to fight. What did the message say? Don't act like it didn't involve me." Her voice lumbered from her throat with as much effort as lifting a boulder.

His eyes flashed with hard emotion, then he banked them. "That's my worry, Hattie. What I've got to say is too important to spring on you when you're too weak to speak your mind. But I'm afraid if I don't do it soon, we'll run out of time."

Her throat dried like the granite rock sticking out of the peak overhead. What could be so urgent except news about her former masters. "Please don't keep it from me, Hugh. I can't stand not knowing what's going to happen."

He sighed and bowed his head, raking his hands through his short hair. He was worried and a knot grew in her stomach.

"Oh Hattie, I don't want to do this to you." He swiped his hands down his face and her heart thumped in her chest. He was going to send her back...abandon her. She wanted to cry but her body refused to give up even a little moisture for the effort.

"That note was from Sheriff Bullock. He can't make it in time for the hearing and he advised your family not to come because of something that's happened locally. He didn't say what. Though, he did say they wanted to come and be with you. His advice—to keep you away from the Garter permanently—" He paused, and she could see the tension pulling the tender skin between his eyes together. "The only way...is to marry."

She misheard him. Certainly. She couldn't have heard him just say they were supposed to get married. Or did he have some other idea? Her heart slammed against her ribs, desperate to beat itself free. She tried to take measured breaths. "And just who am I supposed to marry?" Her head throbbed against the rough fabric of the tick and she closed her eyes against the pain.

"The deputy ordered me to marry you to keep you away from

Lady Ros. She's sent a few wires to lawyers in Pierre in the hopes they'll take her case against you. It means she's desperate and knows they don't have enough to win. We have to act quickly. And we have to do it in Hill City because there isn't even a church in Keystone. Also, we don't want Ros to know."

It wasn't the comforting thought Hugh obviously intended it to be. If losing to a lawyer was such a worry, it was doubtful a certificate of marriage with ink still wet would do much to hold back their case.

"And that's my only option?" Where did that leave Hugh? He'd be stuck with her all his days. A woman almost ten years younger than him and one he didn't want. He'd only signed on to search for her, not save her. How could Bullock even ask such a thing of him?

"As far as I can see it, yes. I may have to pay a fine, but he said your family is willing to cover it. We still have to be here in case there's a trial. If she's looking for lawyers, I'd count on there being one."

She wanted to pull herself up, to look him right in the eye and determine what it was he really wanted. She'd been forced into enough in her life. She wouldn't force the one man who'd shown her a kindness into a life bound to someone he didn't want, only to save her own.

He pulled a chair up beside the bed and sat. "Hattie, I'm willing to do this for you, unless you'd rather have someone else. If you know of someone you'd rather have, tell me and I'll find them." His voice held a tremor she hadn't expected, and his eyes had gone stormy. Would it wound his pride if she said no, even if it was best for him?

"Hugh, if there were any other way to save you from this, from me, I'd do it." She used what strength she could muster and reached out, touching only his knee because she could move no further. He laid his hand on top of hers and squeezed gently, the pressure a sweet reassurance.

"If you're sure. Rest today and try to eat. Get your strength up. As soon as you can stand, we ride out for Hill City."

She nodded and let the warmth of his hand seep into her. His callused thumb wove its way under hers and held tight.

"I'll get you out of this, Hattie. I promised you I would. If you want, as soon as you're home with your family, we can have the marriage annulled. All you have to do is ask."

She closed her eyes and they wanted to stay that way. She struggled but couldn't open them again. "The same...for you, Hugh."

He laid her hand gently down on the bed and tucked the covers up to her chin. Though she couldn't open her eyes, she heard him moving about the cabin. The mere thought of marriage had tempted her for so long, since she'd first heard her father threaten her sisters with it, really. Now, she *would* be. Though, not in truth. Hugh didn't love her. He wouldn't hold her close or say things to her that made her wobbly inside. Those things were for people in love. People who *deserved* to be loved. Not prostitutes or drunks.

A pan hit against the stove with a harsh squeal and a cry tore from her. The pain in her head was unmatched. She tried to shift away from the noise when a cool cloth appeared on her head and Hugh's soft words muttered above her. "I'm sorry. The pan slipped. Try to get some sleep. I'll wake you when the broth is ready."

If only she could sleep. The exhaustion was like a living, breathing demon nibbling on her soul. Yet she couldn't quiet her strange thoughts enough to drift into slumber. Three days ago she'd planned to escape Hugh, to run far away from him, his kindness, and the threat of going back to Deadwood. To Her family. Now, she was going to wed him.

CHAPTER 10

The smell of the broth nipped at Hattie's nose as the steam wafted off the top of the cook pot. Sage and onion with some type of meat and bones. She couldn't tell which animal. For the first time in more days than she could recall, her mouth hungered for the feel of food on her tongue and her belly grumbled at the emptiness.

She'd never known a man who could cook before. Her pa certainly hadn't. Hugh was full of surprises. But of course, everything about him was. She'd only just met him, really. Had he offered to marry her or had that been a dream? And if so, why would her mind play such tricks on her? She hadn't wanted marriage since Roy's betrayal. But what if Hugh *had* offered marriage? How could she go through with it? Roy would be held at bay, but then what? Would they pretend they were a happily married couple with a homestead and a dog...and children? Or, would he quietly annul the marriage and leave her with her sisters to rot as a spinster? Neither option held a world of appeal.

She mentally shook her head, as she couldn't lift her own yet for the motion. She had no business complaining. He was the one strapped to her. A harlot. Tainted. If he did leave her, he'd never be able to comfortably visit his brother again. The marriage was just as much a burden for him as her. Yet he *had* asked her, and she knew—from his character of the last few days—he would do it without complaint.

She forced her eyes open and allowed herself to gaze upon Hugh as he stood by the stove, his back to her. Though he steadily stirred something, he was relaxed, his shoulders broad, but slanting down to strong arms that were neither so large to scare her, nor scrawny. He had most certainly worked many an hour in his life. His hair was dark as coffee and straight, clipped neatly at his neck which was dark from the sun. He turned and glanced back at her and she felt heat creep up her cheeks as his eyes twinkled. It was the closest thing she'd seen to a smile from him. Her heart fluttered at the sight.

"Glad to see your eyes open and getting clearer, if I might say so." He put down the wooden spoon and strode over to her. His hand, still warm from the heat of the stove, touched her forehead gently and he brushed a lock of hair from her temple. "I'd like to move you to a chair, if you'll let me. It'll be easier to get this thin soup into you."

She wanted to sit up, but the weight of her fatigue pulled upon every muscle in her body. He turned her from her side to her back and suddenly his hands slid under her knees and shoulders. He held his breath and slowly lifted her off the bed. Her heart raced so fast within her chest that the lock of hair in front of her eyes quivered with the force.

"Please be calm, Hattie. I won't hurt you." He whispered to the top of her head.

In some ways he was so like his brother Aiden, but in most completely different. Aiden had teased and cajoled her sister Jennie at every turn. It had been obvious from their first meeting that *something* was between them. Hattie had been so very jealous of that, had wanted it so much. Now, she'd never have it.

Gently, he set her down in a narrow rocking chair, then he stuck his foot across the small area and pulled a four-legged ottoman over to them, propping her feet up atop it. She instantly felt less like she would fall forward, and she attempted to smile at him as a thank you. He knelt down next to her until their eyes were level. He flipped his hand palm up and slipped it under hers, weaving their fingers together. Never had a man just held her hand. The solid presence beneath hers brought on a revelation. His touch was welcome.

Her throat felt raw and when she opened her mouth to speak, nothing came but a harsh cough.

"If you feel steady enough for me to go get the soup, squeeze my hand." His warm blue eyes coaxed hers to look at him. The warm pressure on her palm sent a buzzing through her, like fireflies dancing around inside her. She gave his hand as much pressure as she could muster, and the sides of his eyes crinkled in pleasure.

"Good, that's my girl. I'll be right back. I'm only a few steps away. Thank goodness for a small cabin."

Thank goodness, indeed. While she'd struggled to sleep at night, he'd had no such trouble. His steady, heavy breaths from the loft above had been a comfort drifting down to her when she'd been too frightened Roy would come take her away. He'd gone straight up the ladder every night as soon as he'd made sure she was fine in her bed. He kept the lamp on for a while, the soft crinkling of pages turning filtered down once in a while. Then the light would go out and soon his breathing would calm the rough edges of her frantic thoughts.

Hugh appeared in front of her with a cup and spoon. He draped a cloth over her front then brought up a spoonful of something that smelled of herbs and Heaven. The steam wafted toward her as he blew on it gently then held it to her lips. She forced her mouth open and the spoon slid in easily, warming her tongue. After days without food, the broth was like water to a dying man. She let it trickle down her throat, the heat seeping outward as she swallowed. He produced another spoonful and she accepted it as well. Oh, how patient he was!

The spoon clinked softly against the bottom of the enamel cup and he glanced up at her. "How are you feeling?" He wove his hand back into her hers. "Do you want more, Hattie? I don't want to give you more than your stomach will take."

She did want more, but not of the soup. His attention left a fierce desire for more, almost as strong as the drink.

Foolish girl. Stop grasping on dreams you can't have!

She managed to move her head from side to side. He set the cup on the small table next to her and took the towel from where he'd draped it over her, gently wiping the sides of her mouth. Though she hadn't felt anything there. He tossed it to the side as well then gathered her up and nestled her close to his chest. Her breathing calmed. The fear was gone, and only serenity remained.

"I'm proud of you. You are a strong tower, little warrior."

She didn't understand what he meant. But for the first time in days her mind was sated, and she closed her eyes. They were now as heavy as the rest of her.

"Sleep now. There'll be more broth in a few hours, if you want it." He carried her the few steps across the cabin and lowered her onto her bed. Before helping her shoulders to the pillow, he drew all her hair from her neck where it had stuck in the collar of her chemise and laid it gently over her shoulder. Then, his solid, steady hand lowered her head back to the pillow.

HUGH STARED down at Hattie from across the room. She was such a bit of a thing. How was he ever going to explain to his little brother Aiden that Bullock ordered him to marry her in order to keep her safe? After they'd spent days alone in the cabin, it would be better anyway, but he'd never convince Aiden of that. His good name wouldn't stand in Keystone anymore, if it ever had. Yet, a marriage of convenience... He shook his head and let all his air escape the confines of his lungs. His mam would be so disappointed. She'd already lost one son and hoped for the best for her remaining two. She'd been so happy when Aiden had found a helpmate last year. Hattie was about the farthest from what he'd ever figured his wife would be, when he'd taken the time to think on it.

He wouldn't be the one to shame Hattie, though. She'd had enough shame. He wouldn't contribute to it. If—after she was safe from the dogs at the Red Garter—she wanted nothing more to do with him, he'd get the annulment he'd offered her.

The little cabin didn't take long to clean, and he'd already chopped wood that morning to relieve the tension the note had brought. The night had left him sleeping on needles thinking of how to tell Hattie what the letter said without scaring her. The letter itself, he'd burned in the cook stove that morning. If she found it, well, he wasn't quite sure what she'd do. The marriage might protect her. But if Lady Ros got the right lawyer, they could make the marriage void and arrest him. Bullock himself couldn't protect him from that, and Hugh wasn't ready for Hattie to know what they were truly up against. Let her face that at full strength, not the wisp on the wind she was right now.

CHAPTER 11

Velvety darkness crept up to and around the tight little cabin and still Hattie slept. He'd checked on her at least once an hour. Never getting too close, just close enough to see the slight rise and fall of her shoulder as she slept curled on her side. He'd rejoiced when she'd shifted from her back a few hours ago. It had meant the broth and the rest were working. She was healing and slowly getting stronger. The drink might always be an adversary, but she was a fighter. She could do it. He smiled at the description her family had given of her. They'd said she had a mind of her own and was willing to teach anyone just how to heed it. He hadn't been at the brunt of that yet, but her ability to beat such a daunting habit spoke to him in ways her family hadn't of just how bull-headed Hattie could be. He rested his head against the beam that separated the sleeping quarters from the rest of the house and counted her breaths until he was sure she was fine. Sighing heavily, he went back the spot he'd grown accustomed to by the stove.

The soft cadence of her breathing reached him as he banked the stove for the night. It was cool enough to need a blanket, but not enough that he wanted to be up all night feeding a stove. And it made him feel better to stay in his small corner upstairs and give her room to feel comfortable at night. He took one last look around and saw that everything was in order, then grabbed his small oil lamp and took it to the ladder leading to his loft. He hadn't slept in a loft since he was a child, but there was no way Hattie could get up the ladder.

His bed was meant for a child and he had to lay pert-near bent in half to fit, but it was better than the floor. At least a little. He propped himself up against the wall and laid his Bible on his lap. Marrying Hattie should've filled him with a terrible fear, but it didn't. He'd known from the moment he read the note that he was supposed to take care of her. This was the way it had to be done.

He flicked the pages over his thumb, enjoying the sound of the paper as he flipped through them. This book that had given him comfort since he'd changed almost a year before, now felt like lead on his lap. A prayer of supplication fell from his lips, but he couldn't feel a response to his pleas for help. Though the book gave him knowledge and peace, he hadn't heard from the Lord since *that night*.

He'd been working in the barn in Kansas with Aiden trying to finish up the work quickly so his brother could return to Jennie. They'd just finished harvesting the field. Aiden had assumed big brother Hugh followed in Da's footsteps in every way, including in faith. Hugh had let his anger with Aiden cloud all reason, as he usually did, and had called him ten kinds of a fool for following fey tales of long ago. The memory was so clear he could recall it like it happened yesterday. Aiden had challenged him on his lack of belief and Hugh had been ready to punch him. A wind had swept into the barn and swirled around them, but there had been no other wind that day, not even a breeze. It had set the metal tools above their heads clanking together and a giant scythe fell from its hook and landed in a crack just inches from his booted foot. If he'd taken that angry step toward his brother, it would've sliced his skull in two.

Later, they had asked Da about the wind gust but no one else felt it. Though it would've been strong enough to blow things around through the open windows of the house. Mam had told him it was her mam up in heaven, making sure his heart and feet were in the right place. But then, like her mam before her, his had always said little prayers to her parents. It was more like talking to a friend in the room than an actual prayer. Hugh shook his head. That night, he'd picked up the Bible he'd gotten at the old country school for the first time since he'd received it. Now, he couldn't end his day without it. It had fortified him. Until now.

What was wrong with him? He flipped open the pages, trying to remember where he'd been reading. His eye caught on Hosea. He scanned the first chapter, reading that Hosea had received the same message Hugh had. Marry a prostitute. But that wasn't the end. His stomach fell further to the soles of his feet the more he read. He slapped the book shut and set it on his table, turning down the wick and plunging his room into the same darkness as his thoughts.

What if Hattie used him to get free of Ros, but then left him to work somewhere else? Keystone was a growing town, with more than one saloon. Would he, like Hosea, be forced to save her yet again? Would she want to be saved? Could he even make himself do it? If she dishonored him by leaving him and going back to that life, he wasn't so sure. He was only a man.

So was Hosea. The words caressed his aching head and filled him with a warmth he couldn't account for in the chill of the night.

Hugh pulled his boots off his feet and set aside his clothes in the blackness of the loft. The little bed was lumpy and left him shifting to find a comfortable spot. He'd read the Psalms and knew tests of faith were coming, but he hadn't expected a test that would rock him so utterly so soon after choosing to follow Christ. He jammed his knuckles into his eyes and scrubbed.

Okay, I'm listening.

HATTIE'S EYES whipped open as the house collapsed into full darkness. Her pulse raced as she waited for her eyes to adjust to the moonlight caressing the windowpane a few feet away. Hugh's nighttime ritual had been different tonight. He never let his agitation show. Though she knew men well enough to know that at one point, the bits of anger he let slip had ruled him. It had frightened her until he'd proven to her that, while some emotion boiled inside him, he wouldn't release it against her. She shivered and yanked the quilt up around her neck.

She'd fallen asleep in full daylight and now it was night. Her body was rested and though she was as weak as a kitten, it was progress.

She slid to the side of the bed and jammed her feet into her boots, wrapping the house coat around her. It was the house coat Hugh had bought for her to replace the robe she'd brought with her from the Red Garter. The night he'd brought her all the clothes, her old robe had disappeared along with her torn chemise. She wasn't about to ask Hugh about them. If she'd had her way, they'd have burned. The stove seemed far away, but it would still be warm. If she hurried, she could get more of the broth he'd made and maybe even tailor a few of the items Hugh had gotten for her. She could wear a skirt or blouse that didn't fit quite right, but an ill-fitting corset, now that was another matter. Also, she couldn't mend her clothes with him wandering around, since she only had the one corset. She'd have to take it off to fix it.

Pushing herself from the bed to her feet, she wobbled as the cabin shifted precariously around her. She could do this. She was Hattie Arnsby, the stubborn one, or so she'd been told. Just one foot in front of the other until she made it to the small clutch of dishes to the right of the stove. Hugh had already washed everything and put it away neatly. That alone was a prize. How would she ever be worthy of his sacrifice? He was completely self-sufficient, able to cook and clean all on his own. He didn't need her one whit.

Hattie pinched her arm to get her thoughts back in order. She couldn't think about those things now. A lamp next to the stove provided just enough light to see what she was doing, but not enough to rouse Hugh. Or so she hoped. She took the dipper from the water pail and stirred the broth. It had a layer of solid fat on top that protected it. She dipped lower and filled a cup with the barely warm broth, then found a suitable lid for the pan and covered it. The scent of the broth taunted her stomach as she made her way to the same rocker she'd used earlier that day. Somehow, it wasn't half as nice of a seat without a handsome cowboy with dark blue eyes sitting in front of her. Would he still act that way when she was healed...? Or would he abandon her? That little voice of fear would not be quieted. No man had ever proven trustworthy. Why would they start now?

The broth filled her belly and she lay her head back against the chair, rocking for a moment as the quiet of the night hemmed her in. Her skin pricked and her eyes flew open as she scanned the cabin around her. The weak lantern light that a moment before had been inviting, now felt far too inadequate. There were no noises but for the soft snoring of Hugh in the loft, but the feeling remained. She lifted the lantern and slowly walked through the small cabin, but nothing was out of place.

You silly ninny. Afraid of the dark now, are you?

She sighed and tried to smile to wipe away the feeling still lingering in the room when something huge flew through the front window. A scream tore from her throat as the object sprayed glass through the room and ripped a hole in the seat of the wicker rocker she'd just been sitting in.

CHAPTER 12

Hattie stared at the shattered glass glinting off the dim lantern light and a shiver started somewhere near her shoulders and penetrated her whole body. The cabin shook as Hugh landed with a thump a few steps behind her. She gasped and turned as Hugh collected her in his strong, comforting arms. He wore only his undershirt and black cotton trousers. The heat from him seeped through the threadbare cotton of his shirt and into her cheek.

"Are you hurt? What happened?" His steady hand, warm on her back, coaxed the terror from her.

She shook her head and he led her to the couch then left her to check out the damage. His warmth evaporated into thin air, leaving a strange emptiness and distress in its place. He lifted the destroyed rocking chair, revealing a large stone on the floor. It was wrapped in string. Under the string was a note. Hugh pulled it from the binds and growled.

She didn't want to know but if she didn't find out, it would drive her mad. "What does it say."

Hugh's stormy eyes met hers, and she shivered with the intensity.

"It says, '*We're watching you.*'"

She wrapped her arms tightly around her. The cabin had seemed so safe, so separate from Keystone and the people there. Now, the cabin was just as terrifying. She stood and raked her hands up and down her gooseflesh-covered arms. Someone had been watching her. Someone had sat outside the window and waited until she stood. If they hadn't waited, they would've injured her. Hugh strode over to her and turned her to face him. His hand tilted her chin and her breath caught in her throat. Would he kiss her? But he didn't move.

"Hattie, we can do this. Whoever that is can't sit there all the time. We'll make it to Hill City."

She pulled back from his hand and shook her head as she let her fear erupt. "I want to stay there, in Hill City. I don't want to come back here. I never wanted to come here."

Hugh sighed and his eyes turned soft once again. "If we don't, then they could arrest me. You aren't free yet. Not until the circuit judge says you are. Ros will push to get you back. She probably lost money on you." She could picture him talking to a horse in that same gentle, pleading voice…or a child.

Fierce anger welled up to replace the fright. "Once we're married, it shouldn't matter. They can't take a married woman. That note from yesterday said so." A cold seeped into her skin that had nothing to do with the broken window and she couldn't suppress a shiver.

He turned from her. "I wish that were so. I wish I could make that guarantee, but they could just as easily arrest me and take you back."

No, it couldn't be. He'd said marriage would solve the problem. She narrowed her eyes and tried to control the anger pouring through her. "Why didn't you tell me that this morning, before I agreed?"

He scrubbed his hand over the back of his neck. "I wanted you to heal, not worry. But I can't stop you from worrying now. I don't know how I'll get you past whoever's out there. But so help me, I will."

"You're so sure I'll still have you after you kept it from me, that the whole marriage could be for nothing?"

He whipped around to face her, his eyes snapped like fireworks, and that hint of anger flexed through his shoulder muscles in a wave. "The choice is yours. I can't make it for you. But Bullock isn't coming if there's a trial. All I have is the letter from your family saying you were taken. They'll have Roy who'll say you came of your own free will."

"And that's what it comes down to, isn't it?" She pressed herself closer to him, forcing him to meet and hold her gaze. "I did go willingly. I wanted to go. I *needed* to go. But now, because I didn't see what was ahead, we both have to pay the price. Will you hold that against me?"

He flinched then leaned over and grabbed the rock. He crossed the space of the cabin in two strides, throwing it back outside. "Do you have any other ideas? I'd rather not see you returned to Ros. But if that's what you want, by all means, I can take you back."

An icy chill ran down her spine and tingled through her fingers. She most certainly did *not* want to go back, ever. If she were taken now, it would be even worse for her than before, because she'd been free for a time. All the other women would take out their anger on her for trying to get out of that life. Some wanted to be there, others hated it, but they also hated those who tried to escape even more. As if wanting something better was somehow dirtier than the acts they performed. Hattie tried to rub heat into her arms once again but failed.

"No, I don't. Marriage seems to be the only solution. So, now that you have my agreement, what about you? Do you agree with this foolish plan?"

He didn't turn back to her like she'd hoped. Instead he moved to the broken window. "On the contrary, I think it's a fine plan. It just has to be executed properly." She couldn't see his face as he searched out the window into the dark, but there was no hint of sarcasm. His words were steady and his stance as solid as the granite slabs all around the cabin.

How could he be so sure? Her whole life hinged on this one

action, but perhaps that was the problem. He faced possible imprisonment. It would be a short stint, but then he would be out. For her, the term was life. It was much easier to be cocksure when you didn't have much to lose.

He turned from the window. "I'm sure of the plan because I felt it deep within my soul. As soon as I received the note, I knew it was right. The only thing that didn't sit right was wondering how to tell you what the note said."

She tapped her foot against the floor. "When we're through all this and I'm free, please tell me how you manage to speak with your soul. In the meantime, *I* will worry."

"You don't have to. Take it to the Lord and see if He calms your spirit as well."

The Lord? Her ma had told them of the Lord and made them learn the rosary, but it had never become part of her. It had been little more than nonsense to her.

"You can talk to the air if you wish, but I won't."

A slight twitch at the side of Hugh's eye was the only sign he was listening to her at all. The old reverend who'd led them to Deadwood had prayed with them on the way and her sisters had dutifully bowed their heads, but she doubted if any one of them had any idea what he spoke of any more than she did. If there was a God out there, He certainly hadn't shown much interest in her family. If He was even there, she'd given Him no reason pay her any special attention anyway. That was a sure-fire way to get hurt.

HUGH DUG AROUND in his munitions box and pulled out his Colt and six bullets, sliding each one into the cylinder with care. He could feel the burn of Hattie's stare against his back. Her fire was coming back and that was good, but they didn't need to be squabbling just now.

He could picture her stiff stance in his mind, could almost see her tapping her foot.

"Are you going to stay down here? I had a few things I was hoping to get done while you slept."

When he turned, she wouldn't look him in the eye and a sick feeling took up residence in his gut. "And just what were you planning?" he whispered, holding his calm in check. He reminded himself not to draw conclusions. He'd been guilty of that his whole life and it had caused more pain than he could reckon.

"If you must know, I was going to sew my clothes properly. I can't very well do it with you sitting down here."

He closed his eyes and let the relief settle over him. She wasn't hoping to search for something to drink. She just needed a bit of privacy. *Thank you, Lord...*

"I'm sorry, Hattie. I think it best we get the light out as soon as possible. Without the light, they can't see in here."

She threw up her arms. "And just when can I do it? I can't exactly parade around—" Her neck moved ever so slightly as she swallowed back her words.

"I don't expect you to. We haven't seen anyone around the cabin during the day and my horse hasn't sensed anyone. I'll be outside tomorrow so you can get your sewing done then. I think we ought to try to leave the following day though. The longer we wait, the harder it'll be to get back here in time. It's ten miles uphill to Hill City."

She took a delicate breath and held it. Her skin had cleared and was now a soft creamy color. Her eyes looked bluer with each passing day.

"I've slept all day. I finally have a little energy and now I must go back to bed," she huffed, obviously put out. She blew out the lantern, bathing the cabin in darkness. "Are you planning to stay there all night?" Through the darkness, her fear clawed at him. A few days wasn't enough time for her to trust him near her at night. He'd have to stay at least until he was reasonably certain Hattie was safe. "I'm not sure. Just try to rest. Sounds like you have a lot of work ahead of you tomorrow."

"That I do... I have to sew my wedding dress."

413

Her whispered words hit him with the power and accuracy of a marksman. Within the next few days at most, he'd be a married man.

CHAPTER 13

Hattie saw the first creeping rays of light as dawn stole over the window, basking the wall by her bed in a saffron glow. Slowly, everything in the small sleeping area became visible and she pushed herself stiffly out of the bed. What a long night. There had been no way for her to fall asleep. Not after the rock. Not after Hugh came flying down from above to save her. And certainly not after their talk about God.

She pulled on her corset, fastening the busk, then crossing the ties in back and tightening slowly, wiggling until it fit properly. She held her breath and tied them off quickly. Her dress slipped easily over her shoulders and, because it was too big, she didn't have to worry about the buttons.

The wood slatted floor was cool against her stockinged feet, but she'd have the stove lit this morning before Hugh got up—and breakfast made too, if she could find where he kept everything. She hadn't paid much attention the last few days, since her appetite didn't exist. Nosing around the kitchen, she found his stash of eggs and other provender. She smiled, pulling out six of them. Her stomach grumbled as she set them on the counter. Food finally sounded good and she'd prove to Hugh she was worth keeping around. Worth taking as a wife. A little flutter grew in her belly. *Why should I be nervous?*

She heard a soft exhale as she gathered the kindling for the stove and turned to see Hugh, stuffed awkwardly into the small chair where he'd sat sentry when he'd sent her to bed. At some point he'd fallen asleep. His dark hair fell softly over one eyebrow, too short to get in the way, but just long enough to tempt her to push it back up with the rest. He was not the strong man she'd grown accustomed to just then. His sleep made him vulnerable, accessible. He certainly wasn't the first man she'd seen asleep, but he was by far the handsomest.

She padded closer, as quietly as she could manage. He didn't wake as she knelt in front of him, reaching for the gun so he wouldn't be startled awake with it in his hand. As she touched the chilly steel of the sidearm, cold blue eyes opened. His gaze softened immediately, and he held her stare. The slight raise of one side of his mouth told her he knew she'd been staring at him. But still not enough to be a smile. He clicked open the cylinder and lifted it letting the bullets fall into his palm.

"I'm sorry you slept down in the chair. Did you see anything?" Why could she never think of anything to say? It seemed that even days after her last drink her mind was addled.

"I didn't mean to fall asleep here." He rubbed the back of his hand over his forehead then flinched as he rubbed his neck and shoulder. He stood and, with a slight stretch, the thin undershirt fabric pulled taut over his lean waist. *Stop it, you're proving what Roy said was right. Good for nothing calico queen.*

She whipped around back and stomped to the stove. If she weren't careful, she'd snag her stockings on the floor. "The male body isn't interesting in the slightest," she grumbled to herself as Hugh let the door slap closed behind him, covering her grousing. The kindling proved good and dry and she soon had the small cook stove roaring, with the Arbuckle's percolating and some eggs frying.

Hugh came back in after a few minutes and moved in right behind her, brushing her shoulder as he grabbed the coffee pot. He towered above her, but she could feel his breath on her neck. He'd changed his clothes, and his warmth hemmed her in.

Since she was sewing today, she'd make sure he had clean clothes for their wedding, too.

"That smells right fine, Hattie. I'm glad you're feeling up to cooking. I don't know how to make much."

She blazed hot under his compliments. "You cook well. I just wanted to do a little something for you for a change. You've done so much for me. I don't know how I'll ever repay you. I don't think I'll ever be able to." She chattered on, nervous for reasons she couldn't explain. She scraped the eggs out of the pan and onto two plates.

"I'm not doing this for the pay, Hattie. I'd think you know by now I'm doing this for family. Your family is also mine. That connects us."

She felt a small connection growing with him in other ways, too. Ways that frightened her a little. Blast Roy. If not for him, she'd have met Hugh under much different circumstances. *And he wouldn't have given you a second look.* Oh, her thoughts were cruel, but true. He certainly would never entertain thoughts of marrying her. He had to be almost a decade older than her, though he'd never said. He probably wouldn't have thought her much more than a child. He might still.

She rapped the spoon on the pan and slammed it on the table, angry for even thinking about what could've been. Hugh didn't belong strapped to her. He wouldn't even like her. Their marriage would be a farce. How did a God-fearing man stand up before a God he revered and say those vows, yet not mean them?

For her safety, that's how.

He glanced up at her and his eyebrow rose in question at her sudden pique. She bit her tongue. It infuriated her even more that he could read her so easily.

"What crossed your mind that suddenly you want to rip off the head of the spoon?" The side of his eyes crinkled.

"I don't want you to have to marry me, Hugh. I want you to have the life I never will, with happiness and children. I want you to promise me you'll get an annulment the moment the judge says I'm safe." She wanted to reach for his arm, wanted confirmation, or maybe just to sit at his feet and beg him not to ruin his life on account of her. Her own was already destroyed.

A shadow passed over his eyes briefly. "I can't do that to you. And I won't. We'll be married, go through the trial together, then when we're home and you can make a sound decision, we'll decide if we stay married or part. Together."

"Hugh please, my reputation is already ruined. I don't care if people laugh at me and mock me. They already will. I'd rather they not mock *you*."

The muscle by his eye remained still. Hugh wasn't angry with her for saying her piece. He stood and, though she faced him, he turned her body toward him. The soft brush of his hand on her shoulder caught her breath and held it hostage. She no longer wanted to bolt from his touch. There was none gentler.

"Hattie, I would do this for you but not only for you. I do it for me and for my family too. Family is all I have, and *no one* will hurt them." His mouth was but a few inches from hers and his soft words held a terrible threat, but not for her. She would soon be part of this family. Important to Hugh. She wanted to agree, to tell him yes, that she would accept. But the words lodged somewhere within her and she could only stare at the pulse of his heart on the base of his neck where his shirt lay unbuttoned. Would he move in closer? Would he show her he desired her—or maybe he didn't?

She blinked to clear her head. "I believe you."

"Do ya, now?" A slight accent kissed his words as if that phrase had been passed down from generations before.

"I do." She felt the sweet knot tightening in her belly. Those words would soon seal her fate, and his.

CHAPTER 14

The window drew her like a moth to flame and she caught herself staring outside for the third time. The only thing tugging her gaze away was the needle poking her skin. A consequence of her distraction. Hugh was outside, his shirt plastered to his well-muscled shoulders as he moved sections of wood to chop. He'd worked up quite a sweat. She kept telling herself the indomitable heat was the reason she fanned herself, but that was a little white lie. As far as men went, she would get a fine one.

She stood, sucking on her sore finger, and took a look at her handiwork. She'd had to use string to measure herself, then use the string to determine how much she'd need to take in the stays. The same string was a perfect measure for the dress but allowed a little extra room. The effect was a fitted bodice, not a tight one.

Hugh welcomed someone just outside their cabin, and her spine let loose a pack of shivers. No one had visited except whoever had tossed that rock through the window, and any visitor could be the one watching them. She quickly dodged behind the dressing quilt she'd hung in the corner for a screen and wiggled her way into her new fitted stays and gown. It took a few minutes for her to emerge, but she had to know who was out there and what they wanted.

The window nearest where Hugh was talking was open, his rumbling voice like a beacon to her. She peered out the window, attempting to stay as hidden as possible.

"I ain't looking to take on anyone else, Lola. No telling what'll happen to us in the next few days. I have my orders and they don't include you."

"But you ain't heard the talk in town, sugar. I have. I heard tell Ros got herself a humdinger of a lawyer. I used ta do all the laundry there, see, and I heard her tell him they were to arrest you as soon as you show up back in town. For kidnapping."

A cold ache grew like a coating of ice on a window. Soon she shook with it. They would arrest Hugh and leave her all alone to face the trial. She'd have no proof, no family, no chance. "I'm not going back," she whispered to the cobwebs in the corner. Hugh spoke again and she leaned back against the window to hear more clearly.

"I can get you to the stagecoach in Hill City. Take that to Deadwood. When you get there, ask for Aiden Bradly. He'll help you find work and a place to stay. That's the best I can do. I've got other business that needs attending to."

The woman nodded and held out her hand to shake like a man would, which Hugh did. "I thank ye. When I heard what Ros said, I just had to come out here and tell you. Hattie never done me wrong." Her words didn't match her face. She was hiding some-thing, and it had Hattie on edge. She searched her memories of her time at the Garter, but it was difficult, as if it all ran together. She couldn't place this woman.

"She's in the house if you want to go see her." He pointed to the door. "You'll excuse me, I'm trying to get this finished." He nodded and didn't wait for a reply.

The woman turned for the house and a strange feeling crept over Hattie. She should recognize the woman if she'd done the laundry. She'd lived in that awful place for almost a full year. But this woman's face was a complete mystery. How could it be that this woman knew her well enough to risk her life to come tell them of Ros's plan, but no matter how Hattie dug through her memories, she couldn't remember the woman?

Hattie opened the door and tried to remember what Hugh had called the stranger, but her mind simply wouldn't work. The woman stepped inside and looked Hattie up and down.

"Well now, ain't you doing well for yourself? Better than all the ladies you left behind, ain't that the truth. Your man, Roy, he had to provide another girl to take your place. For free."

"No..." She couldn't bear the thought of him taking advantage of anyone else. Her hands shook and something deep inside spoke insidiously in her ear. *You'll handle this news better with a drink.*

Hattie shook her head and turned away.

"Yes. She's older, though, and was much more willing than you to take on the job."

"If they've replaced me, then why do they want me back? I don't understand." Her head pounded in her ears and a headache spiked between her eyes. *Just one. You only need one. Then your head won't hurt, and you'll remember this woman.*

"To set an example. She don't want her girls thinking too hard about cowboys on shining horses who'll whisk them off to the hills to play house."

Now, she couldn't remember if this woman was cheeky by nature, but her words had turned downright insulting.

"We are not *playing house.* We're waiting for the circuit judge."

The woman cackled, throwing her head back. "There'll never be a trial. If you come back to town, that man out there'll be arrested. You'll be marched right back to the Garter. But you won't get your old room back. That was given to the new girl. You get the room in the back of the bar for leftovers too drunk to pay more than pennies."

She clutched her sides to keep the woman from seeing the effect of her words. "Whose side are you on?" Hattie whispered, ready to send the woman back to Keystone.

A gleam lit the woman's eyes as she pulled a metal flask from a bag she carried. Hattie's heart pounded in her chest and her mouth could already feel the warmth flowing down her throat. It had the same look as the flask Roy had when they'd ridden the stage to Keystone. The one that started her back down the road to drowning herself in drink whenever possible. How could this woman have known her greatest weakness?

"I ain't on your side, and I ain't on his side. I'm on my side. Your man, Roy, is offering a reward for you. Enough that I wouldn't have to wash no more. When he heard I was coming out to get you, he sent this as a reminder of what you're missing." She removed the cap and stepped forward, swiftly running it under Hattie's nose. "And when you're back home drowning yourself once again, you can just remember that it was Lola who put you back where you belong." She glanced over her shoulder. "That man out there don't need your trouble. And that's all you are, a passel of trouble. Come back to town right now and save him getting arrested. Because if you don't, it'll be you that puts him there."

Hattie couldn't think or breathe. She stared at the flask and wanted more than anything to pull back just one drink. No one would ever know. Lola smirked and set the flask on the table then sauntered back to the bed. She sat on it, bouncing a little to test it. Then she laid down, pulling Hattie's blankets and quilt over her dusty clothes and boots.

She called from the bed, "You're pretty selfish. He's going to jail if you don't come back with me. Either way, you're going back to the Garter."

Hattie stared at the open flask and a war waged inside her. A few drinks and the remaining fogginess might clear from her mind. She might be able to remember the bits of her life she couldn't from the last year. But it would also make her a failure. Hugh wanted her to stay away from it and he was right. The bottle had never done her any favors. Yet that small metal bottle held her captive in its fragrant promise.

Hugh tromped closer to the house and she snatched up the flask, spun the cap tight, and slid it into one of the large pockets in her skirt. She couldn't have him finding it just sitting there. He might think she'd snuck it in.

Hugh opened the door and strode inside, his frame filling the doorway as he paused to get a dipper of water by the door. He then stepped over to the wash basin and poured a bit of water in the bowl, splashing it over his face. A net full of butterflies took flight in her stomach and the flask weighed heavy against her leg.

His eyes lit when he saw her. "Well now. Don't you just look pretty."

He still wouldn't smile. He must reserve those for very special occasions. "Where did Lola run off to?" He wiped the water from under his eyes and gazed around the cabin.

Would he notice her nerves, could he read her that well yet? "She…was tired. She's resting."

"In your bed? You must have been closer to her than I assumed." Hugh frowned. "Can you come outside with me for a spell and take a walk?"

The fluttering intensified. Did he know what was in her pocket? Could he smell it, or had he seen her hide it away? He strode over to her and stood right in front of her, his penetrating eyes seeing right into her soul. His hands grazed her elbows as he reached for and captured her shoulders, sending a slight shock to her heart.

"What's the matter, Hattie? Was seeing someone from your past too much? I'm sorry. Maybe I should've sent her away, but she sounded as if she genuinely cared about you."

Hattie tried not to scoff at his words. Lola was a viper, but she had to be careful or Lola might tell Hugh too much.

He put his arm around her, and the butterflies stuttered along from her stomach to land across her skin in soft prickles. The sweet scent of evergreen trees tickled her senses, pulling her attention from her pocket to the man next to her. He'd always smelled a little of trees and leather. He led her up a path that wove back and forth but always up, higher and higher until Hattie was sure she couldn't possibly climb any further. But then the trees opened up and light-colored rocks jutted out from the hill. Hugh easily climbed atop the shortest one and held out his hand to her. She waited for a moment, wanting to take his hand, but afraid all the same.

She looked up at him and his warm skin, touched by the sun, invited her. He waited for her hand and when she took it, they climbed the few steps up the side of the rock.

"I'm sorry it isn't real comfortable, but it's the only place I could think of where we'd be out in the open so no one could get close enough to hear us."

The rock had seemed large when she'd looked up at it, but now that she sat upon it, she had to sit right next to Hugh or risk falling off. The back side of the rock was a steeper drop, if she slipped… No, thinking about slipping made her dizzy. She moved a little closer to Hugh, his strong leg next to hers provided a little comfort on the high rock.

Hugh leaned back against his hands, bracing them a few inches behind her, basking in the sun. Her hands shook and she couldn't account for why.

He sighed deeply, as if something bothered him a great deal. "All right, Hattie. Out with it."

CHAPTER 15

Hattie sat rigid and stock-still next to him, her breathing uneven and shallow. The moment he'd stepped inside their cabin he'd known that he'd need to take her here to talk. Her haunted eyes and nervous movements had told him something wasn't right with his future bride. When he walked in, her eyes were huge bright blue pools and her mouth was stuck slightly open as if she'd been caught with her hand in the cookie jar. But what could be the matter? While he enjoyed seeing her surprise, this wasn't a good one. She'd tried to hide it in the folds of her skirt, but her hands were shaking again. He hadn't seen them do that in over a day.

She took a deep breath and faced him. Though she wouldn't look up at him, he could see the soft profile of her cheek. "I'm sure I don't know what you mean, Hugh. If you want to know something, please just ask."

Well, simple enough, he could do that. "I want to know what's got you shaking again. I want to know about Lola sleeping in your bed and not on the couch where she belongs. And I want to know why, after I'd just got you to calm down near me, you're looking at me like I might throw you over my shoulder, drag you to my bed, and ravage you. I've had plenty of opportunity, Hattie. Even after just under a week, I'd think you'd know me better by now."

Her cheeks flamed red. He hadn't been sure she had a blush in her anymore and it did his heart good to see it. She was healing.

Reaching for her was a temptation, but he had to settle for placing his arm just out of reach.

"I...I don't remember her, Hugh. I wish I did. I wish I could tell you more about this woman who's invaded our camp, but I can't. I don't like her. I don't think she should be with us."

Good. At least she was still speaking her mind. He'd thought there had been a faint whiff of drink when he'd walked into the house, but if she'd found a way to get it, she'd be back to her quiet ways. Hiding. Not open and speaking her mind to him.

"I agree with you. But at this point, I'd like to keep her close at hand. If she goes back to town now, we don't know what she'll tell them. I'm not fool enough to think she really came out here to help. Though it's good to know what they're planning. I'll just have to wire Seth Bullock again and insist he come or send help."

"Bullock won't come out here just for me. I'm nothing." She bunched her skirts into her fists then pressed the wrinkles flat.

A board came loose on the corral he'd built around his heart. "That ain't true, Hattie. You don't have to live that life or be that person anymore. You've worked so hard. Don't give up. I won't give up on you." He sat up and wrapped his arm around her. With as close as she'd had to sit next to him to fit on the rock, his arm draped perfectly around her shoulders. She shrieked and scooted away from him the moment his hand touched her hip, and he drew back. Blast it! He'd pushed too far yet again.

Hattie ran her trembling hands down her skirt once more. He picked up the hand closest to him and her other hand went for her hip, then retreated. Her blue eyes glanced up at him and set a fire somewhere deep in his gut. He had to get her back to her family and maybe get away for a while. He'd gotten too close to her, become too protective of her. If he continued, he'd scare her away for sure. He gently pressed his thumb into her palm.

"It's okay that you don't remember. Drink clouds your thinking and makes you do things you wouldn't do without it. I hope there's a lot you don't remember about that place."

She squinted into the sun and shaded her face with her free hand but didn't pull away from him. "I guess that's what's strange. Some things I can remember clearly. As if they scared me so much they're whittled into who I am. Other things are like looking through fog. Fuzzy, distant, like it wasn't me that went through it at all. I know why I can't remember some of it. But the rest, I wish... I wish I'd never met Roy Hayden."

He let his thumb roam in a circle in the palm of her hand, trying to comfort the edge out of her voice. She shuddered in response. *You need to stop now, Hugh Bradly. It doesn't matter that she'll be your wife tomorrow. She isn't yours. Not now, maybe not ever.* He yanked his hand from hers and rested it against the cool rock once more. That, he could handle.

She gave him a knowing glance then frowned. She knew men too well. Did she realize she was gaining a hold over him? A hold he was afraid to inspect too closely. When he'd signed on for this job, he hadn't planned on coming home a married man. His parents waited for him in his brother Aiden's house. But where did he fit? He'd left so quickly. He hadn't thought about it. He, himself, had no home, no place to lay his head. What would he do with a wife?

Hattie shivered next to him and he fought the urge to move closer to her again.

"She said some terrible things to me when she came into the cabin, Hugh. She doesn't care about me or you. She mentioned a reward. She can't be trusted."

He scratched his chin and let her words sink deep. Bullock had to come, that was the only way out of this. Between the watcher and his threats, and Lola, he'd had enough of everything. Getting her home would be the best way out, but how?

Hattie pushed herself to the edge of the rock and as her skirt fell against the rockface he heard a soft *clink*. Hattie's face turned stark white and she glanced quickly at him, then down the side of the rock. She had something hiding in her clothes. He'd gotten closer to her lately, perhaps too close. Had she started carrying a weapon with her? Did she think she needed to defend herself against him? He never should've allowed himself to hold her. He should've known she wouldn't want that.

She jumped the few feet to the ground and clutched her skirts in her fists, rushing away as he pulled himself to the edge. He hadn't done anything, no more than sit near her, and she ran away like a scared rabbit. He'd need to prove to his wife that he was a man she could trust. A man of his word. Maybe even a man she could love, someday. He would protect her above all else. At least until she decided to let him go, and maybe even after that.

There hadn't been many women in his life before Hattie. He hadn't had time while working his fingers to the bone on his father's farm. And even more so after his little brother Peater had paid the ultimate price for serving their father. Now the farm was gone, and he was here in South Dakota with nowhere to call his own.

He let his legs dangle from the edge of the rock, leveraging his hands to push off. A scream tore up the hill followed by the terrifying crack of a gunshot.

CHAPTER 16

Hugh threw himself off the rock and tore down the hill toward the scream. He reached for his gun only to come up empty-handed. He'd been chopping wood before he took Hattie for their walk and he never wore his pistols when chopping. He prayed the scream wasn't from Hattie's lips, but he knew it couldn't be anyone else.

The trail up and down the hill hadn't been well-marked and Hattie hadn't followed it. He skidded to a stop, grabbing a tree to keep from falling headlong down the hill looking for signs of her path. The area was clear, without a person or animal. He reached down and grabbed the knife he'd stuck, wrapped in a leather sheath, into his sock that morning. If it was good enough for his ancestors, it was good enough for him. He'd thought of it when he'd found his da's old *scian* in his gear. He hadn't dared bring the long blade with him or it might scare Hattie, so he'd settled on a short blade, similar to a dirk, though now it seemed woefully inadequate.

He held the knife in front of him, weaving it back and forth as he took careful steps down the hill full of twigs and underbrush that would make noise if he wasn't careful. He heard rustling and a muffled cry ahead. Hugh moved faster, throwing himself down the hill tree by tree. Whoever was ahead wasn't listening for him.

He found Hattie smashed up against the base of a tree with some brute yanking her hands over her head. The lout was pressing himself into her. She had a gun in her hands, but it did little good with her arms in the air. The fear in her eyes enflamed an old anger he'd tamped down over the last eleven months. She pulled her head as far away from the man as she could, and her gaze locked with Hugh's. Tears streamed down her cheeks and she whipped her head to the side as the man pushed closer to her, moving in to kiss her.

Bile rose from his stomach, hot and potent. He plowed toward them, plunging his knife into the man's hand where it was braced against the tree, pinning him in place. The man immediately loosed Hattie's arms and he screeched in pain.

"Hattie, run." Hugh waited only a moment for her to untangle herself before he tore his knife out of the tree and prepared to defend what was his. The man howled again, cradling his hand against his chest.

"What'd you do that for? It ain't nothing I ain't had before." He whined, cradling his hand to his chest.

Hugh's anger thrust from him with more force than the knife. "Get out of here! Make no mistake. If I ever see you again it'll be with a gun in my hand."

"You kilt my good hand!" He held out his quivering, dripping digits for inspection.

"I'll do worse than that if you don't run." He heard the steal edge to his voice, an edge he hadn't heard in a long time. How long had it been since he'd cared about anything enough to defend it to the death?

The man muttered to himself and staggered off through the trees. Hugh turned around to find Hattie waiting a few feet behind him. He wouldn't go to her, not after the moment on the rock when she'd rebuffed his comfort. That would take more from her. It would assume she wanted his touch, his help and support. He held his hand out to her as he lowered himself to sheath his knife. She trembled and stared at his hand. There was a battle going on behind those crystal blue eyes. She took first one tentative step toward him, then another, finally dropping the gun to her feet and rushing at him with the force of a train. She skipped his hand altogether and flung herself at him, wrapping her arms tight around him and clutching him close. A shudder ran down the length of her. He wrapped his arms around her and tried to tell himself that he'd treat his own mam the same way. But it was a lie. His mam wouldn't need healing and support from him. She'd go to his da. No, only Hattie had ever gone straight to him when she needed. *Only Hattie.*

It hit him like a sledgehammer to the gut. He held her close until she pulled away, taking a few steps back. She kept her head bowed and tucked her hands behind her back.

"I'm sorry, Hugh. What must you think of me, throwing myself at you that way?" A lock of hair had come loose from the string she'd used to tie it and she tucked it behind her ear. He'd failed her again. The pins he'd meant to get, he'd completely forgotten. He couldn't admit that he wanted her in his arms. Couldn't admit to her that he'd been terrified a moment ago—first for her, then of her reaction to him.

"Are you all right? Did he hurt you?"

She shook her head but refused to look up at him. He took a step closer to her and she turned and dashed away from him again. He wanted to plant his fist in the tree but that would do neither of them any good. Why was she suddenly running from him? He followed her with his eyes until the tall spruce trees ate every glimpse of her. She'd been acting strangely even before that fool had pinned her to the tree. It had started when Lola came. If she was that bothered by the woman. He'd take his chances and send her back to town.

He picked up the discarded pistol and checked the cylinder. It was empty. How had she gotten it from that man and how had she missed at such close range? He'd have to ask her later once she calmed down. Course, with ousting Lola, then leaving to get married, she might not be good and calm for a long while.

~

HATTIE CLOSED the door behind her and leaned against it. No one would blame her for taking a drink. No one would even know. She touched the heavy flask still in her pocket. Hugh had known she was hiding something and when she'd edged to the side of the rock, it had fallen and made noise, even through all the fabric of her skirts. It had made her run, made her careless... And then... She shuddered at the memory of that man jumping out from behind the tree. He'd trapped her and pinned her shoulders to it. She'd reached for his gun, but he'd forced her arm against the trunk and pulled the trigger. She'd been sure the bullet would find its way to Hugh and in that moment, she'd known more fear than she'd ever experienced. Not for herself, he couldn't take more from her, but for Hugh. He was innocent and if she'd shot him, she'd have to live with that forever. She'd given up and let that man take what he wanted until she saw Hugh pounding through the trees.

Her hand slipped into her pocket. The shape of the flask was so familiar, just like Roy's. Except, Roy had put her in this mess. Hugh had got her out. If Hugh knew it was there, he'd be so disappointed. It was shameful, the way she wanted it, but she could make herself neither take it from her pocket to dispose of it any more than she could take it out to have a drink and be done with it.

Hugh's booted feet tromped up the worn path and she rushed from the door so he could come in. If she didn't look busy, she'd look even more foolish. She went to the stove, but there was nothing on it to stir or tend. He strode through the door and his eyes, so dark and brooding, questioned her without ever saying a word.

She couldn't turn the flask over to him. Couldn't admit she had it and it slammed a wall between them just as solid as the log walls of the cabin. What would he think of her? She had to get rid of it on her own, when she was ready. She could do this. It was the one thing she *could* do all on her own. She sucked in her breath and stood as tall as she could until she heard Lola slip out of the bed and stride over.

"Well. Glad to see you both. Let's make a plan." She smacked her lips and her hands together, making a loud slap and sucking sound that made Hattie cringe. She moved to the fireplace, away from Lola and the trouble she was sure to cause.

Hugh nodded and planted his feet, hands draped casually over his hips, but his glance stuck on her, warming her skin. He looked like the posters of military men she'd seen in Deadwood. Handsome, strong, and ready to fight.

He cleared his throat. "Excellent idea, Lola. I've done some thinking, though. You're still welcome in Keystone, so there's no need for you to come with us. Why don't you go back to Keystone and catch the stage from there? There's no sense in you walking ten miles when you can go right back into town."

Lola smiled and showed a few missing teeth. "I think you're right, Hugh. But you're coming with me." She yanked a pocket derringer from her dress and pointed it at Hugh.

Lola clicked the hammer back and the sound cracked through Hattie's skull. She'd already pictured Hugh bleeding on the ground today. Her gut twisted as she took in the situation. She had to help Hugh. The gun she'd taken from the man outside was tucked into the side of Hugh's trousers.

"Toss that gun in your belt to the chair there. I heard you take care of my man outside. He never puts more'n one bullet in, so I know it ain't loaded."

Hugh carefully drew the weapon and put it on the couch. Hattie wanted to rush Lola, take the gun and beat her over the head with it. How could this be happening? Had she really only had a few days of peace and now she'd have to go back to that other life? Was this what Hugh's prayers for her had done?

Lola waved the gun at Hugh. "Now, let's get us all to Keystone. You've got some people to meet and I've got a stage to catch with the money I get from the reward." She shoved them out the door with the barrel of the gun. "Oh, how I love pay day."

CHAPTER 17

I t was only a short walk but the closer they got, the more she could hear and smell Keystone. The shops, the people, the animals, and the noise grated against her senses. Lola had tied her hands behind her as soon as they'd gotten outside the cabin, making her heart beat rapidly. She'd hoped to stay out of Keystone until the trial. But now they were there, and she and Hugh weren't married yet. She had no protection.

The man who'd attacked her by the tree waited by the mines at the edge of town, his hand wrapped crudely in what appeared to be an old shirt.

Lola laughed at him and handed his pistol back. "Here, I took the liberty of reloading it for you."

Hugh stiffened beside her and his steps slowed. Lola clapped him on the shoulder with her pistol, but he didn't budge. Hattie flinched, remembering just what that felt like. Hattie slowed her steps to match Hugh and crowded close to him. He'd promised to get her out of Keystone. Though she'd laughed at his faith, she banked on it now.

A barber with a mustache comb stuck behind his ear peered out of his front window at them, then strode out on the boardwalk.

He crossed his arms over his chest and hollered to a kid playing in the street.

"Hey, get Peterson down here. I don't like the look of this."

The young boy dashed from his game and rushed off to a building near the other end of the sparse town. Keystone was laid out somewhat haphazardly, with buildings scattered to the winds, not like Deadwood where everything was connected, almost right on top of one another. The barber strode out into the street in front of them, a formidable force with broad shoulders and a barrel chest.

"What's going on here?" He glanced at her for just a moment, but Hattie didn't recognize him.

Lola shoved forward, her man staying behind with the barrel of his pistol in her back. "You just pay no never mind, Horace. I'm bringing in these two for the reward." She shoved Hattie away from Hugh a little. "This one's a runaway." She swung her gun toward Hugh's head and Hattie flinched. "That one helped her."

The barber narrowed his eyes. He was the brawniest barber she'd ever seen. Not that she'd seen more than two in her whole life.

"That isn't the story I heard. I have all the Deputy's wanted posters in my shop, and she isn't on my wall. I heard she was kidnapped."

Lola blustered and stomped, waving the derringer around like a toy. "You don't know anything, Horace Littlefield. I heard Ros say she was wanted. I heard her man say there was a reward."

Horace shook his head and filled his lungs, making him even broader. Though Hattie hadn't thought it possible. "It ain't Ros's fault, but she should know better than to do business with a man she don't know. That Roy's a yellow-bellied side winder. I'm sorry, Lola. I can't let you take these people without the Deputy knowing what's going on. If he says it's fine, then go ahead. But not until then."

Lola seethed, her face turning a deep crimson and her body shook with the tension. "You fancy yourself a deputy, but you ain't.

You keep your nose out of my business. I'll be able to quit washin' with that reward."

Horace took a step closer to her and Hattie stepped back. Even though he was on her side, he made quite a scary picture.

Lola screamed and let off a string of curses fit to make a miner blush. A memory wandered to the front of Hattie's mind. Lola *had* been at Ros's and she'd been mean.

She wore my dress.

The one she'd come to Keystone in. When she'd asked for it back, Lola had cursed her just like she'd just done to the barber and that had earned Hattie two days without food. Roy hadn't come to her defense then.

A woman came out of a small white house. Seeing them, she covered her mouth with her hands and made a noise in her throat of utter indignation. She ran toward Hattie, throwing her arms around her as if they were old friends.

"Oh, that dress looks marvelous on you dear. Get these ropes off them this instant!" The seamstress yanked at the bonds around her wrist and Lola turned and dashed back to her captives to slap the woman away. As her attention was diverted, Hugh lifted his knee and sent the gun flying. Everyone in the street screamed and ducked for cover. Hugh rammed forward, his hands still tied, shoving her to safety with his chest as the small derringer fell back to the ground.

The frowning seamstress picked herself off the ground and dusted off her skirt. She dug a small scissors from the belt about her waist and cut Hattie free. "I'm Ezzy, and Hugh was so sweet to come to me when you needed help. I can't sit by and watch this happen. Here, duck into my store while I free him. She's too crazy to do anything to me."

Hattie rushed up the stairs to Ezzy's small porch, but a wall of a chest stopped her dead in her tracks. She looked up to see Curry, one of Ros's men. She let out every bit of breath in her body and immediately felt faint. He lifted his meaty fist high above his head and his mouth curled in an evil smile.

"I've been waiting to do this for days. No one makes Ros cry."

Deputy Peterson hollered over the commotion, stalling Curry's hand. "What's all this mess about?"

Ros appeared in the street as if she'd just come from afternoon tea. Her gown was impeccable, shimmery and lavender, shining bright in the sun. Her hat was almost demure. "Why Deputy, one of my girls has been missing for almost a whole week," she squeaked. "Now, come to find out this man's been keeping her all for himself. The way I see it—at the rate of five dollars an hour—why, he owes me about five hundred dollars." She batted her unnaturally long eyelashes.

The Deputy rolled his eyes skyward then brought his gaze down and settled it on Hugh, who stood in the street, Ezzy still working on his bonds. "Who are you, son. And why are you here?"

Hugh yanked his hands free and turned to Ezzy. Whatever he said to her made her titter sweetly and Hattie felt an instant dislike for the woman and her pretty feminine features.

Hugh faced Deputy Peterson and squared his shoulders. "My name's Hugh Bradly. I came down here by request of Sheriff Seth Bullock. That there's Hattie Arnsby, she was taken from her home in Deadwood by compulsion and her family wants her back. Ros contested my claim so I agreed to stay just outside of town until the circuit judge could come and I could show him the letters I have showing a crime had been committed." He rubbed his wrists and waited for the Deputy to speak but when he didn't, he continued, "I apologize for not contacting you straight away. I didn't know you were here."

Her fingers clutched the railing until her knuckles were white. Here was Hugh, yet again protecting her. He had been from the moment she'd first laid eyes on him and his badge. He hadn't worn it since he'd brought her to the cabin. Being a deputy had never been his job. She realized that now. He'd only ever been her guardian angel.

"Well, son. I wasn't. We have a small jail here and rooms above, but I work out of Hill City and don't get here often. Do you have that paperwork with you?"

Hugh's shoulders relaxed just a bit. "I don't, sir. This woman," he motioned toward Lola, "decided to take it upon herself to bring us back into town. She mentioned some type of reward."

The Deputy scoffed. "There's no reward for either of you. Leastwise, not a legal one."

Ros's chin notched up just a hair and she narrowed her eyes. "What about my contract that says Hattie will work for me...for life?"

"Hugh, go get your paperwork. We're not going to bother any judge with this silly dispute. Especially since the local circuit judge happens to be a good friend of Bullock. Ros, get your birdcage back where it belongs. We both know any contract you have ain't legal." Peterson glanced around and his eyes warmed on a space just behind Hattie. "Miss Ezzy, I assume you can take care of the girl for a while?"

Ezzy rushed up and squeezed Hattie's shoulders. "I'd be happy to." She turned and pulled Hattie—with more force than she'd thought the woman capable of—toward her store. Hattie paused near the door and glanced over her shoulder at Hugh. He wouldn't have to marry her now. He was free. If the Deputy declared her free, Hugh could take her home. So, why did she feel so alone and scared? Why wasn't she happy about it?

HUGH FELT the burn of the eyes on his back as he left Keystone. He was a no-account stranger in their community, and he'd upset the apple cart. As he turned the bend in the road, a sigh escaped his lungs at the freedom from the prying glances. At least Hattie was safe with the nice seamstress for now. If the letters were found sufficient, he wouldn't need to marry Hattie. She could go right home to her family. She would finally be free. Of everything. Including him.

He shoved the cabin door open and his gaze landed on the dress he'd brought to pack for their wedding trip, the brush on the table by her bed, and the blanket she left by the chair. He shook his head and climbed up to his loft. He couldn't think about what he was losing. What *she* was gaining was the only thing that mattered. He could well remember the feeling of finally signing Da's farm over to the big rancher who'd offered to buy it, relieving him of the burden of managing all the work of a farm meant for three brothers. Freedom was a sweet balm that he wouldn't take from her. Especially when she'd run from him with fear in her eyes, her body trembling.

He lifted his Bible off his nightstand and turned to his favorite passage in Romans. The three documents flipped out and he pulled them loose, tucking them in his vest. She wouldn't want to come back to the cabin and be alone here again. She wouldn't need to. Slowly, he gathered all her things in a flour sack as carefully as he could, trying to ignore the fancy stitches she'd added that morning. It was the dress Hattie had planned to get married in. But now she'd get to marry someone she wanted. In a beautiful dress her sister Ruby would help pick out. Not some cast-off dress that no one else had wanted to buy. With one last look around the cabin, he left closing the door behind him.

Daisy waited for him in the lean-to, as patient as ever. As soon as he showed the papers to Peterson and brought Hattie her clothes, he needed to get away. Get Hattie out of his mind. He could come back for his own things later.

To some, Keystone was a fortress completely protected from the rest of the world. It lay in a slight valley at the crux of a few mountains. Though calling them mountains was an exaggeration. If only Keystone had protected Hattie in its little fortress.

He tied Daisy to a post in front of the sewing shop and spied the mercantile where he'd sent the first telegram to Bullock. He left Hattie's bag tied to his saddle and walked the few blocks over to the store. The man smiled at him as he entered.

"'Lo, friend. What can I get for you today?" He adjusted the garter around his arm then wiped the counter. Though it already gleamed.

His legs felt twitchy, nervous. Men didn't buy women baubles unless they were courting. "I'm looking for hair pins, a mirror, and maybe some pretty ribbon?"

"Hair ribbons? I got a few colors here for you to pick from. Red, arsenic, and this blue one is right pretty."

"That it is. It's about the color of her eyes. I'll go with a length of that."

"The other notions for women's hair are in the back corner, on the bottom. I've got a few mirrors to pick from."

"Thank you." He strode back, glancing at all the wares on the shelves. He found the mirrors. One had a porcelain back, one was a heavy pewter, and the last one looked to be tin. The porcelain one was the most expensive, but also the prettiest. He picked it up and it had a good weight, not too heavy or light. It was perfect for her. He brought them to the front and the man had a telegram laying on the counter face down.

"You wouldn't happen to be Hugh Bradly, would you?" The man raised an eyebrow and his clean clipped mustache danced in a smile.

"Yes, I am. Why?"

"I've had this telegram for you for a few days, but I didn't know who you were and no one I asked knew you, either. I figured the strange telegram might go with the stranger in my store."

"Good thing I stopped by." Had Bullock finally agreed to come help when it was all but too late? The situation was over now. He set down his purchases and picked up the note. The folded sheet was stiff as he flipped it open. His eyes caught the words and his stomach took a plunge.

DEADWOOD IN QUARANTINE. STAY THERE. - AIDEN

CHAPTER 18

The living room was larger than the whole cabin and it was pressing down on her. Hattie sat in a chair the likes of which she'd never seen before and waited for Ezzy to stop flitting about asking nervous questions without waiting for the answers. While she waited for her new friend to calm down, she inspected the chair. It had covered buttons that seemed to pull in bits of the chair to make it softer to sit on and the cushion itself had more give than any bed she'd ever laid on. Ezzy wandered off and back again, still chattering, making tea and fussing over Hattie's hair as she walked by. A warmth crept over her that she hadn't felt in a long time, probably since before her pa died. She didn't mind being fussed over one bit.

The door jingled open and Hattie gasped as a dark cowboy strode through the doorway then stopped, his face obscured by the light behind him. Once the shock of his arrival disappeared, she recognized Hugh and smiled in relief, letting out a long breath. Was he here to get her? They could go back to the cabin and prepare to go back to Deadwood.

"Oh! Mr. Bradly don't scare us so! Come on in." Ezzy darted

over to him and took his hat, batting it against her hand to relieve it of the dust before hanging it on a coat rack by the door.

Hattie held her breath. The soft look in Hugh's eyes told her she was free to go and do what she wanted, so why did she want to go back to that cabin and pretend like nothing had changed? Would he still want her, or would he just take her home and be done with her? Just like everyone else—in her life for a moment, then gone. Her chest burned with tears looking for a reason to spill as he sauntered his way to her. He dropped to one knee and she reminded herself to breathe or she might faint. Would he tell her he still wanted to marry her? She'd agree in a heartbeat, would follow him yet today to Hill City, since there wasn't a preacher or judge in Keystone.

He pulled a flour sack from behind his back and opened it. "I brought your things from the cabin. Didn't figure you'd ever want to go back there."

She reached forward and looked down into the bag. Sure enough, there was her dress and the brush Ezzy had so generously given her.

"I need to go over to the Deputy and give him the papers. I went over to the mercantile to get you a few things." He dug into the bottom of the bag and handed over a wrapped package.

Why was he acting so strange, so cold? She took the package, but she didn't want to look at it yet. He was just sitting there, not saying what she desperately wanted him to say. Why couldn't he say nothing had changed, he cared about her, didn't want to give her up? Why couldn't he just say something! *Unless he felt…free.*

She blinked at him for a moment, then looked down at the package. She carefully opened it and inside she found the pins he'd promised her, and a silky blue hair ribbon. Underneath it was a mirror. Unsuccessfully blinking back the tears, she clutched it to her chest. How could he be so kind and generous when that isn't what she wanted? She wanted only the most precious thing, him.

"Do…you like it?" His eyes, looking straight into her from where he knelt, were knit with worry. She couldn't leave him feeling like his gift wasn't appreciated, but it was so much different than what she'd hoped for.

"It's beautiful, Hugh. Thank you."

"Now you have a glass to go with that brush and you can do your hair all pretty." He reached out as if to pick up a lock of her hair, and she held her breath, hoping. Then he dropped his hand and stood, but not before Hattie noted the red-hot anger that flashed over his face. "I guess I'd best get over to the Deputy. I got a telegram from Aiden when I was at the store. We're to stay here in Keystone until we receive word that it's safe to go back. They're under quarantine. I don't know what kind or how bad, if it's all of Deadwood or just out at the ranch, but Aiden says don't come, so we stay here. If it *is* the town, it's a good thing they live so far away from it or I'd be worried about them."

"They live *outside* of town now?" When she'd left, they lived in a large home owned by the same man who owned the hotel. She couldn't remember if Hugh had ever mentioned they no longer lived there.

"Yes, there's a ranch a few miles out of Deadwood. Though they still consider it Deadwood, where Aiden and Beau work. My da and mam are there, too."

"Your parents are there?" She stood from her seat and set the mirror on the counter. "Hugh, I'd like to meet them when we go back."

He stood and turned from her, his back a rigid line. "I'm sure you will. Can't live on the same place and not see them, probably every day." His voice was rough, hard.

She'd also see him every day, and she'd just made him think of that. She had to reach out, had to let him know that she wanted him near her. "Do you have to go right away? I'm still so out of sorts..."

He held up his hand and turned his head, cutting her off. "I know you'll be fine, Hattie. This is where you belong, not in that tiny cabin and especially not alone with me. Being here with Miss Ezzy will be good until I can figure a way to get you back to Deadwood. You're strong and I'll come into town to see you when I can."

"When you can...?" He didn't want her. She closed her eyes and her tears spilled over. She'd known it deep down. That he was only marrying her to do what Bullock had told him, but to be faced with his rejection was so much harder than she'd expected. She turned from him and dashed her hand over her eye to keep him from seeing her tears. She'd been tossed aside her whole life. Had always been expendable. She should be used to it. But she wasn't. Her heart was torn into a thousand jagged pieces that even Ezzy couldn't mend. The flask again bumped against her leg and she wanted a drink to take the pain away, because it would. It would drown it, deaden it, bury it until she had to face it in the morning. Just one. She just wasn't strong enough to take the pain alone.

Ezzy tilted her head and clicked her tongue as she draped her arm over Hattie's shoulder. "My, my, it's been an emotional day. You should rest dear. I have a spare bed upstairs. You can stay here with me until everything gets sorted out and we can send you back home." Ezzy patted her shoulder and directed her toward the stairs and away from Hugh. The door softly clicked shut and she knew he was gone. It felt as if the goodbye was for forever.

"Now Hattie, I may be a matron, but I've seen those kinds of looks before. I don't care a fig that you were a...*calico queen*, but if you live under my roof, that man won't be buying anything from you. Not for expensive mirrors or anything else." She led Hattie upstairs to a small room with a bureau, a bed, and a small washstand.

"He wasn't trying to buy me. He got me out of there. He was... telling me goodbye." Hattie choked and clutched the mirror close to her heart as she hid the hot tears coursing down her face. But her pain would not remain hidden. The sobs burst from her. "Earlier today, we talked about getting married to avoid trial. Now that the Deputy has taken away that fear, there's no need."

Ezzy led her over to the bed and Hattie let her knees buckle underneath her.

"And you hoped he'd still want to? That he cared for you?"

Hattie pulled the bit of cotton fabric she used for a kerchief from her pocket and dabbed at her nose. "It's silly, really. I've only known him for a week, but he saved me. He cared about me, and he was willing to marry me to protect me from harm. That has to account for something, right?"

Ezzy patted her leg. "Yes dear, it should. But men are strange characters." Ezzy's face held little emotion and she patted Hattie's leg as if comforting someone was a little foreign to her. "Well, it looks like you'll be stuck in Keystone for a bit. You can work here with me until then. Maybe he'll decide he still wants to wed before you go back?"

"Or, he'll just avoid me until then and send me back alone. There's no need for him to stay once the deputy makes his decision. He was only hired to find me. His job is done." She swiped a tear and tried to rein in her breathing.

"Have you tried praying about it?" Ezzy squeezed her hand and Hattie pulled it loose.

Why couldn't people leave her well enough alone? "I have not. Silly stories. Fairy tales, all."

Ezzy shook her head and sighed. "Maybe you think so now, but I want to share something with you that might make you listen. You'll always feel like you don't deserve him if you don't allow the Lord to forgive you for what you've done, and I'm not just talking about at the Garter." Ezzy blushed and looked away.

"We've all done things we regret, Hattie. We all need more grace than we'll ever be able to give."

Hattie wrapped her arms around her stomach to quell the roiling deep inside. This woman didn't know about her past. Hattie'd done too much to even be able to recount it all.

"The Lord knows about what you're hiding in your pocket, Hattie. And He can help you with that, too."

Hattie gasped. How did Ezzy know? She hadn't touched it, had only thought of it.

The side of Ezzy's mouth tipped up slightly. "I'm no spring chicken, Hattie. So your secrets and pains won't surprise me.

When you're ready to talk about the Lord, I'll be here. There's no filth the Lord can't clean."

How dare she say such things? She'd been bad for sure, but *filth*? "What makes you think I'll want to talk?" Hattie's stays bit into her hips as she seethed.

"Because I know my Lord, and you need Him. He leads you through the dark. He listens to your heart. He knows your desires even before you do, but you've got to seek Him first."

CHAPTER 19

Hugh tromped past each building, avoiding everyone he could, then crossed over, avoiding horses and carts as he wove through the busy thoroughfare. The hurt expression on Hattie's face when he'd given her the gift danced before his eyes. Taunting him. She hadn't wanted it. Probably hadn't wanted anything from him that would remind her of Keystone or him. A year ago, he'd have cursed the ground he walked on and took out his anger in a hard days' work. But not today. He roped the fury in and branded it for what it was, sin. Sin that he needed to bring to the Lord when he got a quiet minute.

The Deputy's office was an unmarked, squat brick building near the end of town. He'd have completely missed it if Peterson himself hadn't been sitting in a chair outside. Peterson waved then ducked into the building. Hugh strode in and found the deputy sitting behind his desk, gathering scattered wanted posters.

"Figured I'd sit outside since the only people who know this is my office are people who live here and those to whom I've extended Keystone's finest hospitality." He thumbed behind him at the two cells. "I'm glad to see you want to get this business finished as quickly as we do. Generally, we have no trouble with the Garter.

They keep the riff-raff busy at night which suits me just fine. They have a rule. You leave your gun at the door and if you can't pay your tab before you leave...Ros keeps it."

"I guess that's one way to settle a debt." He didn't much care about Ros or her business sense. He just wanted word that Hattie was free to go, then he could get on his horse and clear his mind in the hills for a while.

"Yup, she hangs them all on her wall. Gal's got spunk." The Deputy smiled then held out his hands for the papers. Hugh dug them out of his vest and handed them over. An unease settled in his chest as the papers cleared his hand. Hattie's future would be determined by this man in the next few minutes. Or rather, his own future, because he *would* take Hattie back to her family and he'd gladly go to prison to keep her away from the Garter.

The man glanced down at the papers and ignored him for a moment, but Hugh couldn't keep his hands still. He flexed and bent his hat, curling the brim in his hands. A small part of him wanted to ride right out of town and far away from Hattie Arnsby. Let her have her family and he'd just live somewhere far away, maybe in New York as he'd originally planned. Someone from Keystone could get her back to Deadwood. But Aiden would take it as a slight and he didn't want to battle with him anymore. They'd spent the better part of their lives fighting, now was not the time to open a fresh wound. He'd hurt his parents if he didn't come back, but he couldn't bear to watch Hattie grow to love someone else.

The Deputy looked over the top two pieces of correspondence. They were the telegrams from Aiden requesting Sheriff Bullock's help. Peterson let those fall to his desk and his eyes got wide as he read the third.

"I didn't think he'd actually get involved in this. I see why they'd ask, but I didn't think he had time for such truck as this. What with Deadwood being so, well, you understand." He collected all three sheets and tapped them on his desk. "I don't see any reason why Hattie shouldn't go home to her family. As much as we hope all the women in those places are there because they want to be, we know it ain't the case. We don't see many cat wagons, but I s'pect even the few we see aren't always full of the willing."

Hugh's mouth ran dry. He'd never even thought about prostitutes or their plight until he'd signed on to search for one. He wasn't there to change the world, only to rescue his brother's sister-by-law. He sighed heavily. "So, Hattie's free then? Good. The plan is to take her back home as soon as I'm able. We were told to hole up here until the outbreak in Deadwood calms down."

"I hadn't heard about any outbreak in Deadwood. Depending on what it is, that could take months. They only have but one doctor, last I heard, and they've got over four thousand people there."

That made sense. The town was huge by western standards and flowed out from the main street like a huge spider whose legs stood poised up the sides of the nearby hills.

The man clasped his hands in front of him. "Now, if you'll be here for a while, I could use some help. As I said, I can't be here every day. The pay wouldn't be great, but it would give you something to do while you're stuck here for a mite."

Hugh sat back in the chair. His days of being a deputy for Bullock were about up and he hadn't planned on signing on for another job. Things got interesting in Deadwood and carrying a badge was dangerous work. He itched to get out of town, but his heart stalled on the chance to stay closer to Hattie.

"I'd be much obliged." Hugh picked up his papers and slipped them back in his vest. For the time being, he was stuck here. He might as well have a good excuse to stay. He'd just have to stay busy and try to give Hattie space and wait for the Lord to fulfil His promise. He'd told Hugh to marry Hattie, that meant a wedding was in their future. He just had to be patient. *Another test, Lord?* It had been easy to stand back when she needed it at the tight cabin. Why did it seem so much harder in the out and open of town?

"There's a small apartment above the jail for our deputies. I live at home with my wife in Hill City, of course. So you'll have the run of the place. You can move up there as soon as you're able. The only thing I ask is that you have no women up there. We don't care if you see anyone, but nothing that'll make us look bad. Ya hear? Oh, and Horace stops by here a few times a day to let out the Deputy."

Hugh didn't even want to know what he meant. He just needed to get himself out of town soon and the daylight was waning. The insinuation that he might bring a woman to his room rankled, but he wouldn't explain to the deputy that he'd never do that. To the town, he already had. He'd lived with a prostitute for five days and he'd do it again if he were ever called to. But Peterson was saying loud and clear he couldn't court a former prostitute and work for the city of Keystone. Not that the only former prostitute in town would have him even if he could. She'd made it plain she was only going through with the marriage because it was the only option.

He swiped his thumb below his nose. "I'll go get my few things from my cabin and move it over later tonight. I've got a little business to tend to first."

"You do that. If I don't see you later, I'll be back bright and early to show you around."

HATTIE RAN her hand over the soft fabrics on large bolts in the back room of Ezzy's house. She'd never had such things to sew. Some of them glided under her hands as if they were made of water, others sturdier, but still better quality than she'd ever worn until Ezzy had given Hugh her dresses.

Ezzy appeared at her side and lifted a butter-colored fabric with a blue pattern. "I think this silk damask would be lovely as an evening gown, don't you?"

Hattie shook her head and brought her thoughts back to the fabric. "I don't know anything about which fabric is what or what would work for an evening gown. I've never had anything but sturdy cotton. I can sew a fine hem and I can do minor tailoring with a little embroidery. I'm just not sure I'll be any good working for you."

Ezzy grabbed the sheers from the loose-fitting belt she wore and pulled down the large bolt of yellow fabric, hefting it to a huge, waist-high table in the center of the room.

"This is the damask. Help me get past the faded edge so we can see it better. Will you? We're going to cut off the yardage we need."

Hattie approached the table, her hands bunched in her skirt. The fabric looked too nice to handle. "Do you have someone to make a dress for?" She touched the fabric gingerly. Everything she laid her fingers on turned to dust and she couldn't afford to replace the fine fabric. The acrid scent of the dye brushed her nostrils with each bounce of the bolt against the table as Ezzy deftly flipped it. After the first turn of the fabric, it become brighter, the pattern clearer.

"It's lovely." Hattie held the bolt straight so Ezzy could cut it with her sheers. Ezzy grabbed the fabric before it fell to the floor and folded it carefully.

"Isn't it though?" Ezzy smiled mischievously and stepped closer to Hattie, lifting a lock of her hair. "Now, I'm going to teach you what I need you to do most. Over here to the sun." She directed with her sheers and Hattie obeyed. "Now, turn around and hold your arms wide." Hattie did as she was told, but it was silly, standing there like a scarecrow. Ezzy's hands reached around her and measured her body from neck to toes. Ezzy's arms snaked around her over and over. Each time a little more invasive.

"Now, take note of what I'm doing because next you'll be doing it if someone comes in. I make most of my dresses using only measurements. You see, I used to work in Minneapolis at a premier dress shop, but I prefer it here. Though, I still get many orders from there every month. There are roughly fifty points you'll need to measure. Most women are quite used to having it done and it isn't a problem."

Most women had the luxury of special order dresses? Hattie wasn't so sure of that. Even the ladies from Cutter's Creek had sewn their own, but then perhaps they were used to measuring themselves.

She tried to remember all the places where Ezzy's arms roped around her, but it was like the woman had sprouted six extra arms for how quickly she measured.

"Now sit. I need a few from a sitting position."

Hattie complied and put up with more of the tape winding around her body. Ezzy disappeared for a moment and pulled out a small notebook. "This is where I keep all my measurements."

Hattie turned back to look at the silk. "Wouldn't that make a nice wedding dress?" She felt her eyes water and she snapped them shut to keep the thought and tears at bay. She'd cried enough for one day.

"I suppose it would make a wonderful dress for a bride who wasn't a new bride. A widow finding new love, perhaps? Since Queen Victoria demanded a white wedding dress, most ladies want to copy her. White dresses for weddings are *en vogue*." Ezzy went back to measuring Hattie's legs and tugging her skirts this way and that.

White gowns were for pure and untouched brides. Her own sister, Ruby, had been married in a walking suit and she *had* been untouched. "There are some who just shouldn't wear white," she whispered.

Ezzy stood and rested a hand on Hattie's arm. "You wear whatever dress you want to wear. A wedding is one special day, a marriage is a lifetime."

"But you spend your life making beautiful dresses. Don't you want them to count?" Hattie dropped her arms and flattened her damp palms against her roiling stomach.

"The fabric will always be there. Whether I make a dress that women wear one day or every other day. What's more special? Which one is more beloved? I have a few women who buy my dresses so they may wear a fresh gown for every occasion. But they are rare. More often, I make a gown that will get worn until the elbows wear through. I'd say the woman who wears the gown until she needs a new one appreciates the work just as much as the one who wants a frock of fancy stitches for just one day." Ezzy draped her measuring tape around her neck and tilted her head, her mouth askew.

"Your life is like that Hattie. You don't have to be the decorated wedding gown. You can be the everyday dress with a good cut, strong fabric, worthy of everyday work and still be beautiful and loved."

"Nobody's going to love a *calico* dress." Especially not the man who had promised to never touch her—but had—more deeply than she'd ever allowed anyone else. Right to her soul.

CHAPTER 20

Daisy struggled up the last of the trail then slowed as they reached the flattened summit. The sky hung overhead in the brightest blue with wisps of clouds. A haze covered the horizon for as far as he could see, spreading further than he could ever guess. The green of the hills against the blue of the sky was a humbling sight, but he couldn't rid his mind of Hattie. Maybe it was because he felt he'd known her long before he'd found her. Or maybe it was just the Lord's way of connecting them. He couldn't explain it except that nothing could take her place in his thoughts.

The heavens didn't open up and direct him and the ground didn't open up and swallow him. He'd ridden until both he and Daisy were worn out and there still wasn't a clear path for what he should do. Everything had been easier when all that mattered was getting Hattie well, then getting her to Hill City. He hadn't even given much thought to what life would be like after that. It hadn't mattered. The Lord would take care of it. But now the apple cart had been upended.

Lord, I'm waiting. I can't stop thinking about her now that the seed has been planted. Was it your plan to open my heart so you could see if I would follow your will, like Abraham? Or did you really mean I should take Hattie as my wife? He shook his head and took one more look at the horizon. Though many of the hills surrounding the one he was on seemed equally high, everything around him steadily faced downward, as if he truly were on the top of the world. The Lord remained silent.

After making a quick stop at the cabin and wandering back into town, he plunged the key into the door on the second floor of the jail house. An old hound dog thumped its tail on the floorboards as Hugh brought in his saddle bags. He'd only brought what he could carry with him on the journey, so moving had been little more than gathering his few things from the cabin and bringing them into town. He'd already rented a spot for Daisy at the livery but being on the road away from his parents for so long had left him weary. How many different places had he slept? He'd lost track after the first few months.

The dog lifted his head, his ears drooping to the floor. Hugh dropped his bags on the bed and a cloud of dust erupted from it. At least it was a full-sized bed. He'd be able to stretch out. Not that he'd begrudged Hattie the other. She'd needed it, but not now. She was strong and full of life, ready to take on new things all on her own. While living within the city might bring back some bad memories, the sounds would likely bother her the most, as she hadn't been allowed to leave the saloon. From her room, she'd probably heard the sounds of the town and pictured what life was like outside those four walls.

Hattie had Ezzy to help her with anything she might face until it was time to leave. He'd really given that some thought on the way back down the mountain. How would he get Hattie and his horse back to Deadwood? He'd ridden Daisy everywhere so far, but now he had Hattie. He couldn't just get another horse, nor could he leave his behind to take the stage. He scratched his jaw. It would take some thought.

He let himself fall to his bunk and the dog raised slowly, one short fat leg at a time, and shoved his cold nose into Hugh's hand.

"You're a real guard dog, I see. You must've been the *deputy*

Peterson spoke of earlier. The one Horace lets out." The dog opened lips much too big for his face and heaved one deep bark. Hugh scratched the dog on the head and the beast grunted his approval. "I don't know what to do, boy. I can't stop thinking about her. Wondering if she's fine… Wondering if she needs anything. Wondering if she needs…me." He shook his head and the dog rested his large chin on Hugh's leg, his soft brown eyes looking up at him through over-large, shifting eyebrows. "You aren't much help, either. And your eyes are just as shifty as Aiden's dog, Jack."

He turned to his bags and unbuckled them, flipping the flap open. All his clothes had been freshly washed and the tears all repaired. Hattie had done the wash earlier that morning, the warm dry air in Keystone had dried them quickly. Now, after being in his bag, they weren't as nice as he'd found them when he'd returned to the cabin. Hattie had slowly begun doing more and more around the cabin. Pride swelled within his chest. She'd come so far. From being dull and forgetful without any energy or fire, to a woman fit for anything she'd want to do. She should be proud of all she'd accomplished.

He stood and shoved the clothes into one side of a drawer and his shaving kit in the other. Tomorrow would be a new day, with a new job. He'd stop thinking about Hattie soon enough. She could move on and when they returned to Deadwood, she could find a good man to marry. She wouldn't need him anymore. Probably stopped needing him days ago. A cold chill seeped its way deep into his bones.

The door swung open and Deputy Peterson moseyed into the room, closing the door behind him. He tossed his hat on the dresser and crossed his arms over his chest.

"You find the accommodations to your liking?" He spread his feet apart and waited.

"It would seem I'm taking someone else's bunk." He patted the dog again, then stood.

"That's Deputy Giblet. He's too old now to do much but we used to walk down the streets of this town when we were both younger, before it was much of a town at all. I'm getting too old to do it and I'm not even here that much. That's one of the things I want you to do, walk through the town each day. The presence of the law will help people feel more secure.

"If people are drunk and causing a ruckus, bring them in to cool off. Any fights should be stopped right away, especially gun fights. We don't want a bad reputation. Keystone is growing, and we want to continue to see growth."

"Do you get many?" Hugh rested his hand on his Colt. He'd learned his lesson in the woods. Never be without it.

"Enough. It's the drunks that'll take most of your job. We *do* get plenty of those. Ever handled a drunk before?"

His gut clenched. He had, but not when she was drinking, only after. His da had never allowed drink on the farm and even at Aiden's wedding they hadn't offered anything stronger than coffee.

"Not really, but I think I can spot one."

"It isn't the spotting that's the trouble. They can be stronger than they look. And for whatever reason, when there's one, four more tend to show up the minute you think you have him under control. I'll take you tomorrow morning and show you around. After that, you'll be on your own. Think you can handle it?"

He wasn't a lawman, despite the badge Bullock had given him. He was a farmer who wanted to get back to the ranch in Deadwood. But for now, sure, he could handle it. The townspeople were already cautious with him, so what was a badge? Not like they'd ever have a chance to know him. "I don't think I'll have too much trouble."

"I've already warned Ros and her men to leave you alone. They're sore over this whole deal to be sure."

"What about Roy? Where's he? I'm more worried about him than Ros. The town would expect her to do something, but no one's been watching Roy." That man had to be kept far from Hattie. He'd be keen on taking her from Keystone and selling her again to make up for his losses. It wouldn't be too tough to get at her, either. With only the seamstress watching.

"Haven't seen Roy in a couple days. He dropped off some

haggard woman about two days ago, according to Horace." He shook his head. "I don't know where he found her, but she wants to be there. So, Ros has forgiven him."

"So the only thing left for them is humiliating Hattie as a way to keep their girls from thinking about running." He frowned. Didn't seem right, but he couldn't let that get to him. He'd have to leave that to God.

"That's about it. I'm glad you've already thought about that. It might just be rumors or they might really try something. I wanted you walking the street for that very reason. They can't get to her with you there. All I ask is, as soon as Deadwood opens, you get yourself and your gal out of here. I'd like things to get back to routine around here."

"Pretty quiet before all this? Horace seems to help you out a fair bit. How come you don't just deputize him?" Hugh couldn't help but wonder how a mining town could be quiet, but this one didn't have that new, wild-town feel. In fact, if the Garter and the other scattered small saloons weren't there, Keystone would be a great place to start over.

Peterson nodded. "Horace is willing to help, but he makes a living giving cuts and shaves. He don't carry a gun and doesn't want to. As to how quiet Keystone is, well, you can see that I'm only here once a week or so and the town is fine. It's a good thing you didn't wait for a judge. They don't have to come often, and you'd have been waiting a long while. I'll be happy to go back to the occasional drunk and disorderly once you're gone. No offense meant."

"None taken. I'll do my best to oblige you. As soon as I hear from Deadwood, you'll be the first to know."

CHAPTER 21

Hugh pulled his hat low to keep the sun off and shrugged on his black coat. The badge Bullock had given him was buried in the bottom of his shaving kit. He hadn't looked at it in a week. It wiped off easy and shone like a new penny. Hugh pinned it to his coat then checked his belt and his munitions pouch, both were loaded and ready. Giblet raised his head and looked at him with knowing eyes then let loose with a deep *woof* that seemed to sap him of what little energy he possessed. Giblet would love to go out and join the patrol, but the poor old dog could hardly make it up and down the stairs to do his business. Soon, they'd have to keep him in the main floor jail.

The dog had proven to be good company for his mercurial mood. Every time he'd closed his eyes, all he could see were bright blue ones. He'd replayed their conversation on the rock and the little clink that had made her run. It couldn't have been a weapon. If it had, she'd have used it against Lola's man in the woods. She was smart and scrappy enough to know that you trusted the weapon you had more than the one you had to take. If she'd already had a weapon, she wouldn't have needed to get close enough to steal the brute's.

Nothing had been missing from the cabin. With the notable exception of the window, they'd left it just as he'd found it. So, she hadn't taken anything from the cabin with her and she had no place to hide anything, so the only explanation was Lola. What could Lola have given her that she'd be nervous about him finding? The only thing he'd come up with had chilled him. Booze.

It wasn't his place to lead her. He wasn't her husband and couldn't take that responsibility. But as the festering thought came back to taunt him, he said another prayer that she could do the right thing and not succumb to drink again. He didn't want to have to arrest Hattie. The jail was no place for her.

He patted Giblet on the head. "You know where I'm going, don't you boy? I know you'd like to come with, but I'll let you know everything that's going on in your town when I get back."

Giblet laid his large head between his huge front feet and sighed.

Hugh closed and locked the door, reminding himself that he'd have to go up and let the poor dog outside later. Probably when he stopped for his lunch. He jogged down the stairs and met Peterson in the front office.

"You ready to really see Keystone? It's our job to check out the businesses, including the mines, and make sure no one's standing about that shouldn't be. Then, we come back here for a short lunch and do the rounds again in the afternoon. The only change is, if you arrest anyone in the morning, then we have some paperwork for you to fill out. You can't do your rounds until the paperwork is done. So you'll have to do a quick job of it."

Hugh nodded, only half listening.

"Why do I get the feeling you'd like to start our rounds at Ezzy's?" Peterson laughed.

Hugh wasn't in the mood to joke. His hand flexed and relaxed. "Why don't we start where you usually do? Then you can show me what I need to know to do my job?" The anger he'd worked so hard to keep tamped down threatened to spill out. No, he wasn't like that anymore. He had to let go.

Peterson threw up his hands in surrender and grabbed his hat.

He clipped a large keyring to his belt and swung the door open, holding it for Hugh.

The town hadn't seemed quite so spread out until he had the job of keeping an eye on all of it. The little seamstress' house was on the far end of town, away from the mines but near the saloons, where he'd probably be the busiest. If Hattie needed him, he'd most likely be near.

"I usually start down here by the mines. All five are pretty close to one another, all along the ridge line. Closest to town is the Holy Terror. We don't need to get too close to them, just make sure no one is loitering about that shouldn't be. Then we'll go on over to the Trading Company mercantile and check for any wires. Then, over to the school. If Mrs. Wheelock is in, she might chat for a bit. Then we'll come back up main street and start at Peggy's."

"What's Peggy's?" He followed Peterson toward the first mine, the Holy Terror, which was only a few yards away.

"Peggy is what we call the blacksmith...on account of his peg leg." Peterson shook his head with disgust, as if that should've been easy to figure out.

"We'll stop at Franklin House for a cup of coffee and see what people are talking about this morning. Mrs. Jennie Franklin makes a mean cup of belly wash. After that, we'll walk by the saloons and the restaurant, finally ending over by the barber and seamstress. They're across from the big Loomis place."

Hugh nodded. Didn't seem to be all that difficult. He could probably do the job faster without stopping for coffee or hanging around, but perhaps that's what people needed in order to feel safe. They needed to see the law in the street. He could also see how the older deputy had grown such a large gut, all the coffee and sweets would turn a man soft in no time.

He followed Peterson around the Holy Terror, then to the Keystone mine, the Bullion, the Lucky Boy and finally the Big Thunder. They were all in a close arc that led right back into town. There wasn't much going on in the small town during the early morning. The teacher had very little to share and, being married, was quick to send Hugh outside because he was a single man. The teachers board was kind to let her teach as a married woman, but there were standards she had to uphold. She was strict about them.

The seamstress' little home was the last place they visited. Ezzy sat in the big front window of her home, draped in fabric and pins. He stood near the front porch, trying to keep from looking suspicious or nervous. But if Hattie really did have some form of drink, he needed to know she wasn't giving in. He prayed for her again.

Peterson spoke to Ezzy for a few minutes and just as they were about to leave, Hattie came down the stairs. She walked slowly and her eyes looked sunken and red. His stomach plummeted to his boots. She hadn't looked that bad off since he'd taken her from the Garter.

He approached her slowly. "Hattie?"

She turned to him with blank eyes, her hands were hidden in her skirts, the very same skirts she'd worn the day before, rumpled from lying in bed. Her skin again was very pale and wane.

"What did you do, Hattie?" he whispered.

She barely looked at him. "Ezzy, you called?"

Ezzy cleared her throat. "Yes dear, about two hours ago."

"Oh. I guess I lost track of time while I was getting ready." She turned around and went back up the stairs. She hadn't even acknowledged Hugh's presence.

Hugh turned on Ezzy. "What's going on with Hattie? How long has she been like this?"

Ezzy narrowed her eyes at him. "She's been drawn like that since just after you left yesterday. She hasn't eaten, nor does she want to talk. She just sits in her room. I showed her how to measure a dress yesterday afternoon. After she castigated herself for her past, she blockaded her door and hasn't come out until now. I suspect I won't be able to get her out again."

"Did you give her anything, or did you see her drink anything?" He had to know for sure. He could only speculate until he did.

"How foolish do you think I am, Mr. Bradly? I know she's hiding something, but I didn't give her anything. Not that I didn't try to give her everything I had to get her to come out last night."

He glanced up the stairs, but he couldn't very well go up to her room. There was no cause. She'd already forgotten him, had looked right past him. He'd never fathomed how much he'd miss that girl.

Ezzy gave them a confused smile as she attempted to stand underneath the yards of yellow fabric. Peterson prodded him with his elbow, and they left the seamstress to her struggle.

"What do you make of Hattie?" he asked Peterson.

"I think the gal's been crying for hours, I don't think she'd done anything wrong. I didn't smell anything and that's hard to hide."

He hadn't considered that. But if it wasn't drink, what would've made her act so out of sorts? It made no sense.

Peterson eyed him. "You were only with that gal for a week. You telling me you fell that hard in *one week*?"

"I don't know what I feel, confused mostly. I wish I knew what Hattie wanted."

Peterson nodded and clasped his hands behind his back, his belt thumping against his leg with every step. "It don't really matter what she wants. You ain't there yet. You need to figure out what *you* want first. Never know. Maybe it's the same thing."

CHAPTER 22

Hattie closed her door, her mind, and her heart with a decisive thud. It had taken all her concentration to avoid Hugh downstairs. To treat him as she would the Deputy. That is, to treat him as if he weren't there at all, except to see Ezzy. Because that was why he *was* there. He wore his badge again. He hadn't worn it since that first day at the cabin. Hadn't needed to since his job for Bullock had been to find her. And he had.

Ezzy would understand her behavior. She'd spoken soft words of reassurance through the door the night before when she'd refused to come down. Her stomach rejected food for wanting a drink. Hattie couldn't open that door and let her in. Hugh was the only one who'd seen her in such a state of need and no one else would be allowed to see her in that state.

The flask on the dresser glinted in the soft sunlight pouring through her window, taunting her. It was Roy's. She could see that now. The small jewel on the front glimmered as it had on the trip from Deadwood to Lead and then to Keystone. He'd always made sure it was full. Now, he was trying to pull her back the only way he knew how. And, if Hugh wouldn't have her, at least Roy would. She sat on the bed, the flask within reach, and the whiskey within compelled her to make a choice.

Roy's attention—if it could even be called that—was more fickle than a warm spring breeze on a Montana morning. Even though Hugh was no longer interested in her, his bits of affection were far superior and left her wanting more. Whereas she'd hid from Roy. Hugh had made her feel as if she was worthy of better. She let her head drop to her chest. She wasn't fit to make a decision like this. To take that drink would be like slapping Hugh in the face and would be giving Roy quarter to do as he pleased again.

You can do better. She looked around the room but saw no one. Her mind had to be agreeing with Hugh. She *could* do better. She could tell Roy straight away that she'd not take his flask or anything else. She was free. Free of drink and free of him. Hattie stood and swiped the flask off her dresser. She shoved it back into her pocket and rushed down the stairs, her feet barely touching the steps.

Hattie paused on the base of the stairs just as Ezzy dashed toward the back of the house. She wasn't about to disrupt her and didn't want Ezzy knowing she'd left at all. She had something to do. Hattie knew where to find Roy if she really wanted to. There was a small cave just a mile outside Keystone where he'd hole up when Ros was angry at him. It had happened frequently enough over the last year. From there, he could walk to town in under a half hour, even with the uneven terrain.

She searched around by the front door for a bonnet. No sense in alerting the town to what she was doing. She'd gotten herself into the mess with Roy and now she'd end it. Near Ezzy's bonnet sat a small box of tools, a couple shiny thimbles, needles stuck into a cushion, a small scissors, and a measuring rope, but nothing she could take to defend herself. Beside it sat Ezzy's mailed-in orders and her pearl handled letter opener. It wasn't incredibly sharp, but she remembered facing Roy all too well, and wouldn't face him again without a weapon. Hugh would be angry if she went into that battle without something to protect herself. She pocketed the letter opener and rushed out the door.

The sun was almost straight overhead and burned down hot on her heavy shoulders. Town was north, so Roy's cabin would be east of town or past all of the businesses and mines and to the right. It was also past the cabin where she'd stayed with Hugh. She slowed her steps. She'd never seen the writing on the note tied to the rock. She'd assumed it had been Lola's man, but it could also have been Roy. She shook her head and began moving again, keeping her head down. If he'd done that, all the more reason to give him back his property and tell him to leave her alone. She was finished with him for good.

Men stood outside the mine, eating their lunch, and she kept as far from them as possible. Though it was as likely as not they were family men, it was still a group of men with a lone woman. Her heart raced as she wrapped her hand around the handle of the letter opener in her pocket. It was certain that, in the small clutch of men, one would be sure to recognize her. She ducked her head further and pressed on. Soon the trees closed in around her and she followed the trail back to the cabin.

It sat lonely where they'd left it the day before. Without the sound of Hugh's ax or his voice, it was just like any other cabin. Desolate and dark. She pressed on deeper into the woods and along the canyon, away from the rock where Hugh had taken her yesterday. When he'd let his guard down and she'd seen beneath his measured surface to the caring and heat beneath. But she'd let her fear lead her. If he'd discovered what she'd carried with her, he would've been so disappointed. But what did it matter? It wasn't worth thinking on if it would only lead to more hurt. She focused on the uneven rock face ahead of her, thoughts of Hugh pushed to the back of her mind. At least for a while.

Roy had said you'd only be able to see the cave if you knew where it was. You could be looking directly at it and not see it because of the shadows of the jutting granite slabs. She approached the rocks, careful to keep as silent as a church mouse on potluck day. The trees rustled around her and the hair on the back of her neck prickled.

"Why, if it isn't Hattie Arnsby come to pay me a visit. Did you miss havin' a real man, Hattie?"

CHAPTER 23

Hugh stood from his chair where he'd been listening to Peterson relay all the laws passed so far in South Dakota that pertained to their small burg. His voice droned on and Hugh couldn't keep Hattie's red rimmed eyes from pressing in on his thoughts. Was it his fault? Had he hurt her in some way? Had he been wrong about the drink?

Hugh pulled back the curtain to watch as the stage rumbled into town and stopped in front of Franklin's. He blinked a few times and shook his head. Could he be imagining the redhead that had stepped off with a dark-haired man? Not many had hair the color of a ruby, but he knew one. Hattie's older sister, who bore the same name as the precious stone.

"Bradly? You listening?"

"I'm sorry, stage just came in. Caught my attention." He glanced out the window again.

The woman held a bundle in her arms and the man wrapped his arm around her back and pointed toward the Red Garter Saloon. They both turned to look around the small town. No doubt about it. It was Beau Rockford and his wife, Ruby. Hattie's oldest sister. They could take her home. His obligation was finished. It sat like a lead weight in his stomach.

"Sir. I think the answer to your prayers just arrived on the stage. Hattie's family is here."

Peterson stood up and started clearing his desk. "Well, go get them son. Don't just stand around here jawing."

Hugh grabbed his hat and went outside to meet Beau and Ruby. Beau saw him first and led Ruby to meet him in the street.

"Hugh, been a while. We just couldn't wait any longer." Beau held out his hand for a shake then pulled him into a one-arm hug as soon as he had hold of him. He'd hoped Aiden had been with them, too. But that wouldn't make any sense since Beau and Ruby were Hattie's guardians. He showed the couple up the short flight of stairs to the Deputy's front door and held it for them. Deputy Peterson made a spectacle of continuing to clear off his desk as he gruffly welcomed them, but neither appeared to care much.

Beau was never one for many words, so he cut right to the chase. "We're here for Hattie. Been pert-near a year since we've seen her."

Hugh nodded and glanced at Peterson. "Mind if I take them over to Ezzy's?"

"Yes well, I've got quite a lot to do. I think that's a fine idea. Send my regards." Hugh had picked up from their earlier visit that Peterson had a soft spot for Ezzy, as if she were a daughter. Though, he and his wife had no children of their own.

Ruby cooed to the little bundle in her arms as they walked the few blocks toward the seamstress. The weather was warm for late July, but the boy didn't fuss. Hugh had pent up so much of what he felt for so long that he didn't know what to say to Hattie's sister. While he was glad to see them, it also meant she'd be leaving much sooner than he'd expected. Somehow home would be different. He just knew Ruby and Beau would worry about her and never let Hattie out of their sight. Even if Hattie accepted him, they wouldn't agree to a courtship after losing her for a year.

He had to say something to break the strange silence. "How's little Joseph? He's such a tiny little guy."

Ruby laughed and nuzzled Joseph's head. "He's supposed to be tiny, Hugh. When was the last time you ever even saw a baby?"

Fair question. He couldn't remember. While Ruby didn't look like Hattie, they still had a similar face and watching her nuzzle her little one reminded him too much of a sweet blond and what he'd prayed for as he'd laid down to sleep the night before.

"I got Aiden's telegram. That's why I didn't bring her right home." They hadn't yet said why they'd come in defiance of a quarantine.

Ruby turned slightly and smiled. "Aiden is finally doing better under Jennie's watchful eye. He was pretty sick for a few weeks. When Bullock got your telegram, he didn't want to come right out and say your brother was sick. He thought it would distract you when you already had a lot on your mind." She stopped in her tracks and turned to look at him, her stance suddenly one to do battle. "When we were at the office, you said Hattie, not *my wife*. Why aren't you married yet?"

He scratched the back of his neck and closed his eyes. Lord knew he wanted to be. "We had planned to head to Hill City yesterday to have it done but, well, it's a long story that I'll let Hattie tell you. We just aren't married. And it doesn't look like we need to be now."

"No. That isn't how it was supposed to happen. I told Bullock to tell you to get married. I spent hours convincing him it was the perfect way to keep Hattie out of that place and secure with a husband. You were supposed to follow the order, right away." Her eyes pierced and challenged him to defy her. Ruby had been a formidable woman before. But as a mother, she wasn't one to be crossed, especially with her gun-toting husband at her shoulder.

He shook his head. "*You* told him? You're asking an awful lot from me, Ruby."

"Am I? You signed on to save Hattie's life. When she gets back to Deadwood, all those old feelings will return. She wanted to be married, to have someone to cherish her. She made a wrong choice and there's no one who'll have her now. Except you."

Beau laid a hand on his wife's shoulder. "I told you not to make trouble, Ruby. You stepped in where you should've let God handle it."

Ruby shook her head and buried her face in Joseph's curls. "I just don't want to see her hurting anymore."

Hugh took a deep breath and let it out slowly to keep from saying what he really wanted. Ruby had no business meddling, and he'd never admit she was right, but he couldn't just let her manipulate his life.

"Ruby, I know you love Hattie and, to be honest, I've grown to love her over the last week. But I don't think forcing marriage is going to make her feel cherished. She never wanted to marry me, not even when it seemed like the only way out. You picked the wrong man." He strode past her and continued toward Ezzy's. His gut was in knots. Beau and Ruby could take Hattie back on tomorrow's stage. For months, he'd thought about finding her and protecting her. So how could he turn that over to Beau? It would be one of the most difficult things he'd been called to do. Could he stay away until his feelings were good and dead?

He knocked on the door and it took Ezzy a full minute to open it. When she did, her eyes were red and her hair was in a frazzle about her head. She dabbed her handkerchief under her eyes and sobbed.

"Oh Hugh! I'm so glad to see you. Hattie's gone! I don't know what happened. She's just gone!"

Hugh turned her back into her house, Beau and Ruby close behind.

"Ezzy, this is Hattie's sister, Ruby, and brother-in-law, Beau. Please tell us exactly what happened." Hugh took to pacing in front of her as Ruby stood to the side, her face a mask. His mind raced in all directions while the older woman pulled her wits about her. Where could Hattie have gone and why?

"I was in the back room, looking for fabrics that would go well with the dress I started yesterday. I didn't hear her come downstairs, didn't hear the door close. I came from the back room around luncheon then went upstairs, determined to get her to come down and eat. I knocked and called, then yelled, finally pushing the door open to an empty room." She let loose with a huge sniffle and Beau handed her his dry kerchief. She blew into it daintily and folded it into her hand. "I searched the house as fast as I could. My bonnet is missing, and my letter opener of all things."

"Why would she take a letter opener?" Ruby interrupted. Hugh strode to the stove. He had to admit he needed to think, and coffee usually did the trick.

Ezzy shuddered. "That girl needs Jesus, Hugh. She was keeping a secret. She fancies you. Did you know? She's sure you don't want her anymore. I told her to turn it over to Jesus and she laughed at me."

Hugh swung his head to Ruby and she gave him a triumphant jab of her chin, but it was short-lived. "So, if you were Hattie. Where would you go with a letter opener and a purpose."

Hugh scratched his chin, afraid to say what he'd really do, but knowing he'd have to be honest with Ruby. "I'd make sure I'd slayed all my demons before leaving town. I'd make sure they could never chase me down again. That would mean either Ros, Roy, or both."

Beau stepped forward and crossed his arms. "Who are Ros and Roy?" Beau always wore an ancient pistol on his hip, claimed it was more accurate than any gun he'd ever owned, and Hugh considered that he might need Beau's assistance. Beau unfurled his long arms and rested his hand atop the old barker as if he knew the direction of Hugh's thoughts. It wasn't bluster, nor a threat. He was ready and Hugh would accept every bit of his help.

"Roy's the man who kidnapped Hattie and used her addiction to convince her she wasn't worth salt. Ros...was her madam."

Ruby gasped and clutched the front of her walking suit. Beau was there in a heartbeat, his arm supporting her. Near enough she could take his strength if she wanted it.

"How long was she with Ros?" Ruby whispered.

"About ten months, far as I can tell. I know she spent a short time in Lead with Roy. I don't know what happened there, but he brought her here before I made it to Lead. I might've caught her there if I'd left right away, instead of waiting for Aiden and

Jennie's wedding, then helping with building their house. I didn't know…"

Ruby's face had gone stark white. "We didn't expect you to leave and many of us assumed that she wanted to be gone, so we thought there was no rush." Joseph fussed and Ruby broke away from them to go retrieve the bundle.

"So, where can we find Roy and Ros?" Beau's voice had a sharp edge and it bolstered Hugh's own anger.

"Ros will be easy to find. She owns the *upstairs* of the Red Garter. Roy… He hasn't been seen in days."

CHAPTER 24

A scream lodged in her throat for a moment too long. She didn't have to turn around to see who it was. That voice would haunt her for a lifetime. Roy clamped one hand over her mouth and hauled her against his body.

"It's been too long Hattie. Five days you've played house with that good for nothing lawman. I had to take matters into my own hands. I had to convince Lola there was a reward for your return. I had to tell her what to do and to get her man involved so she wouldn't foul up." He whipped her around to face him, his eyes angry pools of hatred. "What I don't understand, is why I had to. I gave you everything and you turned on me like a viper the moment he showed up. What did he offer you that I didn't?"

She couldn't answer with his hand covering her mouth and he didn't seem to need an answer badly enough to move it. She had no words that would appease him, anyway. Roy yanked her hair back, pulling the bonnet off and most of the pins out. She yelped at the biting pain. He dug his fingers in her hair and smiled slowly, then crushed his mouth to hers. For the first time, her stomach roiled with something other than fear. If she could only reach her pocket, she could defend herself against him.

Roy shoved her from him, satisfied for now. She resisted the urge to wipe her mouth with her sleeve. That would only enrage him further.

"It was time I brought you here. If you can't make me any more money, no use in putting it off any longer." He grabbed her arm tightly and drug her toward the face of the rocks. It looked as if they would stride right into them until all of a sudden, the dark spot right in front of them looked less than shadow. It was a hole. It wasn't large, not much more than three feet by three feet, and about two feet off the ground. He ducked her head and shoved her into the dark cavern.

Roy's body completely blocked the light. She couldn't see if she was dropping into a hundred-foot cavern or if it was a tunnel that would slowly tighten until she was trapped. Roy shoved at her from behind. "Get in there, gal. Before someone comes along. I don't need people knowing I don't live in no palace." He cackled and a shiver ran down her back as she crawled, holding the front of her skirt so she didn't fall face first in the tunnel. It went along for a while, then opened up. She tried to pull her legs forward so she could swing them down and gradually find her footing, but Roy was right behind her and gave her a mighty shove, spilling her a few feet down into the cave.

"There." He spoke into the dark, and the scratch of a sulfur match against his boot brought a tiny flame to life. He stuck it into a lantern by the cave mouth and it bathed the small area in light. The cave had yellow stone that looked slippery and wet. The whole room felt damp and cold.

"This little room is where I stay. But beware, back there—" he swung the lantern toward the other side of the cavern, "back there is a drop off." He picked up a pebble they'd tracked in and tossed it to the other side of the room. There was no sound for a long time, then finally a faint *plink* as it hit something below. "Don't know how far down it is, but I suspect you wouldn't live if you fell."

Hattie slipped down the wall, clutching her knees to her chest. No one would ever find her here. Roy laughed and set the lantern on a crude table in the middle of the cavern. The lantern shed weak light in the space that was maybe fifteen feet in each direction. The edges of the room hung in darkness. She couldn't see where the floor ended and the expanse began. Her stomach did a loop and her head swam.

Roy strode over to her and yanked her off the floor, dragging her to a pallet of furs along the wall. She saw where he usually built a fire, right by the door, but it would be cold in the cave at night and that little fire wouldn't reach far. He flung her onto the bed and reached for his suspenders.

"I been waiting for this for a long time."

She reached into her pocket and dug for the letter opener. Finding it with her hand she drew it out and held it in front of her. The pearl handle was slippery in her sweaty fingers.

Roy laughed. "You planning to hold me off with that?" He came closer. "I see you've got your spunk back." He lowered one knee onto the furs and she gasped, aiming the blade at his thigh. It wasn't sharp enough to penetrate his trousers. He slapped her hand and she pushed herself up on both knees, holding the opener in front of her with both hands.

"Is that how you're going to be with me? Did you open up for the lawman when you sat there all alone in that cabin? I know you didn't, because I saw you there." He bent low like he would rush at her and she adjusted her weapon, too late realizing that's what he expected her to do. He hit the knife from her hands and was on her in a heartbeat. "I guess, like usual, I need to pay you first. Did you already drink what I sent you? It was good wasn't it. Reminded you of what you'd been missing." He twisted her hair in a vicious grip. "I'll be back. Be ready when I get here." He grabbed a bandana and wrapped it around her eyes. She held out her arms to steady herself as dizziness fell on her and he grabbed them, tying them behind her back.

"Remember, if you move too far you'll go over the edge. That'd be a waste." He bit her ear below the tie, and she yelped as he tossed her back onto the bed.

In a few moments, even the edges of the bandana grew dark.

He'd put out the light. If she crawled around, she could slip. Especially without use of her hands. Cold fear crawled up her spine and the scream she'd swallowed earlier threatened to erupt. Even if anyone missed her, no one would ever know where to look. The cold air of the cave nipped at her hands and face. She sat still, trying to feel the origin of the slight breeze. It had to flow from the mouth of the cave to the opening in the floor. She sat up on her knees and tried to remember which way her letter opener had flown. If she could find it, she might be able to untie her hands.

Roy used his left hand most often, he'd often leave bruises on her right cheek, so she had to look right. But was right toward the opening of the cave? She stopped and tried to remember. No, it was toward the expanse she didn't want to go near. She stood and found the wall with her foot. There was only so far it would take her until the floor disappeared out from under her, but she hoped she'd feel it first and not slip. Could she remember the knife hitting the floor or had it fallen to the depths below?

She swung her leg in a wide arc in front of her, trying to keep her foot from dragging on the floor. She didn't want to kick the letter opener away. After a few steps, her leg tired and she switched to the other. On the tenth step, her slow half-circle found the edge of the deep and she sprang back away from it and wobbled, her head suddenly light as a feather.

She turned back and slowly searched for the letter opener with her foot once again. Time was running short. She could feel it. It would take less than an hour for Roy to walk to town and back. It wouldn't take him long at all to get whiskey from Ros. She loved to sell it. Hattie pinched the skin of her hand. *Stop it. You need your wits about you. Now more than ever.*

A chill spilled down her spine and she shivered. Ezzy had said that she should take her situation to her God—fine. If that's what it took to get her out of this, she'd ask for help. Hattie stood rod straight.

"I don't know you, but Hugh and Ezzy do. When I was little and I needed someone, anyone, to pay attention to me. I prayed and you didn't answer. You weren't there. That's when I took my first drink. The drink was there for me, and it brought me closer to my pa. He didn't care about any of the others, but he cared for me.

"No one else knows it, but it was because of me Jennie wasn't sold off like Ruby. I made him a bet I could drink him under the table and if he lost, Jennie wouldn't have to go with the man he picked. Now, I know I should be sorry for that, but I'm not. I drank myself sick, but he passed out cold. I won. If you're there and you care so much, how come you left a girl to fight that battle? Why weren't you there when he sold off Ruby? How can I believe in a God that ignores those who need Him most?" She yelled and the sound echoed off the walls. Hattie stood up on her toes, trying to make herself bigger in the great expanse of the cave. She lost her balance and fell backward, her tied hands scraping against the smooth handle of the letter opener.

CHAPTER 25

R uby picked up Joseph and cuddled him close. "If Roy hasn't been seen for days then we can count him out." She bounced the tiny bundle on her hip.

Hugh scratched his jaw and considered what to say. If only that were the case, but he didn't have time to explain it to Ruby. "Beau, you ready?" He flipped the strap on his holster, leaving it open for use. If Hattie'd gone to either of those two, there was no telling what kind of trouble she might be in.

Beau nodded and stepped over to his wife. He whispered something in her ear, and she gave a shaky smile and nodded to him. He didn't have to hear what Beau said to know what he was doing. Ruby had been worried about her sister for a year and she'd hoped to be embracing her now. Not sending her husband out to save her.

Hugh closed the door behind them and waited until they were a few paces from the house. "I wish I could say Ruby was right, but I don't think Roy went very far. He's connected to Ros, helps her find new girls. Even if he is gone, he'll be back soon."

Beau kept a steady pace and made almost no noise. "I think we ought to aim for Ros first. Then if she isn't there, we move on to Roy."

The bottle—or whatever it was—in Hattie's pocket, was the only clue. If it had come from Roy, then she'd go to Roy. But since Lola had gotten the reward information from Ros maybe that's where Hattie went. He just couldn't be sure. "I suppose that's a good plan. I don't know where Roy is. He might have a room with Ros. We can ask her. I don't think she'll share, but what have we got to lose?"

Beau nodded and kept pace. "Hugh, what are your intentions with Hattie? I know what Ruby did was rash and if Hattie ever finds out, she'll think Ruby's just as bad as her pa was. She really thought it was the best course, but you did say you'd grown to love her." Beau stopped moving and regarded him with knowing eyes that reminded him of his own father. "So, I need to know what you intend."

Hugh took a deep breath to calm his nerves. Wasn't that the same question he'd wanted to know himself? "I told her I'd marry her when I got the telegram. It was out of duty and I even offered her an annulment as soon as she wanted one." He glanced to the heavens for the right words to finish what he wanted to say. He had to get this right. While Beau wasn't her pa, he was her guardian and had the final say.

Beau crossed his arms. "And now?"

Hugh sighed. "Now? I can't stop thinking about her. I'm worried about her when she isn't with me. I think about her all the time. I know she's young. And I'm, well, quite a few years older than her. But I can't help but hope that she'd want stability after all she's been through. I'd take good care of her, Beau."

"I know you would, but that's not what I'm asking. You said you love her, do you?" His eyes hardened. He wanted answers. He'd always known Beau to be direct. He should've seen this coming, instead it pulled the rug right from under him. "I don't know."

Beau frowned and turned his feet back down the path. "We'll take her back with us and give you some time to think on it. Once we find her."

"You're right. I'm worried for her. But somehow, I know she's all right." And he did. He knew he should be worried, but there was a peace that shouldn't be there, that hadn't been there when he'd searched for her all those months. She was nearby.

Beau gave him a look out of the corner of his eye and a smile lifted the edge of his lip then dropped. "You sure you don't know?"

The question hit him between the shoulders and sent his mind buzzing around like a dragonfly. You couldn't fall in love in such a short time, could you? He certainly felt protective, but that came with the job, didn't it? He was concerned about her feelings and her health, but that could just be Christian charity. He wanted everyone to be healthy. But even as he tried to discount all his feelings as common, Hattie was so much more.

Hugh looked through the front window of the Garter to see how many people would be around. He wondered how many of them would come to Ros's defense. He could see three people plus the bartender, but no Ros. He jerked his head toward the door and Beau opened it just as silently as he walked. Not a person looked up from their drinks as they strode over to the bar. The keeper wiped off two places as Beau and Hugh sat.

"What can I get for ya?" He chewed on a mangled sliver of wood.

"Information. Looking for Hattie, or Ros. Do you have either of them handy?" Hugh asked, drumming his fingers on the bar. A knot of tension coiled in his shoulders, which meant they'd attracted the attention of the men behind them.

"It's four o'clock." The bartender said with a smirk. "Ros is at *tea*."

"Where can we find her?" Beau leaned forward, the growl in his voice an unmistakable threat.

The barkeep thumbed the stairs. "In her *boudoir*, of course." He mocked her with the word. Things weren't as happy at the saloon as people would think.

Hugh pushed himself away from the bar and headed for the stairs, Beau right behind him. The last time he'd gone up those stairs was because he'd heard a scream, but not just that, he'd also heard Hattie was there. Finding her so quickly had been lucky. If only he could be that lucky now. The hallway consisted of a door every few feet, three doors on each side. All of the doors were closed and chained shut on the outside except the one on the very end. They stopped in front of it. This was the point of no return. Making Ros angry could get you more than hurt. Her men could take your life and dump you in some mine where no one would miss you.

Beau raised an eyebrow and shoved the door open with a bang. That was one way to get the job done. Porcelain shattered and sharp shards spread out around the richly dressed Ros. She was having tea, alone. She growled and let loose with a cussing streak.

"That was my best set! What makes you think you can just come on up here and slam into my room. I'm not just a common wench, you know!" Then she eyed them closer and squinted dark kohl-lined eyes. Her cheeks were far too pink, and her lips were dyed a deep red.

"You." Her lips pursed into a deep frown that left creases beside her lips and eyes. "Just because you're with Peterson doesn't give you the right to come in here. Until South Dakota makes what I do illegal, you've got no business here."

Beau pushed on Hugh's back, but he stood his ground. "I'm looking for Hattie. She turned up missing today and you're on the top of my list. Do I need to bust down all those doors out there, or will you cooperate?"

The skin under all the false color went pale. "You won't find her here. Roy was just here looking for whiskey. I sold him some but didn't ask questions. He bought some two days ago as well, so I assumed he'd gotten back together with Hattie. He doesn't drink whiskey himself. He's always been more of a beer drinker." She drew a cigarette and a long holder from a pouch sitting on her table and fitted them together. You can unchain any of those doors you want. Most of my girls are awake now and getting prepared for what we call 'lunch.' Not a one of them has seen Hattie. I can assure you." She took a match from a small box and lit her cigarette. "Now get out. I've got work to do." She brushed past them, her leather boots crunching the porcelain into the rug.

Beau turned as she walked through the door. "Where can we find Roy?"

She glanced over her shoulder, a wicked gleam in her eye. "You'll never get it out of me, cowboy."

CHAPTER 26

Hattie gasped as she twisted and reached to grab the letter opener. She had to scoot around and find it, but the cool smooth handle slid easily into her hand. She slipped it up until the blade rubbed against the rope. The blackness all around her tugged at her every sense, making her feel as if she were in a tiny box, not a cavernous room. The opening was in front of her, by maybe a few feet. She had to get back to the pallet before Roy came back or he would know what she was up to.

She slid backward along the floor until she hit her head against the table in the center. Good, the bed was to her left. It was an almost impossible feat as she struggled upright, still holding her precious yet dull blade. She stumbled against the pallet and fell onto it, struggling again to sit up and work to cut the cord. Her fingers were near numb from holding them behind her back and the blade slipped in her fingers. She dropped it twice, but the cord came free. She pulled her hands forward and rubbed her wrists to relieve the numbness and the bite the rope had left.

A scraping sounded all around her, bouncing off the walls and coming closer. Her heart took up residence in her throat. If that was Roy, she'd have but a moment to put her hands back and pretend she was still bound. Feet slapped against the floor of the cave and Roy's menacing laugh reverberated around her.

He didn't bother with the light. There was no change in the darkness over her eyes. His footfalls strode right up to the pallet. His hand slapped her cheek as he swiped for her in the darkness.

"I don't need no light to get around in here. But you do. I can tell right where I am just by the sound the cave makes with each of my steps." A cold bottle landed in her lap. "Drink up, love. You'll never get another chance." He clutched her shoulder and yanked her forward. His clammy hands followed her arms, the sickening feeling of his flesh against hers made her tremble. She jerked her hands out from behind her and shoved him off.

He fell backward as she pushed to her feet and slid the tie off her eyes.

Go right along the wall! Came a voice she didn't recognize.

She reached out and found the solid wall, moving as fast as she could to find the hole, but Roy was on her before she'd taken more than a few steps. He pinned her there, holding her hands above her head, her face smashed into the cold stone. Hattie pushed and flung her head back into his face to loosen his grip.

"No! Stop!" She screamed and kicked back at him.

He crushed her flat against the cold stone, his whole body trapping her. "You never fought me before." He ground into her ear. "You welcomed my touch when I took you from Deadwood. You danced under me. You wanton little—"

"No! Never! I welcomed the drink, but not you. I hate you!" She wiggled against his strength, but he pinned her harder.

His huge hand wrapped over her mouth. "Too much talk. I never wanted you for your mouth."

She held her breath against his hand. Taking her chances with the opening at the back of the cave would be better than her fate with Roy. She knocked her head back again and heard a satisfying *crack*. He let out a wail like she'd never heard before. She dashed along the wall but her tussle with Roy disoriented her. She didn't know how far off the ground the entry was or where she was looking.

KARI TRUMBO

She heard Roy groan and step toward her. Her heart raced in her chest. Surely he could hear it. She stood still, willing him to stay away from her.

"I know you're still in here. You ain't tall enough to reach the door and get yourself out of here. See, it's the perfect little hold for you. You won't ever get out without my help and I won't help you." He gargled as he cackled at her. She must've broken his nose good. His steps came closer, but he couldn't know where she was. Not as long as she stayed perfectly still. Her lungs burned from a lack of air. But she refused to take a full breath, forcing her body to be satisfied with short shallow breaths through her nose.

She heard the whoosh of his hands through the air and knew if she didn't do something quickly, he'd just light the lamp and then she was done for. He was angry enough to kill. Her body involuntarily shivered and she gasped.

"Ha. I knew you couldn't stay silent for long. I've got you now. You don't dare run because you'll die if you fall down that hole."

He was right. She'd die if she fell. Almost as surely as her heart would die if she gave herself to Roy again. She took a step back and then another. Ezzy's voice whispered in the back of her mind, *"I know my Lord, and you need Jesus."*

I don't want to need Jesus... She could hear Roy advancing on her, his slow steady steps coming closer and closer.

Hattie, jump. Came the strange voice again

She couldn't deny it any longer. Risking the deep was a better option than facing Roy. She took a run for the back, determined to just let her body fall. The ground disappeared from under her feet, and she screamed. The slippery rock caught her, and she slid. She couldn't tell how fast she fell or how far she went. The scream died on her lips as she realized she was not only alive but getting away from Roy, but to where? The cave floor dropped out from under her and she landed in a very cold lake in complete blackness, her skirts and petticoats dragging her down.

CHAPTER 27

Ros shuffled off down the hall and then down the stairs. Hugh had to make a decision. Risk wasting more time by looking in each room or trust Ros. She could easily be bluffing. She hadn't become a successful madam by being honest.

Hugh paused in Ros's doorway as he looked at each door. "We need to find someone who knows Roy's whereabouts."

Beau glanced out beyond him down the hall. "Didn't you say that Roy brings girls to work here? Isn't it likely that Hattie isn't the only one he brought here against their wishes? Might take a while, but no longer than it would to just start looking."

He didn't want to see the insides of those rooms, or those women. Each time he thought about where Hattie had been, it tore him up. He hadn't found her in time to prevent all those terrible things that happened to her. Hattie had wanted freedom and had been too young and impetuous to understand that people could be deceitful. She'd grown into womanhood in the worst possible way. A slave to the man she'd trusted.

Hugh strode to the first door. "Let's get this done with. I don't want to be here any more than you do."

"Yeah, if I want to be welcome in my own room tonight, I'd best buy a bath after this. I can smell the perfume as sure as if a skunk was in the room."

Hugh unhooked the hanging chain on the first door. He knocked and waited for a reply.

"I ain't taking callers yet. I ain't even eaten' yet! If you need something right now, there's a girl behind the bar what can't say no."

Beau frowned and looked away. Hugh's stomach turned at the idea.

"Ma'am, we're aren't here as callers. We're looking for Roy Hayden."

"Good luck. He don't tell no one where he hides. The snake."

The woman didn't open the door and Hugh wasn't willing to open it against her wishes.

"I can help you." A voice called to them from down the hall. Hugh followed it to Hattie's old room. He unlatched the chain as his gut tightened in knots. Who was waiting on the other side of that door?

"Are you going to open the door or just stand out there? I'm not going to bite and I'm as decent as you're liable to find me."

Hugh pushed the door open. The room was just as he'd left it, but a woman who looked to be about ten years older than him sat at the dressing table. She was thin as a rail and her dress hung loosely off her shoulders. The lines on her face were deep and her hair held banners of gray all down her back.

"Did I hear correct that you're looking for Roy?" She dabbed some sort of cream on her face and it accentuated every line but made her pale. She'd somehow managed to avoid getting hit, least as far as he could tell.

"Yes, ma'am. We think he may have taken someone. We want her back."

"If he found her, she'll end up somewhere like this. I was a widow, couldn't pay my rent anymore. This weren't exactly what I wanted to be doing, but it's better than starving. And men who think you're old enough to break, treat you better than they do the young ones."

Hugh shuffled his feet. The longer she talked, the longer Hattie waited.

"I know you think you can save her, but Roy's not one to let her escape. He lives in a hole in the rock a mile or two east of town. You won't find it unless you feel along the rocks. Until you're right in front of it, it looks like you'll walk into stone. I was only outside of it. He didn't want me to climb in and not be able to get out. I hope you *do* find her, but I don't think you will."

Hugh stared at her. "What soured you toward him enough to rat on him?" If she was pretending to hate Roy, she could give them information that would take them in the wrong direction, preventing them from getting to Hattie.

"He told me I'd have money to pay my own rent. That I'd make enough so I wouldn't have to do this for long. He didn't tell me that most of my pay would go to him as a *finder's fee.*" She gritted out the words. "He's a slippery one, that's for sure. What he doesn't know will get him, though. I've been talking to Ros and slowly turning her mind about him. It's all in how you talk to someone. Even more in how you listen. Soon enough, he won't be able to show his face here. Then, I'll get my whole pay and I'll leave this place. I see the Franklin House out my window and every day I think of what it would be like to work there. Not here."

"Thank you, ma'am. I hope you succeed." He didn't know what else to say to the older woman.

"Don't ma'am me until I earn the title back. For now, I'm just Helen."

Beau ducked out of the room and Hugh followed. "East of town. I know that area fairly well. I lived out that way until yesterday."

Beau's eyebrow raised again. He was beginning to hate that questioning tick.

"Yes, Hattie was there too."

"Do you think she could just be hiding out there? Somewhere

she feels safe?" Beau's long-legged stride took them outside of town quickly.

"It's a possibility, though I don't think she felt that safe there the last few days."

Beau whipped around to look at him, his hands bunched right above his gun belt. "And just why is that, Hugh?"

"It's not what you think. Someone tossed a rock through the window when she was up late one night. The next day, she was attacked as she was walking down the mountain." It wasn't worth mentioning that she was running from him. It was only because she was afraid of what she was hiding from him. The fact that she felt she needed to hide something at all still hit him like a punch to the gut. What hurt worse was that she'd rather put herself in danger than tell him.

"While we're here, let's check it just to be sure. Then we can search the rocks. There's a lot of ground to cover and only about four more hours of good light.

Hugh nodded his agreement and prayed Beau was right, that she was curled up in her bed at the cabin and they could all go back to Keystone happy.

Hugh was standing outside the cabin while Beau checked inside when he heard a faint scream drift down the side of the rocks.

"Beau, did you hear that?" He ran behind the cabin and waited to hear more but it was silent. Then, another quick screech that sounded more terrified human than injured animal.

"Hugh, let's go!"

CHAPTER 28

Cold seeped into Hattie until she couldn't control her shivers. There was no light, nothing to give away where she was. And almost worse, she couldn't hear Roy. Would he follow her? Would he dare to jump down the hole? She'd learned to swim in the Yellow Medicine river as a child, but that had been a long time ago. Her boots and skirts were like stones pulling against her. She kicked her feet and pressed forward. There was a solid ledge at the edge of the pond, but her hands were so cold she couldn't grip the edge.

She moved herself along the side of the rock, trying to find a way out of the cold water. She stopped for a moment and listened. Roy was still silent above her head. He hadn't given chase, or she would've heard him splash in the water. If he thought her dead, all the better. Her teeth chattered into the darkness and she clenched them, hoping to stay silent as she moved forward, searching for a way out.

The water became shallow and she walked along the bottom. Soon it was low enough for her to pull herself out and sit on the dry ledge. The air inside the cave raised gooseflesh all down her arms. She collapsed into a heap against the wall. Her heart had been in the same heap the day before when she'd realized Hugh didn't want her.

She gritted her teeth tighter until her gums ached, but what did it matter? What hope did she have of ever getting out of this? What would her life be if she did? She'd be forced to live on a ranch with the man she loved and would watch him live happily without her. Or worse, with someone else.

She clutched her knees to her chest and tried to collect some heat around her. Her arms shook and she scraped her hands up and down them. Speaking out loud would let Roy know she wasn't dead, but she wanted to scream, to call for help. Anything to get free of the dark and cold.

All right. You have my attention, God. The last two times I've wanted to give up, you presented a way of escape. I heard you tell me to jump, now what?

A sliver of light appeared overhead and she squinted up at it.

"Hattie, you down there?" Roy called from above. He let loose with a long string of curses, the likes of which she hadn't heard since her pa was alive. "You fool!" he yelled. "Now I'm gonna have to tell the miners." The mumbled words bounced off the walls around her.

The miners. She was deep under the ground, possibly near the mines. She'd only been by the mines three times, which one was farthest out of town? The Bullion…that was the name? There had been a clutch of men standing outside the mine for lunch when she'd walked by. But how long ago had that been and would they still be there? Most importantly, how could she let them know she was there without alerting Roy? She stood and inched her way about twenty paces around rock formations she could only feel with her hands until she found solid wall. It was wet, just like in Roy's chamber.

She continued to feel along the wall and delved deeper into the cave, or so it felt. It was no darker or lighter, just colder to her skin. She kept moving, listening for the sounds of mining. They used water to mine the area around Keystone and water should make noise, but she could pick out no sounds in the heavy silence.

Her heart would not slow its frantic pace, every movement was frightening as she couldn't see if she would drop into another cavern or her foot would find solid rock. Each new step was a painfully slow process as she slid her feet along the floor of the cave. She wouldn't cry. What good would tears do? They'd never helped her before, and they wouldn't help now.

Hattie. Sit and wait. Be still.

No! She didn't want to be still. If she stopped, she may not find the miners, may never get out of this alive. They may never even find her body down there. She shivered again and moved her foot then yanked it back as the floor opened up beneath her.

Okay. I'm listening. I'll not move anymore. How could she be talking to the Lord and why was He talking to her? Was this what people experienced right before they died? Did they have strange waking dreams with voices?

From far off, a sound tickled her ears. Her name. Someone was screaming her name. It was...*Hugh.*

She sucked back as much air as she could muster and screamed, "I'm down here!" Her voice rose to a deafening crescendo as it echoed up through the cavern.

CHAPTER 29

They'd been searching along the ridge line for what seemed like an hour when Beau motioned for him to come over. There it was. The small entrance to a cave. It was so small that a man much larger than Hugh or Beau wouldn't be able to fit. Hugh drew his gun. "I go first," he whispered. "Follow me."

Once he maneuvered into the opening and started crawling down the shaft, the walls seemed to close in on him. He had to push forward, had to find Hattie. She had to be in here. There was nowhere else for him to look, but what would he do if he found her with Roy? If she was there against her will, he'd want to kill the man. He gritted his teeth and focused on the halo of light ahead of him, getting bigger with each inch. He crept slowly to the edge.

Roy lay on his belly on the other end of the cave, a lantern beside him. He yelled for Hattie down in the floor and Hugh's anger rose to the boiling point. He flung himself through the hole and landed with his gun pointed at Roy, the hammer gave a satisfying crack in the hollow cave.

"Get up and turn around slowly, Roy. You're under arrest."

The man looked over his shoulder at him. His face was filthy and bloody. He growled, "For what? I didn't do nothing. She came here looking for me, then jumped off the edge. Must'a been the drink. I didn't do nothing." He repeated, his eyes not fixed on anything in the room. "What'd you do to her? She was just fine, good working girl until you came to town. I oughta' throw you down that hole." Roy stood and took a run at Hugh.

He heard Beau drop into the cave behind him. Hugh knew he had at least twenty pounds on Roy and a good few inches. But Roy was pert-near crazy. He took his stance and just before Roy hit him, he dropped his shoulder, taking him in the gut. Roy groaned and Hugh wrapped his arms around Roy's stomach, cutting his leg in behind Roy's ankle to bring him down. Beau cocked the hammer on his pistol and the fight went out of Roy. He laid there shaking.

Now that Roy was down, he took a look around. There, on the bed, was the missing letter opener. His anger burst forth like a cannon and he yanked Roy off the floor and shook him.

"Where's Hattie?"

Roy's head flopped around as if he were drunk. "I told you. She jumped. I called down there, but there was no answer. She's dead."

"Heaven have mercy on you if she is. Because I won't have any."

He glanced at the opening in the floor he hadn't seen before. "Beau, you take care of Roy. I'm going to see if I can find her."

Beau didn't say anything, but he didn't have to. He was as dependable as they came. Hugh grabbed a lantern off the wall and lit it, then dangled it down the hole. It was deep, but there was a steady slope a few feet down.

"Hattie? Can you hear me?" His voice sounded too harsh to his own ears. Desperate.

"Hattie?"

"I'm down here!"

"Don't move, sweetie. I'm coming to get you!" *Sweetie?* Where had that come from?

He swung his leg off the edge and just barely caught the slide with his toe. He didn't want to go tumbling down if he could help it. Especially not if he hoped to keep the lantern lit.

495

"Keep talking to me, Hattie. So I can find you." *And so that I don't go crazy with worry.*

"Hugh? That's you. Isn't it?" Her voice was shaky with cold.

"Yes, darlin'. I'm just trying to find a way down to you. Your voice sounds like an angel. Keep talking."

"Careful. If you slip on that slide, you'll land in the water down here." Her voice came stronger now, as if she were coming nearer.

"Thank you, that's good. I have a lantern and I don't want it getting snuffed out."

She laughed but it was shaky and faint.

Hugh edged his way slowly down the formation on the side of the cave. It was slicker than wet clay. After what seemed like a long descent, he came to a slightly level area overlooking a large underground lake. The water was a beautiful turquoise blue in the soft light of the lantern. If circumstances weren't so dire, it would've been almost peaceful.

"Where are you, Hattie? Have I lost you again?" he called out into the cavern.

"I'm over here, along the wall. I don't want to get back in the water. I'm so cold. But I don't know how to get out."

"Just wait there. I'll figure something out." He set the lantern down near the edge to give Hattie light and tried to climb back up the slide. It was treacherous but might be possible with help from Beau.

"Beau! Throw me down some rope. Whatever you can find. The longer the better."

Beau's head appeared above. "I'll see what I can find. Did you find her?"

"I can't see her, but I can hear her. She'll be all right if we can get her out. She's cold."

"It ain't exactly warm in here." Beau tossed down a long coil of rope and it slid down the slide catching on Hugh's feet. He collected the rope and slid carefully back down to the ledge.

"Hattie. I'm sorry, sweetie, but I can't see you. I'll be down there in just a few minutes. Can you wait for me?"

"Hugh." She paused and he could feel the tension in her voice. "I don't want you to see me like this."

"It wasn't your fault. I need to see you to know you're okay."

He tied the end of the rope in a loop and stood in the center, pulling it up his body. He guessed at how much slack he would need to make it to the lake and tied the rope around a pillar so he could lever himself back up after he found Hattie. He held tight to the rope and hung backward for a moment off the edge. Hattie screamed behind him, almost sending him falling off the edge.

"Don't worry, I won't fall. Just hold tight. I'll be there." He jumped back a few feet and let the rope slide through his fingers. He gripped it tightly as he hit the water. The lake was colder than he'd expected. He couldn't blame Hattie for not wanting to jump back in. The rope slid over his head and he tied the end loosely around itself so it would be there when he brought Hattie back. But first, he had to find her.

He bobbed in the water and turned until he saw her huddled along the wall, her pale face above her knees, her hair falling dark and damp around her shoulders. He drank in the sight of her as he swam toward her. He pushed himself up out of the water on the edge of the lake and crawled onto the ledge. Her booted feet made little clicking noises on the rocks as she ran toward him.

Hattie slid to a stop in front of him and he took in her face. Fear made her eyes wide and her lips parted slightly. He didn't want to scare her again. She waited for only a moment before she flung her arms around him and clung to him for dear life. Her body shook with chills and he wrapped his arms around her shoulders, crushing her closer to him. He couldn't seem to get close enough.

She tipped her face up to him and the invitation of her sweet lips was too much to bear. He lowered his face to hers, stopping a breath and waiting.

He could barely speak past his desire. "I'm sorry, Hattie." He cradled her close. "I promised I'd never touch you, but you make me weak-willed."

Her arm reached up over his chest and around his neck, pulling his mouth to hers once more. He wouldn't take, but he'd give. Her lips trembled against his and he pulled her closer, enveloping her. He could think of nothing but the softness of her skin, the velvet of her lips against his and the heat that slowly built between them. She released her hold on his shirt and tangled her fingers in his short hair.

Hattie sucked in a deep breath and buried her face in his chest. "I'm sorry, Hugh. It's just that I —"

He silenced her with a soft kiss and, when he pulled back, she was silent.

"I don't want an apology, sweetie." He caressed her cheeks and she leaned into his hand. "I just want you. I know that now. I can't stand the thought of you ever offering your hand to anyone else. If you can't love me, I won't follow you back to Deadwood. I just couldn't stand it, Hattie. Like I said, when it comes to you, I'm weak."

"Hugh, you're the strongest man I've ever known. I don't want anyone but you ever again."

He ran the tip of his finger along the bottom of her lip. "I'm sorry our first kiss was in the bottom of a hole. I'll make that up to you."

She smiled and returned to her spot, where she fit just perfectly under his chin. "We've got our whole lives for you to show me how it's done right."

He laughed and kissed the top of her head. "Beau is waiting for us. We need to get back up there and I don't know any other way but back through the lake."

"Beau is here? With Ruby?" Her eyes grew wide and a smile lit her face.

"They are. You'll be on your way home before you know it. But first, we have to cross this lake."

Hattie shook her head. "It's so cold and I almost drowned with my petticoats and boots."

"Come." He drew her to his side. "I'll help you. We'll do this together." They stood on the edge of the water. "I'll jump in first, then help you in."

She nodded her agreement and he stepped into the water. It was fairly shallow, and he held his arms up to help her. She sat in front of him and slipped her feet into the water, her knees knocking and teeth chattering almost instantly. When she was in the water, he swam next to her so that if she wasn't strong enough, he could pull her right back up. He reached the looped rope and untied it, then turned to find Hattie. She bobbed next to him, but fatigue lined her face.

"I need you to hold your breath and float for a moment while I put this around you."

She held her breath and tried to float, but it didn't work.

She shook her head. "I can't. My petticoats pull me down. They weigh so much." Her words were gasps for air.

The blasted clothes would be her death. "Hattie, Please. You're more important to me than a petticoat. Take it off."

"I can't do that Hugh!"

He looked around, frantic for something he could do. He kicked as hard as his booted feet would allow and wished he'd have left them up by the lantern. His muscles screamed at holding his own weight and hers. He slipped the loop around her body as quickly as he could then tied the other end around himself. Now she couldn't sink or fall any further than she was. He'd have to carry up a soaking wet Hattie.

He rested her head against his. "I'm going to pull you to the top. As soon as you're on the ledge, I need you take off the rope and toss it back to me."

She nodded and held tight to the rope. His muscles screamed as he began to swim against the weight, away from Hattie, as he slowly pulled her up to the ledge. When she reached the top, he waited, kicking in one place made his legs throb and he was ready to get out of the frigid water, but Hattie was safe now.

She tossed the rope back over the ledge and as he swam back to it, it lowered to him. He threaded it through the loop at his waist and pulled himself up, hand over hand. His muscles protested with each movement, but he couldn't wait any longer, they needed to get out of the cold cave and warm up. Hattie waited for him at the top.

She was stark white. The only color to her was her eyes and her was hair dark from the water. She reached for him as he approached her, and he clasped onto her hand. He sat heavy on the ground next to her, every muscle in his body exhausted. He pulled her softly over on his lap and looked her in the eyes.

She touched his cheek and wiped the moisture from his brow. "You came for me. I didn't think you would." She was shivering against him, the cold air from above pouring over them.

"Why would you ever think that? I'll always be here for you, Hattie. I wish you would've come to me for help, instead of Roy. I thought you trusted me." The betrayal cut the deepest. He'd given up a year of his life to find her, and yet, she hadn't come to him.

"I do trust you. I only went to Roy to tell him to leave me alone. I want nothing to do with him anymore." Her lips were purple, and he wanted to turn them back to their lovely pink the best way he knew how. But now was not the time. He slowly ran his hands down her face, neck and shoulders, then tucked her head under his chin to keep from kissing her senseless. She didn't need another man forcing himself on her and he still couldn't accept that she'd want his kisses.

She sighed and clutched the front of his coat.

He wouldn't let her go, but he could offer her a covering. It was wet, but thicker than what she had on. He lifted her up and shrugged out of his coat, swinging it around her shoulders. "Here, it'll warm you." He couldn't help tipping his chin and kissing her head. He felt her gasp and regretted it immediately. "I'm sorry, Hattie. I shouldn't have."

She lifted her face and searched his eyes in the dim light of the lantern beside them. "Hugh, you don't need to apologize." She shook her head. "I'm yours if you want me." She ducked her face and buried herself in his coat.

He ran his finger under her chin and over her sweet, soft lips. "I've never wanted another," he breathed.

Her eyes met his and she leaned forward, tentatively brushing her lips against his. They were as cold as they looked, and his heart beat faster than a reel at a barn dance. He ached to pull her closer and take the time to show her what a kiss could be like. Because he'd wager she'd never had one from someone who cared. In that respect, she was still as pure as snow.

He smiled down at her and held her cheek, trying to brush warmth into the chill beneath his hand. "You need to hold onto my hand as tightly as you can so I can walk us up. It might take a while. Can you do that?"

She was shivering but managed to nod. "That's my girl. We'll have you up top in no time."

CHAPTER 30

She watched Hugh closely as he moved slowly up the incline, careful so they wouldn't slip. Each step was measured, and she had to make sure she had her footing before they could move on. His patience with her warmed her through. No man had ever treated her with such respect. When they reached the upper ledge, about seven feet from Roy's home, Hugh leaned against the wall to rest and she stood in front of him.

He searched her eyes and the pain in his gaze had her wishing she'd sat closer to him.

"When Roy told me you were dead, I—" He glanced away, and his mouth hardened.

"No you don't, Hugh. You will not block me from hearing." She had to see his eyes, had to read in them what she wanted so desperately to know.

He closed his eyes and his voice turned to a harsh pained whisper. "I thought I'd die right along with you. I couldn't bear even thinking about it." He didn't look at her and she couldn't force him to. She stepped over to his shoulder and gazed up into his darkened eyes. They were stormy, for sure. But she saw more care there than she'd ever seen before.

"Hugh, I don't think I ever thanked you. Not for rescuing me the first time, not for caring for me in the cabin, and not for risking your life to save me just now. Though, a thank you doesn't seem quite adequate."

He sucked in his breath as if she'd punched him. The heat pouring off him was welcoming and she ducked under his arm and held him tight. When his arms fell heavy and solid around her, she finally let the tears escape.

"I'm so sorry, Hugh. I didn't drink anything, I promise. Roy sent Lola to lure me back into town for more. I came out here to tell him to leave me alone. I thought you'd hate me if you found the flask. I couldn't stand that. I hated myself for what that bottle did to me."

"I could never hate you." He rasped in her ear. His mouth was just a breath from her head. He kissed the ear Roy had bitten earlier.

"He'll never touch you again. If I'd known he did this to you when I found him, I'd have flogged him."

She touched the spot on her ear and realized Roy had left a small nick in it. She'd been so terrified, she hadn't noticed.

He sighed and rested his head against hers. "We need to get back up. Beau is waiting."

Beau's voice came from above. "I'm not that far away."

Hattie's cheeks burned and Hugh laughed. "All right, Beau. I'm going to toss this rope up. Can you haul us out of here?"

"I reckon I can."

HUGH CLIMBED out and back into Roy's cave. Hattie, draped in his coat, stood in the corner. As far away from the bound Roy as she could. He was mumbling something, but Hugh didn't care enough to listen.

"Beau, before we go any further. I want to ask permission to court Hattie."

Beau's eyebrow shot up. "Bit late for that. Isn't it?"

Hattie giggled nervously from behind them. "We haven't done a thing, Beau."

Now both eyebrows rose. "You mean you two didn't live together for a week? If you think for one moment I'll let you dishonor my wife's sister, you've got another think coming, Hugh Bradly."

Hugh could see the amusement in Beau's eyes, but Hattie couldn't. She crumpled to the floor. "No. I won't force him. I didn't want him saddled with me in the first place and he shouldn't have to now."

"Saddled with you? Sweetie, I *want* to marry you. Granted, at first it was because I felt led to, but now I want to."

"You were led to?" Her head snapped up and she stared at him.

He held his breath. Hattie always turned defensive when anyone spoke about the Lord. More than anything, he wanted to share his faith with her, just as much as he wanted to share his heart.

"He saved me. When I needed my knife, I asked Him and I found it. When I was scared and couldn't find the way out, He told me which way to go. When Roy came back and I knew he was going to do something awful, He spoke in my ear and told me to jump. So, I did. Fairytales don't talk to you. They don't care if you live. There are two reasons I will never forget my time in the cave. Fear and peace. I was scared the whole time, but every time I heard that voice, I knew what I was doing was right."

Hugh wanted to burst with happiness. It wasn't an admission of belief, but she had admitted to faith. The obedience part was always the hardest, but she'd obeyed the Lord and it saved her life. They could learn about Jesus together. He held out his arms and she dashed toward him, flinging her hands around his neck. He'd never get tired of that.

Beau lifted Roy up off the floor by his arm. "I think it's time we get Roy here to Deputy Peterson."

Hugh relished the feel of Hattie in his arms for one more moment. "And let Hattie see her sister and her new nephew."

Hattie squealed. "Ruby had a baby? Why didn't you tell me?"

He ran his finger under her chin. "You've been gone a long time. Welcome home, Hattie."

CHAPTER 31

Hattie hung her head out the window of the stagecoach and saw Deadwood ahead. Before leaving Keystone, Beau had wired the owner of the ranch, Brody Ferguson, so he could meet them with a wagon. Hugh was nowhere in sight, but she ached to see him. It was the longest they'd been apart in two weeks. He'd warned her that it would take him much longer by horse, since he couldn't keep pace with the stage.

Baby Joseph squirmed in her arms and rooted around for something to eat. Ruby hadn't been able to nurse him at the last stop and now he was fussy and hungry. She handed her nephew back to his mother and her arms immediately ached to hold him again. It would be wonderful to have a child. By the grace of God, she'd managed to avoid pregnancy the year she'd been gone. Now she worried that perhaps she was barren. She stuffed her fear far back in her mind. They'd tarried a week in Keystone to get all the loose ends tied up with Roy, Ros, and Ezzy. The seamstress finished the dress that was to become her wedding gown. During that time, Hugh had shown her the story in Hosea he'd read right after he'd gotten the telegram. It had warmed her heart to know that the Lord could have a plan for a prostitute, even one who *wanted* that life, which she hadn't. Hugh explained that not only was the story real it also paralleled God's redeeming love for His people, Israel. He told her that her past need not hold her back, not from him and not from God.

She smiled as she thought on all Hugh had brought into her life, including this new knowledge of the Lord. Living without Hugh, even for the day or two it would take him to make the trip, weighed heavily on her heart. She tried to remember to give it up to the Lord, but faith was so new and so foreign to her.

Ruby touched her arm and pointed just out the window at the house they'd lived in before she'd foolishly left, romance and whiskey on her mind.

The stage stopped at the station. They let the passengers disembark before Beau stood and took his wife's hand, leading her out. He then waited by the door to help her down. She thanked him and took a look around. The town had grown in the year she'd been gone. More women, though still not many, walked down the street, arm in arm with men. Their smart hats and walking suits were a burst of color in an otherwise drab landscape of browns.

Beau spoke with a man she didn't recognize. He tossed their bags in the back of the wagon and held out his hand to help her up into the back. Apprehension prickled at the back of her neck.

He smiled and held out his hand, "I'm Brody Ferguson and I own the ranch Beau and Aiden work on. Any family of Beau's or Aiden's is welcome there." He took her hand and brushed his lips gently over her knuckles. She couldn't quite move from the spot, afraid to say anything. No one had ever kissed her hand before. Like she was a woman worthy of consideration and respect. A new strength sprouted deep within her. She could be that woman. "Thank you, Mr. Ferguson." He helped her up the side of the wagon.

A tense knot formed in her stomach. Her sisters had false ideas about her and now she'd have to face them and their distrust. She settled herself on the bench seat and Ruby sat next to her, Beau and Brody Ferguson, in front.

The ranch wasn't far from town, not even an hour, which

seemed like nothing after such a long journey. Her knees wobbled as she climbed down. In the doorway of a small cabin stood her twin sister, Eva, and Jennie. She gasped. Eva looked just like her now. Eva had always been more frail, quiet, small. Now, after a year of unbearable food, Hattie looked much the same.

"Oh Eva, I've missed you!" And it was true. She'd grown to miss them all. Even after she'd told herself she hated them for following Beau and Ruby, for always agreeing, for being good and obedient, and mostly for taking her far from her home in Yellow Medicine. Now she knew home was where your family was, and pa had barely been family.

Eva bunched her skirts in her hands and tore off toward Hattie, they collided in a fierce embrace. Jennie stood back. Her hands hidden in the folds of her dress. She looked terrified to come near as if she couldn't quite believe she was seeing the truth.

"Jennie?" Hattie held out her hands, but Jennie stayed rooted to her spot.

Jennie slowly shook her head. "Hattie, I'm so sorry. I should've paid more attention. I should've tried to save you. It's all my fault."

Aiden appeared behind Jennie, a little thinner than she remembered him being. He put his arm around Jennie and kissed her head, then whispered something in her ear. She nodded then stepped off the porch and strode toward her. Hattie chewed her lip. She'd been incredibly unkind to Jennie before she'd left. That hurt had followed her all the way to Keystone and had been one of the few things to break through the fog of her drunken mind.

Jennie stood before her. Her hands were still hidden in the folds of her dress. Hattie reached out and Jennie stepped into her arms. "Jennie, I'm so sorry. I had no right to say the things I did. I'm sure some of those things made you think I wanted to be where I was, but I didn't. I was so selfish, then I couldn't get out once I saw how bad life was going to get. Can you ever forgive me?"

Jennie stiffened and Hattie stepped back, still holding Jennie's arms. She saw the purple color of Jennie's hands and gasped. "What happened to you?"

Jennie shook her hands and pulled them away, shoving them into the pockets of her skirt. "I wanted to save you, but I couldn't."

Hattie shook her head. That made no sense. How could Jennie have saved her? And how did that hurt her hands? "I don't understand."

Aiden appeared beside her and again pulled her close to his side. "Jennie was sleep walking and had a vision of you burning in the house in Deadwood. She reached into the fireplace. Luckily, I pulled her out before she damaged more than her hands."

Hattie's knees went weak under her. She'd hurt those she loved most. How could they ever take her back? She'd be apologizing until she didn't have breath left.

Jennie met her gaze. "It wasn't your fault, Hattie. I was reading about the fires in Deadwood's history, and I missed you so much and felt so guilty after you left." A tear fell down her cheek. "I just wanted my family all together. I'm so glad you're home now."

Hattie's other sisters lined up along the porch waiting for her. All four of them: Francis, Lula, Nora, and Daisy had grown so much since she'd left. She'd lost so much time with them. When Hugh arrived, she'd get married and she'd never get that time with them back. She sighed and hugged each one in turn, blinking back hot tears.

Ruby stood next to her, holding the still fussing Joseph. "You can come on in and take the spot Jennie left when she married. There's barely enough room to turn around in there, but the ranch is huge and you're free to go anywhere up on this ridge. It's hard to get down to Aiden and Jennie's without a horse, so you'll need to learn to ride. Hugh can help you with that when he arrives."

Ruby brushed past them and into the house, probably to go feed Joseph. Hattie sighed and went to pick up her bag. Aiden, Beau, and Brody stood by the wagon. Beau nodded to her. "I'll bring your bag in. Why don't you go rest? It's good to have you home. I'm sure Hugh will be here in the next few days."

CHAPTER 32

F our days.

It had been four days since arriving in Deadwood and she hadn't seen nor heard from Hugh. She'd written a letter to her mother in Cutter's Creek. She'd spent time learning her way around the ranch, and she'd cleaned the cabin she and Hugh would share when he returned. She'd run out of things to do besides letting her gut twist in worry about every possible thing that could go wrong. The one worry that reoc-curred the most was that he came to his senses and just ran away.

Hattie snapped off the end of a green bean and tossed it into the saltwater on her lap. He had to come soon. He just had to. But what if he didn't? Had she been wrong about his feelings? After he'd rescued her from the cave, they'd spent hours together, talking and reading... And trying to avoid situations where they'd be alone. The temptation to kiss him was far too great. Yet all she wanted was to spend more time with him, to never be apart from him.

Eva dropped down next to her on the step with an elaborate sigh. "Still watching for your prince to arrive?" Her soft pale cheeks rose in a slight smile. "He'll be here soon. I told Jennie the same thing and she waited weeks and weeks."

Hattie snapped a bean and tried to look at anything but the trail down the hill. "So, Jennie had to wait too? Why?"

"Aiden had to go back home and make things right with his family. Then he ended up bringing them back with him. Good thing he did, or you'd never have met Hugh."

She stopped snapping and closed her eyes. "If not for Hugh, I'd probably be dead… Or wishing I were."

"You're right. I think our Heavenly Father planned everything, just so you could find Hugh."

Hugh had shown her passages where men had gone through terrible things just to be used by the Lord for good, but that didn't make her any more pleased about being the one chosen for God's purpose. "Please don't talk about that time as a blessing, Eva. It was anything but." Just thinking about what she'd gone through that year left her sick to her stomach.

"I wasn't talking about that. It wasn't God's choice that you should go. But since He knew you would, He brought—not only Aiden for Jennie, but also Hugh. Hugh was meant to come here, and he was meant to go save you. He was meant to love you."

"I don't know about that, Eva. Hugh isn't here. He was supposed to be here two days ago." She snapped her bean with vengeance, and it sent the top flying behind her.

"You have no idea why he's late. I'm excited for him to get here. I've been riding the range out around the fences and I can't wait to show you some wonderful things I've found. I have drawings… There are some things that you can only share with a twin."

"Eva… Once Hugh comes back—if he comes back—we'll get married. I don't know if he'll want to live and work here or if we'll go to Deadwood. I don't want to count on staying here, if I'm not."

Eva's face sagged. "You just came back. I've missed you so much. We all have. Doesn't that account for anything?"

Hattie wrapped her arm around Eva and squeezed. "Of course it does. But Hugh will decide where we live. Not me."

The rumble of a man's voice shocked her out of her thoughts.

"I'm sure if the man's worth his salt he can take his wife's desires under advisement."

The familiar voice vibrated through Hattie's heart and into her soul. She leapt to her feet, spraying beans everywhere. She screamed in surprise and ran to Hugh, throwing her arms around his neck. He lifted her clean off the ground in a crushing squeeze then dropped her to her toes with a light kiss that didn't even come close to fulfilling her need.

"Oh Hugh, where have you been?"

He smiled, the first real smile out of him she'd ever seen—and it was glorious. She'd paint it if she could. His eyes fairly glowed with it. She stared, wanting to remember that sight forever.

"I was in Deadwood for a few extra days setting things right with Bullock and ordering some wood. I can't have my bride and not have a place for her."

Her outburst had brought people from all over the ranch, but she wouldn't let them steal him from her quite yet. "But a house will take a long time to build, are we to wait until it's finished?"

Brody strode up behind Hugh and clapped him on the back. "Nope, I've already told Hugh you prepared the small cabin. It's the same one that Aiden and Jennie lived in while he and Hugh built the house in the valley. If this keeps up, I'm going to end up deeding all my land to you sisters and your husbands!" He laughed.

"You already talked to Brody? When?" He hadn't come to see her first? She pushed aside the hurt, glad he was there at all.

"Brody was in Deadwood picking up supplies. I happened to see him in the street." He clapped Brody on the back. "I also arranged for the new preacher to come here and perform a wedding in two days. If you'll still have me?"

"Of course I'll have you." Heat rose into her cheeks.

Eva squealed in excitement. "Oh, I'm so excited. Another Arnsby married to the right man!"

Hattie turned and smiled slyly at her. "You do realize, you're next?"

Eva shook her head so vigorously pins fell from her hair. "No, not me. The Dakota's don't make my kind of man. Quiet, book learned. My kind of man would be too soft for South Dakota." She turned a deep pink.

Hattie couldn't help but smile at her sweet sister. "Maybe that's what the Lord has in mind for you, maybe not. Either way, you'll be next. Francis will only be sixteen this year."

Hattie laughed as Eva nibbled at her lip. Eva had plenty of time to think about what she wanted. Though Eva would always be her twin, Hattie suddenly felt ages older.

Hugh touched her back, ever so softly, sending a shiver up her spine. "Walk with me?"

She looked at the bowl of scattered beans and the saltwater.

Eva raised an eyebrow and sighed. "I'll wash them up. You go."

Hugh didn't wait for a reply. He directed her toward the stable, his excitement almost palpable. She could feel his pace increase the closer they got.

"I have to show you something." He drew her into the dark barn, and she blinked as her eyes adjusted to the dim interior. Hugh took her hand and led her forward. His breath was warm on the back of her neck and his solid frame behind her reassuring. "Are you ready?" He sounded so happy and excited. How could she not share in it?

She nodded and he moved his hand. There, before her, was a beautiful smoke-colored horse. She knew next to nothing about horses, couldn't even tell if it were male or female, but it was beautiful.

"Oh Hugh! Is it for me?" She glanced back at him, his expression soft. The lines around his eyes and lips had vanished, the strain from the time in Keystone long gone.

"Yes, Hattie. She's all yours. You can name her, and I'll teach you to care for her. You'll learn to ride so that you'll always be able to get where you want to go. I never want to ride alone again. I missed you so much."

"I missed you, too. I was so worried you wouldn't come back, Hugh. I guess that was foolish of me. You've never let me down."

He tucked his finger gently under her chin and lifted her face to look up at him. "I told you I'd never leave you. I meant it. I didn't want to be apart from you, either, but sometimes work has to be done. I thought about you the whole time."

His lips brushed across her cheek, sending a pleasant heat dancing down her body. She opened her eyes and took in everything about him. Memorized every line around his eyes and his soft brown eyelashes, his long straight nose and his strong chin. She wouldn't change a thing about him and, despite what she'd been through, she couldn't wait to be his wife.

"We have to wait two whole days?" She took his hand in hers and he followed her from the barn.

"It gives the family a little time to prepare. And the preacher couldn't come out any sooner. I asked."

She couldn't keep the laughter from bubbling up and Hugh's arm wound around her waist, pulling her into him, squeezing her close. She wanted to see him smile every day of her life. He'd been too long without.

CHAPTER 33

"W hat do you mean, Eva's missing?" Hattie tugged her dress up over her arms and Jennie grabbed the seams and began on the long row of buttons up the back.

Jennie ignored the question. "I hope you don't plan on wearing this gown again. Hugh will have a devil of a time unbuttoning you tonight and he won't ever want to do it again. If it were Aiden... well, never you mind." She laughed. "I'm having enough trouble with my stiff fingers as it is."

Hattie turned around and words escaped her for a moment. "Oh, Jennie. I'm sorry. That was thoughtless of me. Ruby would be glad to do this. You can help me with something else."

Jennie shook her head, her lower lip trembled, and she sucked it into her mouth. "It isn't that I can't, or that I don't want to, it's just difficult. There's a difference."

"Jennie, I'm real sorry for the things I said to you about Aiden. I had no right."

"Oh, fiddle-faddle. It's water under the bridge, gone a million miles from here by now." Jennie wouldn't look up to her eyes.

Hattie turned back around, and Jennie's hands held the two sides together as she sighed deeply. "You need to forgive me, though. It was my fault. I told Beau and Aiden they shouldn't follow you. I assumed you wanted to be where you were. I…" Her voice slid away and her body shuddered with a sob. Hattie spun to embrace her sister, but Jennie held up her hand. "No, hear me out. I assumed you wanted to be…what you would later become. That you wanted the drink bad enough to do anything to get it. I was wrong. I should've sent them after you. If I had, they may have found you in Lead in time."

Hattie sighed. She'd known this was coming, had worried about it the last two days. But everyone had been so busy preparing, no one had spoken about her past.

"Even if they'd found me the very first night I was taken, it would've been too late. Roy used me first, then he convinced me that because I didn't fight back, I liked it and I deserved to be a prostitute. I believed that the whole time I was there. Hugh showed me that Roy tricked me, used me.

"I was with Roy in Lead for about a month, but never outside the little house where he took me. I didn't realize it then, but I was as much a prisoner there as I was at the Red Garter. I doubt they would've found me, and I don't hold it against you. I was angry when I left. Pent up. And you're right. I would've done about anything for a real drink. I was taking nips of Ruby's pain tinctures just to feel well enough to get through the day.

"I don't expect you to understand, but Hugh does, and we can build a life where I never have to have a drink again." She laughed softly as Jennie raised her head. "But I need to get this dress on first. I can't go out there hanging open."

Hattie turned around and after a moment's hesitation Jennie fastened the last few buttons at the base of her neck. The gown itself had a plunging neckline, but a blue lace insert in the front made it look like a high collar. It matched the pattern of the fabric and was set against a buttery yellow background. The blue lace rose in three tiers of ruffles on the front of the gown, sweeping along the back of the bustle as well. It was, by far, the nicest gown she'd ever owned.

The thoughts of her dress turned her mind to the buttons Jennie had mentioned. Sure, she knew the basics of what happened between a man and a woman, but she had the distinct feeling that what went on between husband and wife was different, if not in action, then in emotion. There was nothing for it, she'd find out soon enough. The worry had her tying her fingers in knots.

Ruby came into the room and laid a hand on Hattie's shoulder. "You've forgotten the blue ribbon Hugh got you. It would look lovely woven into your hair."

Hattie sat in front of Ruby's small mirror and watched as Ruby wove the ribbon intricately through her pins.

"We still aren't sure where Eva is, but I'm sure she'll be back soon. If she doesn't come back before the preacher arrives, do you want to start without her? He can only stay for two hours."

Hattie nibbled on her fingernail, then sighed. "Did she go on another one of her rides?" She wanted her twin there but couldn't postpone it. Eva would understand, she hoped.

"I'm sure she did. She's been acting so strange of late." Ruby tucked a pin into Hattie's hair, securing the ribbon.

Hugh appeared at the doorway with a sweet smile on his face. "Ladies. Ruby, would you mind if I spent a few minutes with my beautiful Hattie while we wait for Eva?"

Ruby hesitated. "It isn't usually done, Hugh. And to have you both alone in our room before you're wed, it's just…"

"I promise you nothing will happen, leave the door open if you wish. I just want to spend a few minutes with Hattie before she becomes Mrs. Bradly."

Hattie's stomach fluttered as Hugh stepped closer. He looked more handsome than usual in his tailored black suit and string tie. Jennie left and Ruby followed, giving them a quick glance as she left the door open behind her.

Hugh strode toward her and dropped down on one knee in

front of her. She gazed directly into his deep blue eyes as he rested his hand on her knee. "You are the most precious, beautiful woman I've ever laid eyes on."

Heat rose up her neck and she couldn't hold in a smile.

"I want you to know that in this last few weeks, I've grown to see you as a whole new woman. You aren't the Hattie I found in the Red Garter. You aren't the woman who couldn't even raise her hand after the drink sapped your energy. That Hattie is gone, and in her place is a new creation. That creation is bathed in white, is precious. Is forgiven by the only one that matters."

Her lip quivered and she bit it to keep from crying. "You?"

"No, the one who binds me to you today, the Lord. I have nothing to forgive. You are a spotless and pure bride and I love you."

She stood and stepped into his arms. "Thank you Hugh. For reminding me that this day marks something more important than you or I alone. It marks you and I together as one. And now I wish I did have a white gown."

He cupped her face with his large hand and smiled warmly as he tilted her face to him. He leaned over, coaxing her lips to his own. She slipped her hands around him and tilted her head back to accept him, loving how she fit just perfectly within his arms.

He sighed contentedly as she squeezed him closer. A rumble vibrated against her cheek, first softly, then growing in strength with every breath. She'd never heard him laugh before and her own giggles erupted from her lips.

"I'm sorry, Hattie, I'm just so happy. I can't help it."

She cupped his cheeks. "I never want another day to go by where I don't hear you laugh and see your smile."

He brushed his lips over her forehead. "While I can't promise you that. I can promise you'll never be alone again."

She wanted to tell Hugh how she felt but showing was so much easier than telling. She slid her hand around his neck, guiding him to her. He groaned and pulled her closer to him, his warmth seeping through to her very heart. His lips crushed hers for a moment, then he tensed and pulled back, softening, tempting. She didn't want to stop. She pulled him to her again and this kiss was tender, a sweet nibbling at her lips. Her body felt light as a surge of heat spread like fire.

"My sweet. It's time to see the preacher."

Historical Elements

This book was birthed from a 2016 trip to South Dakota with my family, though it was not my first trip to Keystone. We had such a wonderful time. We visited a lot of delightful towns, and some of them will find their way into this series.

The mines: Keystone has many mines just outside of town. The five mentioned in the story are some of the most popular in the area, though not all of them were active during the time of this book. I included them as a way to pay homage to the rich history of the area, a history you can still experience today, as one of the mines is open for tourists as of this printing. While we think of South Dakota as a gold rush state, the mines there are rich in many minerals, including copper. Though the mining operations in Keystone closed during the first and second World Wars, Keystone still hosts gold panning excursions.

The businesses: I mention quite a few businesses in Kisses in Keystone, some are real, some purely fiction, some a blend of the two. You can take a walking tour of Historic Keystone to see the sites where some of these businesses actually stood. Some people, such as Peggy the blacksmith and Jennie Franklin, were real people; pioneers in the budding town of Keystone. The Red Garter Saloon is fictitious but is based on a restaurant I love to visit when we're in Keystone and the story of Ros and her guns comes from one popular establishment there.

Deputy's in Keystone: I contacted a historian to help me with this. Originally, I'd written Deputy Peterson as the sheriff. When I found out that the only law they had in Keystone in 1893 were deputies from Hill City, I had to revise that part of the story. The jail itself is fiction. As far as I can tell, Keystone didn't have a jail.

Prostitution in the Wild West: It is an unfortunate fact that in almost all growing western towns, prostitution was a part of life. While some western towns were merely stops for cat wagons, (wagon trains that provided services and traveled somewhat like a circus) many had saloons and brothels. While there are documents and photos that suggest some of these women were quite happy in their chosen profession, others, like Hattie, were not.

I'd like to take a moment to thank the Keystone Historical Museum for their help with research for this book. I highly recommend a stop there. Just a few miles from Mount Rushmore, it's a perfect place to spend a relaxing afternoon and learn about the history of mining, the buildings, Mt. Rushmore, and Carrie Ingalls, who lived in Keystone for a time.

Sad to see it end? Join my mailing list to keep up to date on when the next Seven Brides of South Dakota book, Love in Lead, will be released! You can sign up HERE

LOVE IN LEAD

I dedicate this story to my dear mom. I hope the Lord has a library in heaven, so you can finally read my stories as you wanted to. Love and miss you.

CHAPTER 1

Hills outside Lead, South Dakota
September 1893

Eva hid in a cedar thicket. It was a skill she'd honed to perfection. Few things in her short life had served her better. But now, in the hills of South Dakota, on a ranch in Deadwood, it served a vastly different purpose. Her silence came in handy when watching and following the wildlife so she could capture their likeness in her notebook. She loved being out in the open, under the sky and sun, lost amongst the trees and small animals. She felt alive and safe here. As if her whole world were at peace.

The only time she'd ever been frightened while hidden in the trees behind the Brody Ranch had been just a few weeks before. An Indian had appeared, seemingly out of thin air. Eva had never seen so much male skin in all her blessed life. He'd walked right up to her and pointed at her drawing, a sketch of her favorite flower. She'd given it to him as her heart raced, worried he'd want more. He'd waved his arm in a great arc, pointing to the whole valley. She'd nodded as if she had a clue what he was asking for. Then he was gone. She hadn't seen him again, at least not in the flesh. She hadn't been able to keep herself from drawing him—and all that glorious golden-brown skin—in her sketchbook.

The gray rabbit ahead of her scampered further down the hill, as if it knew it was taking her on a merry chase. She stopped, giving the tiny animal—by far the smallest she'd ever seen—a chance to rest so it wouldn't run too fast as she approached it again. Sun dappled down on her head through the smattering of trees. Twigs and leaf litter made moving silently difficult for her, but the rabbit had no trouble escaping her soundlessly.

Her pad of drawing paper and box of pencils bit deeply into the back of her hip. She'd hidden them under the shirt she'd pilfered from Beau, her brother-in-law. It had been on the clothes-line up until she needed it. When she was finished, she'd wash it and put it right back. Eva snickered. Recently, Ruby had commented about how his shirts and trousers were taking a long time to dry, but she never inquired further. Eva stopped and tightened the twine she'd wound around her waist to secure her paper and pencils out of the way.

Her weight shifted, as did the rocks under her. She bit her lip, tasting blood, to keep from screaming and alerting her family. Gravel slid and scraped. Her arms flew about without thought, but her fingers found only air. She tumbled down the hill, faster and faster. Her shoulder met rock, knocking the wind from her. The hill and trees blurred by as she bounced and slipped until the hill's slope gradually widened and she hit the trunk of a tree with a solid *crack*.

She groaned and pushed to raise herself, but all the trees around her danced in a bizarre circle. The tree held her fast as her world stabilized. Pain, mostly in her head, but down through her shoulder as well, kept her from taking deep breaths. Her stomach pitched, and she groaned again. Her hair had come undone and now fell in a tangled, golden mess all around her shoulders. Leaf litter scratched her cheek and swiped against her neck. Eva lifted her arm to inspect her head, and her hand came away sticky.

She blinked until the trees around her finally stopped spinning. She was farther from home than she'd ever allowed herself to go.

Her heart pounded as visions of all the dangerous things Beau had warned her about raced around in her head. She was much further out than the acceptable boundaries drawn by Beau and Ruby, but more importantly, by the owner Brody Ferguson. She'd been warned about the dangers of trespassing on the neighboring properties. She bit her lip and winced at the broken skin. Try as she might, she couldn't push herself to sitting without wanting to retch.

She rested her head against her arm. Beau and Ruby wouldn't miss her for a little while yet. She could wait there until her stomach settled. Then she could return for Hattie's wedding ceremony. Dread cramped her stomach harder. Brody had warned all the girls against venturing too far beyond the houses. He told stories more real and vivid than Beau's, but he'd also fought against the Indians. She thought he'd only been telling stories until she met that Indian before.

If she weren't mistaken, she was now off Brody Ferguson's property and was trespassing on lands owned by Jonas Anders. He wasn't one to be tangled with. It would be bad enough if she were caught, but her twin sister Hattie was to be married as soon as the preacher came out. He could be there even now. Oh, what good was riding a horse if the only place she ever got to ride was the pasture?

Her limbs wouldn't hold her and her pencil case pinched painfully into her back, making movement difficult. After she'd crashed into their world, all the birds and other animals had gone completely silent. Even now, they hadn't resumed their noise. Strange. She glanced around her, but she couldn't see the rabbit or anything else. Her arms appeared fine, but Beau's nice white shirt was torn and ruined. She'd have to explain what she'd been doing with it and try to replace it. There would be no sneaking back, either.

The arm beneath her tingled with the weight of her body. She forced herself to her knees, a most immodest position, for sure. The situation would be funny if she wasn't headed for a heap of trouble.

Unfamiliar dark brown boots appeared in front of her and she gasped. Her gaze followed the feet up to thick, sturdy legs—

thicker than most of the trees around her—covered in well-fitting trousers. A military jacket protected a man's lean stomach, with a gun belt on his hips and a broad chest. His face was darkly tanned and hidden by a wide brimmed hat. How had this man snuck up on her? She hadn't heard a sound. Had the fall rattled her hearing? She blinked up at him from her vulnerable position on the ground.

He leaned down, his face solid as stone. He had a deep cleft in his chin and a heavy forehead under the brim of his hat that completely shaded his eyes. "You certainly are no Indian." His voice dripped with annoyance.

"Of course I'm no Indian! I've never even seen one," she lied, gripping the tree and straining to push herself up. His hand enveloped her arm and yanked her up with more force than was necessary. Her size seemed to surprise even him as her face rushed headlong toward his before he plopped her on her feet. She swayed and gripped the tree as her head wobbled on her shoulders.

"Did you ever think perhaps the reason you've never seen them was because of people like me? People who stay hidden and keep watch after your safety? People who sacrifice a home and hearth to report on what the Indians are doing?"

Because of his vice-like grip on her arm, she couldn't meet his remarks with her typical response of running from confrontation. "How could I possibly know you were there if you've been hidden? It seems like a foolish question to ask."

His eyes raked down her and she felt exposed. No matter how she pulled against his hold, she could not free herself to shield her body, barely concealed in men's clothes, from his gaze.

"I think you're a spy. And if you are, I have ways to make you talk." He spun her so quickly that she lost her balance and he shoved her against the tree. Bile rushed to her throat as his hand snaked around her waist to her flimsy twine belt and yanked. She screeched and grabbed for her trousers before they could end up around her ankles. Her sketch pad and pencils crashed to the ground, scattering at her feet. Beau's shirt billowed out, fluttering around the back of her knees.

He pinned her to the tree as he squatted to pick up the notebook. His hand seemed to cover her whole back. She was going to die, and all for a rabbit.

He flipped through a few pages from where the notebook lay on the ground. Eva closed her eyes and prayed he'd let her go. Her stomach rebelled against all the swinging and treatment as her breakfast made ready to evacuate. Her knees were slowly turning to sand, and soon his hand would be all that kept her upright.

"These are rabbits...endless pictures of rabbits and birds." His confusion would be funny if she didn't feel so sick. He had to let her go. Couldn't he feel the pounding of her heart beneath his hand? Her head swam. Not now, please not now...

"Sir?" She breathed deeply to calm herself. It wasn't working.

"Hush. I need to look at all of these and make sure you aren't hiding anything."

"But, sir?" She closed her eyes and concentrated on keeping her roiling stomach calm.

He pressed her harder against the tree. She twisted her body away from him. He groped for her and grabbed hold of the loose shirt. She yanked to break free as her borrowed trousers dropped around her ankles. They both bent to grab them at the same moment. The crushing pressure of bending forward released her stomach contents all over his linen shirt.

GEORGE HELD OUT HIS ARMS, at a loss for what to say. The stench clung to him and there wasn't anywhere to clean himself. This was one experience he'd never had before. Up until that moment, it would've been a funny little story to tell around the fire back at Fort Crook. But not now. The woman he'd thought was a spy, because of her men's clothing and hidden writing devices, might be nothing more than a waste of his time. She stood in front of him, wobbling and pale as if she might faint, unable to bend far enough to right her trousers and too sick to straighten up. The poor woman was either shocked, in mortification, or something was wrong with her.

He stepped toward her, keeping his hands out of the way in case she vomited again. Her face was as white as his mother's sheets, and the cuts and scrapes on her head hadn't looked that bad until the rest of her face drained of color. Now he wasn't at all sure she could make it back up the hill. Her pants lay within reach and he grabbed the waistband, tugging them up. The huge shirt she wore covered her down to her knees. That was a blessing, at least.

As his hands landed around her waist, he reached for the twine to wind it back around her waist. She came back to her senses and yanked the fabric from his hand, backing against the tree and resting her head there. Her blonde hair pooled over her shoulders, her light blue eyes wary as she waited to see what he'd do next. He picked up the twine and handed it to her slowly, backing away as soon as she had it, and waited while she secured her clothing once again. He'd assumed the twine was only there to hold whatever was contained in the back of her shirt. If he'd known, he wouldn't have removed it.

He backed away and his foot caught the edge of the sketch-book, opening to a page with the image of a Sioux brave, kneeling in the grass. The woman had either lied, or she had a pretty keen imagination. That was no bunny or plant. He kicked the book shut and stepped over it.

"Miss, do you have a way to get home? It isn't safe for you to be out here wandering around. All the noise we've made has alerted anyone for miles of our presence."

The sprite licked her lips and didn't move from the tree. Her voice was hoarse. "Leave me be. I'll find my way back." The little thing had pluck, but not enough to get her home. She was waning by the moment and as light as the wind. He couldn't leave Miss Rabbit there to fend for herself, even if she was a potential spy.

"I'll assume you came from either Ferguson's or Ander's. There aren't any other properties nearby."

She glanced away from him, and her head bobbed as if she was forcing herself to stay upright. He took a chance and knelt by her feet to pick up all the pencils he could find which had scattered when the box and her notebook fell. When he stood, her eyes were closed. This woman was taking his precious time, but he couldn't just leave her out in the open for anyone to find. She might not know or feel the danger, but after scouting the range of these hills for years, he felt eyes on them and knew it was time to move.

"Miss, we need to get you back on your property. Just tell me where I should take you and I'll get you back there, but you can't stay here."

She waved him off. "Just leave me alone. I'm tired. I need a rest. Then I'll walk back for my horse."

He chuckled to himself. Perfect. Horses were smart and he could let the horse do the work for him. He tucked the notebook and pencils in the back of his belt and scooped up the maiden in his arms. She couldn't weigh more than his niece. If she weren't bloody, covered in leaves, sick, and wearing men's clothes, she might be almost pretty. Almost. No time to think of that now.

CHAPTER 2

E va groaned as she reached to touch her throbbing head when someone slapped her fingers.

"Keep your hands off. I'm trying to ice the lump on your head." Ruby's agitated voice cut through the roar of the headache engulfing her from the neck up.

"I can't believe you would do this to Hattie. You, of all the sisters? Just where were you and what were you doing with Captain Roth? Is he who you've been meeting out there? All this time I thought you were drawing pictures. Oh, never mind, don't answer that. I'm just so furious right now."

Eva held up her hand to stop Ruby but it earned her another swat to the wrist. Ruby was in rare form today. She'd taken the role of mother to all the girls very seriously, and now that she *was* a mother to a child of her own, her coddling and grousing reached new heights.

"Ruby, I didn't do anything but fall. I was out drawing and lost my footing. I don't know who Captain Roth is."

"Well, he certainly seemed to know you when he carted your unconscious body back up here. Hattie thought you were dead. She'll forever remember her wedding day. *That* is certain."

Eva opened her eyes and focused on Ruby's face, but it kept dancing away from her. Though Ruby didn't seem to be moving at all. "I didn't mean to hurt her. You know me better than that, Ruby. Please tell me there wasn't a spectacle." From what Ruby already said, it was doubtful. Heat crept up her neck. No, this Captain Roth had put her in that position. Ruby said he'd brought her back.

"I don't know what your intent was, but what happened was Captain Roth carried you out of the barn for all to see. Aiden was furious to find Golden gone, and Beau's work shirt and trousers were ruined! Not to mention what happened to Captain Roth's clothes." Ruby's face scrunched as if there were a foul odor in the room.

"I don't understand..." Eva searched through her memory, but came up with nothing beyond a sweet, tiny bunny she'd wanted to draw. She'd slipped, then...nothing.

"Where are my drawings?" Eva pushed onto her elbow and an ice pack fell off her head and landed, frigid, against her bare arm.

"Girl, you will stop moving right this instant!" Ruby pushed her back down onto the pillow and replaced the ice with a sharp *plop* on her throbbing head. Eva winced.

"I don't know what you mean. You didn't have anything with you and Captain Roth didn't bring anything back."

"No, I'll have to go back and find them! I saved for months for those!" Her drawings. Her precious drawings were all that had given her peace in the last months, and they'd been left out in the wilderness.

"Eva, you're old enough to be married and on your own. You know that I won't push you into that, but I do expect you to follow the rules that Brody and Beau have set for your safety. They don't tell you of all the dangers and they shouldn't have to. If there are rules, you follow them out of respect for those who provide you with a safe roof over your head. They don't ask for much from you in return."

Eva wanted to roll her eyes, but even thinking about the motion hurt. She was eighteen years old and her twin was now married. While she couldn't say she'd met a huge number of men in the last year, she *could* say she wasn't interested in a single one. She refused to marry a man she couldn't talk to about what she'd read, and then encourage her to continue.

She liked quiet time with her animals and with her pencils and paper. It was perfection and there was no room for a man, especially one who would tromp through her place of peace and scare everything away. An educated man might not even want to venture into the woods, and that would be even better. The fewer people out there, the more quiet and tranquil it would remain.

South Dakota men were just a little too wild for her — not that her original home of Montana grew them any tamer. Her own father distilled moonshine until he died in a house fire. Both places were rough and wild. She dreamed of moving east, but that would mean leaving her family. She'd considered begging Beau to send her to school so she could return later and at least be a *learned* spinster. Not that there was much honor in a useless degree.

A knock on the door interrupted her thoughts. Ruby stood and went to the door, opening it, blocking her view, and conversing with whomever was on the other side. There was the low timbre of a man's voice that she didn't recognize. Ruby returned to the bed and frowned.

"Captain Roth is leaving. He just wanted to make sure that the bump on your head wasn't severe. He offered to bring you to the doctor in Lead if it was. That was very kind of him, considering."

She'd lost her chance to see this man who'd *rescued* her and put Ruby in such a foul mood. "Considering what? He already brought me back here. What more do I need to apologize for?" Eva wished she could burrow deeply into the bed to escape Ruby's hot, blue eyes.

"What more? Perhaps you should start with losing your breakfast on him?"

Eva groaned and, this time, she did cover her head with her arm, not caring if Ruby swatted her or not. Of all the things she could've done... That was mortifying enough. Men weren't even supposed to think that you ate, much less that a girl could ever lose it.

"And you were out traipsing about the woods in Beau's clothing, nothing but a bit of twine between you and losing your drawers." Ruby's voice seemed to get louder with each word. Not that it needed to——the image would be branded on her mind forever. If Captain Roth had carried her back, one slip of the twine would have been disastrous... But wait. If her notebook and pencils were gone, the twine would have had to have been removed. She couldn't hold back her gasp and felt the heat crawl up her cheeks. Just what had the Captain done to her while she was out of her right mind?

"You have some explaining to do. I want to know what happened, young lady." Ruby's hands found permanent residence on her hips as she scowled down at her.

"I don't know. I had my notebook and pencils tucked in the back of my shirt so it was easier to walk. It was held up by the twine and tied securely. If my notebook is gone..."

Ruby sucked in her breath. "Heavens, are you saying something happened out there?"

"I'm saying no such thing! I'm saying I don't know where my notebook is. You can't accuse a captain of such things." But her head felt light as a cloud and she couldn't take a deep enough breath to fill her lungs.

"Was there any way for you to lose it without untying the belt, or is it possible you had it out before you met the Captain?" Ruby's voice was so quiet and tight with emotion that Eva feared to answer.

"Ruby, I don't remember. I'm sorry. I was out following a rabbit, and then I was here waking up to Hattie's scream."

"Beau and Brody will not be pleased about this. If he dishonored you, he'll have to make it right." Ruby took to pacing at the side of the bed.

"No. I'm sure I'm fine and I don't want to see the Captain again. Please, Ruby. Don't make a show of this." The covers were the only thing protecting her and she yanked them up to her neck, but she felt no more secure.

"Eva." Ruby sat on the edge of the bed and gently tugged Eva's arm from her eyes. "I don't want to embarrass you. But if he has ruined your chances of marriage, what else would you have me do? You deserve to be a bride. To be loved tenderly and without reservation." She gently combed the wispy locks from Eva's forehead.

"I don't think anything happened, and I would choose to remain alone rather than be forced into something that lasts forever. I would hope that, before you run to Beau or Brody, you would take my feelings into account." While she'd already decided she wanted the life of a spinster, having the door shut against marriage now felt like a heavy weight on her chest.

Ruby clenched her fists in her lap. "I'm not agreeing to this, Eva. But I will wait until after your sister's wedding month has passed before we revisit this."

Ruby stood and left the room.

"Good. I have one whole month to form a plan," Eva murmured into the now cold room.

CHAPTER 3

"Captain Roth? I assume you have something important to tell me or you wouldn't be back from your assignment so soon." The salt and pepper general leaned forward behind his desk, wagging his bushy mustache. His weathered face held hard lines that never softened.

"Yes, sir. I came upon a woman dressed in men's clothes. I didn't realize she was a woman at first. I confiscated this from her." He set the notebook on General Talbot's desk.

The general regarded him for a moment and then flipped open the book. "These are all wildlife pictures. What did you hope to accomplish, Roth?"

George cleared his throat and flipped to the picture of the brave. "Before I saw this, she said she'd never witnessed an Indian. It could be a picture from Deadwood, or it could be someone she's meeting. I'm not sure if the drawings mean anything, sir. I *do* know that many of the Indian peoples, including the Sioux, tell stories with picture drawings and animals play a huge part of that. So, having both in the same notebook is … interesting."

The general flicked through the pictures. "These pictures don't look native at all. Some of them look like they could be from

Culpepper's Herbal Guide, but most of them just look like nature pictures. It isn't our business if she's having some secret tryst with an Indian. Do you really think this could be anything, or are we barking up a tree here?"

George refused to let his anger at the idea of Miss Rabbit cavorting with anyone show on his face. "Permission to speak, sir?" He'd practiced that hard edge to his voice his whole military life and now it came instinctively.

"Granted." The old general leaned back in his seat.

"We haven't seen any action in this territory in some time. If this is some new secret way of passing information, using some hapless female, then I think we should try to figure it out."

"What were you able to find out about this girl?" The general's stone cold eyes regarded his every move.

He hadn't been able to learn anything about her other than she was a slip of a thing, had hit her head hard, and she felt good sleeping in his arms. But he couldn't say any of that to the general. "Her twin said that she wants to go to school, is bored with life in South Dakota, and wishes to get further book learning. She wasn't all that warm to my questions. She thought her sister was dead when I brought her through the barn."

"Hmm." He tapped a thick finger against his temple. "That's interesting. It just so happens, I know about an opportunity that could put this little lady right in the environment she wants. And you would be right there with her. Watching her every move."

"Sir, I don't know that I'm qualified to follow her. I chase Indians, not female spies. How about Hadley? He could fit in easily and would be more than happy to chase a skirt around. Not to mention, she would most likely recognize me."

"Correction, Captain. You follow whoever I tell you to. The rangers may be a secret group, but you've brought the Army nothing recently. So, that means I can give you new orders.

"Mrs. Hearst, in Lead, is putting together a library to give to the community this Christmas. It's to remain secret, but she's looking for help. I'll arrange for both you and this spy to help Mrs. Hearst. Use your time wisely, Roth. It's September. You've got three months to discover what these pictures mean and who they were intended for. Use any means necessary to get to the bottom of it. Understood?"

George nodded and collected the notebook. "You haven't answered my question. What if she recognizes me?"

"Women are excessively dim. Clean up, put on a suit, and use all those history books you grew up reading. As I said, *any means necessary.*"

George swallowed the bile in his throat. Any means necessary when meeting a male adversary meant it was within reason to use lethal force. That wasn't the case with a woman. It had a completely different meaning for the fairer sex, and that directive left his gut tense. A man was an equal foe. It would be difficult to see the blonde girl as an enemy, and perhaps she wasn't. But he had to make sure. There was one drawing the general hadn't seen because he hadn't gotten that far in the notebook. That particular drawing left George wondering even more about Miss Rabbit. It was a drawing of an eagle, soaring over the body of a man, but the man was nothing more than a shadow in her drawing. It had given him chills.

If the girl was a spy, he'd have to deal with her. In the meantime, he'd have to shave off his beard and maybe get a trim. He wouldn't cut much, though. It would take too long to grow back. At least when he met her, he'd been wearing his hat and his face had been hidden. She'd never open up if she didn't trust him.

He wandered to the barracks and tossed the notebook onto his cot. His closest friend Bodie sat across from him.

"What's a ranger got to shave for? I thought that was one of the perks?" Bodie laughed, slapping his knee.

"This ranger has to shave and gets to romance a pretty lady for the job." He dug through the trunk at the end of his cot and dusted off his shaving kit.

Bodie's eyes widened and his mouth went a little slack. "You've got to watch out for them fillies. They hide guns in those big dresses. You'd never see it coming. Buddy a mine got planted because of it."

541

The sick feeling in his gut took root and spread. If this girl had a mind to, she'd have already planted him. Course, she hadn't been wearing any skirts. She'd been wearing men's trousers... At least, most of the time.

"I'll keep my eye on her. That's my job for the next few months. If the general can get her to fall for the bait, we'll be working in a library. And I don't plan on giving her much time to think of shooting me."

"Well, just keep in mind what I said. Women are slippery creatures. They seem all soft and pretty, then they turn on a man." He shivered. "No, sir. You can have your assignment with your woman. I'll stay right here." He slid onto his cot and dropped his hat over his nose.

George stared hard at himself in his shaving mirror. Was this job going to be more dangerous than he thought? That girl couldn't give him any more trouble than the Sioux, could she? She hadn't seemed capable of doing him much harm in the woods, other than messing his shirt. He ran his hand over his cheek and then put the blade to the stubble there. He'd slowly win her trust and ask just the right questions. In a month or two, he'd know if she was a spy or not, and he could get back to his life here at the fort. He could also go to one of the other forts if the general felt he wasn't needed in this area anymore.

Ferguson ranch was quiet. Maybe he wasn't needed in the area anymore but checking on Miss Rabbit would be a good last attempt at gleaning information. Lead had been his home for some time, and if reassigned, all the friends he'd worked to cultivate in the area would be wasted. Staying in Lead and keeping the job he'd given his life to had to be his main objective. That meant he'd have to squeeze every bit of information he could from his little blonde spy.

CHAPTER 4

The letter shook as her hands trembled. Eva swung her glance up at Ruby and Hattie, sitting across from her and waiting to hear what the letter said. It had been three weeks since Hattie's wedding and she now joined them often while her husband, Hugh, worked with the other men around the ranch. None of them had ever received a message from someone so important. It came from Phoebe Hearst, the wife of the owner of the Homestake mine, Senator George Hearst.

Dear Miss Eva Arnsby,

It has come to my attention that you have an interest in bringing culture to the wilds of South Dakota. I share that desire. While I cannot offer you an education at university, I can offer you the chance to work for me. I am in the process of building a library for the people of Lead and hope to give it to them as a Christmas offering.

I am not in Lead often, as our home is in California. To this end, I require the help of a few very exceptional people. You are one of those people. I would require you to live in Lead, in an apartment we will provide for you, to help both procure and curate the books for the library. The apartment would be part of your pay, but I can also offer you some recompense for your time. I have very little time to search for others who would do well for me, so please do me the honor of accepting my offer. This offer is secret in nature as I would like the library to remain a surprise. Your discretion is appreciated.

Cordially,

Mrs. Phoebe Apperson-Hearst

Ruby's mouth snapped shut, and then opened again. "Mrs. Hearst? How does she know of you, Eva? I just don't understand."

Eva shook her head, still unable to grasp what the letter said, and let the beautiful scented stationary fall to the table. "I'm sure I don't know. I never go anywhere. Nor have I told anyone except you that I want to go to university. I wasn't in any school long enough to be considered exceptional. This is perplexing."

Hattie sat back and regarded her twin. Her head tilted and eyes narrowed. "This is terribly funny coming at a time when your drawings disappeared with a man you claim you don't know. You'd been riding off for weeks before that. How often did you meet with Captain Roth? Did you convince him to send off your drawings to encourage help from outside your family so you could attend university?"

Hattie's accusations hit their mark but couldn't be farther from the truth. She still missed her notebook and couldn't remember much of anything about Hattie's wedding day, other than that she'd had to buy a new shirt and trousers out of what little she earned around the ranch. Earning enough to buy a new notebook in the near future would be impossible.

"You know that isn't true. I wouldn't give up that notebook. And my *silly drawings* wouldn't attract the attention of Mrs. Hearst. I can't begin to figure how she got my name or information, but I have no intention to let this slip by. This is my chance to do something important. To be somebody." There were so many volumes she would include in a library of her own, if only she had the means.

Ruby pursed he lips. "And do you intend to ask Beau about this, or just rush off to Lead all on your own?"

"Ruby, forgive me, but you've been acting incredibly bossy since Hattie returned. You aren't my mother and I don't intend to be treated like you are. Yes, I did plan to speak with Beau about this, but if I must, I'll go above his head and ask Ma. She would agree that this is not an opportunity to let pass."

Ruby's mouth hung open. "I don't think I've been bossy at all."

Hattie laughed. "Ruby, you've been doing your best. But you need to remember, we've been through the worst life has to offer. We're strong. Lula, Daisy, Nora, and Frances are still young and might need that kind of mothering, but we just need you to be there for us. For Eva, anyway. Since she'll never marry."

Eva clutched the table and bit her tongue. Hattie hadn't been the same since returning to Deadwood. The bond that had held them for so long was severed. She cast a glance at Ruby, who had promised not to speak to anyone except Beau about what had happened. Or rather, what they assumed happened the day of Hattie's wedding. She'd made it clear that she wanted all her sisters to think she'd made the choice to stay alone of her own will. Not because she could've possibly been defiled by a stranger in the woods. She'd spent countless hours trying to recall what happened that day and was still no closer to knowing. At least her monthly courses had come when expected. So, she wouldn't have to explain *that* or live in shame.

Ruby cast her a scathing glance. "I didn't say a word. Don't glare at me so. Now you'll have Hattie wondering just what you're doing. You've gone and given it away yourself."

Hattie regarded her and it was like looking in a mirror. The only difference between the two was Hattie had always been slightly curvier, but that had changed after she'd been gone for a year. Now, the only noticeable difference was Hattie's happiness and Eva's worry. That was a reversal for certain. Hattie had always been harsher, less apt to smile, but not now. Hugh only had to walk into the room and Hattie's face would glow.

Beau strode into the house, breaking the brewing argument. He laid his hand on Ruby's shoulders and pressed his lips to her cheek. "Good afternoon, wife. Air's as thick as cheese in here. What's the matter?" He tossed a cursory glance at Hattie and Eva, but his eyes sought out Ruby and held there. A nail of longing wedged in Eva's heart. Those knowing glances and heated looks would never be aimed at her.

Ruby glowed under his appraisal. "Eva has received a letter from the estimable Mrs. Hearst of California, wife to George Hearst, U.S. Senator."

Beau's eyebrow rose steadily and Eva pursed her lips. That eyebrow was known to ask more questions than Beau himself.

Ruby continued, "We aren't sure why, but Mrs. Hearst would like our Eva to be a guest of hers in Lead for the purpose of starting a library."

Beau nodded. "Mr. Hearst owns a large portion of the Homestake mine there in Lead. I'd heard his wife had taken some initiative to spruce up the town a bit, but I hadn't heard about a library."

Eva could no longer keep silent. "The letter says that it's to remain a secret until the new year. I'd really like to go and be a part of this. It might be the only chance I ever get to do something so important."

Beau glanced at Hattie. "Can you leave us for a bit, please?"

Hattie's face flushed, and Eva could feel the tension pour off her. She knew the feeling. When a decision was made about one twin, it was hard for the other twin to separate herself from the situation. But Hattie couldn't be part of this. She left the house, closing the door with a telling thud.

Beau sat in the seat Hattie left and regarded Eva with serious eyes, eyes that had begun to crinkle at the edges from time and worry.

"We haven't talked about what happened because Ruby asked me not to. But I think before we decide whether you can go, we need to talk about this. A woman's purity is her protection. No good man wants to be the one to soil a woman. But one who is… Well, there's plenty of men who think that makes her fair game."

Eva couldn't stop the flood of heat up her neck. She hated being the center of attention and talk of this nature only made it worse.

She bit her lip and then let her anger burst like a dam. "It isn't like I'll wear a sign around my neck that says some lout took advantage of me, Beau. I don't know what happened that day. You all know more than I do. All I can tell you is that I was following a rabbit, I fell and hit my head. This Captain Roth found me, and at some point, the twine around my waist came loose and my notebook and pencils were lost. But I also know someone put the twine back. I've also been told I got sick all over him." She couldn't look anyone in the face for the heat of the mortification. "I can't imagine anyone would want to take advantage when he was covered in sick." She whispered, praying it was true. She didn't feel any differently than she had before riding out that morning but asking a question so personal of Ruby would be unheard of. She couldn't ask if the attention of a man changed a girl, but surely it must.

Beau cleared his throat softly. "If it matters, I don't *think* he did anything. He seemed an honorable man and I don't believe he would've done something to then bring you right back up to a house full of armed cowboys. It would make no sense. And as a ranger, he's most likely a sensible man. However, what I think and what may have happened could be two completely different things. Only the Lord and Captain Roth knows what happened out there."

"I'm grateful for your thoughts, but I'd rather never see him again to find out the truth."

"Well, that brings us to your invitation. We can't be there with you, but this would be no different than if you went off to university for a time. Can we trust you?" Beau and Ruby stared at her expectantly.

With her sneaking around and stealing Beau's clothes, she could understand how untrustworthy she seemed, but her heart screamed out for the once in a lifetime chance.

547

CHAPTER 5

The black tailored suit tugged against his shoulders and George shifted to make it as comfortable as the wool coat he always wore. It was as if the suit were made for another man. In truth, it was. It had been made for the man his mother hoped he'd become. A book-learned doctor or some other worthy profession. Not a man who worked with his hands or tracked Indians. Certainly not the man he'd become. She hadn't spoken to him since he'd enlisted. She considered him a wastrel. All he had of her was ten long years of silence and a dusty suit in the bottom of his trunk.

Mrs. Hearst required him to tailor his suit and then order another one. He'd refused to get his hair trimmed, making her plain face pucker in indignation. That was non-negotiable. He'd already cut it more than he'd wanted to. If Eva recognized him because of it, she would've seen through him anyway. Now, the rest was up to him.

Mrs. Hearst leveled him with her gaze, bursting through his thoughts. She had a way about her that was intriguing and beguiling, but aloof as well. Neither tall nor short, she was still a woman who filled a room with her presence. As if she both wanted you with her and hated that you were there all the same. She was on a deadline and Miss Arnsby was running late. In order for the plan to work, Mrs. Hearst had to introduce them. The hope was that Eva wouldn't remember where she'd seen him last, if she recognized him at all without his beard and with his hair pulled back.

"You seem rather nervous, Mr. Roth. Surely you haven't asked me to stay here knowing Miss Arnsby isn't coming?" Mrs. Hearst's lips pursed slightly, the only indication he'd raised her ire.

"She'll come, ma'am. The general assured me she'd be here. I can only assume the stage was late."

As if on cue, Eva dashed into the room looking flushed and touching her hair as she slowed her pace. He knew instinctively that she would be dressed as a woman — it would've been foolish not to — but the sight of her in a dress still shocked him. While the trousers had hugged soft curves, the dress which hid most everything was much more appealing. Mrs. Hearst took her hand and they made their introductions. Eva curtsied and then Mrs. Hearst led her to him.

He held his breath for a moment, waiting to see any sign of recognition. Those blue pools he remembered so well didn't show the slightest recollection of him. Part of him almost hoped she would. But he had a job to do while he was here. If he let her feminine charms wile him, she would succeed in her possible clandestine endeavors. He couldn't allow that. His very livelihood depended on it.

Mrs. Hearst gestured to him. "And this young man will be the head curator. You are to go to him with each new acquisition and he will help you keep excellent records and catalog everything. You two will be working closely together, so I do hope you get along." She fixed him with a piercing glance. "Just not too well. I don't want to hear about this. Understood?" she said with as much force as the General. He bit back a chuckle at the memory.

He held out his hand to Eva, ignoring Mrs. Hearst's warning for now, and bowed slightly, pressing his lips to her knuckles. "My name is Mr. Roth. I'm pleased to meet you." Her eyes widened in what could only be fear as she yanked her hand back and wiped it down the front of her gown.

"Are you well, Miss Arnsby?" She couldn't bolt now. This was why the general had insisted Mrs. Hearst be here. He glanced to her, but she would be of no help.

Eva shoved her hand behind her back as if he'd bitten her. "Fine, it's just that your name reminds me of something I'd rather forget. I do apologize."

He'd considered changing his name, but he knew too many people in Lead. It would've only been a matter of time before someone used his name. Then he would have to find a way to cover his lie.

Mrs. Hearst directed them to her husband's office, a large space with fine wood paneling accentuating the walls. She held her arms wide. "This is the space you may use until the books are all here. I may briefly join you again near the completion of the project if weather permits. If not, I'll send a letter detailing what I would like the library to look like. I have another man working tirelessly to get the room for the library completed as well. He will be assisting you as he can."

He could see Eva holding back, unwilling to ask what she wanted to, afraid of being rude to the senator's wife. He inched closer to her as Mrs. Hearst opened cabinets to show them the space where they could store the books as they came.

He whispered to avoid alerting Mrs. Hearst to Eva's discomfort. "Mrs. Hearst is unable to stay in Lead. Although her husband owns a major stake in the mine, their home is in California." Eva flinched and swung away from him. Once she was safely out of reach, she nodded her chin slightly.

While the time he'd spent with her in the forest hadn't been pleasant, it certainly wasn't anything to bring fear. She hadn't done anything terribly embarrassing. It wasn't as if he'd seen anything of her with the billowing shirt. Since then, he'd been unable to keep the vision of a woman with long blonde hair clad only in one of his shirts from his mind. An image that, once seen, was hard to scour. At the time, he'd been more concerned that she'd faint. Her face came to mind more than anything. Eva stood away from him, hands clutched tightly in front of her.

"Mrs. Hearst, I want to thank you for the opportunity to work on your library. However, I'm a woman alone in Lead. My family only lives a few miles away. Perhaps it would be better for me to stay with them and just travel in by stage every day? I'm not certain my family would like that I'll be working alone with a man." Her eyes darted to him and then back to Mrs. Hearst.

"I'm afraid I have to disagree. The stage got you late here today. Not to mention, you have nothing to fear of Mr. Roth. I've worked with him in the past. I just finished a project with him, actually, and you will not be staying with him."

Eva's eyes registered her shock then confusion. "You *just* finished a project with him?"

This was his chance to fully sink into the lie that he wasn't Captain Roth, that it hadn't been him she'd seen. He stepped toward her. "Yes, we've just finished putting together a program for a school here in Lead."

Mrs. Hearst's lips almost smiled. "Now, I need to be going. I'm already behind schedule and my son awaits me. If you think you must go home, then do so. I'm of a mind that you are a perfectly capable young woman. Mr. Roth has the key to your apartment and he can show you where it is. There are no men allowed in that boarding house, so there's no worry once you're in your room."

He wondered what Eva would choose. If she chose to stay at the ranch, it would make his job much harder. Of course, he could always rent a buggy and offer to take her every day. That would give him more time with her. Mrs. Hearst left the room and a silence surrounded them.

Eva cleared her throat delicately. "Mr. Roth, I'm sorry about my hesitancy earlier. As I said, your name reminded me of someone else. Someone I'd rather not see again. But your assurance that you were working with Mrs. Hearst tells me it couldn't possibly have been you."

The deception ate at him, but it was his job and he was bound to do it. If she were a spy, he had to catch her. No matter how frail and soft she looked. "I'm sure we've never met. I would certainly remember. But alas, I've been working here with Mrs. Hearst. Now, shall I show you the rest of the building, or do you wish to see the place you'll call home for the next few months?" He said a brief prayer that the Lord would not only forgive him, but that Eva would be amenable to staying.

"My trunk is downstairs. I wasn't sure where to send it and the gentleman who brought me here couldn't wait."

He nodded. "Yes. Mrs. Hearst was unsure of where you would stay until yesterday. Now it's all arranged. I hope you enjoy your time in Lead."

Her shoulders softened almost imperceptibly with the acceptance he'd been praying for.

"Yes, Mr. Roth. I think I will."

"Just let me lead the way. You'll do just fine." He smiled as he offered his arm. She hesitated only a moment before laying her hand on his coat sleeve. Success, on the very first day.

CHAPTER 6

I t simply couldn't be him. There had to be other men named
Roth. This one certainly wasn't a military man. Ruby had
said he was a captain. This man was a dandy, with his suit
and manners and talk of books. The Roth she'd met couldn't have
had any manners if he'd untied her belt and stolen her notebook.
No. She wouldn't think of that right now. Her past held no bearing
on today. She'd just keep telling herself that, and those shivers she
kept feeling anytime he came near her might subside.

It should've been funny, the idea of an army captain in a suit,
parading around as an intellectual. Yet, her mind wouldn't be put
at ease. He was, even now, watching her with eyes that were a little
too eager. As if she were a particularly enchanting bread pudding.
She stepped forward and walked around the room, looking at the
cabinets to avoid him. They weren't interesting in the slightest but
the walk served to calm her.

"Miss Arnsby, may I call you Eva?" There he was again, just a
few steps away. Couldn't he maintain any distance?

"If you must. And what might I call you, Mr. Roth?" A first
name would be better. She'd never been told Captain Roth's first

name, and it would separate the two men in her thoughts, calm her, unless he persisted in acting so strangely.

"George. You may call me George." He seemed to be waiting for her to react, and he probably thought she would with how she'd yanked away from him at first.

"George is a pleasant name. Were you named after the king?" Making useless chatter might distract him or remind her of why he was here.

"No, my father's name was George and he was named after a friend. I'm afraid my lineage shows no fealty to a long-dead king." He secured each of the cabinet doors on one end of the room and she went to the other end to help him. When they met, he smiled at her. "Why don't I take you over to your apartment? I'll bring your trunk up for you. But from then on, you'll have to come down if you want to see anyone other than another woman. They have very strict rules there." He laughed as he held out his arm. "They probably wouldn't even let me bring the trunk if there were a way for a woman to do it." He was trying to be pleasant, but it was so false on his lips. As if his voice were not his own.

"I would think Mrs. Hearst would say that there's always a way for a woman to do something she has a mind to."

His gray eyes twinkled and he smiled as he led her down the hall and to the stairs. "That she would. You must've studied her before you came. I can't imagine you learned of her feelings on women just from your short meeting with her."

That she had. In the few weeks since the letter, she'd asked Beau to buy all the old newspapers with Phoebe Hearst in them, and she'd read every single one. She was a woman to emulate and be proud of, but she also loved her husband dearly and respected him. It was wonderful to see, at least in print, the relationship between the two of them. With her educational and enriching projects and his business and governmental acumen, they seemed made for each other.

"Yes, you could say I think quite highly of her. She was a teacher before she married Mr. Hearst, a learned woman who made something of herself. I would love to be like her."

He patted her hand and held the door open for her. "This is a step in the right direction. Mrs. Hearst loves this community and would never do anything to jeopardize it."

His look was puzzling, as if he was asking her two questions at once but hoping she wouldn't understand. She regarded him for a moment to figure out what he could mean. "I would never hurt the community. I will do my best to honor both Mrs. Hearst and Lead by doing a good job." If the question was a test, his face didn't change to let her know if she'd passed or failed. Talking with him had the same effect on her as walking down the hills by her home. They were gravely and prone to landslides. One false move and she would slip.

He led her up into an enclosed carriage. She waited for him to bring her small trunk out and climb in. Outside her window, the town of Lead bustled with life. She'd never dreamed it would be so large. It was a mining town, so she assumed it was smaller than Deadwood. That didn't seem to be the case.

George climbed in across from her and the carriage pulled into the street. The seats were black leather and everything inside shone back at her. It was difficult not to stare at the brass fixtures and shining paint. She'd never ridden in anything so fine.

"Is this your carriage, George?" She ran her hand over the plush seat.

"No. This is one of the benefits of working for Mr. or Mrs. Hearst. This is the carriage they use when they stay here. But since they won't be, you and I are to make use of it."

"And just where are you staying?" She gasped as she realized how cheeky she sounded.

He laughed softly and glanced out the window, giving her a first real chance to look at him without his notice. He was clean shaven with a strong brow. A slight scar above his right eyebrow was the only thing that marred an otherwise devilishly handsome face. His angled jaw was perhaps a little too strong and firm to fit her ideal. He glanced back at her and she quickly averted her eyes.

"Mrs. Hearst has asked me to watch after her personal apartment. I'll be able to get to you quickly, should you need me. I'll be staying just a few blocks away."

Her nerves tingled to life again. "And will you be picking me up in the morning?"

His lip turned up and his gaze sent an unexpected sizzle through her. "I'll be here whenever you wish and won't be here when you do not. I'm not going to be a nursemaid, Eva. We are here to work. I'll teach you tomorrow what you can expect to be doing. After that, you'll be on your own."

She doubted that. As close as he'd kept to her since her arrival, he wanted more than just to teach her. The realization was both worrisome and exciting.

His eyes narrowed, and she puzzled over his quizzical stare. There wasn't much about Mr. Roth that wasn't strange. He acted, looked, and sounded to be just the kind of man she'd been hoping for. Here in South Dakota, which she'd never expected. However, the man himself seemed so false. A complete disappointment. If not in figure, in action. He was nothing like Beau, Aiden, or Hugh. All of them were strong and captivating. They had claimed the hearts of her sisters completely. Holding this learned man against any of the three would leave him sorely lacking. Part of her dream crumbled. Men like her brothers-in-law wouldn't appreciate her books or her art. While Mr. Roth might, his abnormal behavior left her wanting little to do with him. Perhaps his name was still affecting her. There might be other men. Hattie had warned her she was next to be married, but with this man as her companion for the next few months, and her own desire to be a spinster, it didn't seem likely.

George stood as the carriage came to a stop, his muscles flexing against the suit jacket. What she saw in him didn't fit the man he was trying to portray.

"Wait here while I bring up your trunk. The proprietress won't let you up there while I'm inside."

Eva nodded and let him do as he'd suggested. Though she'd quipped about a woman taking her own trunk, she'd tried to lift it and couldn't. It was so odd that he would now know where she slept. When he returned, he handed her a key and then offered his hand to help her out. Her foot caught on the hem of her gown and she tripped on the step. Mr. Roth caught her by the waist and had her righted before she could even cry out.

She stood in shock looking at him. A wispy memory danced just out of reach. Large hands around her waist. She took a steadying breath. "Thank you for delivering me to my temporary home, Mr. Roth. I shall see you in the morning." Her body trembled. She had to get away from him. From everyone.

He nodded and slipped his gloves on, his eyes suddenly distant. "Is there anything you require that would make your stay more comfortable, miss?"

Odd that after he'd touched her he would turn cold. Her heart slowed to a steady patter. It would do no good to analyze him. She shook her head and brought her thoughts back to his question. Dare she ask for the one thing that would make the trip perfect? "Might I have some paper and pencils?"

A slow smile took over his face. "So, you draw? If I provide you with what you ask, would you show some of them to me?"

No one had ever given her drawings a moment's notice. Not even Hattie, whom she'd wanted to share them with. Yet here was this strange man who took interest in her hobby. She knew so few learned men. Maybe they were all this peculiar.

"When I finish something, I don't see why not. Unless you find them silly——then I would hide them away."

He reached for the handle of the carriage and his foot rested on the first step. "I don't think I would find your art silly, Eva. I'll be here in the morning to pick you up."

He swung himself back into the carriage and closed the door. While he'd been with her, Lead hadn't seemed so cold. Now that she was alone at the boarding house, she would call home for the next few months, the loneliness hit her. Tears pricked at the back of her eyes and she read the numbers painted on her key before her vision blurred. Room B7. She noticed nothing about the home as she rushed up the stairs. The key slipped into the lock but wouldn't open, and a sob burst forth as the lock finally gave way. She pushed into the room and closed the door. On the table near the window stood a jar of wildflowers. The same ones she'd drawn in her notebook, now long gone.

CHAPTER 7

S he'd asked for paper. This job might end up going faster than he'd thought, and he could hand the curator job back over to the *true* curator of the library. He could leave behind the suits, the stuffy carriages, and the endless talk of books he hadn't read in ten years. Mrs. Hearst had quizzed him, convinced he was a simpleton. She'd arched an elegant brow his way when he'd answered her questions correctly, reminding him that she'd been a schoolteacher at one time.

When he left to eat for the evening, he'd stop at the mercantile first to pick up the nicest set of pencils and a notebook. If she tried to recreate the pictures from her other one, he could ask her about them. He'd have to think of a way to encourage that without letting her know who he was or what his main objective was. That was the ultimate goal, for her to go through this experience without knowing who he was. If she was in some way feeding information to any of the tribes, she could be watched. Or silenced.

The thought chilled him. No, he'd gotten ahead of himself. If she were found guilty of providing information to the Indians, her punishment would be severe. The United States Government had no intention to let go of their holdings in South Dakota. While they may have attained the land in a less than honorable way, people had moved in and purchased land, worked it, made it their own. If she were found guilty… It didn't bear thinking about.

She was so small and frail. How had he managed to forget that beneath those men's trousers and shirt had been a tiny woman? A woman who would look simply lovely in a dress with her hair done just so in order to meet the admirable Mrs. Hearst. And she had. Her light pink gown had only served to make her hair and skin look lovelier. The billowing white shirt she'd worn the day he'd found her had not shown her subtle curves, but the dress highlighted them excellently. When he'd thought about her and how to set up this elaborate trap, he'd always pictured her in the ragamuffin outfit. Today had been a shock to his senses. And he'd always prided himself on being one step ahead. She'd bested him without ever knowing she was in a contest. That wouldn't happen again.

He'd left a vase of flowers in her room to brighten it. Her favorites had been easy to pick out. Pops of pink and purple color amidst the green foliage and woodland animals were in many of her drawings. He'd taken a brief trip out to the country that morning to get them. It had cleared his mind of all the extra things he'd been working on. He'd focused on Eva and what those pictures could mean. The drawing of the eagle and of the brave held his attention more than the others. The Sioux wouldn't find much interest in pictures of rabbits, common birds, or flowers. The picture of the eagle, however, had a completely different feel. It was both majestic and sad. With the shadow below in the shape of a man, and the soaring raptor above, it looked like a power struggle. Something he was innately familiar with.

The carriage drew up to the Hearst apartments and he stepped down, nodding to the driver that he was finished for now. How very strange to have people around to serve you in a home you rarely visited. The Hearsts didn't come to Lead often. Their main home was near San Francisco, but they were known to travel all over the world. Phoebe's home library was rumored to be quite extensive.

He pulled off his gloves and dropped them on the table by the door. Another servant met him and offered to take his coat. He handed it over as a discordant note passed through him. The person serving him probably made as little as he did. The floors gleamed and his boots clicked loudly as he walked the elaborate hall to the one place Mrs. Hearst had told him he could make use of the spare room. Even that was more well-appointed than any room he'd ever had or ever would.

Eva's notebook lay beside his bed and he sat down, automatically flipping it open to the eagle drawing. The notebook was now creased and opened easily to it.

"Eva. What were you thinking about when you drew this?" He touched the graceful eagle and traced the elegant line of its head. "Are you hiding something, or were you just where you shouldn't have been with something terribly suspicious? And how can I find out the truth without you running away like the little rabbit you are?"

The new notebook would be his key. It would take time, but he was patient. In the meantime, he could gather information about her character by pushing her just a little. Women spies were not known to be conservative. In fact—though no one would ever claim Phoebe Hearst was a spy—if one were to look for a role model, they could find none better. Mrs. Hearst was a believer in the strength of women, that they could attain the highest offices and be whatever they wanted to be. Those feisty traits could easily include aiding the enemy.

The army would want answers quickly. The ranger in him wanted to take the situation for what it was and find out as much as he could. He prayed the general would give him the time he needed. As long as there was no activity, the general should let him be. The man had his own concerns. The United States was in a financial crisis and men couldn't find work, so they looked to the army as a means to find some. The army couldn't take on anymore of the poor, out-of-work men just looking to feed their families. Dragging his feet could be grounds for discharge.

He flipped to the next drawing, a robin sitting on a branch. The orange of its breast was vibrant against the dull brown of the wing and the branch. Its dark eyes searched for something not shown in the drawing, and it hit him. Everything she'd drawn had been watching her. Even though she wasn't in any of the drawings herself, she was a *part* of them...and they were part of her. But where did that leave his investigation?

He flipped the notebook shut and strode over to the window that looked out over Lead. A few blocks away, Eva would be putting away her clothes and preparing to order dinner. Should he surprise her right away, or wait until they'd worked together a few days? The temptation was to move fast, but would that frighten the little rabbit? He hadn't been able to stop thinking of her since their first encounter, and the name rabbit seemed to fit her so much more aptly than Eva.

Smoke plumed from some of the businesses on the other side of town and he watched it rise into the sky. The soft floating clouds calmed him as they dissipated into the blue beyond. He imagined his worries doing just the same. Letting Eva eat on her own for one night might make her more receptive to eating with him in the future. She was used to a large family and one lonely meal might do his cause good. As the sun dipped below the peak of the Home-stake berm, he knew he had a decision to make.

CHAPTER 8

Eva inhaled deeply, the wildflowers the only bit of life in
her room. At the scent, her tears subsided. They smelled
of home. The land around the ranch had become more
soothing to her spirit than the room she shared with all her sisters.
When she followed animals, they calmed once she sat and
remained still for a while, allowing her to take in their likeness.
They went about their natural habits of eating or frolicking about.
She'd learned to draw them without making noise, so she disturbed
them very little. Once George brought the drawing utensils, they
would bring life back to her world.

Her old notebook was long gone. She'd gone out and looked
everywhere. Now she could start over. The library wouldn't take
all of her time, and neither would friends since she didn't have any.
She'd be able to take walks outside of Lead and enjoy the landscape. It was only a little over a mile to the ranch. Walking home
for a meal wouldn't be difficult. She smiled as the thought took
root. Feeling homesick was silly when she was so close by.

The flowers' sweet scent drew her nose once more. She took a
deep breath and sighed. How could someone have known she

would enjoy them? That they would help quiet her nerves? There was no card with them. Perhaps the proprietress did that for all the women who came to stay with her, knowing they would feel more at home. She couldn't know these were her favorites. That must have been just providence.

Wherever they came from, their presence drove her thoughts back to the Ferguson ranch. To Ruby and her cooking. It wasn't that far, and walking to the ranch would clear her thoughts from the day. After eating with her boisterous family her entire life, eating at a table alone would be lonesome. She changed into a comfortable walking dress and pulled her gloves back on. Living in the city meant conforming to rules she'd only read about before. She wouldn't shame Mrs. Hearst by ignoring them, so gloves and a hat would be required.

A dusty wind pulled at her hat as she dodged out of the boarding house. Small huddles of people walked the streets and sun sparkled off the flecks of dust blown about her. Eva held her hat to her head and covered her mouth as she made her way to the edge of town. Just outside the edge of buildings, the grasses and trees ate the breeze and soon she relaxed and breathed deeply of the wonderful scents of spruce, grass, and a coming rain.

On the stage that morning, she'd been nervous enough to bounce right out of her chair, too anxious to look around at the scenery as it flew by. Now, she could stroll along and see all that she'd missed. Her family would certainly be surprised she'd chosen to come home on the very first night. They would all wonder about her first day and Mrs. Hearst. George had been a surprise. She hadn't known anyone else would be there, but she should have. Building a library would take a lot of time and effort. Beau was so protective of them all. He may not like that she would be working so closely with someone he hadn't met, but he wouldn't ask her to leave as long as he trusted her.

Eva stopped in the road and looked back at the cleft in the hills from where she'd just come. She'd never intentionally lied to her family before and keeping Mr. Roth from them would be a lie. The man seemed so benign, even with his behavior. It was silly to worry her family over him.

They weren't expecting her. If she turned around now, she could avoid talking about him altogether. The tug of home pulled her as sure as if a rope were tied about her waist. She accepted the pull a few steps further before she stopped again.

She could invite Beau to come into town. He could then meet Mr. Roth, and she would no longer have to be concerned with Beau's reaction. Best of all, that would mean she didn't have to lie to her family. It would be the best way. Her family would fuss over her for a few minutes, but then she could settle back and let everyone else take over. That was just as she liked it, surrounded by the noise of her large family but never the center of attention.

She made a mental list of the questions she could ask to shift the subject from herself. With Eva gone, Francis would've stepped into the role of oldest sister at home. At sixteen, she was a big help to Ruby and hated change of any sort. Francis would be so pleased to have her home for one last night. She cried on Eva's shoulder when she'd found out Eva was going to Lead. Lula, Nora, and Daisy were getting so big. Daisy was almost ten now.

Eva strode over a small hill and the edge of the Ferguson pastures spread out before her in the valley. Beside the fence stood a girl who seemed neither old, nor young. Her leather dress and leggings hung on wiry shoulders and hips that hadn't seen enough food. Her eyes didn't flinch. Instead, she held up her hand as if she wanted Eva to wait.

Eva stopped and held up her hand the same, hoping the gesture meant hello. The girl nodded and pointed to a plant growing near the fence line. Eva nodded, giving her permission. Mr. Ferguson would never quibble over a few plants that his cattle wouldn't miss anyway. Eva suddenly wished she'd studied more botany books to understand what the woman was looking for.

The woman pulled a few of the flowers from the ground, quickly looking around for more, but not finding any. Eva realized the woman was picking the flowers she loved. The woman stood up tall and stared at her for a moment, then raised her head in a quick acknowledgment and strode off. Eva stared after her.

Brody Ferguson had said there were still bands that lived quite close by, but she'd only ever seen the two. For as much as the newspapers spread fear, her experience had not been frightening. To be fair, the woman wasn't an Indian brave like she'd seen before and like most newspaper men wrote about.

Ferguson Hill jutted up in front of her. It was almost impassable without a horse. How could she have forgotten it would only be easy if she were a goat? The jingle of traces drew her attention just to the north of where she stood, and she picked up her pace. Aiden and Jennie were heading up the hill for supper. She could get a ride with them.

As she rounded the bend, Aiden saw her and he waved, pulling the lines and waiting for her.

"Eva! We didn't expect to see you back so soon!" Jennie called down and moved over to make room, happily trapping her husband to the edge of the bench.

Eva smiled back and climbed up. "It was a long day and I needed both a walk and to eat with my family. Eating alone in my room didn't hold much appeal."

Jennie patted Eva's leg. "I don't blame you. I'm glad you caught us. It would've been quite the walk up the hill."

"Yes, it's much easier on the pasture side." Eva gasped and covered her mouth. She hadn't told anyone but Hattie where she'd gone, and Hattie hadn't cared.

Jennie raised an eyebrow in an expression that was too much like Beau's not to laugh. "Do I want to know how it is you know that?"

"It's probably best that you not." Eva clutched the side of the wagon as they jostled over the uneven rocks.

THE SOFT LEATHER of his gloves slipped through George's hands once again, the familiar motion a reminder that time was both fleeting and laborious all at once. He both had it in his grasp and was letting it go in the very same instant. He pushed to his feet and rang for the servant.

An older man opened the door to his room and stepped inside.

"Tell Jones to get the carriage ready. I'll need to go to the Hearst Mercantile and then to pick up Miss Arnsby for supper."

"Yes, sir." The man bowed slightly and left. This would never fit him. Every second he had to endure living in this house, under these pretenses, just proved how wrong his mother had been. This was not for him. Not any part of it. He longed for the grass under his feet. His horse. The tight jacket pinched at his shoulders and he itched to shrug it off for his own work-worn wool coat.

The butler returned shortly and held the door open. George followed him out and down to the front entrance where the butler helped him with yet another unfamiliar and tight jacket. Playing the part of a wealthy man meant wearing all the useless trappings, clothing that served no purpose but to tell the world you had enough gold lining your pocket to line someone else's. He tightened and straightened his tie and checked his teeth in the mirror. The carriage waited just outside the door. At least he and Eva could talk while inside. That was the only thing about the rig that didn't bother him.

He climbed inside and tapped the ceiling as he sat. The driver responded quickly, and the carriage pulled away. His military wages wouldn't allow him to rent a room of his own and Mrs. Hearst had thought it wasteful to rent two when they had a house George could stay in. He'd agreed then, but now he ran his finger under a collar that was too tight to let him breathe.

The carriage stopped in front of the exchange and George shuffled out without waiting for the driver to climb down and assist him. He'd been able to open his own doors for as long as he could recall. He didn't need to start letting another man do that simple task for him.

The store was large, as its original intent was to provide a mining family with provisions for setting up a new house in the area. It had everything from furniture to farm equipment. He searched the aisles for just what he needed and finally found the stationary and writing utensils stuffed in a bottom corner, out of the way. One pack of colored pencils with a lead pencil wrapped in ribbon looked similar to what Eva had before and the notebook was considerably nicer than the one he'd taken from her. Having the nicer equipment might encourage her to draw quicker. He paid for his purchases and returned to the carriage. It was only a few blocks to the women's boarding house just off Main Street. The whole first level was alight, and he saw many women eating in the front dining area.

It was still early, and he prayed he wasn't too late. If she'd already eaten, he'd have no reason to stay. The proprietress, Mrs. Nelson, cocked her brow at seeing him yet again as he entered. The women at the tables near the door ceased talking and soon silence spread at the interloper in their midst.

"Mr. Roth. I've seen you more today than my own husband. What brings you back?" She pretended interest in her ledger, but her glance dodged up at him through bushy white eyebrows.

"Mrs. Nelson, good evening. I'm looking for the young lady I helped check in earlier, Miss Arnsby."

Her eyes grew wide as her mouth formed a slack 'O' of surprise. "I'm sorry, Mr. Roth. She went out for a walk over an hour past and I haven't seen her return yet. Was she supposed to meet with you?" She leaned forward and stared at him.

Frustration welled up within him. "Did she mention where she might be going? She is new to the area and I'd rather she not end up lost."

Mrs. Nelson shook a head that seemed far too small for the amount of hair atop it. "I'm sorry. She didn't say if she would be a while or not. I figure if a woman is grown up enough to have a room, she can handle herself on a walk. *This* is my place, Mr. Roth. Not out there." She motioned to the door. "Now, if you don't have anything else you need, you'd best make use of the door. I don't want my ladies getting nervous."

He nodded and turned back for the exit. By the look of her *ladies*, her worry was far too late. Where could Eva have gone? She didn't know anyone in Lead as far as he knew. Neither did she know where to go. She'd only just come in on the stage that morning. Now he'd have to rush through his dinner and come back to make sure she made it safely. First, he'd check every place in the area that served food. Drat, how could she be missing already? Was she meeting up with a secret contact? Perhaps his original thoughts of her being a spy weren't so far-fetched.

CHAPTER 9

Eva walked in as the room erupted in cheers. She pulled her coat off, using it as an excuse to turn away from the glowing faces. She only had to survive a few minutes of their attention before it would be diverted to someone else. There were always enough people in the family that no one stayed a topic for long. Arms encircled her waist and she turned into Frances's embrace. At sixteen, she was as tall as Eva and would probably eventually be about Ruby's height. Her hair was blonde, and she had narrow blue eyes but there the similarities ended. Francis was steadfast, never changing. When she was in school or had a schedule, Francis thrived, but throw her into an unexpected situation and she had to search for her strength. The fire that had burned their house to the ground back in Montana had traumatized Frances more than anyone.

Eva rested her hand briefly on Frances's back and just like that, she was gone, off to chase one of their sisters around. She met Ruby's glance across the room. Her eyes smiled as if to say, *let her be young, it won't last long.* The plates lay stacked in the cabinet and Eva used the distraction of her sisters bounding about the small house to skirt the room and get them. She took her time to set the table, easing back into the role she'd given up just the night before.

Beau came in from the back and washed his hands in the basin. "Eva, how'd you get all the way back out here?" he asked as he dried his hands on the towel.

She smiled at his concern. He'd treated them all like his own, more than her own Pa had. "I walked. After being introduced to Mrs. Hearst and the others I'll be working with, I just needed to get out in the open and think. I hope you don't mind." She realized that maybe they hadn't planned for her to be back and maybe they'd find her intrusion rude.

He strode toward her and laid a large work-worn hand on her shoulder, squeezing slightly. "You're always welcome at our table. Don't think for a second that's what I meant. I was just worried about you walking all that way alone. I suppose it's no different than kids going to school, but we tend to worry about young ladies more."

She nodded and forced a smile. His doting warmed her. "I'll be sure to head back before it gets too dark, so you don't have to worry."

Hattie slid into the room followed closely by Hugh, his hand on her back. Something sparked between her and her twin. Something akin to the feelings they'd shared in the distant past. The pain of missing that connection hit her like a frying pan between the eyes. It would never be the same for them. Their lives had moved in opposite directions. Hattie smiled and wrapped her arms around Eva, giving her a quick embrace. "I'll not hear of you walking home in the dark. Hugh and I were planning a trip tonight while the weather was nice, so we'll just make part of that trip back to Lead."

Hugh nodded, his face as somber as ever. Yet when his eyes met Hattie's, there was a softness he didn't share with anyone else. "We'd be happy to take you back. That way we'll know where you're staying. It would put all our minds to ease."

Hugh's rumbling voice was strange to her ears. After growing up with seven sisters, men's voices left her feeling slightly off-center. Beau and Ruby invited everyone to sit at the table, which was two sawhorses and long boards that had to be brought in and out before and after each meal. The small table that came with the house just couldn't seat enough of them at once. Aiden and Jennie often ate at their own home with his parents. Hugh and Hattie were building a home down near Aiden's. When they all gathered, the house was stuffed full.

Everyone sat down and Beau said grace. Chatter erupted all around the table with talk of what everyone had done that day and Eva breathed a deep sigh. This was home. The wonderful babble of all her sisters, and now her brothers by law. Even the occasional cry of her little nephew Joseph. It was loud, but mealtime just wouldn't be the same without it. She said a swift prayer of thanks that she'd walked out to see them.

Beau cleared his throat and the table quieted a little. "So, Eva. We're all surprised to see you here so soon after sending you off this morning. Why don't you tell us about what you'll be doing in Lead? We're all a mite curious." He rested his arms against the table for a moment to lock eyes with her, then went back to his meal.

Now she'd have to tell them about Mr. Roth or not. She swallowed hard. It would be so much easier if she worked with even one other woman, not just one other man. Would Beau ask her to quit? He was like a father to her in every way that mattered. She valued his opinion, but there was no need for him to worry needlessly.

The lamp on the center of the table flickered as everyone quieted. Eva set down her fork. "I met Mrs. Hearst and she was everything I'd thought she would be and more. So intelligent and sophisticated."

Ruby glanced up from her meal and her eyes were alight with questions. "Are you to work with anyone else, or will it just be you and Mrs. Hearst? I'd heard she doesn't spend much time in Lead, but perhaps that was just rumor?"

Of course, Ruby would know that. Ruby probably read the same articles she'd read in order to better judge if Eva should work there in the first place. "Actually...Mrs. Hearst won't be there at all. She left shortly after I arrived this morning."

Beau's head shot up and his mouth turned down. "Are you saying you'll be in Lead without anyone else? Working every day? Didn't your letter say there weren't many others qualified to do the job?" His hand had stalled between his plate and his mouth as he stared at her.

She hastened to answer him. "No, I'm working with others. The boarding house where Mrs. Hearst found me a room is only for women and it is quite nice. The rooms all have a comfortable bed, a bureau, a dressing table, and they even got me flowers for my very first night." *Lord, please don't let Beau ask anything else. I know that hiding this is wrong, but I fear that if I tell him about George, he won't like it if go back. Please let him talk about cattle or whatever else is interesting to him...*

Hattie cleared her throat. "Hugh and I had planned on taking Eva back to Lead tonight so she wouldn't have to walk. If Hugh even suspects for a second that she isn't safe, we could just bring her right back home."

Eva hadn't considered that Hattie hadn't been to Lead since she'd been taken there by force over a year ago. She reached across the table to her twin. "Are you sure you want to go to Lead? I'll understand if you don't. I can walk. I got myself here. I can get myself back."

"Nonsense." Hugh's low voice made her jump once again. She clutched her fist, admonishing herself to stop being so senseless. "If Hattie doesn't want to go, I can take you. Beau needs to have his time with his wife and baby, and Aiden and Jennie should get back for Da and Mam. That leaves us."

Hattie blushed slightly and wove her hand under her husband's arm, holding him close. "I can do it. *We* can do it. I said we would."

He nodded and that familiar jolt went through Eva. She and Hattie had shared feelings in the past. Was that what Hattie felt every time the giant looked at her? A small part of her prayed not. That slight burst made her even more wary of him.

"It's settled then. After we eat and clean up, we'll take Eva back to Lead." Hugh patted Hattie's hand, still wrapped around his arm, and went back to eating.

Eva set to eating once more. At least the direction the conversation had gone naturally left the questions about who she worked with unanswered. But it didn't mean that Beau would forget. The man never forgot anything, and he could be as silent as they come. She'd have to warn Mr. Roth to be on his best behavior or her adopted pa would show up when he least expected it.

THE STREETS of Lead grew steadily darker and the creak of the leather rigging bothered him more with every moment. George wanted to get out of the carriage and make a search himself. He could've done the whole thing much faster if he hadn't brought the cumbersome conveyance. How had Eva managed to dodge him so easily? He'd warned Mrs. Hearst that having her at the boarding house was a foolish mistake. If Eva was guilty, she could meet with any number of people and he'd never know about it. He hadn't expected it to happen so soon. Mrs. Hearst had tut-tutted and refused to have a young, single girl and a ranger staying in her home when she wasn't around to chaperone. And she couldn't leave such a task up to the servants. They weren't paid for such duties. In the end, he'd given up and allowed her to get Eva a room.

He would have to find a better way to keep an eye on her without her knowing she was being watched. He'd taken all her drawings and since she'd asked for more paper, he'd thought himself safe. Now he knew better. He slapped his leather gloves against his hand and tapped the roof. The driver stopped and George opened the small window.

"I'd like to get out and just walk for a bit. Meet me back in front of Miss Arnsby's boarding house in a half hour."

The driver nodded, but George was sure he caught the whites of the man's eyes as he rolled them. So he didn't act like a dandy ought. When had he ever? His own father had been brow-beaten by his mother to act and dress the part of a man without cares. His father was a bank president during the day, and a man afraid to relax in his own home at night. George had decided, even as a young man, that his life wouldn't be that way. He'd avoid every woman before he'd let one cajole him.

His stomach grumbled and he walked into a sandwich shop on the corner with a few tables and the rich smell of fried onions. His mouth watered as he took a seat. A woman in a blue gingham dress and crisp, white apron approached him and smiled.

"The menu card's on the table. Can I get you a cup of coffee?"

He nodded and picked up the card in front of him. The scent from the kitchen was enough to make a man beg and it was only a few blocks away from Eva's room. He could bring her there for a meal sometime. If he ever found her. He cradled his head in his hands. People didn't just trust new surroundings enough to venture out without seeking help. But then, she was a student of Mrs. Hearst's way of thinking, that she was an independent woman with her own mind. That was all fine but reading that mind wouldn't be easy. And to think, the general had predicted she'd be dim.

The woman in gingham appeared with a ceramic cup and a carafe of coffee. She took her time pouring it and then turned back to him. "What can I get for you?"

He hadn't even looked at the card yet. "It smells wonderful in here. Why don't you just bring me whatever is your most popular item." He tried to form his face into some contortion of friendliness, although it had been a long time since he'd had constant company.

She gave him a gentle nod and left him to stew about Eva. He hadn't thought about anything but this day for months. He'd lived the moment in his mind. When she first walked in to meet him. He'd gone over it so many times, nothing should've surprised him. In some versions, she remembered him and ran. In others, she'd slapped him. In some, she pretended that she didn't recognize him only to admit later that she did, but he'd seen through her facade the entire time.

But what happened had never occurred to him. That she *might* not recognize him at all… No, he was certain she *didn't* recognize him. She hadn't faced him for very long that day they met. Was it possible that she hadn't seen his face?

Her lack of reaction put him off his plan. It was what his commanding officer had hoped for, yes, but he'd hoped to have the upper hand. To have her know he knew everything about her and could reach her with ease. Now, he'd have to be subtle, and sneaky. It went against his very nature.

Miss Blue Gingham brought a plate of dark meat that had been slow roasted and stuffed into a loaf of bread bigger than his head, with fried onions atop. "This is the special. You can order it any time if you like it." She set the plate down with another smile and sashayed off to another table.

He ate so much he wasn't sure he'd be able to drag himself from the chair, much less walk the few blocks to check on Eva. As he came around the corner, he spotted his carriage, but behind it was parked a wagon with three people he knew. He ducked back behind the building. Hugh Bradly and his wife Hattie were just climbing back into the wagon and Eva was waving to them. She must've walked back to the ranch. He hadn't even thought about her going that far, but he should've figured it possible. She'd been known to go for walks. That's how he'd found his little rabbit in the first place.

As soon as Hugh pulled away, he dashed around the corner and over to the boarding house to catch Eva before she went up to bed. He called to her when she touched the door. She jumped, turning to look at him with huge, frightened eyes. He held up his hand and halted under the light of the gas streetlamp.

"Don't be frightened. It's me, George. I came by earlier to see if you wanted to go to supper with me, but you'd gone out. I was worried about you."

She cast a nervous glance at his carriage and licked her lips. He had to tear his gaze from her mouth, so soft in the lamplight. "I saw your carriage waiting there when we arrived and wondered." She looked so small in the shadows, hovering near the door, as if she didn't know which way to go. Her pale hair fluttered around her face.

"I brought something for you. Will you wait while I get it out of the carriage?" He held his breath, hoping Hugh and Hattie were far away as they could probably tell who he was, shave and change of clothes or not.

"Of course, and I'm sorry to have worried you. It was such an exciting day, I wanted to share it with my family. I don't really know anyone here in Lead, excepting you. I hope you'll forgive me."

He stepped up into the carriage and found the treasures quickly then returned to her. "Of course I understand, I just didn't realize you'd walk on your own. Next time be sure to ask me. I'd be happy to take you." He didn't want to. He would steer her away from that if he could, but better that he be found out than she meet with anyone on the way.

"It really isn't far and it's a nice walk but thank you."

And just like that, she'd shut him down. He was so used to everyone taking orders from him that it took a moment to realize just what she'd done.

"You would risk yourself for a walk?" He handed her the drawing items he'd purchased.

Her eyes lit up, and a smile bloomed across her lips. "Thank you so much! You don't know how much this means to me."

"Well, your safety means just as much to me. Please, do consider asking me next time."

She shook her head. "If we get a day when we aren't working, I'll take you down the path to where my family lives and show you there's nothing to harm me. That will set your mind at ease."

Far from it. He'd have to try harder with this stubborn woman.

CHAPTER 10

Don't turn around and look back! Her heart beat wildly in her chest. That would only encourage him. She'd left George standing in the street, even though she wanted to throw her arms around his neck and kiss his cheek when he handed her the pencils and paper. Eva dashed inside the large boarding house and up the stairs, clutching her new writing equipment to her chest. The cold metal key in her pocket hit against her leg as she strode to her door. Her heart still feared him. Men always made her nervous. What about this one in particular set her nerves afire?

While she hadn't given George a proper goodbye, it was also improper to come so late in the evening to visit her. They were even, and she'd have to deal with it when he picked her up in the morning. She dug in her pocket, rushing to get out of the open hallway and safe inside the security and privacy of her room. Having seven sisters, it was a luxury she'd always wished for and could now enjoy. Even at the huge house they'd lived in temporarily in Deadwood, she'd shared a room. Now, she wouldn't have to walk out into the open to feel the peace and quiet. But as the thought struck, she banished it. The outdoors drew her like no other place.

She closed her door and waited as her eyes adjusted to the dim light from the moon streaming in the second-story window. It wasn't much, just enough to navigate around the furniture that she was unfamiliar with as yet. A small kerosene lamp sat on a table near the window and she lit it with the flexibles she'd set next to it earlier in the day. She had to be judicious about using it. If she needed oil, it would cost extra. Its light warmed the room with a soft glow, falling right where she needed it. She placed the new notebook on the table and opened the first blank page, touching its pristine, crisp whiteness.

Pulling out a chair, she sat heavily in front of the page. The flowers on the table were beautiful, and she slowly turned the lavender blooms until they were at the perfect angle with the light. A blue ribbon kept all her pencils contained and she tugged on it to loosen them, catching them as they rolled. She lay them flat in an exact line so she could see each color. He'd made an excellent choice. They were very similar to the ones she'd left at home. The ones that hadn't been used in a month. Since *that* day.

No. She wouldn't think about it. *Couldn't* think about it. How often had she attempted to remember where she'd been and what had happened, and just who Captain Roth was? If she met him again, she might just be able to piece everything together, but the idea of meeting him also terrified her. What if he had done the terrible things Ruby suspected? A small voice inside her also wondered if Beau were right, that he hadn't done anything.

As the scattered thoughts hit her, she grabbed the lead pencil and with swift motions on paper, eyes appeared, then a strong jaw, the hard line of a mouth, and a small scar... No. She flung the pencil and shook her head. Her mind was confusing Captain Roth with George yet again. She ripped out the page and tossed it in the waste basket. No more thinking about that day. It wasn't gainful.

The common gray lead pencil almost called to her from the floor, like the blank page in front of her. She picked it up, placing it perfectly in the center. Her strokes were slow at first, then built in confidence and soon a vase of flowers was clear on the page where once had been nothing but fragmented lines. She sighed, realizing it was probably well past the time she should retire if she were going to get up in time. She would have to add the color to it another day.

Her heart felt free and she turned down the wick of the lamp until it doused the light. She'd gotten dressed and undressed in the dark her whole life. It made no sense to start a new habit today. Her sleeping gown was a comfortable, soft cotton flannel that made her think once again of home and all her sisters. They were probably enjoying the extra room they would have on the bed without her there. She spread her arms wide as she lay down and sighed. She wouldn't feel guilty about enjoying the extra space either.

The visit home had been nice, but she'd felt like a guest. An outsider among them. Hattie and she had always been inseparable, but now her sister was married and had little time. The old connection they'd shared was all but gone. Those few short bursts of feeling from earlier were more frightening than the comfort she'd always taken from their bond. The loss hadn't seemed to affect Hattie at all. She had Hugh. It left Eva feeling alone in a field, nothing nearby to comfort her, with an approaching wolf in an army coat.

THE STARS WERE MISSING. George searched the sky from the window in his private room, but the bright lamps on every corner deadened the twinkling lights he was so accustomed to. It had been days since he'd stayed out beneath them and let the animals and insects talk him to sleep. The noises of the city did little to calm his busy mind. He'd have to get out of town for the Sabbath and follow some of his old trails, just to make sure he didn't lose the feel of the ground beneath his feet.

The assignment held little interest for him now. It was difficult to push Eva into doing things just as he'd like, although he knew it was best. Her eyes spoke louder than words that she didn't find him honest, and he wasn't. Every passing hour with her was torturous, acting the weak and soft man the general had asked him to be. He'd spent his whole life in secret and saying what needed to be said to keep peace between two nations who wanted the same commodity. But this woman, with the slight tilt of her head, could convince him he was a fool for trying.

The only time she looked on him with anything warmer than suspicion had been when he'd handed her the notebook. Then she'd smiled. He'd stared at the soft curve of her mouth and a glow of wonder had passed over him. As if he'd witnessed an eclipse and not some flitting emotion on a woman he'd tried hard to paint as the enemy. But was she? Yesterday had gone quickly. And yet, the minutes he'd spent hadn't left him with the impression she wanted to harm what she was building. If she weren't the enemy, what good would he do wasting his time following her? Better to just disappear and let her work with the actual curator of the library and let the experience of working on something wonderful be his apology.

He'd have to see some sign of her spying before the week's end, or he'd tell the general this was a dead end. He'd learn more from following the Indians themselves, and quicker, than following Eva around. Strange that the people he wasn't allowed to trust thought more of him than Eva.

George slipped his leather gloves off his hands and the familiar worn leather slipping through his fingers calmed his thoughts. Argus would be happy to fill his nose with a little fresh air, and the run would do him good after a few days of being penned in. The stable was no place for such a spirited, rugged horse. An excitement built within him. He quickly changed into his old gear, the ease of the denims and wool coat like family welcoming him home. He saddled Argus and swung his leg over, the liveryman left puffing in indignation.

George let Argus pick the pace as they left the confines of the city and entered into the dark of night. His heart raced wildly as Argus pushed faster along the barren road and veered off over a rise and down into a small valley. The darkness closed in around him, but he trusted Argus. Always had. He slowed and then stopped, swinging down, leaving Argus pawing at the ground, hoping for more.

A little stream trickled through the lowest point between two small mounds at the base between hills, where flat land was at a premium. Thick, green grass grew at the edge. He sat down, leaning back on his elbows, and searched the night sky for familiar constellations. He breathed in deeply, the cool air filling his lungs as the scent of wildflowers and fresh grass filled his nose. This was where he belonged. Not in a stuffy room with a rich bed, but here, on the lumpy ground near a river, listening to his horse chomp the grass.

A slight shuffling to his left drew his glance from the sky and a man stood where only air had been before. George pressed into the ground to lift himself, but the man held up one hand for him to be still. The hair on the back of his neck stood at attention as he figured in his head how fast he'd have to move to reach his gun if it were necessary. The Indian knelt by the stream, keeping his dark eyes focused on George, then dipped something in the water.

The Indian stood back up and pulled a folded paper from a pouch at his belt and handed it to George. The paper was heavy and familiar. He unfolded it and turned it toward the moonlight. Though it was dark, he'd studied her work so well he recognized the style of drawing immediately from Eva's notebook. The man pointed to the flower in the drawing, the same purple blooms he'd noticed in many of her drawings. The man pointed again, then at the ground around them.

What could he want with flowers? That couldn't be what this was all about, could it? Wildflowers? What danger could there be in telling him? George pointed toward Lead and the man nodded. He disappeared as quickly and silently as he came, but he left George with a sense of unease. As Captain Roth, he could ask Eva about the picture he now held. As George Roth, curator of a library, he should have no interest and no reason to be out meeting with Indians in the depths of the night. But he had to know. If his little rabbit was entangled in a snare, he'd get her out.

CHAPTER 11

Two weeks flew by with books in crates arriving from all over. Friday found her exhausted. Eva watched as George pried open another crate full of books Mrs. Hearst had ordered. His strength was easy to watch, which caused her to forget what else she was doing.

Mrs. Hearst had been ordering books even before she and George had arrived. She was not there, of course, but she was obviously concerned about which books ended up in her library. So far, they had done little more than open and arrange crates of books.

George glanced up and caught her watching him. His eyes softened as he stood fully upright, his arms flexing out a little as if to give her a better view. "Why don't you start cataloguing these like I showed you?"

She ducked her head until her cheeks cooled and approached him slowly, taking a stack from near him. Though he'd never done anything to make her distrust him, she couldn't relax when he was nearby. She couldn't even pinpoint what it was about him that made her nervous, other than something about him felt…off.

The task of cataloguing the books gave her the chance to sit in a corner and be alone. His company was enjoyable, but there were times she simply couldn't puzzle him. He was unlike any man she'd ever known.

Part of her wanted to argue that he was exactly the man she'd always wanted, the kind she jokingly said couldn't be found in South Dakota. Now that she'd met him, she realized Hattie had been right. What she thought she wanted and what she realized she now wanted were two separate things. Mr. Roth was *boring*. Jennie and Hattie had told her of how Aiden and Hugh made their hearts race with just a look, or how they loved seeing their husbands come home from a difficult day's work, knowing he'd done that work to support them as a family. She'd yet to see Mr. Roth work up a sweat, even opening all those crates, and his strange questions of her only made her wary of his company. At least she didn't fear him anymore. He was nothing like the Captain Roth that continued to stomp into her dreams with his shadowy, bearded face. That much she could remember. A thick beard peeking out from under a low-slung hat. She shivered and looked up to find George watching her.

He smiled slightly. "Eva, it's about time for us to take a break. Maybe I could show you around Lead? Have you been?"

She glanced around to her various piles of books and the deep shadows in the corners told her she'd been there for hours. It was well past when she should've taken lunch. There would be no acceptable excuse to say no. "That sounds lovely. Let me get my gloves and hat."

As she stood, so did he. He nodded at her and followed her to the cloak hall to help her shrug into her thin coat. As he opened the door, the light flashed against her eyes, over-bright after being inside in the darkly paneled room for so long.

"Blink for a bit. It will help your eyes adjust," George whispered behind her ear as he took her hand and guided it to his arm. His suit always seemed to shrink him. Touching his arm was palpable evidence that he was so much stronger than he had any right to be, another conundrum for the mysterious Mr. Roth. Even moving books all day long wouldn't make a man muscled like that.

"Mr. Roth, forgive my curiosity, but were you always a scholar?"

He laughed beside her, but even as she batted her lashes against the glaring sun, she still couldn't see much of his face to gauge his response.

"Why do you ask? Are my manners not quite up to expectations?" He turned them down Baltimore Street and the shadow of a building finally allowed her to see his slight smirk.

"Don't tease. It isn't that at all." She felt heat rim her ears and hoped he would think it was the sun. "It's just that...you seem much stronger than a man who has spent his life studying."

He patted her hand and chuckled again, but his face shifted. He avoided her gaze. "You're quite observant and more forthright than I expected. I should've known—with your artist's eye—that I couldn't hide my secret from you. I had to work my way through university."

It could be another lie. His eyes still wouldn't meet hers.

She chewed on her bottom lip. That was more information than he'd shared with her before. Dare she ask for more? If that were true, that he worked to put himself through school, then he couldn't be as old as she assumed. She'd thought he had to be near Hugh's age, by looks.

"So, you recently finished then?" If he refused to answer, she'd at least have gotten closer to the truth of who Mr. George Roth really was.

This time he laughed outright. "No, Eva. I finished almost ten years ago. Now," he said as he led her across the street and down another block, "this is Hill Street. Just like Main Street, if you follow it, you'll end up down at the mines. We won't venture there today, but this is a great place to start a tour. Right across this street is a wonderful place I found that first night you were in town. It's quite good. May I?" He gestured across the street.

Eva rimmed her eyes, shading them from the sun, and squinted to where he indicated. There was a squat building on the corner that looked a little like a rail car. The street was narrow and crowded with great carts of lumber rumbling down the street toward the mine. People, horses, oxen, and wagons made the street noisy and she understood why her room was loud at night. She lived only a few blocks away.

"Yes, please." She nodded and he led the way, watching for traffic and guiding her through the mess. A fire wagon rolled by pulled by two large horses and followed closely by a large tank full of water. George wrapped his arm around her waist, drawing her off the street and out of the way. The clanging bell on the back sounded long after the large rig had turned.

Eva glanced at George, whose gaze remained fixed at the rooftops. Worry lined his brow.

"I'm sure they'll put it out."

His lips pinched. "We haven't had rain in a week. Everything's dry. I hope it's small and not near the grass. Could be bad if it catches."

There again, he surprised her. Why notice the rain if he were cloistered away in a library?

He glanced at her and his look immediately shifted back to that of the scholar. The false face she was growing to dislike.

"Come, it's just over here." He released her waist and offered his arm again.

Now that she was close enough to get a good look, the little diner *was* a little red dining car. The smells coming from it taunted her nose and her empty stomach. They sat in a small padded booth just like she'd imagined a dining car would look like, and she couldn't help squeezing George's hand in excitement.

"Look at all the benches! Is this what it looks like inside a train? I've never been in one before."

His expression warmed as he looked around the little car. "Yes, this is actually a quite well-appointed one. Some of them have wooden seats."

She ran her fingers over the velvety, deep red fabric of the plush booth. "Someday..." She couldn't finish. Someday, she'd still be living in Deadwood on the Ferguson ranch collecting eggs for Ruby, because she'd remain alone for life. Someday would be just like any other day.

George touched her fingers lightly where they lay on the table, sending a strange jolt through her hand and bringing her back to the present. "Why does the thought of what could be make you so sad? You were just excited." George's face held that pinched look of interest as it often did when she gave away a little bit about herself. As if he might pounce on any new bit about her.

"It's nothing. I was going to say, perhaps someday I will ride in one like this. But that isn't likely. There won't be cars like this by the time I have the chance."

"Surely there is some young man waiting for you to come back from your trip. You will marry and can travel all over, just like Mrs. Hearst."

Eva slowly shook her head. "No, that life isn't for me. I don't come from wealth. I can't even explain to you how Mrs. Hearst heard about me to offer me this opportunity. There's no one waiting for me except my family, and there never will be." She was saved from explaining further when the server arrived.

"Mr. Roth. Can I get you both the special?" The server rested her hand on a rounded hip.

He smiled at the server and the genuine action sent jealousy spiking through Eva. How could he be himself with a woman he could hardly know, but treat *her* so strangely? The soft lines around his eyes framed a smile that would warm a February in Montana. Was he sweet on their server?

"Yes, that sounds wonderful." He turned back to Eva and, too late, she tried to school the anger from her face. He tilted his head. "I'm sorry, Eva. I should've asked. It's just that the special is quite good."

"I'm sure it is. Thank you." She nodded at the server, who took that as her cue to go and dashed off to the next table.

George took a deep breath and fidgeted with his gloves. She couldn't fathom how sitting with her could make him uncomfortable. It wasn't as if she could do anything. The disquiet between them grew until she had to say something to fill it.

"So, you showed me where the mine offices are. Where did you plan to take me next?"

His shoulders relaxed and his mouth quirked up on one side. He was handsome when he let his guard down. *And when that server came by...* That thought sneaked up on her. But analyzing it, she saw it for the truth that it was. While his look was far from conventional, his longer hair framed a strong face with even eyes and a handsomely chiseled nose that some might call overlarge, but had it been any smaller within his face, it would have been abnormal.

"There are a few special places I want to show you. Mostly, I want you to see where they're working on the library. Mrs. Hearst took me there first thing and didn't have a chance to show you since you arrived a little late your first day."

Her excitement returned and she leaned in closer to him, pushing herself forward on the seat. "It's being built already? But, of course it must. It's already October. How are all the books going to arrive here in time?"

"Don't worry about that. Many of them Mrs. Hearst ordered ahead of time. Volumes she wanted to make sure the people of Lead had access to. The plan is to eventually also offer an opera house. Patrons will have to buy tickets to see those performances, but the library will be free for everyone to use. You may even use it, since you live nearby."

"I do plan to make use of it. A mile is not a long walk. It makes me even more curious as to why I'm even here. I can't figure out how or where Mrs. Hearst would've learned of me. It isn't as if my name is on some school ledger somewhere. Nor am I really needed here. With many of the books already ordered and you here, it wasn't necessary for me to come."

He backed away from her, leaning into the back of the seat, and frowned. "You're here because Mrs. Hearst requested you. Isn't that all the reason that matters?"

"But how? I am no one. Don't you see how strange it is that she would know who I am?" She sighed, folding and unfolding her napkin. "How did Mrs. Hearst hear of *you*? Perhaps if I knew how she found you, I might find some connection in how she found me?" She turned her own worry on him. Knowing how such a notable woman had come across her name had bothered her since she'd gotten the letter, but it was such an honor. She'd cherish that letter, signed by Mrs. Hearst, for as long as she lived.

George hesitated and folded his hands in front of him. "I work for a very influential man who knew of the Hearst library. He thought the opportunity would be perfect for me and sent me here straight away."

"And what do you do for this influential man?" She was finally cracking through the surface, getting to know the man who'd only been interested in asking her questions, not answering them. His answer didn't help her solve her own problem, since she knew no influential men. At least she could find out more about George.

"That would be difficult to talk about. And rather boring, I'm afraid. You're curious, I can see that." He sighed and glanced around the diner then back to her eyes. "I didn't grow up here in South Dakota, obviously. I was born and raised in Missouri. My father was a banker. He helped run a small savings and loan. My mother always wanted me to do even greater things than my father. To be educated and wealthy, without having to work as hard as her parents."

Eva smiled to encourage him. "Isn't that what most parents want for their children, to see them succeed?"

"I suppose. Honestly, I strained under their rules. They *would* be proud of this project. They don't think much of the rest of my life."

The emotion peeling away his false layer took her breath away. "Are you saying they wouldn't be proud that you work with such an influential man, whoever that man is?"

His face darkened. It was time to bring him back to a more pleasant topic or she'd lose all the ground she'd gained with him. He avoided her question and searched the diner again.

"Where is our food? Does it usually take this long?" She sighed, thinking back on how the conversation had progressed and where it had gone wrong. That was all he'd divulge to her. If she pushed him for more information, it would make the remainder of the day uncomfortable. She hated inviting him into her life, but it would at least bring him back to the table with her. "Well, as long as we're here and you've answered a few of my questions, we both know I've been dodging yours. Go ahead and ask one or two." She smiled with as much warmth as she could manage to encourage him.

He yanked his sleeves down to each wrist and pursed his lips. His tan was dark against the white of his shirt, starker than she'd realized.

"What got you started drawing?" he began, staring at her hands folded in front of her.

She should've known. He rarely asked about anything else. "You're so interested in my silly drawings. They're nothing more than doodles, really. But if you want to know, a little over a year ago my twin was taken. It was like half my heart was gone." Eva pulled her handkerchief from her sleeve. She still couldn't talk about Hattie's kidnapping without crying. "She was found a few months ago and is even happily married now, but what we shared... It's like it's severed permanently. She changed so much. When she first left, my drawings were a way to look at myself, because I didn't know who I was without Hattie." A tear ran down her cheek and she rushed to dab it away, afraid that she'd said too much.

"I'm sorry. I had no idea." His eyes softened in true concern, his fingers loosening from their fists before clenching again. "I'm glad she's back with you, but why are you here if you miss her so much?"

"As I said, she's married now. She had a whole year where she had to be independent. Whereas I had a year of needing my twin. I never learned how to *not* need that. It's almost harder now, because she's right there but not the same." Why couldn't that server come back and save her now?

"Are you lonely, Eva?" His question brought her attention right back to him. No one had ever bothered to ask her that question, but that was the root of her struggle. Having it said aloud by someone little more than a stranger struck her.

"Yes. No one understands me like Hattie did. So, after she

came back, I started wandering further than I should've around our ranch. I wanted to be near the animals, feel the air, smell the grass. When I draw, it fills in the missing places. So, now you know all there is to know about my drawings."

George's face transformed. The questioning pinch between his eyebrows relaxed, his cheek muscles smoothed out, and he unclenched his hand and reached out for her. Eva hesitated. She'd never trusted a man enough to allow such a familiarity. But, if she wanted to see more of this genuine George, she had to encourage it. She wove her hand within his, and a warmth settled between them.

"I'm sorry, Eva. You seem like a lovely woman and far too young to give up on hope. You'll find someone who'll know you even better than Hattie. Someday. For now, don't forget there's One who knows you even better than Hattie ever could, and you don't ever have to feel alone." He squeezed her hand so gently, then slid his away.

The server arrived with the food, interrupting them. And for the second time that day, she wanted to stomp the poor woman's foot.

CHAPTER 12

Eva finished as much of her meal as he expected and daintily wiped her mouth. She'd enjoyed her food and that gave him a sense of pride he had no right to feel. He paid the server and waited as Eva slipped her gloves back on over her slender fingers.

"Now, let's go take a look at that library and stroll around the town just a bit. I'm sorry you've worked so long, and we haven't made the time to see Lead. There is a little church back on Baltimore, not far from your boarding house, if you're looking for a church on Sunday."

She held his arm above his elbow, giving him an odd sense of protecting her as they walked back out into the street and toward Baltimore. He'd spent his whole adult life protecting people, but this felt different, personal...wonderful. "It's the one I'd planned to go to, since it's also the closest to me. Can I pick you up on Sunday?"

She hesitated slightly, her lips bunching in concentration as he held his breath, waiting for her answer. "I could do that. There's no harm in going to a service with you. I don't think my family would disagree with that."

A laugh rumbled within him that he tamped down. "Certainly, and Mrs. Hearst would encourage it. She gives to that church often." He wasn't below using Mrs. Hearst's name to spend more time with her.

Eva's soft blue eyes glanced around the street and he slowed their pace so she could see everything. He pointed to the little white church with the stained-glass windows, at the end of the block. "That's the one. The town is growing so quickly. There are quite a few churches now, but that is the closest for us."

"It's lovely." Her glance flitted from the church to the meat market and further down the street, where homes took over the businesses. Lead had grown out of its own skin quite quickly, changing from an ugly brown burrowing caterpillar into a huge colorful moth draped over the gulch. Many of the homes that had once been at the edge of town were now firmly in the middle, surrounded by other businesses.

Eva interrupted his thoughts. "I'd heard there was a plan to put in a huge hotel. How will they do that when the streets aren't level?" She tilted her head, looking at a few homes that climbed up the side of a slanting street.

Her sweet innocence belayed what he had to think about her. He had to remember she could very well be a spy, but perhaps not of her own choice. But did that matter? "Well, let me show you." He gripped her hand gently and squeezed it. No one before had looked at him with such trust. How could he dupe her? How could he continue to see her as false?

"This is Ellison road. See the fire station? How it's cut into the ground just off the street? That way, the building is level, but the street is not. You can walk around the building, but that corner is cut into the ground."

"Some of the city seems so flat, but..." She shook her head. "Why are some streets left hilly while others are not?"

Taking her on this walk was so much more enjoyable than sitting in the stuffy office. "The black hills are covered in massive slabs of stone. Buried under this city are huge granite deposits. At least I'd guess that, since the mountains are full of granite."

She looked up the street to the sweeping open cut of the Homestake mine, with its shoots and rail trams festooned before it. "The Homestake is mined differently than the ones in Deadwood, yes?"

He could get used to her curiosity as long as it wasn't about him. He'd had a tough time not answering her earlier. She had honest eyes that begged a man to swim in them and tell her everything. Dangerous eyes for his profession.

"Yes, the Homestake is different. How much do you know about the mining process?" He didn't wish to insult her, but he knew enough men who couldn't tell the difference between a placer mine and a load.

"Not much, I just noticed how different it looks."

"Did you know the town of Lead takes its name from a mining term?"

She turned to him and smiled, interest lighting her eyes.

He directed her to the shade of an awning. How nice that after so many days of trying to get her to come out of her shell and failing, lunch and a little relaxation had done it. "Lead is another term for lode, which is the type of mine Homestake is, and it's an outcropping of ore that *leads* you to the vein."

She smiled and stared at the rock face that dominated one whole side of town. "I wish I could say it was pretty."

"Well, to the people that make a living from that mine, it is." He turned her and headed them back toward the new library, back on Main street, to the offices where they worked every day. "Now for the part I wanted to show you. Down here in the Miner's Union Hall, is where the library will be housed."

He led her down the street and past their offices. As he held the door for her, he held his breath also. He wanted her to be impressed, to love it. It would be worth it if she at least could look back at her time spent in Lead as being worthwhile. Why it mattered, he couldn't say, but he wanted to hear her gasp and see the light of approval on her lovely oval face.

They entered the room and the first thing Eva noticed was exactly the first thing Mrs. Hearst had wanted people to notice: a grand, rounded desk where the librarian could sit. In front of that was a card catalogue, waiting for all the cards that he and Eva had been working on as they organized the books. There were gleaming wood tables and chairs along the walls, waiting to be placed.

"Oh, George. It's simply beautiful. I hope the people of Lead love it." She fingered the wood of a nearby bookcase. "And it's to be a Christmas present?"

"Yes, as I understand it, that's her goal. She'll be sending large numbers of foreign texts as well. They will go here." He pointed along the wall. "You mentioned once that you lived in Deadwood for a time. Well, Lead is much the same. It has people from all over who come here to work in the mines and provide for their families. Mrs. Hearst even has a college scholarship fund for the children of people who work in the mine."

Eva turned to him, her eyes wide. "She does so much. I don't think I'll ever be able to fill such shoes." She shook her head. "I mean, I don't think I'd ever be able to do near as much."

Her sudden change pierced him. "Eva, she doesn't ask you to do as she has done. You do what *you* are called to do to make the world better. Be it raising children who follow the Lord, or humanitarian aid, even the library. You are doing what she can't be here to do."

Eva frowned as she turned from him. "It isn't the same, and I'm not educated as she is. I'll never be a teacher, nor marry a wealthy man to give the way she does. My time here might be the only thing I can ever give to the community."

Her shoulder beaconed for his touch and he couldn't hold back. Her shirt was even softer than he'd imagined it would be, and he had to school his voice back to normalcy. "Eva don't ever try to be someone else. You are the woman the Lord made you to be and that is perfect for someone."

Her breath caught in her throat and she glanced back, searching his eyes for a moment. Then she closed herself off from him and stepped away.

~

HOW OFTEN HAD she placed her hand on his arm and it had been safe? Not so when he'd touched her. The slight caress on her shoulder had been meant to pull her out of distressing thoughts, but what it had done was drive them into other places. Places she'd never allowed them to go.

When he'd touched her, her eyes had sought out his lips of all places, and they had been slightly parted, looked soft, and so completely masculine it had made her pulse race. She could hear him following her up the street but turning or waiting for him would be folly before she could tame the wild thoughts chasing her even faster.

Where had they come from? She'd only worked with him two weeks. He'd only just opened up and talked to her today. Perhaps that was all it was. She'd been so curious about him that when he finally opened up, her mind had confused it for attraction. But he *was* attractive...

George finally caught her and touched her arm to halt her progress, the slight tingle on her arm assuring her it was him and no one else. Even *that* confused her.

"Eva, I apologize. I didn't mean to send you running." His dark blue eyes searched hers, the concern in them real, his words genuine. Why couldn't he be *this* George all the time? Why did he keep switching from this man to the one constantly asking her questions with subtle points and pushing her to answer?

"You did nothing wrong, George. I simply felt it was time to get back to the office." His slight smirk said he knew she lied, but what did it matter? She couldn't tell him her true thoughts.

"We'd mostly concluded our tour, anyway." He held out his arm to her once again and she took it. Walking with him was becoming more comfortable, as was talking with him. When he was like this, talking with him was as natural as talking with Beau. Though different, because Beau didn't make her stomach flip strangely. If he'd only acted like this from the start... If he had though, she would've had to tell Beau about working with him. Honest George was much more dangerous, and Beau would most likely want to be told if he was a potential suitor. She'd been living under his roof for three years and he deserved that respect.

He held the door open for her once again and she ducked down the cloak hall to hang her hat and gloves before returning to work. The darkness gave her a few minutes to stop the fluttering in her belly. Ruby would not approve of her enjoying the company of the man she worked with. Especially not after the episode on the hillside with Captain Roth. Beau might not even give his permission unless she agreed to let him speak to George about it. And once George knew she'd been so reckless as to run around alone in the forest... Heat filled her cheeks and she covered them with her cool hands, remembering that Beau wasn't as sure about what happened with the Captain as Ruby seemed to be. And Eva was nineteen, a woman who didn't necessarily need permission.

Pish-posh. She and George probably didn't have a future anyway. Worrying about what might've happened when Mr. Roth had not shown much interest in her at all was frivolous, and she'd always prided herself on being as salt of the earth as she could manage. No. Mr. Roth wasn't interested in *her* in the slightest, only her drawings. She'd go right back out there and work just as she always did, forgetting about the jarring heat his touch kindled, or the fluttering in her belly when he favored her with a rare smile.

She tucked her head to her chest and strode out of the hall, right into Mr. Roth waiting by the door.

"There you are. I didn't want to follow you in as it was dark in there and thought I might frighten you. I certainly don't want that." His lip crept up on one side, the slight stubble on his chin drew both her eye and her hand. She clenched it in her skirt to make it mind.

"I'm sorry, I just needed a moment to put my things away." *And make my heart stop thumping in my chest so...*

Her desk suddenly seemed so far away from his, all the way across the room. "I've got work to do. I suppose I should get back to it." She prayed a silent prayer that she had work to do near him, preferably at his desk. When had she become desirous of any man's attention? It was foolish and she had to control her thoughts.

"Did you want to join me in cataloging these? I could use your help." He gestured to his own desk.

Flip went her heart. "Sure. Let me pull my chair over."

"Nonsense, I'll get it for you." He strode over and moved the stool she'd been using right next to his own. Her palms moistened and she dashed them down the front of her skirt.

He sat down and waited for her to lower herself onto the stool. He brought out large catalogs of books, setting them in stacks on his desk. "I'm looking through these to decide which of the books would be most appreciated here, which books would fit this city the best. We do have limited space and of course a budget to stick to."

She warmed under his words. Most men seemed rather hesitant to speak of money matters with a woman. Perhaps the fact that it was a woman funding the library changed his way of thinking. Or perhaps Mr. Roth was simply an uncommon man. She was beginning to think she'd been wrong about him.

She lifted the heavy book nearest her and opened it to the section marked *science*. She ran her finger down the columns, looking with awe at each one and calculating how much of her pay could be spent here alone.

His hand brushed hers as he reached to point at a title on horticulture. "Forgive me for looking over your shoulder, but I think that one is a book we need to order."

Her hand shook slightly as she took down the order number and wrote all the relevant information as neatly as she could.

She turned yet another page but her eyes either couldn't or wouldn't see anything in the book. The intoxicating scent of printed pages, leather binding, and George's subtle clean soap that smelled a bit like lemon played with her sensibilities.

"Eva, are you feeling all right? You look a little tired. Perhaps today has been long enough and I should walk you home." The usual pucker between his eyebrow that indicated he was going to be pushy was replaced by a slight drawing of concern and it amazed her that she could, with certainty, tell the difference.

"Yes, I do think I've had quite a long day. Perhaps it would be time to go home and rest."

"I'll get your things. Why don't you wait here? Do you need me to have the carriage brought around?"

She smiled, unable to remember the last time anyone had made such a fuss over her. "No, I'm sure I can walk the few blocks. The air will do me good. I've come to prefer the outdoors."

His frown deepened. "Perhaps on a normal evening. But with the direction the wind is blowing, the cyanide smell might make you feel worse. Let me get the driver."

She contemplated his request and stood to step back from him. "If you insist, then thank you."

He smiled and nodded as he ducked out the door. It would take him a few minutes to get to the livery and have the carriage brought over, giving her time to think. He'd been so different today, so accommodating and pleasant. If she weren't careful, she could find herself attracted to such a man. But where had the boring, pushy George gone and when should she expect his return?

CHAPTER 13

E va had managed to get more out of him Friday than he'd *ever* planned to say. He'd found himself enjoying the conversation far more than he ever should've allowed. After a weekend away from her, thinking about her, he'd been ready to join her at the office again. He brushed his long hair, which had come loose in the breeze, back from his face. He used the motion as an excuse to glance over at Eva. How had she managed to break through his reserve, get him to talk, when he was under orders to keep quiet? He'd never failed at a mission, but this one would fail if he didn't rein himself in.

She sat in her seat going through her stacks of books, never complaining though her slender neck was bent over and her shoulders tense. He'd assumed that she'd be so swept up in the idea of Mrs. Hearst inviting her here that she'd never question why. That had been a miscalculation on both General Talbot's and his part. They'd both assumed her frivolous and silly, two things she wasn't. There hadn't been a single thing he'd assumed right about her and his unease grew with each passing hour. Was he wasting his time? Somewhere, out on his trail, things were happening that he wasn't seeing because he was here. And it was his own fault, because he'd brought the notebook to the general's attention.

Eva heaved a sigh and tried to rub her shoulders without it looking obvious. That protective feeling from last week reared its head again, and he refused to fight it. Today had been a long day, even with the short break they'd taken for lunch. He'd promised to take her on another tour because their lunch break hand been shorter than either of them had planned. And he had to admit it had been nice. Eva had a quick wit and a big heart. Too big. Except for looking daggers at the poor waitress, he'd never seen her be less than kind to anyone. Where did her fear come in? And how did that kindness translate to her activities with the Indians? Whether he wanted to admit it or not, she had drawn a picture of a brave, and a very similar brave had had a picture of hers. Those were connections he couldn't deny.

He'd been pondering over everything for the last two days and nothing came to mind. Those thoughts got him nowhere. All that mattered was finding answers and then getting back on the trail where he belonged, out of these clothes that felt like a false skin, and away from Miss Rabbit before she made him stumble.

Eva glanced up and caught him staring. She turned a delicate shade of pink, visible in the light filtering in from the high windows. He cleared his throat. He had to either go over and talk with her or get out of the room. There could be no other option.

"I think we should call it a day. I can take you home in the carriage."

"No, thank you. I think I'd like a walk today, if you don't mind." She stood and stretched delicately onto the tips of her toes and rubbed her neck again. Her movements were showing curves he had no business noticing.

"I think I need to move a bit. I've been sitting too long."

"I could walk with you. I hate for you to have to walk alone." His lips acted of their own accord. He needed to get away from her, so why did he insist on prolonging the connection?

She smiled faintly. "One is never very alone on the streets of

Lead, but you may join me if you wish," she said, as she strode to the coat hall and quickly reappeared, pinning her hat in place.

He waited for her to gather her fan and gloves from her desk before he held the door open for her. The evening air was much cooler than it had been at lunch and she shivered slightly as the breeze hit her. George offered his arm and to take her basket. While he never would have said he missed having a woman on his arm before this mission, finally having one there, it was obvious to him why men would desire it. She was so small in comparison to him, fragile, like a butterfly. And for all his dressing up, he felt like a buffalo next to her.

Her lip curled up slightly as if she could read his thoughts. "It's much more pleasant to walk in the evening. The heat isn't so pressing, and the air is nice and brisk."

He couldn't agree more and wished they had more than just a few blocks to walk. "Would you care to take the long way back? There's something I'd like to show you." He couldn't stay away. This charade would tear him apart if he had to keep it up much longer.

Her eyes widened and her face glowed with excitement. "Can we drop my basket off so I can grab my shawl? If it gets much cooler, I'll need it."

Her excitement was contagious. He had to show her everything. He had to spend every minute with her she would allow, but he couldn't push too hard or she could flee. He nodded, thinking ahead to how cool the evening might get. "I don't want you to think I'm trying to monopolize you. Why don't you sup and change into something more suitable for a short hike, and I'll do the same? I'll come back and get you in, say, an hour? That way you won't think I must join you for every meal, as much as I'd like to."

She glanced away, hiding the brief look of pure joy he'd seen. Was the joy because of what he'd said or was is simply the excitement of spending time outside? "A hike? That sounds wonderful. I'll be ready. And, thank you. I don't mind that you monopolize me." She laughed nervously. "I don't know anyone else."

Not that he'd been allowing her much time or opportunity to

meet anyone. She looked on him with the trust he'd been hoping for since the beginning The trust he'd tried and failed to build as the dandy scholar. Being himself had worked where he'd thought hiding would. A connection passed between the two of them as she smiled up at him and a weak thread of trust formed as she softened against his arm.

"Then it's settled. I know it might be unexpected, but I prefer the outdoors to anywhere else."

Her grip tightened on his arm and she stepped a little livelier. "I do too, and I've missed it. It will be too dark to bring my notebook, but I'll enjoy the air and the walk."

He couldn't help but hope she enjoyed the company as well.

CLOTHES... What could she wear? She tapped her fingers against the table while considering her few options. When she'd gone hiking at home, she always took Beau's clothing. That wasn't available here and she couldn't wear pants in front of George anyway. The closest thing she had was a split riding skirt that Ruby had thought she might need. It was brown and boring but would work better than her other clothing. It would be easier to climb with than any of her walking skirts. If they went hiking anywhere close by, there would be some climbing. Her heart raced at the idea of getting away from the walls and the buildings for a little while. Even if her heart also tripped at the thought of going for a walk in the evening with George. Heat crawled up her face as she pictured him the way he'd sat with her at lunch both today and the last. How had she not noticed his high cheekbones or strong brow before? Not until he opened up to her a little. He'd suddenly become a man to her instead of an annoyance.

His strength had come through in his willingness to talk with her and it had been both exhilarating and attractive. And why shouldn't she enjoy his company for the few weeks that she would be in Lead? When the library was completed, she would go home and he back to wherever his job was. He hadn't wanted to talk about it much, but that was just as well. An attachment to George would only lead to hurt since they couldn't see each other again after Christmas. A picture of Ruby glaring with her arms crossed over her chest floated before Eva's eyes.

"Not tonight, Ruby," Eva said to the room. "Tonight, I will dash convention and just be myself. Tonight, I will enjoy myself as if I were allowed a future to court." Her heart was light, and her fingers fumbled as she buttoned the front of her shirtwaist.

She buckled the split skirt in place and ate the last of the lunch she'd bought but had not eaten earlier that day, since George had taken her to lunch once again. The small mirror by the washstand was only large enough to see bits of her at a time, but it was sufficient to see that she appeared about as well as she could. She tilted her head and stared at the glass, wishing she could do something to make herself prettier. It was odd that she and Hattie were identical, but if asked, she would whole-heartedly say that Hattie was the prettier of the two. Eva's own eyebrows were bunched in the center and no matter how hard she tried, they never seemed to relax.

Her little watch read five minutes to the hour. Better to be early and waiting for him than to make him wait or rush down late and appear over-eager. She gathered her warmest shawl and wrapped it around her shoulders, pinning it in place so she could have use of her arms. Her steps were as gentle as rain when she descended the stairs. Though she was sure she was still early, George sat waiting for her by the front desk, his long legs stretched out in front of him, crossed at the ankles, and his broad shoulders dwarfed the dainty chair. His face brightened and he stood as soon as he saw her.

"I know I'm a little early. I hope you don't think I'm too forward." He hitched his thumb in the front of his denims and waited for her. The motion was so much more masculine than any the George she knew would make that she couldn't help her gaze fixing to it.

"I don't think that at all, as I'm also a few minutes early. Shall we?"

He opened the door but didn't offer his arm. It would be difficult to hike hanging onto him and she was glad he understood, so she wouldn't have to refuse it. He led her down a darkening, empty street and behind the city livery, where the land opened up. The twilight made the grass a dark green and after a few yards, trees hemmed them in. She could make out a path to their left and she followed George as he took it.

Because so many people had used it before them, the trail was easy enough at first. But after a bit, it became rockier and more difficult to follow. Eva's slippery shoes wouldn't grip the rocks and she struggled to catch up to George. He waited ahead of her and when she reached him, he moved over on the rock he used as a seat and patted it for her to sit. "Take off your boots. One at a time."

She couldn't see enough of his face to tell if he were serious. Why would he need her boots? She took a step back.

He reached out his hand. "Come, sit. I can make it easier for you to walk, but I can't do it if they're on your feet. Can you trust me?" His voice was as soft as the breeze and she sighed, taking a seat next to him on the rock. How she'd managed to open up to him wasn't something to examine that night. She pulled her leg across her knee and then released the buttons on her first boot. She'd left her sturdy work boots at the ranch as she'd had to be choosy with each thing she brought. They had seemed unnecessary for a librarian. She handed him her boot, glad of the dim light of the fading sun so he couldn't see her face.

George pulled a small knife from his pocket and flipped it open. He scored the bottom of the boot and handed it back to her. Running her fingers over the shallow grooves, she could feel that it would grip better than the flat, slippery soles before. She handed him her other boot and he made quick work of that one as well.

"How did you know to do that?" she asked.

He avoided the question and handed her the second boot. "There, now I don't have to worry about you tripping and hurting yourself. I'd rather not have to carry you down the mountain. I suppose I could've just offered to hold your hand."

Heat raced up her cheeks and spread further. Both at the

thought of his strong arms holding her close and even at the idea of holding his hand, as lovers would. Would she have let him if he'd offered? It didn't bear thinking about, because he hadn't. Her voice was quiet to her own ears. "Well, now you don't need to worry on such things. You took care of the problem." She fumbled with the boot buttons and propelled herself off the rock. The cool air calmed her frayed nerves and she drew in a few more calming breaths. George stood. She let him pass and followed, anxious to get to wherever he was planning to take her.

He stopped and brushed off the front of his pants, taking a moment to find the path once more before he continued. It must have been well-known to him, because without his bright white shirt to guide the way, she would've been lost in the dark.

The rocks gave way under her and she screeched as the world tumbled forward. George spun, reaching out, and grabbed her hands before she could fall down the hill. Warmth, contentment, and safety flooded her every sense as he held her hands in the dark. Once she got her feet under her, she couldn't force herself to let go. Instead, she held tighter, worried he'd release her. If he let go, all those feelings of fear and unease would drown her.

"I've got you. I won't let you go." He grasped her tightly and eased her forward toward him. A memory slammed her. Booted feet, strong legs, fear, large hands that held her against a tree... Her breath came too fast and she couldn't stop it any more than she could stop those hands. The memories spun around within her.

"Eva?" George's voice was filled with concern, bringing her back to the moment. She'd gripped him so hard that her hands ached, and she shoved him away, losing her footing on the steep incline. He grabbed hold of her waist as she threw her arms out to find her balance. George pulled her to him, wrapping his strong arm around her.

Her stomach roiled and another memory pushed forward, the scent of pine woods, blood, and vomit. She'd gotten sick on Captain Roth, but why were her memories coming back now, on an evening she'd just been relishing? Would she never enjoy the company of any man again? Captain Roth had ruined her, perhaps not in the sense she'd originally thought, but he'd ruined her capacity to enjoy time with men. She pushed against him, but George rested her head against his chest. His steadily beating heart calmed her until hers matched his rhythm.

He released her as soon as she relaxed, and she almost wished he couldn't read her so well. How had he managed to soothe the fears when even her family hadn't? And how did he both cause and know how to relieve them?

"What I wanted to show you is just up ahead, if you still want to see it?" His face was cloaked in shadow, but she could hear the hope in it. Hope that whatever had bothered her was now past and they could continue to enjoy the evening.

Clenching her fists, she refused to give in to the old fears. She nodded and pushed forward on the dark trail, but soon had to drop back behind him. While he seemed capable of picking the way easily, she couldn't see it. He reached out to her and she didn't hesitate to take his offer. The moment they touched, the fear of losing the trail disappeared and she could just trust him and walk. Nothing mattered. Not the sounds creeping in from the trees around them nor the deep darkness, just her hand in his.

They came to a clearing at the top of the hill, but George led her toward the ledge. The closer she got to the edge of the mountain, the more of Lead she could see twinkling below them in the dark like stars. She'd never seen anything like it. It took her breath away. She wanted to remember every line and hollow but knew it would be impossible to recreate.

"You see, Eva? The mine and the town around it can be beautiful," he whispered from behind her as he stared over the expanse.

"The lights in my room bother me at night. I must close the curtain when I'm ready to sleep because I'm so used to living where the only light is the moon. But this is so beautiful." She realized she hadn't let go of him and he hadn't moved to release her.

"It's one of the few things about city life I like," George said as he glanced down at her.

"I guess I figured you to be a city man, but you keep surprising me, George."

He lifted her hand and brushed his warm lips over her knuckles, sending a glorious shiver through her. Hattie had said that the first time anyone did that it would leave you blooming with new, womanly sensations. Hattie was not wholly correct. She definitely felt a new, womanly sensation but other, more interesting feelings took over quickly. Like the strange lightning bolt down to her belly and then back to her heart. At nineteen, she'd never felt a man's lips until that moment, and if she decided to remain single, she might never have another chance for them at all. It was now or never. This Mr. Roth had already taken the first step, but could she leap?

Eve bit her lip hard to keep the feeling at bay, but it pressed on her. George was there, right next to her, staring down at the beautiful city, holding her hand as if she belonged to him. Would he run from her if she put her lips on his, as he'd just put his on her hand? Her heart beat a staccato rhythm in her ear, and she tried to keep the shaking in her hands from giving her away. He tucked himself in fully behind her, blocking the chill breeze as it blew over the mountain tops around them. The sky went from rose to orchid, then dark blue to black, as the stars blazed their way into view. Lord, forgive her for wanting what she couldn't have, but all she had to do was turn around and look up to get it.

CHAPTER 14

The general had said to discover the truth of the drawings by any means necessary and he'd agreed, as long as he could be someone else. Now George would have to look in the mirror and know that he was leading the lovely Eva down a trail he had no business on. His heart was owned by the Rangers and there wasn't room for any soft, delicate, beautiful distractions. Her hand had fit far too comfortably within his and, even now, he wanted to wrap his arms around her and just enjoy the feel of her soft curves against him. It would be enough. It had to be.

Eva's hand shook and she gently tugged it away from him. Had she somehow read his thoughts yet again? The moon cast her hair in wisps of silver silk. They were alone. The mountain could be theirs for as quiet as it was. He reached for her and she spun to face him before stretching up on her toes and brushing her whisper soft lips against his. She pressed into him and tangled her hands in his hair. His breath caught as his hands found her hips. Before he could even react, it was over. She dropped back on her heels and hid her face in his chest. He stopped and let his world quit spinning. His little rabbit had surprised him once again.

"Now where did that come from?" He tried to bring her face to the light, but the stubborn woman dodged his hand and pulled herself closer to him, wrapping her arms around him tighter than he'd thought she could. He'd have to right this situation. If he didn't, she'd be mighty uncomfortable with him at the library tomorrow and working there was hard enough without going back to silence. He couldn't get her to tell him anything he needed to know about the drawings and her intentions, if any, if she wasn't talking.

"I didn't figure you for a woman who'd just take everything she wanted." He hoped teasing her a little would draw her out from her hiding spot. She stepped back and looked up at him. Her lower lip trembled, and he reached up, caressing its velvetiness with the pad of his thumb. The heat of her breath did strange things to his senses. Things he'd have trouble saying no to.

She closed her eyes. "Not everything. If I could, I wouldn't have stopped." The movement of her lips against his thumb burst the weak dam of his restraint and he guided her lips to his. The trembling stopped and she fisted his shirt in her hands. His lips tasted hers for just a moment. He'd had every intention of making his kiss as brief and as innocent as hers, but starved of attention, he feasted on her sweetness. She responded in kind, exploring his lips, learning him as she stoked his hunger. He brushed her cheek with his hand and its coolness brought him back to where they were, to just who he was and why he had to stop. Not because he was Mr. Roth who'd been given permission to do as he was doing, but because he was George Roth who couldn't play with Eva's heart.

His breath was ragged to his own ears as he pulled away from her. "I fear what you'll think of this in the morning, Eva. Of what you'll think of me. After a night of considering all that happened here, will you think I brought you up here to take advantage of you? Will you hate me?" She fit perfectly to him, so small and soft pressed against him. But not for long. As much as he could willingly stay in the moment for eternity, it wasn't real. She hadn't kissed him. She'd kissed a man who didn't exist. She wanted a man he could never be, a man he had thrown off like an old coat. A man that reminded him far too much of his browbeaten father.

Her voice was muffled by his shirt. "We'll deal with tomorrow when it comes. I... I've never done that before."

He wanted to laugh. Of course she hadn't. Her sweet attempt had been angelic, but not meant to convey anything. He was certainly the one who had crossed the line from harmless to stimulating. Now he had to let her down easy without offending her in the process. He drew her face out of his chest for the second time and pulled her shawl tighter around her narrow shoulders.

He kissed the edge of her eye and the warm tear he tasted there brought reality crashing in. He framed her face with his hands as he tilted it up. "Why tears?" He kissed them away, unable to stop.

"Because I'm not who you think I am, George. I'm poor, an orphan really. My father distilled moonshine until it killed him. I said that I'd never done that before, but the fact is, I don't *remember* doing that. It's possible I did." The tears streamed down her cheeks and he drew her back to his chest. Her shaking sobs drove their way right to his heart and split it in two.

"I don't think so, Eva. While your darling lips are wonderful, they were innocent." He brushed her hair with his fingers, hoping his coarse calluses didn't somehow roughen the silken threads, like the Midas Touch gone horribly wrong.

She reached up on her toes once more and brushed her lips over his again, as if to prove his thoughts wrong. She had to stop. She had no idea what she was putting him through.

Her eyes found his and they glistened in the moonlight. "If that's true, is that better?"

He sucked in his breath. No woman had ever tested him so. "Yes, dear Eva."

"And do I have your permission to practice as I'd like?"

He couldn't look away from those eyes, the moon shining back at him from within each sparkling one. How could he tell her no? No would be right. It would be honorable. When it came time to tell her the truth, they both would suffer. But he couldn't do it. He needed to taste her again, and often. "As you'd like."

She smiled at him. "Well then, I don't think we'll have a problem with how I'll feel in the morning." She turned away from him and leaned back into his chest. His traitorous heart rejoiced at her nearness as he wrapped his arms around her. He closed his eyes against the twinkling town laid out before him, even as his head clanged a warning.

~

SHE'D DONE IT. Her first, and second, third … and maybe her last kisses had been glorious, and she would spend the whole day with her lips pressed to his, if he let her. He *had* given her permission… No, she couldn't be greedy. Her time with him would eventually draw to an end. And then what? Her heart sang a song she hoped to compose into a familiar melody, but he was still a mystery to her.

While he'd become more handsome as he'd allowed her glimpses of himself, most of who he was still lay in shadow, and she didn't need more shadows chasing her. While this night had possibly been the best she'd ever had, the power to continue their flirtation or end it sat with her. He hadn't asked for permission to court her, nor had he asked for the permission to kiss *her* as he'd like. If she chose to never set her lips to his again, this relationship, or whatever it was, would end. She shivered and his hands moved from the fingertip hold he had on her waist, up her arms, and finally rested on her shoulders.

"Eva, it's getting late. I should get you back to the boarding house. The proprietress will already wonder what you've been up to with me." She wove her fingers through his but didn't turn. She wasn't ready to give up on the night just yet. How could she? It had been better than her most extravagant Christmas. She'd been given what she'd been sure she'd never have, but now she wanted it more than she should ask for.

"You're right, of course. But I don't want to go. Life is so easy up here on the hill without anyone else. Without the pressure of what anyone else thinks or demands."

His lips brushed her fingers and her heart sped once again.

"Life isn't easy, but at least we were given this time, this brief time, to enjoy."

She nodded and forced her feet to step out of his embrace, but she let him hold her hand as he led her away from the beautiful cliff and its twinkling stars and gas lights. Everything about this night had been perfect—the outdoors, the slight chill, the scent of the trees, and him. But why hadn't he said anything? He'd agreed her lips were innocent, but did that mean she just didn't know what to do, or had he some way of knowing he was her first kiss? Had her naiveté bothered him? It couldn't have, for it had made him come back for more. Heat rose up her cheeks at the difference in the two kisses, hers slight and only to experience the fleeting moment, his to savor it. If she could store that moment in a bottle, she'd taste of it every day.

The way down the hill went much quicker than the way up, and all too soon they stood in a halo of light outside her boarding house. If Mrs. Hearst were in town and heard of their capriciousness, she would censure them for sure. George hesitated, giving her fingers a slight squeeze.

"I hope I won't get you in too much trouble in there. Mrs. Daphne can be rather strict." His hair wisped in the breeze and her hand ached to tuck it behind his ear. It was much longer than was currently stylish, and his rejection of convention made him even more handsome.

"If I am, so be it. I wouldn't change anything." It wouldn't be proper to say goodnight as she wanted to, not here in the street in front of anyone who could be watching. "I will see you in the morning?" She couldn't keep the hope from her voice.

"Yes, I'll have the carriage come pick you up. Goodnight, sweet Eva." He moved away, directly under the light so she wouldn't be tempted further, or maybe so that *he* wouldn't. It didn't much matter. It worked. She dashed into the building and was saved any embarrassment as there was no one waiting for her.

The whole main level of the boarding house was dark and quiet, and she did her best to keep it that way as she dug in her pocket for her key and removed her boots to go up the stairs. There was no need for the whole house to know she was arriving back so late. She'd stuck to herself so much that Mrs. Daphne probably didn't even remember her.

Once in her room, she lit the lamp and brought it to the window. George was no longer under the streetlamp and she couldn't see him in the street. She set down the lamp and flipped her notebook open to a fresh page. Quickly, she drew his image. She remembered every line around his eyes, the slight scar above his right eyebrow, his strong nose and chin, and those thin lips that had fit perfectly against her own. It was as if his face were right before hers, even now.

He'd been right. Her blood already tingled at the thought of working with him tomorrow. They were often alone as they worked and trusting herself to behave would be difficult. Perhaps he would take her to the library so they might be around people. The idea both excited and dismayed her, because kissing him had been so exciting, new, and tempting.

She stood and pulled the shawl from around her shoulders. She had so few dresses, but one was her favorite. It made her feel pretty and that would be the one she'd wear tomorrow. A twinge of guilt nibbled at her. She wasn't acting as she should, not like Ruby would want her to. Ruby would advise her to pray about her feelings, to slow down and think before she did anything rash. How often had Ruby said that the Lord could heal any hurt? Would the Lord understand desire? Perhaps, but He wouldn't understand her tempting a man she could never have.

CHAPTER 15

Either her stays were too tight, or she just couldn't breathe properly. Eva shifted her lunch basket and notebook to her other arm as she waited for the carriage the next morning. He wasn't late. She'd been unable to sleep thinking about how she would greet him, what he would say, or if nothing would change at all. Her one—perhaps rash—move *had* changed everything, just as George had predicted.

The black carriage turned the corner and her heart leapt. In a few moments, she'd know just how he felt. The tingles in her stomach quivered to a fever pitch as the horses stopped in front of her and the door swung open. George moved quickly to get out and help her. He'd also worn his best clothes and had shaved the slight stubble on his jaw that had scratched at her chin the night before. His eyes were bright as they lit on her with an appreciative smile.

"Good morning," he whispered just for her ears. "I trust you slept well."

She wondered if *he* had. If he hadn't, he hid it well. She'd had to use a bit of flour under her eyes to hide the dark circles. "And you. I wish I could say that I did. As you predicted, I was a little worried about today. About what you might think of me."

He glanced around them. "Best get into the carriage before we speak plainly. There are curious ears all around."

She'd been so concerned about talking with him she hadn't noticed the women milling about behind her.

"Come, let's get in the carriage." He held out his hand to assist her up.

He climbed in, and then closed the door and sat across from her. She hoped he would've chosen the seat next to her at least this time, but his manners won out.

"I confess, I had a difficult night as well. How do you propose we move forward?" His eyes trailed their way from her hair down to her lips and back to her eyes. Heat crept up her neck at his blatant appreciation.

"I think it best that, at least at the library, we go back to being just as we were before last night." She licked her suddenly parched lips. The words were difficult to push past the lump in her throat. They didn't want to come, but it would be wrong to continue. They'd get little accomplished if they continued as they did last night.

"I would have to agree, although I do hope you'll consider spending time with me in the evenings. I find that I'm suddenly rather attached to you."

Her heart did a little flip. "And I'm looking forward to getting to know you further, George."

His mouth quirked on one side as they turned the corner just a few blocks from the offices. "I can see an idea turning in your head, Eva. What is it?"

"Oh, I wasn't thinking anything." She refused to let him see her discomfort. He was a temptation and it was never a good idea to get too close to the flame. They both knew time was fleeting, but her returning memories of Captain Roth kept her from taking that extra step.

He chuckled, drawing her attention to his lips. "Here we are." He hesitated a moment before standing to open the door, and too late she realized he was waiting for her to say something. He stepped down and reached for her hand. A soft, pleasant heat infused hers where he touched it. But it just as quickly disappeared when he let her go. Would she spend her days wishing for the slightest touch from him? Would her eyes betray her wish for his attention? Without Beau's approval, even considering another night like their time on the hill would be wrong.

His touch was warm against her back as he led her up the stairs to the offices. They'd almost reached the door when she turned to him. She was unable to go back into the office where they'd met—where the old George always seemed to reappear— without speaking her heart.

"George, what we did on the mountain... I don't regret it, but it wasn't right for me to act in such a manner. My sister and brother, who are my guardians, wouldn't approve." She swallowed the knot forming in her throat and prayed George would make an excuse she hadn't thought of. "It's probably best if we don't allow ourselves to do that again until you talk to them. If that is your intention?"

What if a relationship hadn't been his intention at all? She hadn't really considered that. Her wanton behavior put her into an even tighter bind. He'd never mentioned the future, and now she'd pushed him away and slammed the door on any further enjoyment. She'd forced him right into a corner. What a fool. How could she fix the damage without throwing herself at him?

All desire to go into the office left her. A few thoughtless minutes had changed her life entirely. She gathered her courage and straightened her spine. George waited for her outside the cloak hall.

His brow raised slightly as a smile played at the corner of his mouth. "In order to ask, I would need to know whom to ask." His voice was quiet, and he searched her face with eyes only for her. She relished it, for it would be fleeting. Once he spoke to Beau and found out about the other time she'd gone off to the mountain alone, George would be gone.

"I'll take you to meet them. If that is your wish."

617

The tips of George's rough fingers traced up her cheek and her breath caught. She prayed he'd been as affected by their evening as she had. That he wanted more just as she did.

He closed his eyes and let his hand fall. "I do wish. Perhaps some Sunday we can join your family for church. If you live close enough to walk home, you must go to services close by."

"My family has always gone to Deadwood, but I can send them a note to join us here on a Sunday soon."

He leaned against the wall near her, as if to keep his hand from touching her again. "That would be good. I'd like to meet them."

He glanced to the door of the office and his mask fell in place again. She wanted to yell and shake him. His face clouded and he pushed away from the wall, entering the office she'd begun to hate.

HIS TIME RAN SHORT. Especially now that he'd agreed to meet Eva's family. A family who would recognize him straight away and wonder why Eva didn't. That was still a mystery. She'd hit her head hard enough that day to make her sick. But it hadn't seemed so bad as to confuse her memories. He'd avoided pushing her too hard whenever she'd brought up anything hinting at Captain Roth. He had to keep his true self away from the one he'd built for this assignment or he'd never find out about her drawings. Not that he'd cared much recently. He had ample opportunity to push her for information, but he couldn't do it. He couldn't ask the tough questions he needed to.

She'd brought her notebook today. His hand had brushed against it outside the office, reminding him of exactly why he was here. And it wasn't for a pleasant afternoon of exploring Eva's willing mouth. She was too eager, almost desperate for him. Most women knew that—at some point in their future—a man would slake that need, so they held their desire in check. Eva drank from the fountain of pleasure as if she'd never have that chance again. It could only be her age and inexperience. Despite the general's orders, he'd make sure she didn't experience any more desire than she had thus far. She needed a man who could take her on walks and show her wildlife, teach her to camp under the stars. She needed a man who would give her a brood of children who loved to draw and couldn't be penned in by four walls. Children like he and Eva could create, if not for this mission.

He arranged his desk as she walked in, fingering her lips. She glanced at him for a moment and set her notebook on his desk. It was close, so close.

"You've been so curious about what I've done, but I can only show you one today. The other one is personal."

His heart did a jig. This was it. She was ready to let him in. Would it be worth it? Did he even want it to be? He didn't have to dig that far to find what he hoped was some simple explanation that would free her from suspicion. He sat down and folded his hands in front of him to keep from seeming too interested. Every time he'd mentioned her drawings in the past, she'd shut him out.

She flipped to the first page and there were the flowers he'd left for her in her room at the boarding house. Or rather, the flowers he'd given to Mrs. Daphne to leave in her room.

"They are lovely. These are the wildflowers that grow around here in the spring and linger in the valleys."

She nodded and bit the edge of her lip. A groan leapt into his chest, but he swallowed it back.

"They are my favorites. After the spring, you have to search for them. I found some in a small covered, secret glade at the edge of our property. It was always cool there and the air was fresh with their fragrance. It was as if the Lord had made that special place, just for me."

He had to focus on the picture, not the woman, or he'd lose all concentration. "They are certainly lovely. What makes them your favorite?" If he knew that, perhaps he could figure out the connection to her and the Indians? Was it the flowers or the covered, secret location she spoke of?

"I just love them. They are delicate and small, yet just a few of them can make a whole room smell wonderful."

He searched the drawing closely, but it was just a vase of

flowers on a table. As much as he looked to find some secret meaning, it wasn't there. Perhaps the private picture held something more, but he'd have to secret the notebook away to see it.

"I wish you wouldn't look like that."

He glanced up at her and the worry etched across her face threw all thoughts of the drawing away. "Look like what?" All that mattered was wiping the concern off her face.

"Like you're pained by my drawing." She pressed the notebook closed. "I warned you they weren't very good."

He'd offended her. In maintaining his silence and distance, he'd hurt her. He couldn't let that stand. George stood and leaned toward her over the desk. He could just barely smell the scent of her lavender soap tantalizing his nose.

"I was looking closely, not pained. Your drawing is quite good. I not only knew it was a flower, but exactly which kind and where to find it. I'd say that makes your drawing quite good."

She collected the notebook and turned from him as she clutched it to her chest, leaning against his desk. "I thank you for that. I'm still not sure why you were so interested in seeing it, but now you have. Has it tempered your curiosity, George?"

It felt as if his last chance to make the mission worth anything was steadily slipping from his grasp. "More like tempted it. Have you ever shown them to anyone else?"

Eva stiffened. "I tried to show them to Hattie. She had little interest. And one man took my first notebook from me. It's silly. I shouldn't miss them. They were just drawings of flowers and animals, but there was one drawing... A special one. It was a picture of who I am, and I miss it."

He forced himself to stay behind the desk, to hang back from her and let her alone. Did she mean the eagle...or the brave? "Can you draw a new copy?" he whispered. "Would that help you?"

"It wouldn't be the same." She pushed away from the desk and retreated to her little stool, closing herself off from him as she always did. He'd yet to figure out if it was simple artist's fear or something more sinister. Now his emotions were too wound up in this situation.

"Eva, on Saturday would you like to visit the countryside? I know I could stand a day out of doors. I promise to keep to my own side of the wagon." He laughed, praying she would return to her pleasant demeanor.

She glanced up and smiled slightly. "Getting outside would be wonderful, but where would we go?"

"There's a great place just outside of town, to the west." He had to tempt her, had to take her back where she was comfortable, even though it put him at risk. His papa had always said that the truth should never hurt, but then his papa had never told mama the truth about how he'd felt.

She sighed and her eyes registered that he'd be taking her close to home. Maybe she'd finally tell him the truth, and then he could shed these lies. The longer it took, it was less likely she'd forgive him and the more likely he'd miss her. And he *would* miss her. Miss what might have been if they had met under different circumstances, and if he were not owned by the army.

CHAPTER 16

The week passed so slowly, but Saturday had finally come. The Hearst's liveryman was happy to help him find a suitable small buckboard, but Argus was less happy about being hitched to the light rig. He couldn't tear his mind from Eva. It had been a full week since their walk up the mountain and he was more than ready to get out of the city again. But would it matter? Eva had been chilly and formal ever since.

The little buckboard would be perfect for a quick trip out to the countryside. Every man needed a day of rest and they'd worked hard the last few days, cataloging books that would both interest and enhance the culture. But she'd worked even harder to avoid him. His feet fairly danced at the chance to get out of the city and get sweet Eva back where she was comfortable. He kept telling himself the pull he felt for Eva was just him getting closer to her secrets, but it sounded false even to his own ears. He was plum sick of falsehoods. Both days, he'd held back from talking to her or reaching out and touching her arm. More than once he'd stopped himself from crossing the room and kissing some life back into her.

He pulled up in front of the boarding house and found her waiting outside. She wore a pretty lavender walking skirt and matching hat. The sun shone off the tendrils of golden hair that slipped free. A basket tucked over her arm held her notebook and what looked like the makings of a picnic. He hadn't even considered eating, only getting her out of the city where they both could relax.

Her face was radiant, a nice change from her stuffy determination to avoid him. He'd half expected to find Beau waiting with her. She hadn't wanted to go out of town with him again before he'd talked to Beau. He reminded himself again that he wasn't even supposed to know Beau's name. The day of reckoning was still on the horizon.

As he pulled the brake to hold the wagon, she slid the basket along the floorboards between them and climbed up before he could even wrap the lines around the brake. She seated herself on the narrow bench, barely touching him. He told himself they were out in the open, that she had to remain away from him, almost aloof. It wasn't that she'd chilled toward him. Was it? She arranged her skirts and shifted her feet to brace herself.

"It's good to see you, George. You're looking handsome today."

He grinned. "I was just thinking to myself how handsome I am."

She laughed and shook her head. The softness of her neck was a temptation almost too much to bear.

"You look like a summer flower, sweet Eva." She glowed under his praise but said nothing more.

He picked up the lines and flicked them, contemplating just where along the trail he would take her. Part of him wanted to be caught. He was tired of the lies to Eva. If he took her to the edge of the Ferguson ranch, there was a chance one of her brothers-in-law would be out riding and see them, or even Brody himself. Then he'd be saved from the deceit. There was also the possibility she might recall him. Deep in his gut, he knew she wouldn't ever tell him the truth of what she was doing. *Captain* Roth knew about the picture she'd given to the Indians. *Mr.* Roth couldn't ask about that. He shouldn't know about it at all. The longer he had to be Mr. Roth, the less he liked the man. It was also clear that while Eva thought she'd kissed Mr. Roth, she only responded when he allowed who he was as Captain Roth to come through.

He pulled off the road where he'd met the Indian by the little creek, just a few hills away from Ferguson land. They probably wouldn't be discovered there. If they were, he'd deal with it. Eva glanced over at him as he pulled the lines and the horses slowed.

"This is a pretty spot. What made you choose it?"

"It's not too far out of town in case we tire of one another's company." He glanced at her and the slight look of hurt in her eyes stopped him short. "Aw, don't look at me that way. We've been rushing away from each other for five straight days."

A pink tinge colored her cheeks. "I didn't mean to be rude. I... haven't, that is, I didn't know how to deal with..."

He picked up her hand and caressed the soft flesh on top. "I didn't expect you to. It's been a bit of a touch to my pride, that's all. I've never actually chased a woman across the room with a mere look before." He turned from her and forced himself to watch his feet as he climbed down to give her a moment to let her color subside. That had been unexpected. They'd joked to break the tension before, but the few days of avoiding her had made him prickly, too.

He came around to her side of the small rig as she stood to climb down. He held her loosely at the waist until her feet touched the ground and released her immediately, though his hands didn't want to. She glanced at him for a moment, her brow crinkled in confusion, and turned from him. She strode off toward the small creek, shielding her eyes even with the pretty hat while he unhitched Argus. The temperamental horse tried to take a hunk out of his leg for hooking him up to the noisy contraption. A giggle from behind drew him around.

Eva stood watching him, her slight hand covering her mouth and her eyes bright with mirth.

"So you think Argus is funny, do you?"

She approached, slow but confident, brushing Argus's forelock from his eyes and rubbing the star she exposed.

"Now, aren't you handsome," she whispered, her soft voice sending tension singing through him.

Argus leaned forward, pushing his whole head into her for more attention.

"Hey, no being greedy there." George pulled back on the harness to keep Argus from shoving her into the ground. "He must like you. Generally, he only tolerates people. Even then, only if it suits him."

"Strange. Like when I first met you, it feels like I've met him before. But that can't be." She petted Argus's cheeks and then turned to face him, her eyes seeking to know more than he could tell. "Can it?"

He'd been given the chance. If he told her now who he was, he could ask her straight out what she was up to—if anything—and get back to his life as a ranger. Doing so might mean losing what they'd started. He might not even be able to go back to what he loved. If he told her the truth, he'd be disobeying a direct order. While he wasn't directly under the command of the army, in this case, he was doing army business.

"No, I'm sure it can't be." The lie felt like acid in his throat. "Why don't I show you something?" Changing her thoughts would help her forget Argus. "There's a flat rock you can sit on and the view of the water is pretty."

She seemed thrown off balance by his change of subject. Confusion clouded her eyes, and she glanced from Argus to the creek as if she didn't quite know where she should go. He held out his hand. She smiled warmly and took it, walking alongside him. He allowed himself the pleasant pressure of her hand in his.

"I'm sorry, George. I know I've behaved strangely. You must think I'm incredibly silly." She stopped and her face darkened in concern. "You see, I've...met another Mr. Roth not so long ago. He took something from me that can never be replaced, and I find myself very unsure when I'm with you. Unsure that I'm acting the way I should. Perhaps worried that what he took will make what we have begun impossible. I'm sure I'm just confusing you more." Her face pinched as she looked away.

His heart lurched, and then raced. She really did suspect him of taking her notebook but, obviously, something far more precious as well. "Surely whatever he took couldn't have been so important? Important enough to ruin this?" He reached for her face.

She flashed an angry glare at him, and he dropped his hand. She moved over to the flat rock on her own. "I'd rather not speak of what he took from me. But suffice it to say, it sometimes makes being with you uncomfortable. I get these flashes of memory, like just now with Argus. I only tell you so that you understand and perhaps won't condemn me when or if I trust myself to tell you someday."

She wasn't talking about a notebook. There was no way that much anger could come from missing a few drawings. Here was more information that only Captain Roth could glean, but would she even speak to him if she knew who he really was? Could he take that chance?

"I'm sorry." He laid his hands on her shoulders and she tensed. "I hope you know that I mean you no harm. Our friendship will be, unfortunately, most temporary if you are unsure of how we should continue. Only while we work together for Mrs. Hearst. Then you won't have to hear the name Roth again. If you desire it, I'll disappear back to my home and never see you again."

She shivered. "I will miss you, George. I'll give you that. But the completion of this project will not spare me hearing your name. My family doesn't know the extent of what happened. But should Captain Roth show his face again, he'll have to answer for what he did." He stepped around the rock to face her and her face was pale, eyes distant. The pencil she pinched between her finger and thumb bounced nervously off her leg.

He'd taken nothing from her but her drawings. What could her family think he did? "I'll give you a few minutes alone. Seems like you might need it." George turned back to Argus so Eva could let steam off. What could she possibly mean? He'd *done* nothing to her that day. Well, aside from holding her against the tree to get to what she was hiding. He hadn't realized she hit her head so hard that she wasn't thinking, and it would make her sick. What else could she be missing?

She couldn't think he'd done anything to her...not when she was barely conscious and covered in... No. There had to be something else she feared. He'd never taken advantage of a woman. Even when he'd been given the direct order to use any means necessary to get the information from Eva, he hadn't. He'd stopped that night on the cliff where, if he'd followed orders, he wouldn't have. His stomach pitched at the thought. No wonder she didn't trust him. He was her worst nightmare.

George stood over by his horse, but it did little to relieve the tension bunching Eva's shoulders. Her own distrust showed him the way. He couldn't tell her the truth. Not today.

Argus was an amazing horse, one that wouldn't easily be forgotten, but could he convince her that she'd seen the horse with him, as Mr. Roth? The thought of another lie twisted his gut. The horse's roan coat shone in the sun and his white star was bright and clean. Even when he was dirty after living on the trail, he'd be hard to forget.

There was no way she could sit comfortably on the rock and hold her paper. From the corner of his eye, he watched her shift her position and stretch her back. He could foster temporary trust between them by being of service. Allow himself to pack away Mr. Roth and be himself for a while. Enjoy the free day with a beautiful woman. It would come to an end soon enough.

He strode back and shaded her from the sun to let her know he was there. "I can sit behind you. You can lean against me, rest a little. Sitting on a rock isn't like sitting on a stool." She glanced up. He captured her gaze and held it. Eva didn't reply and he sat behind her, pushing himself close, enjoying even the feel of her back against his. "Just relax for a minute."

Her muscles bunched and flexed as she leaned against him until she pushed away, dragging a deep breath from her lungs.

He leaned back and touched her shoulder with his, the slight contact making her jump. "No sense in rushing off. You haven't even had a chance to draw anything yet." He turned back and waited as she settled back against him but couldn't relax. Every bit of her was rigid. This outing wasn't going near how he'd planned. The heat from her back poured into his, adding to the warmth of the sweltering sun. She flexed her wrists in circles and raked her hand across her forehead. A girl's head appeared out of the grass just within his view and Eva gasped.

"George, she's back," Eva whispered, tilting her head. "What do I do?"

He had no idea what she meant and didn't want to scare either Eva or the girl. He looked over their shoulders again. "What do you mean, back?" He matched his tone to hers.

"She was here when I walked home that first night. She was looking for flowers. My flowers." Her voice wasn't nervous. Eva was more scared of him than the Indian and that rocked him.

Eva stood and he moved along with her, mimicking her movement. While the girl might not be a brave, there could be one hiding anywhere.

"How do you know all she wanted was flowers?" His mind raced. He hadn't brought his guns, thinking it would give away his cover. He squinted and the girl saw him, they both exchanged a glance of recognition. No. How could she be from Sitting Bear's village? Why way over here?

"She pointed to the flowers. I told her she could take them."

The young woman drew closer and pulled a rough leather pouch from around her neck. She handed it to Eva. The nearer the woman got, the more he could feel the tension coil inside Eva. She wanted to bolt. He reached around and grasped her hand both to calm her and keep her from running. Though he couldn't see them, he sensed there were more nearby, and they may not only take her flight as an insult, but as cause to chase them.

"Hold still, Eva. Look her in the eyes. She won't harm you. She's giving you a gift. You must've done something that helped her greatly or she wouldn't have risked coming back here for you." He wanted to tell her that the woman's name was Sun on River and her father was a close friend of the chief.

"I did nothing." She shook her head and the Indian stopped, confusion narrowing her eyes.

George squeezed Eva's hand. "No, don't do that. Let her know, with your eyes, that you accept her gift. The Sioux rely on gifts as a way to thank people. If you don't accept it, you'll offend her."

"How do you know?" Eva hissed under her breath.

"I just do. Now nod and hold out your hand."

She waited, but the action followed. Good. She could trust him when it was important.

"I don't know what it is…"

"Don't worry about that and don't look unless you can be sure you can look absolutely thankful for it. If you can't, don't open it. Now, hold her eye contact."

"I'm scared."

He pressed her hand. "She won't hurt you."

The woman nodded and held up her hand, backing away as soundlessly as she'd come.

Eva let out a huge rush of air. "I haven't been so frightened since…" She shook her head and dropped his hand, moving away from him and over to the river. She didn't have to say the words. He wasn't sure when he'd learned to read her so well, but he knew she was talking about the first time they'd met. She just didn't know it.

CHAPTER 17

Her breath came hard and fast and she fluttered her lashes to keep the tears where they belonged—behind her eyes. She wouldn't cry in front of George. How silly she must seem to him. He hadn't been frightened at all. How had he known just what to do? How to react? Those things hadn't been in anything she'd ever read. In fact, the newspaper accounts she'd read had only incited fear. She still wanted to run back to the ranch where she felt safe with her family. She reminded herself again that it was impossible. They couldn't give her back what the captain had taken. *Possibly taken,* Beau's voice rang loud and clear in her thoughts.

George's steady hand softly touched her shoulder. She wanted to soak up his reassurance, wanted to take the comfort he offered, but she couldn't. As badly as her heart wanted to melt into him, her mind was fixed. The mountaintop had been her first and last kiss. After their kiss, he'd gone back to his strange false self. Being near him was like looking through a warped mirror. Nothing was as it appeared.

She took a deep, steadying breath. "How did you know? I don't understand how you knew just what she was doing and what would happen." She stepped back away from his touch as he reached for her. If she let him touch her, she would accept whatever he said. She had to know the truth, finally.

"Some things you just can't learn from books." He rested his hands on his hips and his silhouette was too strong, too masculine to be a scholar. And she'd known the strength of him because she'd leaned against him and drawn from that strength on the top of the mountain. He couldn't be who he said he was. Her mind and heart both knew what was true and that Mr. Roth was false.

"Who are you, George Roth? I want the truth."

"I could ask the same of you." His eyes pinned her where she stood. "You've met that woman here before? How many times? Do you realize that helping them carries a heavy penalty? If the army thinks you are aiding an uprising..."

"Why would I do that? We're less than a mile from the place I call home! Why would I endanger my family? Both from the army and the Indians? How foolish do you think I am?" Her heart pounded harder against her chest and her head felt faint. How could he accuse her of such things? Only a few days ago, he'd been so tender. "It was just flowers, George. Would you turn me in because of that?"

"If whatever you did was important enough for her to seek you out in the light of day, then I'd say it was more than flowers." Anger narrowed his eyes. "How did she know you'd be here? Have you told them where to find you, where to watch for you?"

Hurt and anger pierced down to her soul. "Take me home. I don't want to be out here with you anymore." She hadn't even known where he was going to take her. How could she have told *them*, if she hadn't known herself? George's words clenched around her heart, choking her.

His face had shut again like a mask. Hard, false. "I don't know if you can be trusted. Would you put the project at risk?"

"Why can't you believe me? I've only ever had contact with that woman once before, for mere moments on my way home."

He grabbed her arm and led her back to the wagon. She shoved against him, yanking her arm free. Though he didn't hurt her, she didn't want him touching her. Not in anger, and maybe not ever again.

"You wait just a moment, George Roth. You ask me who *I* am and what have *I* done? What about you? You have knowledge of how the Indians act and react. You weren't even frightened. I was next to you. It didn't quicken your pulse at all. I was terrified. You accuse me when maybe you're trying to shift blame from yourself." She seethed that he would dare accuse her of treachery. She would never harm her family or Mrs. Hearst. The idea was preposterous.

He stood back and stared at her for a moment, his jaw clamped tightly as his chest rose and fell. He stared at her as if she sickened him.

The silence became unbearable. "Well, have you nothing to say for yourself? You were so quick to accuse me, yet if I turn the favor around, it bothers you?"

"You have no idea what you accuse me of." His voice was quiet, sharp.

"I do. She could've just as easily been looking for you. It was just that I was closest." She handed the pouch to him, but he only stared it at.

"You would swear on a Bible that you aren't helping them?"

"I couldn't do that. Obviously, they needed those plants for something. You're just trying to trap me in circles. Could you make the same oath?"

The deceit fell momentarily from his eyes and she could see clearly that he couldn't. For the first time that day, George was himself and she stepped closer to him, curious about what this change could mean.

He backed away and the mask slammed back in place. "I'll take you back, just wait for me to hitch Argus."

Her writing pad and pencils lay in the grass next to the basket lunch she'd packed. It would be a waste now. She wasn't hungry and wouldn't be. Her hands shook with anger as she shoved all her belongings back into the basket and carried it to the buckboard. George cinched the breech straps at Argus's hind quarters as she shoved the basket under the seat. He came

632

around to help her up, but she didn't want his hands anywhere near her. Tossing him a glare over her shoulder, she clutched her skirt and climbed into the rig. She heard him mutter as he went around the back and climbed up on his side. Her anger exploded like a shot.

"Mr. Roth, you have no right to be angry. You accused me of treachery against my country when all I'm guilty of is human decency. If you're angry that I turned that accusation back on you, then you know exactly how I feel."

He turned on her, his voice thrummed with tension. "I have entrusted my very *life* to this country, Eva. You couldn't possibly understand."

"I would if you'd tell me! One moment I think I've begun to break through the false face you wear, then the next you slap it back in place and become whoever it is you're trying to be. I want to know the man who so gently held me at the precipice of the mountain. I want to be with *him* and hope he'll come back every day. I have no idea if George Roth even exists. If he does, he seems to be made of duplicities beyond my comprehension."

His arm next to hers on the short seat tensed until she thought he'd strike out. She'd pushed too far and was glad he said nothing as he pulled the horse to a stop in front of her boarding house. She scrambled down the wheel and rushed away from him and all that coiled anger. Her heart raced as she watched him drive away. Only after he'd gone more than a block did she remember the basket. Her heart sunk. He'd find the drawing of himself if he dared to look. And why wouldn't he? The drawings and her supposedly suspicious actions were all he seemed to care about. Part of herself rode away on that wagon. This time, it had nothing to do with the notebook.

ARGUS SOMEHOW FELT the tension George couldn't contain as he fumbled with the chest straps of the harness. The great beast stomped his foot and puffed great blasts of air at him.

"Sorry, old boy." George rubbed Argus's flank. "She raked me good and I shouldn't take it out on you."

Argus notched his head higher in agreement.

"Sad thing, she's too close to the truth. I've never had someone read me like that before. Not even my own mother could see through me like that." George reached for the comb and gently brushed over Argus's coat to calm them both.

"All these facts just don't line up. The notebook, the picture from that Indian... I know it was one of hers. She said she'd met that woman before today, but for what? None of this makes sense and I won't be able to figure it out if she doesn't trust me."

Argus blasted him again.

"I guess it's time Eva became reacquainted with Captain Roth, but I have to visit the general first. We'll take a little ride in a bit, eh? When I've had a chance to return to reasonable?"

He backed away, narrowly missing a nip in the leg. "That's my boy." He patted the horse's rump as he strode toward the rig. He shoved it back in place and reached for the cover when the handle of the basket caught his eye. He lifted it out and couldn't stop from pulling out the notebook.

She'd only drawn in the first three pages. The first drawing was the vase of flowers he'd left her at the boarding house. The second was a sketch of himself that he didn't want to think about. The third was Argus, almost finished, from today. His regal head took up most of the page, but what drew his attention almost immediately, was a shadow figure in the back, sitting on the ground far away, small.

He rushed up to his room and flipped open the other notebook to the eagle picture to see the two next to one another. Both had shadowy people, both had the same short strokes and use of color. The shadow figures looked so similar, almost as if he could concentrate or squint just enough, he would manage to somehow pull the person close enough to see. But no matter how he looked, the answer wouldn't come to him. Maybe he wouldn't wait to call on the general.

The butler stood at the doorway to his room. "Mr. Roth,

General Talbot has sent a telegram requesting your presence. I requested Anderson get the carriage ready."

"The carriage? I can't go meet the general in a carriage. I'll ride my horse."

The butler frowned and backed up a step. "Yes, sir."

George ripped the string tie from his throat and unbuttoned his shirt. If he had to meet with the general, he'd be wearing his own clothes as Captain Roth. After he shrugged on his wool coat, the butler appeared in the door once again.

"Your horse is ready, sir."

George gave him a smile, something he hadn't felt comfortable doing until that moment. "Don't worry, the house is yours until the Hearsts come back. After my meeting with the general, I doubt I'll be back."

"That is too bad, sir," he said, though his face said he wouldn't miss George a bit. George failed at being a refined gentleman, just like he told his mother. He wasn't cut out to live this life. And just like Eva had accused of him, it was false. It was a lie and he'd make it right after the trip to the general.

"Most of my clothes here, I won't miss. But could you put them in my trunk for me. I'll pick them up soon."

"Most assuredly, sir."

He strode out to the stable with the two notebooks and shoved them into his saddle bag. He rolled his shoulders at the thought of a good, long ride. A confrontation with the general was never something to look forward to, but he'd have the ride all the way to Camp Crook to think about just what to say and how to say it to get what he wanted.

Argus made quick work of the miles. He only realized once he got there that he hadn't paid attention to anything. Eva was the only thing on his mind. He had to make this right. He had to be honest with her so he could stop accusing her and just ask about the drawings and the Indians. It all hinged on this meeting.

He paced outside the general's roughhewn office until a corporal let him in.

"I'm impressed you came right away, Roth. What've you learned? It's been over three weeks with no report."

George strode to the front of the desk. He couldn't sit, so he wouldn't ask for permission. He had to feel in control. "Sir, after spending as much time as possible with the girl, I have my doubts that she's done anything. Permission to break cover and ask her a few more questions before I exit the situation?"

General Talbot leaned back in his chair and cocked his head as he crossed his arms over his chest. "Did you use any and all means necessary?"

"Of course, sir. I follow orders, even when I don't agree with them." He stood perfectly still, eyes locked forward, hands straight at his sides.

"Is that so? Then why do you need permission to break cover? If you had this girl wrapped around you like you were supposed to, you wouldn't need to. Do I need to send someone else in there to do the job? Anderson is more than willing."

Hot anger bolted through him at the thought of any of the men even speaking to Eva. "You don't trust my word? I just said I have my doubts that she knows anything."

"And can you explain away the drawings, then?"

"They are nothing. She was trying out a new hobby because she misses her sister. A sister who is now married." Normally, he'd never give the general such useless information, but if the general knew that he'd paid close attention to Eva, he might let George complete his mission and not chase her into the lion's den with one of his other men.

"I saw two natives while in Lead, neither hostile. Both were looking for the giliweed plant."

"What purpose could the plant serve? Can it poison people?" The general sat forward in his seat and his narrowed eyes bored into George, making his skin tighten.

"No, sir. It's relatively safe. I've heard it's used to clear the system, and you'd need a large amount to do harm. I never saw them with more than a few plants and this late in the season, they're rare. Giliweed is a spring plant, sir." It also happened to be Eva's favorite.

"I'll write a letter to Mrs. Hearst and let her know you're finished, and I'll send a telegram to Eva's family to come pick her up. There is no sense in her staying on."

"Sir, she's doing a good job. I don't think Mrs. Hearst will like having to find someone else to finish. She doesn't want to have to come back here."

"Mrs. Hearst is none of your concern. You're not telling me everything, Roth."

"I'm not under your command anymore, sir. You just relieved me of my mission."

Talbot slammed his fists on the desk in front of him. "Roth, I'm more than a little tired of your attitude. I think it's about time the rangers disbanded. You've got one week to gather them all. In that time, I expect a decision. You either join us here or resign. I won't have any more rogue militia thinking they can just do as they please. Dismissed."

CHAPTER 18

S he'd gone to the church the day before and confessed the sin of throwing herself at a man, so why didn't she feel better? As she waited for George's carriage, her thoughts kept returning to the argument with him on Saturday. A day that should've been fun had gone horribly wrong. Worse, her notebook had been left in the carriage and now he'd know about her silly drawings. The one of him would be the worst. Terribly embarrassing. Perhaps it would make his mood better and they could get back to being, well, whatever it was they were.

He'd been so angry with her. But to be fair, she'd been angry too. Never had she been accused of something so terrible. Treason. Her heart squeezed tightly within her just thinking about the words he'd said. How could anyone believe, even for a moment, she'd be capable of such? But he'd also shown her a little bit of himself that he'd never shared before. He'd given his life to serving his country and that little bit of information had left her unable to sleep. *Captain* Roth had also given his life to serving his country. He couldn't possibly be the same person.

He'd said they'd never met. He had even claimed she'd never met his horse before. How could he play her for such a fool and why? Had he assumed she wouldn't recognize him, or had he changed his appearance just to trick her? It couldn't be. The more she thought on it, the more it twisted its way deep inside. Whenever her crippling fear occurred, he'd been there every time. It seemed likely that he was, at least in part, the cause.

And now she was waiting for him to arrive in the carriage so she could confront him. The longer she waited, the more her unease grew until her stomach felt like a ship lost at sea. He'd picked her up every morning last week, but the argument had changed everything. If he didn't come soon, she'd resume walking to the office. The late October wind bit at her face, but she wouldn't go back into the boarding house.

The bustling city of Lead went on without her as she waited, but the carriage didn't arrive. The sun beat down on her neck, warming the chill wind. George hadn't come for her. Was he really so very angry with her that he'd report her, or get her removed from the project? Was there even a project, or was that just another ruse? Tears threatened at the back of her eyes. A wagon pulled up in front of her. Immediately, she recognized her brother-in-law Beau.

"Beau, what're you doing here? Is everything all right at the ranch?" Why would he be there unless something was wrong? And would George finally show up? Beau had met Captain Roth. He could prove her fears or dispel them.

His eyebrow cocked slightly. "I came here to get you. We got a telegram this morning saying you needed to come home. That the job was done. I had to arrange for all the ranch work to get done before I could come. I'm sorry for keeping you waiting."

"But...no." She shook her head. "The work *isn't* done." She shook her head slowly as her heart sank into her feet. "He wouldn't have. He doesn't even know who you are." It just wasn't possible that George could've sent such a telegram. He hadn't known anything about her life away from Lead. Unless...

"Who?" Beau climbed down and held onto her elbow, the only thing keeping her from sinking onto the ground. She clung to him and he held her close. "Eva, dear. What's wrong? The telegram was short, just that your job was done and to pick you up with an address."

She couldn't catch her breath. Her world spun out of control. What had he done? Would she go to prison? Or worse? Her knees buckled.

George's voice penetrated her tumbling thoughts. "Eva, are you all right? Eva, answer me."

She turned to see his eyes. Concern deepened the ridge of his forehead. He'd returned, the real George. He reached for her hand.

"You stop right there, Captain." Beau growled and pulled her away from him. Her heart lurched and she couldn't catch her breath. Everything around her seemed to slow unnaturally yet come into crystal focus.

"Captain?" She looked first at Beau for confirmation, then to George. So, it *was* true. This whole last three weeks had been a lie and she'd kissed the man who'd taken everything from her. She had literally thrown herself in his arms.

"Oh, George. What have you done?" She couldn't be in the street anymore. Couldn't face the bright sun. The doors to the boarding house were only a few feet away but her steps seemed to take her through clay to get to them. Beau called her name and she ignored his calls. She needed her bed, to close her eyes, to forget. But how could she? The very man who had tormented her dreams at night, she'd desired during the day. He'd taken her for a fool. Her own Jekyll and Hyde. She could never trust him, or herself, again.

Beau would have to return with one of her sisters. She wouldn't come down again and risk facing George. The safety of the all-women boarding house had never been more welcome.

HER STAGGERED footsteps spoke of how much he'd hurt her and each one felt like stomping on his own heart. He'd never seen a woman push ahead when her body would rather crumple.

Strength beyond measure. George watched her until she made the door and then turned to face the man who he'd prayed would take away his deception. Now, too late, he saw how foolish that prayer was.

"Why are you here, Captain? The last time we met should've been the last." Beau's quiet tenor might've been lost on a weaker man, a man who couldn't sense a battle coming.

"General Talbot sent me. He felt Eva knew things she shouldn't. I was finally relieved of that mission yesterday." Beau would require nothing less than his honesty. If he gave it, he may have a friend in his corner, someone who might understand duty and honor. But only the full truth would bring that.

"You lied to her."

"I was required to. If she'd remembered me when we met, it wouldn't have been necessary."

There were no other words. He'd known that playing his role would push her away, but he'd convinced himself it was important more than anything. If he could go back, he'd have done things *his* way. He'd have watched her as she ventured into the woods by her home without her ever knowing about his presence until he was sure she was innocent. She never would've even known he was there. He strode over to Argus and pulled the notebooks from within his saddlebag. Beau followed him, and he handed the books off to Beau.

"Please tell her I'm sorry. That I didn't want to lie to her, and that the army has cleared her of any clandestine activities. That I... wish her well." It was so inadequate and not all of what he felt, but he refused to analyze or name what his genuine feelings were. Those words would never make up for what he'd done. "I only hope she can forgive me."

Beau's voice shifted to a low growl. "Is that all you have to apologize for, Captain?"

George rested his arm against Argus's neck and leaned forward, resting his head as he took a deep breath. "Eva told me that she thinks I did something way back there at the ranch. I didn't. She was hiding that notebook, and I did take it from her, but I never took advantage of her. You have my word. I'm nothing without that."

"And what about later, while she was here for weeks with apparently no other chaperone but you? How can I trust your word when—it would seem—that the army has brought my sister-in-law, my *daughter* in every way that matters, out of our home to be investigated most insidiously? How do I know you haven't led her completely astray?"

His anger flared, mostly because Beau was right and what he'd been asked to do was inexcusable, but he'd never dishonored her. "Did *you* watch her? Did you know where she was going or that she'd attracted the attention of at least one Indian village while she was out drawing pictures? What if it hadn't been me out there that day she hit her head, but rather the brave that found me just outside of your fence-line a few weeks ago? Yes, the army was wrong, but we couldn't take the chance that because she was a woman she didn't know anything. Battles less important have been lost because of assumptions like that." Even as he said the words, knowing they were true, they rang hollow. His heart hated the man he'd had to become.

Beau took a step forward, crowding him by Argus. "How about because you knew Ferguson, and you'd met me and my family? You were there for Eva's twin's wedding. We aren't traitors. Ferguson fought with Custer."

Tension coiled in his arms. Beau was too close, and he wouldn't be bullied. Not even by Eva's father. "Yes, he did. But Ferguson also has a very weak spot when it comes to those who are hated by society. Eva's been at that ranch for well over a year, plenty of time to learn those habits from Ferguson."

Beau's lips flatted into a hard line and he glared. "I'm not going to stand here in the street and argue with you, but if I ever see you near Eva again…"

George turned and shoved Beau back out of his space. "Don't threaten what you can't follow through on." He slipped his foot in the stirrup and Argus was off without looking back. Eva's crystal blue eyes filling with tears wouldn't disappear from his thoughts.

What had he done? He'd destroyed the only woman who'd ever truly wanted to know *him*. She had even argued with him to bring out who he really was. The rangers had been his home since he left his real home ten years before. If Talbot disbanded the rangers, George wouldn't give his life to the army, not after what they'd asked of him. Not after taking his sweet Eva.

CHAPTER 19

Nothing was right. The two weeks since she'd been home had been almost unbearable. The gaping hole she felt when Hattie had left was now so much worse. Her sisters left her be, and that also hurt. No one wanted to talk about Lead or what she'd been doing, or with whom, or why her heart was so inexplicably broken after so short a time.

George had tricked her. She'd given him her most precious moment and he'd twisted that too, turning it into something she didn't want to think on. That one man had managed to take more from her than any other. She wanted to hate him, but her heart rebelled.

Ruby sat down next to her on the couch in the small sitting room. Her son Joseph was tucked in one arm and some notebooks in the other. She drew the books from under her arm and handed them to Eva. They were the ones she'd lost. She grabbed them, clutching them to her chest. How had Ruby come to have these? George was the last one to have them.

Eva felt her breath come faster. "How did you get these? George had one of them..."

"George? You mean Captain Roth?"

Eva closed her eyes. Ruby wouldn't understand just how close she and the captain had become, and it would only hurt more to tell her. She had to stop thinking of him as George. *He* didn't even exist. He was Captain Roth, the one who thought she could commit treason. The enemy. "Yes, the captain. How did you get them?"

"He gave them to Beau outside of your boarding house the day Beau came in to get you."

That whole exchange had become so blurry in her mind. First Beau was there, then suddenly George had been there and she'd learned the hideous truth.

"Beau is still too angry with the captain to talk to you himself, so he asked me to bring these to you and to talk to you about what happened. You were there for three weeks, virtually unchaperoned. Beau is furious. Not that you wouldn't want him to meet someone, but that you didn't trust him enough to tell him. You may be old enough to make those decisions on your own, but Beau sees you as his daughter. Precious. More precious than anything. And no man should get to your heart without passing Beau's muster first." Ruby rested her hand on Eva's arm, soft and soothing, but not soothing enough to take the edge off her anger at herself and her heart. Let Beau be angry. His anger couldn't match her own.

"George wanted you to know that he's sorry. He was asked to do a job and he did it, but he never wanted to hurt you. He claims that he did take the notebook from you, but that was it. He didn't hurt you any other way. And he didn't touch you." Ruby nestled her face in Joseph's neck to hide the red that, even now, tinged her ears.

Eva closed her eyes and remembered his words on the hill, that she would hate him in the morning, and she had still run headlong into his arms. Oh, he'd hurt her all right, but she'd handed him the knife.

"And you believe him? You were the one so sure I'd been ruined."

Ruby flinched at the accusation and pulled her hand back, cradling her son against her. "When a man brings a woman, tousled from head to foot and battered—you tell me what *you* would've assumed? My husband, whom I trust, says he believes Roth. So I must."

"But he's also still angry." Eva lay the notebooks in her lap. They both looked much more used than when she'd last seen them.

"As I said, he's angry because he was kept in the dark. You must realize that if you'd let him know that very first night, this could've all been avoided. Beau knew Captain Roth. He would've insisted on meeting him and the lie would've ended."

"I'm sorry I didn't trust Beau as you do." How could it be so easy for Ruby? "I was growing to trust George, but there was a side to him that I didn't trust. Whenever *that* man was with me, I'd avoid him. That man seemed harmless, which is why I said nothing to Beau. However, when the man I thought was the real George would show, the man that loved the trees and nature, the man that smiled with a glint in his eye——that man I trusted. And yet, he lied to me."

"He also asked for forgiveness. Despite what you say, there's only one Captain Roth. And, to be fair, I need to ask forgiveness of you as well. I fed you a lie which could tarnish a man's repu-tation. Proverbs says a good reputation and respect is worth more than silver and gold. I was sure he'd dishonored you and I didn't even allow you to question it. Though I believed what I said was truth, it made what Roth did even worse. I'm so sorry, Eva."

"It doesn't matter anymore. He's long gone, and the lie will remain. Whether I forgive him or not…he'll never know the difference."

"But you will. Trust me on this, Eva.

She stared into the dancing fire in the fireplace. "It's passing strange to me that I can forgive you easily, but George…my heart fights."

"You called what you feel trust, Eva. But I would question that word. Just how much did you *trust* Captain Roth? You called him by his first name. Even just now, after I'd reminded you to call him captain." Ruby glanced at her from nuzzling her son and the eyes, so like her mother Maeve's, looked deep into her. She could never tell an outright lie to those eyes.

"When he acted in truth, all my fears fell away. I..." She couldn't tell Ruby just how far they'd fallen, would never admit that she'd thrown herself in his arms, felt actual comfort there, and more. She'd felt...loved.

"I won't push you. Just know that you need to talk to Beau, to make it right with him. He loves you as a father and he feels betrayed." Ruby pulled a letter from her front apron pocket. "Mrs. Hearst sent you a letter."

Eva took it from her and glanced at the neat script on the front. Before she'd worked in the library, and even during, a letter from Mrs. Hearst would've been incredibly exciting. But nothing could pull her from her heart's pit.

She stood and climbed to the small loft area she shared with her sisters Francis, Lula, Nora, and Daisy. Now that both Jennie and Hattie were married, the loft had slightly more space, although they'd never all shared it together at the same time.

Eva opened the letter and sat on her bed, laying the notebooks next to her.

Dear Miss Arnsby,

I trust you are feeling better after taking a few weeks to rest. Captain Roth wrote to inform me that you had become ill and had to go home. I do hope you mend quickly. I want to thank you for giving so generously of your time in helping me find the collections of books that will most benefit and enrich the people of Lead. Being so close to the city, I hope they also benefit you. I will not be able to be there for the giving of the library to the people of Lead, but I'm hoping that all of those who have been integral in the process to make this happen can come and join the festivities. This, of course, includes you.

Captain Roth also tells me that you have a philanthropic heart and wish to continue to give to those in need. I hope you do. We, as women who naturally nurture, teach, and enrich, have it within us to change the world for the better. Through education, giving, and work, we can.

Sincerely,

Mrs. Phoebe Apperson-Hearst

Captain Roth had covered for her. He hadn't told Mrs. Hearst that she'd been under investigation. How they'd gotten Mrs. Hearst to agree to contact her was still a mystery. It had been a wonderful experience and not many could say they'd ever get to meet such an amazing woman. She could at least look on that with fondness.

As to the festivities, they were out of the question. Captain Roth would be there, and her heart wasn't ready to see him yet. Not in the flesh anyway. She flipped through the notebook to see the drawing she'd done of him and gasped at the small note on the bottom in his blocky, clean print.

Eva, you make me better than I ever could be. George.

A tear formed at the edge of her eye. She blotted it before it escaped down her cheek to smudge her drawing. She feverishly shoved aside everything on the little table and sat, grabbing for her pencils, blue first. His eyes needed emotion, like the longing she'd seen as he'd looked at her in the library the day after their walk up the mountain. That same longing she'd felt in her own soul. Blue eyes took shape with flecks of gold at the center.

Next, she shaded the area of his forehead. Then she paused. If she added more, he'd be pinched and calculating, the false man she couldn't trust. She shifted her attention to the structure of his cheek bones. Strong, prominent. She hadn't seen them as handsome at first because they were so sharp, but now they formed a face that wouldn't stray from her thoughts.

The more she added, the more lifelike the picture became. Francis approached from behind and rested her hand on Eva's shoulder. "I don't know how you do it. You've drawn him from memory? Those eyes!" She shook her head. "How did you keep control of yourself with those eyes following you every day?" She smiled slightly and pressed her skirt. "He looks as I picture the heroes in the romances I read. Looks. Intense, handsome, dangerous."

"Frances, you're too young to be reading such things. You don't know a thing about romance." Frances had been saving her money and buying dime novels for a long time. She had a trunk full of them in the corner. Ruby never asked about the types of books Frances bought, but if she had, Frances might have had to be sneakier.

"I've read enough to know that you're pining for Captain Roth. It was so romantic how he carried you back through the barn that day, draped over his arms. He was strong and courageous." She sighed deeply. "I couldn't have written it better. Handsome stranger rescues damsel from dangerous mountain fall!" She clutched the bodice of her dress and fluttered her lashes.

"You keep me and Captain Roth out of your little stories. I know what you do at night, Frances. Ruby and Beau would never agree. Especially if they found the story you wrote about *them*."

Frances rolled her eyes. "I can write what I wish." She narrowed her eyes with a slight gleam. "But, after being alone for a few weeks with the Captain, I bet you can tell me what a kiss is like. It's the one thing I have to guess about when I write."

Eva gasped and covered her mouth before thinking.

"I knew it! He kissed you! Tell me about it. I must know. Research." She dashed for her trunk and flung it open, gathering pencil and paper.

"Hold your voice down! Why don't you go ask Ruby, Jennie, or Hattie? They are all married and much more well-versed on kissing than I'll ever be."

"Oh now, that's just sad. Don't you think you'll ever see your captain again?" She twirled, her skirts filling the small space, and flopped backward on the bed. "Oh captain, my captain!" She dissolved into a fit of giggles.

Eva touched the edge of her drawing and a tear fell off her chin to mar the corner. "No, Frances. I don't," she whispered.

CHAPTER 20

R uby had been right, of course, about speaking to Beau.
Eva had been thinking about the apology and just what
she'd say for an entire day. Knowing that Beau deserved
an apology and admitting it to him humbly were two different
things. Eva took a deep breath and strode out to the barn where
Beau would be working, hopefully alone. Though he was roughly
Hugh's age, taking on the responsibility of all the Arnsby girls had
aged him in the last few years, adding silver streaks to the black
hair at his temples. He sat on a three-legged stool in the back of the
barn, balancing papers on his lap, pencil in hand.

He glanced up and stopped his figuring. His eyes were hard,
almost as black as gun-metal in the dim shadows of the barn.

"Beau." She stopped in front of him, praying for the right
words. "I'm sorry. I should've told you I was working alone with
Mr. Roth. He seemed so bookish and harmless..." She sighed.
That wasn't a good enough excuse for taking away his right to
protect her. A right he'd never asked for but taken on gladly. "I
know you care, and that you worry. I thought...that if I told you,
you wouldn't let me stay. Working in that library was the most
important thing I'll ever do. Don't you see?"

He didn't answer. Instead he set the papers to the side and leaned over, his fingers of his left hand, meeting those of his right. His head was bent. Her stomach clenched as she waited for him to respond. He had to, somehow. She couldn't just walk away now.

"Those are fine excuses, Eva. But the fact is, that's all they are. You lied by omission, and that lie cost you. You could've been spared whatever it was you and Captain Roth shared during your time in Lead. I had the information you needed. You kept saying you knew Mr. Roth was dealing false with you, but that didn't concern you sufficiently to tell me about it. You haven't lived long enough to make a discerning decision like that. I was here to help you, and very willing."

She opened her mouth to protest. He couldn't know that they'd shared anything.

He held up his hand and the set of his jaw silenced her. "Don't treat me like a fool, Eva. I saw how you reacted when he showed up in front of your boarding house. I spoke to him after you went back inside. There was *something* between you two."

Fury flashed red before her eyes. "It doesn't matter now. Does it? It was all a lie. He wasn't interested in me. He thought I knew something. He used my emotions. I've paid for my transgressions. I'll never be the same."

"No, you won't. You'll be less trusting now, and while that's good it's also sad. I'm not angry with you, just with what you did—"

She had to get away, couldn't listen to another word. She had to get back out to the serenity of the hillside, in her glade, but how? Stealing Beau's pants would be discovered immediately, and she couldn't afford to replace them again. There had to be a way, as long as she was patient.

LEI, Ferguson's housekeeper, had turned into her biggest ally. She had no issue helping Eva sew pants. She even knew how to do it. Lei had found some sturdy canvas and they hid for short hours in the back of the ranch house kitchen working on a pair of work trousers for Eva. She'd have to wear one of her own shirts, but the waiting was becoming unbearable. She needed to get out in the open, to follow her rabbits and visit the eagle.

It took days to finally complete them in secret, but they'd finished the pants. Lei wished her well and Eva brought them out to the back of their small house to wash them. For a family that had so much laundry, there was still the worry someone would see the pants out on the line and wonder whom they belonged to, for other than Beau and Joseph, it was a family of girls.

She scrubbed all the other clothes first until the lye burned her hands, and then Eva dunked her new trousers into the water and scrubbed the fabric clean. As she pegged them to the line, the skin on the back of her neck prickled. Beau had offered to teach all the girls to shoot as Ruby did, but not a one of them had been interested at the time. A sick feeling now in the pit of her stomach had her wishing she could go back and change her mind. A chill skidded up her back that had nothing to do with the early November wind. Eva hugged her arms close around her and stood on her toes to peer over the clothesline and around her, but she could find nothing out of place nor anything strange about what she saw. Still, she'd tell Beau about it.

Eva collected her basket and brought it back into the house. The strange feeling left as she closed the door behind her, and she sighed at the release of the tension.

"Eva, what's the matter? You look like you've gotten quite the surprise." Ruby stood at the stove as Joseph played with a small wooden horse at her feet.

"It was very strange. I was out doing the wash and felt like someone was watching me. I couldn't see anyone, but I couldn't shake the feeling, either."

Ruby dried off her hands. "Aiden and Hugh are both down the range checking on strays. If it had been them coming back, they would've called out to you and waved to let you know."

"I didn't go anywhere near the pastures, just in the back yard to do the wash by the line."

"I best go tell Beau. He'd want to let Ferguson know, and he may even want to go check it out. We haven't had any trouble since Aiden was shot, but you just never know. Watch Joseph for me?"

Eva nodded and moved her little nephew to the floor in the sitting room. He was a happy boy and the change in scenery, even so slight, made him squeal in delight. Eva's heart did a little flip as she saw a shadow by the kitchen window. She strode toward it and stopped when she realized it was one of the hands striding behind the house to toss some waste water.

She'd made shadows into monsters. Who would be out wandering around the ranch? It made no sense. Her hands needed something to do, so she whisked Joseph off the floor and set him on her hip. What a wonderful child he was, and how she wished to someday have one of her own.

A knock on the front door made her jump. She rushed to open it. If Ferguson were here, he'd want to know where to find Ruby and Beau. She opened the door, but no one was there. On the step lay a dried lavender giliweed flower.

THE BRAVE DUCKED behind a copse of birch trees and disappeared momentarily. George checked his compass again. Fool take it, they were headed right for the Ferguson ranch. He'd thought about that ranch and the woman who lived there pert-near every waking moment. She sometimes came into his dreams since he'd last seen her in Lead almost three weeks ago. He'd stayed away while work had kept him busy catching up with all the rangers. He'd told every one of them what had happened with General Talbot and how Talbot hadn't trusted him and threatened to go after Eva himself. Not a single ranger had chosen to join the army after that, leastwise not under General Talbot.

He'd gone rogue now, or at least that's what any record of his activities would say. There was no cover of the rangers anymore, but that didn't mean he wouldn't keep an eye on them and let

653

someone in charge know if anything came up. The brave he was following was up to something. He moved in shadows, wanting to remain hidden. He'd catch glimpses of the man as he followed him through the trees, never close enough to be seen or caught. That's how he'd end up dead and his remains never found.

The brave climbed a tree and looked out over the hill. At the back of Eva's house sat a woman doing wash. He couldn't tell which sister it was, hunched over the wash basin. With the blonde hair, it could be Jennie, Hattie, or Eva. She rose and pressed her fist into her back and his heart catapulted into his throat. He'd never forget that familiar motion. It was Eva, and the brave took notice of her, too. He made quick work of climbing down the tree and moving quickly under cover, closer and closer.

Eva stopped and searched, shading her eyes and scanning the forest. George ducked behind a tree to avoid being seen. As much as he wanted her to see the man sneaking up on her, he didn't want her to think it was him.

He chanced a look around the tree and she'd disappeared, but so had the brave. He gulped down a lungful of air and rested his hand on his Colt. If that man hurt Eva, he'd pay in spades. Passing information was one thing. Touching her was a far greater sin. He ducked closer to the house and watched as the man crept around to the front of the house. A ranch hand headed right toward him from his right. He couldn't move, or he'd be spotted.

Ruby dashed toward the barn from the front of the house. He'd seen her for but an instant. The laborer got closer, close enough that he couldn't risk running. He was maybe thirty yards away and closing. The man tossed a bucket of water over the fence-line and turned back. The brave melded himself against the back corner of the house, becoming almost invisible, and the ranch hand, though he walked right by him, didn't see.

George bit back a curse as Eva ran from the front of the house to the back along the opposite side as the brave, carrying an infant on her hip. The sight yanked on his heart. He couldn't let anything happen to Eva, but with a child, this brave could unknowingly start a war! The Sioux man was now trapped. He just didn't know it. George stayed hidden. His eyes wanted to drink in Eva with her windswept hair. She held something small and purple in her hand as the small boy reached for it and she searched the tree line, wiping a tear from her cheek.

The brave glanced around and made a dash for the trees. If George had ever thought Eva was guilty of collusion, how she looked just then would've dispelled that notion. She screamed as the Indian shifted direction and disappeared in moments. Eva's legs gave way under her and he raced toward her as fast as his feet could fly.

Nothing mattered except making sure Eva was all right. He knelt beside her and lifted the child from her arms, settling him on the ground. She'd landed with the babe on her stomach. He gently lay her head in his lap. His fingers quivered as he brushed the tangled locks from her face.

"Eva, do you hear me?"

"George?" Her eyes fluttered open. "I was hoping it was you, but..." She reached up and grabbed her throat. "It wasn't you, though. I saw..." Her eyes narrowed and she sat up like a shot. "Get off our land, Captain." She got up as gracefully as her full skirt would allow and reached for the boy on the grass, planting him back on her hip as he squirmed.

"Eva, I mean you no harm. I was following that Indian to see what he was doing."

Her eyes narrowed. "Were you? Or did you chase him here to make it look like I was meeting with him?" She threw the dried flower at his chest. "You failed. If anyone asks me, I'll never admit I saw him here. If you can lie to me, then I'll lie to keep you away from me." She whipped around and stomped back to the house.

The flower lay at his feet and he picked it up. It was a dried giliweed, just as he'd told the general the Indians were looking for. It was time to take this to one of his friends on the inside. Red Eagle was always a last resort, but he would know what was going on.

CHAPTER 21

Red Eagle sat in front of his teepee, his son beside him. Though it was cold, neither seemed to notice the wind as it plowed down the hills into their village. It wasn't safe for George to enter and speak. He'd have to wait until Red Eagle came to him. In the ten years he'd followed this band, he'd never had to report them. That could all change if that brave was with them. They were a quiet group, small, and set apart from some of the main Sioux tribes. Most of them knew him by sight, but he was still an outsider. An outsider who worked for the army who kept them from the lands they had known long before white men ever showed up.

He waited by the edge of the camp until it was dark and small fires lit areas around the large twelve-foot-tall teepees. Red Eagle's wife took their son in to bed and the man strode out right to where George lay waiting. He marveled at how the man could know he was there, exactly where he lay. It didn't even matter that he'd been hiding.

"Why have you come, Roth? We haven't seen you in many months and now that the chief's son improves, you come back?

You could have used that time to garner favor with Sitting Bear. I heard you were seen near the city of cut stone."

"I was in Lead. But I didn't recognize the man who met me there."

"Neither did he recognize you. If not for your long hair, I would've thought he spoke of someone else. Most men like you wear short hair on your head and long hair above your mouth."

The man had him there. He did stick out among the white population. Men wore their hair short, above the collar, with bushy mustaches. But not him. He couldn't stand the feel of the growth above his lip, and wearing his hair longer seemed to help him fit in a little better as a ranger, so he hadn't cut it. Still couldn't bring himself to cut it, even weeks after the end of the rangers.

"What ails the chief's son?" He'd bet the giliweed did something these people knew about that others didn't, and that was why they'd been watching Eva. Giliweed was Eva's flame.

"He couldn't make water, was bloated like a fish. The plant is out of season and we'd used all that we'd saved to help him. It sometimes grows where the heat can't get to it and the frost doesn't reach it, like in the valleys of high mountains."

"You weren't looking for Eva at all. You were looking for the flower she loves."

"Our people were drawn to the same meadows as the white woman. She even helped Gray Dawn find more."

"Will he heal?" If the chief's son were in danger of dying, it could mean the whole village should be watched at least for a while. People, no matter where they came from, did regrettable things in grief.

"Yes, he is well."

"You will stay away from the white woman now then?" His heart raced. He'd never given Red Eagle a direct order before, always asking questions or giving answers, but never telling him what to do. He had to at least try, for her sake.

"Hawk's Tail is interested in the woman. She amuses him."

"He can't have her. She's mine." A show of strength would

either be seen as worthy or cause a fight. He had no way of knowing which one.

The man chuckled. The sound so strange from such a stoic man. "A woman isn't worth fighting over, Roth."

"Perhaps for you. You have many beautiful women to pick from. This one is special to me." If bravado wouldn't work, flattery might. For Eva's safety, he'd do what he could, including risking his tentative friendship with Red Eagle.

"I will speak to Hawk's Tail."

That was the best he would get out of the man. "Thank you. She was quite frightened by his presence today."

"And what will you do, Roth? If you see him again, looking after your woman? Is she worth starting a battle over? Is she worth the army following us? Is she worth your life?" His dark eyes, made darker by the setting sun behind him, pierced him like arrows.

"No. She's worth fighting a war and winning."

Red Eagle chuckled into the night once more as he turned from George. "You surprise me, Roth. Go to your woman and make her yours. We cannot take that which isn't ours." Red Eagle glanced at him over his shoulder and strode back into camp, leaving George to look at the stars and listen to the soft noises of the people as they prepared their watch.

When the camp was silent, he rose off the ground and made his way back to where he'd tethered Argus. Red Eagle had made him think long and hard. What he said was true. No one could take from him what he'd claimed as his own. Not really. Was he willing to take that leap and make Eva his? Was it even an option? Even if she accepted him, Beau might not.

He had to find a way to convince her to give him another chance, to make all the wrongs he'd done right. Those few stolen moments on the hillside over Lead still flamed his blood. The memory of her eyes when she'd found out who he really was haunted his dreams. There had to be a way to erase it all and start over.

First, he had to see her. He had seen a pair of trousers on the clothesline that had to belong to someone other than Beau. No ranch hand was that small. It had to mean that Eva was out wandering the hillside again. If she was, and Hawk's Tail was looking for her, it could be dangerous. He'd just have to find her first and tell her of the danger, convince her to be wary. Most of all, convince her that the right place for her was in his arms.

He kicked himself for allowing her to get in his blood and wondered if she was suffering as he was. Or did her anger with him keep her from feeling the same stirring as he did whenever he thought on her name?

He'd have to deal with his future soon. He'd never had a home, never needed one. Even if he continued to do as he had been doing, he'd need a place for his wife to lay her head at night that was a sight more comfortable than the crook of his arm. He might first have to talk to Beau, get permission to talk to her, and then find a nice, quiet place where she could yell at him and no one would hear. The image of his little rabbit yelling at him and pounding out her anger against his chest only made him want to see her more.

CHAPTER 22

Phoebe Hearst had come through again. When he'd sent her a letter to tell her of how the army had treated Eva, she'd sent him a telegram wanting to also know what had happened to him. He'd hesitated, but then he told her vaguely that his position was no longer needed. When she replied, it was with an address. He'd gone there and his trunk from her house had already been waiting for him. She'd paid for his room and board until he could find employment elsewhere and had even offered to contact the Homestake supervisor for him. Though it was generous, his heart was in the wide open, not in the bottom of the earth.

Now that he had a place for his few things, he could focus on fixing what his own poor judgment and the army had taken. He looked critically at his face in the mirror and just couldn't see what Eva had seen. He'd recognized himself immediately in the rough pencil drawing, but her rendition was better. As if she'd added something to the image he couldn't name. So he'd left her a note. That was another regret. He shouldn't have touched her drawing. She'd probably burned it to be rid of him.

He yanked his hair back into a low tail and tied it with a leather cord. At least from the front, he'd appear like every other man in the street. The trousers from the trunk reminded him too much of what he'd done, but they were in better condition than what he usually wore. Beau shouldn't see him as either a dandy or a ranger. He was neither anymore. He slipped on suspenders and decided against a tie. He wasn't looking for a job, just approval.

Argus waited for him and blasted him with a great puff of breath as he took him from the stall.

"I know. This isn't the Hearst house and they don't baby you here like they did there. I think you'll be all right, ol' boy." He patted Argus's neck.

The horse flung his head from side to side in protest. George mounted and set Argus off for the gulch at the base of Ferguson hill. It wasn't far, only a mile. Argus wasn't even ready to slow down when they reached the fence line.

He drew rein and waited, looking up the hill to the house on the top, gleaming like a frontier castle in the sun. *Lord, I don't pray near enough, and certainly not enough recently, but I need your help today. Guide me in my words. Help me keep my anger to myself, and most of all, help me to remember that I hurt them and they have a right to be sore about it. Help them to forgive me. Amen.*

Argus passed two homes snug against the chill with smoke pouring out of each chimney. That was what Eva deserved. A little home with a hearth at the base of a hill. Lots of space to roam and do as she pleased. He pushed Argus to climb the hill. They slowly wound their way up until the level area at the top that opened before him.

Beau shut the door to the barn and stood as if waiting for George to decide what to do. He couldn't have asked for better timing. *Thank you, Lord.*

He dismounted and walked Argus, holding to the bridle.

"Beau, I think it's time I talk with you about what happened out in that valley with Eva. Man to man."

Beau notched his chin up slightly. "I always thought you'd be a fool to pull anything with her and then bring her back here, but now I'm not so sure. You lied to Eva for three whole weeks. That don't sit well with me."

"I know. Is there somewhere we can talk about this?" He glanced around. He couldn't feel anyone watching them, but that was never certain. "Eva may be in danger. This isn't just about me or her anymore."

Beau's mouth flattened and he turned, opening the barn door again. "Follow me." He shoved it wide so he and Argus could both fit through. "Put the big guy in here. Everyone else is down the hill or out on the range right now. It's just me in here, so you can say what you'd like."

He sat on a bale of hay and Beau followed suit, crossing his arms over his chest. He'd have been good in the army, hard to read. "You know the end of what happened that day, and I told you most of it a few weeks ago. I always assumed that Eva would tell you the rest. I never dreamed she'd hit her head hard enough that she wouldn't remember. I heard her crash down the hill from where I was hidden in the valley, but I didn't think she was a girl until I went over to make sure she was all right. Her hair had fallen out of her braid. That's how I knew. Her face was scuffed up from the fall, but she didn't seem hurt otherwise."

Here's where the story got embarrassing. He sucked in his breath and plowed forward. "I saw that she was hiding something in her shirt. I assumed she wore a belt with her trousers. How was I to know that when I pulled on the bit of twine holding what was hiding in the back of her shirt that everything would come loose?" He shook his head and Beau's face hardened into a tense ball of anger. "I took the notebook and helped her get fastened again. That's when she got sick on me."

"Why did you take what wasn't yours and why did you keep it?" Beau stared at him, steady and hot as the sun.

"She was out wandering beyond your property line, dressed up like a man, and carrying something in secret. I looked at a few of the drawings while I was out there. There was a picture of a Sioux warrior in there, just after she'd told me she'd never seen an Indian. I was concerned she was passing information to them. At least two Indians know of her. One of them now wants to make her his wife."

A squealing gasp ripped through the barn. Both he and Beau turned to see Eva standing at the end of the barn, her face white.

"I never! I will never!" She slashed at the tears rolling down her face as she whipped around and rushed from the barn.

George took off only to be hauled back by Beau.

"Now, you wait just a minute. You're telling me that you lied to her. Hoped that she wouldn't remember you, so you could find out about these drawings, and now she's in danger of being found by an Indian and taken for a wife?"

"Yes, and if she's run off your property again, she's in danger. Please. Let me go talk to her."

"While I might understand why you did it, Eva won't. She believed you did far more than you told me and the fact that you lied will only make that fear worse."

George wanted to burst from Beau's hold and run after her. "I won't lie to you, Beau. I'm falling for that girl. I want your permission to make this right, but I can't come around here without your permission, and I won't beg. I can protect her, but you need to say so."

Beau let his hand drop. "Eva has been tender as a baby rabbit since Hattie left, and as much as I don't like it, I can see she feels something for you. If you can help her to feel whole again, I can't take that chance from her. Don't make me regret it."

Eva tore away from the barn and down the mountain through the trees. She couldn't see where to run, just that she needed to get away. As George recounted the events of that long-ago day to Beau, it all came back to her. Every last second flooded back as he spoke. He was telling the truth, but it had been so much scarier to her. He'd handled her so roughly, not anywhere near the gentleness he'd shown her during that one sweet week. The week that had changed her life.

Her feet slid down the broken rocks and she grabbed hold of a tree. Below was the spot. The very spot where she'd met George a few months before. She slid down the steep hill to the bottom and knelt by the tree. A few of her pencils still lay at the base of it. Her heart raced beneath her bodice as she knelt and gathered each one from the leaf litter. The crashing of someone following her careened down the hill. She glanced over her shoulder to see George. She'd almost hoped Beau would be with him, but it wasn't to be. He was alone. Now she'd have to face her fears, and her desires.

Eva sat on the ground and cleaned off the pencils with her fingers. George stayed a few yards away from her and sat on a rocky outcropping, folding his hands in front of him and waiting for her to speak.

"Why are you here, George? You never had any interest in me besides my drawings and what you thought they meant. You used me. You lied to me. And I hate you for it." It broke her heart to lie, but he would never use her again. It was like a knife to her own soul just to say it.

To his credit, he flinched at her words. "I did lie to you. I'll take my lumps for that. But the rest just isn't true. I'm sorry, Eva. I stole your notebook, not knowing who you were. But I'm suspicious of everyone. I have to be. That's my job. At least, it was."

She glared at him, clutching her pencils to her chest. His job was no excuse for what he'd done. "You blame your job. Did the army tell you to look at me like that, to kiss my hand? Did the army tell you that taking me far away from everyone I knew and treating me to lunch and dinner would ply me into telling you everything?" She had to know. "Did they tell you to kiss me?" she whispered.

He pursed strong, handsome lips and furrowed his brow. "You want to cut me down, so be it. If you must know, they asked me to do much more than that to get everything out of you that I could. For the good of the country, you see. Problem with that was, the closer I got to you, the harder it was to look myself in the eye in the mirror. I was supposed to get to you, but you got to me instead. The only lies were words, Eva. My kiss wasn't a lie. Ever."

Eva propelled herself off the ground and turned from him. His frank declarations were true. In fact, she'd known from the start when he'd been lying and when not. She just hadn't known what he was being false about. But what good was his truth now?

"You haven't answered me, George. Why are you here?"

"I don't know if it was my attentions, or if you brought it on yourself with your wanderings, but you're in danger. An Indian brave, Hawk's Tail, has found you interesting and now wishes to take you for a wife. The flowers you helped them find, they saved the chief's son. So even the chief is pleased with the match."

Fear spiked down her spine. "And if I don't want to go?"

"I can't say. I don't know if you'll have a choice or not. It would be best for you to stay near your house for a while until this sorts out. But he already visited your house yesterday. He knows just where to find you."

"That was him? The Indian you brought to my house?" She flinched at the screech in her voice.

"I didn't bring him. I *followed* him."

"But…George Roth, why are *you* here? You haven't said why the army would send you."

"As I alluded to earlier, I'm no longer with the army. Nor am I a ranger. I'm here because I don't want to see you hurt."

A man grunted, and Eva spun to see a man just slightly shorter than George standing a few feet behind him. George's hand went to his gun belt. She hadn't even noticed he'd been wearing them. Hawk's Tail pointed at her, then at George and himself.

George took great deep breaths. "He wants you to go with him. He wants you to make a choice between the two of us. He's being more diplomatic than he has to be."

She took a step backward. "No. I don't want either of you right now."

Hawk's Tail stepped forward. George flung his arm in the man's way. "No. *Mithawa!*"

The Indian shoved him away and stared at Eva.

"Eva, you must choose. He will not take my word for it and he will not leave you alone."

"What did you say to him?" Her voice was stronger than she

felt. But as he'd defended her, something deep within her had cracked.

"I called you *mine*." George still stared at the Indian, giving him no chance to attack when George was distracted.

"How do I choose you? How do I tell him no?" She didn't have to agree to George either, but if it got the Indian to go away, she'd do it. George was much easier to deal with.

"Come here. Show him you choose me. My friend Red Eagle said that they wouldn't take that which isn't theirs."

She took one step, then another, until she was within reach of George. Now she had to figure out a way to tell the man, without words, that she belonged to George. For at least the next few minutes. Her heart pounded as she looked from Hawk's Tail's dark eyes to George and his great blue ones. So different. Both desired her, but in vastly different ways.

She reached for George and he glanced at her. A blur flew from the Indian's belt and to George's head. Blood splattered over his face and she screamed, reaching for him as he crumpled to the ground. Hawk's Tail grabbed her about the waist and tossed her over his shoulder. She kicked and screamed but his hold was fast. George lay there bleeding. She could see the glint of red spreading as Hawk's Tail jostled her away.

It was her fault. She'd helped this man, had invited him into her life by giving him the picture of the flowers and showing him where to find them. She should've run. She'd been scared then too, but it had done no harm. Until now.

"George!" She screamed his name, but he didn't move from his prone spot on the ground. Eva prayed that Beau would hear her and come running. If he did, the Indian might not get far. "Beau!" She kicked harder and Hawk's Tail grunted as her foot connected with some part of his body. He grabbed the fabric of her skirt by the rear and she screeched in protest. She wouldn't let him do anything to her. She'd just learned that she was untouched. She wouldn't let him take her innocence from her. He'd have to kill her first.

CHAPTER 23

He'd have a new scar above his eye. George tentatively touched the gash above his left brow and flinched. Beau hovered over his head as if he were swimming.

"Can you walk?"

Why did it sound like Beau was speaking through water? George managed to groan as he pulled himself to his feet. "He nailed me with the back of his axe." He yanked his bandanna from his pocket and dabbed at the rough, sticky patch of skin above his eye.

Beau faced him. "Heard Eva scream and came down here quick as I could. Which way'd he take her?"

"I can take you right to them. I know the village, unless they're on the move."

"And would a new prisoner make them move?" Beau searched the trees as George tied the bandanna around his head to protect it from the band of his hat.

"Don't know. They've never been hostile before. Pretty quiet."

"My horse is up the hill and so is yours. Let's go."

George clenched his teeth against the pain and then followed Beau up the hill. They had to find her fast. Hawk's Tail might not be willing to wait to make her his bride, and then Eva would be lost to them.

Argus stomped his hooves. He'd never been fond of the smell of blood. George couldn't blame him. He swung up in the saddle and followed Beau out of the barn. He pointed to the north.

"Follow the ridge line and keep going north."

Beau nodded. "I'll follow you."

"He'd have had a horse hidden over here, so he's probably there by now."

"Then let's stop jawing and go." Beau heeled his horse and Argus was quick to gain the lead. The camp wasn't far off and they dismounted on the side of the mountain, looking down into it.

"This is where I left Argus last time."

"I hope you have a plan. You know these people. Use what you know to get her out of this." Beau's chin hardened.

"My plan is to see if Red Eagle has seen Eva and knows where we can find her. I don't think he'll actually help us, but he may give us information."

"And what if he just tries to kill us for trespassing?" Beau rested his hands on his gun belt.

"He's never been aggressive in the past. This band is small and stays somewhat separate from the main Sioux tribe."

"I'll believe that when we get out of this with our hides intact." Beau flipped the little leather strap on his holster, allowing quick access to his gun.

George ground tied Argus and led Beau down the hill, keeping to the shadows. Red Eagle would know they were there. He always did, but would the others?

He knelt on the ground and watched the few people go about their business, preparing for the winter, which would be on them soon. Some were stretching hides over what looked like a large loom. Some were drying meat. The scent of smoking meat mixed with the waste on the edge of camp soured his stomach.

Red Eagle stood from his spot by the fire and approached them. "You shouldn't have come, Roth. You lost. You need to leave now. Hawk's Tail has already presented her as his."

"I didn't lose. He took her against her will," George spat, standing face to face with the Indian.

"I warned you to take what you wanted, but instead, you gave the choice to her. Her choice matters not to us."

"I'll ask you what you asked me, Red Eagle. Is she worth starting a war? This is kidnapping. You might not see it that way, but the army will. You took her against her will. After she helped you, this is how you thank her?"

"A sufficient thank you was already given. She should be proud to be accepted by Hawk's Tail. She is a good woman for helping us. Sitting Bear wants her with Hawk's Tail."

"Then I guess we have no choice but to take this to the army. Your band is small. The fight won't last long."

Red Eagle made a noise like a growl. "You would threaten me with your guns and your wars?"

"I want Eva back. She's mine. *Mithawa.*" He clapped himself on the chest.

Red Eagle shook his head. "She's in the far teepee. You won't get her out easily. She's in with Hawk's Tail's mother, preparing her."

The words froze in his head. "Thank you."

"Don't thank me. I won't help you further. You are no longer welcome here."

THE SMOKE in the teepee burned her nose and eyes. An older woman brushed her hair and plaited it, petting it and murmuring words that seemed impossible to say.

"I don't want to be here." Eva looked to her and the woman chuckled, patting her hand.

The words meant nothing to the woman. They were as much gibberish to her as the language the woman spoke was to Eva. She sighed. Was George dead? Had her small act killed him? How much worse was that than a lie? And now, it wasn't a lie at all. She *had* unknowingly been aiding them. If she'd only helped George to begin with, she might not be here now. She'd probably be in some army prison, but not here.

When they arrived, she on the front of his horse, Hawk's Tail's arms possessively surrounded her. He'd used the same word George had. *Mithawa.* Coming from Hawk's Tail, that word struck fear in her from her head to the tips of her toes. From George, it had been thrilling. If she'd believed him, had followed him back to the house, Hawk's Tail wouldn't have her now and George wouldn't be laying in his own blood under the tree.

Her head throbbed with the foul smoke filling her lungs. The man who brought her opened the flap of the tent and sent the woman out.

"You hungry?" he asked.

Eva clamped her mouth shut. He'd understood what George had said, *and* what she'd said. He'd understood that she didn't want either of them.

"You knew." She narrowed her eyes. "You knew he was trying to save me from you."

"You said you didn't want him. That meant you chose me." He eyed her appreciatively and lifted one of the braids the woman had put in. Eva stood and moved to the far end of the teepee. His attention turned her stomach.

"I didn't pick you. I don't want to be here."

"But here you are and here you'll stay."

"What if I love him?"

Hawk's Tail laughed. "You have a strange way of showing it. It doesn't matter. He won't be getting up anytime soon and by then, you will have lain with me as my wife."

"I will not!"

"You have no choice."

The flap flew open once again and George pushed his way in, his gun drawn. "I don't think you understand. She's mine," he growled.

Eva ran to him as Beau ducked into the small space. The three men filled the tent.

Hawk's Tail narrowed his eyes at her. "Just how many men are after you, Little Flower?"

Eva found her voice and rested her hand on George's arm, claiming him. "Only one that matters."

"And of the lies he told you, the ones you were fighting about when I found you?"

A small weight pressed on her shoulders. *If you would deny me before men...*

"George asked my forgiveness. My faith requires I forget what he'd done to me and return to a relationship with him. You caught us working through that back in the woods. It was wrong of me not to give him the forgiveness he asked for."

"And who requires that of you?" The man spread his feet and crossed his arms, though he was the shortest of the men, he was also the most fearsome.

Eva swallowed hard. She'd only been attending church for a year. She wasn't prepared to be a missionary, to tell him the gospel or how forgiveness worked. Her heart begged for the words to say.

"The Holy Spirit presses upon my heart that I must."

"And who does your spirit tell you to accept?"

She couldn't lie while speaking of the Lord. If she chose George in that moment it had to be because she felt certain of it. Eva closed her eyes and rested her head against George's solid arm. While the Lord was silent in that moment, her heart reached out to George, a string between the two of them, beating as one.

"George." It was all she could say.

Hawk's Tail straightened back to his full height. "I could slay these men where they stand and take what I want." He approached her, fearless of the other men, and lifted her braid once again, fanning the end over his thumb.

She held her breath. "I'll never be happy with you. I'd never give you what you want, not willingly."

"You could've had a powerful warrior, but you would choose that man instead. I gave you a choice back there. I didn't have to."

George's arm tensed as she leaned against him. She gripped his arm to stay his hand. "I know." She stood tall, forcing strength into

671

her limbs. "I helped you. I showed you what you needed. You owe me."

"You were given a powerful medicine. I owe you nothing."

George raised his gun.

"No, George, there has to be a way out of this without shooting him." She stepped forward and her hand shook as she touched his sunbaked bare arm. "Please. I'm asking you to let me go. There is someone else that will make you happy. Someone who will keep your home and give you strong children, but that woman is not me."

Another man ducked in through the flap. George took a step back, pulling her to his side. "Red Eagle. Are you here as friend or foe?" George's whole body was coiled and ready, tense as he held her.

"Hawk's Tail. Your mother has asked that you let the girl go from her teepee."

Hawk's Tail growled. "I will not forget this theft." His movements were stiff as he followed Red Eagle outside.

George holstered his gun and grabbed her hand. Beau held open the flap and they both ducked out. The old woman standing outside had a sad look on her face, and a young boy stood in front of her, clutching her hand. The two braves were already out of sight.

The boy came forward and reached for her hand. She couldn't fear the child as he came for her she knelt to him.

"Thank you. My father said it was your help that saved me."

She did just as George had advised her. She looked the boy in the eye and nodded. "You are welcome, and I hope you continue to get better and stronger."

The boy smiled and then bounded off to play with other children. The old woman touched her forehead and turned away.

"Come, Argus is waiting up the hill." George wrapped his hand around her arm and tugged on her, pulling her thoughts from the camp. How could these people weather the winter? How could they survive? While she wouldn't offer to stay, they were thriving, strong, even with the dangers of life in the hills.

Eva followed Beau and George up to where the horses waited, and a heavy silence settled between them. Beau glanced at her, as if checking her over to make sure every bit of her was still there, but he didn't come near her.

George held back, winding the reins around his hands.

Beau cleared his throat. "I'm going to ride on ahead just a bit. I won't be far. Don't take too long."

Eva glanced between Beau and George and caught the strained emotion between them. She let the hoof beats of Beau's horse clear before she turned to George. He was hesitant. Dried blood marred his face. She stepped forward and took off his hat. The stain on the bandana stole the strength from her legs. She laid her hand against his chest and pressed him down to his knees. He let her, landing with a thud as a groan fell from his lips. He'd held up well, but now she was concerned he wouldn't be able to sit a horse long enough to get back.

She reached around his head and untied the caked-on wrap, wishing she could just pull him close and cradle him. "Oh, George. This is worse than I thought. I'm so sorry. I should've stayed back." There were no streams or water near them. How could she clean the wound? He didn't even have a canteen on his saddle.

He grimaced. "I told you to come. I forced your hand. Made you choose. It doesn't take a scholar to know you were pressed into what you said back there. But I thank you for it. At least I got to hear it once." His head bobbed forward and his eyes looked distant. "Take Argus. Catch up with Beau."

"Don't you dare!" she yelled. "I didn't lie to you." Eva cupped his pale cheeks and tipped his head, forcing him to look up into her eyes. "I didn't lie, George."

He pushed away from her and his knees buckled as he stood. He was slipping away as sure as he had back in the office in Lead.

"George." Her voice trembled. "Don't just walk away. Don't put up that wall again. I'm trying. Can't you? Please. Don't make me go through losing you again."

His shoulders locked. "It killed you back there. You didn't

want to have to do it and you wouldn't have if you hadn't been trapped into it." He panted, grabbing at his head.

"No, it's not true."

He collected Argus's reins and walked him toward her. The gash on his brow had opened and the bandana she still held was useless. Her petticoat would have to do. She gripped the seam and tore it. George whipped his head up at the sound and gripped Argus as he closed his eyes against the pain. Argus pawed the rocky earth under his hooves.

He handed her the reins. "What are you doing?"

She yanked a wide strip off the bottom of her slip until it came free. "You're going to let me fix you up, and then we're going to ride back to the ranch together where Ruby can take care of that."

"You always did take what you want," he whispered, and the mention of that night tightened that sweet, curling tension to her heart.

She pressed him back to his knees. He didn't have the strength to protest as she wiped away what she could with the ruined bandana and wrapped the strip of clean cloth around his head. "With your hat on, no one will know it isn't a bandage. Well, Ruby will know when she takes it off..." The expanse between them had to be filled with something, the silence would swallow her whole if she didn't.

"I'm not going in, Eva. You can ride Argus back home, and I'm going to try to get back to Lead."

"No. I won't let you. You can stay with us. There's a small cabin behind ours that you can stay in while you mend. Beau might even have a job for you." A tear coursed its way down to her chin and hung there. He reached up and wiped it away. She wanted to insist, to order him around, to make him understand, but somehow, she'd always known that browbeating him would turn him away.

"You won't let me, eh?" He gently pushed her hands away and plopped his hat back on his head. "Haven't I done enough in your life? Do you remember when I asked if you'd hate me in the morning? If you'd feel like I led you up to that hill to take advantage of you?"

She nodded, unable to look away from his eyes. He raised back to his feet and towered over her. "You would feel the same way in a day or two after insisting I stay. You'd wish I'd just kept riding. As much as I want to have you next to me for the rest of my life, I can't shackle you to regret. You aren't the only one who can see when someone's telling you a falsehood. When you look at me, you still see the guy in the library, not the one who'd rather sleep on the prairie."

"George, he's part of you. He's part of the man I see in front of me." She reached for him and he stepped back, stopping her. He put his foot in the stirrup and swung up. George held out his hand to her and moved his foot so she could mount in front of him. He wrapped his arms loosely around her. Oh, how she wished he would hold her as possessively as Hawk's Tail had. He gave Argus a slight heel, leaving the cold hillside behind.

675

CHAPTER 24

He'd relished every moment of the ride with Eva pressed closely to him, but they were coming up on the Ferguson ranch and he'd have to let her go. He'd never forget the look in her eyes when Hawk's Tail had made her choose. Such pain, hesitation, resignation. He'd never wanted a bride before her, and he wouldn't force her. Nor would he ever want another. Eva would be his only. He'd never take what he wanted or celebrate over words said under duress.

If she changed her mind, it would trap her. But how he prayed her words were true. If they were, the Lord would find a way. He pulled Argus to a stop in front of her home, where Beau waited for her. He strode up and helped Eva down, leaving George cold and his chest aching for her against him.

"Want to come in sit for a spell, Roth? Think we need to talk." Beau said.

Eva's mouth flattened and she glared up at him. "He won't stay. Doesn't want to. Can you at least follow him to Lead and make sure he gets back to his room?"

George shook his head. "I don't need a nanny. I'm a grown man." He twisted and Argus turned, heading back down the trail.

His head had him a little woozy in the saddle as Beau rode up next to him.

"You might not think we need to have a chat, but I do."

George closed his eyes against the roiling in his stomach. If he didn't get to a doc soon, it'd be hard to keep upright.

"I don't get you, Roth. You come to our place to set things right with Eva, I'm assuming so you could court her, then when you get things good and set right with Eva...you leave? I know where you're at. Loving an Arnsby is never easy. They are strong women, been through a lot, and I love every last one of them. You'll understand if I'm not ready to just let you ride off to Lead and disappear."

George yanked on the reins and Argus squealed in protest. "Yes, I do think you should just let me ride off, because Eva needs me to. She hated me until today. Me. The man who found her crumpled at the bottom of that hill. Thinking about me terrified her. I can't be the scholar she wants. Why is it every female wants that for me? It isn't the mold I was made for. I'm not cut out for it."

"So you really aren't riding off for her at all. You're riding off for you. You're riding off because you're afraid of letting her know you." Beau turned his horse around. "When Eva first met you, I would've agreed with you. Captain Roth was just the opposite of the kind of man she wanted. Now, she doesn't need or want some milksop. When you're ready to court like a man and not a cheat, you're welcome on the ranch. I may even have a job for you. Until then, stay out."

Beau's horse leapt into action, taking him back to the ranch. George's head pounded, but so did his heart. The George Eva knew was weak, but no more. He'd get stitched up, go back and court her proper. Eva deserved it. She deserved to feel like a woman who was sought after, not one who'd been given a choice between two evils and chosen the lesser.

He stopped in front of the small doctor's office on Main and wandered inside. Doc sat behind his desk with a pipe hanging from his mouth.

677

"I guess I don't need to ask what you're in for." He pushed open a narrow door that led back to an exam room. "Come along."

Facing the brave *might* have been more daunting, but the doctor was a close second. He clenched his teeth and followed the old man's smoke trail to the little room. A bed with white sheets and a small table sat off to one side of the room. The other half was dominated by a shelf of jars. Most of the things inside he couldn't begin to name. A two-headed calf stared back at him with blank eyes.

"Now, if you'll just sit there, I'll get you cleaned up real quick, and right back to work with you."

"Right. Back to work." George clutched the edge of the bed as he sat. It was barely wide enough to hold him.

The doctor threaded a needle with black catgut. "Just close your eyes. Might take a minute." He unwound the fabric from the gash and clicked his tongue. "You sure made a mess of your head. What did you get hit with, a crane?"

Of course, he'd assume it was an injury from the mine. "No, sir. An axe head."

The doctor took some gauze, put it over an amber bottle, flipped it over and back again, and then poked his skull with it. The burn about unseated him. He sucked his breath and the oath he wanted to scream back inside.

"That'll smart a bit." The doctor prodded around until he felt the cut oozing again, forcing him to close his eyes.

"There now, clean. Let's get you patched so you don't bleed all over my table."

After the first few pokes, he focused on how much his teeth hurt as he tightened his jaw.

"Done. That'll be five dollars."

He couldn't even disagree with the man. If someone made you hurt that bad, he'd probably earned it.

"You need a minute to rest here?"

George fished around in his belt for his money clip and handed the man five dollars, but he couldn't bring himself to stand.

"Just sit here and rest until you regain your head. It might take a minute."

George nodded and laid back against the pillow. If he could do the day over, he'd have seen that axe coming. It wasn't like Hawk's Tail hadn't waited until the exact moment he was distracted. But if he had, Eva never would've said those words. She'd chosen him and if she never did again, he'd heard her say it. That was all that mattered, that and hearing it again.

EVA STARED after Beau and yanked the braids from her hair. Exhaustion sucked at her very bones. How different the day had gone from how it started out. Yesterday, Hawk's Tail had delivered a flower and she'd accused George of bringing him to her. Part of her reveled in looking up into those amazing blue eyes from the comfort of his lap. Then today, he'd proved he told the truth when he came for her.

Ruby stood on the front stoop and gripped the post holding up the overhang.

"Eva? What in the world's happened to you? I heard screaming, dreadful screaming, then nothing. No one bothered to come tell me what had happened. Everyone, just gone." Ruby hadn't been that pale since she'd been pregnant with Joseph.

Eva combed the remainder of the plait out with her fingers. "It's too long of a story to tell." She sighed. "I'm sorry they scared you, but I imagine they were trying to be quick."

She followed Ruby into the house and plopped down at the table, cradling her pounding head in her arms. "I don't understand, Ruby. I told him I wanted him, and he left anyway."

"Who?" She splashed water on her face. "Long story or not, I need to know what's happened the last few hours. How many of my sisters do I have to lose?"

Eva swallowed the lump in her throat. She hadn't considered how Ruby would react after Hattie had been taken. Ruby must've been beside herself.

She couldn't bring her legs to hold her weight. "Ruby, I'm so sorry. George came. He told Beau what happened, and what didn't, back in August. I got angry and ran. I was taken by an Indian, but by the grace of God, George and Beau were able to free me quickly." She looked up to see the wide-eyed shock on Ruby's face. "That's the long and short of it."

Ruby pulled herself together and came around behind her, squeezing Eva's shoulders. She collected her hair back with gentle fingers and wound it into a bun. "Eva, let me tell you something you wouldn't have been open to hearing until perhaps now. Men aren't like you or me. They like the pursuit, the hunt. They like to feel as if they've caught you. Wooed you away from the sensible choice, and claimed the most valuable prize imaginable. Your heart. Telling a man you choose him is taking all that away from him. Don't get me wrong. He wants to hear it, but not yet."

"But we had our time in Lead…"

"A time when he wasn't being himself. What if he's convinced you love a lie?"

"He is."

"Then let the real Captain Roth tenderly draw you in. There's nothing else like the first breath of love, Eva. It's heat and swirling, drawing and giddiness in your belly that nothing else quite brings."

Eva shoved herself away from the table and her hair tumbled back down her shoulders. "He left. He isn't coming back."

"He'll come back, and when he does, start over. No more worry about the shadowy man who delivered you back here. No more worry about truth and falsehoods."

"What if he decided he doesn't approve of me? You forget, he's only known me at the library as well. I don't dress or act here like I did there. There's no place for fine culture on a dusty ranch."

Ruby laughed and her hands draped her hips. "You two are well-suited for one another. He was a ranger, sleeping under the stars and observing nature. *You* would never come inside if we didn't make you. You both love books and learning, but living is more important."

"You're sure he'll be back." Her heart hoped, but her mind wouldn't latch on to it.

"Absolutely. Now, didn't you get a letter about a gala on Christmas when they will open the library?"

"Yes, but I hadn't planned on attending."

"I think you should, so we'd better start sewing a dress for you right away."

Frances swung down out of the attic. "I can help. It'll be *so* romantic."

"You think everything is romantic." Eva turned to avoid hurting Frances as she rolled her eyes. Frances thought everything was a romance novel waiting to happen.

"It should be blue, to go with your eyes, so that when he looks at you, your eyes will be even brighter." Frances did a twirl, holding out her skirt and fanning her face with an imaginary fan.

Ruby frowned. "And just where are we going to get the fabric?"

Frances narrowed her eyes and giggled. "The same place Eva found fabric for trousers, with Lei."

Ruby's eyes widened. "What? Eva, you wouldn't!"

Eva shook her head. "No, not after today. I'm not going out alone again."

Frances pouted and crossed her arms over her bodice. "I'm not going to find out what happened, am I?"

Ruby laughed. "No dear, we can't tell you anything without worrying it will end up in one of your notebooks." She glanced at Eva. "At least you know you'll have a chance to use the trousers with George."

Eva considered the two very different walks she'd had with him. He'd been so wonderful that night, so real. No, her trousers wouldn't go to waste. If he ever came back.

681

CHAPTER 25

S now piled heavy along the trail to the Ferguson ranch. It had taken a full week to build his strength back after the wound to his head left him weak. It gave him seven days to think of little other than Eva. He held out hope she would visit to check on him, but Beau would've never allowed it.

The catgut puckered his head and would leave a terrible ugly scar. He ran his finger along the itchy ridge. Just one more thing to frighten Eva. As if the sight of him before didn't cause her to run fast enough. He carefully pulled his hat over the wound and belted his holsters over his hips. Today was the day he'd take Beau up on that offer. The economy had left jobs as scarce as water in the desert and he'd found exactly two jobs, the mine through Mrs. Hearst, and the ranch with Beau. Working outside with cattle would at least be close to what he was used to.

His legs were stiff under him from lack of use, and Argus seemed just as antsy to get out of the stall. "Don't worry, boy. You'll get to stretch your legs in just a minute." Argus stomped as George quickly finished with the saddle.

During the time he worked with Eva and after, Lead had begun to feel like home. The noise of the mine, the diverse people, even the way it seemed to sit precariously on the edge of the hill, as if the Lord himself were keeping it from sliding away. If he and Eva ever got past their rocky start, he'd find work in Lead. It would be a good home for Eva, close to the library and schools, yet with just a short walk the city disappeared. It was perfect for them.

Eva exited her house as he crested the hill. She stopped, clutching the basket over her arm and staring at him. He had to stop himself from smiling under her frank gaze. She came a little closer, just a few steps, as he swung down.

"Eva. Good morning. It's good to see you."

A brief smile teased her lips, then evaporated. "Is it?" She took a step forward and snatched off his hat, leaving him as exposed as a rock in the sun.

Seeing the wound on his forehead, she gasped. "George. I'm so sorry." She covered her lips with shaking hands.

He couldn't stop from covering the ugly gash, hiding it from her. "It's nothing." He reached for his hat and she swung it around her back.

"I didn't lie, George," she whispered.

He wanted to believe her. Wanted to reach around her with both hands under the guise of taking back his hat just to hold her against him again.

"Did you miss me, Eva?"

She nodded, her eyes shining.

"If Beau has work for me, I'll be here every day. Unless you don't want me around." This was her chance. She wasn't being held by an Indian or given a lie. This was him, just him.

She took a step back, still clutching his hat behind her. He made it up the steps in one leap and reached around her. She gasped, her basket hitting the porch. He clutched the hat behind her, but he didn't tug it from her grip. Her breath quickened, the slight wisp of hair by her temple quivering with her heartbeat.

"Just tell me to stay or go, Eva. That's all I ask."

She toed forward, so close to him that his breath weighed like gold in his lungs, his arm now draped leisurely over her hip.

She stood up on her toes, just inches from his lips, yet it was her eyes that held him.

"Stay," she whispered and dropped back to her heels, handing him his hat.

"I'm going to ask Beau to court you." He slipped his hat back in place. She hadn't stared at his wound at least.

Eva nodded. "I'll look forward to it."

"Will you?" he teased, hoping to see her smile at least once.

Pay dirt. A brief but enchanting smile kissed her lips. She leaned over, collecting her basket, and slipped around him. She threw a smile over her shoulder as she strode off to the hen house, leaving his heart racing like a horse after a good run.

Beau strode out the barn door and waited for him to bring Argus over.

"I see you finally came to your senses."

George chuckled. "It didn't take half as long as it seemed. He hit me hard enough to put me on my back for a while, but not hard enough to make me forget why I wanted to get back up again."

"And why was that?" Beau shuffled his feet apart.

"I'm here to work, but also for Eva, if you give the go-ahead, that is."

Beau nodded. "I figured as much. You know Ferguson, but how well do you know his land?"

He'd been wandering this area for ten years. There wasn't much he didn't know about it. "I know it well enough."

"Good. You'll need to talk to Ferguson quickly, then take your horse out to the west pasture. They're driving the herd back to this hill for winter. Easier to keep track of them when they're close by. Your head healed enough for that?"

He wouldn't have said no even if he weren't. This was a job, and one that would allow him to see Eva every day again. "I'll manage."

"Welcome to the gang."

~

HER HANDS SHOOK as she shooed the chickens from off their nests to collect the bounty underneath. Ruby had been right. It had taken a week, but George was back. The gash on his head had been a horrible reminder of what he'd done for her. All because she'd been too afraid to examine her feelings when he followed her down the hill. If she'd listened, accepted, forgiven... *If only* wasn't going to change things. Actions would.

She felt down to her boot-clad feet that no other man interested her more than he did. With his love of both nature and books, not to mention his strength, he was perfect. How could she have ever thought less of her brothers in law simply because they were less well-read than others? A hasty judgment, certainly.

Eva rushed back to the house and caught the twinkle in Ruby's eye as she sat, giving Joseph his morning feeding in the rocking chair.

"Was that George I saw ride up?"

Eva felt her face flame, and for what? She was guilty of nothing. "Yes, it would seem he wants to work here."

"And why wouldn't he? Frances took me into confidence that you and George might already be more acquainted than either Beau or I realized." Her brow arched up, reminiscent of her husband. "Is that so?"

"Frances likes to tell tales. There was a moment, very brief, where I succumbed and let my feelings drive me. Is that so terrible?"

Ruby nodded to the chair next to her. "It may be, it may not be. It depends on just what you did. Would you regret your moment of lapse if you and George do not end up as husband and wife? Will you regret letting him kiss you if you compare his kiss to your husband's your whole life? Or was it more than a kiss? That is why the church expects purity. It isn't because they don't understand temptation, or even that they don't understand how wonderful a budding relationship can be. Including the stolen kisses. No. They understand all too well how good it feels and how seductive desire can be. The Lord expects you to remain pure for other reasons.

Your body is a temple and should be for you and your husband only."

Eva flamed hot. "We certainly didn't let it go that far."

"I didn't think you did but remember where those delicious kisses lead." Joseph took that moment to suck loudly on Ruby's breast.

"I trust you, Eva. You have a good head on your shoulders. It's one of the reasons we never said anything when Beau's clothing would wind up missing. You were so lonely without Hattie that we decided not to take that from you when you'd proven you could be trusted. Just be mindful of your heart. It can lead you astray, but the Lord never will."

Ruby patted her hand, and then focused her attention back on her son. Eva took the eggs to the kitchen to brush them off. George rode by with Aiden and Hugh on his way out to the pasture. He would work hard and prove himself to her whole family, but when would he have time to see her? He was still living in Lead. When the workday was done, what would he do? How did she fit into his plan?

Frances came in with a bowl of potatoes she'd washed outside and grabbed the paring knife.

"That's quite the bowlful you have there." Eva washed her hands and wiped them dry.

"Beau says we're to set up the table for lunch from now on and he wants all of us to eat the noon meal together." She shrugged. "I just do what he tells me to do." Frances heaved a heavy, burdensome sigh.

"That's very strange. We've lived here over a year and he's always had the men eat out in the outdoor kitchen. It's just so difficult to pack everyone in here."

Frances leveled her with a look. "For being so book learned, you sure don't see much."

"What do you mean?"

Frances rolled her eyes. "You didn't notice that on the *very* day Captain Roth starts working here, he finds an excuse to bring the hired hands into the house?"

"I can only assume my other sisters are happy about this. I'm sure Ruby is." She glanced over her shoulder at Ruby.

"She doesn't know yet. Beau just told me when I was out making sure the remuda had enough water."

Ruby stood and tucked her son into a blanket on the floor. "So we're supposed to make a big lunch every day? I may have to go out and ask Beau about this." She crossed her arms. "This house just isn't big enough." Beau strode in the door and Ruby turned her glare on him. "Just what is this nonsense all about, eating here in the house? Do you know the mess that'll make? Just the boots alone!"

He smiled at her, his eyes twinkling. He sauntered up to her and took her hands. "Here I thought you wanted to do everything you could to find good husbands for your sisters. Isn't that what you told me before we even got married... The very day we got married?"

She sighed. "Well, of course I do. But Beau, this house is just too small to have all of you here every day."

"You have plenty of help. I already talked to Lula and Nora. They gave up their outdoor chores to help you." He laid a kiss on the tip of her nose and she swatted him away.

"Beau Rockford, don't think for a second I can be bribed."

He laughed and ran his finger under her chin, tipping it slightly. "I'm pretty sure I already did."

Frances sighed. "How romantic..."

Eva tossed a potato at her and she screeched, making Beau and Ruby laugh, breaking the moment.

Beau kissed Ruby's cheek. "You'll do it? For Eva?"

"No, I'll do it for you, husband. But you owe me."

Beau laughed and walked back out with a strange spring in his step.

CHAPTER 26

The table was set and ready for the men to come in for the noon meal. Eva made herself busy dashing between the table and kitchen, getting work done because the longer she stood still, the more she wanted to jitter right out of her skin.

Ruby sighed and glanced over the makeshift table. "I think we've got everything here, Eva. Why don't you go on up and fix your hair? You've been working hard all morning."

Eva touched her hair to realize the heat from the stove and all her work had made a mess of it. The door swung open and Beau sauntered in, followed by Aiden, Hugh, and then George. Eva ducked behind Ruby.

"I didn't think he'd come in so quickly!" she gasped.

Ruby's laugh floated back to her. "Duck into my room. You can fix your hair there but be quick. This is for you and the men won't be able to stay around for long."

Eva ducked over to the one actual bedroom in the little cabin. A bed sat against one wall with one bureau, a chair, the stand that held a pitcher of water and bowl, and a small vanity that Beau had built for Ruby last Christmas. She sat down in front of the glass at the vanity and picked up the brush.

The work of cooking a rushed lunch for so many had taken its toll. She looked like a frazzled chicken. The pins were easy to remove, and she made quick work of combing out her long blonde hair. It would take time to get it all back in order, time she didn't have. Splitting the hair into three sections, she quickly whipped it into a braid and rushed back out to the table.

Hattie and Jennie arrived, and all eyes turned to see them, except George. His were fixed on her, unwavering. She smiled slightly and his face brightened, though it was pale. His eyes were strained with creases next to them. He'd overdone his first day, or perhaps her brothers-by-law were giving him a hard time. They, especially Aiden, were known for their teasing.

Beau directed everyone to sit and she was placed directly across from George. Though he looked dead on his feet, he waited for all the women to sit before he slumped down in his own. There would be no staying late tonight. He'd want to get home to his bunk.

Ruby handed a large bowl of fried chicken to Beau and smiled at George. "It's good to have you here, George. Will you be moving out to the small cabin, then? I can't imagine making that ride every day in the winter, even if it is only a mile."

George accepted the bowl from Beau and dished himself out a bit before answering, then passed it across to Eva. He glanced at her for just a moment and then folded his hands in front of him. "I like Lead. I think it's a good place to make a start."

Beau nodded. "I agree, but unless you've already purchased land, I'd advise you stay here. You can always go back in the spring if you choose. The pass gets pretty deep. I'd hate to be worrying everyday if you'll make it here or not. Not to mention the weather can blow in mighty fast. Sunny one minute, blizzard the next."

George nodded, his lips a strained line.

Eva gently cleared her throat. "Beau, if he doesn't feel right about staying here, then he'll ride. I'm sure he has his reasons."

His face softened. As their eyes met, a powerful jolt went

straight to her heart, similar to what she'd felt between Hattie and Hugh, but strong enough to give her pause.

"I'm sure you're right, Eva. But it'd be rude not to give him the option."

Eva pushed her food around on her plate, unable to take a bite. A silly smile kept creeping to her face and as hard as she tried to douse it, the wretched thing would come right back. George moved his foot slightly under the table and bumped hers. She glanced up at him and he smiled, giving her a quick wink. The smile returned and she wiped her mouth to hide it.

George's foot found hers once more and he gently tapped the bottom a few times while he continued to eat, pretending to ignore her. His laughing eyes gave him away. She moved her foot slightly and watched as he found hers once more.

She cleared her throat and wiped her mouth. "Beau, may I be excused?"

He looked at her plate and his forehead bunched. "You spent all that time cooking it and nary ate a bite."

"Yes, well, perhaps the preparation was just a bit too much. May I go sit on the front step for some air?"

She caught George's glance and he looked at her plate with worry knitting his brow. She couldn't wink at him as he had at her now that everyone was looking at her.

"Yes, by all means. I hope when you're feeling better, you can return to your plate."

She very much doubted that. Food didn't hold any appeal to her swirling stomach. Her shawl hung on one of the pegs by the door and she whipped it around her shoulders, again remembering when she'd worn it with George up on the mountaintop. There would be more days like that, and more nights, too. She ducked out into the brisk afternoon December air to chill her cheeks. A breeze bit across her neck. She pulled her shawl up closer as she sat on the top step of the porch.

The scuff of boots thudded behind her and George sighed as he sat next to her. His eyes were pinched and his shoulders tense.

"Eva, I can't stay here if the sight of me turns your stomach so bad you can't eat. You worked hard all morning on that meal, and I didn't see you take a bite." He leaned forward, avoiding her eyes and blocking her from the wind. He was so thoughtful, her George. And she had come to think of him as hers, because she could never love another.

He sighed and her heart twisted. He'd worked hard all morning. Hattie and Jennie had been right. There was nothing quite so handsome or alluring as a man who'd worked himself into exhaustion for you. And it *had* been for her. He'd come here just to be near her.

"You don't turn my stomach, George. You turn my head. I can't think straight when you're close by. My belly flutters. I can't stop smiling. This is the silliest I've ever felt. Not even as a child did my mind go so fanciful."

His shoulders shifted and he looked at her. "I don't know what you've got to be nervous about. It's just me and there's not much to me."

Oh, how wrong he was. There was more to him than she could bear. "No, you don't understand. There's more to you than I ever gave you credit for. The Lord used you to show me that a man who works hard can be just as intelligent and thoughtful as a man whose hardest job is lifting a book. I thought I'd be alone forever because I was so sure that brawn…meant no brains." She ducked her head to avoid his eyes.

"Don't hide from me, Eva. You've shown me that reading, and education wasn't a waste. I never wanted that life, but that doesn't mean it wasn't profitable or worthwhile. Without that past, I never would've been able to be the one with you in Lead."

Her eyes met his and that strain was still there, bunching the edges. She reached up and formed her hands to his cool cheeks. "You once said 'as you wish.'" She paused, gathering her courage. "George, I wish." She didn't know how to direct his face to hers or how to move her mouth, but it didn't matter. She hovered closer, just a whisper away from him. His breath stopped short. She took the invitation. His mouth was softer than she remembered, softer than any of the rest of him. His muscles bunched around her, drawing her into his heated embrace. His mouth moved over hers and her head swam with the wave of energy zipping through her.

Her hands wandered from his cheeks back into his hair and over the hard muscles of his neck and shoulders. His hand ran up her spine and wove under her braid. She had to get closer, nearer. George broke the kiss, a fire in his eyes, more alive than she'd seen him all day.

He shook his head and pulled her to him, cradling her to his chest. "I'm so afraid, Eva. That our beginning will be our undoing and I don't want this to end."

"It doesn't have to. Not ever. I forgive you." She backed away and cupped his cheeks again. "George, forgiveness means we've thrown out the rubbish, burned it. Stop taking the rubbish from the ashes and making us look at it again. It's gone. Do you hear me? Gone. That's what forgiveness means."

"I don't deserve it." His eyes shone bright.

"No one does. That's the beauty of it."

"I'm sorry I didn't believe you." He caressed her palms as he lowered her hands from his face.

"I'm sorry I didn't tell you sooner. You never would've doubted if I'd told you before Hawk's Tail showed up. You doubted because I didn't listen. I wanted a fight. It was easier to be hurt than to forgive, when I should've been glad that my fears weren't real. But I was so angry. Hurt that you were so different that first day."

"I'm not proud of that, either. I had no idea you'd hit your head so hard. I shouldn't have been so rough with you."

"Well, I'm not proud of that day for a completely separate reason." Her face flamed, remembering just what she'd done to him when her head had throbbed her stomach contents loose.

"I deserved it. I hadn't seen anything from the Indians in a long time and finding you wandering alone in the woods, dressed like you were... It was easy to be suspicious. But I had you tried and found guilty. I treated you as such and that wasn't right."

The door swung open behind them. Beau, Aiden, and Hugh

strode out onto the short porch. "Time to get back to work, George."

He pressed her palm. "Come to the library opening with me?"

Her face melted into the silly smile she couldn't seem to control anymore. "I'd love to."

CHAPTER 27

E va ran her fingers over the cool stones of the bracelet circling her wrist. George had given it to her for Christmas eve, the night before. The quartz was smooth and had a soft sparkle. He'd also found her a copy of *Tess of the D'Urbervilles*, which he claimed had been a best-seller a few years before. Ruby's mirror was far too small to see how her sky-blue dress looked, but her sisters had helped her put it on and do her hair. She felt as pretty as a picture, even if she couldn't see herself.

Ruby notched open the door and peeked inside. "Are you ready? George just pulled up with the rig."

Eva sighed and touched her hair one last time. The front door opened with a soft thud, then closed again. George was waiting. Tonight, he'd wear a suit and look like the man from the library. While she'd forgiven the lie, *that* George wasn't her favorite. He wasn't the one she wanted to spend the evening with. Maybe if she asked, they could just stay home and talk into the night as they'd done every night for the past week. Boring talks for anyone else, but to them, it had been like exploring a cave of treasure. The more bits she found about him, the more she wanted to be by his side forever.

Frances dashed into the room, tears streaming down her face. She clutched a dime novel to her chest and flopped on the bed.

"It's not fair. You getting to go off to the party alone. They should send me with you. I'd make a good chaperone." She sighed heavily and raked the damp from her cheeks. "Jennie found Aiden on the trail. Hattie was off alone with Hugh in Keystone, and you were alone with George in Lead. And I'm stuck here."

Eva smiled and sat next to Frances. "Beau trusts us to go because he knows just how long it takes to get there, how long we are supposed to be there, and how long it will take to come back. Perhaps you missed him winding the clock in the sitting room earlier? That was my warning that I'd better not be late or he'd come to town after me." She giggled. "No one could ever claim he doesn't care."

"Far too much! I'm fairly stifled!" She flung back on the bed and covered her eyes with her arm.

"You are also only sixteen. Give yourself time, Frances. You want so much to experience the love you write about but wait. It'll be all the sweeter if it comes when it's supposed to."

"I should've known you wouldn't understand." She rolled off the bed and stomped out, slamming the door. Ruby's voice rose, chastising Frances for her behavior. Eva flinched at the words. Frances would need a guiding hand, but Ruby had done well so far, much better than she ever should've had to.

She pulled the door open and her breath caught painfully somewhere between her lungs and throat. George stood by the door, in a black string tie and a suit stretched snuggly across his wide frame. Though the clothes were similar to what he wore in the library, his hair was down as she liked it and there was no mask, no hiding in his eyes. They were open and searching her just as she was searching him. Chatter droned on around her, but what they said wasn't important. Nothing mattered but the appreciation on George's face.

He took a few steps toward her. "You're beautiful."

"So are you." No, that wasn't what she'd meant to say. So stupid.

He chuckled and touched the puckered scar on his head. She stepped forward and drew his hand away, clutching it tightly in her own. "What I meant to say was that you look so different from usual, and it was unexpected."

"I was worried, but then I remembered what you said about forgiveness. It calmed my nerves a bit."

"You should always remember what I say." She smiled and a laugh bubbled from her, drawing a smile from him.

"I'd say that's pretty fair advice." He wrapped her coat around her, and she slid her arms into the sleeves.

Beau stepped forward, his face serious. "You know what time you need to have her home, Roth, or that axe to your head will be the least of your worries."

George gave Beau a perfect salute. "Understood."

HIS HANDS WRAPPED EASILY around her waist as he helped her into the small buckboard. Soft skin, curled hair, curving waist, every bit of her was supple to the harsh reality of his roughness. She was everything he wasn't, in a tiny package that was perfection to his eyes. The way she sat, even the way she closed her eyes drew him closer.

She rested her hand on his arm. "Thank you for inviting me, George. I didn't want to go until you did."

"You deserve to go. We might have only helped for a few weeks, but your mark will always be there."

"As will yours. Thank you for the bracelet. I've never owned anything so beautiful."

She certainly had. The bracelet was a false beauty to him compared to her. "It belongs with you." He smiled. When had he become so sappy?

She leaned her head against his shoulder as he flicked the lines. They'd had a slight warm snap and he was glad of it. He hadn't wanted to bring Eva out in her finery if it were too cold, not to mention the horse. He'd left Argus back at the ranch, opting for an older horse who wouldn't mind a short job, nor would he try to take a bite out of his trousers. There wouldn't be room at the livery and, being Christmas day, it might not even be open. They would have to go to the opening, enjoy a few minutes, and then return the horse to his warm stall.

Eva's hand wrapped around his arm and the light pressure of her head against him was a dream. That she would trust him that much, was a gift he'd never understand. They crested a small hill outside of Lead and looked down over the town. He pulled up on the lines as the city twinkled back at them.

She breathed in deeply. "I'll never tire of looking at the city."

"Eva... I want to buy a house, in Lead. Would you help me find one?" He waited, holding his breath. He hadn't a clue how to tell her just how he felt, how seeing her at the end of the day was like coming home, but it wasn't enough. How he hated leaving her in the evening. None of his words measured up to the pretty ones she read in books. They sounded so foolish and inadequate.

"What kind of house are you looking for?" Her voice was quiet in the soft darkness and her warm breath mingled with his as it curled in a cloud above their heads.

"A good sized one. Maybe on the edge of town, so it isn't far to the trees and hills. I want a back yard. But most important, I think I need one of those new big houses. The Queen Anne style, with lots of bedrooms." He looked at her, holding his breath against the rattle of his heart in his chest. He'd face down Hawk's Tail with his bare hands and be less afraid than he was waiting for her to answer.

She reached for his hand and he gave it to her, letting her wrap both of her tiny ones around his. "And just what do you plan on doing with all that space, George?"

She was tormenting him with such sweetness. The grand opening would start soon and he found that he didn't care. Nothing was as important as that moment.

"I want to fill it with beautiful children who like to draw and who take on the world with a fierce hunger. Who are honest and hard-working." Her shoulders trembled. He gathered her in his arms. His sweet Eva, though he dared not think he deserved her. "Will you help me, Eva? Help me find a house and then help me make it a home?"

"And can we have a library?" She tilted her head back. Her lips were a scant few inches from him, drawing him to her heat. He'd promise her the sun if she'd be his forever, and he'd deliver it on a platter with a smile.

"As long as we can have a stable, too."

She stretched her body up and pressed her lips against his, that promise she'd asked to kiss him 'as she'd like' would be one he'd never regret. She could kiss him whenever and he would never tire of it.

"I wouldn't have it any other way." She laughed and smoothed her skirt back in place. "We'd best get to the library. If Beau finds out we didn't make it, we'll have some explaining to do."

"As soon as it's warm again, we'll start looking for a home." He flicked the lines, because she was right, they needed to get around people before he took her in his arms and kissed her as *he'd* like. "Let's pray for an early spring."

CHAPTER 28

Frances held Eva's short train off the floor as she walked up the aisle. She and George had been attending the church together for four months, through the deep snow, because they wanted to be part of the congregation once they'd wed. She strode past her ma, Maeve, sitting in the front pew of the church, clutching her kerchief to her nose. A tear ran down ma's cheek. She'd only been able to stay for a brief visit, but since she hadn't been there for Hattie's wedding, she wanted to come.

It was April. Ruby had picked tulips and giliweed for her to hold, bright red with splashes of pink and purple, tied with a large white ribbon. Her dress had been lovingly assembled by all eight sisters in their spare hours after chores. Ruby had promised to keep it in her special chest for Frances, for when it was her time. As everyone had expected, Frances thought it was romantic. Eva said a quick prayer that her sister would wait and not run head-long into love. She'd always been afraid of change, but if she wanted something bad enough, she'd be willing to face her fears to get it. Frances would be headstrong, but then, which of the Arnsbys hadn't been?

George waited for her at the front of the church. His parents sat in the front row behind where he stood. His mother sat with her back rigid, looking down her nose at everyone. She couldn't help but feel she hadn't made a good impression on her, but George had assured her *he* was the only one that mattered, not his mama. His father was a picture of how George would look in twenty years, except perhaps less dapper. He'd still have the strong chin she loved to run her thumb over, and his high cheek bones would be smooth, his hair thick. She smiled and turned her focus back to the man who would be her husband in a few minutes.

No one else would suspect he was nervous, he stood with such strength as he waited for her. The only slight sign that his knees might be knocking as much as hers was his hand, gripping his wrist a little too tight. White knuckles shown against the tan of skin too long outside.

Each of them had thought they would end this life alone, which made them perfect for one another. She reached him, and he took both her trembling hands in his and her nerves fled as he relaxed. Alone, she'd been afraid. Next to him, she could face anything, including changing who she was. From Eva Arnsby, to wife, Eva Roth.

The service was a blur. Suddenly George tenderly kissed her and she prayed she'd said everything when she was supposed to. He led her out of the church and over to the small diner where they'd had their first lunch together. Their guests laughed and chatted, but nothing they said made it to her ears. It was as if her mind were too active, her skin too sensitive, and all too soon, she'd said goodbye to their last guest.

George spoke to the man at the till and she waited for him to finish. When he turned to her, his eyes devoured every inch of her. Her stays were all that kept her from melting into the floor under his heavy gaze. He strode toward her and held out his hand. "Ready to go home, my rabbit?"

She giggled at the name he'd begun calling her in their private moments together in the evening. Her hand fit perfectly in his. He led her out into the sunshine and to the white carriage Mrs. Hearst had rented for them for the day. She hadn't been able to make the wedding but sent her happy tidings. Her heart beat wildly. They were going home, to the place they had picked. Their home.

George helped her up, his hands lingering briefly on her, and then he sat next to her. She settled into his side. It wasn't far but she would enjoy every moment of this day. The day she'd been sure would never happen for her.

"I've done a little work on the house. I hope you don't mind." He wrapped his arm around her shoulder and pulled her nearer still.

"I'm sure it's wonderful. I haven't seen it since the bank handed you the key." She'd helped him in his search for the perfect home for them. It hadn't taken long. His dream had become hers and they'd found the exact house he'd described to her on Christmas night. He bought it and moved from the ranch the week before the wedding, leaving her feeling alone without him. Ruby had said it was for the best, that seeing him for the first time in a week on their wedding day would make her remember each moment. Ruby, as usual, had been right. But all week it had been torture.

He pulled Argus to a stop in front of the large white house that was now theirs. It had three floors and a large rounded tower like a castle on the right side. The room at the very top of that rounded area was to be her library, its massive windows providing brilliant light for reading. It had four porches, a gabled roof, and small dormer windows on the top floor. Even knowing what it looked like, she was still left in awe of it.

George came around as a young man approached them. "I'll take care of the horse, sir." He tipped his page-boy hat slightly. George nodded. He reached up, pulling her easily from her seat and cradling her against his chest. His heart was like a racehorse under her hand. He carried her up the stairs and through the door of her new home.

Every surface gleamed back at her. He'd polished the floors and painted, making every surface perfect. Furniture hugged the rooms and pictures hung on the walls—her pictures. He set her down and she walked up to the drawing of the eagle. The picture didn't fit her new life, not who she was now. Not with the peace she'd found. She took it down and held it in front of her.

"I used to love this drawing, but I don't want it anymore." He wrapped his arms around her, and she leaned back into his strength. "See that shadow? That's me. That's how I felt without Hattie. Like I was only a smudge of myself. I don't feel like that anymore, George. You make me whole."

He took the framed drawing from her hands and set it on the shelf. "Then we'll make new pictures. Together."

～

GEORGE HELD her hand tightly as they crested the hill overlooking Lead. They came often, but tonight she couldn't wait to reach *their* spot. He stopped and held her close, leaning over and breathing deeply as if he couldn't get enough of her.

"There's something different about you tonight, Eva. But I can't put my finger on it." He traced her jaw with a gentle finger, sending a shiver down her spine.

She drew his hand away and waited until his gaze met hers.

"What's the matter, Eva?" He cupped her cheek and, at his tender touch, she closed her eyes.

"Christmas," she whispered past the lump in her throat.

"Eva?" His voice was heavy with worry.

"Our first baby. It should come by Christmas." She opened her eyes to see his mouth drop open in shock. "I had to tell you here, at our spot. I'm so tired, I didn't think I'd make it, but the doctor said that it was normal."

"Baby..." His eyes were wide and a smile grew until it covered his whole face. He kissed her forehead and her cheek, finally taking her lips as he lifted her off her feet, leaving her toes to dangle.

As he let her slide back to the earth, he rested his head against hers. "I've never been so happy and scared all at the same time."

She drew his hand and placed it over her heart. "Neither have I, but I suspect we can do anything we set our mind to." She looked out over the ledge and found their white house on the edge of town, so small from way up on the hill. "The house looks a lot easier to fill from up here."

He cradled her against his chest and kissed the top of her head. "Let's start with one room at a time."

Historical Elements

We can't really start a section on the historical elements of the book without first correcting the language a bit. Most "foreigners" pronounce Lead incorrectly. It is pronounced "leed," not "led."

I researched the Phoebe Hearst library extensively for this book. You can find a picture of the original library on my Pinterest page: www.pinterest.com/kari_trumbo/. The library is what originally fascinated me, and the timing was almost perfect, as Mrs. Hearst donated the library the year after I was writing about, 1894 vs. 1893 as the date of the story. However, the story is fiction. Much of the work of putting together the library was actually completed, as I understand it, by the man who presented the library to the community, T. J. Grier.

This story took a turn from my original vague notes when I started researching rangers of that period. I wasn't sure if there were men who were the equivalent to park rangers at that time. There weren't, but I still needed a rugged man who loved the outdoors. As I researched rangers, I came upon some information about a very secret band of militia who may or may not have been part of the army in that area of South Dakota. They were trackers tasked with the job of keeping an eye on all the tribes, to watch for unrest. Because of the secret nature of the group, I have no idea if they were able to stop any violence, and, let's face it, that was a particularly bloody time in our history. But they did exist and they worked perfectly for this story.

The streets mentioned are actual streets in Lead, and some places are just as they were then. However, the little railcar restaurant is fiction. The fire station, church, and even the big hotel that was to be built in two years, the Bullock Hotel, named after the first sheriff of Laurence County, Seth Bullock, are real.

The giliweed mentioned in the story is a native weed from the area and does have the properties described in the book, although it is a spring plant and finding them as prevalently as they do in the story would be difficult. It would grow better in the lowlands, as described. It comes in three colors: lavender, pink, and white.

Mrs. Phoebe Apperson-Hearst was the wife of one of the owners of the Homestake mine. He was also a senator and the owner of the mercantile in Lead. As hinted at in the book, she was not born rich. She met George Hearst, an old family friend, and when she was just 19, she defied the wishes of her parents and married him.

She gave heavily to churches, schools, and other projects that she deemed worthy in a successful attempt to tear Lead away from its boomtown origins to a true city, which seemed to happen overnight. One of these was her program to offer scholarships to children of parents who worked in the mines. In addition to the library, she also donated an opera house which would open years later. Though she spent very little time there, her impression was a lasting one.

I've done my best to bring the spirit of who she was to the people of Lead to life, but this story is completely fiction. I would like to thank Karen of the Lead Area Chamber of Commerce for her help in finding just the right people and just the right websites.

Sad to see it end? Join my mailing list to keep up-to-date on when the next book will be released! You can also get a free book when you sign up at www.KariTrumbo.com.

Loved this book? Leave me a review!

Don't miss the spin-off series, **Brothers of Belle Fourche**

starting with *Teach Me to Love*, Izzy Lawson's story

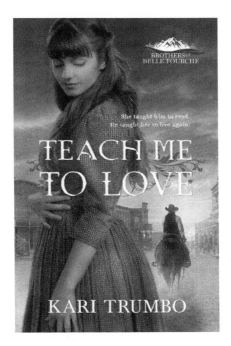

Can a widow find love in the arms of a man so different from her husband?

Looking for another series? Try Millie and the Marksman

Find my complete list of titles at www.KariTrumbo.com

Kari Trumbo is a writer of Christian Historical Romance and a stay-at-home mom to four vibrant children. She does freelance developmental editing and blogging. When she isn't writing or editing, she homeschools her children and pretends to keep up with them. Kari loves reading, listening to contemporary Christian music, singing with the worship team, and curling up near the wood stove when winter hits. She makes her home in central Minnesota with her husband of eighteen years, two daughters, two sons, and two cats.

Thank you, dear reader, for joining me on this adventure. I hope you've enjoyed it and that you'll continue reading the other books I have available, listed on the next page.

Be sure to join my special reader list to find out when my next novel will be released. You can also get a free book at www. KariTrumbo.com.

Made in the USA
Coppell, TX
06 August 2020

32484470R00414